RANDOM
HOUSE

LARGE
PRINT

Also by Donna Tartt
available from Random House Large Print

The Little Friend

THE

SECRET

HISTORY

DONNA TARTT

THE

SECRET

HISTORY

RANDOM HOUSE
LARGE PRINT

Published in the United States of America by
Random House Large Print in association with
Vintage Books, New York.
Distributed by Random House, Inc., New York.

**The Library of Congress has established
a Cataloging-in-Publication record for
this title.**

0-375-43496-8

www.randomlargeprint.com

FIRST LARGE PRINT EDITION

10 9 8 7 6 5 4 3 2 1

This Large Print edition published in accord
with the standards of the N.A.V.H.

For Bret Easton Ellis, whose generosity will never cease to warm my heart; and for Paul Edward McGloin, muse and Maecenas, who is the dearest friend I will ever have in this world.

I enquire now as to the genesis of a philologist and assert the following:
1. A young man cannot possibly know what Greeks and Romans are.
2. He does not know whether he is suited for finding out about them.

—FRIEDRICH NIETZSCHE,
Unzeitgemässe Betrachtungen

Come then, and let us pass a leisure hour in storytelling, and our story shall be the education of our heroes.

—PLATO,
Republic, BOOK II

ACKNOWLEDGMENTS

Thanks to Binky Urban, whose dauntless efforts on behalf of this book leave me speechless; to Sonny Mehta, who made everything possible; to Gary Fisketjon **il miglior fabbro**; and to Garth Battista and Marie Behan, whose patience with me sometimes makes me want to weep.

And—despite the risk of sounding like a Homeric catalog of ships—the following people must all be thanked for their aid, inspiration and love: Russ Dallen, Greta Edwards-Anthony, Claude Fredericks, Cheryl Gilman, Edna Golding, Barry Hannah, Ben Herring, Beatrice Hill, Mary Minter Krotzer, Antoinette Linn, Caitlin McCaffrey, Joe McGinniss, Paul and Louise McGloin, Mark McNairy, Willie Morris, Erin "Maxfield" Parish, Delia Reid, Pascale Retourner-Raab, Jim and Mary Robison, Elizabeth Seelig, Mark Shaw, Orianne Smith, Maura Spiegel, Richard Stilwell, Mackenzie Stubbins, Rebecca Tartt, Minnie Lou Thompson, Arturo Vivante, Taylor Weatherall, Alice Welsh, Thomas Yarker and, most of all, that dear old bad old Boushé family.

T H E

S E C R E T

H I S T O R Y

PROLOGUE

THE SNOW in the mountains was melting and Bunny had been dead for several weeks before we came to understand the gravity of our situation. He'd been dead for ten days before they found him, you know. It was one of the biggest manhunts in Vermont history—state troopers, the FBI, even an army helicopter; the college closed, the dye factory in Hampden shut down, people coming from New Hampshire, upstate New York, as far away as Boston.

It is difficult to believe that Henry's modest plan could have worked so well despite these unforeseen events. We hadn't intended to hide the body where it couldn't be found. In fact, we hadn't hidden it at all but had simply left it where it fell in hopes that some luckless passerby would stumble over it before anyone even noticed he was missing. This was a tale that told itself simply and well: the loose rocks, the body at the bottom of the ravine with a clean break in the neck, and the muddy skidmarks of dug-in heels pointing the way down; a hiking accident, no more, no less, and it might have been left at that, at quiet tears and a small funeral, had it not been for the snow that fell that night; it covered him without a trace, and ten days later, when the thaw finally came, the state troopers and the FBI and the searchers from the town all saw that they had been walking back and forth over his body until the snow above it was packed down like ice.

———

It is difficult to believe that such an uproar took place over an act for which I was partially responsible, even more difficult to believe I could have walked through it—the cameras, the uniforms, the black crowds sprinkled over Mount Cataract like ants in a sugar bowl—without incurring a blink of suspicion. But walking through it all was one thing; walking away, unfortunately, has proved to be quite another, and though once I thought I had left that ravine forever on an April afternoon long ago, now I am not so sure. Now the searchers have departed, and life has grown quiet around me, I have come to realize that while for years I might have imagined myself to be somewhere else, in reality I have been there all the time: up at the top by the muddy wheel-ruts in the new grass, where the sky is dark over the shivering apple blossoms and the first chill of the snow that will fall that night is already in the air.

What are you doing up here? said Bunny, surprised, when he found the four of us waiting for him.

Why, looking for new ferns, said Henry.

And after we stood whispering in the under-brush—one last look at the body and a last look round, no dropped keys, lost glasses, everybody got everything?—and then started single file through the woods, I took one glance back through the saplings that leapt to close the path behind me. Though I remember the walk back and the first lonely flakes of snow that came drifting through the pines, re-member piling gratefully into the car and starting down the road like a family on vaca-tion, with Henry driving clench-jawed through the potholes and the rest of us leaning over the seats and talking like children, though I re-member only too well the long terrible night that lay ahead and the long terrible days and nights that followed, I have only to glance over my shoulder for all those years to drop away and I see it behind me again, the ravine, rising all green and black through the saplings, a pic-ture that will never leave me.

I suppose at one time in my life I might have had any number of stories, but now there is no other. This is the only story I will ever be able to tell.

BOOK I

CHAPTER

1

DOES SUCH a thing as "the fatal flaw," that showy dark crack running down the middle of a life, exist outside literature? I used to think it didn't. Now I think it does. And I think that mine is this: a morbid longing for the picturesque at all costs.

A moi. L'histoire d'une de mes folies.

My name is Richard Papen. I am twenty-eight years old and I had never seen New England or Hampden College until I was nineteen. I am a Californian by birth and also, I have recently discovered, by nature. The last is something I admit only now, after the fact. Not that it matters.

I grew up in Plano, a small silicon village in the north. No sisters, no brothers. My father ran a gas station and my mother stayed at home until I got older and times got tighter and she went to work, answering phones in the office of one of the big chip factories outside San Jose.

Plano. The word conjures up drive-ins, tract

homes, waves of heat rising from the blacktop. My years there created for me an expendable past, disposable as a plastic cup. Which I suppose was a very great gift, in a way. On leaving home I was able to fabricate a new and far more satisfying history, full of striking, simplistic environmental influences; a colorful past, easily accessible to strangers.

The dazzle of this fictive childhood—full of swimming pools and orange groves and dissolute, charming show-biz parents—has all but eclipsed the drab original. In fact, when I think about my real childhood I am unable to recall much about it at all except a sad jumble of objects: the sneakers I wore year-round; coloring books and comics from the supermarket; little of interest, less of beauty. I was quiet, tall for my age, prone to freckles. I didn't have many friends but whether this was due to choice or circumstance I do not now know. I did well in school, it seems, but not exceptionally well; I liked to read—**Tom Swift**, the Tolkien books—but also to watch television, which I did plenty of, lying on the carpet of our empty living room in the long dull afternoons after school.

I honestly can't remember much else about those years except a certain mood that permeated most of them, a melancholy feeling that I associate with watching "The Wonderful World of Disney" on Sunday nights. Sunday was a sad day—early to bed, school the next morning, I was constantly worried my homework was wrong—but as I watched the fireworks go off in the night sky, over the floodlit castles of Disneyland, I was consumed by a more general sense of dread, of imprisonment within the dreary round of school and home: circumstances which, to me at least, presented sound empirical argument for gloom. My father was mean, and our house ugly, and my mother didn't pay much attention to me; my clothes were cheap and my haircut too short and no one at school seemed to like me that much; and since all this had been true for as long as I could remember, I felt things would doubtless continue in this depressing vein as far as I could foresee. In short: I felt my existence was tainted, in some subtle but essential way.

I suppose it's not odd, then, that I have trouble reconciling my life to those of my friends, or at least to their lives as I perceive them to be. Charles and Camilla are orphans (how I longed to be an orphan when I was a child!) reared by grandmothers and great-aunts in a house in Virginia: a childhood I like to think about, with horses and rivers and sweet-gum trees. And Francis. His mother, when she had him, was only seventeen—a thin-blooded, capricious girl with red hair and a rich daddy, who ran off with the drummer for Vance Vane and his Musical Swains. She was home in three weeks, and the marriage was annulled in six; and, as Francis is fond of saying, the grandparents brought them up like brother and sister, him and his mother, brought them up in such a magnanimous style that even the gossips were impressed—English nannies and private schools, summers in Switzerland, winters in France. Consider even bluff old Bunny, if you would. Not a childhood of reefer coats and dancing lessons, any more than mine was. But an American childhood. Son of a Clemson football star turned banker. Four brothers, no sisters, in a big noisy house in the suburbs, with sailboats and tennis rackets and golden retrievers; summers on Cape Cod, boarding schools near Boston and tailgate picnics during football season; an upbringing vitally present in Bunny in every respect, from the way he shook your hand to the way he told a joke.

I do not now nor did I ever have anything in common with any of them, nothing except a knowledge of Greek and the year of my life I spent in their company. And if love is a thing held in common, I suppose we had that in common, too, though I realize that might sound odd in light of the story I am about to tell.

How to begin.

After high school I went to a small college in my home town (my parents were opposed, as it had been made very plain that I was expected to help my father run his business, one of the many reasons I was in such an agony to escape) and, during my two years there, I studied ancient Greek. This was due to no love for the language but because I was majoring in pre-med (money, you see, was the only way to improve my fortunes, doctors make a lot of money, **quod erat demonstrandum**) and my counselor had suggested I take a language to fulfill the humanities requirement; and, since the Greek classes happened to meet in the afternoon, I took Greek so I could sleep late on Mondays. It was an entirely random decision which, as you will see, turned out to be quite fateful.

I did well at Greek, excelled in it, and I even won an award from the Classics department my last year. It was my favorite class because it was the only one held in a regular classroom— no jars of cow hearts, no smell of formaldehyde, no cages full of screaming monkeys. Initially I had thought with hard work I could overcome a fundamental squeamishness and distaste for my subject, that perhaps with even harder work I could simulate something like a talent for it. But this was not the case. As the months went by I remained uninterested, if not downright sickened, by my study of biology; my grades were poor; I was held in contempt by teacher and classmate alike. In what seemed even to me a doomed and Pyrrhic gesture, I switched to English literature without telling my parents. I felt that I was cutting my own throat by this, that I would certainly be very sorry, being still convinced that it was better to fail in a lucrative field than to thrive in one that my father (who knew nothing of either finance or academia) had assured me was most unprofitable; one which would inevitably result in my hanging around the house for the rest of my life asking him for money; money which, he assured me forcefully, he had no intention of giving me.

So I studied literature and liked it better. But I didn't like home any better. I don't think I can explain the despair my surroundings inspired in me. Though I now suspect, given the circumstances and my disposition, I would've been unhappy anywhere, in Biarritz or Caracas or the Isle of Capri, I was then convinced that my unhappiness was indigenous to that place. Perhaps a part of it was. While to a certain extent Milton is right—the mind is its own place and in itself can make a Heaven of Hell and so forth—it is nonetheless clear that Plano was modeled less on Paradise than that other, more dolorous city. In high school I developed a

habit of wandering through shopping malls after school, swaying through the bright, chill
mezzanines until I was so dazed with con-
sumer goods and product codes, with prome-
nades and escalators, with mirrors and Muzak
and noise and light, that a fuse would blow in
my brain and all at once everything would become unintelligible: color without form, a
babble of detached molecules. Then I would
walk like a zombie to the parking lot and drive
to the baseball field, where I wouldn't even get
out of the car, just sit with my hands on the
steering wheel and stare at the Cyclone fence
and the yellowed winter grass until the sun
went down and it was too dark for me to see.

Though I had a confused idea that my dis-
satisfaction was bohemian, vaguely Marxist in
origin (when I was a teenager I made a fatuous
show of socialism, mainly to irritate my father), I couldn't really begin to understand it;
and I would have been angry if someone had
suggested that it was due to a strong Puritan
streak in my nature, which was in fact the case.
Not long ago I found this passage in an old
notebook, written when I was eighteen or so:
"There is to me about this place a smell of rot,
the smell of rot that ripe fruit makes. Nowhere, ever, have the hideous mechanics of
birth and copulation and death—those monstrous upheavals of life that the Greeks call

miasma, defilement—been so brutal or been painted up to look so pretty; have so many people put so much faith in lies and mutability and death death death."

This, I think, is pretty rough stuff. From the sound of it, had I stayed in California I might have ended up in a cult or at the very least practicing some weird dietary restriction. I remember reading about Pythagoras around this time, and finding some of his ideas curiously appealing—wearing white garments, for instance, or abstaining from foods which have a soul.

But instead I wound up on the East Coast.

I lit on Hampden by a trick of fate. One night, during a long Thanksgiving holiday of rainy weather, canned cranberries, ball games droning from the television, I went to my room after a fight with my parents (I cannot remember this particular fight, only that we always fought, about money and school) and was tearing through my closet trying to find my coat when out it flew: a brochure from Hampden College, Hampden, Vermont.

It was two years old, this brochure. In high school a lot of colleges had sent me things because I did well on my SATs, though unfortunately not well enough to warrant much in the way of scholarships, and this one I had kept in my Geometry book throughout my senior year.

I don't know why it was in my closet. I suppose I'd saved it because it was so pretty. Senior year, I had spent dozens of hours studying the photographs as though if I stared at them long enough and longingly enough I would, by some sort of osmosis, be transported into their clear, pure silence. Even now I remember those pictures, like pictures in a storybook one loved as a child. Radiant meadows, mountains vaporous in the trembling distance; leaves ankle-deep on a gusty autumn road; bonfires and fog in the valleys; cellos, dark windowpanes, snow.

Hampden College, Hampden, Vermont. Established 1895. (This alone was a fact to cause wonder; nothing I knew of in Plano had been established much before 1962.) Student body, five hundred. Coed. Progressive. Specializing in the liberal arts. Highly selective. "Hampden, in providing a well-rounded course of study in the Humanities, seeks not only to give students a rigorous background in the chosen field but insight into all the disciplines of Western art, civilization, and thought. In doing so, we hope to provide the individual not only with facts, but with the raw materials of wisdom."

Hampden College, Hampden, Vermont.

Even the name had an austere Anglican cadence, to my ear at least, which yearned hopelessly for England and was dead to the sweet dark rhythms of the little mission towns. For a long time I looked at a picture of the building they called Commons. It was suffused with a weak, academic light—different from Plano, different from anything I had ever known—a light that made me think of long hours in dusty libraries, and old books, and silence.

My mother knocked on the door, said my name. I didn't answer. I tore out the information form in the back of the brochure and started to fill it in. **Name:** John Richard Papen. **Address:** 4487 Mimosa Court; Plano, California. Would you like to receive information on Financial Aid? Yes. And I mailed it the following morning.

The months subsequent were an endless dreary battle of paperwork, full of stalemates, fought in trenches. My father refused to complete the financial aid papers; finally, in desperation, I stole the tax returns from the glove compartment of his Toyota and did them myself. More waiting. Then a note from the Dean of Admissions. An interview was required, and when could I fly to Vermont? I could not afford to fly to Vermont, and I wrote and told him so. Another wait, another letter. The college would reimburse me for my travel expenses if their scholarship offer was accepted. Meanwhile the financial aid packet had come in. My family's contribution was more than my father said he could afford and he would not pay it. This sort of guerrilla warfare dragged on for eight months. Even today I do not fully understand the chain of events that brought me to Hampden. Sympathetic professors wrote letters; exceptions of various sorts were made in my case. And less than a year after I'd sat down on the gold shag carpet of my little room in Plano and impulsively filled out the questionnaire, I was getting off the bus in Hampden with two suitcases and fifty dollars in my pocket.

I had never been east of Santa Fe, never north of Portland, and—when I stepped off the bus after a long anxious night that had begun somewhere in Illinois—it was six o'clock in the morning, and the sun was rising over mountains, and birches, and impossibly green meadows; and to me, dazed with night and no sleep and three days on the highway, it was like a country from a dream.

The dormitories weren't even dorms—or at any rate not like the dorms I knew, with cinderblock walls and depressing, yellowish light—but white clapboard houses with green shutters, set back from the Commons in groves of maple and ash. All the same it never occurred to me that my particular room, wherever it might be, would be anything but ugly and disappointing and it was with something of a shock that I saw it for the first time—a white room with big north-facing windows, monkish and bare, with scarred oak floors and a ceiling slanted like a garret's. On my first night there, I sat on the bed during the twilight while the walls went slowly from gray to gold to black, listening to a soprano's voice climb dizzily up and down somewhere at the other end of the hall until at last the light was completely gone, and the faraway soprano spiraled on and on in the darkness like some angel of death, and I can't remember the air ever seeming as high and cold and rarefied as it was that night, or ever feeling farther away from the low-slung lines of dusty Plano.

Those first days before classes started I spent alone in my whitewashed room, in the bright meadows of Hampden. And I was happy in those first days as really I'd never been before, roaming like a sleepwalker, stunned and drunk with beauty. A group of red-cheeked girls playing soccer, ponytails flying, their shouts and laughter carrying faintly over the velvety, twilit field. Trees creaking with apples, fallen apples red on the grass beneath, the heavy sweet smell of apples rotting on the ground and the steady thrumming of wasps around them. Commons clock tower: ivied brick, white spire, spellbound in the hazy distance. The shock of first seeing a birch tree at night, rising up in the dark as cool and slim as a ghost. And the nights, bigger than imagining: black and gusty and enormous, disordered and wild with stars.

———

I was planning to sign up for Greek again, as it was the only language at which I was at all proficient. But when I told this to the academic counselor to whom I had been assigned—a French teacher named Georges Laforgue, with olive skin and a pinched, long-nostriled nose like a turtle's—he only smiled, and pressed the tips of his fingers together. "I am afraid there may be a problem," he said, in accented English.

"Why?"

"There is only one teacher of ancient Greek here and he is very particular about his students."

"I've studied Greek for two years."

"That probably will not make any difference. Besides, if you are going to major in English literature you will need a modern language. There is still space left in my Elementary French class and some room in German and Italian. The Spanish"—he consulted his list—"the Spanish classes are for the most part filled but if you like I will have a word with Mr. Delgado."

"Maybe you could speak to the Greek teacher instead."

"I don't know if it would do any good. He accepts only a limited number of students. A **very** limited number. Besides, in my opinion, he conducts the selection on a personal rather than academic basis."

His voice bore a hint of sarcasm; also a suggestion that, if it was all the same to me, he would prefer not to continue this particular conversation.

"I don't know what you mean," I said.

Actually, I thought I did know. Laforgue's answer surprised me. "It's nothing like that," he said. "Of course he is a distinguished scholar. He happens to be quite charming as well. But he has what I think are some very odd ideas about teaching. He and his students have virtually no contact with the rest of the division. I don't know why they continue to list his courses in the general catalogue—it's misleading, every year there is confusion about it—because, practically speaking, the classes are closed. I am told that to study with him one must have read the right things, hold similar views. It has happened repeatedly that he has turned away students such as yourself who

have done prior work in classics. With me"—
he lifted an eyebrow—"if the student wants to
learn what I teach and is qualified, I allow him
in my classes. Very democratic, no? It is the
best way."

"Does that sort of thing happen often here?"

"Of course. There are difficult teachers at
every school. And plenty"—to my surprise, he
lowered his voice—"and **plenty** here who are
far more difficult than him. Though I must ask
that you do not quote me on that."

"I won't," I said, a bit startled by this sudden
confidential manner.

"Really, it is quite essential that you don't."
He was leaning forward, whispering, his tiny
mouth scarcely moving as he spoke. "I must
insist. Perhaps you are not aware of this but I
have several formidable enemies in the Literature Division. Even, though you may scarcely
believe it, **here in my own department**. Besides," he continued in a more normal tone,
"he is a special case. He has taught here for
many years and even refuses payment for his
work."

"Why?"

"He is a wealthy man. He donates his salary
to the college, though he accepts, I think, one
dollar a year for tax purposes."

"Oh," I said. Even though I had been at
Hampden only a few days, I was already ac-

customed to the official accounts of financial hardship, of limited endowment, of corners cut.

"Now me," said Laforgue, "I like to teach well enough, but I have a wife and a daughter in school in France—the money comes in handy, yes?"

"Maybe I'll talk to him anyway."

Laforgue shrugged. "You can try. But I advise you not to make an appointment, or probably he will not see you. His name is Julian Morrow."

I had not been particularly bent on taking Greek, but what Laforgue said intrigued me. I went downstairs and walked into the first office I saw. A thin, sour-looking woman with tired blond hair was sitting at the desk in the front room, eating a sandwich.

"It's my lunch hour," she said. "Come back at two."

"I'm sorry. I'm just looking for a teacher's office."

"Well, I'm the registrar, not the switchboard. But I might know. Who is it?"

"Julian Morrow."

"Oh, him," she said, surprised. "What do you want with him? He's upstairs, I think, in the Lyceum."

"What room?"

"Only teacher up there. Likes his peace and quiet. You'll find him."

Actually, finding the Lyceum wasn't easy at all. It was a small building on the edge of campus, old and covered with ivy in such a manner as to be almost indistinguishable from its landscape. Downstairs were lecture halls and classrooms, all of them empty, with clean blackboards and freshly waxed floors. I wandered around helplessly until finally I noticed the staircase—small and badly lit—in the far corner of the building.

Once at the top I found myself in a long, deserted hallway. Enjoying the noise of my shoes on the linoleum, I walked along briskly, looking at the closed doors for numbers or names until I came to one that had a brass card holder and, within it, an engraved card that read JULIAN MORROW. I stood there for a moment and then I knocked, three short raps.

A minute or so passed, and another, and then the white door opened just a crack. A face looked out at me. It was a small, wise face, as alert and poised as a question; and though certain features of it were suggestive of youth—the elfin upsweep of the eyebrows, the deft lines of nose and jaw and mouth—it was by no means a young face, and the hair was snow white.

I stood there for a moment as he blinked at me.

"How may I help you?" The voice was reasonable and kind, in the way that pleasant adults sometimes have with children.

"I—well, my name is Richard Papen—"

He put his head to the side and blinked again, bright-eyed, amiable as a sparrow.

"—and I want to take your class in ancient Greek."

His face fell. "Oh. I'm sorry." His tone of voice, incredibly enough, seemed to suggest that he really was sorry, sorrier than I was. "I can't think of anything I'd like better, but I'm afraid there isn't any room. My class is already filled."

Something about this apparently sincere regret gave me courage. "Surely there must be some way," I said. "One extra student—"

"I'm terribly sorry, Mr. Papen," he said, almost as if he were consoling me on the death of a beloved friend, trying to make me understand that he was powerless to help me in any substantial way. "But I have limited myself to five students and I cannot even think of adding another."

"Five students is not very many."

He shook his head quickly, eyes shut, as if entreaty were more than he could bear.

"Really, I'd love to have you, but I mustn't

even consider it," he said. "I'm terribly sorry. Will you excuse me now? I have a student with me."

———

More than a week went by. I started my classes and got a job with a professor of psychology named Dr. Roland. (I was to assist him in some vague "research," the nature of which I never discovered; he was an old, dazed, disordered-looking fellow, a behavioralist, who spent most of his time loitering in the teachers' lounge.) And I made some friends, most of them freshmen who lived in my house. **Friends** is perhaps an inaccurate word to use. We ate our meals together, saw each other coming and going, but mainly were thrown together by the fact that none of us knew anybody—a situation which, at the time, did not seem necessarily unpleasant. Among the few people I had met who'd been at Hampden awhile, I asked what the story was with Julian Morrow.

Nearly everyone had heard of him, and I was given all sorts of contradictory but fascinating information: that he was a brilliant man; that he was a fraud; that he had no college degree; that he had been a great intellectual in the forties, and a friend to Ezra Pound and T. S. Eliot; that his family money had come from a partnership in a white-shoe banking firm or, conversely, from the purchase of foreclosed property during the Depression; that he had dodged the draft in some war (though chronologically this was difficult to compute); that he had ties with the Vatican; a deposed royal family in the Middle East; Franco's Spain. The degree of truth in any of this was, of course, unknowable but the more I heard about him, the more interested I became, and I began to watch for him and his little group of pupils around campus. Four boys and a girl, they were nothing so unusual at a distance. At close range, though, they were an arresting party—at least to me, who had never seen anything like them, and to whom they suggested a variety of picturesque and fictive qualities.

Two of the boys wore glasses, curiously enough the same kind: tiny, old-fashioned, with round steel rims. The larger of the two—and he was quite large, well over six feet—was dark-haired, with a square jaw and coarse, pale skin. He might have been handsome had his features been less set, or his eyes, behind the glasses, less expressionless and blank. He wore dark English suits and carried an umbrella (a bizarre sight in Hampden) and he walked stiffly through the throngs of hippies and beatniks and preppies and punks with the self-conscious formality of an old ballerina, surprising in one so large as he. "Henry Winter," said my friends when I pointed him out, at a distance, making a wide circle to avoid a group of bongo players on the lawn.

The smaller of the two—but not by much—was a sloppy blond boy, rosy-cheeked and gum-chewing, with a relentlessly cheery demeanor and his fists thrust deep in the pockets of his knee-sprung trousers. He wore the same jacket every day, a shapeless brown tweed that was frayed at the elbows and short in the sleeves, and his sandy hair was parted on the left, so a long forelock fell over one bespectacled eye. Bunny Corcoran was his name, Bunny being somehow short for Edmund. His voice was loud and honking, and carried in the dining halls.

The third boy was the most exotic of the set. Angular and elegant, he was precariously thin, with nervous hands and a shrewd albino face and a short, fiery mop of the reddest hair I had ever seen. I thought (erroneously) that he dressed like Alfred Douglas, or the Comte de Montesquiou: beautiful starchy shirts with French cuffs; magnificent neckties; a black greatcoat that billowed behind him as he walked and made him look like a cross between a student prince and Jack the Ripper. Once, to my delight, I even saw him wearing pince-nez. (Later, I discovered that they weren't real pince-nez, but only had glass in them, and that his eyes were a good deal sharper than my own.) Francis Abernathy was his name. Further inquiries elicited suspicion from male acquaintances, who wondered at my interest in such a person.

And then there were a pair, boy and girl. I saw them together a great deal, and at first I thought they were boyfriend and girlfriend, until one day I saw them up close and realized they had to be siblings. Later I learned they were twins. They looked very much alike, with heavy dark-blond hair and epicene faces as clear, as cheerful and grave, as a couple of Flemish angels. And perhaps most unusual in the context of Hampden—where pseudo-intellects and teenage decadents abounded, and where black clothing was **de rigueur**— they liked to wear pale clothes, particularly white. In this swarm of cigarettes and dark sophistication they appeared here and there like figures from an allegory, or long-dead celebrants from some forgotten garden party. It was easy to find out who they were, as they shared the distinction of being the only twins on campus. Their names were Charles and Camilla Macaulay.

All of them, to me, seemed highly unapproachable. But I watched them with interest whenever I happened to see them: Francis, stooping to talk to a cat on a doorstep; Henry dashing past at the wheel of a little white car, with Julian in the passenger's seat; Bunny leaning out of an upstairs window to yell something at the twins on the lawn below. Slowly, more information came my way. Francis Abernathy was from Boston and, from most accounts, quite wealthy. Henry, too, was said to be wealthy; what's more, he was a linguistic genius. He spoke a number of languages, ancient and modern, and had published a translation of Anacreon, with commentary, when he was only eighteen. (I found this out from Georges Laforgue, who was otherwise sour and reticent on the topic; later I discovered that Henry, during his freshman year, had embarrassed Laforgue badly in front of the entire literature faculty during the question-and-answer period of his annual lecture on Racine.) The twins had an apartment off campus, and were from somewhere down south. And Bunny Corcoran had a habit of playing John Philip Sousa march tunes in his room, at full volume, late at night.

Not to imply that I was overly preoccupied with any of this. I was settling in at school by this time; classes had begun and I was busy with my work. My interest in Julian Morrow and his Greek pupils, though still keen, was starting to wane when a curious coincidence happened.

It happened the Wednesday morning of my second week, when I was in the library making some Xeroxes for Dr. Roland before my eleven o'clock class. After about thirty minutes, spots of light swimming in front of my eyes, I went back to the front desk to give the Xerox key to the librarian and as I turned to leave I saw them, Bunny and the twins, sitting at a table that was spread with papers and pens and bottles of ink. The bottles of ink I remember particularly, because I was very charmed by them, and by the long black straight pens, which looked incredibly archaic and troublesome. Charles was wearing a white tennis sweater, and Camilla a sun dress with a sailor collar, and a straw hat. Bunny's tweed jacket was slung across the back of his chair, exposing several large rips and stains in the lining. He was leaning his elbows on the table, hair in eyes, his rumpled shirtsleeves held up with striped garters. Their heads were close together and they were talking quietly.

I suddenly wanted to know what they were saying. I went to the bookshelf behind their table—the long way, as if I wasn't sure what I was looking for—all the way down until I was so close I could've reached out and touched Bunny's arm. My back to them, I picked a book at random—a ridiculous sociological text, as it happened—and pretended to study the index. Secondary Analysis. Secondary Deviance. Secondary Groups. Secondary Schools.

"I don't know about that," Camilla was saying. "If the Greeks are sailing **to** Carthage, it should be accusative. Remember? Place whither? That's the rule."

"Can't be." This was Bunny. His voice was nasal, garrulous, W. C. Fields with a bad case of Long Island lockjaw. "It's not place whither, it's place to. I put my money on the ablative case."

There was a confused rattling of papers.

"Wait," said Charles. His voice was a lot like his sister's—hoarse, slightly southern. "Look at this. They're not just sailing to Carthage, they're sailing to **attack** it."

"You're crazy."

"No, they are. Look at the next sentence. We need a dative."

"Are you sure?"

More rustling of papers.

"Absolutely. **Epi tō karchidona.**"

"I don't see how," said Bunny. He sounded like Thurston Howell on "Gilligan's Island." "Ablative's the ticket. The hard ones are always ablative."

A slight pause. "Bunny," said Charles, "you're mixed up. The ablative is in Latin."

"Well, **of course**, I know that," said Bunny irritably, after a confused pause which seemed to indicate the contrary, "but you know what I mean. Aorist, ablative, all the same thing, really . . ."

"Look, Charles," said Camilla. "This dative won't work."

"Yes it will. They're sailing to attack, aren't they?"

"Yes, but the Greeks sailed over the sea **to** Carthage."

"But I put that **epi** in front of it."

"Well, we can attack and still use **epi**, but we have to use an accusative because of the first rules."

Segregation. Self. Self-concept. I looked down at the index and racked my brains for the case they were looking for. The Greeks sailed over the sea to Carthage. To Carthage. Place whither. Place whence. Carthage.

Suddenly something occurred to me. I closed the book and put it on the shelf and turned around. "Excuse me?" I said.

Immediately they stopped talking, startled, and turned to stare at me.

"I'm sorry, but would the locative case do?"

Nobody said anything for a long moment.

"Locative?" said Charles.

"Just add **zde** to **karchido**," I said. "I think it's **zde**. If you use that, you won't need a preposition, except the **epi** if they're going to war. It implies 'Carthage-ward,' so you won't have to worry about a case, either."

Charles looked at his paper, then at me. "Locative?" he said. "That's pretty obscure."

"Are you sure it exists for Carthage?" said Camilla.

I hadn't thought of this. "Maybe not," I said. "I know it does for Athens."

Charles reached over and hauled the lexicon towards him over the table and began to leaf through it.

"Oh, hell, don't bother," said Bunny stridently. "If you don't have to decline it and it doesn't need a preposition it sounds good to me." He reared back in his chair and looked up at me. "I'd like to shake your hand, stranger." I offered it to him; he clasped and shook it firmly, almost knocking an ink bottle over with his elbow as he did so. "Glad to meet you, yes, yes," he said, reaching up with the other hand to brush the hair from his eyes.

I was confused by this sudden glare of attention; it was as if the characters in a favorite painting, absorbed in their own concerns, had looked up out of the canvas and spoken to me. Only the day before Francis, in a swish of black cashmere and cigarette smoke, had brushed past me in a corridor. For a moment, as his arm touched mine, he was a creature of

flesh and blood, but the next he was a hallucination again, a figment of the imagination
stalking down the hallway as heedless of me as
ghosts, in their shadowy rounds, are said to be
heedless of the living.

Charles, still fumbling with the lexicon, rose
and offered his hand. "My name is Charles
Macaulay."

"Richard Papen."

"Oh, you're the one," said Camilla suddenly.

"What?"

"You. You came by to ask about the Greek
class."

"This is my sister," said Charles, "and this
is—Bun, did you tell him your name already?"

"No, no, don't think so. You've made me a
happy man, sir. We had ten more like this to
do and five minutes to do them in. Edmund
Corcoran's the name," said Bunny, grasping
my hand again.

"How long have you studied Greek?" said
Camilla.

"Two years."

"You're rather good at it."

"Pity you aren't in our class," said Bunny.

A strained silence.

"Well," said Charles uncomfortably, "Julian
is funny about things like that."

"Go see him again, why don't you," Bunny
said. "Take him some flowers and tell him you

love Plato and he'll be eating out of your hand."

Another silence, this one more disagreeable than the first. Camilla smiled, not exactly at me—a sweet, unfocused smile, quite impersonal, as if I were a waiter or a clerk in a store. Beside her Charles, who was still standing, smiled too and raised a polite eyebrow—a gesture which might have been nervous, might have meant anything, really, but which I took to mean **Is that all?**

I mumbled something and was about to turn away when Bunny—who was staring in the opposite direction—shot out an arm and grabbed me by the wrist. "Wait," he said.

Startled, I looked up. Henry had just come in the door—dark suit, umbrella, and all.

When he got to the table he pretended not to see me. "Hello," he said to them. "Are you finished?"

Bunny tossed his head at me. "Look here, Henry, we've got someone to meet you," he said.

Henry glanced up. His expression did not change. He shut his eyes and then reopened them, as if he found it extraordinary that someone such as myself should stand in his path of vision.

"Yes, yes," said Bunny. "This man's name is Richard—Richard what?"

"Papen."

"Yes, yes. Richard Papen. Studies Greek."

Henry brought his head up to look at me. "Not here, surely," he said.

"No," I said, meeting his gaze, but his stare was so rude I was forced to cut my eyes away.

"Oh, Henry, look at this, would you," said Charles hastily, rustling through the papers again. "We were going to use a dative or an accusative here but he suggested locative?"

Henry leaned over his shoulder and inspected the page. "Hmm, archaic locative," he said. "Very Homeric. Of course, it would be grammatically correct but perhaps a bit off contextually." He brought his head back up to scrutinize me. The light was at an angle that glinted off his tiny spectacles, and I couldn't see his eyes behind them. "Very interesting. You're a Homeric scholar?"

I might have said yes, but I had the feeling he would be glad to catch me in a mistake, and that he would be able to do it easily. "I like Homer," I said weakly.

He regarded me with chill distaste. "I love Homer," he said. "Of course we're studying things rather more modern, Plato and the tragedians and so forth."

I was trying to think of some response when he looked away in disinterest.

"We should go," he said.

Charles shuffled his papers together, stood up again; Camilla stood beside him and this time she offered me her hand, too. Side by side, they were very much alike, in similarity less of lineament than of manner and bearing, a correspondence of gesture which bounced and echoed between them so that a blink seemed to reverberate, moments later, in a twitch of the other's eyelid. Their eyes were the same color of gray, intelligent and calm. She, I thought, was very beautiful, in an unsettling, almost medieval way which would not be apparent to the casual observer.

Bunny pushed his chair back and slapped me between the shoulder blades. "Well, sir," he said, "we must get together sometime and talk about Greek, yes?"

"Goodbye," Henry said, with a nod.

"Goodbye," I said. They strolled off and I stood where I was and watched them go, walking out of the library in a wide phalanx, side by side.

———

When I went by Dr. Roland's office a few minutes later to drop off the Xeroxes, I asked him if he could give me an advance on my work-study check.

He leaned back in his chair and trained his watery, red-rimmed eyes on me. "Well, you know," he said, "for the past ten years, I've made it my practice not to do that. Let me tell you why that is."

"I know, sir," I said hastily. Dr. Roland's discourses on his "practices" could sometimes take half an hour or more. "I understand. Only it's kind of an emergency."

He leaned forward again and cleared his throat. "And what," he said, "might that be?"

His hands, folded on the desk before him, were gnarled with veins and had a bluish, pearly sheen around the knuckles. I stared at them. I needed ten or twenty dollars, needed it badly, but I had come in without first deciding what to say. "I don't know," I said. "Something has come up."

He furrowed his eyebrows impressively. Dr. Roland's senile manner was said to be a facade; to me it seemed quite genuine but sometimes, when you were off your guard, he would display an unexpected flash of lucidity, which—though it frequently did not relate to the topic at hand—was evidence that rational processes rumbled somewhere in the muddied depths of his consciousness.

"It's my car," I said, suddenly inspired. I didn't have a car. "I need to get it fixed."

I had not expected him to inquire further but instead he perked up noticeably. "What's the trouble?"

"Something with the transmission."

"Is it dual-pathed? Air-cooled?"

"Air-cooled," I said, shifting to the other foot. I did not care for this conversational turn. I don't know a thing about cars and am hard-pressed to change a tire.

"What've you got, one of those little V-6 numbers?"

"Yes."

"I'm not surprised. All the kids seem to crave them."

I had no idea how to respond to this.

He pulled out his desk drawer and began to pick things up and bring them close to his eyes and put them back in again. "Once a transmission goes," he said, "in my experience the car is gone. Especially on a V-6. You might as well take that vehicle to the junk heap. Now, myself, I've got a '98 Regency Brougham, ten years old. With me, it's regular checkups, new filter every fifteen hundred miles, and new oil every three thousand. Runs like a dream. Watch out for these garages in town," he said sharply.

"Pardon?"

He'd found his checkbook at last. "Well, you ought to go to the Bursar but I guess this'll be all right," he said, opening it and beginning to write laboriously. "Some of these places in Hampden, they find out you're from the college, they'll charge you double. Redeemed Repair is generally the best—they're a bunch of born-agains down there but they'll still shake you down pretty good if you don't keep an eye on them."

He tore out the check and handed it to me. I glanced at it and my heart skipped a beat. Two hundred dollars. He'd signed it and everything.

"Don't you let them charge you a penny more," he said.

"No sir," I said, barely able to conceal my joy. What would I do with all this money? Maybe he would even forget he had given it to me.

He pulled down his glasses and looked at me over the tops of them. "That's Redeemed Repair," he said. "They're out on Highway 6. The sign is shaped like a cross."

"Thank you," I said.

I walked down the hall with spirits soaring, and two hundred dollars in my pocket, and the first thing I did was to go downstairs to the pay phone and call a cab to take me into Hampden town. If there's one thing I'm good at, it's lying on my feet. It's sort of a gift I have.

———

And what did I do in Hampden town? Frankly, I was too staggered by my good fortune to do much of anything. It was a glorious day; I was sick of being poor, so, before I thought better of it, I went into an expensive men's shop on the square and bought a couple of shirts. Then I went down to the Salvation Army and poked around in bins for a while and found a Harris tweed overcoat and a pair of brown wingtips that fit me, also some cufflinks and a funny old tie that had pictures of men hunting deer on it. When I came out of the store I was happy to find that I still had nearly a hundred dollars. Should I go to the bookstore? To the movies? Buy a bottle of Scotch? In the end, I was so swarmed by the flock of possibilities that drifted up murmuring and smiling to crowd about me on the bright autumn sidewalk that—like a farm boy flustered by a bevy of prostitutes—I brushed right through them, to the pay phone on the corner, to call a cab to take me to school.

Once in my room, I spread the clothes on my bed. The cufflinks were beaten up and had someone else's initials on them, but they looked like real gold, glinting in the drowsy autumn sun which poured through the window and soaked in yellow pools on the oak floor—voluptuous, rich, intoxicating.

I had a feeling of déjà vu when, the next afternoon, Julian answered the door exactly as he had the first time, by opening it only a crack and looking through it warily, as if there were something wonderful in his office that needed guarding, something that he was careful not everyone should see. It was a feeling I would come to know well in the next months. Even now, years later and far away, sometimes in dreams I find myself standing before that white door, waiting for him to appear like the gatekeeper in a fairy story: ageless, watchful, sly as a child.

When he saw it was me, he opened the door slightly wider than he had the first time. "Mr. Pepin again, isn't it?" he said.

I didn't bother to correct him. "I'm afraid so."

He looked at me for a moment. "You have a wonderful name, you know," he said. "There were kings of France named Pepin."

"Are you busy now?"

"I am never too busy for an heir to the French throne if that is in fact what you are," he said pleasantly.

"I'm afraid not."

He laughed and quoted a little Greek epigram about honesty being a dangerous virtue, and, to my surprise, opened the door and ushered me in.

It was a beautiful room, not an office at all, and much bigger than it looked from outside—airy and white, with a high ceiling and a breeze fluttering in the starched curtains.

In the corner, near a low bookshelf, was a big round table littered with teapots and Greek books, and there were flowers everywhere, roses and carnations and anemones, on his desk, on the table, in the windowsills. The roses were especially fragrant; their smell hung rich and heavy in the air, mingled with the smell of bergamot, and black China tea, and a faint inky scent of camphor. Breathing deep, I felt intoxicated. Everywhere I looked was something beautiful—Oriental rugs, porcelains, tiny paintings like jewels—a dazzle of fractured color that struck me as if I had stepped into one of those little Byzantine churches that are so plain on the outside; inside, the most paradisal painted eggshell of gilt and **tesserae**.

He sat in an armchair by the window and motioned for me to sit, too. "I suppose you've come about the Greek class," he said.

"Yes."

His eyes were kind, frank, more gray than blue. "It's rather late in the term," he said.

"I'd like to study it again. It seems a shame to drop it after two years."

He arched his eyebrows—deep, mischievous—and looked at his folded hands for a moment. "I'm told you're from California."

"Yes, I am," I said, rather startled. Who had told him that?

"I don't know many people from the West," he said. "I don't know if I would like it there." He paused, looking pensive and vaguely troubled. "And what do you do in California?"

I gave him the spiel. Orange groves, failed movie stars, lamplit cocktail hours by the swimming pool, cigarettes, ennui. He listened, his eyes fixed on mine, apparently entranced by these fraudulent recollections. Never had my efforts met with such attentiveness, such keen solicitude. He seemed so utterly enthralled that I was tempted to embroider a little more than perhaps was prudent.

"How **thrilling**," he said warmly when I, half-euphoric, was finally played out. "How very romantic."

"Well, we're all quite used to it out there, you see," I said, trying not to fidget, flushed with the brilliance of my success.

"And what does a person with such a romantic temperament seek in the study of the classics?" He asked this as if, having had the good fortune to catch such a rare bird as myself, he was anxious to extract my opinion while I was still captive in his office.

"If by romantic you mean solitary and introspective," I said, "I think romantics are frequently the best classicists."

He laughed. "The great romantics are often failed classicists. But that's beside the point, isn't it? What do you think of Hampden? Are you happy here?"

I provided an exegesis, not as brief as it might have been, of why at the moment I found the college satisfactory for my purposes.

"Young people often find the country a bore," said Julian. "Which is not to say that it isn't good for them. Have you traveled much? Tell me what it was that attracted you to this place. I should think a young man such as yourself would be at a loss outside the city, but perhaps you feel tired of city life, is that so?"

So skillfully and engagingly that I was quite disarmed, he led me deftly from topic to topic, and I am sure that in this talk, which seemed only a few minutes but was really much longer, he managed to extract everything about me he wanted to know. I did not suspect that his rapt interest might spring from anything less than the very richest enjoyment of my own company, and though I found myself talking with relish on a bewildering variety of topics— some of them quite personal, and with more frankness than was customary—I was convinced that I was acting of my own volition. I wish I could remember more of what was said that day—actually, I do remember much of what **I** said, most of it too fatuous for me to recall with pleasure. The only point at which he differed (aside from an incredulous eyebrow raised at my mention of Picasso; when I came to know him better I realized that he must have thought this an almost personal affront) was on the topic of psychology, which was, after all, heavy on my mind, working for Dr. Roland and everything. "But do you really think," he said, concerned, "that one can call psychology a science?"

"Certainly. What else is it?"

"But even Plato knew that class and conditioning and so forth have an inalterable effect on the individual. It seems to me that psychology is only another word for what the ancients called fate."

"Psychology **is** a terrible word."

He agreed vigorously. "Yes, it is terrible, isn't it?" he said, but with an expression that indicated that he thought it rather tasteless of me even to use it. "Perhaps in certain ways it is a helpful construct in talking about a certain kind of mind. The country people who live around me are fascinating because their lives are so closely bound to fate that they really are predestined. But"—he laughed—"I'm afraid my students are never very interesting to me because I always know exactly what they're going to do."

I was charmed by his conversation, and despite its illusion of being rather modern and digressive (to me, the hallmark of the modern mind is that it loves to wander from its subject) I now see that he was leading me by circumlocution to the same points again and again. For if the modern mind is whimsical and discursive, the classical mind is narrow, unhesitating, relentless. It is not a quality of intelligence that one encounters frequently these days. But though I can digress with the best of them, I am nothing in my soul if not obsessive.

We talked a while longer, and presently fell silent. After a moment Julian said courteously, "If you'd like, I'd be happy to take you as a pupil, Mr. Papen."

I, looking out the window and having half-forgotten why I was there, turned to gape at him and couldn't think of a thing to say.

"However, before you accept, there are a few conditions to which you must agree."

"What?" I said, suddenly alert.

"Will you go to the Registrar's office tomorrow and put in a request to change counselors?" He reached for a pen in a cup on his desk; amazingly, it was full of Montblanc fountain pens, Meisterstücks, at least a dozen of them. Quickly he wrote out a note and handed it to me. "Don't lose it," he said, "because the Registrar never assigns me counselees unless I request them."

The note was written in a masculine, rather

nineteenth-century hand, with Greek **e**'s. The ink was still wet. "But I have a counselor," I said.

"It is my policy never to accept a pupil unless I am his counselor as well. Other members of the literature faculty disagree with my teaching methods and you will run into problems if someone else gains the power to veto my decisions. You should pick up some drop-add forms as well. I think you are going to have to drop all the classes you are currently taking, except the French, which would be as well for you to keep. You appear to be deficient in the area of modern languages."

I was astonished. "I can't drop **all** my classes."

"Why not?"

"Registration is over."

"That doesn't matter at all," said Julian serenely. "The classes that I want you to pick up will be with me. You will probably be taking three or four classes with me per term for the rest of your time here."

I looked at him. No wonder he had only five students. "But how can I do that?" I said.

He laughed. "I'm afraid you haven't been at Hampden very long. The administration doesn't like it much, but there's nothing they can do. Occasionally they try to raise problems with distribution requirements but that's never caused any real trouble. We study art, history, philosophy, all sorts of things. If I find you are deficient in a given area, I may decide to give you a tutorial, perhaps refer you to another teacher. As French is not my first language, I think it wise if you continue to study that with Mr. Laforgue. Next year I'll start you on Latin. It's a difficult language, but knowing Greek will make it easier for you. The most satisfying of languages, Latin. You will find it a delight to learn."

I listened, a bit affronted by his tone. To do what he asked was tantamount to my transferring entirely out of Hampden College into his own little academy of ancient Greek, student body five, six including me. "All my classes with you?" I said.

"Not quite all of them," he said seriously, and then laughed when he saw the look on my face. "I believe that having a great diversity of teachers is harmful and confusing for a young mind, in the same way I believe that it is better to know one book intimately than a hundred superficially," he said. "I know the modern world tends not to agree with me, but after all, Plato had only one teacher, and Alexander."

Slowly I nodded, trying as I did so to think of a tactful way to withdraw, when my eyes met his and suddenly I thought: **Why not?** I was slightly giddy with the force of his personality but the extremism of the offer was appealing as well. His students—if they were any mark of his tutelage—were imposing enough, and different as they all were they shared a certain coolness, a cruel, mannered charm which was not modern in the least but had a strange cold breath of the ancient world: they were magnificent creatures, such eyes, such hands, such looks—**sic oculos, sic ille manus, sic ora ferebat**. I envied them, and found them attractive; moreover this strange quality, far from being natural, gave every indication of having been intensely cultivated. (It was the same, I would come to find, with Julian: though he gave quite the opposite impression, of freshness and candor, it was not spontaneity but superior art which made it seem unstudied.) Studied or not, I wanted to be like them. It was heady to think that these qualities were acquired ones and that, perhaps, this was the way I might learn them.

This was all a long way from Plano, and my father's gas station. "And if I do take classes with you, will they all be in Greek?" I asked him.

He laughed. "Of course not. We'll be studying Dante, Virgil, all sorts of things. But I wouldn't advise you to go out and buy a copy of **Goodbye, Columbus**" (required, notoriously, in one of the freshman English classes) "if you will forgive me for being vulgar."

———

Georges Laforgue was disturbed when I told him what I planned to do. "This is a serious business," he said. "You understand, don't you, how limited will be your contact with the rest of the faculty and with the school?"

"He's a good teacher," I said.

"No teacher is that good. And if you should by chance have a disagreement with him, or be treated unjustly in any way, there will be nothing anyone on the faculty can do for you. Pardon me, but I do not see the point of paying a thirty-thousand-dollar tuition simply to study with one instructor."

I thought of referring that question to the Hampden College Endowment Fund, but I said nothing.

He leaned back in his chair. "Forgive me, but I should think the elitist values of such a man would be repugnant to you," he said. "Frankly, this is the first time I have ever heard of his accepting a pupil who is on such considerable financial aid. Being a democratic institution, Hampden College is not founded on such principles."

"Well, he can't be all that elitist if he accepted me," I said.

He didn't catch my sarcasm. "I am willing to

speculate that he isn't aware you are on assistance," he said seriously.

"Well, if he doesn't know," I said, "I'm not going to tell him."

———

Julian's classes met in his office. They were very small classes, and besides, no classroom could have approached it in terms of comfort, or privacy. He had a theory that pupils learned better in a pleasant, non-scholastic atmosphere; and that luxurious hothouse of a room, flowers everywhere in the dead of winter, was some sort of Platonic microcosm of what he thought a schoolroom should be. ("Work?" he said to me once, astonished, when I referred to our classroom activities as such. "Do you really think that what we do is work?"

"What else should I call it?"

"**I** should call it the most glorious kind of **play**.")

As I was on my way there for my first class, I saw Francis Abernathy stalking across the meadow like a black bird, his coat flapping dark and crowlike in the wind. He was preoccupied, smoking a cigarette, but the thought that he might see me filled me with an inexplicable anxiety. I ducked into a doorway and waited until he had passed.

When I turned on the landing of the Lyceum stairs, I was shocked to see him sitting in the windowsill. I glanced at him quickly, and then quickly away, and was about to walk into the hall when he said, "Wait." His voice was cool and Bostonian, almost British.

I turned around.

"Are you the new **neanias**?" he said mockingly.

The new young man. I said that I was.

"Cubitum eamus?"

"What?"

"Nothing."

He transferred the cigarette to his left hand and offered the right one to me. It was bony and soft-skinned as a teenage girl's.

He did not bother to introduce himself. After a brief, awkward silence, I told him my name.

He took a last drag of the cigarette and tossed it out the open window. "I know who you are," he said.

Henry and Bunny were already in the office; Henry was reading a book and Bunny, leaning across the table, was talking to him loudly and earnestly.

". . . tasteless, that's what it is, old man. Disappointed in you. I gave you credit for a little more **savoir faire** than that, if you don't mind my saying so. . . ."

"Good morning," said Francis, coming in behind me and closing the door.

Henry glanced up and nodded, then went back to his book.

"Hi," said Bunny, and then "Oh, hello there" to me. "Guess what," he continued to Francis. "Henry bought himself a Montblanc pen."

"Really?" said Francis.

Bunny nodded at the cup of sleek black pens that sat on Julian's desk. "I told him he better be careful or Julian will think he stole it."

"He was with me when I bought it," said Henry without looking up from his book.

"How much are those things worth, anyway?" said Bunny.

No answer.

"Come on. How much? Three hundred bucks a pop?" He leaned all of his considerable weight against the table. "I remember when you used to say how ugly they were. You used to say you'd never write with a thing in your life but a straight pen. Right?"

Silence.

"Let me see that again, will you?" Bunny said.

Putting his book down, Henry reached in his breast pocket and pulled out the pen and put it on the table. "There," he said.

Bunny picked it up and turned it back and forth in his fingers. "It's like the fat pencils I used to use in first grade," he said. "Did Julian talk you into getting this?"

"I wanted a fountain pen."

"That's not why you got this one."

"I am sick of talking about this."

"I think it's tasteless."

"You," said Henry sharply, "are not one to speak of taste."

There was a long silence, during which Bunny leaned back in his chair. "Now, what kind of pens do we all use here?" he said conversationally. "François, you're a nib-and-bottle man like myself, no?"

"More or less."

He pointed to me as if he were the host of a panel discussion on a talk show. "And you, what's-your-name, Robert? What sort of pens did they teach you to use in California?"

"Ball points," I said.

Bunny nodded deeply. "An honest man, gentlemen. Simple tastes. Lays his cards on the table. I like that."

The door opened and the twins came in.

"What are you yelling about, Bun?" said Charles, laughing, kicking the door shut behind him. "We heard you all the way down the hall."

Bunny launched into the story about the Montblanc pen. Uneasily, I edged into the corner and began to examine the books in the bookcase.

"How long have you studied the classics?" said a voice at my elbow. It was Henry, who had turned in his chair to look at me.

"Two years," I said.

"What have you read in Greek?"

"The New Testament."

"Well, of course you've read **Koine**," he said crossly. "What else? Homer, surely. And the lyric poets."

This, I knew, was Henry's special bailiwick. I was afraid to lie. "A little."

"And Plato?"

"Yes."

"All of Plato?"

"Some of Plato."

"But all of it in translation."

I hesitated, a moment too long. He looked at me, incredulous. **"No?"**

I dug my hands into the pockets of my new overcoat. "Most of it," I said, which was far from true.

"Most of what? The dialogues, you mean? What about later things? Plotinus?"

"Yes," I lied. I have never, to this day, read a word by Plotinus.

"What?"

Unfortunately my mind went blank, and I could not think of a single thing I knew for sure Plotinus had written. The **Eclogues**?

No, dammit, that was Virgil. "Actually, I don't much care for Plotinus," I said.

"No? Why is that?"

He was like a policeman with the questions. Wistfully, I thought of my old class, the one I'd dropped for this one: Intro to Drama, with jolly Mr. Lanin, who made us lie on the floor and do relaxation exercises while he walked around and said things like: "Now imagine that your body is filling with a cool orange fluid."

I had not answered the Plotinus question soon enough for Henry's taste. He said something rapidly in Latin.

"I beg your pardon?"

He looked at me coldly. "Never mind," he said, and bent back over his book.

To hide my consternation, I turned to the bookshelf.

"Happy now?" I heard Bunny say. "I guess you raked him over the coals pretty good, eh?"

To my intense relief, Charles came over to say hello. He was friendly and quite calm, but we had scarcely more than exchanged greetings when the door opened and a hush fell as Julian slipped in and closed the door quietly behind him.

"Good morning," he said. "You've met our new student?"

"Yes," said Francis in what I thought a bored tone, as he held out Camilla's chair and then slid into his own.

"Wonderful. Charles, would you put on water for tea?"

Charles went into a little anteroom, no bigger than a closet, and I heard the sound of running water. (I never did know exactly what was in that anteroom or how Julian, upon occasion, was miraculously able to convey four-course meals out of it.) Then he came out, closing the door behind him, and sat down.

"All right," said Julian, looking around the table. "I hope we're all ready to leave the phenomenal world, and enter into the sublime?"

———

He was a marvelous talker, a magical talker, and I wish I were able to give a better idea what he said, but it is impossible for a mediocre intellect to render the speech of a superior one—especially after so many years—without losing a good deal in the translation. The discussion that day was about loss of self, about Plato's four divine madnesses, about madness of all sorts; he began by talking about what he called the burden of the self, and why people want to lose the self in the first place.

"Why does that obstinate little voice in our heads torment us so?" he said, looking round the table. "Could it be because it reminds us that we are alive, of our mortality, of our individual souls—which, after all, we are too afraid to surrender but yet make us feel more miserable than any other thing? But isn't it also pain that often makes us most aware of self? It is a terrible thing to learn as a child that one is a being separate from all the world, that no one and no **thing** hurts along with one's burned tongues and skinned knees, that one's aches and pains are all one's own. Even more terrible, as we grow older, to learn that no person, no matter how beloved, can ever truly understand us. Our own selves make us most unhappy, and that's why we're so anxious to lose them, don't you think? Remember the Erinyes?"

"The Furies," said Bunny, his eyes dazzled and lost beneath the bang of hair.

"Exactly. And how did they drive people mad? They turned up the volume of the inner monologue, magnified qualities already present to great excess, made people so much **themselves** that they couldn't stand it.

"And how can we lose this maddening self, lose it entirely? Love? Yes, but as old Cephalus once heard Sophocles say, the least of us know that love is a cruel and terrible master. One loses oneself for the sake of the other, but in doing so becomes enslaved and miserable to the most capricious of all the gods. **War?** One can lose oneself in the joy of battle, in fighting for a glorious cause, but there are not a great many glorious causes for which to fight these days." He laughed. "Though after all your Xenophon and Thucydides I dare say there are not many young people better versed in military tactics. I'm sure, if you wanted to, you'd be quite capable of marching on Hampden town and taking it over by yourselves."

Henry laughed. "We could do it this afternoon, with six men," he said.

"How?" said everyone at once.

"One person to cut the phone and power lines, one at the bridge over the Battenkill, one at the main road out, to the north. The rest of us could advance from the south and west. There aren't many of us, but if we scattered we'd be able to close off all other points of entry"—here he held out his hand, fingers spread wide—"and advance to the center from all points." The fingers closed into a fist. "Of course, we'd have the advantage of surprise," he said, and I felt an unexpected thrill at the coldness of his voice.

Julian laughed. "And how many years has it been since the gods have intervened in human wars? I expect Apollo and Athena Nike would come down to fight at your side, 'invited or uninvited,' as the oracle at Delphi said to the Spartans. Imagine what heroes you'd be."

"Demigods," said Francis, laughing. "We could sit on thrones in the town square."

"While the local merchants paid you tribute."

"Gold. Peacocks and ivory."

"Cheddar cheese and common crackers more like it," Bunny said.

"Bloodshed is a terrible thing," said Julian hastily—the remark about the common crackers had displeased him—"but the bloodiest parts of Homer and Aeschylus are often the most magnificent—for example, that glorious speech of Klytemnestra's in the **Agamemnon** that I love so much—Camilla, you were our Klytemnestra when we did the **Oresteia**; do you remember any of it?"

The light from the window was streaming directly into her face; in such strong light most people look somewhat washed out, but her clear, fine features were only illuminated until it was a shock to look at her, at her pale and radiant eyes with their sooty lashes, at the gold glimmer at her temple that blended gradually into her glossy hair, warm as honey. "I remember a little," she said.

Looking at a spot on the wall above my head, she began to recite the lines. I stared at her. Did she have a boyfriend, Francis maybe? He and she were fairly chummy, but Francis didn't look like the sort who would be too interested in girls. Not that I stood much of a chance, surrounded as she was by all these clever rich boys in dark suits; me, with my clumsy hands and suburban ways.

Her voice in Greek was harsh and low and lovely.

> Thus he died, and all the life struggled
>   out of him;
> and as he died he spattered me with the
>   dark red
> and violent-driven rain of bitter-savored
>   blood
> to make me glad, as gardens stand among
>   the showers
> of God in glory at the birthtime of the
>   buds.

There was a brief silence after she had finished; rather to my surprise, Henry winked solemnly at her from across the table.

Julian smiled. "What a beautiful passage," he said. "I never tire of it. But how is it that such a ghastly thing, a queen stabbing her husband in his bath, is so lovely to us?"

"It's the meter," said Francis. "Iambic trimeter. Those really hideous parts of **Inferno**, for instance, Pier de Medicina with his nose hacked off and talking through a bloody slit in his windpipe—"

"I can think of worse than that," Charles said.

"So can I. But that passage is lovely and it's because of the **terza rima.** The music of it. The trimeter tolls through that speech of Klytemnestra's like a bell."

"But iambic trimeter is fairly common in Greek lyric, isn't it?" said Julian. "Why is that particular section so breathtaking? Why do we not find ourselves attracted to some calmer or more pleasing one?"

"Aristotle says in the **Poetics**," said Henry, "that objects such as corpses, painful to view in themselves, can become delightful to contemplate in a work of art."

"And I believe Aristotle is correct. After all, what are the scenes in poetry graven on our memories, the ones that we love the most? Precisely these. The murder of Agamemnon and the wrath of Achilles. Dido on the funeral pyre. The daggers of the traitors and Caesar's blood—remember how Suetonius describes his body being borne away on the litter, with one arm hanging down?"

"Death is the mother of beauty," said Henry.

"And what is beauty?"

"Terror."

"Well said," said Julian. "Beauty is rarely soft

or consolatory. Quite the contrary. Genuine beauty is always quite alarming."

I looked at Camilla, her face bright in the sun, and thought of that line from the **Iliad** I love so much, about Pallas Athene and the terrible eyes shining.

"And if beauty is terror," said Julian, "then what is desire? We think we have many desires, but in fact we have only one. What is it?"

"To live," said Camilla.

"To live for**ever**," said Bunny, chin cupped in palm.

The teakettle began to whistle.

———

Once the cups were set out, and Henry had poured the tea, somber as a mandarin, we began to talk about the madnesses induced by the gods: poetic, prophetic, and, finally, Dionysian.

"Which is by far the most mysterious," said Julian. "We have been accustomed to thinking of religious ecstasy as a thing found only in primitive societies, though it frequently occurs in the most cultivated peoples. The Greeks, you know, really weren't very different from us. They were a very formal people, extraordinarily civilized, rather repressed. And yet they were frequently swept away **en masse** by the wildest enthusiasms—dancing, frenzies, slaughter, visions—which for us, I suppose, would seem clinical madness, irreversible. Yet the Greeks—some of them, anyway—could go in and out of it as they pleased. We cannot dismiss these accounts entirely as myth. They are quite well documented, though ancient commentators were as mystified by them as we are. Some say they were the results of prayer and fasting, others that they were brought about by drink. Certainly the group nature of the hysteria had something to do with it as well. Even so, it is hard to account for the extremism of the phenomenon. The revelers were apparently hurled back into a non-rational, pre-intellectual state, where the personality was replaced by something completely different—and by 'different' I mean something to all appearances not mortal. Inhuman."

I thought of the **Bacchae**, a play whose violence and savagery made me uneasy, as did the sadism of its bloodthirsty god. Compared to the other tragedies, which were dominated by recognizable principles of justice no matter how harsh, it was a triumph of barbarism over reason: dark, chaotic, inexplicable.

"We don't like to admit it," said Julian, "but the idea of losing control is one that fascinates controlled people such as ourselves more than almost anything. All truly civilized people— the ancients no less than us—have civilized themselves through the willful repression of the old, animal self. Are we, in this room, really very different from the Greeks or the Romans? Obsessed with duty, piety, loyalty, sacrifice? All those things which are to modern tastes so chilling?"

I looked around the table at the six faces. To modern tastes they were somewhat chilling. I imagine any other teacher would've been on the phone to Psychological Counseling in about five minutes had he heard what Henry said about arming the Greek class and marching into Hampden town.

"And it's a temptation for any intelligent person, and especially for perfectionists such as the ancients and ourselves, to try to murder the primitive, emotive, appetitive self. But that is a mistake."

"Why?" said Francis, leaning slightly forward.

Julian arched an eyebrow; his long, wise nose gave his profile a forward tilt, like an Etruscan in a bas-relief. "Because it is dangerous to ignore the existence of the irrational. The more cultivated a person is, the more intelligent, the more repressed, then the more he needs some method of channeling the primitive impulses he's worked so hard to subdue. Otherwise those powerful old forces will mass and strengthen until they are violent enough to break free, more violent for the delay, often strong enough to sweep the will away entirely. For a warning of what happens in the absence of such a pressure valve, we have the example of the Romans. The emperors. Think, for example, of Tiberius, the ugly stepson, trying to live up to the command of his stepfather Augustus. Think of the tremendous, impossible strain he must have undergone, following in the footsteps of a savior, a god. The people hated him. No matter how hard he tried he was never good enough, could never be rid of the hateful self, and finally the floodgates broke. He was swept away on his perversions and he died, old and mad, lost in the pleasure gardens of Capri: not even happy there, as one might hope, but miserable. Before he died he wrote a letter home to the Senate. 'May all the Gods and Goddesses visit me with more utter destruction than I feel I am daily suffering.' Think of those who came after him. Caligula. Nero."

He paused. "The Roman genius, and perhaps the Roman flaw," he said, "was an obsession with order. One sees it in their architecture, their literature, their laws—this fierce denial of darkness, unreason, chaos." He laughed. "Easy to see why the Romans, usually so tolerant of foreign religions, persecuted the Christians mercilessly—how absurd to think a common criminal had risen from the dead, how appalling that his followers celebrated him by drinking his blood. The illogic of it frightened them and they did everything they could to crush it. In fact, I think the reason they took such drastic steps was because they were not only frightened but also terribly attracted to it. Pragmatists are often strangely superstitious. For all their logic, who lived in more abject terror of the supernatural than the Romans?

"The Greeks were different. They had a passion for order and symmetry, much like the Romans, but they knew how foolish it was to deny the unseen world, the old gods. Emotion, darkness, barbarism." He looked at the ceiling for a moment, his face almost troubled. "Do you remember what we were speaking of earlier, of how bloody, terrible things are sometimes the most beautiful?" he said. "It's a very Greek idea, and a very profound one. Beauty is terror. Whatever we call beautiful, we quiver before it. And what could be more terrifying and beautiful, to souls like the Greeks or our own, than to lose control completely? To throw off the chains of being for an instant, to shatter the accident of our mortal selves? Euripides speaks of the Maenads: head thrown back, throat to the stars, 'more like deer than human being.' To be absolutely free! One is quite capable, of course, of working out these destructive passions in more vulgar and less efficient ways. But how glorious to release them in a single burst! To sing, to scream, to dance barefoot in the woods in the dead of night, with no more awareness of mortality than an animal! These are powerful mysteries. The bellowing of bulls. Springs of honey bubbling from the ground. If we are strong enough in our souls we can rip away the veil and look that naked, terrible beauty right in the face; let God consume us, devour us, unstring our bones. Then spit us out reborn."

We were all leaning forward, motionless. My mouth had fallen open; I was aware of every breath I took.

"And that, to me, is the terrible seduction of Dionysiac ritual. Hard for us to imagine. That fire of pure being."

———

After class, I wandered downstairs in a dream, my head spinning, but acutely, achingly conscious that I was alive and young on a beautiful day; the sky a deep deep painful blue, wind scattering the red and yellow leaves in a whirlwind of confetti.

Beauty is terror. Whatever we call beautiful, we quiver before it.

That night I wrote in my journal: "Trees are schizophrenic now and beginning to lose control, enraged with the shock of their fiery new colors. Someone—was it van Gogh?—said that orange is the color of insanity. **Beauty is terror.** We want to be devoured by it, to hide ourselves in that fire which refines us."

———

I went into the post office (blasé students, business as usual) and, still preposterously lightheaded, scribbled a picture postcard to my mother—fiery maples, a mountain stream. A sentence on the back advised: **Plan to see Vermont's fall foliage between Sept. 25 and Oct. 15th when it is at its vivid best.**

As I was putting it in the out-of-town mail slot, I saw Bunny across the room, his back to me, scanning the row of numbered boxes. He stopped at what was apparently my own box and bent to stick something in it. Then he straightened surreptitiously and walked out quickly, his hands in his pockets and his hair flopping everywhere.

I waited until he was gone, then went to my mailbox. Inside, I found a cream-colored envelope—thick paper, crisp and very formal—but the handwriting was crabbed and childish as a fifth-grader's, in pencil. The note within was in pencil, too, tiny and uneven and hard to read:

Richard old Man

What do you Say we have Lunch on
Saturday, maybe about 1? I know this
Great little place. Cocktails, the business.
My treat. Please come.

Yours,
Bun

p.s. wear a Tie. I am Sure you would have
anyway but they will drag some godawful
one out of the back and meke (s.p.) you
Wear it if you Dont.

I examined the note, put it in my pocket,
and was walking out when I almost bumped
into Dr. Roland coming in the door. At first he
didn't seem to know who I was. But just when
I thought I was going to get away, the creaky
machinery of his face began to grind and a
cardboard dawn of recognition was lowered,
with jerks, from the dusty proscenium.
"Hello, Doctor Roland," I said, abandon-
ing hope.
"How's she running, boy?"
He meant my imaginary car. Christine.
Chitty-Chitty-Bang-Bang. "Fine," I said.
"Take it to Redeemed Repair?"
"Yes."

"Manifold trouble."

"Yes," I said, and then realized I'd told him earlier it was the transmission. But Dr. Roland had now begun an informative lecture concerning the care and function of the manifold gasket.

"And that," he concluded, "is one of your major problems with a foreign automobile. You can waste a lot of oil that way. Those cans of Penn State will add up. And Penn State doesn't grow on trees."

He gave me a significant look.

"Who was it sold you the gasket?" he asked.

"I can't remember," I said, swaying in a trance of boredom but edging imperceptibly towards the door.

"Was it Bud?"

"I think so."

"Or Bill. Bill Hundy is good."

"I believe it was Bud," I said.

"What did you think about that old blue jay?"

I was uncertain if this referred to Bud or to a literal blue jay, or if, perhaps, we were heading into the territory of senile dementia. It was sometimes difficult to believe that Dr. Roland was a tenured professor in the Social Science Department of this, a distinguished college. He was more like some gabby old codger who would sit next to you on a bus and try to show you bits of paper he kept folded in his wallet.

He was reviewing some of the information he had previously given me on the manifold gaskets and I was waiting for a good moment to remember, suddenly, that I was late for an appointment, when Dr. Roland's friend Dr. Blind struggled up, beaming, leaning on his walker. Dr. Blind (pronounced "Blend") was about ninety years old and had taught, for the past fifty years, a course called "Invariant Subspaces" which was noted for its monotony and virtually absolute unintelligibility, as well as for the fact that the final exam, as long as anyone could remember, had consisted of the same single yes-or-no question. The question was three pages long but the answer was always "Yes." That was all you needed to know to pass Invariant Subspaces.

He was, if possible, even a bigger windbag than Dr. Roland. Together, they were like one of those superhero alliances in the comic books, invincible, an unconquerable confederation of boredom and confusion. I murmured an excuse and slipped away, leaving them to their own formidable devices.

CHAPTER

2

I HAD HOPED the weather would be cool for my lunch with Bunny, because my best jacket was a scratchy dark tweed, but when I woke on Saturday it was hot and getting hotter.

"Gonna be a scorcher today," said the janitor as I passed him in the hall. "Indian summer."

The jacket was beautiful—Irish wool, gray with flecks of mossy green; I had bought it in San Francisco with nearly every cent I'd saved from my summer job—but it was much too heavy for a warm sunny day. I put it on and went to the bathroom to straighten my tie.

I was in no mood for talk and I was unpleasantly surprised to find Judy Poovey brushing her teeth at the sink. Judy Poovey lived a couple of doors down from me and seemed to think that because she was from Los Angeles we had a lot in common. She cornered me in hallways; tried to make me dance at parties; had told several girls that she was going to sleep with me, only in less delicate terms. She had wild clothes, frosted hair, a red Corvette with California plates bearing the legend JUDY P. Her voice was loud and rose frequently to a screech, which rang through the house like the cries of some terrifying tropical bird.

"Hi, Richard," she said, and spit out a mouthful of toothpaste. She was wearing cut-off jeans that had bizarre, frantic designs drawn on them in Magic Marker and a spandex top which revealed her intensely aerobicized midriff.

"Hello," I said, setting to work on my tie.

"You look cute today."

"Thanks."

"Got a date?"

I looked away from the mirror, at her. "What?"

"Where you going?"

By now, I was used to her interrogations. "Out to lunch."

"Who with?"

"Bunny Corcoran."

"You know Bunny?"

Again, I turned to look at her. "Sort of. Do you?"

"Sure. He was in my art history class. He's hilarious. I hate that geeky friend of his, though, the other one with the glasses, what's his name?"

"Henry?"

"Yeah, him." She leaned towards the mirror

and began to fluff out her hair, swiveling her head this way and that. Her nails were Chanel red but so long they had to be the kind you bought at the drugstore. "I think he's an asshole."

"I kind of like him," I said, offended.

"I don't." She parted her hair in the center, using the curved talon of her forefinger as a comb. "He's always been a bastard to me. I hate those twins, too."

"Why? The twins are nice."

"Oh yeah?" she said, rolling a mascaraed eye at me in the mirror. "Listen to this. I was at this party last term, really drunk, and sort of slam-dancing, right? Everybody was crashing into everybody else, and for some reason this girl twin was walking through the dance floor and pow, I slammed right into her, really hard. So then she says something rude, like totally uncalled for, and first thing I knew I'd thrown my beer in her face. It was that kind of a night. I'd already had about six beers thrown on **me**, and it just seemed like the thing to do, you know?

"So anyway, she starts yelling at me and in about half a second there's the other twin and that Henry guy standing over me like they're about to beat me up." She pulled her hair back from her face in a ponytail and inspected her profile in the mirror. "So anyway. I'm drunk, and these two guys are leaning over me in this menacing way, and you know that Henry, he's really **big**. It was kind of scary but I was too drunk to care so I just told them to fuck off." She turned from the mirror and smiled brilliantly. "I was drinking Kamikazes that night. Something terrible always happens to me when I drink Kamikazes. I wreck my car, I get into fights . . ."

"What happened?"

She shrugged and turned back to the mirror. "Like I said, I just told them to fuck off. And the boy twin, he starts **scream**ing at me. Like he really wants to kill me, you know? And that Henry just standing there, right, but to me he was scarier than the other one. So anyway. A friend of mine who used to go here and who's really tough, he was in this motorcycle gang, into chains and shit—ever heard of Spike Romney?"

I had; in fact I'd seen him at my first Friday-night party. He was tremendous, well over two hundred pounds, with scars on his hands and steel toe-clips on his motorcycle boots.

"Well, anyway, so Spike comes up and sees these people abusing me, and he shoves the twin on the shoulder and tells him to beat it, and before I knew it, the two of them had jumped on him. People were trying to pull that Henry off, too—lots of them, and they

couldn't do it. **Six guys** couldn't pull him off.
Broke Spike's collarbone and two of his ribs,
and fucked up his face pretty bad. I told Spike
he should've called the cops, but he was in
some kind of trouble himself and wasn't supposed to **be** on campus. It was a bad scene,
though." She let her hair fall back around her
face. "I mean, Spike is tough. And **mean**.
You'd think he'd be able to beat the shit out of
both those sissy guys in suits and ties and
stuff."

"Hmm," I said, trying not to laugh. It was
funny to think of Henry, with his little round
glasses and his books in Pali, breaking Spike
Romney's collarbone.

"It's weird," said Judy. "I guess when uptight
people like that get mad, they get **really** mad.
Like my father."

"Yeah, I guess so," I said, looking back into
the mirror and adjusting the knot on my tie.

"Have a good time," she said listlessly, and
started out the door. Then she stopped. "Say,
aren't you going to get hot in that jacket?"

"Only good one I have."

"You want to try on this one I've got?"

I turned and looked at her. She was a major
in Costume Design and as such had all kinds
of peculiar clothing in her room. "Is it yours?"
I said.

"I stole it from the wardrobe at the Costume

shop. I was going to cut it up and make, like, a **bustier** out of it."

Great, I thought, but I went along with her anyway.

The jacket, unexpectedly, was wonderful—old Brooks Brothers, unlined silk, ivory with stripes of peacock green—a little loose, but it fit all right. "Judy," I said, looking at my cuffs. "This is wonderful. You sure you don't mind?"

"You can have it," said Judy. "I don't have time to do anything with it. I'm too busy sewing those dammed costumes for fucking **As You Like It**. It goes up in three weeks and I don't know what I'm going to do. I've got all these freshmen working for me this term that don't know a sewing machine from a hole in the ground."

———

"By the way, love that jacket, old man," Bunny said to me as we were getting out of the taxi. "Silk, isn't it?"

"Yes. It was my grandfather's."

Bunny pinched a piece of the rich, yellowy cloth near the cuff and rubbed it back and forth between his fingers. "Lovely piece," he said importantly. "Not quite the thing for this time of year, though."

"No?" I said.

"Naw. This is the East Coast, boy. I know they're pretty **laissez-faire** about dress in your neck of the woods, but back here they don't let you run around in your bathing suit all year long. Blacks and blues, that's the ticket, blacks and blues. . . . Here, let me get that door for you. You know, I think you'll like this place. Not exactly the Polo Lounge, but for Vermont it's not too bad, do you think?"

It was a tiny, beautiful restaurant with white tablecloths and bay windows opening onto a cottage garden—hedges and trellised roses, nasturtiums bordering the flagstone path. The customers were mostly middle-aged and prosperous: ruddy country-lawyer types who, according to the Vermont fashion, wore gumshoes with their Hickey-Freeman suits; ladies with frosted lipstick and challis skirts, nice looking in a kind of well-tanned, low-key way. A couple glanced up at us as we came in, and I was well aware of the impression we were making—two handsome college boys, rich fathers and not a worry in the world. Though the ladies were mostly old enough to be my mother, one or two were actually quite attractive. Nice work if you could get it, I thought, imagining some youngish matron with a big house and nothing to do and a husband out of town on business all the time. Good dinners, some pocket money, maybe even something really big, like a car . . .

A waiter sidled up. "You have a reservation?"

"Corcoran party," said Bunny, hands in his pockets, rocking back and forth on his heels. "Where's Caspar keeping himself today?"

"On vacation. He'll be back in two weeks."

"Well, good for him," said Bunny heartily.

"I'll tell him you asked for him."

"**Do** that, wouldja?"

"Caspar's a super guy," Bunny said as we followed the waiter to the table. "Maître d'. Big old fellow with moustaches, Austrian or something. And not"—he lowered his voice to a loud whisper—"not a fag, either, if you can believe that. Queers love to work in restaurants, have you ever noticed that? I mean, **every single fag**—"

I saw the back of our waiter's neck stiffen slightly.

"—I have ever known has been obsessed with food. I wonder, why is that? Something psychological? It seems to me that—"

I put a finger to my lips and nodded at the waiter's back, just as he turned and gave us an unspeakably evil look.

"Is this table all right, **gentlemen?**" he said.

"Sure," said Bunny, beaming.

The waiter presented our menus with affected, sarcastic delicacy and stalked off. I sat down and opened the wine list, my face burning. Bunny, settling in his chair, took a sip of water and looked around happily. "This is a great place," he said.

"It's nice."

"But not the Polo." He rested an elbow on the table and raked the hair back from his eyes. "Do you go there often? The Polo, I mean."

"Not much." I'd never even heard of it, which was perhaps understandable as it was about four hundred miles from where I lived.

"Seems like the kinda place you'd go with your father," said Bunny pensively. "For man-to-man talks and stuff. My dad's like that about the Oak Bar at the Plaza. He took me and my brothers there to buy us our first drink when we turned eighteen."

I am an only child; people's siblings interest me. "Brothers?" I said. "How many?"

"Four. Teddy, Hugh, Patrick and Brady." He laughed. "It was terrible when Dad took me because I'm the baby, and it was such a big thing, and he was all 'Here, son, have your first drink' and 'Won't be long before you're sitting in my place' and 'Probably I'll be dead soon' and all that kind of junk. And the whole time there I was scared stiff. About a month before, my buddy Cloke and I had come up from Saint Jerome's for the day to work on a history project at the library, and we'd run up a huge bill at the Oak Bar and slipped off without paying. You know, boyish spirits, but there I was again, with my **dad**."

"Did they recognize you?"

"Yep," he said grimly. "Knew they would. But they were pretty decent about it. Didn't say anything, just tacked the old bill onto my dad's."

I tried to picture the scene: the drunken old father, in a three-piece suit, swishing his Scotch or whatever it was he drank around in the glass. And Bunny. He looked a little soft but it was the softness of muscle gone to flesh. A big boy, the sort who played football in high school. And the sort of son every father secretly wants: big and good-natured and not awfully bright, fond of sports, gifted at back-slapping and corny jokes. "Did he notice?" I said. "Your dad?"

"Naw. He was three sheets to the wind. If I'd of been the **bar**tender at the Oak Room he wouldn't have noticed."

The waiter was heading towards us again.

"Look, here comes Twinkletoes," said Bunny, busying himself with the menu. "Know what you want to eat?"

———

"What's in that, anyway?" I asked Bunny, leaning to look at the drink the waiter had brought him. It was the size of a small fishbowl, bright coral, with colored straws and paper parasols and bits of fruit sticking out of it at frenetic angles.

Bunny pulled out one of the parasols and licked the end of it. "Lots of stuff. Rum, cranberry juice, coconut milk, triple sec, peach brandy, creme de menthe, I don't know what all. Taste it, it's good."

"No thanks."

"C'mon."

"That's okay."

"**C'mon.**"

"No thank you, I don't want any," I said.

"First time I ever had one of these was when I was in Jamaica, two summers ago," said Bunny reminiscently. "Bartender named Sam cooked it up for me. 'Drink three of these, son,' he said, 'and you won't be able to find the door' and bless me, I couldn't. Ever been to Jamaica?"

"Not recently, no."

"Probably you're used to palm trees and coconuts and all that sort of thing, in California and all. **I** thought it was wonderful. Bought a pink bathing suit with flowers on it and everything. Tried to get Henry to come down there with me but he said there was no culture, which I don't think is true, they did have some kind of a little museum or something."

"You get along with Henry?"

"Oh, sure thing," said Bunny, reared back

in his chair. "We were roommates. Freshman year."

"And you like him?"

"Certainly, certainly. He's a hard fellow to live with, though. Hates noise, hates company, hates a mess. None of this bringing your date back to the room to listen to a couple Art Pepper records, if you know what I'm trying to get at."

"I think he's sort of rude."

Bunny shrugged. "That's his way. See, his mind doesn't work the same way yours and mine do. He's always up in the clouds with Plato or something. Works too hard, takes himself too seriously, studying Sanskrit and Coptic and those other nutty languages. Henry, I tell him, if you're going to waste your time learning something besides Greek—that and the King's English are all I think a man **needs**, personally—why don't you buy yourself some Berlitz records and brush up on your French. Find a little can-can girl or something. Voolay-voo coushay avec moi and all that."

"How many languages does he know?"

"I lost count. Seven or eight. He can read **hieroglyphics**."

"Wow."

Bunny shook his head fondly. "He's a genius, that boy. He could be a translator for the UN if he wanted to be."

"Where's he from?"

"Missouri."

He said this in such a deadpan way I thought he was joking, and I laughed.

Bunny raised an amused eyebrow. "What? You thought he was from Buckingham Palace or something?"

I shrugged, still laughing. Henry was so peculiar, it was hard to imagine him being from anyplace.

"Yep," said Bunny. "The Show-Me State. St. Louis boy like old Tom Eliot. Father's some kind of a construction tycoon—and not quite aboveboard, either, so my cousins in St. Lou tell me. Not that Henry will give you the slightest clue what his dad does. Acts like he doesn't know and certainly doesn't care."

"Have you been to his house?"

"Are you kidding? He's so secretive, you'd think it was the Manhattan Project or something. But I met his mother one time. Kind of by accident. She stopped in Hampden to see him on her way to New York and I bumped into her wandering around downstairs in Monmouth asking people if they knew where his room was."

"What was she like?"

"Pretty lady. Dark hair and blue eyes like Henry, mink coat, too much lipstick and stuff if you ask me. Awfully young. Henry's her only chick and she **adores** him." He leaned forward and lowered his voice. "Family's got money like you wouldn't **belie**ve. Millions and millions. Course it's about as new as it comes, but a buck's a buck, know what I mean?" He winked. "By the way. Meant to ask. How does your pop earn his filthy lucre?"

"Oil," I said. It was partly true.

Bunny's mouth fell open in a little round o. "You have oil wells?"

"Well, we have one," I said modestly.

"But it's a good one?"

"So they tell me."

"Boy," said Bunny, shaking his head. "The Golden West."

"It's been good to us," I said.

"Geez," Bunny said. "**My** dad's just a lousy old bank president."

I felt it necessary to change the subject, however awkwardly, as we were heading here towards treacherous waters. "If Henry's from St. Louis," I said, "how did he get to be so smart?"

This was an innocuous question but, unexpectedly, Bunny winced. "Henry had a bad accident when he was a little boy," he said. "Got hit by a car or something and nearly died. He was out of school for a couple years, had tutors and stuff, but for a long time he couldn't do much but lie in bed and read. I guess he was one of those kids who can read at college level when they're about two years old."

"Hit by a car?"

"I **think** that's what it was. Can't think what else it could've been. He doesn't like to talk about it." He lowered his voice. "Know the way he parts his hair, so it falls over the right eye? That's because there's a scar there. Almost lost the eye, can't see out of it too good. And the stiff way he walks, sort of a limp. Not that it matters, he's strong as an ox. I don't know what he did, lift **weights** or what, but he certainly built himself back up again. A regular Teddy Roosevelt, overcoming obstacles and all. You got to admire him for it." He brushed his hair back again and motioned to the waiter for another drink. "I mean, you take somebody like Francis. You ask me, he's as smart as Henry. Society boy, tons of money. He's had it too easy, though. He's lazy. Likes to play. Won't do a thing after school but drink like a fish and go to parties. Now **Henry**." He raised an eyebrow. "Couldn't beat him away from Greek with a stick— Ah, thank you, there, sir," he said to the waiter, who was holding out another of the coral-colored drinks at arm's length. "You want another?"

"I'm fine."

"Go ahead, old man. On me."

"Another martini, I guess," I said to the waiter, who had already turned away. He turned to glare at me.

"Thanks," I said weakly, looking away from his lingering, hateful smile until I was sure he had gone.

"You know, there's nothing I hate like I hate an officious fag," said Bunny pleasantly. "You ask me, I think they ought to round them all up and burn them at the stake."

I've known men who run down homosexuality because they are uncomfortable with it, perhaps harbor inclinations in that area; and I've known men who run down homosexuality and mean it. At first I had placed Bunny in the first category. His glad-handing, varsity chumminess was totally alien and therefore suspect; then, too, he studied the classics, which are certainly harmless enough but which still provoke the raised eyebrow in some circles. ("You want to know what Classics are?" said a drunk Dean of Admissions to me at a faculty party a couple of years ago. "I'll tell you what Classics are. **Wars and homos**." A sententious and vulgar statement, certainly, but like many such gnomic vulgarities, it also contains a tiny splinter of truth.)

The more I listened to Bunny, however, the more apparent it became that there was no affected laughter, no anxiety to please. Instead, there was the blithe unselfconciousness of some crotchety old Veteran of Foreign Wars—married for years, father of multitudes—who finds the topic infinitely repugnant and amusing.

"But your friend Francis?" I said.

I was being snide, I suppose, or maybe I just wanted to see how he would wriggle out of that one. Though Francis might or might not have been homosexual—and could just as easily have been a really dangerous type of ladies' man—he was certainly of that vulpine, well-dressed, unflappable sort who, to someone with Bunny's alleged nose for such things, would rouse a certain suspicion.

Bunny raised an eyebrow. "That's nonsense," he said curtly. "Who told you that?"

"Nobody. Just Judy Poovey," I said, when I saw he wasn't going to take nobody for an answer.

"Well, I can see why she'd say it but nowadays everybody's gay this and gay that. There's still such a thing as an old-fashioned mama's boy. All Francis needs is a girlfriend." He squinted at me through the tiny, crazed glasses. "And what about you?" he said, a trifle belligerently.

"What?"

"You a single man? Got some little cheer-leader waiting back home for you at Holly-wood High?"

"Well, no," I said. I didn't feel like explaining my own girlfriend problems, not to him. It was only quite recently that I had managed to extricate myself from a long, claustrophobic relationship with a girl in California whom we will call Kathy. I met her my first year of college, and was initially attracted to her because she seemed an intelligent, brooding malcontent like myself; but after about a month, during which time she'd firmly glued herself to me, I began to realize, with some little horror, that she was nothing more than a lowbrow, pop-psychology version of Sylvia Plath. It lasted forever, like some weepy and endless made-for-TV movie—all the clinging, all the complaints, all the parking-lot confessions of "inadequacy" and "poor self-image," all those banal sorrows. She was one of the main reasons I was in such an agony to leave home; she was also one of the reasons I was so wary of the bright, apparently innocuous flock of new girls I had met my first weeks of school.

The thought of her had turned me somber. Bunny leaned across the table.

"Is it true," he said, "that the gals are prettier in California?"

I started laughing, so hard I thought my drink was going to blow out my nose.

"Bathing beauties?" He winked. **"Beach Blanket Bingo?"**

"You bet."

He was pleased. Like some jolly old dog of an uncle, he leaned across the table even further and began to tell me about his own girlfriend, whose name was Marion. "I know you've seen her," he said. "Just a little thing. Blond, blue-eyed, about so high?"

Actually, this rang a bell. I had seen Bunny in the post office, in the first week of school, talking rather officiously to a girl of this description.

"Yep," said Bunny proudly, running his finger along the edge of his glass. "She's my gal. Keeps **me** in line, I can tell you."

This time, caught in mid-swallow, I laughed so hard I was close to choking.

"And she's an elementary-education major, too, don't you love it?" he said. "I mean, she's a real **girl**." He drew his hands apart, as if to indicate a sizable space between them. "Long hair, got a little meat on her bones, isn't afraid to wear a dress. I like that. Call me old-fashioned, but I don't care much for the brainy ones. Take Camilla. She's fun, and a good guy and all—"

"Come on," I said, still laughing. "She's really pretty."

"That she is, that she is," he agreed, holding up a conciliatory palm. "Lovely girl. I've always said so. Looks just like a statue of Diana in my father's club. All she lacks is a mother's firm hand, but still, for my money, she's what you call a bramble rose, as opposed to your hybrid tea. Doesn't take the pains she ought, you know. And runs around half the time in her brother's sloppy old clothes, which maybe some girls could get away with—well, frankly I don't think **any** girls can **really** get away with it, but she certainly can't. Looks too much like her brother. I mean to say, Charles is a handsome fellow and a sterling character all around, but I wouldn't want to marry him, would I?"

He was on a roll and was about to say something else; but then, quite suddenly, he stopped, his face souring as if something unpleasant had occurred to him. I was puzzled, yet a little amused; was he afraid he'd said too much, afraid of seeming foolish? I was trying to think of a quick change of subject, to let him off the hook, but then he shifted in his chair and squinted across the room.

"Look there," he said. "Think that's us? It's about time."

———

Despite the vast amount we ate that afternoon—soups, lobsters, pâtés, mousses, an array appalling in variety and amount—we
drank even more, three bottles of Taittinger on
top of the cocktails, and brandy on top of that,
so that, gradually, our table became the sole
hub of convergence in the room, around
which objects spun and blurred at a dizzying
velocity. I kept drinking from glasses which
kept appearing as if by magic, Bunny propos-
ing toasts to everything from Hampden College to Benjamin Jowett to Periclean Athens,
and the toasts becoming purpler and purpler
as time wore on until, by the time the coffee
arrived, it was getting dark. Bunny was so
drunk by then he asked the waiter to bring us
two cigars, which he did, along with the check,
face down, on a little tray.

The dim room was whirling at what was
now an incredible rate of speed, and the cigar,
so far from helping that, made me see as well
a series of luminous spots that were dark
around the edges, and reminded me unpleasantly of those horrible one-celled creatures
that I used to have to blink at through a mi-
croscope till my head swam. I put it out in the
ashtray, or what I thought was the ashtray but
was in fact my dessert plate. Bunny took off
his gold-rimmed spectacles, unhooking them

carefully from behind each ear, and began to polish them with a napkin. Without them, his eyes were small and weak and amiable, watery with smoke, crinkled at the edges with laughter.

"Ah. That was some lunch, wasn't it, old man?" he said around the cigar clamped in his teeth, holding the glasses to the light to inspect them for dust. He looked like a very young Teddy Roosevelt, sans moustache, about to lead the Rough Riders up San Juan Hill or go out and track a wildebeest or something.

"It was wonderful. Thanks."

He blew out a ponderous cloud of blue, foul-smelling smoke. "Great food, good company, lotsa drinks, couldn't ask for much more, could we? What's that song?"

"What song?"

"I want my dinner," sang Bunny, **"and conversation, and . . .** something, dum-te-dum."

"Don't know."

"I don't know, either. Ethel Merman sings it."

The light was growing dimmer and, as I struggled to focus on objects outside our immediate area, I saw the place was empty except for us. In a distant corner hovered a pale shape which I believed to be our waiter, a being obscure, faintly supernatural in aspect, yet without that preoccupied air which shadows are said to possess: we were the sole focus of its attention; I felt it concentrating towards us its rays of spectral hate.

"Uh," I said, shifting in my chair with a movement that almost made me lose my balance, "maybe we should go."

Bunny waved his hand magnanimously and turned over the check, rummaging in a pocket as he studied it. In a moment he looked up and smiled. "I say, old horse."

"Yes?"

"Hate to do this to you, but why don't you stand me lunch this time."

I raised a drunken eyebrow and laughed. "I don't have a cent on me."

"Neither do I," he said. "Funny thing. Seem to have left my wallet at home."

"Oh, come on. You're joking."

"Not at all," he said lightly. "Haven't a dime. I'd turn out my pockets for you, but Twinkle-toes'd see."

I became aware of our malevolent waiter, lurking in the shadows, no doubt listening to this exchange with interest. "How much is it?" I said.

He ran an unsteady finger down the column of figures. "Comes to two hundred and eighty-seven dollars and fifty-nine cents," he said. "That's without tip."

I was stunned at this amount, and baffled at his lack of concern. "That's a lot."

"All that booze, you know."

"What are we going to do?"

"Can't you write a check or something?" he said casually.

"I don't have any checks."

"Then put it on your card."

"I don't have a card."

"Oh, come on."

"I **don't**," I said, growing more irritated by the second.

Bunny pushed back his chair and stood up and looked around the restaurant with a studied carelessness, like a detective cruising a hotel lobby, and for one wild moment I thought he was going to make a dash for it. Then he clapped me on the shoulder. "Sit tight, old man," he whispered. "I'm going to make a phone call." And then he was off, his fists in his pockets, the white of his socks flashing in the dim.

He was gone a long time. I was wondering if he was going to come back at all, if he hadn't just crawled out a window and left me to foot the bill, when finally a door shut somewhere and he sauntered back across the room.

"Worry not, worry not," he said as he slid into his chair. "All's well."

"What'd you do?"

"Called Henry."

"He's coming?"

"In two shakes."

"Is he mad?"

"Naw," said Bunny, brushing off this thought with a slight flick of the hand. "Happy to do it. Between you and me, I think he's damned glad to get out of the house."

———

After maybe ten extremely uncomfortable minutes, during which we pretended to sip at the dregs of our ice-cold coffee, Henry walked in, a book beneath his arm.

"See?" whispered Bunny. "Knew he'd come. Oh, hello," he said, as Henry approached the table. "Boy am I glad to see—"

"Where's the check," said Henry, in a toneless and deadly voice.

"Here you are, old pal," said Bunny, fumbling among the cups and glasses. "Thanks a million. I really owe you—"

"Hello," said Henry coldly, turning to me.

"Hello."

"How are you?" He was like a robot.

"Fine."

"That's good."

"Here you go, old top," said Bunny, producing the check.

Henry looked hard at the total, his face motionless.

"Well," said Bunny chummily, his voice booming in the tense silence, "I'd apologize for dragging you away from your book if you hadn't brought it with you. What you got there? Any good?"

Without a word, Henry handed it to him. The lettering on the front was in some Oriental language. Bunny stared at it for a moment, then gave it back. "That's nice," he said faintly.

"Are you ready to go?" Henry said abruptly.

"Sure, sure," said Bunny hastily, leaping up and nearly knocking over the table. "Say the word. **Undele, undele.** Any time you want."

Henry paid the check while Bunny hung behind him like a bad child. The ride home was excruciating. Bunny, in the back seat, kept up a sally of brilliant but doomed attempts at conversation, which one by one flared and sank, while Henry kept his eyes on the road and I sat in the front beside him, fidgeting with the built-in ashtray, snapping it in and out till finally I realized how irritating this was and forced myself, with difficulty, to stop.

He stopped at Bunny's first. Bellowing a chain of incoherent pleasantries, Bunny slapped me on the shoulder and leapt out of the car. "Yes, well, Henry, Richard, here we are. Lovely. Fine. Thank you so much—beautiful lunch— well, toodle-oo, yes, yes, goodbye—" The door slammed and he shot up the walk at a rapid clip.

Once he was inside, Henry turned to me. "I'm very sorry," he said.

"Oh, no, please," I said, embarrassed. "Just a mix-up. I'll pay you back."

He ran a hand through his hair and I was surprised to see it was trembling. "I wouldn't dream of such a thing," he said curtly. "It's his fault."

"But—"

"He told you he was taking you out. Didn't he?"

His voice had a slightly accusatory note. "Well, yes," I said.

"And **just happened** to leave his wallet at home."

"It's all right."

"It's not all right," Henry snapped. "It's a terrible trick. How were you to know? He takes it on faith that whoever he's with can produce tremendous sums at a moment's notice. He never thinks about these things, you know, how awkward it is for everyone. Besides, what if I hadn't been at home?"

"I'm sure he really just forgot."

"You took a taxi there," said Henry shortly. "Who paid for that?"

Automatically I started to protest, and then

stopped cold. Bunny had paid for the taxi. He'd even made sort of a big deal of it.

"You see," said Henry. "He's not even very clever about it, is he? It's bad enough he does it to anyone but I must say I never thought he'd have the nerve to try it on a perfect stranger."

I didn't know what to say. We drove to the front of Monmouth in silence.

"Here you are," he said. "I'm sorry."

"It's fine, really. Thank you, Henry."

"Good night, then."

I stood under the porch light and watched him drive away. Then I went inside and up to my room, where I collapsed on my bed in a drunken stupor.

———

"We heard all about your lunch with Bunny," said Charles.

I laughed. It was late the next afternoon, a Sunday, and I'd been at my desk nearly all day reading the **Parmenides**. The Greek was rough going but I had a hangover, too, and I'd been at it so long that the letters didn't even look like letters but something else, indecipherable, bird footprints on sand. I was staring out the window in a sort of trance, at the meadow cropped close like bright green velvet and billowing into carpeted hills at the horizon, when

I saw the twins, far below, gliding like a pair of ghosts on the lawn.

I leaned out the window and called to them. They stopped and turned, hands shading brows, eyes screwed up against the evening glare. "Hello," they called, and their voices, faint and ragged, were almost one voice floating up to me. "Come down."

So now we were walking in the grove behind the college, down by the scrubby little pine forest at the base of the mountains, with one of them on either side of me.

They looked particularly angelic, their blond hair wind-blown, both in white tennis sweaters and tennis shoes. I wasn't sure why they'd asked me down. Though polite enough, they seemed wary and slightly puzzled, as if I were from some country with unfamiliar, eccentric customs, which made it necessary for them to take great caution in order not to startle or offend.

"How'd you hear about it?" I said. "The lunch?"

"Bun called this morning. And Henry told us about it last night."

"I think he was pretty mad."

Charles shrugged. "Mad at Bunny, maybe. Not at you."

"They don't care for each other, do they?"

They seemed astonished to hear this.

"They're old friends," said Camilla.

"Best friends, I would say," said Charles. "At one time you never saw them apart."

"They seem to argue quite a bit."

"Well, of course," said Camilla, "but that doesn't mean they're not fond of each other all the same. Henry's so serious and Bun's so sort of—well, **not** serious—that they really get along quite well."

"Yes," said Charles. "L'Allegro and Il Penseroso. A well-matched pair. I think Bunny's about the only person in the world who can make Henry laugh." He stopped suddenly and pointed into the distance. "Have you ever been down there?" he said. "There's a graveyard on that hill."

I could see it, just barely, through the pines—a flat, straggled line of tombstones, rickety and carious, skewed at such angles that they gave a hectic, uncanny effect of motion, as if some hysterical force, a poltergeist perhaps, had scattered them only moments before.

"It's old," said Camilla. "From the 1700s. There was a town there too, a church and a mill. Nothing left but foundations, but you can still see the gardens they planted. Pippin apples and wintersweet, moss roses growing where the houses were. God knows what happened up there. An epidemic, maybe. Or a fire."

"Or the Mohawks," said Charles. "You'll have to go see it sometime. The cemetery especially."

"It's pretty. Especially in the snow."

The sun was low, burning gold through the trees, casting our shadows before us on the ground, long and distorted. We walked for a long time without saying anything. The air was musty with far-off bonfires, sharp with the edge of a twilight chill. There was no noise but the crunch of our shoes on the gravel path, the whistle of wind in the pines; I was sleepy and my head hurt and there was something not quite real about any of it, something like a dream. I felt that at any moment I might start, my head on a pile of books at my desk, and find myself in a darkening room, alone.

Suddenly Camilla stopped and put a finger to her lips. In a dead tree, split in two by lightning, were perched three huge, black birds, too big for crows. I had never seen anything like them before.

"Ravens," said Charles.

We stood stock-still, watching them. One of them hopped clumsily to the end of a branch, which squeaked and bobbed under its weight and sent it squawking into the air. The other two followed, with a battery of flaps. They sailed over the meadow in a triangle formation, three dark shadows on the grass.

Charles laughed. "Three of them for three of us. That's an augury, I bet."

"An omen."

"Of what?" I said.

"Don't know," said Charles. "Henry's the ornithomantist. The bird-diviner."

"He's such an old Roman. He'd know."

We had turned towards home and, at the top of a rise, I saw the gables of Monmouth House, bleak in the distance. The sky was cold and empty. A sliver of moon, like the white crescent of a thumbnail, floated in the dim. I was unused to those dreary autumn twilights, to chill and early dark; the nights fell too quickly and the hush that settled on the meadow in the evening filled me with a strange, tremulous sadness. Gloomily, I thought of Monmouth House: empty corridors, old gas-jets, the key turning in the lock of my room.

"Well, see you later," Charles said, at the front door of Monmouth, his face pale in the glow of the porch lamp.

Off in the distance, I saw the lights in the dining hall, across Commons; could see dark silhouettes moving past the windows.

"It was fun," I said, digging my hands in my pockets. "Want to come have dinner with me?"

"Afraid not. We ought to be getting home."

"Oh, well," I said, disappointed but relieved. "Some other time."

"Well, you know . . . ?" said Camilla, turning to Charles.

He furrowed his eyebrows. "Hmnn," he said. "You're right."

"Come have dinner at our house," said Camilla, turning impulsively back to me.

"Oh, no," I said quickly.

"Please."

"No, but thanks. It's all right, really."

"Oh, come on," said Charles graciously. "We're not having anything very good but we'd like you to come."

I felt a rush of gratitude towards him. I did want to go, rather a lot. "If you're sure it's no trouble," I said.

"No trouble at all," said Camilla. "Let's go."

———

Charles and Camilla rented a furnished apartment on the third floor of a house in North Hampden. Stepping inside, one found oneself in a small living room with slanted walls and dormer windows. The armchairs and the lumpy sofa were upholstered in dusty brocades, threadbare at the arms: rose patterns on tan, acorns and oak leaves on mossy green. Everywhere were tattered doilies, dark with age. On the mantel of the fireplace (which I later discovered was inoperable) glittered a pair of lead-glass candelabra and a few pieces of tarnished silver plate.

Though not untidy, exactly, it verged on being so. Books were stacked on every available surface; the tables were cluttered with papers, ashtrays, bottles of whiskey, boxes of chocolates; umbrellas and galoshes made passage difficult in the narrow hall. In Charles's room clothes were scattered on the rug and a rich confusion of ties hung from the door of the wardrobe; Camilla's night table was littered with empty teacups, leaky pens, dead marigolds in a water glass, and on the foot of her bed was laid a half-played game of solitaire. The layout of the place was peculiar, with unexpected windows and halls that led nowhere and low doors I had to duck to get through, and everywhere I looked was some fresh oddity: an old stereopticon (the palmy avenues of a ghostly Nice, receding in the sepia distance); arrowheads in a dusty glass case; a staghorn fern; a bird's skeleton.

Charles went into the kitchen and began to open and shut cabinets. Camilla made me a drink from a bottle of Irish whiskey which stood on top of a pile of **National Geographics**.

"Have you been to the La Brea tar pits?" she said, matter-of-factly.

"No." Helplessly perplexed, I gazed at my drink.

"Imagine that. Charles," she said, into the kitchen, "he lives in California and he's never been to the La Brea tar pits."

Charles emerged in the doorway, wiping his hands on a dishtowel. **"Really?"** he said, with childlike astonishment. "Why not?"

"I don't know."

"But they're so interesting. Really, just think of it."

"Do you know many people here from California?" said Camilla.

"No."

"You know Judy Poovey."

I was startled: how did she know that? "She's not my friend," I said.

"Nor mine," she said. "Last year she threw a drink in my face."

"I heard about that," I said, laughing, but she didn't smile. "Don't believe everything you hear," she said, and took another sip of her drink. "Do you know who Cloke Rayburn is?"

I knew of him. There was a tight, fashionable clique of Californians at Hampden, mostly from San Francisco and L.A.; Cloke Rayburn was at its center, all bored smiles and sleepy eyes and cigarettes. The girls from Los

Angeles, Judy Poovey included, were fanatically devoted to him. He was the sort you saw in the men's room at parties, doing coke on the edge of the sink.

"He's a friend of Bunny's."

"How's that?" I said, surprised.

"They were at prep school together. At Saint Jerome's in Pennsylvania."

"You know Hampden," said Charles, taking a large gulp of his drink. "These progressive schools, they love the problem student, the underdog. Cloke came in from some college in Colorado after his first year. He went skiing every day and failed every class. Hampden's the last place on earth—"

"For the worst people in the world," said Camilla, laughing.

"Oh, come on now," I said.

"Well, in a way, I think it's true," said Charles. "Half the people here are here because nowhere else would let them in. Not that Hampden's not a wonderful school. Maybe that's why it's wonderful. Take Henry, for instance. If Hampden hadn't let him in, he probably wouldn't have been able to go to college at all."

"I can't believe that," I said.

"Well, it does sound absurd, but he never went past tenth grade in high school and, I mean, how many decent colleges are likely to take a tenth-grade dropout? Then there's the business of standardized tests. Henry refused to take the SATs—he'd probably score off the charts if he did, but he's got some kind of aesthetic objection to them. You can imagine how that looks to an admissions board." He took another sip of his drink. "So, how did you end up here?"

The expression in his eyes was hard to read. "I liked the catalogue," I said.

"And to the admissions board I'm sure that seemed a perfectly sensible reason for letting you in."

I wished I had a glass of water. The room was hot and my throat was dry and the whiskey had left a terrible taste in my mouth, not that it was bad whiskey; it was actually quite good, but I had a hangover and I hadn't eaten all day, and I felt, all at once, very nauseous.

There was a knock at the door and then a flurry of knocks. Without a word, Charles drained his drink and ducked back into the kitchen while Camilla went to answer it.

Before it was even open all the way I could see the glint of little round glasses. There was a chorus of hellos, and there they all were: Henry; Bunny, with a brown paper bag from the supermarket; Francis, majestic in his long black coat, clutching, with a black-gloved hand, the neck of a bottle of champagne. The last inside, he leaned to kiss Camilla—not on the cheek, but on the mouth, with a loud and satisfied smack. "Hello, dear," he said. "What a happy mistake we have made. I've got champagne, and Bunny brought stout, so we can make black and tans. What have we got to eat tonight?"

I stood up.

For a fraction of a second they were struck silent. Then Bunny shoved his paper bag at Henry and stepped forward to shake my hand. "Well, well. If it isn't my partner in crime," he said. "Haven't had enough of going out to dinner, eh?"

He slapped me on the back and started to babble. I felt hot, and rather sick. My eyes wandered around the room. Francis was talking to Camilla. Henry, by the door, gave me a small nod and a smile, nearly imperceptible.

"Excuse me," I said to Bunny. "I'll be back in just a minute."

I found my way to the kitchen. It was like a kitchen in an old person's house, with shabby red linoleum and—in keeping with this odd apartment—a door that led onto the roof. I filled a glass from the tap and bolted it, a case of too much, too quickly. Charles had the oven open and was poking at some lamb chops with a fork.

I—due largely to a rather harrowing tour my

sixth-grade class took through a meat-packing plant—have never been much of a meat eater; the smell of lamb I would not have found appealing in the best of circumstances, but it was particularly repulsive in my current state. The door to the roof was propped open with a kitchen chair, a draft blowing through the rusty screen. I filled my glass again and went to stand by the door: **deep breaths**, I thought, **fresh air, that's the ticket . . .** Charles burned his finger, cursed, and slammed the oven shut. When he turned around he seemed surprised to find me.

"Oh, hi," he said. "What is it? Can I get you another drink?"

"No, thanks."

He peered at my glass. "What've you got? Is that gin? Where did you dig that up?"

Henry appeared in the door. "Do you have an aspirin?" he said to Charles.

"Over there. Have a drink, why don't you."

Henry shook a few aspirins into his hand, along with a couple of mystery pills from his pocket, and washed them down with the glass of whiskey Charles gave him.

He had left the aspirin bottle on the counter and surreptitiously I went over and got a couple for myself, but Henry saw me do it. "Are you ill?" he said, not unkindly.

"No, just a headache," I said.

"You don't have them often, I hope?"

"What?" said Charles. "Is everybody sick?"

"Why is everybody in here?" Bunny's pained voice came booming from the hallway. "When do we eat?"

"Hold on, Bun, it'll only be a minute."

He sauntered in, peering over Charles's shoulder at the tray of chops he'd just removed from the broiler. "Looks done to me," he said, and he reached over and picked up a tiny chop by the bone end and began to gnaw on it.

"Bunny, don't, really," said Charles. "There won't be enough to go around."

"I'm starving," said Bunny with his mouth full. "Weak from hunger."

"Maybe we can save the bones for you to chew on," Henry said rudely.

"Oh, shut up."

"Really, Bun, I wish you would wait just a minute," said Charles.

"Okay," Bunny said, but he reached over and stole another chop when Charles's back was turned. A thin trickle of pinkish juice trickled down his hand and disappeared into the cuff of his sleeve.

———

To say that the dinner went badly would be an exaggeration, but it didn't go all that well, either. Though I didn't do anything stupid, exactly, or say anything that I shouldn't, I felt dejected and bilious, and I talked little and ate even less. Much of the talk centered around events to which I was not privy, and even Charles's kind parenthetical remarks of explanation did not help much to clarify it. Henry and Francis argued interminably about how far apart the soldiers in a Roman legion had stood: shoulder to shoulder (as Francis said) or (as Henry maintained) three or four feet apart. This led into an even longer argument—hard to follow and, to me, intensely boring—about whether Hesiod's primordial Chaos was simply empty space or chaos in the modern sense of the word. Camilla put on a Josephine Baker record; Bunny ate my lamb chop.

I left early. Both Francis and Henry offered to drive me home, which for some reason made me feel even worse. I told them I'd rather walk, thanks, and backed out of the apartment, smiling, practically delirious, my face burning under the collective gaze of cool, curious solicitude.

It wasn't far to school, only fifteen minutes, but it was getting cold and my head hurt and the whole evening had left me with a keen sense of inadequacy and failure which grew keener with every step. I moved relentlessly over the evening, back and forth, straining to remember exact words, telling inflections, any subtle insults or kindnesses I might've missed, and my mind—quite willingly—supplied various distortions.

When I got to my room it was silver and alien with moonlight, the window still open and the **Parmenides** open on the desk where I had left it; a half-drunk coffee from the snack bar stood beside it, cold in its styrofoam cup. The room was chilly but I didn't shut the window. Instead, I lay down on my bed, without taking off my shoes, without turning on the light.

As I lay on my side, staring at a pool of white moonlight on the wooden floor, a gust of wind blew the curtains out, long and pale as ghosts. As though an invisible hand were leafing through them, the pages of the **Parmenides** rippled back and forth.

———

I had meant to sleep only a few hours, but I woke with a start the next morning to find sunlight pouring in and the clock reading five of nine. Without stopping to shave or comb my hair or even change my clothes from the night before, I grabbed my Greek Prose composition book and my Liddell and Scott and ran to Julian's office.

Except for Julian, who always made a point of arriving a few minutes late, everyone was there. From the hall I heard them talking, but when I opened the door they all fell quiet and looked at me.

No one said anything for a moment. Then Henry said: "Good morning."

"Good morning," I said. In the clear northern light they all looked fresh, well rested, startled at my appearance; they stared at me as I ran a self-conscious hand through my disheveled hair.

"Looks like you didn't meet up with a razor this morning, chap," said Bunny to me. "Looks like—"

Then the door opened and Julian walked in.

There was a great deal to do in class that day, especially for me, being so far behind; on Tuesdays and Thursdays it might be pleasant to sit around and talk about literature, or philosophy, but the rest of the week was taken up in Greek grammar and prose composition and that, for the most part, was brutal, bludgeoning labor, labor that I—being older now, and a little less hardy—would scarcely be able to force myself to do today. I had certainly plenty to worry about besides the coldness which apparently had infected my classmates once again, their crisp air of solidarity, the cool way their eyes seemed to look right through me. There had been an opening in their ranks, but now it was closed; I was back, it seemed, exactly where I'd begun.

————

That afternoon, I went to see Julian on the pretext of talking about credit transfers, but with something very different on my mind. For it seemed, quite suddenly, that my decision to drop everything for Greek had been a rash and foolish one, and made for all the wrong reasons. What had I been thinking of? I liked Greek, and I liked Julian, but I wasn't sure if I liked his pupils or not and anyway, did I really want to spend my college career and subsequently my life looking at pictures of broken **kouroi** and poring over the Greek particles? Two years before, I had made a similar heedless decision which had plummeted me into a nightmarish, year-long round of chloroformed rabbits and day trips to the morgue, from which I had barely escaped at all. This was by no means as bad (with a shudder I remembered my old zoology lab, eight in the morning, the bobbing vats of fetal pigs), by no means—I told myself—as bad as that. But still it seemed like a big mistake, and it was too late in the term to pick up my old classes or change counselors again.

I suppose I'd gone to see Julian in order to revive my flagging assurance, in hopes he would make me feel as certain as I had that first day. And I am fairly sure he would have done just that if only I had made it in to see him. But as it happened, I didn't get to talk to him at all. Stepping onto the landing outside his office, I heard voices in the hall and stopped.

It was Julian and Henry. Neither of them had heard me come up the stairs. Henry was leaving; Julian was standing in the open door. His brow was furrowed and he looked very somber, as if he were saying something of the gravest importance. Making the vain, or rather paranoid, assumption that they might be talking about me, I took a step closer and peered as far as I could risk around the corner.

Julian finished speaking. He looked away for a moment, then bit his lower lip and looked up at Henry.

Then Henry spoke. His words were low but deliberate and distinct. "Should I do what is necessary?"

To my surprise, Julian took both Henry's hands in his own. "You should only, ever, do what is necessary," he said.

What, I thought, **the hell is going on?** I stood at the top of the stairs, trying not to make a sound, wanting to leave before they saw me but afraid to move.

To my utter, utter surprise Henry leaned

over and gave Julian a quick little businesslike
kiss on the cheek. Then he turned to leave, but
fortunately for me he looked over his shoulder
to say one last thing; I crept down the stairs as
quietly as I could, breaking into a run when I
was at the second landing and out of earshot.

———

The week that followed was a solitary and surreal one. The leaves were changing; it rained a
good deal and got dark early; in Monmouth
House people gathered around the downstairs
fireplace, burning logs stolen by stealth of
night from the faculty house, and drank warm
cider in their stocking feet. But I went straight
to my classes and straight back to Monmouth
and up the stairs to my room, bypassing all
these homey firelit scenes and hardly speaking
to a soul, even to the chummier sorts who invited me down to join in all this communal
dorm fun.

I suppose I was only a little depressed, now
the novelty of it had worn off, at the wildly
alien character of the place in which I found
myself: a strange land with strange customs
and peoples and unpredictable weathers. I
thought I was sick, though I don't believe I
really was; I was just cold all the time and unable to sleep, sometimes no more than an hour
or two a night.

Nothing is lonelier or more disorienting

than insomnia. I spent the nights reading Greek until four in the morning, until my eyes burned and my head swam, until the only light burning in Monmouth House was my own. When I could no longer concentrate on Greek and the alphabet began to transmute itself into incoherent triangles and pitchforks, I read **The Great Gatsby**. It is one of my favorite books and I had taken it out of the library in hopes that it would cheer me up; of course, it only made me feel worse, since in my own humorless state I failed to see anything except what I construed as certain tragic similarities between Gatsby and myself.

———

"I'm a survivor," the girl at the party was saying to me. She was blond and tan and too tall—almost my height—and without even asking I knew she was from California. I suppose it was something in her voice, something about the expanse of reddened, freckled skin, stretched taut over a bony clavicle and a bonier sternum and ribcage and entirely unrelieved by breasts of any sort—which presented itself to me through the lacuna of a Gaultier corselet. It was Gaultier, I knew, because she'd sort of casually let that slip. To my eyes it looked only like a wet suit, laced crudely up the front.

She was shouting at me over the music. "I guess I've had a pretty hard life, with my injury and all" (I had heard about this previously: loose tendons; dance world's loss; performance-art's gain) "but I guess I just have a very strong sense of myself, of my own needs. Other people are important to me, sure, but I always get what I want from them, you know." Her voice was brusque with the staccato Californians sometimes affect when they're trying too hard to be from New York, but there was a bright hard edge of that Golden State cheeriness, too. A Cheerleader of the Damned. She was the kind of pretty, burnt-out, vacuous girl who at home wouldn't have given me the time of day. But now I realized she was trying to pick me up. I hadn't slept with anybody in Vermont except a little red-haired girl I met at a party on the first weekend. Somebody told me later she was a paper-mill heiress from the Midwest. Now I cut my eyes away whenever we met. (The gentleman's way out, as my classmates used to joke.)

"Do you want a cigarette?" I shouted at this one.

"I don't smoke."

"I don't, either, except at parties."

She laughed. "Well, sure, give me one," she yelled in my ear. "You don't know where we can find any pot, do you?"

While I was lighting the cigarette for her, someone elbowed me in the back and I lurched forward. The music was insanely loud and people were dancing and there was beer puddled on the floor and a rowdy mob at the bar. I couldn't see much but a Dantesque mass of bodies on the dance floor and a cloud of smoke hovering near the ceiling, but I could see, where light from the corridor spilled into the darkness, an upturned glass here, a wide lipsticked laughing mouth there. As parties go, this was a nasty one and getting worse—already certain of the freshmen had begun to throw up as they waited in dismal lines for the bathroom—but it was Friday and I'd spent all week reading and I didn't care. I knew none of my fellow Greek students would be there. Having been to every Friday night party since school began, I knew they avoided them like the Black Death.

"Thanks," said the girl. She had edged into a stairwell, where things were a little quieter. Now it was possible to talk without shouting but I'd had about six vodka tonics and I couldn't think of a thing to say to her, I couldn't even remember her name.

"Uh, what's your major," I said drunkenly at last.

She smiled. "Performance art. You asked me that already."

"Sorry. I forgot."

She looked at me critically. "You ought to loosen up. Look at your hands. You're very tense."

"This is about as loose as I get," I said, quite truthfully.

She looked at me, and a light of recognition began to dawn in her eyes. "I know who you are," she said, looking at my jacket and my tie that had the pictures of the men hunting deer on it. "Judy told me all about you. You're the new guy who's studying Greek with those creepos."

"Judy? What do you mean, Judy told you about me?"

She ignored this. "You had better watch out," she said. "I have heard some weird shit about those people."

"Like what?"

"Like they worship the fucking Devil."

"The Greeks have no Devil," I said pedantically.

"Well, that's not what I heard."

"Well, so what. You're wrong."

"That's not all. I've heard some other stuff, too."

"What else?"

She wouldn't say.

"Who told you this? Judy?"

"No."

"Who, then?"

"Seth Gartrell," she said, as if that settled the matter.

As it happened, I knew Gartrell. He was a bad painter and a vicious gossip, with a vocabulary composed almost entirely of obscenities, guttural verbs, and the word "postmodernist." "That swine," I said. "You know him?"

She looked at me with a glitter of antagonism. "Seth Gartrell is my good friend."

I really had had a bit much to drink. "Is he?" I said. "Tell me, then. How does his girlfriend get all those black eyes? And does he really piss on his paintings like Jackson Pollock?"

"Seth," she said coldly, "is a genius."

"Is that so? Then he's certainly a master of deception, isn't he?"

"He is a wonderful painter. Conceptually, that is. Everybody in the art department says so."

"Well then. If **everybody** says it, it must be true."

"A lot of people don't like Seth." She was angry now. "I think a lot of people are just jealous of him."

A hand tugged at the back of my sleeve, near the elbow. I shrugged it off. With my luck it could only be Judy Poovey, trying to hit up on me as she inevitably did about this time every Friday night. But the tug came again, this time sharper and more impatient; irritably I turned, and almost stumbled backwards into the blonde.

It was Camilla. Her iron-colored eyes were all I saw at first—luminous, bemused, bright in the dim light from the bar. "Hi," she said.

I stared at her. "He**llo**," I said, trying to be nonchalant but delighted and beaming down at her all the same. "How are you? What are you doing here? Can I get you a drink?"

"Are you busy?" she said.

It was hard to think. The little gold hairs were curled in a very engaging way at her temples. "No, no, I'm not busy at all," I said, looking not at her eyes but at this fascinating area around her forehead.

"If you are, just say so," she said in an undertone, looking over my shoulder. "I don't want to drag you away from anything."

Of course: Miss Gaultier. I turned around, half-expecting some snide comment, but she'd lost interest and was talking pointedly to someone else. "No," I said. "I'm not doing a thing."

"Do you want to go to the country this weekend?"

"What?"

"We're leaving now. Francis and me. He has a house about an hour from here."

I was really drunk; otherwise I wouldn't have

just nodded and followed her without a single question. To get to the door, we had to make our way through the dance floor: sweat and heat, blinking Christmas lights, a dreadful crush of bodies. When finally we stepped outside, it was like falling into a pool of cool, still water. Shrieks and depraved music throbbed, muffled, through the closed windows.

"My God," said Camilla. "Those things are hellish. People being sick all over the place."

The pebbled drive was silver in the moonlight. Francis was standing in the shadows under some trees. When he saw us coming he stepped suddenly onto the lighted path. "Boo," he said.

We both jumped back. Francis smiled thinly, light glinting off his fraudulent pince-nez. Cigarette smoke curled from his nostrils. "Hello," he said to me, then glanced at Camilla. "I thought you'd run off," he said.

"You should have come in with me."

"I'm glad I didn't," said Francis, "because I saw some interesting things out here."

"Like what?"

"Like some security guards handing out a girl on a stretcher and a black dog attacking some hippies." He laughed, then tossed his car keys in the air and caught them with a jingle. "Are you ready?"

———

He had a convertible, an old Mustang, and we drove all the way to the country with the top down and the three of us in the front seat. Amazingly, I had never been in a convertible before, and it is even more amazing that I managed to fall asleep when both momentum and nerves should've kept me awake but I did, fell asleep with my cheek resting on the padded leather of the door, my sleepless week and the six vodka tonics hitting me as hard as an injection.

I remember little of the ride. Francis drove at a reasonable clip—he was a careful driver, unlike Henry, who drove fast and often recklessly and whose eyes were none too good besides. The night wind in my hair, their indistinct talk, the songs on the radio all mingled and blurred in my dreams. It seemed we'd been driving for only a few minutes when suddenly I was conscious of silence, and of Camilla's hand on my shoulder. "Wake up," she said. "We're here."

Dazed, half dreaming, not quite sure where I was, I shook my head and inched up in my seat. There was drool on my cheek and I wiped it off with the flat of my hand.

"Are you awake?"

"Yes," I said, though I wasn't. It was dark and I couldn't see a thing. My fingers finally closed on the door handle and only then, as I was climbing out of the car, the moon came out from behind a cloud and I saw the house. It was tremendous. I saw, in sharp, ink-black silhouette against the sky, turrets and pikes, a widow's walk.

"Geez," I said.

Francis was standing beside me, but I was scarcely aware of it till he spoke, and I was startled by the closeness of his voice. "You can't get a very good idea of it at night," he said.

"This belongs to you?" I said.

He laughed. "No. It's my aunt's. Way too big for her, but she won't sell it. She and my cousins come in the summer, and only a caretaker the rest of the year."

The entrance hall had a sweet, musty smell and was so dim it seemed almost gaslit; the walls were spidery with the shadows of potted palms and on the ceilings, so high they made my head reel, loomed distorted traces of our own shadows. Someone in the back of the house was playing the piano. Photographs and gloomy, gilt-framed portraits lined the hall in long perspectives.

"It smells terrible in here," said Francis. "Tomorrow, if it's warm, we'll air it out, Bunny gets asthma from all this dust. . . . That's my great-grandmother," he said, pointing at a photograph which he saw had caught my attention. "And that's her brother next to her—

he went down on the **Titanic**, poor thing. They found his tennis racket floating around in the North Atlantic about three weeks afterward."

"Come see the library," said Camilla.

Francis close behind us, we went down the hall and through several rooms—a lemon-yellow sitting room with gilt mirrors and chandeliers, a dining room dark with mahogany, rooms I wanted to linger in but got only a glimpse of. The piano music got closer; it was Chopin, one of the preludes, maybe.

Walking into the library, I took in my breath sharply and stopped: glass-fronted bookcases and Gothic panels, stretching fifteen feet to a frescoed and plaster-medallioned ceiling. In the back of the room was a marble fireplace, big as a sepulchre, and a globed gasolier—dripping with prisms and strings of crystal beading—sparkled in the dim.

There was a piano, too, and Charles was playing, a glass of whiskey on the seat beside him. He was a little drunk; the Chopin was slurred and fluid, the notes melting sleepily into one another. A breeze stirred the heavy, moth-eaten velvet curtains, ruffling his hair.

"Golly," I said.

The playing stopped abruptly and Charles looked up. "Well there you are," he said. "You're awfully late. Bunny's gone to sleep."

"Where's Henry?" said Francis.

"Working. He might come down before bed."

Camilla went to the piano and took a sip from Charles's glass. "You should have a look at these books," she said to me. "There's a first edition of **Ivanhoe** here."

"Actually, I think they sold that one," said Francis, sitting in a leather armchair and lighting a cigarette. "There are one or two interesting things but mostly it's Marie Corelli and old **Rover Boys**."

I walked over to the shelves. Something called **London** by somebody called Pennant, six volumes bound in red leather—massive books, two feet tall. Next to it **The Club History of London**, an equally massive set, bound in pale calfhide. The libretto of **The Pirates of Penzance**. Numberless **Bobbsey Twins**. Byron's **Marino Faliero**, bound in black leather, with the date 1821 stamped in gold on the spine.

"Here, go make your own drink if you want one," Charles was saying to Camilla.

"I don't want my own. I want some of yours."

He gave her the glass with one hand and, with the other, wobbled up a difficult backwards-and-forwards scale.

"Play something," I said.

He rolled his eyes.

"Oh, come on," said Camilla.

"No."

"Of course, he can't **really** play anything," Francis said in a sympathetic undertone.

Charles took a swallow of his drink and ran up another octave, trilling nonsensically on the keys with his right hand. Then he handed the glass to Camilla and, left hand free, reached down and turned the fibrillation into the opening notes of a Scott Joplin rag.

He played with relish, sleeves rolled up, smiling at his work, tinkling from the low ranges to the high with the tricky syncopation of a tap dancer going up a Ziegfeld staircase. Camilla, on the seat beside him, smiled at me. I smiled back, a little dazed. The ceilings had set off a ghostly echo, giving all that desperate hilarity the quality of a memory even as I sat listening to it, memories of things I'd never known.

Charlestons on the wings of airborne bi-planes. Parties on sinking ships, the icy water bubbling around the waists of the orchestra as they sawed out a last brave chorus of "Auld Lang Syne." Actually, it wasn't "Auld Lang Syne" they'd sung, the night the **Titanic** went down, but hymns. Lots of hymns, and the Catholic priest saying Hail Marys, and the first-class salon which had really looked a lot like this: dark wood, potted palms, rose silk lampshades with their swaying fringe. I really had had a bit much to drink. I was sitting sideways in my chair, holding tight to the arms **(Holy Mary, Mother of God)**, and even the floors were listing, like the decks of a foundering ship; like we might all slide to the other end with a hysterical **wheeee!** piano and all.

There were footsteps on the stair and Bunny, his eyes screwed up and his hair standing on end, tottered in wearing his pajamas. "What the hell," he said. "You woke me up." But nobody paid any attention to him, and finally he poured himself a drink and tottered back up the stairs with it, in his bare feet, to bed.

———

The chronological sorting of memories is an interesting business. Prior to this first weekend in the country, my recollections of that fall are distant and blurry: from here on out, they come into a sharp, delightful focus. It is here that the stilted mannequins of my initial acquaintance begin to yawn and stretch and come to life. It was months before the gloss and mystery of newness, which kept me from seeing them with much objectivity, would wear entirely off—though their reality was far more interesting than any idealized version could possibly be—but it is here, in my memory, that they cease being totally foreign and begin to appear, for the first time, in shapes very like their bright old selves.

I too appear as something of a stranger in these early memories: watchful and grudging, oddly silent. All my life, people have taken my shyness for sullenness, snobbery, bad temper of one sort or another. "Stop looking so superior!" my father sometimes used to shout at me when I was eating, watching television, or otherwise minding my own business. But this facial cast of mine (that's what I think it is, really, a way my mouth has of turning down at the corners, it has little to do with my actual moods) has worked as often to my favor as to my disadvantage. Months after I got to know the five of them, I found to my surprise that at the start they'd been nearly as bewildered by me as I by them. It never occurred to me that my behavior could seem to them anything but awkward and provincial, certainly not that it would appear as enigmatic as it in fact did; why, they eventually asked me, hadn't I told anyone **any**thing about myself? Why had I gone to such lengths to avoid them? (Startled, I realized my trick of ducking into doorways wasn't as clandestine as I'd thought.) And why hadn't I returned any of their invitations? Though I had believed they were snubbing me, now I realize they were only waiting, politely as maiden aunts, for me to make the next move.

At any rate, this was the weekend that things started to change, that the dark gaps between the street lamps begin to grow smaller and smaller, and farther apart, the first sign that one's train is approaching familiar territory, and will soon be passing through the well-known, well-lighted streets of town. The house was their trump card, their fondest treasure, and that weekend they revealed it to me slyly, by degrees—the dizzy little turret rooms, the high-beamed attic, the old sleigh in the cellar, big enough to be pulled by four horses, astring with bells. The carriage barn was a caretaker's house. ("That's Mrs. Hatch in the yard. She's very sweet but her husband is a Seventh-Day Adventist or something, quite strict. We have to hide all the bottles when he comes inside."

"Or what?"

"Or he'll get depressed and start leaving little tracts all over the place.")

In the afternoon we wandered down to the lake, which was shared, discreetly, by several adjoining properties. On the way they pointed out the tennis court and the old summerhouse, a mock **tholos**, Doric by way of Pompeii, and Stanford White, and (said Francis, who was scornful of this Victorian effort at classicism) D. W. Griffith and Cecil B. De

Mille. It was made of plaster, he said, and had come in pieces from Sears, Roebuck. The grounds, in places, bore signs of the geometric Victorian trimness which had been their original form: drained fish-pools; the long white colonnades of skeleton pergolas; rock-bordered parterres where flowers no longer grew. But for the most part, these traces were obliterated, with the hedges running wild and native trees—slippery elm and tamarack—outnumbering the quince and Japanese maple.

The lake, surrounded by birches, was bright and very still. Huddled in the rushes was a small wooden rowboat, painted white on the outside and blue within.

"Can we take it out?" I said, intrigued.

"Of course. But we can't all go, we'll sink."

I had never been in a boat in my life. Henry and Camilla went out with me—Henry at the oars, his sleeves rolled to the elbow and his dark jacket on the seat beside him. He had a habit, as I was later to discover, of trailing off into absorbed, didactic, entirely self-contained monologues, about whatever he happened to be interested in at the time—the Catuvellauni, or late Byzantine painting, or headhunting in the Solomon Islands. That day he was talking about Elizabeth and Leicester, I remember: the murdered wife, the royal barge, the queen on a white horse talking to the troops at Tilbury

Fort, and Leicester and the Earl of Essex holding the bridle rein. . . . The swish of the oars
and the hypnotic thrum of dragonflies blended
with his academic monotone. Camilla, flushed
and sleepy, trailed her hand in the water. Yellow birch leaves blew from the trees and
drifted down to rest on the surface. It was
many years later, and far away, when I came
across this passage in **The Waste-Land**:

> Elizabeth and Leicester
> Beating oars
> The stern was formed
> A gilded shell
> Red and gold
The brisk swell
Rippled both shores
Southwest wind
Carried down stream
The peal of bells
White towers
> Weialala leia
> Wallala leilala

We went to the other side of the lake and returned, half-blinded by the light on the water,
to find Bunny and Charles on the front porch,
eating ham sandwiches and playing cards.

"Have some champagne, quick," Bunny
said. "It's going flat."

"Where is it?"

"In the teapot."

"Mr. Hatch would be beside himself if he saw a bottle on the porch," said Charles.

They were playing Go Fish: it was the only card game that Bunny knew.

———

On Sunday I woke early to a quiet house. Francis had given my clothes to Mrs. Hatch to be laundered; putting on a bathrobe he'd lent me, I went downstairs to sit on the porch for a few minutes before the others woke up.

Outside, it was cool and still, the sky that hazy shade of white peculiar to autumn mornings, and the wicker chairs were drenched with dew. The hedges and the acres and acres of lawn were covered in a network of spider web that caught the dew in beads so that it glistened white as frost. Preparing for their journey south, the martins flapped and fretted in the eaves, and, from the blanket of mist hovering over the lake, I heard the harsh, lonely cry of the mallards.

"Good morning," a cool voice behind me said.

Startled, I turned to see Henry sitting at the other end of the porch. He was without a jacket but otherwise immaculate for such an ungodly hour: trousers knife-pressed, his white shirt crisp with starch. On the table in front of him were books and papers, a steaming espresso pot and a tiny cup, and—I was surprised to see—an unfiltered cigarette burning in an ashtray.

"You're up early," I said.

"I always rise early. The morning is the best time for me to work."

I glanced at the books. "What are you doing, Greek?"

Henry set the cup back into its saucer. "A translation of **Paradise Lost**."

"Into what language?"

"Latin," he said solemnly.

"Hmm," I said. "Why?"

"I am interested to see what I will wind up with. Milton to my way of thinking is our greatest English poet, greater than Shakespeare, but I think in some ways it was unfortunate that he chose to write in English—of course, he wrote a not inconsiderable amount of poetry in Latin, but that was early, in his student days; what I'm referring to is the later work. In **Paradise Lost** he pushes English to its very limits but I think no language without noun cases could possibly support the structural order he attempts to impose." He laid his cigarette back in the ashtray. I stared at it burning. "Will you have some coffee?"

"No, thank you."

"I hope you slept well."

"Yes, thanks."

"I sleep better out here than I usually do," said Henry, adjusting his glasses and bending back over the lexicon. There was a subtle evidence of fatigue, and strain, in the slope of his shoulders which I, a veteran of many sleepless nights, recognized immediately. Suddenly I realized that this unprofitable task of his was probably nothing more than a method of whiling away the early morning hours, much as other insomniacs do crossword puzzles.

"Are you always up this early?" I asked him.

"Almost always," he said without looking up. "It's beautiful here, but morning light can make the most vulgar things tolerable."

"I know what you mean," I said, and I did. About the only time of day I had been able to stand in Plano was the very early morning, almost dawn, when the streets were empty and the light was golden and kind on the dry grass, the chain-link fences, the solitary scrub-oaks.

Henry looked up from his books at me. "You're not very happy where you come from, are you?" he said.

I was startled at this Holmes-like deduction. He smiled at my evident discomfiture.

"Don't worry. You hide it very cleverly," he said, going back to his book. Then he looked up again. "The others really don't understand that sort of thing, you know."

He said this without malice, without empathy, without even much in the way of interest. I was not even sure what he meant, but, for the first time, I had a glimmer of something I had not previously understood: why the others were all so fond of him. Grown children (an oxymoron, I realize) veer instinctively to extremes; the young scholar is much more a pedant than his older counterpart. And I, being young myself, took these pronouncements of Henry's very seriously. I doubt if Milton himself could have impressed me more.

———

I suppose there is a certain crucial interval in everyone's life when character is fixed forever; for me, it was that first fall term I spent at Hampden. So many things remain with me from that time, even now: those preferences in clothes and books and even food—acquired then, and largely, I must admit, in adolescent emulation of the rest of the Greek class—have stayed with me through the years. It is easy, even now, for me to remember what their daily routines, which subsequently became my own, were like. Regardless of circumstance they lived like clockwork, with surprisingly little of that chaos which to me had always seemed so inherent a part of college life—irregular diet and work habits, trips to the Laundromat at one a.m. There were certain times of the day or night, even when the world was falling in, when you could always find Henry in the all-night study room of the library, or when you knew it would be useless to even look for Bunny, because he was on his Wednesday date with Marion or his Sunday walk. (Rather in the way that the Roman Empire continued in a certain fashion to run itself even when there was no one left to run it and the reason behind it was entirely gone, much of this routine remained intact even during the terrible days after Bunny's death. Up until the very end there was always, always, Sunday-night dinner at Charles and Camilla's, except on the evening of the murder itself, when no one felt much like eating and it was postponed until Monday.)

I was surprised by how easily they managed to incorporate me into their cyclical, Byzantine existence. They were all so used to one another that I think they found me refreshing, and they were intrigued by even the most mundane of my habits: by my fondness for mystery novels and my chronic movie-going; by the fact that I used disposable razors from the supermarket and cut my own hair instead of going to the barber; even by the fact that I read papers and watched news on television from time to time (a habit which seemed to them an outrageous eccentricity, peculiar to

me alone; none of them were the least bit interested in anything that went on in the world,
and their ignorance of current events and even
recent history was rather astounding. Once,
over dinner, Henry was quite startled to learn
from me that men had walked on the moon.
"No," he said, putting down his fork.

"It's true," chorused the rest, who had somehow managed to pick this up along the way.

"I don't believe it."

"I saw it," said Bunny. "It was on television."

**"How did they get there? When did this
happen?"**).

They were still overwhelming as a group,
and it was on an individual basis that I really
got to know them. Because he knew I kept late
hours, too, Henry would sometimes stop by
late at night, on his way home from the library.
Francis, who was a terrible hypochondriac and
refused to go to the doctor alone, frequently
dragged me along and it was, oddly enough,
during those drives to the allergist in Manchester or the ear-nose-and-throat man in Keene
that we became friends. That fall, he had to
have a root canal, over about four or five
weeks; each Wednesday afternoon he would
show up, white-faced and silent, at my room,
and we would go together to a bar in town and
drink until his appointment, at three. The os-
tensible purpose of my coming was so I could

drive him home when he got out, woozy with laughing gas, but as I waited for him at the bar while he went across the street to the dentist's office, I was generally in no better condition to drive than he was.

I liked the twins most. They treated me in a happy, offhand manner which implied I'd known them much longer than I had. Camilla I was fondest of, but as much as I enjoyed her company I was slightly uneasy in her presence; not because of any lack of charm or kindness on her part, but because of a too-strong wish to impress her on mine. Though I looked forward to seeing her, and thought of her anxiously and often, I was more comfortable with Charles. He was a lot like his sister, impulsive and generous, but more moody; and though he sometimes had long gloomy spells, he was very talkative when not suffering from these. In either mood, I got along with him well. We borrowed Henry's car, drove to Maine so he could have a club sandwich in a bar he liked there; went to Bennington, Manchester, the greyhound track in Pownal, where he ended up bringing home a dog too old to race, in order to save it from being put to sleep. The dog's name was Frost. It loved Camilla, and followed her everywhere: Henry quoted long passages about Emma Bovary and her greyhound: **"Sa pensée, sans but d'abord,**

vagabondait au hasard, comme sa levrette, qui faisait des cercles dans la campagne. . . ." But the dog was weak, and highly strung, and suffered a heart attack one bright December morning in the country, leaping from the porch in happy pursuit of a squirrel. This was by no means unexpected; the man at the track had warned Charles that she might not live the week; still, the twins were upset, and we spent a sad afternoon burying her in the back garden of Francis's house, where one of Francis's aunts had an elaborate cat cemetery, complete with headstones.

The dog was fond of Bunny, too. It used to go with Bunny and me on long, grueling rambles through the countryside every Sunday, over fences and streams, through bogs and pastures. Bunny was himself as fond of walks as an old dog—his hikes were so exhausting, he had a hard time finding anyone to accompany him except me and the dog—but it was because of those walks that I became familiar with the land around Hampden, the logging roads and hunter's trails, all his hidden waterfalls and secret swimming holes.

Bunny's girlfriend, Marion, was around surprisingly little; partially, I think, because he didn't want her there but also, I think, because she was even less interested in us than we were in her. ("She likes to be with her girlfriends a lot," Bunny would say boastfully to Charles and me. "They talk about clothes and boys and all that kind of malarkey. You know.") She was a small, petulant blonde from Connecticut, pretty in the same standard, round-faced way in which Bunny was handsome, and her manner of dress was at once girlish and shockingly matronly—flowered skirts, monogrammed sweaters with bags and shoes to match. From time to time I would see her at a distance in the playground of the Early Childhood Center as I walked to class. It was some branch of the Elementary Education department at Hampden; kids from the town went to nursery school and kindergarten there, and there she would be with them, in her monogrammed sweaters, blowing a whistle and trying to make them all shut up and get in line.

No one would talk about it much, but I gathered that earlier, abortive attempts to include Marion in the activities of the group had ended in disaster. She liked Charles, who was generally polite to everyone and had the unflagging capacity to carry on conversations with anyone from little kids to the ladies who worked in the cafeteria; and she regarded Henry, as did most everyone who knew him, with a kind of fearful respect; but she hated Camilla, and between her and Francis there had been some catastrophic incident which was so frightful that no one would even talk about it. She and Bunny had a relationship the likes of which I had seldom seen except in couples married for twenty years or more, a relationship which vacillated between the touching and the annoying. In her dealings with him she was very bossy and businesslike, treating him in much the same way she handled her kindergarten pupils; he responded in kind, alternately wheedling, affectionate, or sulky. Most of the time he bore her nagging patiently, but when he did not, terrible fights ensued. Sometimes he would knock on my door late at night, looking haggard and wild-eyed and more rumpled than usual, mumbling, "Lemme in, old man, you gotta help me, Marion's on the warpath. . . ." Minutes later, there would be a neat report of sharp knocks at the door: **rat-a-tat-tat**. It would be Marion, her little mouth tight, looking like a small, angry doll.

"Is Bunny there?" she would say, stretching up on tiptoe and craning to look past me into the room.

"He's not here."

"Are you sure?"

"He's not here, Marion."

"Bunny!" she would call out ominously.

No answer.

"**Bun**ny!"

And then, to my acute embarrassment, Bunny would emerge sheepishly in the doorway. "Hello, sweetie."

"Where have you been?"

Bunny would hem and haw.

"Well, I think we need to talk."

"I'm busy now, honey."

"Well"—she would look at her tasteful little Cartier watch—"I'm going home now. I'll be up for about thirty minutes and then I'm going to sleep."

"Fine."

"I'll see you in about twenty minutes, then."

"Hey, wait just a second there. I never said I was going to—"

"See you in a little while," she would say, and leave.

"I'm not going," Bunny would say.

"No, I wouldn't."

"I mean, who does she think she is."

"Don't go."

"I mean, gotta teach her a lesson sometime. I'm a busy man. On the move. My time's my own."

"Exactly."

An uneasy silence would fall. Finally Bunny would get up. "Guess I better go."

"All right, Bun."

"I mean, I'm not gonna go over to Marion's, if that's what you think," he'd say defensively.

"Of course not."

"Yes, yes," Bunny would say distractedly, and bluster away.

The next day, he and Marion would be having lunch together or walking down by the playground. "So you and Marion got everything straightened out, huh?" one of us would ask when next we saw him alone.

"Oh, yeah," Bunny would say, embarrassed.

———

The weekends at Francis's house were the happiest times. The trees turned early that fall but the days stayed warm well into October, and in the country we spent most of our time outside. Apart from the occasional, half-hearted game of tennis (overhead volley going out of court; poking dispiritedly in the tall grass with the ends of our rackets for the lost ball) we never did anything very athletic; something about the place inspired a magnificent laziness I hadn't known since childhood.

Now that I think about it, it seems while we were out there we drank almost constantly— never very much at once, but the thin trickle of spirits which began with the Bloody Marys at breakfast would last until bedtime, and that, more than anything else, was probably responsible for our torpor. Bringing a book outside to read, I would fall asleep almost immediately in my chair; when I took the boat out I soon tired

of rowing and allowed myself to drift all afternoon. (That boat! Sometimes, even now, when
I have trouble sleeping, I try to imagine that I
am lying in that rowboat, my head pillowed on
the cross-slats of the stern, water lapping hollow through the wood and yellow birch leaves
floating down to brush my face.) Occasionally,
we would attempt something a little more ambitious. Once, when Francis found a Beretta
and ammunition in his aunt's night table, we
went through a brief spate of target practice
(the greyhound, jumpy from years of the starting gun, had to be secluded in the cellar),
shooting at mason jars that were lined on a
wicker tea-table we'd dragged into the yard.
But that came to a quick end when Henry,
who was very nearsighted, shot and killed a
duck by mistake. He was quite shaken by it
and we put the pistol away.

The others liked croquet, but Bunny and I
didn't; neither of us ever quite got the hang of
it, and we always hacked and sliced at the ball
as if we were playing golf. Every now and then,
we roused ourselves sufficiently to go on a
picnic. We were always too ambitious at the
outset—the menu elaborate, the chosen spot
distant and obscure—and they invariably
ended with all of us hot and sleepy and slightly
drunk, reluctant to start the long trudge home
with the picnic things. Usually we lay around

on the grass all afternoon, drinking martinis from a thermos bottle and watching the ants crawl in a glittering black thread on the messy cake plate, until finally the martinis ran out, and the sun went down, and we had to straggle home for dinner in the dark.

It was always a tremendous occasion if Julian accepted an invitation to dinner in the country. Francis would order all kinds of food from the grocery store and leaf through cookbooks and worry for days about what to serve, what wine to serve with it, which dishes to use, what to have in the wings as a backup course should the soufflé fall. Tuxedos went to the cleaners; flowers came from the florists; Bunny put away his copy of **The Bride of Fu Manchu** and started carrying around a volume of Homer instead.

I don't know why we insisted on making such a production of these dinners, because by the time Julian arrived we were invariably nervous and exhausted. They were a dreadful strain for everyone, the guest included, I am sure—though he always behaved with the greatest good cheer, and was graceful, and charming, and unflaggingly delighted with everyone and everything—this despite the fact that he only accepted on the average about one of every three such invitations. I found myself less able to conceal the evidences of stress, in my uncomfortable borrowed tuxedo, and with my less-than-extensive knowledge of dining etiquette. The others were more practiced at this particular dissimulation. Five minutes before Julian arrived, they might be slouched in the living room—curtains drawn, dinner simmering on chafing dishes in the kitchen, everyone tugging at collars and dull-eyed with fatigue—but the instant the doorbell rang their spines would straighten, conversation would snap to life, the very wrinkles would fall from their clothes.

Though, at the time, I found those dinners wearing and troublesome, now I find something very wonderful in my memory of them: that dark cavern of a room, with vaulted ceilings and a fire crackling in the fireplace, our faces luminous somehow, and ghostly pale. The firelight magnified our shadows, glinted off the silver, flickered high upon the walls; its reflection roared orange in the windowpanes as if a city were burning outside. The whoosh of the flames was like a flock of birds, trapped and beating in a whirlwind near the ceiling. And I wouldn't have been at all surprised if the long mahogany banquet table, draped in linen, laden with china and candles and fruit and flowers, had simply vanished into thin air, like a magic casket in a fairy story.

There is a recurrent scene from those dinners

that surfaces again and again, like an obsessive undercurrent in a dream. Julian, at the head of the long table, rises to his feet and lifts his wineglass. "Live forever," he says.

And the rest of us rise too, and clink our glasses across the table, like an army regiment crossing sabres: Henry and Bunny, Charles and Francis, Camilla and I. "Live forever," we chorus, throwing our glasses back in unison.

And always, always, that same toast. Live for**ever**.

———

I wonder now that I was around them so much and yet knew so little of what was happening at the end of that term. Physically, there was very little indication that anything was happening at all—they were too clever for that— but even the tiny discrepancies that squeaked through their guard I met with a kind of willful blindness. That is to say: I wanted to maintain the illusion that their dealings with me were completely straightforward; that we were all friends, and no secrets, though the plain fact of it was that there were plenty of things they didn't let me in on and would not for some time. And though I tried to ignore this I was aware of it all the same. I knew, for instance, that the five of them sometimes did things—what, exactly, I didn't know—without inviting me, and that if put on the spot they would all stick together and lie about it, in a casual and quite convincing fashion. They were so convincing, in fact, so faultlessly orchestrated in the variations and counterpoint of falsehood (the twins' unblinking carelessness striking a bright true note against Bunny's tomfoolery, or Henry's bored irritation at rehashing a trivial sequence of events) that I usually found myself believing them, often against evidence to the contrary.

Of course, I can see traces of what went on—to their credit, quite small traces—in retrospect; in the way they would sometimes disappear, very mysteriously, and hours later be vague about their whereabouts; in private jokes, asides in Greek or even Latin which I was well aware were meant to go over my head. Naturally, I disliked this, but there seemed nothing alarming or unusual about it; though some of those casual remarks and private jokes assumed a horrific significance much later. Towards the end of that term, for instance, Bunny had a maddening habit of breaking out into choruses of "The Farmer in the Dell"; I found it merely annoying and could not understand the violent agitation to which it provoked the rest of them: not knowing then, as I do now, that it must have chilled them all to the bone.

Of course I noticed things. I suppose, being

around them as much as I was, it would have been impossible not to. But they were mostly quirks, discrepancies, most of them so minor that it will perhaps show you how little reason I had to imagine that anything was wrong. For instance: All five of them seemed unusually accident-prone. They were always getting scratched by cats, or cutting themselves shaving, or stumbling over footstools in the dark—reasonable explanations, certainly, but for sedentary people they had an odd excess of bruises and small wounds. There was also a strange preoccupation with the weather; strange, to me, because none of them seemed to be involved in activity which might be aided or impeded by weather of any sort. And yet they were obsessed with it, Henry in particular. He was concerned, primarily, with rapid drops in temperature; sometimes, in the car, he would punch around as frantically on the radio as a sea captain before a storm, searching for barometric readings, long-range forecasts, data of any sort. The news that the mercury was sinking would plunge him into a sudden, inexplicable gloom. I wondered what he would do when winter came; but by the first snowfall, the preoccupation had vanished, never to return.

Little things. I remember waking up once in the country at six o'clock, while everyone was still in bed, and going downstairs to find the kitchen floors freshly washed, still wet, immaculate except for the bare, mysterious footprint of a Man Friday in the clean sandbank between water heater and porch. Sometimes I woke nights out there, half-dreaming, but vaguely conscious of something; muffled voices, movement, the greyhound whining softly and pawing at my bedroom door. . . . Once I heard a muttered exchange between the twins about some bed sheets. "Silly," Camilla was whispering—and I caught a glimpse of ragged, fluttering cloth, streaked with mud—"you took the wrong ones. We can't bring them back like this."

"We'll substitute the others."

"But they'll know. The Linen Service ones have a stamp. We'll have to say we lost them."

Though this exchange did not remain in my mind for long, I was puzzled, and even more so by the twins' unsatisfactory manner when I asked about it. Another oddity was my discovery, one afternoon, of a large copper pot bubbling on the back burner of the stove, a peculiar smell emanating from it. I lifted the lid and a cloud of pungent, bitter steam hit me in the face. The pot was filled with limp, almond-shaped leaves, boiling away in about half a gallon of blackish water. What in God's name, I thought, perplexed but also amused, and when I asked Francis he said, curtly, "For my bath."

It is easy to see things in retrospect. But I was ignorant then of everything but my own happiness, and I don't know what else to say except that life itself seemed very magical in those days: a web of symbol, coincidence, premonition, omen. Everything, somehow, fit together; some sly and benevolent Providence was revealing itself by degrees and I felt myself trembling on the brink of a fabulous discovery, as though any morning it was all going to come together—my future, my past, the whole of my life—and I was going to sit up in bed like a thunderbolt and say **oh! oh! oh!**

We had so many happy days in the country that fall that from this vantage they merge into a sweet and indistinct blur. Around Halloween the last, stubborn wildflowers died away and the wind became sharp and gusty, blowing showers of yellow leaves on the gray, wrinkled surface of the lake. On those chill afternoons when the sky was like lead and the clouds were racing, we stayed in the library, banking huge fires to keep warm. Bare willows clicked on the windowpanes like skeleton fingers. While the twins played cards at one end of the table, and Henry worked at the other, Francis sat curled in the window seat with a plate of little sand-

wiches in his lap, reading, in French, the
Mémoires of the Duc de Saint-Simon, which
for some reason he was determined to get
through. He had gone to several schools in Europe and spoke excellent French, though he
pronounced it with the same lazy, snob accent
as his English; sometimes I got him to help me
with my own lessons in first-year French,
tedious little stories about Marie and Jean-
Claude going to the **tabac**, which he read
aloud in a languishing, hilarious drawl (**"Marie
a apporté des légumes à son frère"**) that sent
everyone into hysterics. Bunny lay on his
stomach on the hearth rug, doing his homework; occasionally he would steal one of Francis's sandwiches or ask a pained question.
Though Greek gave him so much trouble, he'd
actually studied it far longer than any of the
rest of us, since he was twelve, a circumstance
about which he perpetually boasted. He suggested slyly that this had simply been a childish whim of his, a manifestation of early genius
à la Alexander Pope; but the truth of the matter (as I learned from Henry) was that he suffered from fairly severe dyslexia and the Greek
had been a mandatory course of therapy, his
prep school having theorized it was good to
force dyslexic students to study languages like
Greek, Hebrew, and Russian, which did not
utilize the Roman alphabet. At any rate, his

talent as a linguist was considerably less than he led one to believe, and he was unable to wade through even the simplest assignments without continual questions, complaints, and infusions of food. Towards the end of term he had a flare-up of asthma and wandered wheezing around the house in pajamas and bathrobe, hair standing on end, gasping theatrically at his inhaler. The pills he took for it (I was informed, behind his back) made him irritable, kept him up at night, made him gain weight. And I accepted this explanation for much of Bunny's crabbiness at the end of the term, which subsequently I was to find was due to entirely different reasons.

What should I tell you? About the Saturday in December that Bunny ran around the house at five in the morning, yelling "First snow!" and pouncing on our beds? Or the time Camilla tried to teach me the box step; or the time Bunny turned the boat over—with Henry and Francis in it—because he thought he saw a water snake? About Henry's birthday party, or about the two instances when Francis's mother—all red hair and alligator pumps and emeralds—turned up on her way to New York, trailing the Yorkshire terrier and the second husband? (She was a wild card, that mother of his; and Chris, her new husband, was a bit player in a soap opera, barely older than Francis. Olivia was her name. At the time I first met her, she had just been released from the Betty Ford Center after having been cured of alcoholism and an unspecified drug habit, and was launching merrily down the path of sin again. Charles once told me that she had knocked on his door in the middle of the night and asked if he would care to join her and Chris in bed. I still get cards from her at Christmas.)

One day, however, remains particularly vivid, a brilliant Saturday in October, one of the last summery days we had that year. The night before—which had been rather cold—we'd stayed up drinking and talking till almost dawn, and I woke late, hot and vaguely nauseated, to find my blankets kicked to the foot of the bed and sun pouring through the window. I lay very still for a long time. The sun filtered through my eyelids a bright, painful red, and my damp legs prickled with the heat. Beneath me, the house was silent, shimmering and oppressive.

I made my way downstairs, my feet creaking on the steps. The house was motionless, empty. Finally I found Francis and Bunny on the shady side of the porch. Bunny had on a T-shirt and a pair of Bermuda shorts; Francis, his face flushed a blotchy albino pink, and his eyelids closed and almost fluttering with pain, was wearing a ratty terry-cloth bathrobe that was stolen from a hotel.

They were drinking prairie oysters. Francis pushed his over to me without looking at it. "Here, drink this," he said, "I'll be sick if I look at it another second."

The yolk quivered, gently, in its bloody bath of ketchup and Worcestershire. "**I** don't want it," I said, and pushed it back.

He crossed his legs and pinched the bridge of his nose between thumb and forefinger. "I don't know why I make these things," he said. "They never work. I have to go get some Alka-Seltzer."

Charles closed the screen door behind him and wandered listlessly onto the porch in his red-striped bathrobe. "What you need," he said, "is an ice-cream float."

"You and your ice-cream floats."

"They **work**, I tell you. It's very scientific. Cold things are good for nausea and—"

"You're always saying that, Charles, but I just don't think it's true."

"Would you just listen to me for a second? The ice cream slows down your digestion. The Coke settles your stomach and the caffeine cures your headache. Sugar gives you energy. And besides, it makes you metabolize the alcohol faster. It's the perfect food."

"Go make me one, would you?" said Bunny.

"Go make it yourself," said Charles, suddenly irritable.

"Really," Francis said, "I think I just need an Alka-Seltzer."

Henry—who had been up, and dressed, since the first wink of dawn—came down shortly, followed by a sleepy Camilla, damp and flushed from her bath, and her gold chrysanthemum of a head curled and chaotic. It was almost two in the afternoon. The greyhound lay on its side, drowsing, one chestnut-colored eye only partly closed and rolling grotesquely in the socket.

There was no Alka-Seltzer, so Francis went in and got a bottle of ginger ale and some glasses and ice and we sat for a while as the afternoon got brighter and hotter. Camilla—who was rarely content to sit still but was always itching to do something, anything, play cards, go for a picnic or a drive—was bored and restless, and made no secret of it. She had a book, but she wasn't reading; her legs were thrown over the arm of her chair, one bare heel kicking, with obstinate, lethargic rhythm, at the wicker side. Finally, as much to humor her as anything, Francis suggested a walk to the lake. This cheered her instantly. There was nothing else to do, so Henry and I decided to go along. Charles and Bunny were asleep, and snoring in their chairs.

The sky was a fierce, burning blue, the trees ferocious shades of red and yellow. Francis, barefoot and still in his bathrobe, stepped precariously over rocks and branches, balancing his glass of ginger ale. Once we got to the lake he waded in, up to his knees, and beckoned dramatically like Saint John the Baptist.

We took off our shoes and socks. The water near the bank was a clear, pale green, cool over my ankles, and the pebbles at the bottom were dappled with sunlight. Henry, in coat and tie, waded out to where Francis stood, his trousers rolled to the knee, an old-fashioned banker in a surrealist painting. A wind rustled through the birches, blowing up the pale undersides of the leaves, and it caught in Camilla's dress and billowed it out like a white balloon. She laughed, and smoothed it down quickly, only to have it blow out again.

The two of us walked near the shore, in the shallows barely covering our feet. The sun shimmered off the lake in bright waves—it didn't look like a real lake but a mirage in the Sahara. Henry and Francis were further out: Francis talking, gesticulating wildly in his white robe and Henry with his hands clasped behind his back, Satan listening patiently to the rantings of some desert prophet.

We walked a good distance around the lake's edge, she and I, then started back. Camilla, one hand shading her light-dazzled eyes, was telling me a long story about something the dog had done—chewing up a sheepskin rug that belonged to the landlord, their efforts to disguise and finally to destroy the evidence— but I wasn't following her very closely: she looked so much like her brother, yet his straightforward, uncompromising good looks were almost magical when repeated, with only slight variations, in her. She was a living reverie for me: the mere sight of her sparked an almost infinite range of fantasy, from Greek to Gothic, from vulgar to divine.

I was looking at the side of her face, listening to the sweet, throaty cadences of her voice, when I was jolted from my musing by a sharp exclamation. She stopped.

"What is it?"

She was staring down at the water. "Look."

In the water, a dark plume of blood blossomed by her foot; as I blinked, a thin red tendril spiraled up and curled over her pale toes, undulating in the water like a thread of crimson smoke.

"Jesus, what did you do?"

"I don't know. I stepped on something sharp." She put a hand on my shoulder and I held her by the waist. There was a shard of green glass, about three inches long, stuck in her foot just above the arch. The blood pulsed thickly with her heartbeat; the glass, stained with red, glittered wickedly in the sun.

"What is it?" she said, trying to lean over to see. "Is it bad?"

She had cut an artery. The blood was spurting out strong and fast.

"Francis?" I yelled. "Henry?"

"Mother of God," said Francis when he got close enough to see, and started splashing towards us, holding the skirt of his robe out of the water with one hand. "What have you done to yourself? Can you walk? Let me see," he said, out of breath.

Camilla tightened her grip on my arm. The bottom of her foot was glazed with red. Fat droplets ticked off the edge, spreading and dispersing like drops of ink in the clear water.

"Oh, God," said Francis, closing his eyes. "Does it hurt?"

"No," she said briskly, but I knew it did; I could feel her trembling and her face had gone white.

Suddenly Henry was there, too, leaning over her. "Put your arm around my neck," he said; deftly he whisked her up, as lightly as if she were made of straw, one arm under her head and the other beneath her knees. "Francis, run get the first-aid kit out of your car. We'll meet you halfway."

"All right," said Francis, glad to be told what to do, and started splashing for the bank.

"Henry, **put me down**. I'm bleeding all over you."

He didn't pay any attention to her. "Here, Richard," he said, "get that sock and tie it around her ankle."

It was the first time I had even thought of a tourniquet; some kind of doctor I would have made. "Too tight?" I asked her.

"That's fine. Henry, I wish you'd put me down. I'm too heavy for you."

He smiled at her. There was a slight chip in one of his front teeth I'd never noticed before; it gave his smile a very engaging quality. "You're light as a feather," he said.

Sometimes, when there's been an accident and reality is too sudden and strange to comprehend, the surreal will take over. Action slows to a dreamlike glide, frame by frame; the motion of a hand, a sentence spoken, fills an eternity. Little things—a cricket on a stem, the veined branches on a leaf—are magnified, brought from the background in achingly clear focus. And that was what happened then, walking over the meadow to the house. It was like a painting too vivid to be real—every pebble, every blade of grass sharply defined, the sky so blue it hurt me to look at it. Camilla was limp in Henry's arms, her head thrown back like a dead girl's, and the curve of her throat beautiful and lifeless. The hem of her dress fluttered abstractly in the breeze. Henry's trousers were spattered with drops the size of quarters, too red to be blood, as if he'd had a paintbrush slung at him. In the overwhelming stillness, between our echoless footsteps, the pulse sang thin and fast in my ears.

Charles skidded down the hill, barefoot, still in his bathrobe, Francis at his heels. Henry knelt and set her on the grass, and she raised herself on her elbows.

"Camilla, are you dead?" said Charles, breathless, as he dropped to the ground to look at the wound.

"Somebody," said Francis, unrolling a length of bandage, "is going to have to take that glass out of her foot."

"Want me to try?" said Charles, looking up at her.

"Be careful."

Charles, her heel in his hand, caught the glass between thumb and forefinger and pulled gently. Camilla caught her breath in a quick, wincing gasp.

Charles drew back like he'd been scalded. He made as if to touch her foot again, but he couldn't quite bring himself to do it. His fingertips were wet with blood.

"Well, go on," said Camilla, her voice fairly steady.

"I can't do it. I'm afraid I'll hurt you."

"It hurts anyway."

"I can't," Charles said miserably, looking up at her.

"Get out of the way," said Henry impatiently, and he knelt quickly and took her foot in his hand.

Charles turned away; he was almost as white as she was, and I wondered if that old story was true, that one twin felt pain when the other was injured.

Camilla flinched, her eyes wide; Henry held up the curved piece of glass in one bloody hand. **"Consummatum est,"** he said.

Francis set to work with the iodine and the bandages.

"My God," I said, picking up the red-stained shard and holding it to the light.

"Good girl," said Francis, winding the bandages around the arch of her foot. Like most hypochondriacs, he had an oddly soothing bedside manner. "Look at you. You didn't even cry."

"It didn't hurt that much."

"The hell it didn't," Francis said. "You were really brave."

Henry stood up. "She was brave," he said.

———

Late that afternoon, Charles and I were sitting on the porch. It had turned suddenly cold; the sky was brilliantly sunny but the wind was up. Mr. Hatch had come inside to start a fire, and I smelled a faint tang of wood smoke. Francis was inside, too, starting dinner; he was singing, and his high, clear voice, slightly out of key, floated out the kitchen window.

Camilla's cut hadn't been a serious one. Francis drove her to the emergency room—Bunny went, too, because he was annoyed at having slept through the excitement—and in an hour she was back, with six stitches in her foot, a bandage, and a bottle of Tylenol with codeine. Now Bunny and Henry were out playing croquet and she was with them, hopping around on her good foot and the toe of the other with a skipping gait that, from the porch, looked oddly jaunty.

Charles and I were drinking whiskey and soda. He had been trying to teach me to play piquet ("because it's what Rawdon Crawley plays in **Vanity Fair**") but I was a slow learner and the cards lay abandoned.

Charles took a sip of his drink. He hadn't bothered to dress all day. "I wish we didn't have to go back to Hampden tomorrow," he said.

"I wish we never had to go back," I said. "I wish we lived here."

"Well, maybe we can."

"What?"

"I don't mean now. But maybe we could. After school."

"How's that?"

He shrugged. "Well, Francis's aunt won't sell the house because she wants to keep it in the family. Francis could get it from her for next to nothing when he turns twenty-one. And even if he couldn't, Henry has more money than he knows what to do with. They could go in together and buy it. Easy."

I was startled by this pragmatic answer.

"I mean, all Henry wants to do when he finishes school, if he finishes, is to find some place where he can write his books and study the Twelve Great Cultures."

"What do you mean, **if** he finishes?"

"I mean, he may not want to. He may get bored. He's talked about leaving before. There's no reason he's got to be here, and he's surely never going to have a job."

"You think not?" I said, curious; I had always pictured Henry teaching Greek, in some forlorn but excellent college out in the Midwest.

Charles snorted. "Certainly not. Why should he? He doesn't need the money, and he'd make a terrible teacher. And Francis has never worked in his life. I guess he could live with his mother, except he can't stand that husband of hers. He'd like it better here. Julian wouldn't be far away, either."

I took a sip of my drink and looked out at the faraway figures on the lawn. Bunny, hair falling into his eyes, was preparing to make a shot, flexing the mallet and shifting back and forth on his feet like a professional golfer.

"Does Julian have any family?" I said.

"No," said Charles, his mouth full of ice. "He has some nephews but he hates them. Look at this, would you," he said suddenly, half rising from his chair.

I looked. Across the lawn, Bunny had finally made his shot; the ball went wide of the sixth and seventh arches but, incredibly, hit the turning stake.

"Watch," I said. "I bet he'll try for another shot."

"He won't get it, though," said Charles, sitting down again, his eyes still on the lawn. "Look at Henry. He's putting his foot down."

Henry was pointing at the neglected arches and, even at that distance, I could tell he was quoting from the rule book; faintly, we could hear Bunny's startled cries of protest.

"My hangover's about gone," Charles said presently.

"Mine, too," I said. The light on the lawn was golden, casting long velvety shadows, and the cloudy, radiant sky was straight out of

Constable; though I didn't want to admit it, I was about half-drunk.

We were quiet for a while, watching. From the lawn I could hear the faint **pock** of mallet against croquet ball; from the window, above the clatter of pots and the slamming of cabinets, Francis was singing, as though it was the happiest song in the world: " 'We are little black sheep who have gone astray . . . Baa **baa** baa . . .' "

"And if Francis buys the house?" I said finally. "Think he'd let us live here?"

"Sure. He'd be bored stiff if it was just him and Henry. I guess Bunny might have to work in the bank but he could always come up on weekends, if he leaves Marion and the kids at home."

I laughed. Bunny had been talking the night before about how he wanted eight children, four boys and four girls; which had prompted a long, humorless speech from Henry about how the fulfillment of the reproductive cycle was, in nature, an invariable harbinger of swift decline and death.

"It's terrible," said Charles. "Really, I can just see him. Standing out in a yard wearing some kind of stupid apron."

"Cooking hamburgers on the grill."

"And about twenty kids running around him and screaming."

"Kiwanis picnics."

"La-Z-Boy recliners."

"Jesus."

A sudden wind rustled through the birches; a gust of yellow leaves came storming down. I took a sip of my drink. If I had grown up in that house I couldn't have loved it more, couldn't have been more familiar with the creak of the swing, or the pattern of the clematis vines on the trellis, or the velvety swell of land as it faded to gray on the horizon, and the strip of highway visible—just barely—in the hills, beyond the trees. The very colors of the place had seeped into my blood: just as Hampden, in subsequent years, would always present itself immediately to my imagination in a confused whirl of white and green and red, so the country house first appeared as a glorious blur of watercolors, of ivory and lapis blue, chestnut and burnt orange and gold, separating only gradually into the boundaries of remembered objects: the house, the sky, the maple trees. But even that day, there on the porch, with Charles beside me and the smell of wood smoke in the air, it had the quality of a memory; there it was, before my eyes, and yet too beautiful to believe.

It was getting dark; soon it would be time for dinner. I finished my drink in a swallow. The idea of living there, of not having to go back ever again to asphalt and shopping malls and modular furniture; of living there with Charles and Camilla and Henry and Francis and maybe even Bunny; of no one marrying or going home or getting a job in a town a thousand miles away or doing any of the traitorous things friends do after college; of everything remaining exactly as it was, that instant—the idea was so truly heavenly that I'm not sure I thought, even then, it could ever really happen, but I like to believe I did.

Francis was working up to a big finish on his song. " 'Gentlemen songsters **off** on a spree . . . Doomed from here to e**ter**nity . . .' "

Charles looked at me sideways. "So, what about you?" he said.

"What do you mean?"

"I mean, do you have any plans?" He laughed. "What are you doing for the next forty or fifty years of your life?"

Out on the lawn, Bunny had just knocked Henry's ball about seventy feet outside the court. There was a ragged burst of laughter; faint, but clear, it floated back across the evening air. That laughter haunts me still.

CHAPTER

3

FROM THE first moment I set foot in Hampden, I had begun to dread the end of term, when I would have to go back to Plano, and flat land, and filling stations, and dust. As the term wore on, and the snow got deeper and the mornings blacker and every day brought me closer to the date on the smeared mimeograph ("December 17—All Final Papers Due") taped inside my closet door, my melancholy began to turn into something like alarm. I did not think I could stand a Christmas at my parents' house, with a plastic tree and no snow and the TV going constantly. It was not as if my parents were so anxious to have me, either. In recent years they had fallen in with a gabby, childless couple, older than they were, called the MacNatts. Mr. MacNatt was an auto-parts salesman; Mrs. MacNatt was shaped like a pigeon and sold Avon. They had got my parents doing things like taking bus trips to factory outlets and playing a dice game called "bunko" and hanging around the piano bar at the Ramada Inn. These activities picked up considerably around holidays and my presence, brief and irregular as it was, was regarded as a hindrance and something of a reproach.

But the holidays were only half the trouble. Because Hampden was so far north, and because the buildings were old and expensive to heat, the school was closed during January and February. Already I could hear my father complaining beerily about me to Mr. MacNatt, Mr. MacNatt slyly goading him on with remarks insinuating that I was spoiled and that **he** wouldn't allow any son of his to walk all over him, if he had one. This would drive my father into a fury; eventually he would come busting dramatically into my room and order me out, his forefinger trembling, rolling his eyes like Othello. He had done this several times when I was in high school and in college in California, for no reason really except to display his authority in front of my mother and his co-workers. I was always welcomed back as soon as he tired of the attention and allowed my mother to "talk some sense" into him, but what about now? I didn't even have a bedroom in California anymore; in October, my mother had written to say that she had sold the furniture and turned it into a sewing room.

Henry and Bunny were going to Italy over the winter vacation, to Rome. I was surprised at this announcement, which Bunny had made at the beginning of December, especially since the two of them had been out of sorts for over a month, Henry in particular. Bunny, I knew, had been hitting him hard for money in the past weeks, but though Henry complained about this he seemed oddly incapable of refusing him. I was fairly sure that it wasn't the money **per se**, but the principle of it; I was also fairly sure that whatever tension existed, Bunny was oblivious of it.

The trip was all Bunny talked about. He bought clothes, guidebooks, a record called **Parliamo Italiano** which promised to teach the listener Italian in two weeks or less ("Even to those who've never had luck with other language courses!" boasted the jacket) and a copy of Dorothy Sayers's translation of **Inferno**. He knew I had nowhere to go for the winter vacation and enjoyed rubbing salt in my wounds. "I'll be thinking of you while I'm drinking Campari and riding the gondolas," he said, winking. Henry had little to say about the trip. As Bunny rattled on he would sit smoking with deep, resolute drags, pretending not to understand Bun's fallacious Italian.

Francis said he'd be happy to have me to Christmas in Boston and then travel on with him to New York; the twins phoned their grandmother in Virginia and she said she'd be glad to have me there, too, for the entire winter break. But there was the question of money. For the months until school began I would have to have a job. I needed money if I wanted to come back in the spring, and I couldn't very well work if I was gallivanting around with Francis. The twins would be clerking, as they always did during holidays, with their uncle the lawyer, but they had quite a time stretching the job to fit the two of them, Charles driving Uncle Orman to the occasional estate sale and to the package store, Camilla sitting around the office waiting to answer a phone that never rang. I am sure it never occurred to them that I might want a job, too—all my tales of Californian **richesse** had hit the mark harder than I'd thought. "What'll I do while you're at work?" I asked them, hoping they would get my drift, but of course they didn't. "I'm afraid there's not much **to** do," said Charles apologetically. "Read, talk to Nana, play with the dogs."

My only choice, it seemed, was to stay in Hampden town. Dr. Roland was willing to keep me on, though at a salary that wouldn't cover a decent rent. Charles and Camilla were subletting their apartment and Francis had a teenaged cousin staying in his; Henry's, for all I knew, was standing empty, but he didn't offer its use and I was too proud to ask. The house in the country was empty, too, but it was an hour from Hampden and I didn't have a car. Then I heard about an old hippie, an ex–Hampden student, who ran a musical-instrument workshop in an abandoned warehouse. He would let you live in the warehouse for free if you carved pegs or sanded a few mandolins now and again.

Partly because I did not wish to be burdened with anyone's pity or contempt, I concealed the true circumstances of my stay. Unwanted during the holidays by my glamorous, good-for-nothing parents, I had decided to stay alone in Hampden (at an unspecified location) and work on my Greek, spurning, in my pride, their craven offers of financial help.

This stoicism, this Henrylike dedication to my studies and general contempt for the things of this world, won me admiration from all sides, particularly from Henry himself. "I wouldn't mind being here myself this winter," he said to me one bleak night late in November as we were walking home from Charles and Camilla's, our shoes sunk to the ankles in the sodden leaves that covered the path. "The school is boarded up and the stores in town close by three in the afternoon. Everything's white and empty and there's no noise but the wind. In the old days the snow would drift up to the eaves of the roofs, and people would be trapped in their houses and starve to death. They wouldn't be found until spring." His voice was dreamy, quiet, but I was filled with uncertainty; in the winters where I lived it did not even snow.

The last week of school was a flurry of packing, typing, plane reservations and phone calls home, for everybody but me. I had no need to finish my papers early because I had nowhere to go; I could pack at my leisure, after the dorms were empty. Bunny was the first to leave. For three weeks he had been in a panic over a paper he had to write for his fourth course, something called Masterworks of English Literature. The assignment was twenty-five pages on John Donne. We'd all wondered how he was going to do it, because he was not much of a writer; though his dyslexia was the convenient culprit the real problem was not that but his attention span, which was as short as a child's. He seldom read the required texts or supplemental books for any course. Instead, his knowledge of any given subject tended to be a hodgepodge of confused facts, often strikingly irrelevant or out of context, that he happened to remember from classroom discussions or believed himself to have read somewhere. When it was time to write a paper he would supplement these dubious fragments by cross-examination of Henry (whom he was in the habit of consulting, like an atlas) or with information from either **The World Book Encyclopedia** or a reference work entitled **Men of Thought and Deed**, a six-volume work by E. Tipton Chatsford, Rev., dating from the 1890s, consisting of thumbnail sketches of great men through the ages, written for children, full of dramatic engravings.

Anything Bunny wrote was bound to be alarmingly original, since he began with such odd working materials and managed to alter them further by his befuddled scrutiny, but the John Donne paper must have been the worst of all the bad papers he ever wrote (ironic, given that it was the only thing he ever wrote that saw print. After he disappeared, a journalist asked for an excerpt from the missing young scholar's work and Marion gave him a copy of it, a laboriously edited paragraph of which eventually found its way into **People** magazine).

Somewhere, Bunny had heard that John Donne had been acquainted with Izaak Walton, and in some dim corridor of his mind this friendship grew larger and larger, until in his mind the two men were practically interchangeable. We never understood how this fatal connection had established itself: Henry blamed it on **Men of Thought and Deed**, but no one knew for sure. A week or two before the paper was due, he had started showing up in my room about two or three in the morning, looking as if he had just narrowly escaped some natural disaster, his tie askew and his eyes wild and rolling. "Hello, hello," he would say, stepping in, running both hands through his disordered hair. "Hope I didn't wake you, don't mind if I cut on the lights, do you, ah, here we go, yes, yes. . . ." He would turn on the lights and then pace back and forth for a while without taking off his coat, hands clasped behind his back, shaking his head. Finally he would stop dead in his tracks and say, with a desperate look in his eye: "Metahemeralism. Tell me about it. Everything you know. I gotta know something about metahemeralism."

"I'm sorry. I don't know what that is."

"I don't either," Bunny would say brokenly. "Got to do with art or pastoralism or something. That's how I gotta tie together John Donne and Izaak Walton, see." He would resume pacing. "Donne. Walton. Metahemeralism. That's the problem as I see it."

"Bunny, I don't think 'metahemeralism' is even a word."

"Sure it is. Comes from the Latin. Has to do with irony and the pastoral. Yeah. That's it. Painting or sculpture or something, maybe."

"Is it in the dictionary?"

"Dunno. Don't know how to spell it. I

mean"—he made a picture frame with his hands—"the poet and the fisherman. **Parfait**. Boon companions. Out in the open spaces. Living the good life. Metahemeralism's gotta be the glue here, see?"

And so it would go, for sometimes half an hour or more, with Bunny raving about fishing, and sonnets, and heaven knew what, until in the middle of his monologue he would be struck by a brilliant thought and bluster off as suddenly as he had descended.

He finished the paper four days before the deadline and ran around showing it to everyone before he turned it in.

"This is a nice paper, Bun—," Charles said cautiously.

"Thanks, thanks."

"But don't you think you ought to mention John Donne more often? Wasn't that your assignment?"

"Oh, Donne," Bunny had said scoffingly. "I don't want to drag him into this."

Henry refused to read it. "I'm sure it's over my head, Bunny, really," he said, glancing over the first page. "Say, what's wrong with this type?"

"Triple-spaced it," said Bunny proudly.

"These lines are about an **inch apart**."

"Looks kind of like free verse, doesn't it?"

Henry made a funny little snorting noise

through his nose. "Looks kind of like a menu," he said.

All I remember about the paper was that it ended with the sentence "And as we leave Donne and Walton on the shores of Metahemeralism, we wave a fond farewell to those famous chums of yore." We wondered if he would fail. But Bunny wasn't worried: the approaching trip to Italy, now close enough to cast the dark shadow of the Tower of Pisa over his bed at night, had thrown him into a state of high agitation and he was anxious to leave Hampden as soon as possible and dispense with his familial obligations so that he could embark.

Brusquely he asked me, since I didn't have anything to do, would I come over and help him pack? I said I would, and arrived to find him dumping the contents of entire drawers into suitcases, clothes everywhere. I reached up and carefully took a framed Japanese print from the wall and laid it down on his desk: "Don't touch that," he shouted, dropping his nightstand drawer on the floor with a bang and darting over to snatch up the print. "That thing's two hundred years old." As a matter of fact, I knew that it was no such thing, since I happened a few weeks before to have seen him carefully razoring it from a book in the library; I said nothing, but I was so irritated that I left immediately, amidst what gruff excuses his pride permitted him. Later, after he had gone, I found an awkward note of apology in my mailbox, wrapped around a paperback copy of the poems of Rupert Brooke and a box of Junior Mints.

Henry departed quickly and quietly. One night he told us he was leaving and the next day he was gone. (To St. Louis? ahead to Italy? none of us knew.) Francis left the day after that and there were many elaborate and prolonged goodbyes—Charles, Camilla, and I standing by the side of the road, noses raw and ears half-frozen, while Francis shouted at us with the window rolled down and the motor idling and great clouds of white smoke billowing all around the Mustang for what must have been a good forty-five minutes.

Perhaps because they were the last to leave, I hated to see the twins go most of all. After Francis's horn honks had faded into the snowy, echoless distance, we walked back to their house, not saying much, taking the path through the woods. When Charles turned on the light, I saw that the place was heartbreakingly neat—sink empty, floors waxed, and a row of suitcases by the door.

The dining halls had closed at noon that day; it was snowing hard and getting dark and we didn't have a car; the refrigerator, freshly cleaned and smelling of Lysol, was empty. Sitting around the kitchen table we had a sad, makeshift dinner of canned mushroom soup, soda crackers, and tea without sugar or milk. The main topic of conversation was Charles and Camilla's itinerary—how they would manage the baggage, what time they should call the taxi in order to make a six-thirty train. I joined in this travel-talk but a deep melancholy that would not lift for many weeks had already begun to settle around me; the sound of Francis's car, receding and then disappearing in the snowy, muffled distance, was still in my ears, and for the first time I realized how lonely the next two months would really be, with the school closed, the snow deep, everyone gone.

They'd told me not to bother seeing them off the next morning, they were leaving so early, but all the same I was there again at five to tell them goodbye. It was a clear, black morning, encrusted with stars; the thermometer on the porch of Commons had sunk to zero. The taxi, idling in a cloud of fume, was already waiting in front. The driver had just slammed the lid on a trunkful of luggage and Charles and Camilla were locking the door behind them. They were too worried and preoccupied to take much pleasure at my presence. Both of them were nervous travelers: their parents had been killed in a car accident, on a weekend drive up to Washington, and they were edgy for days before they had to go anywhere themselves.

They were running late, as well. Charles put down his suitcase to shake my hand. "Merry Christmas, Richard. You will write, won't you?" he said, then ran down the walk to the cab. Camilla—struggling with two enormous carpetbags—dropped them both in the snow and said: "Dammit, we'll never get all this luggage on the train."

She was breathing hard, and deep circles of red burned high on her bright cheeks; in all my life I had never seen anyone so maddeningly beautiful as she was at that moment. I stood blinking stupidly at her, the blood pounding in my veins, and my carefully rehearsed plans for a goodbye kiss forgotten, when unexpectedly she flew up and threw her arms around me. Her hoarse breath was loud in my ear and her cheek was like ice when she put it against mine a moment later; when I took her gloved hand, I felt the quick pulse of her slender wrist beneath my thumbs.

The taxi honked and Charles put his head out the window. "Come **on**," he shouted.

I carried her bags down to the sidewalk and stood under the street lamp as they pulled away. They were turned around in the back seat and waving to me through the rear window and I stood watching them, and the ghost of my own distorted reflection receding in the curve of the dark glass, until the cab turned a corner and disappeared.

I stood in the deserted street until I could no longer hear the sound of the motor, only the hiss of the powdery snow that the wind kicked up in little eddies on the ground. Then I started back to campus, hands deep in pockets and the crunch of my feet unbearably loud. The dorms were black and silent, and the big parking lot behind the tennis court was empty except for a few faculty cars and a lone green truck from Maintenance. In my dorm the hallways were littered with shoe boxes and coat hangers, doors ajar, everything dark and quiet as the grave. I was as depressed as I have ever been in my life. I pulled down the shades and lay down on my unmade bed and went back to sleep.

———

I had so few belongings it was possible to take them in one trip. When I woke again, around noon, I packed my two suitcases and, dropping my key off at the security booth, hauled them down the deserted, snowy road into town and to the address the hippie had given me over the telephone.

It was a longer walk than I'd expected, and it soon took me off the main road and through some particularly desolate country near Mount Cataract. My way ran parallel to a rapid, shallow river—the Battenkill—spanned by covered bridges here and there along its course. There were few houses, and even those grim, terrifying house trailers one frequently sees in the backwoods of Vermont, with tremendous piles of wood to the side and black smoke pouring out the stovepipes, were few and far between. There were no cars at all, except for the occasional derelict vehicle propped on cinderblocks in someone's front yard.

It would have been a pleasant, if demanding walk even in the summertime but in December, in two feet of snow and with two heavy suitcases to carry, I found myself wondering if I would make it at all. My toes and fingers were cramped with cold, and more than once I had to stop to rest, but gradually the countryside began to look less and less deserted and finally the road came out where I had been told it would: Prospect Street in East Hampden.

It was a part of town I had never seen, and worlds away from the part I knew—maple trees and clapboard storefronts, village green and courthouse clock. This Hampden was a bombed-out expanse of water towers, rusted railroad tracks, sagging warehouses and factories with the doors boarded up and the windows broken out. All of it looked as though it had stood abandoned since the Depression, except for a seedy little bar at the end of the street, which, judging from the scrum of trucks out front, was doing a good brisk business, even this early in the afternoon. Strings of Christmas lights and plastic holly hung above the neon beer lights; glancing inside, I saw a line of men in flannel shirts at the bar, all with shot glasses or beers before them, and— towards the back—a younger set running more to baseball caps and fat clustered around a pool table. I stood outside the red, padded-vinyl door and looked in through the porthole at the top for an instant longer. Should I go in and ask directions, have a drink, get warm? I decided I should, and my hand was on the greasy brass door handle when I saw the name of the place in the window: Boulder Tap. I had heard of the Boulder Tap from the local news. It was the epicenter of what little crime there was in Hampden—knifings, rapes, never a single witness. It was not the type of place where you'd want to stop in alone for a drink if you were a lost college boy from up on the hill.

But it wasn't so hard to find where the hippie lived, after all. One of the warehouses, right on the river, was painted bright purple.

The hippie looked angry, as though I'd woken him up, when he finally came to the door. "Just let yourself in next time, man," he said sullenly. He was a short fat man with a sweat-stained T-shirt and a red beard, who looked as if he'd spent many fine evenings with his friends around the pool table at the Boulder Tap. He pointed out the room where I was to live, at the top of a flight of iron stairs (no railing, naturally), and disappeared without a word.

I found myself in a cavernous, dusty room with a plank floor and high, exposed rafters. Besides a broken dresser, and a high chair standing in the corner, it was completely unfurnished except for a lawn mower, a rusted oil drum, and a trestle table which was scattered with sandpaper and carpentry tools and a few curved pieces of wood which were perhaps the exoskeletons of mandolins. Sawdust, nails, food wrappers and cigarette butts, **Playboy** magazines from the 1970s littered the floor; the many-paned windows were furry with frost and grime.

I let one suitcase and then the other fall from my numb hands; for a moment my mind was numb, too, agreeably registering these impressions without comment. Then, all at once, I became aware of an overwhelming roaring, rushing noise. I went over and looked out the back windows behind the trestle table and was startled to see an expanse of water, hardly three feet below. Farther down, I could see it pounding over a dam, and the spray flying. As I tried to clear a circle on the window with my hand so I could see better, I noticed that my breath was still white, even then, indoors.

Suddenly, something that I can only describe as an icy blast swept over me, and I looked up. There was a large hole in the roof; I saw blue sky, a swift cloud moving from left to right, through the jagged black edge. Below it was a thin powdery dusting of snow, stenciled perfectly on the wooden floor in the shape of the hole above it, and undisturbed except for the sharp line of a solitary footprint, my own.

———

A good many people asked me later if I had realized what a dangerous thing this was, attempting to live in an unheated building in upstate Vermont during the coldest months of the year; and to be frank, I hadn't. In the back of my mind were the stories I'd heard, of drunks, of old people, of careless skiers freezing to death, but for some reason none of this seemed to apply to me. My quarters were uncomfortable, certainly, they were foully dirty and bitterly cold; but it never occurred to me that they were actually unsafe. Other students had lived there; the hippie lived there himself; a receptionist at the Student Referral Office had told me about it. What I didn't know was that the hippie's own quarters were properly heated, and that the students who had lived there in the past had come there well armed with space heaters and electric blankets. The hole in the roof, moreover, was a recent development, unknown to the Student Referral Office. I suppose anyone who knew the whole story would have warned me off, but the fact was, nobody did know. I was so embarrassed at having such living quarters that I had told no one where I was staying, not even Dr. Roland; the only person who knew all was the hippie, and he was supremely unconcerned with anyone's welfare but his own.

Early in the morning, while it was still dark, I would wake up in my blankets on the floor (I slept in two or three sweaters, long underwear, wool trousers **and** overcoat) and walk just as I was to Dr. Roland's office. It was a long walk and, if it was snowing or the wind was up, sometimes a harrowing one. I would arrive at Commons, chilled and exhausted, just as the janitor was unlocking the building for the day. I would then go downstairs and shave and shower in the cellar, in a disused and rather sinister-looking room—white tiles, exposed piping, a drain in the middle of the floor— that had been part of a makeshift infirmary during World War II. The janitors used the taps to fill the wash buckets, so the water was still on and there was even a gas heater; I kept a razor, soap, an inconspicuously folded towel towards the back of one of the empty, glass-fronted cabinets. Then I would go make myself a can of soup and some instant coffee on the hot plate in the Social Science office, and by the time Dr. Roland and the secretaries arrived, I already had quite a start on the day's work.

Dr. Roland, accustomed as he was by this time to my truancy and my frequent excuses and my failure to complete tasks by the deadline, was startled and rather suspicious of this abrupt spurt of industry. He praised my work, questioned me closely; on several occasions I heard him in the hall discussing my metamorphosis with Dr. Cabrini, the head of the psychology department, the only other teacher in the building who hadn't left for the winter. At the first, no doubt, he thought it was all some new trick of mine. But as the weeks rolled by and each new day of enthusiastic labor added another gold star to my shining record he began to believe: timidly at first but at last triumphantly. Around the first of February he even gave me a raise. Perhaps he was hoping in his Behavioralist way that this would spur me to even greater heights of motivation. He came to regret this mistake, however, when the winter term ended and I went back to my comfortable little room in Monmouth House and all my old incompetent ways.

I worked as late at Dr. Roland's as I decently could and then went to the snack bar in Commons for dinner. On certain fortunate nights there were even places to go afterwards, and I scanned the bulletin boards eagerly for these meetings of Alcoholics Anonymous, these performances of **Brigadoon** by the local high school. But usually there was nothing at all, and Commons closed at seven, and I was left my long walk home in the snow and dark.

The cold in the warehouse was like nothing I've known before or since. I suppose if I'd had any sense I'd have gone out and bought an electric heater, but only four months before I had come from one of the warmest climates in America and I had only the dimmest awareness that such appliances existed. It never occurred to me that half the population of Vermont wasn't experiencing pretty much what I put myself through every night—bone-cracking cold that made my joints ache, cold so relentless I felt it in my dreams: ice floes, lost expeditions, the lights of search planes swinging over whitecaps as I floundered alone in black Arctic seas. In the morning, when I woke, I was as stiff and sore as if I'd been beaten. I thought it was because I was sleeping on the floor. Only later did I realize that the true cause of this malady was hard, merciless shivering, my muscles contracting as mechanically as if by electric impulse, all night long, every night.

Amazingly, the hippie, whose name was Leo, was quite angry that I didn't spend more time carving mandolin struts or warping boards or whatever it was I was supposed to be doing up there. "You're taking advantage, man," he would say threateningly whenever he happened to see me. He had some idea that I had studied instrument building and was in fact able to do all sorts of complex, technical work, though I had never told him any such thing. "Yes, you did," he said, when I pled my ignorance. "You did. You said you lived in the Blue Ridge Mountains one summer and made dulcimers. In Kentucky."

I had nothing to say to this. I am not unused to being confronted with my own lies, but those of others never fail to throw me for a loop. I could only deny it and say, quite honestly, that I didn't even know what a dulcimer was. "Carve pegs," he said insolently. "Sweep up." To which I replied, in so many words, that I could hardly carve pegs in rooms too cold for me to take my gloves off. "Cut the fingertips off them, man," said Leo, unperturbed. These occasional collarings in the front hall were as far as my contact with him went. It eventually became evident to me that Leo, for all his professed love for mandolins, never actually set foot in the workshop and had apparently not done so for months before I came to live there. I began to wonder if perhaps he was even unaware of the hole in the roof; one day I made so bold as to mention it to him. "I thought that was one of the things you could fix around the place," he said. It stands as a testimony to my misery that one Sunday I actually attempted to do this, with a few odd scraps of mandolin wood that I found around, and nearly lost my life in the attempt; the grade of the roof was wickedly sharp and I lost my balance and nearly fell into the dam, catching myself only at the last moment on a length of tin drainpipe which, mercifully, held. I managed with effort to save myself—my hands were cut on the rusted tin, and I had to get a tetanus shot—but Leo's hammer and saw and the pieces of mandolin wood tumbled into the dam. The tools all sank and Leo probably does not know to this day that they are missing, but unfortunately the mandolin pieces floated and managed to lodge themselves in a cluster at the top of the spillway, right outside Leo's bedroom window. Of course he had plenty to say about this, and about college kids who didn't care about other people's things, and everybody trying to rip him off all the time.

Christmas came and went without notice, except that with no work and everything closed there was no place to go to get warm except, for a few hours, to church. I came home afterwards and wrapped myself in my blanket and rocked back and forth, ice in my very bones, and thought of all the sunny Christmases of my childhood—oranges, bikes and Hula Hoops, green tinsel sparkling in the heat.

Mail arrived occasionally, in care of Hampden College. Francis sent me a six-page letter about how bored he felt, and how sick he was, and virtually everything he'd had to eat since I'd seen him last. The twins, bless them, sent boxes of cookies their grandmother had made and letters written in alternating inks—black for Charles, red for Camilla. Around the second week of January I got a postcard from Rome, no return address. It was a photograph of the Primaporta Augustus; beside it, Bunny had drawn a surprisingly deft cartoon of himself and Henry in Roman dress (togas, little round eyeglasses) squinting off curiously in the direction indicated by the statue's outstretched arm. (Caesar Augustus was Bunny's hero; he had embarrassed us all by cheering loudly at the mention of his name during the reading of

the Bethlehem story from Luke 2 at the literature division's Christmas party. "Well, what of
it," he said, when we tried to shush him. "All
the world **shoulda** been taxed.")

I still have this postcard. Characteristically,
the writing is in pencil; over the years it's become a bit smudged but it's still quite legible.
There is no signature, but there is no mistaking the authorship:

Richard old Man

are you Frozen? it is quite warm here. We
live in a Penscione (sp.) I ordered Conche
by mistake yesterday in a restaurant it was
awful but Henry ate it. Everybody here is
a damn Catholic. Arrivaderci see you
soon.

Francis and the twins had asked me, rather
insistently, my address in Hampden. "Where
are you living?" said Charles in black ink. "Yes,
where?" echoed Camilla in red. (She used a
particular morocco shade of ink that to me,
missing her terribly, brought back in a rush of
color all the thin, cheerful hoarseness of her
voice.) As I had no address to give them, I ignored their questions and padded my replies
with broad references to snow, and beauty, and
solitude. I often thought how peculiar my life

must look to someone reading those letters, far away. The existence they described was detached and impersonal, all-embracing yet indefinite, with large blanks that rose to halt the reader at every turn; with a few changes of date and circumstance they could have been as easily from the Gautama as myself.

I wrote these letters in the mornings before work, in the library, during my sessions of prolonged loitering in Commons, where I remained every evening until asked to leave by the janitor. It seemed my whole life was composed of these disjointed fractions of time, hanging around in one public place and then another, as if I were waiting for trains that never came. And, like one of those ghosts who are said to linger around depots late at night, asking passersby for the timetable of the Midnight Express that derailed twenty years before, I wandered from light to light until that dreaded hour when all the doors closed and, stepping from the world of warmth and people and conversation overheard, I felt the old familiar cold twist through my bones again and then it was all forgotten, the warmth, the lights; I had never been warm in my life, ever.

I became expert at making myself invisible. I could linger two hours over a coffee, four over a meal, and hardly be noticed by the waitress. Though the janitors in Commons rousted me every night at closing time, I doubt they ever realized they spoke to the same boy twice. Sunday afternoons, my cloak of invisibility around my shoulders, I would sit in the infirmary for sometimes six hours at a time, placidly reading copies of **Yankee** magazine ("Clamming on Cuttyhunk") or **Reader's Digest** ("Ten Ways to Help That Aching Back!"), my presence unremarked by receptionist, physician, and fellow sufferer alike.

But, like the Invisible Man in H. G. Wells, I discovered that my gift had its price, which took the form of, in my case as in his, a sort of mental darkness. It seemed that people failed to meet my eye, made as if to walk through me; my superstitions began to transform themselves into something like mania. I became convinced that it was only a matter of time before one of the rickety iron steps that led to my room gave and I would fall and break my neck or, worse, a leg; I'd freeze or starve before Leo would assist me. Because one day, when I'd climbed the stairs successfully and without fear, I'd had an old Brian Eno song running through my head ("In New Delhi / And Hong Kong / They all know that it won't be long . . ."), I now had to sing it to myself each trip up or down the stairs.

And each time I crossed the footbridge over the river, twice a day, I had to stop and scoop around in the coffee-colored snow at the road's edge until I found a decent-sized rock. I would then lean over the icy railing and drop it into the rapid current that bubbled over the speck-led dinosaur eggs of granite which made up its bed—a gift to the river-god, maybe, for safe crossing, or perhaps some attempt to prove to it that I, though invisible, did exist. The water ran so shallow and clear in places that some-times I heard the dropped stone click as it hit the bed. Both hands on the icy rail, staring down at the water as it dashed white against the boulders, boiled thinly over the polished stones, I wondered what it would be like to fall and break my head open on one of those bright rocks: a wicked crack, a sudden limp-ness, then veins of red marbling the glassy water.

If I threw myself off, I thought, who would find me in all that white silence? Might the river beat me downstream over the rocks until it spat me out in the quiet waters, down be-hind the dye factory, where some lady would catch me in the beam of her headlights when she pulled out of the parking lot at five in the afternoon? Or would I, like the pieces of Leo's mandolin, lodge stubbornly in some quiet place behind a boulder and wait, my clothes washing about me, for spring?

This was, I should say, about the third week

in January. The thermometer was dropping; my life, which before had been only solitary and miserable, became unbearable. Every day, in a daze, I walked to and from work, sometimes during weather that was ten or twenty below, sometimes during storms so heavy that all I could see was white, and the only way I made it home at all was by keeping close to the guard rail on the side of the road. Once home, I wrapped myself in my dirty blankets and fell on the floor like a dead man. All my moments which were not consumed with efforts to escape the cold were absorbed with morbid Poe-like fancies. One night, in a dream, I saw my own corpse, hair stiff with ice and eyes wide open.

I was at Dr. Roland's office every morning like clockwork. He, an alleged psychologist, noticed not one of the Ten Warning Signs of Nervous Collapse or whatever it was that he was educated to see, and qualified to teach. Instead, he took advantage of my silence to talk to himself about football, and dogs he had had as a boy. The rare remarks he addressed to me were cryptic and incomprehensible. He asked, for example, since I was in the Drama department, why hadn't I been in any plays? "What's wrong? Are you shy, boy? Show them what you're made of." Another time he told me, in an offhand manner, that when he was at

Brown he had roomed with the boy who lived down the hall from him. One day, he said he didn't know my friend was in Hampden for the winter.

"I don't have any friends here for the winter," I said, and I didn't.

"You shouldn't push your friends away like that. The best friends you'll ever have are the ones you're making right now. I know you don't believe me, but they start to fall away when you get to be my age."

When I walked home at night, things got white around the edges and it seemed I had no past, no memories, that I had been on this exact stretch of luminous, hissing road forever.

I don't know what exactly was wrong with me. The doctors said it was chronic hypothermia, with bad diet and a mild case of pneumonia on top of it; but I don't know if that accounts for all the hallucinations and mental confusion. At the time I wasn't even aware I was sick: any symptom, any fever or pain, was drowned by the clamor of my more immediate miseries.

For I was in a bad fix. It was the coldest January on record for twenty-five years. I was terrified of freezing to death but there was absolutely nowhere I could go. I suppose I might've asked Dr. Roland if I could stay in the apartment he shared with his girlfriend, but the embarrassment of that was such that death, to me, seemed preferable. I knew no one else, even slightly, and short of knocking on the doors of strangers there was little I could do. One bitter night I tried to call my parents from the pay phone outside the Boulder Tap; sleet was falling and I was shivering so violently I could hardly get the coins in the slot. Although I had some desperate, half-baked hope that they might send money or a plane ticket, I didn't know what I wanted them to say to me; I think I had some idea that I, standing in the sleet and winds of Prospect Street, would feel better simply by hearing the voices of people far away, in a warm place. But when my father picked up the telephone on the sixth or seventh ring, his voice, beery and irritated, gave me a hard, dry feeling in my throat and I hung up.

Dr. Roland mentioned my imaginary friend again. He'd seen him uptown this time, walking on the square late at night as he was driving home.

"I told you I don't have any friends here," I said.

"You know who I'm talking about. Great big boy. Wears glasses."

Someone who looked like Henry? Bunny? "You must be mistaken," I said.

The temperature plummeted so low that I

was forced to spend a few nights at the Catamount Motel. I was the only person in the place, besides the snaggle-toothed old man who ran it; he was in the room next to mine and kept me awake with his loud hacking and spitting. There was no lock on my door, only the antique sort that can be picked with a hairpin; on the third night I woke from a bad dream (nightmare stairwell, steps all different heights and widths; a man going down ahead of me, really fast) to hear a faint, clicking noise. I sat up in bed and, to my horror, saw my doorknob turning stealthily in the moonlight: "Who's there?" I said loudly, and it stopped. I lay awake in the dark for a long time. The next morning, I left, preferring a quieter death at Leo's to being murdered in my bed.

A terrible storm came around the first of February, bringing with it downed power lines, stranded motorists, and, for me, a bout of hallucinations. Voices spoke to me in the roar of the water, in the hissing snow: **"Lie down,"** they whispered, and **"Turn left. You'll be sorry if you don't."** My typewriter was by the window of Dr. Roland's office. Late one afternoon, as it was getting dark, I looked down into the empty courtyard and was startled to see that a dark, motionless figure had materialized under the lamp, standing with its hands in the pockets of its dark overcoat and looking up at my window. It was shadowy and heavy snow was falling: "Henry?" I said, and squeezed my eyes shut until I saw stars. When I opened them again, I saw nothing but snow whirling in the bright cone of emptiness beneath the light.

At night I lay shivering on the floor, watching the illuminated snowflakes sift in a column through the hole in the ceiling. On the margin of stupefaction, as I was sliding off the steep roof of unconsciousness, something would tell me at the last instant that if I went to sleep I might never wake: with a struggle I would force my eyes open and all of a sudden the column of snow, standing bright and tall in its dark corner, would appear to me in its true whispering, smiling menace, an airy angel of death. But I was too tired to care; even as I looked at it I would feel my grasp slackening, and before I knew it I had tumbled down the slanted edge, and into the dark abyss of sleep.

Time was beginning to blur. I still dragged myself to the office, but only because it was warm there, and I somehow performed the simple tasks that I had to do, but I honestly do not know how much longer I would have been able to keep this up had not a very surprising thing happened.

I'll never forget this night as long as I live. It

was Friday, and Dr. Roland was going to be out of town until the following Wednesday. For me, that meant four days in the warehouse, and even in my clouded state it was clear I might freeze to death for real.

When Commons closed I started for home. The snow was deep, and before long my legs to the knees were prickling and numb. By the time the road came around into East Hampden I was wondering seriously if I could make it to the warehouse, and what I would do when I got there. Everything in East Hampden was dark and deserted, even the Boulder Tap; the only light for miles around seemed to be the light shimmering around the pay phone in front. I made my way towards it as though it were a mirage in the desert. I had about thirty dollars in my pocket, more than enough to call a taxi to take me to the Catamount Motel, to a nasty little room with an unlocked door and whatever else might await me there.

My voice was slurred and the operator wouldn't give me the number of a taxi company. "You have to give me the name of a **specific** taxi service," she said. "We're not allowed to—"

"I don't know the name of a specific taxi service," I said thickly. "There's not a phone book here."

"I'm sorry, sir, but we're not allowed to—"

"Red Top?" I said desperately, trying to guess at names, make them up, anything. "Yellow Top? Town Taxi? Checker?"

Finally I guess I got one right, or maybe she just felt sorry for me. There was a click, and a mechanical voice came on and gave me a number. I dialed it quickly so I wouldn't forget, so quickly that I got it wrong and lost my quarter.

I had one more quarter in my pocket; it was my last one. I took off my glove and groped in my pocket with my numbed fingers. Finally I found it, and I had it in my hand and was about to bring it up to the slot, when suddenly it slipped from my fingers and I pitched forward after it, hitting my forehead on the sharp corner of the metal tray beneath the phone.

I lay face down in the snow for a few minutes. There was a rushing noise in my ears; in falling, I had grabbed for the phone and knocked it off the hook, and the busy signal the receiver made as it swung back and forth sounded as if it were coming from a long way off.

I managed to get up on all fours. Staring at the place where my head had been, I saw a dark spot on the snow. When I touched my forehead with my ungloved hand the fingers came away red. The quarter was gone; besides, I had forgotten the number. I would have to come back later, when the Boulder Tap was open and I could get change. Somehow I struggled to my feet, leaving the black receiver dangling from its cord.

I made it up the stairs half walking, half on my hands and knees. Blood was trickling down my forehead. At the landing I stopped to rest and felt my surroundings slide out of focus: static, between stations, everything snowy for a moment or two before the black lines wavered and the picture snapped back; not quite clear, but recognizable. Jerky camera, nightmare commercial. Leo's Mandolin Warehouse. Last stop, down by the river. Low rates. Remember us, too, for all your meat-locker needs.

I pushed the workshop door open with my shoulder and began to fumble for the light switch when suddenly I saw something by the window that made me reel with shock. A figure in a long black overcoat was standing motionless across the room by the windows, hands clasped behind the back; near one of the hands I saw the tiny glow of a cigarette coal.

The lights came on with a crackle and a hum. The shadowy figure, now solid and visible, turned around. It was Henry. He seemed on the verge of making some joking remark, but when he saw me his eyes got wide and his mouth fell open into a small round o.

We stood staring at each other across the room for a moment or two.

"Henry?" I said at last, my voice scarcely more than a whisper.

He let the cigarette fall from his fingers and took a step towards me. It really was him— damp, ruddy cheeks, snow on the shoulders of his overcoat. "Good God, Richard," he said, "what's happened to you?"

It was as much surprise as I ever saw him show. I stood where I was, staring, unbalanced. Things had got too bright. I reached for the door frame, and the next thing I knew I was falling, and Henry had jumped forward to catch me.

He eased me onto the floor and took off his coat and spread it over me like a blanket. I squinted up at him and wiped my mouth with the back of my hand. "Where did you come from?" I said.

"I left Italy early." He was brushing the hair back from my forehead, trying to get a look at my cut. I saw blood on his fingertips.

"Some little place I've got here, huh?" I said, and laughed.

He glanced up at the hole in the ceiling. "Yes," he said brusquely. "Like the Pantheon." Then he bent to look at my head again.

———

I remember being in Henry's car, and lights and people bending over me, and having to sit up when I didn't want to, and I also remember someone trying to take my blood, and me complaining sort of feebly about it; but the first thing I remember with any clarity was sitting up and finding myself in a dim, white room, lying in a hospital bed with an IV in my arm.

Henry was sitting in a chair by my bed, reading by the table lamp. He put down his book when he saw me stir. "Your cut wasn't serious," he said. "It was very clean and shallow. They gave you a few stitches."

"Am I in the infirmary?"

"You're in Montpelier. I brought you to the hospital."

"What's this IV for?"

"They say you have pneumonia. Would you like something to read?" he said courteously.

"No thank you. What time is it?"

"One in the morning."

"But I thought you were in Rome."

"I came back about two weeks ago. If you want to go back to sleep I'll call the nurse to give you a shot."

"No thanks. Why haven't I seen you before now?"

"Because I didn't know where you lived. The

only address I had for you was in care of the
college. This afternoon I asked around at the
offices. By the way," he said, "what's the name
of the town where your parents live?"

"Plano. Why?"

"I thought you might want me to call them."

"Don't bother," I said, sinking back into my
bed. The IV was like ice in my veins. "Tell me
about Rome."

"All right," he said, and he began to talk very
quietly about the lovely Etruscan terra-cottas
in the Villa Giulia, and the lily pools and the
fountains in the nymphaeum outside it; about
the Villa Borghese and the Colosseum, the
view from the Palatine Hill early in the morning, and how beautiful the Baths of Caracalla
must have been in Roman times, with the
marbles and the libraries and the big circular
calidarium, and the frigidarium, with its great
empty pool, that was there even now, and
probably a lot of other things besides but I
don't remember because I fell asleep.

––––––

I was in the hospital for four nights. Henry
stayed with me almost the whole time, bringing me sodas when I asked for them, and a
razor and a toothbrush, and a pair of his
own pajamas—silky Egyptian cotton, cream-
colored and heavenly soft, with HMW (M for
Marchbanks) embroidered in tiny scarlet let-

ters on the pocket. He also brought me pencils and paper, for which I had little use but which I suppose he would have been lost without, and a great many books, half of which were in languages I couldn't read and the other half of which might as well have been. One night— head aching from Hegel—I asked him to bring me a magazine; he looked rather startled, and when he came back it was with a trade journal **(Pharmacology Update)** he had found in the lounge. We talked hardly at all. Most of the time he read, with a concentration that astonished me; six hours at a stretch, scarcely glancing up. He paid me almost no attention. But he stayed up with me on the bad nights, when I had a hard time breathing and my lungs hurt so I couldn't sleep; and once, when the nurse on duty was three hours late with my medicine, he followed her expressionless into the hall and there delivered, in his subdued monotone, such a tense and eloquent reprimand that the nurse (a contemptuous, hard-bitten woman, with dyed hair like an aging waitress, and a sour word for everyone) was somewhat mollified; and afterwards she—who ripped off the bandages around my IV with such callousness, and poked me black and blue in her desultory search for veins—was much gentler in her handling of me, and once, while taking my temperature, even called me "hon."

The emergency room doctor told me that Henry had saved my life. This was a dramatic and gratifying thing to hear—and one which I repeated to a number of people—but secretly I thought it was an exaggeration. In subsequent years, however, I've come to feel that he might well have been right. When I was younger I thought that I was immortal. And though I bounced back quickly, in a short-term sense, in another I never really quite got over that winter. I've had problems with my lungs ever since, and my bones ache at the slightest chill, and I catch cold easily now, whereas I never used to.

I told Henry what the doctor had said. He was displeased. Frowning, he made some curt remark—actually, I'm surprised I've forgotten it, I was so embarrassed—and I never mentioned it again. I think he did save me, though. And someplace, if there is a place where lists are kept, and credit given, I am sure there is a gold star by his name.

But I am getting sentimental. Sometimes, when I think about these things, I do.

———

On Monday morning I was able to leave at last, with a bottle of antibiotics and an arm full of pinpricks. They insisted on pushing me to Henry's car in a wheelchair, though I was perfectly able to walk and humiliated at being rolled out like a parcel.

"Take me to the Catamount Motel," I told him as we pulled into Hampden.

"No," he said. "You're coming to stay with me."

Henry lived on the first floor of an old house on Water Street, in North Hampden, just around the block from Charles and Camilla's and closer to the river. He didn't like to have people over and I had been there only once, and then only for a minute or two. It was much larger than Charles and Camilla's apartment, and a good deal emptier. The rooms were big and anonymous, with wide-plank floors and no curtains on the windows and plaster walls painted white. The furniture, while obviously good, was scarred and plain and there wasn't much of it. The whole place had a ghostly, unoccupied look; and some of the rooms had nothing in them at all. I had been told by the twins that Henry disliked electric lights, and here and there I saw kerosene lamps in the windowsills.

His bedroom, where I was to stay, had been closed off rather pointedly during my previous visit. In it were Henry's books—not as many as you might think—and a single bed, and very little else, except a closet with a large, conspicuous padlock. Tacked on the closet door was a black and white picture from an old magazine—**Life**, it said, 1945. It was of Vivien Leigh and, surprisingly, a much younger Julian. They were at a cocktail party, glasses in hand; he was whispering something in her ear, and she was laughing.

"Where was that taken?" I said.

"I don't know. Julian says he can't remember. Every now and then one runs across a photograph of him in an old magazine."

"Why?"

"He used to know a lot of people."

"Who?"

"Most of them are dead now."

"Who?"

"I really don't know, Richard." Then, relenting: "I've seen pictures of him with the Sitwells. And T. S. Eliot. Also—there's rather a funny one of him with that actress—I can't remember her name. She's dead now." He thought for a minute. "She was blond," he said. "I think she was married to a baseball player."

"Marilyn Mon**roe**?"

"Maybe. It wasn't a very good picture. Only newsprint."

Some time during the past three days, Henry had gone over and moved my things from Leo's. My suitcases stood at the foot of the bed.

"I don't want to take your bed, Henry," I said. "Where are you going to sleep?"

"One of the back rooms has a bed that folds out from the wall," said Henry. "I can't think what they're called. I've never slept in it before."

"Then why don't you let me sleep there?"

"No. I am rather curious to see what it is like. Besides, I think it's good to change the place where one sleeps from time to time. I believe it gives one more interesting dreams."

———

I was only planning on spending a few days with Henry—I was back at work for Dr. Roland the following Monday—but I ended up staying until school started again. I couldn't understand why Bunny had said he was hard to live with. He was the best roommate I've ever had, quiet and neat, and usually off in his own part of the house. Much of the time he was gone when I got home from work; he never told me where he went, and I never asked. But sometimes when I got home he would have made dinner—he wasn't a fancy cook like Francis and only made plain things, broiled chickens and baked potatoes, bachelor food—and we would sit at the card table in the kitchen and eat it and talk.

I had learned better by then than to pry into his affairs, but one night, when my curiosity had got the better of me, I asked him: "Is Bunny still in Rome?"

It was several moments before he answered. "I suppose so," he said, putting down his fork. "He was there when I left."

"Why didn't he come back with you?"

"I don't think he wanted to leave. I'd paid the rent through February."

"He stuck you with the rent?"

Henry took another bite of his food. "Frankly," he said, after he had chewed and swallowed, "no matter what Bunny tells you to the contrary, he hasn't a cent and neither does his father."

"I thought his parents were well off," I said, jarred.

"I wouldn't say that," said Henry calmly. "They may have had money once, but if so they spent it long ago. That terrible house of theirs must have cost a fortune, and they make a big show of yacht clubs and country clubs and sending their sons to expensive schools, but that's got them in debt to the eyebrows. They may look wealthy, but they haven't a dime. I expect Mr. Corcoran is about bankrupt."

"Bunny seems to live pretty well."

"Bunny's never had a cent of pocket money the entire time I've known him," said Henry tartly. "And he has expensive tastes. That is unfortunate."

We resumed eating in silence.

"If I were Mr. Corcoran," said Henry after a long while, "I would have set Bunny up in business or had him learn a trade after high school. Bunny has no business being in college. He couldn't even read until he was about ten years old."

"He draws well," I said.

"I think so, too. He certainly has no gift for scholarship. They should've apprenticed him to a painter when he was young instead of sending him to all those expensive schools for learning disabilities."

"He sent me a very good cartoon of you and he standing by a statue of Caesar Augustus."

Henry made a sharp, exasperated sound. "That was in the Vatican," he said. "All day long he made loud remarks about Dagos and Catholics."

"At least he doesn't speak Italian."

"He spoke it well enough to order the most expensive thing on the menu every time we went to a restaurant," said Henry curtly, and I thought it wise to change the subject and did.

———

On the Saturday before school was to begin, I was lying on Henry's bed reading a book.

Henry had been gone since before I woke up. Suddenly I heard a loud banging at the front door. Thinking Henry had forgotten his key, I went to let him in.

It was Bunny. He was wearing sunglasses and—in contrast to the shapeless, tweedy rags he generally wore—a sharp and very new Italian suit. He had also gained about ten or twenty pounds. He seemed surprised to see me.

"Well, hello there, Richard," he said, shaking my hand heartily. "**Buenos días**. Good to see ya. Didn't see the car out front but just got into town and thought I'd stop by anyway. Where's the man of the house?"

"He's not home."

"Then what are you doing? Breaking and entering?"

"I've been staying here for a while. I got your postcard."

"Staying here?" he said, looking at me in a peculiar way. "Why?"

I was surprised he didn't know. "I was sick," I said, and I explained a little of what had happened.

"Hmnpf," said Bunny.

"Do you want some coffee?"

We walked through the bedroom to get to the kitchen. "Looks like you've made quite a little home for yourself," he said brusquely, looking at my belongings on the night table and my suitcases on the floor. "American coffee all you have?"

"What do you mean? Folger's?"

"No **espresso**, I mean?"

"Oh. No. Sorry."

"I'm an espresso man myself," he said expansively. "Drank it all the time over in Italy. They have all kind of little places where you sit around and do that, you know."

"I've heard."

He took off his sunglasses and sat down at the table. "You don't have anything decent in there to eat, do you?" he said, peering into the refrigerator as I opened the door to take out the cream. "Haven't had my lunch yet."

I opened the door wider so he could see.

"That cheese'll be all right," he said.

I cut some bread and made him a cheese sandwich, as he showed no inclination of getting up and making anything himself. Then I poured the coffee and sat down. "Tell me about Rome," I said.

"Gorgeous," he said through his sandwich. "Eternal City. Lots of art. Churches every which way."

"What'd you see?"

"Tons of things. Hard to remember all the names now, you know. Was speaking the lingo like a native by the time I left."

"Say something."

He obliged, pinching his thumb and forefinger together and shaking them in the air for emphasis, like a French chef on a TV commercial.

"Sounds good," I said. "What does it mean?"

"It means 'Waiter, bring me your local specialties,' " he said, going back to his sandwich.

I heard the slight sound of a key being turned in the lock and then I heard the door shut. Footsteps went quietly toward the other end of the apartment.

"Henry?" bellowed Bun. "That you?"

The footsteps stopped. Then they came very rapidly towards the kitchen. When he got to the door he stood in it and stared down at Bunny, with no expression on his face. "I thought that was you," he said.

"Well, hello to you, too." Bunny, his mouth full, reared back in his chair. "How's the boy?"

"Fine," said Henry. "And you?"

"I hear you've been taking in the sick," said Bunny, winking at me. "Conscience been hurting you? Thought you'd better rack up a couple good deeds?"

Henry didn't say anything, and I'm sure that at that moment he would have looked perfectly impassive to anyone who didn't know him, but I could tell he was quite agitated. He pulled out a chair and sat down. Then he got up again and went to pour himself a cup of coffee.

"I'll have some more, thanks, if you don't mind," Bunny said. "Good to be back in the good old U.S. of A. Hamburgers sizzling on an open grill and all that. Land of Opportunity. Long may she wave."

"How long have you been here?"

"Flew into New York late last night."

"I'm sorry I wasn't here when you arrived."

"Where were you?" said Bunny suspiciously.

"At the market." This was a lie. I didn't know where he'd been but certainly he hadn't been grocery shopping for four hours.

"Where are the groceries?" said Bunny. "I'll help you bring them in."

"I'm having them delivered."

"The Food King has delivery?" said Bunny, startled.

"I didn't go to the Food King," said Henry.

Uneasily, I got up and headed back to the bedroom.

"No, no, don't go," said Henry, taking a long gulp of his coffee and putting the cup in the sink. "Bunny, I wish I'd known you were coming. But Richard and I have got to leave in a few minutes."

"Why?"

"I have an appointment in town."

"With a lawyer?" Bunny laughed loudly at his own joke.

"No. With the optometrist. That's why I came by," he said to me. "I hope you don't mind. They're going to put drops in my eyes and I can't see to drive."

"No, sure," I said.

"I won't be long. You don't have to wait, just drop me off and come back to get me."

Bunny walked us out to the car, our footsteps crunching in the snow. "Ah, Vermont," he said, breathing deep and slapping his chest, like Oliver Douglas in the opening sequence of "Green Acres." "Air does me good. So when d'ya think you'll be back, Henry?"

"I don't know," said Henry, handing me the keys and walking over to the passenger's side.

"Well, I'd like to have a little **chat** with you."

"Well, that's fine, but really, I'm a little late now, Bun."

"Tonight, then?"

"If you like," said Henry, getting in the car and slamming the door.

————

Once in the car, Henry lit a cigarette and didn't say a word. He'd been smoking a lot since he got back from Italy, almost a pack a day, which was rare for him. We started into town, and it wasn't until I pulled in at the eye doctor's office that he shook himself and looked at me blankly. "What is it?"

"What time should I come back to get you?"

Henry looked out, at the low gray building, at the sign in front that said OPTOMETRY GROUP OF HAMPDEN.

"Good God," he said, with a snort and a surprised, bitter little laugh. "Keep driving."

———

I went to bed early that night, around eleven; at twelve I was awakened by a loud persistent banging at the front door. I lay in bed and listened for a minute, then got up to see who it was.

In the dark hallway I met Henry, in his bathrobe, fumbling with his glasses; he was holding one of his kerosene lanterns and it cast long, weird shadows on the narrow walls. When he saw me, he put a finger to his lips. We stood in the hall, listening. The lamplight was eerie, and, standing there motionless in our bathrobes, sleepy, with shadows flickering all around, I felt as though I had woken from one dream into an even more remote one, some bizarre wartime bomb shelter of the unconscious.

We stood there for a long time, it seemed, long after the banging stopped and we heard footsteps crunching away. Henry looked over at me, and we were quiet for a bit longer. "It's all right now," he said at last, and he turned away abruptly, the lamplight bobbing crazily about him as he went back to his room. I waited a moment or two longer in the dark, and then went back to my own room and to bed.

———

The next day, around three in the afternoon, I was ironing a shirt in the kitchen when there was another knock at the door. I went into the hall and found Henry standing there.

"Does that sound like Bunny to you?" he said quietly.

"No," I said. This knock was fairly light; Bunny always beat on the door as if to bash it in.

"Go around to the side window and see if you can see who it is."

I went to the front room and advanced cautiously to the side; there were no curtains and it was hard to get to the far windows without exposing oneself to view. They were at an odd angle and all I could see was the shoulder of a black coat, with a silk scarf blown out in the wind behind it. I crept back through the kitchen to Henry. "I can't really see, but it might be Francis," I said.

"Oh, you can let him in, I suppose," said

Henry, and he turned and went back towards his part of the house.

I went to the front room and opened the door. Francis was looking back over his shoulder, wondering, I suppose, if he should leave. "Hi," I said.

He turned around and saw me. "Hello!" he said. His face seemed to have got much thinner and sharper since I'd seen him last. "I thought nobody was home. How are you feeling?"

"Fine."

"You look pretty bad to me."

"You don't look so good yourself," I said, laughing.

"I drank too much last night and gave myself a stomachache. I want to see this tremendous **head** wound of yours. Are you going to have a scar?"

I led him into the kitchen and shoved aside the ironing board so he could sit down. "Where's Henry?" he said, pulling off his gloves.

"In the back."

He began to unwind his scarf. "I'll just run say hello to him and I'll be right back," he said briskly, and slid away.

He was gone a long time. I had got bored and had almost finished ironing my shirt when suddenly I heard Francis's voice rise, with a hysterical edge. I got up and went into the bedroom so I could hear better what he was saying.

"—thinking about? My God, but he's in a state. You can't tell me you know what he might—"

There was a low murmur now, Henry's voice, then Francis's voice came back to me again.

"I don't care," he said hotly. "Jesus, but you've done it now. I've been in town two hours and already—I don't **care**," he said in reply to another murmur from Henry. "Besides, it's a bit late for that, isn't it?"

Silence. Then Henry began to talk, too indistinctly for me to hear.

"**You** don't like it? **You?**" said Francis. "What about me?"

His voice dropped suddenly and then resumed, too quietly for me to hear.

I walked quietly back to the kitchen and put on water for tea. I was still thinking about what I'd heard when, several minutes later, there were footsteps and Francis emerged in the kitchen, edging his way around the ironing board to gather his gloves and scarf.

"Sorry to run," he said. "I've got to unpack the car and start cleaning my apartment. That cousin of mine tore it all to pieces. I don't believe he took out the garbage once the whole time he was there. Let me see your head wound."

I pulled back the hair on my forehead and showed him the place. I'd had the stitches out long ago and it was nearly gone.

He leaned forward to peer at it through his pince-nez. "Goodness, I must be blind, I can't see a thing. When do classes start? Wednesday?"

"Thursday, I think."

"See you then," he said, and he was gone.

I put my shirt on a hanger and then went into the bedroom and started to pack my things. Monmouth House opened that afternoon; maybe Henry would drive me to school with my suitcases later on.

I was just about finished when Henry called me from the back of the apartment. "Richard?"

"Yes?"

"Would you come here for a moment, please?"

I went back to his room. He was sitting on the side of the fold-out bed, his sleeves rolled up to the elbows and a game of solitaire spread out on the blanket at the foot. His hair had fallen to the wrong side and I could see the long scar at his hairline, all dented and puckered, with ridges of white flesh cutting across it to the browbone.

He looked up at me. "Will you do a favor for me?" he said.

"Sure."

He took a deep breath through the nostrils and pushed his glasses up on the bridge of his nose. "Will you call Bunny and ask him if he'd like to come over for a few minutes?" he said.

I was so surprised that I didn't say anything for half a second. Then I said: "Sure. Fine. I'll be glad to."

He closed his eyes and rubbed his temple with his fingertips. Then he blinked at me. "Thank you," he said.

"No, really."

"If you want to take some of your things back to school this afternoon, you're more than welcome to borrow the car," he said evenly.

I got his drift. "Sure," I said, and it was only after I'd loaded my suitcases in the car and driven them to Monmouth and got Security to unlock my room that I called Bunny from the pay phone downstairs, a safe half hour later.

CHAPTER

4

SOMEHOW I thought that when the twins returned, when we were settled in again, when we were back at our Liddell and Scotts and had suffered through two or three Greek Prose Composition assignments together, we would all fall back into the comfortable routine of the previous term and everything would be the same as it had been before. But about this I was wrong.

Charles and Camilla had written to say they would arrive in Hampden on the late train, around midnight on Sunday, and on Monday afternoon, as students began to straggle back to Monmouth House with their skis and their stereos and their cardboard boxes, I had some idea that they might come to see me, but they didn't. On Tuesday I didn't hear from them either, or from Henry or anybody but Julian, who had left a cordial little note in my post-office box welcoming me back to school and asking me to translate an ode of Pindar's for our first class.

On Wednesday I went to Julian's office to ask him to sign my registration cards. He seemed happy to see me. "You look well," he said, "but not as well as you ought. Henry's been keeping me up to date on your recovery."

"Oh?"

"It was a good thing, I suppose, that he came back early," said Julian, glancing through my cards, "but I was surprised to see him, too. He showed up at my house straight from the airport, in the middle of a snowstorm, in the middle of the night."

This was interesting. "Did he stay with you?" I said.

"Yes, but only a few days. He'd been ill himself, you know. In Italy."

"What was the matter?"

"Henry's not as strong as he looks. His eyes bother him, he has terrible headaches, sometimes he has a difficult time. . . . I didn't think he was in a proper condition to travel, but it was lucky he didn't stay on or he wouldn't have found **you**. Tell me. How did you end up in such a dreadful place? Wouldn't your parents give you money, or didn't you want to ask?"

"I didn't want to ask."

"Then you are more of a stoic than I am," he said, laughing. "But your parents do not seem very fond of you, am I correct?"

"They're not that crazy about me, no."

"Why is that, do you suppose? Or is it rude of me to ask? I should think that they would be quite proud, yet you seem more an orphan than our real orphans do. Tell me," he said, looking up, "why is it that the twins haven't been in to see me?"

"I haven't seen them, either."

"Where can they be? I haven't even seen Henry. Only you and Edmund. Francis telephoned but I only spoke to him for a moment. He was in a hurry, he said he would stop by later, but he hasn't. . . . I don't think Edmund's learned a word of Italian, do you?"

"I don't speak Italian."

"Nor do I, not anymore. I used to speak it rather well. I lived in Florence for a while but that was nearly thirty years ago. Will you be seeing any of the others this afternoon?"

"Maybe."

"Of course, it's a matter of small importance, but the registration slips should be at the Dean's office this afternoon and he will be irritated that I haven't sent them. Not that I care, but he is certainly in a position to make things unpleasant for any of you, if he chooses."

———

I was somewhat annoyed. The twins had been in Hampden three days and hadn't called once. So when I left Julian's I stopped by their apartment, but they weren't home.

They weren't at dinner that night, either. Nobody was. Though I had expected at least to see Bunny, I stopped by his room on the way to the dining hall and found Marion locking his door. She told me, rather officiously, that the two of them had plans and would not be in until late.

I ate alone and walked back to my room in the snowy twilight, with a sour, humorless feeling as if I were the victim of a practical joke. At seven I called Francis, but there was no answer. There was no answer at Henry's, either.

I read Greek till midnight. After I'd brushed my teeth and washed my face and was almost ready for bed, I went downstairs and called again. Still no answer anywhere. I got my quarter back after the third call and tossed it up in the air. Then, on a whim, I called Francis's number in the country.

There was no answer there, either, but something made me hold the line longer than I should have and finally, after about thirty rings, there was a click and Francis said gruffly into the receiver, "Hullo?" He was making his voice deep in an attempt to disguise it but he didn't fool me; he couldn't bear to leave a phone unanswered, and I had heard him use that silly voice more than once before.

"Hullo?" he said again, and the forced deep-

ness of his voice broke into a quaver at the end.
I pressed the receiver hook and heard the line
go dead.

————

I was tired but I couldn't sleep; my irritation
and perplexity were growing stronger, kept
in motion by a ridiculous sense of unease. I
turned on the lights and looked through my
books until I found a Raymond Chandler
novel I had brought from home. I had read it
before, and thought that a page or two would
put me to sleep, but I had forgotten most of
the plot and before I knew it I'd read fifty
pages, then a hundred.

Several hours passed and I was wide awake.
The radiators were on full blast and the air in
my room was hot and dry. I began to feel
thirsty. I read until the end of a chapter, and
then I got up and put my coat on over my pajamas and went to get a Coke.

Commons was spotless and deserted. Everything smelled of fresh paint. I walked through
the laundry room—pristine, brightly lit, its
creamy walls alien without the tangle of graf-
fiti which had accumulated during the term
before—and bought a can of Coke from the
phosphorescent bank of machines which
hummed at the end of the hall.

Walking around the other way, I was startled
to hear a hollow, tinny music coming from the

common rooms. The television was on; Laurel and Hardy, obscured by a blizzard of electronic snow, were trying to move a grand piano up a great many flights of stairs. At first I thought they were playing to an empty room, but then I noticed the top of a shaggy blond head, lolling against the back of the lone couch that faced the set.

I walked over and sat down. "Bunny," I said. "How are you?"

He looked over at me, eyes glazed, and it took him a second or two to recognize me. He stank of liquor. "Dickie boy," he said thickly. "Yes."

"What are you doing?"

He burped. "Feeling pretty sick, to tell you the God's honest truth."

"Drink too much?"

"Naah," he said crossly. "Stomach flu."

Poor Bunny. He never would own up to being drunk; he'd always say he had a headache or needed to get the prescription for his glasses readjusted. He was like that about a lot of things, actually. One morning after he'd had a date with Marion, he showed up at breakfast with his tray full of milk and sugar doughnuts and when he sat down I saw that there was a big purple hickey on his neck above the collar. "How'd you get **that**, Bun?" I asked him. I was only joking, but he was very offended. "Fell down some stairs," he said brusquely, and ate his doughnuts in silence.

I played along with the stomach-flu ruse. "Maybe it's something you picked up overseas," I said.

"Maybe."

"Been to the infirmary?"

"Nope. Nothing they can do. Got to let it run its course. Better not sit so close to me, old man."

Though I was all the way at the opposite end of the couch, I shifted down even further. We sat looking at the television for a while without saying anything. The reception was terrible. Ollie had just pushed Stan's hat down over his eyes; Stan was wandering in circles, bumping into things, tugging desperately at the brim with both hands. He ran into Ollie and Ollie smacked him on the head with the heel of his palm. Glancing over at Bunny, I saw that he was gripped by this. His gaze was fixed and his mouth slightly open.

"Bunny," I said.

"Yeah?" he said without looking away.

"Where is everybody?"

"Asleep, probably," he said irritably.

"Do you know if the twins are around?"

"I guess."

"Have you seen them?"

"No."

"What's wrong with everybody? Are you mad at Henry or something?"

He didn't answer. Looking at the side of his face, I saw that it was absolutely blank. For a moment I was unnerved and I glanced back at the television. "Did you have a fight in Rome, or what?"

All of a sudden, he cleared his throat noisily, and I thought he was going to tell me to mind my own business, but instead he pointed at something and cleared his throat again. "Are you going to drink that Coke?" he said.

I had forgotten all about it. It lay sweating and unopened on the sofa. I handed it to him and he cracked it open and took a large greedy drink and burped.

"Pause that refreshes," he said, and then: "Let me give you a little tip about Henry, old man."

"What?"

He took another swig and turned back to the TV. "He's not what you think he is."

"What does that mean?" I said after a long pause.

"I mean, he's not what you think," he said, louder this time. "Or what Julian thinks or anybody else." He took another slug of the Coke. "For a while there he had me fooled but good."

"Yeah," I said uncertainly, after another long

moment. The uncomfortable assumption had begun to dawn on me that maybe this was all some sex-related thing I was better off not knowing. I looked at the side of his face: petulant, irritable, glasses low on the tip of his sharp little nose and the beginnings of jowls at his jawline. Might Henry have made a pass at him in Rome? Incredible, but a possible hypothesis. If he had, certainly, all hell would have broken loose. I could not think of much else that would involve this much whispering and secrecy, or that would have so strong an effect on Bunny. He was the only one of us who had a girlfriend and I was pretty sure he slept with her, but at the same time he was incredibly prudish—touchy, easily offended, at root hypocritical. Besides, there was something unquestionably odd about the way Henry was constantly shelling out money to him: paying his tabs, footing his bills, doling out cash like a husband to a spendthrift wife. Perhaps Bunny had allowed his greed to get the better of him, and was angry to discover that Henry's largesse had strings attached.

But did it? There were certainly strings somewhere, though—easy as it seemed on the face of it—I wasn't sure that this was where those particular strings led. There was of course that thing with Julian in the hallway; still, that had been very different. I had lived with Henry for a month, and there hadn't been the faintest hint of that sort of tension, which I, being rather more disinclined that way than not, am quick to pick up on. I had caught a strong breath of it from Francis, a whiff of it at times from Julian; and even Charles, who I knew was interested in women, had a sort of naive, prepubescent shyness of them that a man like my father would have interpreted alarmingly—but with Henry, zero. Geiger counters dead. If anything, it was Camilla he seemed fondest of, Camilla he bent over attentively when she spoke, Camilla who was most often the recipient of his infrequent smiles.

And even if there was a side of him of which I was unaware (which was possible) was it possible that he was attracted to **Bunny**? The answer to this seemed, almost unquestionably, No. Not only did he behave as if he wasn't attracted to Bunny, he acted as if he were hardly able to stand him. And it seemed that he, disgusted by Bunny in what appeared to be virtually all respects, would be far more disgusted in that particular one than even I would be. It was possible for me to recognize, in a general sort of way, that Bunny was handsome, but if I brought the lens any closer and tried to focus on him in a sexual light, all I got was a repugnant miasma of sour-smelling shirts and muscles gone to fat and dirty socks. Girls didn't seem to mind that sort of thing, but to me he was about as erotic as an old football coach.

All at once I felt very tired. I stood up. Bunny stared at me, his mouth open.

"I'm getting sleepy, Bun," I said. "See you tomorrow, maybe."

He blinked at me. "Hope you're not coming down with this damn bug, old man," he said curtly.

"Me, too," I said, feeling sorry for him, unaccountably so. "Good night."

———

I awoke at six on Thursday morning, intending to do some Greek, but my Liddell and Scott was nowhere to be found. I looked and looked and, with a sinking feeling, remembered: it was at Henry's house. I had noticed its absence while I was packing; for some reason it wasn't with my other books. I had made a hurried but diligent search which I finally abandoned, telling myself I'd be back for it later. This put me in a fairly serious fix. My first Greek class wasn't till Monday, but Julian had given me a good deal of work and the library was still closed, as they were changing the catalogues from Dewey decimal to Library of Congress.

I went downstairs and dialed Henry's number, and got, as I expected, no answer. Radiators clanged and hissed in the drafty hall. As I listened to the phone ring for about the thirtieth time, suddenly it occurred to me: why not just run up to North Hampden and get it? He wasn't there—at least I didn't think he was—and I had the key. It would be a long drive for him from Francis's. If I hurried I could be there in fifteen minutes. I hung up and ran out the front door.

In the chilly morning light, Henry's apartment looked deserted, and his car was neither in the drive nor in any of the places up and down the street where he liked to park when he didn't want anyone to know he was home. But just to make sure I knocked. **Pas de réponse.** Hoping I wouldn't find him standing in the front hall in his bathrobe, peering around a door at me, I turned the key gingerly and stepped inside.

No one was there, but the apartment was a mess—books, papers, empty coffee cups and wineglasses; there was a slight film of dust on everything, and the wine in the glasses had dried to a sticky purplish stain at the bottom. The kitchen was full of dirty dishes and the milk had been left out of the refrigerator and turned bad. Henry, generally, was clean as a cat, and I'd never even seen him take off his coat without hanging it up immediately. A dead fly floated in the bottom of one of the coffee cups.

Nervous, feeling as if I'd stumbled on the scene of a crime, I searched the rooms quickly, my footsteps ringing loud in the silence. Before long I saw my book, lying on the hall table, one of the most obvious places I could have left it. **How could I have missed it?** I wondered; I'd looked all over the day I'd left; had Henry found it, left it out for me? I grabbed it up quickly and had started out— jittery, anxious to leave—when my eye was caught by a scrap of paper also on the table.

The handwriting was Henry's:

TWA   219

795 × 4

A telephone number with a 617 area code had been added in Francis's hand, at the bottom. I picked the sheet up and studied it. It was written on the back of an overdue notice from the library dated only three days before.

Without quite knowing why, I set down my Liddell and Scott and took the paper with me to the telephone in the front room. The area code was Massachusetts, probably Boston; I checked my watch and then dialed the number, reversing the charges to Dr. Roland's office.

A wait, two rings, a click. "You have reached the law offices of Robeson Taft on Federal Street," a recording informed me. "Our switchboard is now closed. Please call within the hours of nine to—"

I hung up, and stood staring at the paper. I was remembering, with some unease, the crack Bunny had made about Henry needing a lawyer. Then I picked up the phone again and dialed directory assistance for the information number of TWA.

"This is Mr. Henry Winter," I told the operator. "I'm calling, um, to confirm my reservation."

"Just a moment, Mr. Winter. Your reservation number?"

"Uh," I said, trying to think fast, pacing back and forth, "I don't seem to have my information handy right now, maybe you could just—" Then I noticed the number in the upper right-hand corner. "Wait. Maybe this is it. 219?"

There was the sound of keys being punched in on a computer. I tapped my foot impatiently and glanced out the window for Henry's car. Then I remembered, with a shock, that Henry didn't have his car. I hadn't taken it back to him after I borrowed it on Sunday and it was still parked behind the tennis courts where I'd left it.

In a panicky reflex, I nearly hung up—if Henry didn't have his car I couldn't hear him, he might be halfway up the walk that instant—but just then the operator came back on. "All set, Mr. Winter," she said briskly. "Didn't the agent who sold you the tickets tell you it wasn't necessary to confirm on tickets purchased less than three days in advance?"

"No," I said impatiently, and was about to hang up when I was struck by what she'd said. "Three days?" I repeated.

"Well, generally your reservations are confirmed at date of purchase, especially on non-refundable fares such as these. The agent should have informed you of this when you purchased the tickets on Tuesday."

Date of purchase? Non-refundable? I stopped pacing. "Let me make sure I have the correct information," I said.

"Certainly, Mr. Winter," she said crisply. "TWA flight 401, departing Boston tomorrow from Logan Airport, gate 12, at 8:45 p.m., arriving Buenos Aires, Argentina, at 6:01 a.m. That's with a stopover in Dallas. Four fares at seven hundred and ninety-five dollars one way, let's see"—she punched in some more numbers on the computer—"that comes to a total of three thousand one hundred and eighty dollars plus tax, and you chose to pay for that with your American Express card, am I correct?"

My head began to swim. Buenos **Aires**? Four tickets? One way? Tomorrow?

"I hope you and your family have a pleasant flight on TWA, Mr. Winter," said the operator cheerily, and hung up. I stood there, holding the receiver, until a dial tone came droning on the other end.

Suddenly something occurred to me. I put down the telephone and went back to the bedroom and threw open the door. The books on the book shelf were gone; the padlocked closet stood open, empty; the unfastened lock swung open from the hasp. For a moment I stood staring at it, at the raised Roman capitals that said YALE across the bottom, and then went back to the spare bedroom. The closets there were empty, too, nothing but coat hangers jingling on the metal rod. I turned quickly and almost stumbled over two tremendous pigskin suitcases, strapped in black leather, just inside the doorway. I picked one of them up, and the weight nearly toppled me.

My God, I thought, **what are they doing?** I went back to the hall, replaced the paper, and hurried out the front door with my book.

———

Once out of North Hampden I walked slowly, extremely puzzled, an undertow of anxiety tugging at my thoughts. I felt as if I needed to do something, but I didn't know what. Did Bunny know anything about this? Somehow, I thought not, and somehow I thought it better not to ask him. **Argentina.** What was in Argentina? Grasslands, horses, cowboys of some sort who wore flat-crowned hats with pom-poms hanging from the brim. Borges, the writer. Butch Cassidy, they said, had gone into hiding there, along with Dr. Mengele and Martin Bormann and a score of less pleasant characters.

It seemed that I remembered Henry telling a story, one night at Francis's house, about some South American country—maybe Argentina, I wasn't sure. I tried to think. Something about a trip with his father, a business interest, an island off the coast . . . But Henry's father traveled a good deal; besides, if there was a connection, what could it possibly be? Four tickets? One way? And if Julian knew about it—and he seemed to know everything about Henry, even more so than the rest—why had he been inquiring about everyone's whereabouts only the day before?

My head ached. Emerging from the woods near Hampden, into an expanse of snow-covered meadow that sparkled in the light, I saw twin threads of smoke coming from the age-blacked chimneys at either end of Commons. Everything was cold and quiet except for a milk truck that idled at the rear entrance as two silent, sleepy-looking men unloaded the wire crates and let them fall with a clatter on the asphalt.

The dining halls were open, though at that hour of the morning there were no students, only cafeteria workers and maintenance men eating breakfast before their shifts began. I went upstairs and got myself a cup of coffee and a couple of soft-boiled eggs, which I ate alone at a table near a window in the empty main dining room.

Classes started today, Thursday, but my first class with Julian wasn't until the next Monday. After breakfast I went back to my room and began to work on the irregular second aorists. Not until almost four in the afternoon did I finally close my books, and when I looked out my window over the meadow, the light fading in the west and the ashes and yews casting long shadows on the snow, it was as if I'd just woken up, sleepy and disoriented, to find it was getting dark and I had slept through the day.

It was the big back-to-school dinner that night—roast beef, green beans almondine, cheese soufflé and some elaborate lentil dish for the vegetarians. I ate dinner alone at the same table where I'd had my breakfast. The halls were packed, everyone smoking, laughing, extra chairs wedged in at full tables, people with plates of food roaming from group to group to say hello. Next to me was a table of art students, branded as such by their ink-grimed fingernails and the self-conscious paint spatters on their clothes; one of them was drawing on a cloth napkin with a black felt marker; another was eating a bowl of rice using inverted paintbrushes for chopsticks. I had never seen them before. As I drank my coffee and gazed around the dining room, it struck me that Georges Laforgue had been right, after all: I really was cut off from the rest of the college—not that I cared to be on intimate terms, by and large, with people who used paintbrushes for cutlery.

There was a life-or-death attempt being made near my table by a couple of Neanderthals looking to collect money for a beer blast in the sculpture studio. Actually, I did know these two; it was impossible to attend Hampden and not to. One was the son of a famous West Coast racket boss and the other was the son of a movie producer. They were, respectively, president and vice-president of the Student Council, offices they utilized principally in order to organize drinking contests, wet-T-shirt competitions, and female mud-wrestling tournaments. They were both well over six feet—slack-jawed, unshaven, dumb dumb dumb, the sort who I knew would never go indoors at all after daylight savings in the spring but instead would lounge bare-chested on the lawn with the Styrofoam cooler and the tape deck from dawn till dusk. They were widely held to be good guys, and maybe they were decent enough if you lent them your car for beer runs or sold them pot or something; but both of them—the movie producer's kid in particular—had a piggish, schizophrenic glitter about the eye that I did not care for at all. Party Pig, people called him, and not entirely with affection, either; but he liked this name and took a kind of a stupid pride in living up to it. He was always getting drunk and doing things like setting fires, or stuffing freshmen down chimneys, or throwing beer kegs through plate glass windows.

Party Pig (a.k.a. Jud) and Frank were making their way to my table. Frank held out a paint can full of change and crumpled bills. "Hi, guy," he said. "Keg party in the sculpture studio tonight. Want to give something?"

I put down my coffee and fished in my

jacket pocket and found a quarter and some pennies.

"Oh, come on, man," Jud said, rather menacingly I thought. "You can do better than that."

Hoi polloi. Barbaroi. "Sorry," I said, and pushed back from the table and got my coat and left.

I went back to my room and sat at my desk and opened my lexicon, but I didn't look at it. "Argentina?" I said to the wall.

———

On Friday morning I went to my French class. Several students dozed in the back, overcome no doubt by the previous evening's festivities. The odor of disinfectant and chalkboard cleaner, combined with vibrating fluorescents and the monotonous chant of conditional verbs, put me into kind of a trance, too, and I sat at my desk swaying slightly with boredom and fatigue, hardly aware of the passage of time.

When I got out I went downstairs to a pay phone and called Francis's number in the country and let the phone ring maybe fifty times. No answer.

I walked back to Monmouth House through the snow and went to my room and thought, or, rather, didn't think, but sat on my bed and stared out the window at the ice-rimed yews below. After a while I got up and went to my desk, but I couldn't work, either. One-way tickets, the operator had said. Nonrefundable.

It was eleven a.m. in California. Both my parents would be at work. I went downstairs to my old friend the pay phone and called the number of Francis's mother's apartment in Boston, reversing the charges to my father.

"Well, **Rich**ard," she said when she finally figured out who I was. "Darling. How nice of you to call us. I thought you were going to come spend Christmas with us in New York. Where are you, dear? Can I send somebody to pick you up?"

"No, thank you. I'm in Hampden," I said. "Is Francis there?"

"Dear, he's at **school**, isn't he?"

"Excuse me," I said, suddenly flustered; it had been a mistake to call like this, without planning what to say. "I'm sorry. I think I've made a mistake."

"I beg your pardon?"

"I thought he'd said something about going to Boston today."

"Well, if he's here, sweetheart, I haven't seen him. Where did you say you were? Are you sure you don't want me to send Chris around to get you?"

"No thank you. I'm not in Boston. I'm—"

"You're calling all the way from **school**?" she said, alarmed. "Is anything wrong, dear?"

"No, ma'am, of course not," I said; for a moment I had my customary impulse to hang up but it was too late for that now. "He came by last night while I was really sleepy, and I could've sworn he said he was going down to Boston—oh! **Here he is now!**" I said stupidly, hoping she wouldn't call my bluff.

"Where, dear? **There?**"

"I see him coming across the lawn. Thank you so much, Mrs. er, Abernathy," I said, badly flustered and unable to remember the name of her present husband.

"Call me Olivia, dear. You give that bad boy a kiss for me and tell him to call me on Sunday."

I made my goodbyes quickly—by now I'd broken out in a sweat—and was just turning to go back up the stairs when Bunny, dressed in one of his smart new suits and chewing briskly on a large wad of gum, came striding down the rear hall towards me. He was the last person I was ready to talk to, but I couldn't get away. "Hello, old man," he said. "Where's Henry got off to?"

"I don't know," I said, after an uncertain pause.

"I don't either," he said belligerently. "Haven't

seen him since Monday. Nor François or the twins, either. Say, who was that on the phone?"

I didn't know what to say. "Francis," I said. "I was talking to Francis."

"Hmn," he said, leaning back with his hands in his pockets. "Where was he calling from?"

"Hampden, I guess."

"Not long distance?"

My neck prickled. What did he know about this? "No," I said. "Not that I know of."

"Henry didn't say anything to you about going out of town, did he?"

"No. Why?"

Bunny was silent. Then he said: "There hasn't been a single light on at his house the last few nights. And his car is gone. It's not parked anywhere on Water Street."

For some strange reason, I laughed. I walked over to the back door, which had a window at the top that faced the parking lot behind the tennis courts. Henry's car was there, right where I'd parked it, plain as day. I pointed it out to him. "There it is, right there," I said. "See?"

Bunny's jaw slowed at its work, and his face clouded with the effort of thinking. "Well, that's funny."

"Why?"

A thoughtful pink bubble emerged from his

lips, grew slowly, and burst with a pop. "No reason," he said briskly, resuming his chewing.

"Why would they have gone out of town?"

He reached up and flipped the hair out of his eyes. "You'd be surprised," he said cheerily. "What are you up to now, old man?"

We went upstairs to my room. On the way he stopped at the house refrigerator and peered inside, stooping down myopically to inspect the contents. "Any of this yours, old soak?" he said.

"No."

He reached in and pulled out a frozen cheesecake. Taped to the box was a plaintive note: "Please do not steal this. I am on financial aid. Jenny Drexler."

"This'd hit the spot about now," he said, glancing quickly up and down the hall. "Anybody coming?"

"No."

He stuck the box underneath his coat and, whistling, walked ahead to my room. Once inside, he spat out his gum and stuck it on the inside rim of my garbage can with a quick, feinting motion, as if he hoped I wouldn't see him do it, then sat down and began to eat the cheesecake straight from the box with a spoon he'd found on my dresser. "Phew," he said. "This is terrible. Want some?"

"No thanks."

He licked thoughtfully at the spoon. "Too lemony, is what the problem is. And not enough cream cheese." He paused—thinking, I believed, about this handicap—and then said abruptly: "Tell me. You and Henry spent a lot of time together last month, huh?"

I was suddenly watchful. "I guess."

"Do much talking?"

"Some."

"He tell you much about when we were in Rome?" he said, looking at me keenly.

"Not a whole lot."

"He say anything about leaving early?"

At last, I thought, relieved. At last we were going to get to the bottom of this business. "No. No, he didn't tell me much at all," I said, which was the truth. "I knew he'd left early when he showed up here. But I didn't know you were still there. Finally I asked him about it one night, and he said you were. That's all."

Bunny took a jaded bite of the cheesecake. "He say why he left?"

"No." Then, when Bunny didn't respond, I added: "It had something to do with money, didn't it?"

"Is that what he told you?"

"No." And then, since he had gone mute again: "But he did say you were short on cash, that he had to pay the rent and stuff. Is that right?"

Bunny, his mouth full, made a brushing, dismissive motion with one hand.

"That Henry," he said. "I love him, and you love him, but just between the two of us I think he's got a little bit of Jew blood."

"What?" I said, startled.

He had just taken another big bite of cheesecake, and it took him a moment to answer me.

"I never heard anybody complain so much about helping out a pal," he finally said. "I tell you what it is. He's afraid of people taking advantage of him."

"How do you mean?"

He swallowed. "I mean, somebody probably told him when he was little, 'Son, you have a load of money, and someday people are going to try to weasel it out of you.'" His hair had fallen over one eye; like an old sea captain, he squinted at me shrewdly through the other. "It's not a question of the money, y'see," he said. "He don't need it himself, it's the principle of the thing. He wants to know that people like him not for his money, you know, but for himself."

I was surprised by this exegesis, which was at odds with what I knew to be Henry's frequent and—by my standards of reckoning—extravagant generosity.

"So it's not about money?" I said at last.

"Nope."

"Then what is it about, if you don't mind my asking?"

Bunny leaned forward, his face thoughtful, and for a moment almost transparently frank; and when he opened his mouth again I thought he was going to come right out and say what he meant; but instead, he cleared his throat and said, if I didn't mind, would I go make him a pot of coffee?

———

That night, as I was lying on my bed reading Greek, I was startled by a flash of remembrance, almost as if a hidden spotlight had been trained without warning on my face. **Argentina.** The word itself had lost little of its power to startle and had, due to my ignorance of the physical place it occupied on the globe, assumed a peculiar life of its own. There was the harsh Ar at the beginning, which called up gold, idols, lost cities in the jungle, which in turn led to the hushed and sinister chamber of Gen, with the bright interrogative Tina at the end—all nonsense, of course, but then it seemed in some muddled way that the name itself, one of the few concrete facts available to me, might itself be a cryptogram or clue. But that wasn't what made me bolt upright, but the sudden realization of what time it must be—nine-twenty, I saw, when I looked at my watch. So they were all on the plane now (or were they?) hurtling towards the bizarre Argentina of my imagination through the dark skies.

I put down my book and went over and sat in a chair by the window, and didn't work for the rest of the night.

———

The weekend passed, as they will do, and for me it went by in Greek, solitary meals in the dining hall, and more of the same old puzzlement back in my room. My feelings were hurt, and I missed them more than I would have admitted. Bunny was behaving oddly besides. I saw him around a couple of times that weekend, with Marion and her friends, talking importantly as they stared in goony admiration (they were Elementary Education majors, for the most part, who I suppose thought him terribly erudite because he studied Greek and wore some little wire-rimmed glasses). Once I saw him with his old friend Cloke Rayburn. But I didn't know Cloke well, and I was hesitant to stop and say hello.

I awaited Greek class, on Monday, with acute curiosity. I woke that morning at six. Not wanting to arrive insanely early, I sat around my room fully dressed for quite some time, and it was with something of a thrill that I looked at my watch and realized that if I didn't hurry, I'd be late. I grabbed my books and dashed out; halfway to the Lyceum, I realized I was running, and forced myself to slow to a walk.

I had caught my breath by the time I opened the back door. Slowly, I climbed the stairs, feet moving, mind oddly blank—the way I'd felt as a kid on Christmas morning when, after a night of almost insane excitement, I would walk down the hall to the closed door behind which my presents lay as if the day were nothing special, suddenly drained of all desire.

They were all there, all of them: the twins, poised and alert in the windowsill; Francis, with his back to me; Henry beside him; and Bunny across the table, reared back in his chair. Telling a story of some sort. "So get this," he said to Henry and Francis, turning his face sideways to glimpse the twins. Everyone's eyes were riveted on him; no one had seen me come in. "The warden says, 'Son, your pardon hasn't come through from the governor and it's already five after. Any last words?' So the guy thinks for a minute, and as they're leading him into the chamber"—he brought his pencil up close to his eyes and studied it for a moment—

"he looks over his shoulder and says, 'Well, Governor So-and-So has certainly lost **my** vote in the next election!' " Laughing, he tipped back even further in his chair; then he looked up and saw me standing like an idiot in the doorway. "Oh, come in, come in," he said, bringing the front legs of the wooden chair down with a thump.

The twins glanced up, startled as a pair of deer. Except for a certain tightness around the jaw, Henry was as serene as the Buddha, but Francis was so white he was almost green.

"We're just chucking around a couple jokes before class," said Bunny genially, leaning back in his chair. He tossed the hair out of his eyes. "Okay. Smith and Jones commit an armed robbery and they both get death row. Of course, they go through all the usual channels of appeal but Smith's runs out first and he's slotted for the chair." He made a resigned, philosophical gesture and then, unexpectedly, winked at me. "So," he continued, "they let Jones out to see the execution and he's watching them strap his buddy in"—I saw Charles, his eyes blank, biting down hard into his lower lip—"when the warden comes up. 'Heard anything on your appeal, Jones?' he says. 'Not much, Warden,' says Jones. 'Well, then,' says the warden, looking at his watch, 'hardly worth going back to your cell then, is it?' " He threw back his head and laughed, pleased as all get-out, but no one else even smiled.

When Bunny started in again ("And then there's the one about the Old West—this is when they still hung folks . . .") Camilla edged over on the windowsill and smiled nervously at me.

I went over and sat between her and Charles. She gave me a quick kiss on the cheek. "How are you?" she said. "Did you wonder where we were?"

"I can't believe we haven't seen you," said Charles quietly, turning towards me and crossing his ankle over his knee. His foot was trembling violently, as if it had a life of its own, and he put a hand on it to still it. "We had a terrible mishap with the apartment."

I didn't know what I'd expected to hear from them, but this was not it. "What?" I said.

"We left the key back in Virginia."

"Aunt Mary-Gray had to drive all the way to Roanoke to Federal Express it."

"I thought you had someone subletting," I said suspiciously.

"He left a week ago. Like idiots we told him to mail us the key. The landlady is in Florida. We've been in the country at Francis's the whole time."

"Trapped like rats."

"Francis drove us out there and about two miles from the house something terrible happened to the car," said Charles. "Black smoke and grinding noises."

"The steering went out. We ran into a ditch."

They were both talking very rapidly. For a moment, Bunny's voice rose stridently above them. ". . . Now this judge had a particular system he liked to follow. He'd hang a cattle thief on a Monday, a card cheat on a Tuesday, murderers on Wednesday—"

". . . so after that," Charles was saying, "we had to walk to Francis's and for **days** we called Henry to come get us. But he wasn't answering the phone—you know what it's like to try to get in touch with him—"

"There was **no food** at Francis's house except some cans of black olives and a box of Bisquick."

"Yes. We ate olives and Bisquick."

Could this be true? I wondered suddenly. Briefly I was cheered—my God, how silly I had been—but then I remembered the way Henry's apartment had looked, the suitcases by the door.

Bunny was working up to a big finish. "So the judge says, 'Son, it's a Friday, and I'd like to go on and hang you today, but I'm going to have to wait until next Tuesday because—' "

"There wasn't any milk, even," said Camilla. "We had to mix the Bisquick with water."

There was the slight sound of a throat being cleared and I looked up and saw Julian closing the door behind him.

"Goodness, you magpies," he said into the abrupt silence that fell. "Where have you all **been**?"

Charles coughed, his eyes fixed on a point across the room, and began rather mechanically to tell the story of the apartment key and the car in the ditch and the olives and the Bisquick. The wintry sun, coming in at a slant through the window, gave everything a frozen, precisely detailed look; nothing seemed real, and I felt as though this were some complicated film I'd started watching in the middle and couldn't quite get the drift of. Bunny's jailhouse jokes had for some reason unsettled me, though I remembered him telling an awful lot of jokes like that, back in the fall. They had been met, then as now, with a strained silence, but then they were silly, bad jokes. I had always assumed the reason he told them was because he had some corny old Lawyer's Joke Book up in his room or something, right up there on the shelf with Bob Hope's autobiography, the Fu Manchu novels, and **Men of Thought and Deed.** (Which, as it eventually turned out, he did.)

"Why didn't you call **me**?" said Julian, perplexed and perhaps a little slighted, when Charles finished his story.

The twins looked at him blankly.

"We never thought of it," Camilla said.

Julian laughed and recited an aphorism from Xenophon, which was literally about tents and soldiers and the enemy nigh, but which carried the implication that in troubled times it was best to go to one's own people for help.

————

I walked home from class alone, in a state of bewilderment and turmoil. By now my thoughts were so contradictory and disturbing that I could no longer even speculate, only wonder dumbly at what was taking place around me; I had no classes for the rest of the day and the thought of going back to my room was intolerable. I went to Commons and sat in an armchair by the window for maybe forty-five minutes. Should I go to the library? Take Henry's car, which I still had, and go for a drive, maybe see if there was a matinee at the movie house in town? Should I go ask Judy Poovey for a Valium?

I decided, finally, that the last of these would be a prerequisite for any other plan. I walked back to Monmouth House and up to Judy's room, only to find a note in gold paint-marker on the door: "Beth—Come to Manchester for lunch with Tracy and me? I'm in the costume shop till eleven. J."

I stood staring at Judy's door, which was adorned with photographs of automobile crashes, lurid headlines cut from the **Weekly World News**, and a nude Barbie doll hanging from the doorknob by a noose. By now it was one o'clock. I walked back to my pristine white door at the end of the hall, the only one in the suite unobscured by taped-up religious propaganda and posters of the Fleshtones and suicidal epithets from Artaud, and wondered how all these people were able to put up all this crap on their doors so fast and why they did it in the first place.

I lay on my bed and looked at the ceiling, trying to guess when Judy would return, trying to think of what to do in the meantime, when there was a knock at the door.

It was Henry. I opened the door a little wider and stared at him and said nothing.

He gazed back at me with a fixed and patient unconcern. He was level-eyed and calm and had a book tucked under his arm.

"Hello," he said.

There was another pause, longer than the first. "Hi," I said, after a while.

"How are you?"

"Fine."

"That's good."

There was another long silence.

"Are you doing anything this afternoon?" he said politely.

"No," I said, taken aback.

"Would you like to go on a drive with me?"

I got my coat.

———

Once well out of Hampden, we turned off the main highway and onto a stretch of gravel road that I had never seen. "Where are we going?" I said, rather uneasy.

"I thought we might go out and take a look at an estate sale on the Old Quarry Road," said Henry, unperturbed.

———

I was as surprised as I've ever been at anything in my life when the road finally did bring us out, about an hour later, to a large house with a sign in front that said ESTATE SALE.

Though the house itself was magnificent, the sale turned out not to be much: a grand piano covered with a display of silver and cracked glassware; a grandfather clock; several boxes full of records, kitchen implements, and toys; and some upholstered furniture badly scratched by cats, all out in the garage.

I leafed through a stack of old sheet music, keeping Henry in the corner of my eye. He poked around unconcernedly in the silver; played a disinterested bar of "Träumerei" on

the piano with one hand; opened the door of
the grandfather clock and had a look at the
works; had a long chat with the owner's niece,
who had just come down from the big house,
about when was the best time to put out tulip
bulbs. After I had gone through the sheet music twice, I moved to the glassware and then
the records; Henry bought a garden hoe for
twenty-five cents.

———

"I'm sorry to have dragged you all the way out
here," he said on the way home.

"That's all right," I said, slouched down in
my seat very close to the door.

"I'm a bit hungry. Are you hungry at all?
Would you like to have something to eat?"

———

We stopped at a diner on the outskirts of
Hampden. It was virtually deserted this early
in the evening. Henry ordered an enormous
dinner—pea soup, roast beef, a salad, mashed
potatoes with gravy, coffee, pie—and ate it
silently and with a great deal of methodical relish. I picked erratically at my omelet and had
a hard time keeping my eyes off him as we ate.
I felt as though I were in the dining car of a
train and had been seated by the steward with
another solitary male traveler, some kindly
stranger, someone who didn't even speak my
language, perhaps, but who was still content to

eat his dinner with me, exuding an air of calm acceptance as if he'd known me all his life.

When he'd finished he took his cigarettes out of his shirt pocket (he smoked Lucky Strikes; whenever I think of him I think of that little red bull's-eye right over his heart) and offered me one, shaking a couple out of the pack and raising an eyebrow. I shook my head.

He smoked one and then another, and over our second cup of coffee he looked up. "Why have you been so quiet this afternoon?"

I shrugged.

"Don't you want to know about our trip to Argentina?"

I set my cup in its saucer and stared at him. Then I began to laugh.

"Yes," I said. "**Yes**, I do. Tell me."

"Don't you wonder how I know? That you know, I mean?"

That hadn't occurred to me, and I guess he saw it in my face because now he laughed. "It's no mystery," he said. "When I called to cancel the reservations—they didn't want to do it, of course, non-refundable tickets and all that, but I think we've got it worked out now—anyway, when I called the airline they were rather surprised, as they said I'd called to confirm only the day before."

"How did you know it was me?"

"Who else could it have been? You had the

key. I know, I know," he said when I tried to interrupt him. "I left you that key on purpose. It would have made things easier later on, for various reasons, but by sheer chance you happened in at just the wrong time. I had only left the apartment for a few hours, you see, and I never dreamed that you'd happen in between midnight and seven a.m. I must have missed you by only a few minutes. If you'd happened in an hour or so later everything would have been gone."

He took a sip of his coffee. I had so many questions it was useless to try to sort them into any coherent order. "Why did you leave me the key?" I said at last.

Henry shrugged. "Because I was pretty sure you wouldn't use it unless you had to," he said. "If we'd actually gone, someone would eventually have had to open the apartment for the landlady, and I would have sent you instructions on who to contact and how to dispose of the things I'd left, but I forgot all about that damned Liddell and Scott. Well, I won't say that. I knew you'd left it there, but I was in a hurry and somehow I never thought you'd come back for it **bei Nacht und Nebel**, as it were. But that was silly of me. You have as much trouble sleeping as I do."

"Let me get this straight. You didn't go to Argentina at all?"

Henry snorted, and motioned for the check. "Of course not," he said. "Would I be here if we had?"

Once he'd paid the check he asked me if I wanted to go to Francis's. "I don't think he's there," he said.

"So why go there?"

"Because my apartment is a mess and I'm staying with him until I can get somebody in to clean it up. Do you happen to know of a good maid service? Francis said the last time he had someone from the employment office in town, they stole two bottles of wine and fifty dollars from his dresser drawer."

———

On the way into North Hampden, it was all I could do to keep from deluging Henry with questions, but I kept my mouth shut until we got there.

"He isn't here, I'm sure," he said as he unlocked the front door.

"Where is he?"

"With Bunny. He took him to Manchester for dinner and then I think to some movie that Bunny wanted to see. Would you like some coffee?"

Francis's apartment was in an ugly 1970s building owned by the college. It was roomier and more private than the old oak-floored houses we lived in on campus, and as a conse-

quence was much in demand; as a trade-off
there were linoleum floors, ill-lit halls, and
cheap, modern fixtures like at a Holiday Inn.
Francis didn't seem to mind it much. He had
his own furniture there, brought out from the
country house, but he'd chosen it carelessly
and it was an atrocious mix of styles, uphol-
stery, light and dark woods.

A search revealed that Francis had neither
coffee nor tea ("He needs to go to the grocery
store," said Henry, looking over my shoulder
into yet another barren cabinet), only a few
bottles of Scotch and some Vichy water. I got
some ice and a couple of glasses and we took a
fifth of Famous Grouse with us into the shadowy living room, our shoes clicking across the
ghastly wilderness of white linoleum.

"So you didn't go," I said, after we'd sat
down and Henry had poured us each a glass.

"No."

"Why not?"

Henry sighed, and reached into his breast
pocket for a cigarette. "Money," he said, as the
match flared brightly in the dim. "I don't have
a trust like Francis, you see, only a monthly allowance. It's much more than I generally need
to live on, and for years I've put most of it into
a savings account. But Bunny's just about
cleaned that out. There was no way I could put

my hands on more than thirty thousand dollars, even if I sold my car."

"Thirty thousand dollars is a lot of money."

"Yes."

"Why would you need that much?"

Henry blew a smoke ring half into the yellowy circle of light beneath the lamp, half into the surrounding dark. "Because we weren't coming back," he said. "None of us have work visas. Whatever we took would've had to last the four of us for a long time. Incidentally," he said, raising his voice as if I'd tried to interrupt him—actually, I hadn't, I was only making a sort of inarticulate noise of stupefaction—"incidentally, Buenos Aires wasn't our destination at all. It was only a stop along the way."

"What?"

"If we'd had the money, I suppose we would have flown to Paris or London, some gateway city with plenty of traffic, and once there to Amsterdam and eventually on to South America. That way we'd have been more difficult to trace, you see. But we didn't have that kind of money, so the alternative was to go to Argentina and from there take a roundabout course to Uruguay—a dangerous and unstable place in its own right, to my way of thinking, but suitable for our purposes. My father has an interest in some developing property down there. We'd have had no problem finding a place to live."

"Did he know about this," I said, "your father?"

"He would have eventually. As a matter of fact I was hoping to ask you to get in touch with him once we were there. Had something unforeseen happened he would've been able to help us, even get us out of the country if need be. He knows people down there, people in the government. Otherwise, no one would know."

"He would do that for you?"

"My father and I are not close," said Henry, "but I am his only child." He drank the rest of his Scotch and rattled the ice around in his glass. "But anyway. Even though I didn't have much ready cash, my credit cards were more than adequate, leaving only the problem of raising a sum large enough to live on for a while. Which is where Francis came in. He and his mother live off the income of a trust, as I expect you know, but they also have the right to withdraw as much as three percent of the principal per year, which would amount to a sum of about one hundred and fifty thousand dollars. Generally this isn't touched when it turns up, but in theory either of them can take it out whenever they like. A law firm in Boston serves as the trustees, and on Thursday morning we left the country house, came into Hampden for a few minutes so the twins and I could get our things, and then we all went to Boston and checked into the Parker House. That's a lovely hotel, do you know it? No? Dickens used to stay there when he came to America.

"At any rate, Francis had an appointment with his lawyers, and the twins had some things to straighten out with the passport office. It takes more planning than you might think to pick up and leave the country, but everything was pretty much taken care of; we were leaving the next night and there seemed no way things could go wrong. We were a bit worried about the twins, but of course it wouldn't have posed a problem even if they'd had to wait ten days or so and follow us down later. I had some things to do myself, but not many, and Francis had assured me that getting the money was a simple matter of going downtown and signing some papers. His mother would find out he'd taken it, but what could she do once he was gone?

"But he wasn't back when he said he would be, and three hours passed, then four. The twins came back, and the three of us had just ordered up some lunch from room service when Francis burst in, half-hysterical. The money for that year was all gone, you see. His mother had checked out every cent of the principal at the first of the year and hadn't told him about it. It was a nasty surprise, but even nastier given the circumstances. He'd tried everything he could think of—to borrow money on the trust itself, even to assign his interests, which is, if you know anything about trusts, about the most desperate thing one can do. The twins were all for going ahead and taking our chances. But . . . It was a difficult situation. Once we left we couldn't come back and anyway, what were we supposed to do when we got there? Live in a treehouse like Wendy and the Lost Boys?" He sighed. "So there we were, with our suitcases packed and passports ready, but no money. I mean, literally none. Between the four of us we had hardly five thousand dollars. There was quite a bit of discussion, but in the end we decided our only choice was to come back to Hampden. For the time being, at least."

He said this all quite calmly but I, listening to him, felt a lump growing in the pit of my stomach. The picture was still wholly obscure, but what I saw of it I didn't like at all. I said nothing for a long time, only looked at the shadows the lamp cast on the ceiling.

"Henry, my God," I said at last. My voice was flat and strange even to my own ears.

He raised an eyebrow and said nothing, empty glass in hand, face half in shadow.

I looked at him. "My God," I said. "What have you done?"

He smiled wryly, and leaned forward out of the light to pour himself some more Scotch. "I think you already have a pretty good idea," he said. "Now let me ask you something. Why have you been covering up for us?"

"What?"

"You knew we were leaving the country. You knew it all the time and you didn't tell a soul. Why is that?"

The walls had fallen away and the room was black. Henry's face, lit starkly by the lamp, was pale against the darkness and stray points of light winked from the rim of his spectacles, glowed in the amber depths of his whiskey glass, shone blue in his eyes.

"I don't know," I said.

He smiled. "No?" he said.

I stared at him and didn't say anything.

"After all, we hadn't confided in **you**," he said. His gaze on mine was steady, intense. "You could have stopped us any time you wanted and yet you didn't. Why?"

"Henry, what in God's name have you done?"

He smiled. "You tell me," he said.

And the horrible thing was, somehow, that I did know. "You killed somebody," I said, "didn't you?"

He looked at me for a moment, and then, to my utter, utter surprise, he leaned back in his chair and laughed.

"Good for you," he said. "You're just as smart as I thought you were. I knew you'd figure it out, sooner or later, that's what I've told the others all along."

The darkness hung about our tiny circle of lamplight as heavy and palpable as a curtain. With a rush of what was almost motion sickness, I experienced for a moment both the claustrophobic feeling that the walls had rushed in towards us and the vertiginous one that they receded infinitely, leaving both of us suspended in some boundless expanse of dark. I swallowed, and looked back at Henry. "Who was it?" I said.

He shrugged. "A minor thing, really. An accident."

"Not on purpose?"

"Heavens, no," he said, surprised.

"What happened?"

"I don't know where to begin." He paused, and took a drink. "Do you remember last fall, in Julian's class, when we studied what Plato calls telestic madness? **Bakcheia?** Dionysiac frenzy?"

"Yes," I said, rather impatiently. It was just like Henry to bring up something like this right now.

"Well, we decided to try to have one."

For a moment I thought I hadn't understood him. "What?" I said.

"I said we decided to try to have a bacchanal."

"Come on."

"We did."

I looked at him. "You must be joking."

"No."

"That's the weirdest thing I've ever heard."

He shrugged.

"Why would you want to do something like that?"

"I was obsessed with the idea."

"Why?"

"Well, as far as I knew, it hadn't been done for two thousand years." He paused, when he saw he hadn't convinced me. "After all, the appeal to stop being yourself, even for a little while, is very great," he said. "To escape the cognitive mode of experience, to transcend the accident of one's moment of being. There are other advantages, more difficult to speak of, things which ancient sources only hint at and which I myself only understood after the fact."

"Like what?"

"Well, it's not called a mystery for nothing,"

said Henry sourly. "Take my word for it. But one mustn't underestimate the primal appeal—to lose one's self, lose it utterly. And in losing it be born to the principle of continuous life, outside the prison of mortality and time. That was attractive to me from the first, even when I knew nothing about the topic and approached it less as potential **mystes** than anthropologist. Ancient commentators are very circumspect about the whole thing. It was possible, with a great deal of work, to figure out some of the sacred rituals—the hymns, the sacred objects, what to wear and do and say. More difficult was the mystery itself: how did one propel oneself into such a state, what was the catalyst?" His voice was dreamy, amused. "We tried **everything**. Drink, drugs, prayer, even small doses of poison. On the night of our first attempt, we simply overdrank and passed out in our chitons in the woods near Francis's house."

"You wore **chitons**?"

"Yes," said Henry, irritated. "It was all in the interests of science. We made them from bed sheets in Francis's attic. At any rate. The first night nothing happened at all, except we were hung over and stiff from having slept on the ground. So the next time we didn't drink as much, but there we all were, in the middle of the night on the hill behind Francis's house, drunk and in chitons and singing Greek hymns like something from a fraternity initiation, and all at once Bunny began to laugh so hard that he fell over like a ninepin and rolled down the hill.

"It was rather obvious that drink alone wasn't going to do the trick. Goodness. I couldn't tell you all the things we tried. Vigils. Fasting. Libations. It depresses me even to think about it. We burned hemlock branches and breathed the fumes. I knew the Pythia had chewed laurel leaves, but that didn't work either. You found those laurel leaves, if you recall, on the stove in Francis's kitchen."

I stared at him. "Why didn't I know about any of this?" I said.

Henry reached into his pocket for a cigarette. "Well, really," he said, "I think that's kind of obvious."

"What do you mean?"

"**Of course** we weren't going to tell you. We hardly knew you. You would have thought we were crazy." He was quiet for a moment. "You see, we had almost nothing to go on," he said. "I suppose in a certain way I was misled by accounts of the Pythia, the **pneuma enthusiastikon**, poisonous vapors and so forth. Those processes, though sketchy, are more well documented than Bacchic methods, and I thought for a while that the two must be related. Only after a long period of trial and error did it become evident that they were not, and that what we were missing was something, in all likelihood, quite simple. Which it was."

"And what might that have been?"

"Only this. To receive the god, in this or any other mystery, one has to be in a state of **euphemia**, cultic purity. That is at the very center of Bacchic mystery. Even Plato speaks of it. Before the Divine can take over, the mortal self—the dust of us, the part that decays—must be made clean as possible."

"How is that?"

"Through symbolic acts, most of them fairly universal in the Greek world. Water poured over the head, baths, fasting—Bunny wasn't so good about the fasting nor about the baths, either, if you ask me but the rest of us went through the motions. The more we did it, though, the more meaningless it all began to seem, until, one day, I was struck by something rather obvious—namely, that any religious ritual is arbitrary unless one is able to see past it to a deeper meaning." He paused. "Do you know," he said, "what Julian says about the **Divine Comedy**?"

"No, Henry, I don't."

"That it's incomprehensible to someone who isn't a Christian? That if one is to read Dante, and understand him, one must become a Christian if only for a few hours? It was the same with this. It had to be approached on its own terms, not in a voyeuristic light or even a scholarly one. At the first, I suppose, it was impossible to see it any other way, looking at it as we did in fragments, through centuries. The vitality of the act was entirely obfuscated, the beauty, the terror, the sacrifice." He took one last drag of his cigarette and put it out. "Quite simply," he said, "we didn't believe. And belief was the one condition which was absolutely necessary. Belief, and absolute surrender."

I waited for him to continue.

"At this point, you must understand, we were on the verge of giving up," he said calmly. "The enterprise had been interesting, but not that interesting; and besides, it was a good deal of trouble. You don't know how many times you almost stumbled on us."

"No?"

"No." He took a drink of his whiskey. "I don't suppose you remember coming downstairs one night in the country, about three in the morning," he said. "Down to the library to get a book. We heard you on the stairs. I was hidden behind the draperies; I could have reached out and touched you if I'd wanted. Another time you woke up before we even got home. We had to slip around to the back door, sneak up the stairs like cat burglars—it was

very tiresome, all that creeping around barefoot in the dark. Besides, it was getting cold.
They say that the **oreibasia** took place in mid-
winter, but I daresay the Peloponnesus is
considerably milder that time of year than Vermont.

"We'd worked on it so long, though, and it
seemed senseless, in light of our revelation, not
to try once more before the weather turned.
Everything got serious all of a sudden. We
fasted for three days, longer than we ever had
before. A messenger came to me in a dream.
Everything was going beautifully, on the brink
of taking wing, and I had a feeling that I'd
never had, that reality itself was transforming
around us in some beautiful and dangerous
fashion, that we were being driven by a force
we didn't understand, towards an end I did
not know." He reached for his drink again.
"The only problem was Bunny. He didn't
grasp, in some fundamental way, that things
had changed significantly. We were closer than
we'd ever been, and every day counted; already
it was terribly cold, and if it snowed, which it
might have any day, we'd have had to wait till
spring. I couldn't bear the thought that, after
everything we'd done, he'd ruin it at the last
minute. And I knew he would. At the crucial
moment he'd start to tell some asinine joke
and ruin everything. By the second day I was

having my doubts, and then, on the afternoon
of the night itself, Charles saw him in Commons having a grilled cheese sandwich and a
milk shake. That did it. We decided to slip
away without him. To go out on the weekends
was too risky, since you'd almost caught us several times already, so we'd been driving out late
on Thursday and getting back about three or
four the next morning. Except this time we left
early, before dinner, and didn't say a word to
him about it."

He lit a cigarette. There was a long pause.

"So?" I said. "What happened?"

He laughed. "I don't know what to say."

"What do you mean?"

"I mean that it worked."

"It **worked**?"

"Absolutely."

"But how could—?"

"It worked."

"I don't think I understand what you mean
when you say 'it worked.' "

"I mean it in the most literal sense."

"But how?"

"It was heart-shaking. Glorious. Torches,
dizziness, singing. Wolves howling around us
and a bull bellowing in the dark. The river ran
white. It was like a film in fast motion, the
moon waxing and waning, clouds rushing
across the sky. Vines grew from the ground so

fast they twined up the trees like snakes; seasons passing in the wink of an eye, entire years for all I know. . . . I mean we think of phenomenal change as being the very essence of time, when it's not at all. Time is something which defies spring and winter, birth and decay, the good and the bad, indifferently. Something changeless and joyous and absolutely indestructible. Duality ceases to exist; there is no ego, no "I," and yet it's not at all like those horrid comparisons one sometimes hears in Eastern religions, the self being a drop of water swallowed by the ocean of the universe. It's more as if the universe expands to fill the boundaries of the self. You have no idea how pallid the workday boundaries of ordinary existence seem, after such an ecstasy. It was like being a baby. I couldn't remember my name. The soles of my feet were cut to pieces and I couldn't even feel it."

"But these are fundamentally **sex** rituals, aren't they?"

It came out not as a question but as a statement. He didn't blink, but sat waiting for me to continue.

"Well? Aren't they?"

He leaned over to rest his cigarette in the ashtray. "Of course," he said agreeably, cool as a priest in his dark suit and ascetic spectacles. "You know that as well as I do."

We sat looking at each other for a moment.

"What exactly did you do?" I said.

"Well, really, I think we needn't go into that now," he said smoothly. "There was a certain carnal element to the proceedings but the phenomenon was basically spiritual in nature."

"You saw Dionysus, I suppose?"

I had not meant this at all seriously, and I was startled when he nodded as casually as if I'd asked him if he'd done his homework.

"You saw him **corporeally**? Goatskin? Thyrsus?"

"How do **you** know what Dionysus is?" said Henry, a bit sharply. "What do you think it was we saw? A cartoon? A drawing from the side of a vase?"

"I just can't believe you're telling me you **actually saw**—"

"What if you had never seen the sea before? What if the only thing you'd ever seen was a child's picture—blue crayon, choppy waves? Would you know the real sea if you only knew the picture? Would you be able to recognize the real thing even if you saw it? You don't know what Dionysus looks like. We're talking about God here. God is serious business." He leaned back in his chair and scrutinized me. "You don't have to take my word for any of this, you know," he said. "There were four of us. Charles had a bloody bite-mark on his arm that he had no idea how he'd got, but it wasn't a human bite. Too big. And strange puncture marks instead of teeth. Camilla said that during part of it, she'd believed she was a deer; and that was odd, too, because the rest of us remember chasing a deer through the woods, for miles it seemed. Actually, it **was** miles. I know that for a fact. Apparently we ran and ran and ran, because when we came to ourselves we had no idea where we were. Later we figured out that we had got over at least four barbed-wire fences, though how I don't know, and were well off Francis's property, seven or eight miles into the country. This is where I come to the rather unfortunate part of my story.

"I have only the vaguest memory of this. I heard something behind me, or someone, and I wheeled around, almost losing my balance, and swung at whatever it was—a large, indistinct, yellow thing—with my closed fist, my left, which is not my good one. I felt a terrible pain in my knuckles and then, almost instantly, something knocked the breath right out of me. It was dark, you understand; I couldn't really see. I swung out again with my right, hard as I could and with all my weight behind it, and this time I heard a loud crack and a scream.

"We're not too clear on what happened after that. Camilla was a good deal ahead, but

Charles and Francis were fairly close behind and had soon caught up with me. I have a distinct recollection of being on my feet and seeing the two of them crash through the bushes—God. I can see them now. Their hair was tangled with leaves and mud and their clothes virtually in shreds. They stood there, panting, glassy-eyed and hostile—I didn't recognize either of them, and I think we might have started to fight had not the moon come from behind a cloud. We stared at each other. Things started to come back. I looked down at my hand and saw it was covered with blood, and worse than blood. Then Charles stepped forward and knelt at something at my feet, and I bent down, too, and saw that it was a man. He was dead. He was about forty years old and he had on a yellow plaid shirt—you know those woolen shirts they wear up here—and his neck was broken, and, unpleasant to say, his brains were all over his face. Really, I do not know how that happened. There was a dreadful mess. I was drenched in blood and there was even blood on my glasses.

"Charles tells a different story. He remembers seeing me by the body. But he says he also has a memory of struggling with something, pulling as hard as he could, and all of a sudden becoming aware that what he was pulling at was a man's arm, with his foot braced in the armpit. Francis—well, I can't say. Every time you talk to him, he remembers something different."

"And Camilla?"

Henry sighed. "I suppose we'll never know what really happened," he said. "We didn't find her until a good bit later. She was sitting quietly on the bank of a stream with her feet in the water, her robe perfectly white, and no blood anywhere except for her hair. It was dark and clotted, completely soaked. As if she'd tried to dye it red."

"How could that have happened?"

"We don't know." He lit another cigarette. "Anyway, the man was dead. And there we were in the middle of the woods, half-naked and covered with mud with this body on the ground in front of us. We were all in a daze. I was fading in and out, nearly went to sleep; but then Francis went over for a closer look and had a pretty violent attack of the dry heaves. Something about that brought me to my senses. I told Charles to find Camilla and then I knelt down and went through the man's pockets. There wasn't much—I found something or other that had his name on it—but of course that wasn't any help.

"I had no idea what to do. You must remember that it was getting cold, and I hadn't slept or eaten for a long time, and my mind wasn't at its clearest. For a few minutes—goodness, how confusing this was—I thought of digging a grave but then I realized that would be madness. We couldn't linger around all night. We didn't know where we were, or who might happen along, or even what time it was. Besides, we had nothing to dig a grave with. For a moment I nearly panicked—we couldn't just leave the body in the open, could we?—but then I realized it was the only thing we could do. My God. We didn't even know where the car was. I couldn't picture dragging this corpse over hill and dale for goodness knows how long; and even if we got it to the car, where would we take it?

"So when Charles came back with Camilla, we just left. Which, in retrospect, was the smartest thing we could have done. It's not as if teams of expert coroners are crawling all over upstate Vermont. It's a primitive place. People die violent natural deaths all the time. We didn't even know who the man was; there was nothing to tie us to him. All we had to worry about was finding the car and then making our way home without anyone seeing us." He leaned over and poured himself some more Scotch. "Which is exactly what we did."

I poured myself another glass, too, and we sat without speaking for a minute or more.

"Henry," I said at last. "Good God."

He raised an eyebrow. "Really, it was more upsetting than you can imagine," he said. "Once I hit a deer with my car. It was a beautiful creature and to see it struggling, blood everywhere, legs broken . . . And this was even more distressing but at least I thought it was over. I never dreamed we'd hear anything else about it." He took a drink of his Scotch. "Unfortunately, that is not the case," he said. "Bunny has seen to that."

"What do you mean?"

"You saw him this morning. He's driven us half mad over this. I am very nearly at the end of my rope."

There was the sound of a key being turned in the lock. Henry brought up his glass and drank the rest of his whiskey in a long swallow. "That'll be Francis," he said, and turned on the overhead light.

CHAPTER
5

WHEN THE lights came on, and the circle of darkness leapt back into the mundane and familiar boundaries of the living room—cluttered desk; low, lumpy sofa; the dusty and modishly cut draperies that had fallen to Francis after one of his mother's decorating purges—it was as if I'd switched on the lamp after a long bad dream; blinking, I was relieved to discover that the doors and windows were still where they were supposed to be and that the furniture hadn't rearranged itself, by diabolical magic, in the dark.

The bolt turned. Francis stepped in from the dark hall. He was breathing hard, pulling with dispirited jerks at the fingertips of a glove.

"Jesus, Henry," he said. "What a night."

I was out of his line of vision. Henry glanced at me and cleared his throat discreetly. Francis wheeled around.

I thought I looked back at him casually enough, but evidently I didn't. It must have been all over my face.

He stared at me for a long time, the glove half on, half off, dangling limply from his hand.

"Oh, no," he said at last, without moving his eyes away from mine. "Henry. You didn't."

"I'm afraid I did," Henry said.

Francis squeezed his eyes tight shut, then reopened them. He had got very white, his pallor dry and talcumy as a chalk drawing on rough paper. For a moment I wondered if he might faint.

"It's all right," said Henry.

Francis didn't move.

"Really, Francis," Henry said, a trifle peevishly, "it's all right. Sit down."

Breathing hard, he made his way across the room and fell heavily into an armchair, where he rummaged in his pocket for a cigarette.

"He knew," said Henry. "I told you so."

Francis looked up at me, the unlit cigarette trembling in his fingertips. "Did you?"

I didn't answer. For a moment I found myself wondering if this was all some monstrous practical joke. Francis dragged a hand down the side of his face.

"I suppose everybody knows now," he said. "I don't even know why I feel bad about it."

Henry had stepped into the kitchen for a glass. Now he poured some Scotch in it and handed it to Francis. **"Deprendi miserum est,"** he said.

To my surprise Francis laughed, a humorless little snort.

"Good Lord," he said, and took a long drink. "What a nightmare. I can't imagine what you must think of us, Richard."

"It doesn't matter." I said this without thinking, but as soon as I had, I realized, with something of a jolt, that it was true; it really didn't matter that much, at least not in the preconceived way that one would expect.

"Well, I guess you could say we're in quite a fix," said Francis, rubbing his eyes with thumb and forefinger. "I don't know what we're going to do with Bunny. I wanted to slap him when we were standing in line for that damned movie."

"You took him to Manchester?" Henry said.

"Yes. But people are so nosy and you never do really know who might be sitting behind you, do you? It wasn't even a good movie."

"What was it?"

"Some nonsense about a bachelor party. I just want to take a sleeping pill and go to bed." He drank off the rest of his Scotch and poured himself another inch. "Jesus," he said to me. "You're being so nice about this. I feel awfully embarrassed by this whole thing."

There was a long silence.

Finally I said: "What are you going to do?"

Francis sighed. "We didn't **mean** to do anything," he said. "I know it sounds kind of bad, but what can we do about it now?"

The resigned note in his voice simultaneously angered and distressed me. "**I** don't know," I said. "Why for God's sake didn't you go to the police?"

"Surely you're joking," said Henry dryly.

"Tell them you don't know what happened? That you found him lying out in the woods? Or, God, I don't know, that you hit him with the car, that he ran out in front of you or something?"

"That would have been a very foolish thing to do," Henry said. "It was an unfortunate incident and I am sorry that it happened, but frankly I do not see how well either the taxpayers' interests or my own would be served by my spending sixty or seventy years in a Vermont jail."

"But it was an **accident**. You said so yourself."

Henry shrugged.

"If you'd gone right in, you could've got off on some minor charge. Maybe nothing would have happened at all."

"Maybe not," Henry said agreeably. "But remember, this is Vermont."

"What the hell difference does that make?"

"It makes a great deal of difference, unfortunately. If the thing went to trial, we'd be tried here. And not, I might add, by a jury of our peers."

"So?"

"Say what you like, but you can't convince me that a jury box of poverty-level Vermonters would have the remotest bit of pity for four college students on trial for murdering one of their neighbors."

"People in Hampden have been hoping for years that something like this would happen," said Francis, lighting a new cigarette off the end of the old one. "We wouldn't be getting off on any **man**slaughter charges. We'd be lucky if we didn't go to the chair."

"Imagine how it would look," Henry said. "We're all young, well educated, reasonably well off; perhaps most importantly, not Vermonters. And I suppose that any equitable judge might make allowances for our youth, and the fact that it was an accident and so forth—"

"Four rich college kids?" said Francis. "Drunk? On drugs? On this guy's land in the middle of the night?"

"You were on his land?"

"Well, apparently," said Henry. "That's where the papers said his body was found."

I hadn't been in Vermont very long, but I'd been there long enough to know what any Vermonter worth his salt would think of **that**. Trespassing on someone's land was tantamount to breaking into his house. "Oh, God," I said.

"That's not the half of it, either," said Francis. "For Christ's sake, we were wearing **bed** sheets. Barefoot. Soaked in blood. Stinking drunk. Can you imagine if we'd trailed down to the sheriff's office and tried to explain all **that**?"

"Not that we were in any condition to explain," Henry said dreamily. "Really. I wonder if you understand what sort of state we were in. Scarcely an hour before, we'd all been really, truly **out of our minds.** And it may be a superhuman effort to lose oneself so completely, but that's nothing compared to the effort of getting oneself **back** again."

"It certainly wasn't as if something snapped and there we were, our jolly old selves," said Francis. "Believe me. We might as well have had shock treatments."

"I really don't know how we got home without being seen," Henry said.

"No way could we have patched together a plausible story from this. Good Lord. It was weeks before I got over it. Camilla couldn't even talk for three days."

With a small chill, I remembered: Camilla, her throat wrapped in a red muffler, unable to speak. Laryngitis, they'd said.

"Yes, that was very strange," said Henry. "She was thinking clearly enough, but the words wouldn't come out right. As if she'd had a stroke. When she started to speak again, her high-school French came back before her English **or** her Greek. Nursery words. I remember sitting by her bed, listening to her count to ten, watching her point to **la fenêtre, la chaise** . . ."

Francis laughed. "She was so funny," he said. "When I asked her how she felt she said, **'Je me sens comme Hélène Keller, mon vieux.'** "

"Did she go to the doctor?"

"Are you kidding?"

"What if she hadn't got any better?"

"Well, the same thing happened to all of us," said Henry. "Only it more or less wore off in a couple of hours."

"You couldn't talk?"

"Bitten and scratched to pieces?" Francis said. "Tongue-tied? Half mad? If we'd gone to the police they would have charged us with every unsolved death in New England for the last five years." He held up an imaginary newspaper. " 'Crazed Hippies Indicted for Rural Thrill-Killing.' 'Cult Slaying of Old Abe So-and-So.' "

"Teen Satanists Murder Longtime Vermont Resident," said Henry, lighting a cigarette.

Francis started to laugh.

"It would be one thing if we had even a chance at a decent hearing," said Henry. "But we don't."

"And I personally can't imagine much worse than being tried for my life by a Vermont circuit-court judge and a jury box full of telephone operators."

"Things aren't marvelous," said Henry, "but they could certainly be worse. The big problem now is Bunny."

"What's wrong with him?"

"Nothing's **wrong** with him."

"Then what's the problem?"

"He just can't keep his mouth shut, that's all."

"Haven't you talked to him?"

"About ten million times," Francis said.

"Has he tried to go to the police?"

"If he goes on like this," said Henry, "he won't have to. They'll come right to us. Reasoning with him does no good. He just doesn't grasp what a serious business this is."

"Surely he doesn't want to see you go to jail."

"If he thought about it, I'm sure he'd realize he didn't," said Henry evenly. "And I'm sure he'd realize that he doesn't particularly want to go to jail himself, either."

"Bunny? But why—?"

"Because he's known about this since November and he hasn't gone to the police," Francis said.

"But that's beside the point," said Henry. "Even he has sense enough not to turn us in. He doesn't have much of an alibi for the night of the murder, and if it ever came to prison for the rest of us I think he must know that I, at least, would do everything in my power to see he came along with us." He stubbed out his cigarette. "The problem is he's just a fool, and sooner or later he's going to say the wrong thing to the wrong person," he said. "Perhaps not intentionally, but I can't pretend to be too concerned with motive at this point. You heard him this morning. He'd be in quite a spot himself if this got back to the police but of course he thinks those ghastly jokes are all terribly subtle and clever and over everyone's head."

"He's only just smart enough to realize what a mistake turning us in would be," said Francis, pausing to pour himself another drink. "But we can't seem to pound it into him that it's even more in his own self-interest not to go around talking like he does. And, really, I'm not at all sure he won't just come out and **tell** someone, when he's in one of these confessional moods."

"Tell someone? Like who?"

"Marion. His father. The Dean of Studies." He shuddered. "Gives me the creeps just to think about it. He's just the sort who always stands up in the back of the courtroom during the last five minutes of 'Perry Mason.' "

"Bunny Corcoran, Boy Detective," said Henry dryly.

"How did he find out? He wasn't with you, was he?"

"As a matter of fact," said Francis, "he was with **you**." He glanced at Henry, and to my surprise the two of them began to laugh.

"What? What's so funny?" I said, alarmed.

This sent them into fresh peals of laughter. "Nothing," said Francis at last.

"Really, it is nothing," said Henry, with a bemused little sigh. "The oddest things make me laugh these days." He lit another cigarette. "He was with you that night, early in the evening, anyway. Remember? You went to the movies."

"The Thirty-Nine Steps," Francis said.

With something of a start, I did remember: a windy autumn night, full moon obscured by dusty rags of cloud. I'd worked late in the library and hadn't gone to dinner. Walking home, a sandwich from the snack bar in my pocket, and the dry leaves skittering and dancing on the path before me, I'd run into Bunny on his way to the Hitchcock series, which the Film Society was showing in the auditorium.

We were late and there were no seats left so we sat on the carpeted stairs, Bunny leaning back on his elbows with his legs stretched in front of him, cracking pensively with his rear molars at a little Dum-Dum sucker. The high wind rattled the flimsy walls; a door banged open and shut until somebody propped it open with a brick. On the screen, locomotives screaming across a black-and-white nightmare of iron-bridged chasms.

"We had a drink afterwards," I said. "Then he went to his room."

Henry sighed. "I wish he had," he said.

"He kept asking if I knew where you were."

"He knew himself, very well. We'd threatened half a dozen times to leave him at home if he didn't behave."

"So he got the bright idea of coming around to Henry's to scare him," said Francis, pouring himself another drink.

"I was so angry about that," said Henry abruptly. "Even if nothing had happened, it was a sneaky thing to do. He knew where the spare key was, and he just got it and let himself in."

"Even so, nothing might have happened. It was just a horrible string of coincidences. If we'd stopped in the country to get rid of our clothes, if we'd come here or to the twins', if Bunny only hadn't fallen asleep . . ."

"He was asleep?"

"Yes, or otherwise he would have got discouraged and left," Henry said. "We didn't get back to Hampden until six in the morning. It was a miracle we found our way to the car, over all those fields and things in the dark. . . . Well, it **was** foolish to drive to North Hampden in those bloody clothes. The police could have pulled us over, we could have had a wreck, anything. But I felt ill, and I wasn't thinking clearly, and I suppose I drove to my own apartment by instinct."

"He left my room around midnight."

"Well, then, he was alone in my apartment from about twelve-thirty to six a.m. And the coroner reckoned the time of death between one and four. That's one of the few decent cards fate dealt us in the whole hand. Though Bunny wasn't with us, he'd have a hard time proving he wasn't. Unfortunately, that's not a card we can play except in the direst circumstances." He shrugged. "If only he'd left the lamp on, anything to tip us off."

"But that was going to be the big surprise, you see. Jumping out at us from the dark."

"We walked in and turned on the light, and then it was too late. He woke up instantly. And there we were—"

"—all white robes and bloody like something from Edgar Allan Poe," Francis said gloomily.

"Jesus, what did he do?"

"What do you think? We scared him half to death."

"It served him right," said Henry.

"Tell him about the ice cream."

"Really, this was the last straw," Henry said crossly. "He took a quart of ice cream out of my freezer to eat while he waited—he couldn't bother to get a bowl of it, you understand, he had to have the whole quart—and when he fell asleep it melted all over him **and** on my chair and on that nice little Oriental rug I used to have. Well. It was quite a good antique, that rug, but the dry cleaners said there was nothing they could do. It came back in shreds. And my **chair**." He reached for a cigarette. "He screamed like a banshee when he saw us—"

"—and he would not shut up," said Francis. "Remember, it was six o'clock in the morning, the neighbors sleeping . . ." He shook his head. "I remember Charles taking a step towards him, trying to talk to him, and Bunny yelling bloody murder. After a minute or two—"

"It was only a few seconds," Henry said.

"—after a minute, Camilla picked up a glass ashtray and threw it at him and hit him square in the chest."

"It wasn't a hard blow," said Henry thought-fully, "but it was quite judiciously timed. In-stantly he shut up and stared at her and I said to him, 'Bunny, shut up. You'll wake the neighbors. We've hit a deer in the road on the way home.' "

"So then," said Francis, "he wiped his brow and rolled his eyes and went through the whole Bunny routine—boy you guys scared me and must've been half-asleep and just on and on and on—"

"And meanwhile," Henry said, "the four of us were standing there in the bloody sheets, the lights on, no curtains, in full view of any-one who might happen to drive by. He was talking so loudly, and the lights were so bright, and I felt so faint with exhaustion and shock that I couldn't do much more than stare at him. My God—we were covered with this man's blood, we'd tracked it into the house, the sun was coming up, and here, to top it all off, was Bunny. I couldn't force myself to think what to do. Then Camilla, quite sensibly, flicked off the light and all of a sudden I real-ized no matter how it looked, no matter who was there, we had to get out of our clothes and wash up without losing another second."

"I practically had to rip the sheet off," said Francis. "The blood had dried and it was stuck to me. By the time I'd managed that, Henry and the others were in the bathroom. Spray was flying; the water in the bathtub was backed up red; rusty splashes on the tile. It was a nightmare."

"I can't tell you how unfortunate it was that Bunny happened to be there," said Henry, shaking his head. "But for heaven's sake, we couldn't just stand around and wait for him to leave. There was blood everywhere, the neighbors would soon be up, for all I knew the police would be pounding at the door any second. . . ."

"Well, it was too bad we alarmed him, but then, it wasn't like we thought we were doing this in front of J. Edgar Hoover, either," said Francis.

"Exactly," said Henry. "I don't want to convey the impression that Bunny's presence seemed like a tremendous **menace** at that point. It was just a nuisance, because I knew he wondered what was going on, but at the moment he was the least of our troubles. If there'd been time, I would have sat him down and explained things to him the instant we got in. But there wasn't time."

"Good God," Francis said, and shuddered. "I still can't go in Henry's bathroom. Blood smeared on the porcelain. Henry's straight razor swinging from a peg. We were bruised and scratched to pieces."

"Charles was the worst by far."

"Oh, my God. Thorns stuck all over him."

"And that **bite**."

"You've never seen anything like it," said Francis. "Four inches around and the teeth marks just gouged in. Remember what Bunny said?"

Henry laughed. "Yes," he said. "Tell him."

"Well, there we all were, and Charles was turning to get the soap—I didn't even know Bunny was there, I suppose he was looking in the door—when all of a sudden I heard him say, in this weird businesslike way, 'Looks like that deer took a plug out of your **arm**, Charles.'"

"He was standing there for part of the time, making comments of various sorts," said Henry, "but the next thing I knew he wasn't. I was disturbed by how suddenly he'd left but glad he was out of the way. We had a great deal to do and not too much time."

"Weren't you afraid he'd tell somebody?"

Henry looked at me blankly. "Who?"

"Me. Marion. Anybody."

"No. At that point I had no reason to think he'd do anything of the sort. He'd been with us on previous tries, you understand, so our appearance didn't seem as extraordinary to him as it might have to you. The whole thing was deadly secret. He'd been involved in it with us for months. How could he have told anyone without explaining the whole thing and making himself look foolish? Julian knew what we were trying to do, but I was still pretty certain Bunny wouldn't talk to him without checking it with us first. And, as it happened, I was right."

He paused and lit a cigarette. "It was almost daybreak, and things were still a dreadful mess—bloody footprints on the porch, the chitons lying where we'd dropped them. The twins put on some old clothes of mine and went out to take care of the porch and the inside of the car. The chitons, I knew, should be burnt, but I didn't want to start a big fire in the back yard; nor did I want to burn them inside and risk setting off the fire alarm. My landlady is constantly warning me not to use the fireplace, but I'd always suspected it worked. I took a chance and as luck would have it, it did."

"I was no help at all," said Francis.

"No, you certainly weren't," said Henry crossly.

"I couldn't help it. I thought I was going to throw up. I went back to Henry's room and went to sleep."

"I think we all would have liked to go to sleep but somebody had to clean up," Henry said. "The twins came in around seven. I was still having a terrible time with the bathroom. Charles's back was stuck full of thorns like a pincushion. For a while Camilla and I worked on him with a pair of tweezers; then I went back in the bathroom to finish up. The worst of it was over, but I was so tired I couldn't keep my eyes open. The towels weren't so bad— we'd pretty much avoided using them—but there were stains on some of them so I put them in the washing machine and dumped in some soap. The twins were asleep, on that fold-out bed in the back room, and I shoved Charles over and was out like a light."

"Fourteen hours," said Francis. "I've never slept that long in my life."

"Nor have I. Like a dead man. No dreams."

"I can't tell you how disorienting this was," Francis said. "The sun was coming up when I went to sleep, and it seemed like I'd just closed my eyes when I opened them again, and it was dark, and a phone was ringing, and I had **no** idea where I was. It kept ringing and ringing, and finally I got up and found my way into the hall. Somebody said don't answer it but—"

"I've never seen anybody like you for an-swering a phone," said Henry. "Even in some-body else's house."

"Well, what am I supposed to do? Just let it ring? Anyway, I picked it up, and it was Bunny, cheery as a lark. Boy, the four of us had really been messed up, and were we turning into a bunch of nudists or what, and how about if we all went to the Brasserie and had some dinner?"

I sat up in my chair. "Wait," I said. "Was that the night—?"

Henry nodded. "You came too," he said. "Remember?"

"Of course," I said, unaccountably excited that the story was at last beginning to dovetail with my own experience. "Of course. I met Bunny on his way to your place."

"If you don't mind my saying so, we were all a little surprised when he showed up with you," said Francis.

"Well, I suppose eventually he wanted to get us alone and find out what happened, but it was nothing that couldn't wait," said Henry. "You'll recall that our appearance wouldn't have seemed so odd to him as it might. He'd been with us before, you know, on nights very nearly as—what is the word I'm looking for?"

"—when we'd been sick all over the place," said Francis, "and fallen in mud, and didn't get home till dawn. There was the blood—he might have wondered exactly **how** we'd killed that deer—but still."

Uncomfortably, I thought of the **Bacchae**: hooves and bloody ribs, scraps dangling from the fir trees. There was a word for it in Greek:

omophagia. Suddenly it came back to me:
walking into Henry's apartment, all those tired
faces, Bunny's snide greeting of "**Khairei,**
deerslayers!"

They'd been quiet that evening, quiet and
pale, though not more than seemed remarkable for people suffering particularly bad
hangovers. Only Camilla's laryngitis seemed
unusual. They'd been drunk the night before,
they told me, drunk as bandicoots; Camilla
had left her sweater at home and caught cold
on the walk back to North Hampden. Outside, it was dark and raining hard. Henry gave
me the car keys and asked me to drive.

It was a Friday night, but the weather was so
bad the Brasserie was nearly deserted. We ate
Welsh rarebits and listened to the rain beating
down in gusts on the roof. Bunny and I drank
whiskey and hot water; the others had tea.

"Feeling queasy, **bakchoi**?" said Bunny slyly
after the waiter took our drink orders.

Camilla made a face at him.

When we went out to the car after dinner
Bunny walked around it, inspected the headlights, kicked at the tires. "This the one
you were in last night?" he said, blinking in
the rain.

"Yes."

He brushed the damp hair from his eyes and
bent to examine the fender. "German cars," he

said. "Hate to say it but I think the Krauts have got Detroit metal beat. I don't see a scratch."

I asked him what he meant.

"Aw, they were driving around drunk. Making a nuisance of themselves on the public road. Hit a deer. Did you kill it?" he asked Henry.

Walking around to the passenger's side, Henry looked up. "What's that?"

"The deer. Didja kill it?"

Henry opened the door. "It looked pretty dead to me," he had said.

———

There was a long silence. My eyes were smarting from all the smoke. A thick gray haze of it hung near the ceiling.

"So what's the problem?" I said.

"What do you mean?"

"What happened? Did you tell him about it or not?"

Henry took a deep breath. "No," he said. "We might have, but obviously the fewer people who knew the better. When I first saw him alone, I broached it carefully, but he seemed satisfied with the deer story and I let it go at that. If he hadn't figured it out on his own there was certainly no reason to tell him. The fellow's body was found, an article ran in the Hampden **Examiner**, no problem at all.

But then—by some rotten stroke of luck—I suppose in Hampden they don't get many stories like this—they published a follow-up story two weeks later. 'Mysterious Death in Battenkill County.' And that was the one Bunny saw."

"It was the stupidest thing," Francis said. "He **never** reads the newspaper. None of this would have happened if it wasn't for that blasted Marion."

"She has a subscription, something to do with the Early Childhood Center," said Henry, rubbing his eyes. "Bunny was with her in Commons before lunch. She was talking to one of her friends—Marion, that is—and Bunny I suppose had got bored and started to read her paper. The twins and I went up to say hello and the first thing he said, practically across the room, was 'Look here, you guys, some chicken farmer got killed out by Francis's house.' Then he read a bit of the article out loud. Fractured skull, no murder weapon, no motive, no leads. I was trying to think of some way to change the subject when he said: 'Hey. November **tenth**? That's the night you guys were out at Francis's. The night you ran over that deer.'

" 'I don't see,' I said, 'how that could be right.'

" 'It was the tenth. I remember because it

was the day before my mom's birthday. That's really something, isn't it?'

" 'Why yes,' we said, 'it certainly is.'

" 'If I had a suspicious mind,' he said, 'I'd guess you'd done it, Henry, coming back from Battenkill County that night with blood from head to toe.' "

He lit another cigarette. "You have to remember that it was lunch time, Commons was packed, Marion and her friend were listening to every word, and besides, you know how his voice carries. . . . We laughed, naturally, and Charles said something funny, and we'd just managed to get him off the topic when he looked at the paper again. 'I can't believe this, guys,' he said. 'An honest-to-God murder, out in the woods too, not three miles from where you were. You know, if the cops had pulled you over that night, you'd probably be in jail right now. There's a phone number to call if anybody's got any information. If I wanted to, I bet I could get you guys in a heck of a lot of trouble . . .' et cetera, et cetera.

"Of course, I didn't know what to think. Was he joking, did he really suspect? Eventually I got him to drop it but still I had an awful feeling that he'd felt how uneasy he'd made me. He knows me so well—he has a sixth sense about that kind of thing. And I **was** uneasy. Goodness. It was right before lunch, all these security guards were standing around, half of them are connected with the police force in Hampden . . . I mean, there was no way our story could stand up to even peremptory examination and I knew it. **Ob**viously we hadn't hit a deer. There wasn't a scratch on either of the cars. And if anyone made even a casual connection between us and the dead man . . . So, as I say, I was glad when he dropped it. But even then I had a feeling we hadn't heard the last of it. He teased us about it—quite innocently, I believe, but in public as well as private—for the rest of the term. You know how he is. Once he gets something like that on the brain he won't give it up."

I did know. Bunny had an uncanny ability to ferret out topics of conversation that made his listener uneasy and to dwell upon them with ferocity once he had. In all the months I'd known him he'd never ceased to tease me, for instance, about that jacket I'd worn to lunch with him that first day, and about what he saw as my flimsy and tastelessly Californian style of dress. To an impartial eye, my clothes were in fact not at all dissimilar from his own but his snide remarks upon the subject were so inexhaustible and tireless, I think, because in spite of my good-natured laughter he must have been dimly aware that he was touching a nerve, that I was in fact incredibly self-conscious about these virtually imperceptible differences of dress and of the rather less imperceptible differences of manner and bearing between myself and the rest of them. I am gifted at blending myself into any given milieu—you've never seen such a typical California teenager as I was, nor such a dissolute and callous pre-med student—but somehow, despite my efforts, I am never able to blend myself in entirely and remain in some respects quite distinct from my surroundings, in the same way that a green chameleon remains a distinct entity from the green leaf upon which it sits, no matter how perfectly it has approximated the subtleties of the particular shade. Whenever Bunny, rudely and in public, accused me of wearing a shirt which contained a polyester blend, or remarked critically that my perfectly ordinary trousers, indistinguishable from his own, bore the taint of something he called a "Western cut," a large portion of the pleasure this sport afforded him was derived from his unerring and bloodhoundish sense that this, of all topics, was the one which made me most truly uncomfortable. He could not have failed to notice what a sore spot his mention of the murder had touched in Henry; nor, once he sensed its existence, could he have restrained himself from continuing to jab at it.

"Of course, he didn't know a thing," Francis

said. "Really, he didn't. It was all a big joke to him. He liked to throw out references to that farmer we'd gone and murdered, just to see me jump. One day he told me he'd seen a policeman out in front of my house, asking my landlady questions."

"He did that to me, too," said Henry. "He was always joking about calling the tips number in the newspaper, and the five of us splitting the reward money. Picking up the telephone. Pretending to dial."

"You can understand how thin that wore after a time. My God. Some of the things he said in front of **you**— The terrible thing was, you could never tell when it was coming. Right before school let out he stuck a copy of that newspaper article under the windshield wiper of my car. 'Mysterious Death in Battenkill County.' It was horrible to know that he'd saved it in the first place, and kept it all that time."

"Worst of all," said Henry, "there was absolutely nothing we could do. For a while we even thought of telling him outright, throwing ourselves on his mercy so to speak, but then we realized, at that late date, it was impossible to predict how he'd react. He was grouchy, and sick, and worried about his grades. And the term was nearly over too. It seemed that the best thing to do was to stay on his good side until the Christmas break—take him places, buy him things, pay a lot of attention to him—and hope it would blow over during the winter." He sighed. "At the end of virtually every school term I've been through with Bunny, he's suggested that the two of us go on a trip, meaning by this that we go to some place of his choosing and that I pay for it. He hasn't the money to get to Manchester on his own. And when the subject came up, as I knew it would, about a week or two before school was out, I thought: why not? In this way, at least, one of us could keep an eye on him over the winter; and perhaps a change of scenery might prove beneficial. I should also note that it didn't seem to be such a bad thing if he were to feel a bit under obligation to me. He wanted to go to either Italy or Jamaica. I knew I couldn't bear Jamaica, so I bought two tickets for Rome and arranged for some rooms not far from the Piazza di Spagna."

"And you gave him money for clothes and all those useless Italian books."

"Yes. All in all it was a considerable outlay of money but it seemed like a good investment. I even thought it might be a bit of fun. But never, in my wildest dreams . . . Really, I don't know where to begin. I remember when he saw our rooms—actually, they were quite charming, with a frescoed ceiling, beautiful old balcony, glorious view, I was rather proud of myself for having found them—he was incensed, and began to complain that it was shabby, that it was too cold and the plumbing was bad; and, in short, that the place was completely unsuitable and he wondered how I had been duped into taking it. He'd thought I knew better than to stumble into a lousy tourist trap, but he guessed that he was wrong. He insinuated that our throats would be cut in the night. At that point, I was more amenable to his whims. I asked him, if he didn't like the rooms, where would he prefer to stay? and he suggested why didn't we just go down and get a suite—not a room, you understand, but a suite—in the Grand Hotel?

"He kept on, and finally I told him we would do nothing of the sort. For one thing, the exchange rate was bad and the rooms— besides being paid in advance, and with **my** money—were already rather more than I could afford. He sulked for days, feigning asthma attacks, moping around and honking at his inhaler and nagging me constantly—accusing me of being cheap, and so forth, and when **he** traveled he liked to do it right—and finally I lost my temper. I told him that if the rooms were satisfactory to me, they were certainly better than what he was used to—I mean, my God, it was a palazzo, it belonged to a **countess**, I'd paid a fortune for it—and, in short, there was no possibility of my paying 500,000 lire a night for the company of American tourists and a couple of sheets of hotel stationery.

"So we stayed on at the Piazza di Spagna, which he proceeded to transform into a living Hell. He needled me ceaselessly—about the carpet, about the pipes, about what he felt was his insufficient supply of pocket money. We were living just a few steps from the Via Condotti, the most expensive shopping street in Rome. **I** was lucky, he said. No wonder **I** was having such a good time, since I could buy whatever I wanted, while all he could do was lie wheezing in the garret like a poor stepchild. I did what I could to placate him, but the more I bought him, the more he wanted. Besides which, he would hardly let me out of his sight. He complained if I left him alone for even a few minutes; but if I asked him to come along with me, to a museum or a church—my God, we were in **Rome**—he was dreadfully bored and kept at me constantly to leave. It got so I couldn't even read a book without his sailing in. Goodness. He'd stand outside the door and jabber at me while I was having my bath. I caught him going through my suitcase. I mean"—he paused delicately—"it's slightly annoying to have even an unobtrusive person sharing such close quarters with one. Perhaps I'd only forgotten what it was like when we lived together freshman year, or perhaps I've simply become more accustomed to living alone, but after a week or two of this I was a nervous wreck. I could hardly bear the sight of him. And I was worried about other things as well. You know, don't you," he said abruptly to me, "that sometimes I get headaches, rather bad ones?"

I did know. Bunny—fond of recounting his own illnesses and those of others—had described them in an awed whisper: Henry, flat on his back in a dark room, ice packs on his head and a handkerchief tied over his eyes.

"I don't get them so often as I once did. When I was thirteen or fourteen I had them all the time. But now it seems that when they do come—sometimes only once a year—they're much worse. And after I'd been a few weeks in Italy, I felt one coming on. Unmistakable. Noises get louder; objects shimmer; my peripheral vision darkens and I see all sorts of unpleasant things hovering at its edges. There's a terrible pressure in the air. I'll look at a street sign and not be able to read it, not understand the simplest spoken sentence. There's not much that can be done when it comes to that but I did what I could—stayed in my room with the shades pulled, took medicine, tried to keep quiet. At last I realized I would have to cable my doctor in the States. The drugs they give me are too powerful to dispense in prescription form; generally I go to the emergency room for a shot. I wasn't sure what an Italian doctor would do if I showed up gasping at his office, an American tourist, asking for an injection of phenobarbital.

"But by then it was too late. The headache was on me in a matter of hours and after that, I was quite incapable either of finding my way to a doctor or making myself understood if I had. I don't know if Bunny tried to get me one or not. His Italian is so bad that when he tried to speak to anyone he would generally just end up insulting them. The American Express office was not far from where we lived, and I'm sure they could have given him the name of an English-speaking doctor, but of course that's not the sort of thing that would occur to Bunny.

"I hardly know what happened for the next few days. I lay in my room with the shades down and sheets of newspaper taped over the shades. It was impossible even to have any ice sent up—all one could get were lukewarm pitchers of **acqua semplice**—but then I had a hard time talking in English, much less Italian. God knows where Bunny was. I have no memory of seeing him, nor much of anything else.

"Anyway. For a few days I lay flat on my back, hardly able to blink without feeling like my forehead was splitting open, and everything sick and black. I swung in and out of consciousness until finally I became aware of a thin seam of light burning at the edge of the shade. How long I'd been looking at it I don't know, but gradually I became aware that it was morning, that the pain had receded somewhat, and that I could move around without awful difficulty. I also realized that I was extraordinarily thirsty. There was no water in my pitcher, so I got up and put on my dressing gown and went to get a drink.

"My room and Bunny's opened from opposite ends to a rather grand central room—fifteen-foot ceilings, with a fresco in the manner of Carracci; glorious sculptured-stuccoed framework; French doors leading to the balcony. I was almost blinded by the morning light, but I made out a shape which I took to be Bunny, bent over some books and papers at my desk. I waited until my eyes cleared, one hand on the doorknob to steady myself, and then I said, 'Good morning, Bun.'

"Well, he leapt up as if he'd been scalded, and scrabbled in the papers as if to hide something, and all of a sudden I realized what he had. I went over and snatched it from him. It was my diary. He was always nosing around trying to get a look at it; I'd hidden it behind a radiator but I suppose he'd come digging in my room while I was ill. He'd found it once before, but since I write in Latin I don't suppose he was able to make much sense of it. I didn't even use his real name. **Cuniculus molestus**, I thought, denoted him quite well. And he'd never figure **that** out without a lexicon.

"Unfortunately, while I was ill, he'd had ample chance to avail himself of one. A lexicon, that is. And I know we make fun of Bunny for being such a dreadful Latinist, but he'd managed to eke out a pretty competent little English translation of the more recent entries. I must say, I never dreamed he was capable of such a thing. It must have taken him days.

"I wasn't even angry. I was too stunned. I stared at the translation—it was sitting right there—and then at him, and then, all of a sudden, he pushed back his chair and began to bellow at me. We had killed that fellow, he said, killed him in cold blood and didn't even bother to tell him about it, but he knew there was something fishy all along, and where did I get off calling him Rabbit, and he had half a mind to go right down to the American consulate and have them send over some police. . . . Then—this was foolish of me—I slapped him in the face, hard as I could." He sighed. "I shouldn't have done that. I didn't even do it from anger, but frustration. I was sick and exhausted; I was afraid someone would hear him; I just didn't think I could stand it another second.

"And I'd hit him harder than I meant to. His mouth fell open. My hand had left a big white mark across his cheek. All of a sudden the blood rushed back into it, bright red. He began to shout at me, cursing, quite hysterical, throwing wild punches at me. There were rapid footsteps on the stairs, followed by a loud banging at the door and a delirious burst of Italian. I grabbed the diary and the translation and threw them in the stove—Bunny went for them, but I held him back until they started to go up—and then I yelled for whoever it was to come in. It was the chambermaid. She flew into the room, screaming in Italian so fast I couldn't understand a word she said. At first I thought she was angry about the noise. Then I understood it wasn't it at all. She'd known I was ill; there'd been hardly a sound from the room for days and then, she said excitedly, she'd heard all the screaming; she had thought I'd died in the night, perhaps, and the other young **signor** had found me, but as I was standing now in front of her, that was obviously not the case; did I need a doctor? An ambulance? **Bicarbonato di soda?**

"I thanked her and said no, I was perfectly

all right, and then I sort of **dunque-dunque**d around, trying to think of some explanation for the disturbance, but she seemed perfectly satisfied and went away to fetch our breakfast. Bunny looked rather stunned. He had no idea what it had been about, of course. I suppose it seemed rather sinister and inexplicable. He asked me where she was going, and what she'd said, but I was too sick and angry to answer. I went back to my bedroom and shut the door, and stayed there until she came back with our breakfast. She laid it out on the terrace, and we went outside to eat.

"Curiously, Bunny had little to say. After a bit of a tense silence, he inquired about my health, told me what he'd done while I was ill, and said nothing about what had just happened. I ate my breakfast, and realized all I could do was try to keep my head. I had hurt his feelings, I knew—really, there were several very unkind things in the diary—so I resolved to be as pleasant to him from then on out as I could, and to hope no more problems would arise."

He paused to take a drink of his whiskey. I looked at him.

"You mean, you thought problems might **not** arise?" I said.

"I know Bunny better than you do," Henry said crossly.

"But what about what he said—about the police?"

"I knew he wasn't prepared to go to the police, Richard."

"If it were simply a question of the dead man, things would be different, don't you see?" said Francis, leaning forward in his chair. "It's not that his conscience bothers him. Or that he feels any compelling kind of moral outrage. He thinks he's been somehow **wronged** by the whole business."

"Well, frankly, I thought I was doing him a favor by not telling him," Henry said. "But he was angry—**is** angry, I should say—because things were kept from him. He feels injured. Excluded. And my best chance was to try to make amends for that. We're old friends, he and I."

"Tell him about those things Bunny bought with your credit cards while you were sick."

"I didn't find out about that until later," said Henry gloomily. "It doesn't make much difference now." He lit another cigarette. "I suppose, right after he found out, he was in a kind of shock," he said. "And, too, he was in a strange country, unable to speak the language, without a cent of his own. He was all right for a little while. Nonetheless, once he caught on to the fact—and it didn't take him long—that, circumstances to the contrary, I was actually

pretty much at his mercy, you can't imagine
what torture he put me through. He talked
about it **all the time.** In restaurants, in shops,
in taxicabs. Of course, it was the off season,
and not many English around, but for all I
know there are entire families of Americans
back home in Ohio wondering if . . . Oh,
God. Exhaustive monologues in the Hosteria
dell'Orso. An argument in the Via dei Cestari.
An abortive re-en**actment** of it in the lobby of
the Grand Hotel.

"One afternoon at a cafe, he was going on
and on and I noticed that a man at the next
table was hanging on every word. We got up
to leave. He got up too. I wasn't sure what to
think. I knew he was German, because I'd
heard him talking to the waiter, but I had no
idea if he had any English or if he'd been able
to hear Bunny distinctly enough to understand. Perhaps he was only a homosexual, but
I didn't want to take any chances. I led the way
home through the alleys, turning this way and
that, and I felt quite certain we'd lost him but
apparently not, because when I woke up the
next morning and looked out the window he
was standing by the fountain. Bunny was
elated. He thought it was just like a spy picture. He wanted to go out and see if this fellow
would try to follow us, and I had practically to
restrain him by force. All morning I watched

from the window. The German stood around, had a few cigarettes, and drifted away after a couple of hours; but it wasn't until about four o'clock when Bunny, who'd been complaining steadily since noon, began to raise such a ruckus that we finally went to get something to eat. But we were only a few blocks from the piazza when I thought I saw the German again, walking behind us at quite a distance. I turned and started back, in hopes of confronting him; he disappeared, but in a few minutes I turned around and he was there again.

"I'd been worried before, but then I began to feel really afraid. Immediately we went off into a side street, and made our way home by a roundabout route—Bunny never did get his lunch that day, he almost drove me crazy—and I sat by the window until it got dark, telling Bunny to shut up and trying to think what to do. I didn't think he knew exactly where we lived—otherwise, why roam around the piazza, why not come directly to our apartment if he had something to say? At any rate. We left our rooms pretty much in the middle of the night and checked into the Excelsior, which was fine with Bunny. Room service, you know. I watched quite anxiously for the German the rest of my time in Rome—goodness,

I dream about him still—but I never saw him again."

"What do you suppose he wanted? Money?"

Henry shrugged. "Who knows. Unfortunately at that point I had very little money to give him. Bunny's jaunts to the tailors and so forth had just about cleaned me out, and then having to move to this hotel—I didn't care about the money, really I didn't, but he was nearly driving me crazy. Never once was I alone. It was impossible to write a letter or even to make a telephone call without Bunny lurking somewhere in the background, **arrectis auribus**, trying to listen in. While I was having a bath, he'd go in my room and root through my things; I'd come out to find my clothes all wadded up in the bureau and crumbs in the pages of my notebooks. Everything I did made him suspicious.

"I stood it as long as I could but I was beginning to feel desperate and, frankly, rather unwell too. I knew that leaving him in Rome might be dangerous but it seemed every day that things got worse and eventually it became obvious that staying on was no solution. Already I knew that the four of us could under no circumstances go back to school as usual in the spring—though look at us now—and that we'd have to devise a plan, probably a rather

Pyrrhic and unsatisfactory one. But I needed time, and quiet, and a few weeks' grace period in the States if I was to do anything of the sort. So one night at the Excelsior when Bunny was drunk and sleeping soundly I packed my clothes—leaving him his ticket home and two thousand American dollars and no note—and took a taxi to the airport and got on the first plane home."

"You left him two thousand dollars?" I said, aghast.

Henry shrugged. Francis shook his head and snorted. "That's nothing," he said.

I stared at them.

"Really, it is nothing," said Henry mildly. "I can't tell you how much that trip to Italy cost me. And my parents are generous, but they're not **that** generous. I've never had to ask for money in my life until the last few months. As it is, my savings are virtually gone and I don't know how much longer I can keep feeding them these stories about elaborate car repairs and so forth. I mean, I was prepared to be reasonable with Bunny, but he doesn't seem to understand that after all I'm just a student on an allowance and not some bottomless well of money. . . . And the horrible thing is, I don't see an end to it. I don't know what would happen if my parents got disgusted and cut me off, which is extremely likely to happen at some point in the near future if things go on as they are."

"He's blackmailing you?"

Henry and Francis looked at each other.

"Well, not exactly," said Francis.

Henry shook his head. "Bunny doesn't think of it in those terms," he said wearily. "You'd have to know his parents to understand. What the Corcorans did with their sons was to send them all to the most expensive schools they could possibly get into, and let them fend for themselves once they were there. His parents don't give him a cent. Apparently they never have. He told me when they sent him off to Saint Jerome's they didn't even give him money for his schoolbooks. Rather an odd child-rearing method, in my opinion—like certain reptiles who hatch their young and abandon them to the elements. Not surprisingly, this has inculcated in Bunny the notion that it is more honorable to live by sponging off other people than it is to work."

"But I thought his folks were supposed to be such bluebloods," I said.

"The Corcorans have delusions of grandeur. The problem is, they lack the money to back them up. No doubt they think it very aristocratic and grand, farming their sons off on other people."

"He's shameless about it," said Francis.

"Even with the twins, and they're nearly as poor as he is."

"The bigger the sums, the better, and never a thought of paying it back. Of course, he'd rather die than get a job."

"The Corcorans would rather see him dead," said Francis sourly, lighting his cigarette and coughing as he exhaled. "But this squeamishness about work wears a bit thin when one is forced to assume his upkeep oneself."

"It's unthinkable," said Henry. "I'd rather have any job, six jobs, than beg from people. Look at you," he said to me. "Your parents aren't particularly generous with you, are they? But you're so scrupulous about not borrowing money that it's rather silly."

I said nothing, embarrassed.

"Heavens. I think you might have died in that warehouse rather than wire one of us for a couple of hundred dollars." He lit a cigarette and blew out an emphatic plume of smoke. "That's an infinitesimal sum. I'm sure we shall have spent two or three times that on Bunny by the end of next week."

I stared. "You're kidding," I said.

"I wish I were."

"I don't mind lending money either," Francis said, "if I've got it. But Bunny borrows beyond all reason. Even in the old days he thought nothing of asking for a hundred dollars at the drop of a hat, for no reason at all."

"And never a word of thanks," said Henry irritably. "What can he spend it on? If he had even a shred of self-respect he'd go down to the employment office and get himself a job."

"You and I may be down there in a couple of weeks if he doesn't let up," said Francis glumly, pouring himself another glass of Scotch and sloshing a good deal of it on the table. "I've spent thousands on him. **Thousands,**" he said to me, taking a careful sip from the trembling brim of his glass. "And most of it on restaurant bills, the pig. It's all very friendly, why don't **we** go out to dinner and that sort of thing, but the way things are, how can I say no? My mother thinks I'm on drugs. I don't suppose there's much else she can think. She's told my grandparents not to give me any money and since January I haven't gotten a damn thing except my dividend check. Which is fine as far as it goes, but I can't be taking people out for hundred-dollar dinners every night."

Henry shrugged. "He's always been like this," he said. "Always. He's amusing; I liked him; I felt a little sorry for him. What was it to me, to lend him money for his schoolbooks and know he wouldn't pay it back?"

"Except now," Francis said, "it's not just

money for schoolbooks. And now we can't say no."

"How long can you keep this up?"

"Not forever."

"And when the money's gone?"

"I don't know," said Henry, reaching up behind his spectacles to rub his eyes again.

"Maybe I could talk to him."

"No," said Henry and Francis, one on top of the other, with an alacrity that surprised me.

"Why—?"

There was an awkward pause, finally broken by Francis.

"Well, you may or may not know this," he said, "but Bunny is a little jealous of you. Already he thinks we've all ganged up on him. If he gets the impression you're siding with the rest of us . . ."

"You mustn't let on you know," said Henry. "Ever. Unless you want to make things worse."

For a moment no one spoke. The apartment was blue with smoke, through which the broad expanse of white linoleum was arctic, surreal. Music from a neighbor's stereo was filtering through the walls. The Grateful Dead. Good Lord.

"It's a terrible thing, what we did," said Francis abruptly. "I mean, this man was not **Voltaire** we killed. But still. It's a shame. I feel bad about it."

"Well, of course, I do too," said Henry matter-of-factly. "But not bad enough to want to go to jail for it."

Francis snorted and poured himself another shot of whiskey and drank it straight off. "No," he said. "Not that bad."

No one said anything for a moment. I felt sleepy, ill, as if this were some lingering and dyspeptic dream. I had said it before, but I said it again, mildly surprised at the sound of my own voice in the quiet room. "What are you going to do?"

"I don't know what we're going to do," said Henry, as calmly as if I'd asked him his plans for the afternoon.

"Well, I know what **I'm** going to do," said Francis. He stood up unsteadily and pulled with his forefinger at his collar. Startled, I looked at him, and he laughed at my surprise.

"I want to sleep," he said, with a melodramatic roll of his eye, " **'dormir plutôt que vivre'!**"

" **'Dans un sommeil aussi doux que la mort . . .'** " said Henry with a smile.

"Jesus, Henry, you know everything," said Francis, "you make me sick." He turned unsteadily, loosening his tie as he did it, and swayed out of the room.

"I believe he is rather drunk," said Henry, as a door slammed somewhere and we heard taps running furiously in the bathroom. "It's early still. Do you want to play a hand or two of cards?"

I blinked at him.

He reached over and got a deck of cards from a box on the end table—Tiffany cards, with sky-blue backs and Francis's monogram on them in gold—and began to shuffle through them expertly. "We could play bezique, or euchre if you'd rather," he said, the blue and gold dissolving from his hands in a blur. "I like poker myself—of course, it's rather a vulgar game, and no fun at all with two—but still, there's a certain random element in it which appeals to me."

I looked at him, at his steady hands, the whirring cards, and suddenly an odd memory leapt to mind: Tōjō, at the height of the war, forcing his top aides to sit up and play cards with him all night long.

He pushed the deck over to me. "Do you want to cut?" he said, and lit a cigarette.

I looked at the cards, and then at the flame of the match burning with an unwavering clarity between his fingers.

"You're not too worried about this, are you?" I said.

Henry drew deeply on the cigarette, exhaled, shook out the match. "No," he said, looking thoughtfully at the thread of smoke that curled from the burnt end. "I can get us out of it, I think. But that depends on the exact opportunity presenting itself and for that we'll have to wait. I suppose it also depends to a certain extent on how much, in the end, we are willing to do. Shall I deal?" he said, and he reached for the cards again.

———

I awoke from a heavy, dreamless sleep to find myself lying on Francis's couch in an uncomfortable position, and the morning sun streaming through the bank of windows at the rear. For a while I lay motionless, trying to remember where I was and how I had come to be there; it was a pleasant sensation which was abruptly soured when I recalled what had happened the night before. I sat up and rubbed the waffled pattern the sofa cushion had left on my cheek. The movement made my head ache. I stared at the overflowing ashtray, the three-quarters-empty bottle of Famous Grouse, the game of poker solitaire laid out upon the table. So it had all been real; it wasn't a dream.

I was thirsty. I went to the kitchen, my footsteps echoing in the silence, and drank a glass of water standing at the sink. It was seven a.m. by the kitchen clock.

I filled my glass again and took it to the living room with me and sat on the couch. As I drank, more slowly this time—bolting the first glass had made me slightly sick—I looked at Henry's solitaire poker game. He must have laid it out while I was asleep. Instead of going all out for flushes in the columns, and full houses and fours on the rows, which was the prudent thing to do in this game, he'd tried for a couple of straight flushes on the rows and missed. Why had he done that? To see if he could beat the odds? Or had he only been tired?

I picked up the cards and shuffled them and laid them out again one by one, in accordance with the strategic rules that he himself had taught me, and beat his score by fifty points. The cold, jaunty faces stared back at me: jacks in black and red, the Queen of Spades with her fishy eye. Suddenly a wave of fatigue and nausea shuddered over me, and I went to the closet, got my coat, and left, closing the door quietly behind me.

The hall, in the morning light, had the feel of a hospital corridor. Pausing unsteadily on the stairs, I looked back at Francis's door, indistinguishable from the others in the long faceless row.

I suppose if I had a moment of doubt at all it was then, as I stood in that cold, eerie stairwell looking back at the apartment from which I had come. Who were these people? How well did I know them? Could I trust any of them, really, when it came right down to it? Why, of all people, had they chosen to tell me?

It's funny, but thinking back on it now, I realize that this particular point in time, as I stood there blinking in the deserted hall, was the one point at which I might have chosen to do something very different from what I actually did. But of course I didn't see this crucial moment then for what it was; I suppose we never do. Instead, I only yawned, and shook myself from the momentary daze that had come upon me, and went on my way down the stairs.

———

Back in my room, dizzy and exhausted, I wanted more than anything to pull the shades and lie down on my bed—which seemed suddenly the most enticing bed in the world, musty pillow, dirty sheets, and all. But that was impossible. Greek Prose Composition was in two hours, and I hadn't done my homework.

The assignment was a two-page essay, in Greek, on any epigram of Callimachus that we chose. I'd done only a page and I started to hurry through the rest in impatient and slightly dishonest fashion, writing out the English and translating word by word. It was something Julian asked us not to do. The value

of Greek prose composition, he said, was not
that it gave one any particular facility in the
language that could not be gained as easily by
other methods but that if done properly, off
the top of one's head, it taught one to think in
Greek. One's thought patterns become different, he said, when forced into the confines of
a rigid and unfamiliar tongue. Certain common ideas become inexpressible; other, previously undreamt-of ones spring to life, finding
miraculous new articulation. By necessity, I
suppose, it is difficult for me to explain in English exactly what I mean. I can only say that
an **incendium** is in its nature entirely different
from the **feu** with which a Frenchman lights
his cigarette, and both are very different from
the stark, inhuman **pur** that the Greeks knew,
the **pur** that roared from the towers of Ilion or
leapt and screamed on that desolate, windy
beach, from the funeral pyre of Patroklos.

Pur: that one word contains for me the
secret, the bright, terrible clarity of ancient
Greek. How can I make you see it, this strange
harsh light which pervades Homer's landscapes
and illumines the dialogues of Plato, an alien
light, inarticulable in our common tongue?
Our shared language is a language of the in-
tricate, the peculiar, the home of pumpkins
and ragamuffins and bodkins and beer, the
tongue of Ahab and Falstaff and Mrs. Gamp;

and while I find it entirely suitable for reflections such as these, it fails me utterly when I attempt to describe in it what I love about Greek, that language innocent of all quirks and cranks; a language obsessed with action, and with the joy of seeing action multiply from action, action marching relentlessly ahead and with yet more actions filing in from either side to fall into neat step at the rear, in a long straight rank of cause and effect toward what will be inevitable, the only possible end.

In a certain sense, this was why I felt so close to the others in the Greek class. They, too, knew this beautiful and harrowing landscape, centuries dead; they'd had the same experience of looking up from their books with fifth-century eyes and finding the world disconcertingly sluggish and alien, as if it were not their home. It was why I admired Julian, and Henry in particular. Their reason, their very eyes and ears were fixed irrevocably in the confines of those stern and ancient rhythms—the world, in fact, was not their home, at least not the world as I knew it—and far from being occasional visitors to this land which I myself knew only as an admiring tourist, they were pretty much its permanent residents, as permanent as I suppose it was possible for them to be. Ancient Greek is a difficult language, a very difficult language indeed, and it is eminently possible to study it all one's life and never be able to speak a word; but it makes me smile, even today, to think of Henry's calculated, formal English, the English of a well-educated foreigner, as compared with the marvelous fluency and self-assurance of his Greek—quick, eloquent, remarkably witty. It was always a wonder to me when I happened to hear him and Julian conversing in Greek, arguing and joking, as I never once heard either of them do in English; many times, I've seen Henry pick up the telephone with an irritable, cautious "Hello," and may I never forget the harsh and irresistible delight of his **"Khairei!"** when Julian happened to be at the other end.

I was a bit uncomfortable—after the story I'd just heard—with the Callimachean epigrams having to do with flushed cheeks, and wine, and the kisses of fair-limbed youths by torchlight. I'd chosen instead a rather sad one, which in English runs as follows: "At morn we buried Melanippus; as the sun set the maiden Basilo died by her own hand, as she could not endure to lay her brother on the pyre and live; and the house beheld a twofold woe, and all Cyrene bowed her head, to see the home of happy children made desolate."

I finished my composition in less than an hour. After I'd gone through it and checked the endings, I washed my face and changed my shirt and went, with my books, over to Bunny's room.

Of the six of us, Bunny and I were the only two who lived on campus, and his house was across the lawn on the opposite end of Commons. He had a room on the ground floor, which I am sure was inconvenient for him since he spent most of his time upstairs in the house kitchen: ironing his pants, rummaging through the refrigerator, leaning out the window in his shirtsleeves to yell at passers-by. When he didn't answer his door I went to look for him there, and I found him sitting in the windowsill in his undershirt, drinking a cup of coffee and leafing through a magazine. I was a little surprised to see the twins there, too: Charles, standing with his left ankle crossed over his right, stirring moodily at his coffee and looking out the window; Camilla—and this surprised me, because Camilla wasn't much of one for domestic tasks—ironing one of Bunny's shirts.

"Oh, hello, old man," said Bunny. "Come on in. Having a little kaffeeklatsch. Yes, women are good for one or **two** things," he added, when he saw me looking at Camilla and the ironing board, "though, being a gentleman"— he winked broadly—"I don't like to say what the other thing is, mixed company and all.

Charles, get him a cup of coffee, would you? No need to wash it, it's clean enough," he said stridently, as Charles got a dirty cup from the drain board and turned on the tap. "Do your prose composition?"

"Yeah."

"Which epigram?"

"Twenty-two."

"Hmn. Sounds like everybody went for the tearjerkers. Charles did that one about the girl who died, and all her friends missed her, and you, Camilla, you picked—"

"Fourteen," said Camilla, without looking up, pressing rather savagely on the collar band with the tip of the iron.

"Hah. I picked one of the racy ones myself. Ever been to France, Richard?"

"No," I said.

"Then you better come with us this summer."

"Us? Who?"

"Henry and me."

I was so taken aback that all I could do was blink at him.

"France?" I said.

"May wee. Two-month tour. A real doozy. Have a look." He tossed me the magazine, which I now saw was a glossy brochure.

I glanced through it. It was a lollapalooza of a tour, all right—a "luxury hotel barge cruise" which began in the Champagne country and then went, via hot air balloon, to Burgundy for more barging, through Beaujolais, to the Riviera and Cannes and Monte Carlo—it was lavishly illustrated, full of brightly colored pictures of gourmet meals, flower-decked barges, happy tourists popping champagne corks and waving from the basket of their balloon at the disgruntled old peasants in the fields below.

"Looks great, doesn't it?" said Bunny.

"Fabulous."

"Rome was all right but actually it was kind of a sinkhole when you get right down to it. Besides, I like to gad about a little more myself. Stay on the move, see a few of the native customs. Just between you and me, I bet Henry's going to have a ball with this."

I bet he will, too, I thought, staring at a picture of a woman holding up a stick of French bread at the camera and grinning like a maniac.

The twins were studiously avoiding my eye, Camilla bent over Bunny's shirt, Charles with his back to me and his elbows on the sideboard, looking out the kitchen window.

"Of course, this balloon thing's great," Bunny said conversationally, "but you know, I've been wondering, where do you go to the bathroom? Off the side or something?"

"Look here, I think this is going to take several minutes," said Camilla abruptly. "It's almost nine. Why don't you go ahead with Richard, Charles. Tell Julian not to wait."

"Well, it's not going to take you **that** much longer, is it?" said Bunny crossly, craning over to see. "What's the big problem? Where'd you learn how to iron, anyway?"

"I never did. **We** send our shirts to the laundry."

Charles followed me out the door, a few paces behind. We walked through the hall and down the stairs without a word, but once downstairs he stepped close behind me and, catching my arm, pulled me into an empty card room. In the twenties and thirties, there had been a bridge fad at Hampden; when the enthusiasm faded, the rooms were never subsequently put to any function and no one used them now except for drug deals, or typing, or illicit romantic trysts.

He shut the door. I found myself looking at the ancient card table—inlaid at its four corners with a diamond, a heart, a club and a spade.

"Henry called us," said Charles. He was scratching at the raised edge of the diamond with his thumb, his head studiously down.

"When?"

"Early this morning."

Neither of us said anything for a moment.

"I'm sorry," said Charles, glancing up.

"Sorry for what?"

"Sorry he told you. Sorry for everything. Camilla's all upset."

He seemed calm enough, tired but calm, and his intelligent eyes met mine with a sad, quiet candor. All of a sudden I felt terribly upset. I was fond of Francis and Henry but it was un-thinkable that anything should happen to the twins. I thought, with a pang, of how kind they had always been; of how sweet Camilla was in those first awkward weeks and how Charles had always had a way of showing up in my room, or turning to me in a crowd with a tranquil assumption—heartwarming to me—that he and I were particular friends; of walks and car trips and dinners at their house; of their letters—frequently unacknowledged on my part—which had come so faithfully over the long winter months.

From somewhere overhead I heard the shriek and groan of water pipes. We looked at each other.

"What are you going to do?" I said. It seemed the only question I had asked of any-one for the last twenty-four hours, and yet no one had given me a satisfactory answer.

He shrugged, a funny little one-shouldered

shrug, a mannerism he and his sister had in common. "Search me," he said wearily. "I guess we should go."

———

When we got to Julian's office, Henry and Francis were already there. Francis hadn't finished his essay. He was scratching rapidly at the second page, his fingers blue with ink, while Henry proofread the first one, dashing in subscripts and aspirants with his fountain pen.

He didn't look up. "Hello," he said. "Close the door, would you?"

Charles kicked at the door with his foot. "Bad news," he said.

"Very bad?"

"Financially, yes."

Francis swore, in a quick hissing under-breath, without pausing in his work. Henry dashed in a few final marks, then fanned the paper in the air to dry it.

"Well for goodness' sakes," he said mildly. "I hope it can wait. I don't want to have to think about it during class. How's that last page coming, Francis?"

"Just a minute," said Francis, laboriously, his words lagging behind the hurried scrawl of his pen.

Henry stood behind Francis's chair and leaned over his shoulder and began to proofread the top of the last page, one elbow resting on the table. "Camilla's with him?" he said.

"Yes. Ironing his nasty old shirt."

"Hmnn." He pointed at something with the end of his pen. "Francis, you need the optative here instead of the subjunctive."

Francis reached up quickly from his work— he was nearly at the end of the page—to change it.

"And this labial becomes pi, not kappa."

———

Bunny arrived late, and in a foul temper. "Charles," he snapped, "if you want this sister of yours to ever get a husband, you better teach her how to use an iron." I was exhausted and ill prepared and it was all I could do to keep my mind on the class. I had French at two, but after Greek I went straight back to my room and took a sleeping pill and went to bed. The sleeping pill was an extraneous gesture; I didn't need it, but the mere possibility of restlessness, of an afternoon full of bad dreams and distant plumbing noises, was too unpleasant to even contemplate.

So I slept soundly, more soundly than I should have, and the day slipped easily away. It was almost dark when somewhere, through great depths, I became aware that someone was knocking at my door.

It was Camilla. I must have looked terrible,

because she raised an eyebrow and laughed at me. "All you ever do is sleep," she said. "Why is it you're always sleeping when I come to see you?"

I blinked at her. My shades were down and the hall was dark and to me, half-drugged and reeling, she seemed not at all her bright unattainable self but rather a hazy and ineffably tender apparition, all slender wrists and shadows and disordered hair, the Camilla who resided, dim and lovely, in the gloomy boudoir of my dreams.

"Come in," I said.

She did, and closed the door behind her. I sat on the side of the unmade bed, feet bare and collar loose, and thought how wonderful it would be if this really were a dream, if I could walk over to where she sat and put my hands on either side of her face and kiss her, on the eyelids, on the mouth, on the place at her temple where the honey-colored hair graded into silky gold.

We looked at each other for a long time.

"Are you sick?" she said.

The gleam of her gold bracelet in the dark. I swallowed. It was hard to think what to say.

She stood up again. "I'd better go," she said. "I'm sorry to have bothered you. I came to ask if you wanted to go on a drive."

"What?"

"A drive. It's all right, though. Some other time."

"Where?"

"Somewhere. Nowhere. I'm meeting Francis at Commons in ten minutes."

"No, wait," I said. I felt sort of marvelous. A narcotic heaviness still clung deliciously to my limbs and I imagined what fun it would be to wander with her—drowsy, hypnotized—up to Commons in the fading light, the snow.

I stood up—it took forever to do it, the floor receding gradually before my eyes as if I were simply growing taller and taller by some organic process—and walked to my closet. The floor swayed as gently beneath me as the deck of an airship. I found my overcoat, then a scarf. Gloves were too complicated to bother with.

"Okay," I said. "Ready."

She raised an eyebrow. "It's sort of cold out," she said. "Don't you think you should wear some shoes?"

———

We walked to Commons through slush and cold rain, and when we got there Charles, Francis, and Henry were waiting for us. The configuration struck me as significant, in some way that was not entirely clear, everyone except for Bunny—"What's going on?" I said, blinking at them.

"Nothing," said Henry, tracing a pattern on the floor with the sharp, glinting ferrule of his umbrella. "We're just going for a drive. I thought it might be fun"—he paused delicately—"if we got away from school for a while, maybe had some dinner . . ."

Without Bunny, that is the subtext here, I thought. Where was he? The tip of Henry's umbrella glittered. I glanced up and noticed that Francis was looking at me with lifted eyebrows.

"What is it?" I said irritably, swaying slightly in the doorway.

He exhaled with a sharp, amused sound. "Are you **drunk**?" he said.

They were all looking at me in kind of a funny way. "Yes," I said. It wasn't the truth, but I didn't feel much like explaining.

———

The chill sky, misty with fine rain near the treetops, made even the familiar landscape around Hampden seem indifferent and remote. The valleys were white with fog and the top of Mount Cataract was entirely obscured, invisible in the cold haze. Not being able to see it, that omniscient mountain which grounded Hampden and its environs in my senses, I found it difficult to get my bearings, and it seemed as if we were heading into strange and unmarked territory, though I had been down this road a hundred times in all weathers. Henry drove, rather fast as he always did, the tires whining on the wet black road and water spraying high on either side.

"I looked at this place about a month ago," he said, slowing as we approached a white farmhouse on a hill, forlorn bales of hay dotting the snowy pasture. "It's still for sale, but I think they want too much."

"How many acres?" said Camilla.

"A hundred and fifty."

"What on earth would you do with that much land?" She raised her hand to clear the hair from her eyes and again I caught the gleam of her bracelet: **blown hair is sweet, brown hair over the mouth blown. . . .** "You wouldn't want to farm it, would you?"

"To my way of thinking," Henry said, "the more land the better. I'd love to have so much land that from where I lived I couldn't see a highway or a telephone pole or anything I didn't want to see. I suppose that's impossible, this day and age, and that place is practically on the road. There was another farm I saw, over the line in New York State . . ."

A truck shot past in a whine of spray.

Everyone seemed unusually calm and at ease and I thought I knew why. It was because Bunny wasn't with us. They were avoiding the topic with a deliberate unconcern; he must be somewhere now, I thought, doing something, what I didn't want to ask. I leaned back and looked at the silvery, staggering paths the raindrops made as they blew across my window.

"If I bought a house anywhere I'd buy one here," said Camilla. "I've always liked the mountains better than the seashore."

"So have I," said Henry. "I suppose in that regard my tastes are rather Hellenistic. Landlocked places interest me, remote prospects, wild country. I've never had the slightest bit of interest in the sea. Rather like what Homer says about the Arcadians, you remember? **With ships they had nothing to do**. . . ."

"It's because you grew up in the Midwest," Charles said.

"But if one follows that line of reasoning, then it follows that I would love flat lands, and plains. Which I don't. The descriptions of Troy in the **Iliad** are horrible to me—all flat land and burning sun. No. I've always been drawn to broken, wild terrain. The oddest tongues come from such places, and the strangest mythologies, and the oldest cities, and the most barbarous religions—Pan himself was born in the mountains, you know. And Zeus. **In Parrhasia it was that Rheia bore thee,**" he said dreamily, lapsing into Greek, **"where was a hill sheltered with the thickest brush. . . ."**

It was dark now. Around us, the countryside lay veiled and mysterious, silent in the night and fog. This was remote, untraveled land, rocky and thickly wooded, with none of the quaint appeal of Hampden and its rolling hills, its ski chalets and antique shops, but high and perilous and primitive, everything black and desolate even of billboards.

Francis, who knew this territory better than we did, had said there was an inn nearby but it was hard to believe there was anything habitable for fifty miles around. Then we rounded a bend and our headlights swept across a rusted metal sign pockmarked with shotgun pellets, that informed us that the Hoosatonic Inn, straight ahead, was the original birthplace of Pie à la Mode.

The building was ringed by a rickety porch—sagging rockers, peeling paint. Inside, the lobby was an intriguing jumble of mahogany and moth-eaten velvet, interspersed with deer heads, calendars from filling stations, and a large collection of Bicentennial commemorative trivets, mounted and hung upon the wall.

The dining room was empty except for a few country people eating their dinners, all of whom looked up at us with innocent, frank curiosity as we came in, at our dark suits and spectacles, at Francis's monogrammed cufflinks and his Charvet tie, at Camilla with her boyish haircut and sleek little Astrakhan coat. I was a bit surprised at this collective openness of demeanor—neither stares nor disapproving looks—until it occurred to me that these people probably didn't realize we were from the college. Closer in, we would have been pegged instantly as rich kids from up on the hill, kids likely to make a lot of noise and leave a bad tip. But here we were only strangers, in a place where strangers were rare.

No one even came by to take an order. Dinner appeared with instantaneous magic: pork roast, biscuits, turnips and corn and butternut squash, in thick china bowls that had pictures of the presidents (up to Nixon) around their rims.

The waiter, a red-faced boy with bitten nails, lingered for a moment. Finally he said, shyly: "You folks from New York City?"

"No," said Charles, taking the plate of biscuits from Henry. "From here."

"From Hoosa**ton**ic?"

"No. Vermont, I mean."

"Not New York?"

"No," said Francis cheerily, carving at the roast. "I'm from Boston."

"I went there," said the boy, impressed.

Francis smiled absently and reached for a dish.

"You folks must like the Red Sox."

"Actually I do," said Francis. "Quite a bit. But they never seem to win, do they?"

"Some of the time they do. I guess we'll never see 'em win the Series, though."

He was still loitering, trying to think of something else to say, when Henry glanced up at him.

"Sit down," he said unexpectedly. "Have some dinner, won't you?"

After a bit of awkward demurral, he pulled up a chair, though he refused to eat anything; the dining room closed at eight, he told us, and it wasn't likely that anyone else would come in. "We're off the highway," he said. "Most folks go to bed pretty early around here." His name, we discovered, was John Deacon; he was my age—twenty—and had graduated from Equinox High School, over in Hoosatonic proper, only two years before. Since graduation, he said, he'd been working on his uncle's farm; the waiter's job was a new thing, something to fill the winter hours. "This is only my third week," he said. "I like it here, I reckon. Food's good. And I get my meals free."

Henry, who generally disliked and was disliked by **hoi polloi**—a category which in his view expanded to include persons ranging from teenagers with boom boxes to the Dean of Studies of Hampden, who was independently wealthy and had a degree in American Studies from Yale—nonetheless had a genuine knack with poor people, simple people, country folk; he was despised by the functionaries of Hampden but admired by its janitors, its gardeners and cooks. Though he did not treat them as equals—he didn't treat anyone as an equal, exactly—neither did he resort to the condescending friendliness of the wealthy. "I think we're much more hypocritical about illness, and poverty, than were people in former ages," I remember Julian saying once. "In America, the rich man tries to pretend that the poor man is his equal in every respect but money, which is simply not true. Does anyone remember Plato's definition of Justice in the **Republic**? Justice, in a society, is when each level of a hierarchy works within its place and is content with it. A poor man who wishes to rise above his station is only making himself needlessly miserable. And the wise poor have always known this, the same as do the wise rich."

I'm not entirely sure now that this is true—because if it is, where does that leave me? still wiping down windshields in Plano—? but there is no doubt that Henry was so confident of his own abilities and position in the world, and so comfortable with them, that he had the strange effect of making others (including my-self) feel comfortable in their respective, lesser positions, whatever they might happen to be. Poor people for the most part were unim-pressed by his manner, except in the most hazy and admiring fashion; and as a consequence they were able to see past it to the real Henry, the Henry I knew, taciturn, polite, in many re-spects as simple and straightforward as they themselves were. It was a knack he shared with Julian, who was greatly admired by the coun-try people who lived around him, much as one likes to imagine that kindly Pliny was held in affection by the poor folk of Comum and Tifernum.

Through most of the meal, Henry and the boy talked in the most intimate and, to me, baffling terms, about the land around Hamp-den and Hoosatonic—zoning, developments, price per acre, uncleared land and titles and who owned what—as the rest of us ate our dinners and listened. It was a conversation one might overhear at any rural filling station or feed store; but hearing it made me feel curi-ously happy, and at ease with the world.

———

In retrospect, it is odd how little power the dead farmer exercised over an imagination as morbid and hysterical as my own. I can well imagine the extravagance of nightmares such a thing might provoke (opening the door to a dream-classroom, the flannel-shirted figure without a face propped ghoulishly at a desk, or turning from its work at the blackboard to grin at me), but I suppose it is rather telling that I seldom thought of it at all and then only when I was reminded in some way. I believe the others were troubled by it as little as or less than I was, as evidenced by the fact that they all had carried on so normally and in such good humor for so long. Monstrous as it was, the corpse itself seemed little more than a prop, something brought out in the dark by stage-hands and laid at Henry's feet, to be discovered when the lights came up; the picture of it, staring and dumb in all its gore, never failed to provoke an anxious little **frisson** but still it seemed relatively harmless compared to the very real and persistent menace which I now saw that Bunny presented.

Bunny, for all his appearance of amiable, callous stability, was actually a wildly erratic character. There were any number of reasons for this, but primary among them was his complete inability to think about anything before he did it. He sailed through the world guided only by the dim lights of impulse and habit, confident that his course would throw up no obstacles so large that they could not be plowed over with sheer force of momentum.

But his instincts had failed him in the new set of circumstances presented by the murder. Now that the old trusted channel-markers had, so to speak, been rearranged in the dark, the automatic-pilot mechanism by which his psyche navigated was useless; decks awash, he floundered aimlessly, running on sandbars, veering off in all sorts of bizarre directions.

To the casual observer, I suppose, he seemed pretty much his jolly old self—slapping people on the back, eating Twinkies and HoHos in the reading room of the library and dropping crumbs all down in the bindings of his Greek books. But behind that bluff facade some distinct and rather ominous changes were taking place, changes of which I was already dimly aware but which made themselves more evident as time went on.

In some respects, it was as if nothing had happened at all. We went to our classes, did our Greek, and generally managed to pretend among one another and everybody else that things were all right. At the time it heartened me that Bunny, in spite of his obviously disturbed state of mind, nonetheless continued to follow the old routine so easily. Now, of course, I see that the routine was all that held him together. It was his one remaining point of reference and he clung to it with a fierce Pavlovian tenacity, partly through habit and partly because he had nothing with which to replace it. I suppose the others sensed that the continuation of the old rituals was in some respects a charade for Bunny's benefit, kept up in order to soothe him, but I did not, nor did I have any idea how disturbed he really was until the following event took place.

We were spending the weekend at Francis's house. Aside from the barely perceptible strain which manifested itself in all dealings with Bunny at that time, things seemed to be going smoothly and he'd been in a good mood at dinner that night. When I went to bed he was still downstairs, drinking wine left from dinner and playing backgammon with Charles, to all appearances his usual self; but some time in the middle of the night I was awakened by a loud, incoherent bellowing, from down the corridor in Henry's room.

I sat up in bed and switched on the light.

"You don't care about a goddamn thing, do you?" I heard Bunny scream; this was followed by a crash, as if of books being swept from desk to floor. "Not a thing but your own fucking self, you and all the rest of them—I'd like to know just what Julian would think, you bastard, if I told him a couple of— **Don't touch me,**" he shrieked, "get away—!"

More crashing, as of furniture overturned, and Henry's voice, quick and angry. Bunny's rose above it. **"Go ahead!"** he shouted, so loudly I'm sure he woke the house. "Try and stop me. I'm not scared of you. You make me sick, you fag, you Nazi, **you dirty lousy cheapskate Jew—"**

Yet another crash, this time of splintering wood. A door slammed. There were rapid footsteps down the hall. Then the muffled noise of sobs—gasping, terrible sobs which went on for a long while.

About three o'clock, when everything was quiet and I was just about to go back to sleep, I heard soft footsteps in the hall and, after a pause, a knock at my door. It was Henry.

"Goodness," he said distractedly, looking around my room, at the unmade four-poster bed and my clothes scattered on the rug beside it. "I'm glad you're awake. I saw your light."

"Jesus, what was all that about?"

He ran a hand through his rumpled hair. "What do you suppose?" he said, looking up at me blankly. "I don't know, really. I must have done something to set him off, though for the life of me I don't know what. I was reading in my room, and he came in and wanted a dictionary. In fact, he asked me to look something up, and— You wouldn't happen to have an aspirin, would you?"

I sat on the side of my bed and rustled through the drawer of the night table, through the tissues and reading glasses and Christian Science leaflets belonging to one of Francis's aged female relatives. "I don't see any," I said. "What happened?"

He sighed and sat down heavily in an arm-chair. "There's aspirin in my room," he said. "In a tin in my overcoat pocket. Also a blue enamel pillbox. And my cigarettes. Will you go get them for me?"

He was so pale and shaken I wondered if he was ill. "What's the matter?" I said.

"I don't want to go in there."

"Why not?"

"Because Bunny's asleep on my bed."

I looked at him. "Well, Jesus," I said. "**I'm** not going to—"

He waved away my words with a tired hand. "It's all right. Really. I'm just too upset to go myself. He's fast asleep."

I went quietly out of my room and down the hall. Henry's door was at the end. Pausing out-side with one hand on the knob, I heard dis-tinctly from within the peculiar huffing noise of Bunny's snores.

In spite of what I'd heard earlier, I was un-prepared for what I saw: books were scattered in a frenzy across the floor; the night table was knocked over; against the wall lay the splay-legged remains of a black Malacca chair. The shade of the pole lamp was askew and cast a crazy irregular light over the room. In the middle of it was Bunny, his face resting on the tweed elbow of his jacket and one foot, still in its wing-tipped shoe, dangling off the edge of the bed. Mouth open, his eyes swollen and unfamiliar without their spectacles, he puffed and grumbled in his sleep. I grabbed up Henry's things and left as fast as I could.

Bunny came down late the next morning, puff-eyed and sullen, while Francis and the twins and I were eating our breakfasts. He ignored our awkward greetings and went straight to the cabinet and made himself a bowl of Sugar Frosted Flakes and sat down wordlessly at the table. In the abrupt silence which had fallen, I heard Mr. Hatch come in the front door. Francis excused himself and hurried away, and I heard the two of them murmuring in the hall as Bunny crunched morosely at his cereal. A few minutes passed. I was looking, obliquely, at Bunny slumped over his bowl when all of a sudden, in the window behind his head, I saw the distant figure of Mr. Hatch, walking across the open field beyond the garden, carrying the dark, curlicued ruins of the Malacca chair to the rubbish heap.

———

As troubling as they were, these eruptions of hysteria were infrequent. But they made it plain how upset Bunny was, and how disagreeable he might make himself if provoked. It was Henry he was angriest at, Henry who had betrayed him, and Henry who was always the subject of these outbursts. Yet in a funny way, it was Henry he was best able to tolerate on a daily basis. He was more or less constantly irritated with everyone else. He might explode at Francis, say, for making some remark he found pretentious, or become inexplicably enraged if Charles offered to buy him an ice-cream; but he did not pick these petty fights with Henry in quite the same trivial, arbitrary way. This was in spite of the fact that Henry did not take nearly the pains to placate him that everyone else did. When the subject of the barge tour came up—and it came up fairly often—Henry played along in only the most perfunctory way, and his replies were mechanical and forced. To me, Bunny's confident anticipation was more chilling than any outburst; how could he possibly delude himself into thinking that the trip would come about, that it would be anything but a nightmare if it did? But Bunny, happy as a mental patient, would rattle for hours about his delusions of the Riviera, oblivious to a certain tightness about Henry's jaw, or to the empty, ominous silences which fell when he was talked out and sat, chin in hand, staring dreamily into space.

It seemed, for the most part, that he sublimated his anger towards Henry into his dealings with the rest of the world. He was insulting, rude, quick to start a quarrel with virtually everyone he came in contact with. Reports of his behavior drifted back to us through various channels. He threw a shoe at some hippies playing Hackysack outside his window; he threatened to beat up his neighbor for playing the radio too loudly; he called one of the ladies in the Bursar's office a troglodyte. It was fortunate for us, I suppose, that his wide circle of acquaintance included few people whom he saw on a regular basis. Julian saw as much of Bunny as anyone, but their relation did not extend much beyond the classroom. More troublesome was his friendship with his old schoolmate Cloke Rayburn; and most troublesome of all, Marion.

Marion, we knew, recognized the difference in Bunny's behavior as clearly as we did, and was puzzled and angered by it. If she'd seen the way he was around us, she doubtless would have realized that she was not the cause; but as it was she saw only the broken dates, the mood swings, the sullenness and the quick irrational angers which apparently were directed solely at her—Was he seeing another girl? Did he want to break up? An acquaintance at the Early

Childhood Center told Camilla that one day at work Marion had called Bunny six times, and the last time he had hung up on her.

"God, please God, let her give him the old heave-ho," said Francis, turning his eyes to heaven, when he heard this bit of intelligence. Nothing more was said of it, but we watched them carefully and prayed that it would be so. If he had his wits about him Bunny surely would keep his mouth shut; but now, with his subconscious mind knocked loose from its perch and flapping in the hollow corridors of his skull as erratically as a bat, there was no way to be sure of anything he might do.

Cloke he saw rather less frequently. He and Bunny had little in common besides their prep school, and Cloke—who ran with a fast crowd, and took a lot of drugs besides—was fairly self-preoccupied, not likely to concern himself with Bunny's behavior or even to take much notice of it. Cloke lived in the house next door to mine, Durbinstall (nicknamed, by campus wags, "Dalmane Hall," it was the bustling center of what the administration chose to refer to as "narcotics-related activity" and one's visits there were occasionally punctuated with explosions and small fires, incurred by lone free-basers or the student chemists who worked in the basement) and, fortunately for us, he lived in the front, on the ground floor. Since his shades were always up and there were no trees in the immediate area, it was possible to sit safely on the porch of the library, some fifty feet away, and enjoy a luxurious and unobscured view of Bunny, framed in a bright window as he gazed open-mouthed at comic books or talked, arms waving, with an invisible Cloke.

"I just like to have an idea," Henry explained, "where he goes." But actually it was quite simple to keep tabs on Bunny: I think because he, too, was unwilling to let the others, and Henry in particular, out of his sight for very long.

If he treated Henry with deference, it was the rest of us who were forced to bear the wearing, day-to-day brunt of his anger. Most of the time he was simply irritating: for example, in his ill-informed and frequent tirades against the Catholic Church. Bunny's family was Episcopalian, and my parents, as far as I knew, had no religious affiliation at all; but Henry and Francis and the twins had been reared as Catholics; and though none of them went to church much, Bunny's ignorant, tireless stream of blasphemies enraged them. With leers and winks he told stories about lapsed nuns, sluttish Catholic girls, pederastic priests ("So then, this Father What's-His-Name, he said to the altar boy—this kid is nine years old, mind you,

he's in my Cub Scout troop—he says to Tim
Mulrooney, 'Son, would you like to see where
me and all the other fathers sleep at night?' ").
He invented outrageous stories of the perversions of various Popes; informed them of little-
known points of Catholic doctrine; raved
about Vatican conspiracies, ignoring Henry's
bald refutations and Francis's muttered asides
about social-climbing Protestants.

What was worse was when he chose to zero
in on one person in particular. With some pre-
ternatural craftiness he always knew the right
nerve to touch, at exactly the right moment, to
wound and outrage most. Charles was good-
natured, and slow to anger, but he was sometimes so disturbed by these anti-Catholic
diatribes that his very teacup would clatter
upon its saucer. He was also sensitive to remarks about his drinking. As a matter of fact,
Charles did drink a lot. We all did: but still,
though he didn't indulge in any very conspicuous excess, I'd frequently had the experience
of smelling liquor on his breath at odd hours
or dropping by unexpectedly in the early afternoon to find him with a glass in his hand—
which was perhaps understandable, things
being what they were. Bunny made a show of
fraudulent, infuriating concern, peppered with
snide comments about drunkards and sots. He
kept exaggerated tallies of Charles's cocktail

consumption. He left questionnaires ("Do you sometimes feel you need a drink to get through the day?") and pamphlets (freckle-faced child gazing plaintively at parent, asking, "Mommy, what's 'drunk'?") anonymously in Charles's box, and once went so far as to give his name to the campus chapter of Alcoholics Anonymous, whereupon Charles was deluged with tracts and phone calls and even a personal visit from a well-meaning Twelfth-Stepper.

With Francis, on the other hand, things were more pointed and unpleasant. Nobody said anything about it, ever, but we all knew he was gay. Though he was not promiscuous, every so often he would disappear quite mysteriously at a party and once, very early in our acquaintance, he'd made a subtle but unmistakable pass at me one afternoon when we were drunk and by ourselves in the rowboat. I'd dropped an oar, and in the confusion of retrieving it I felt his fingertips brush in a casual yet deliberate fashion along my cheek near the jawbone. I glanced up, startled, and our eyes met in that way that eyes will, and we looked at each other for a moment, the boat wobbling around us and the lost oar forgotten. I was dreadfully flustered; embarrassed, I looked away; when suddenly, and to my great surprise, he burst out laughing at my distress.

"No?" he said.

"No," I said, relieved.

It might seem that this episode would have imposed a certain coolness upon our friendship. While I don't suppose that anyone who has devoted much energy to the study of Classics can be very much disturbed by homosexuality, neither am I particularly comfortable with it as it concerns me directly. Though I liked Francis well enough, I had always been nervous around him; oddly, it was this pass of his that cleared the air between us. I suppose I knew it was inevitable, and dreaded it. Once it was out of the way I was perfectly comfortable being alone with him even in the most questionable situations—drunk, or in his apartment, or even wedged in the back seat of a car.

With Francis and Bunny it was a different story. They were happy enough to be together in company, but if one was around either of them for too long it became obvious that they seldom did things with each other and almost never spent time alone. I knew why this was; we all did. Still, it never occurred to me that they weren't genuinely fond of each other on some level, nor that Bunny's gruff jokes concealed, however beguilingly, a keen and very pointed streak of malice toward Francis in particular.

I suppose the shock of recognition is one of the nastiest shocks of all. I'd never considered, though I should have, that these crackpot prejudices of Bunny's which I found so amusing were not remotely ironic but deadly serious.

Not that Francis, in normal circumstances, wasn't perfectly able to take care of himself. He had a quick temper, and a sharp tongue, and though he could've put Bunny in his place pretty much any time he chose, he was understandably apprehensive about doing so. We were all of us painfully aware of that metaphoric vial of nitroglycerine which Bunny carried around with him day and night, and which, from time to time, he allowed us a glimpse of, unless anyone forget it was always with him, and he had the power to dash it to the floor whenever he pleased.

I don't really have the heart to recount all the vile things he said and did to Francis, the practical jokes, the remarks about faggots and queers, the public, humiliating stream of questions about his preference and practices: clinical and incredibly detailed ones, having to do with such things as enemas, and gerbils, and incandescent light bulbs.

"Just once," I remember Francis hissing, through clenched teeth. "Just once I'd like to . . ."

But there was absolutely nothing that anyone could say or do.

One might expect that I, being at that time

perfectly innocent of any crime against either Bunny or humanity, would not myself be a target of this ongoing sniper fire. Unfortunately I was, perhaps more unfortunately for him than for me. How could he have been so blind as not to see how dangerous it might be for him to alienate the one impartial party, his one potential ally? Because, as fond as I was of the others, I was fond of Bunny, too, and I would not have been nearly so quick to cast in my lot with the rest of them had he not turned on me so ferociously. Perhaps, in his mind, there was the justification of jealousy; his position in the group had started to slip at roughly the same time I'd arrived; his resentment was of the most petty and childish sort, and doubtless would never have surfaced had he not been in such a paranoid state, unable to distinguish his enemies from his friends.

By stages I grew to abhor him. Ruthless as a gun dog, he picked up with rapid and unflagging instinct the traces of everything in the world I was most insecure about, all the things I was in most agony to hide. There were certain repetitive, sadistic games he would play with me. He liked to entice me into lies: "Gorgeous necktie," he'd say, "that's a Hermès, isn't it?"—and then, when I assented, reach quickly across the lunch table and expose my poor tie's humble lineage. Or in the middle of a conversation he would suddenly bring himself up short and say: "Richard, old man, why don't you keep any pictures of your folks around?"

It was just the sort of detail he would seize upon. His own room was filled with an array of flawless family memorabilia, all of them perfect as a series of advertisements: Bunny and his brothers, waving lacrosse sticks on a luminous black-and-white playing field; family Christmases, a pair of cool, tasteful parents in expensive bathrobes, five little yellow-haired boys in identical pajamas rolling on the floor with a laughing spaniel, and a ridiculously lavish train set, and the tree rising sumptuous in the background; Bunny's mother at her debutante ball, young and disdainful in white mink.

"What?" he'd ask with mock innocence. "No cameras in California? Or can't you have your friends seeing Mom in polyester pants suits? Where'd your parents go to school anyway?" he'd say, interrupting before I could interject. "Are they Ivy League material? Or did they go to some kind of a State U?"

It was the most gratuitous sort of cruelty. My lies about my family were adequate, I suppose, but they could not stand up under these glaring attacks. Neither of my parents had finished high school; my mother did wear pants suits, which she purchased at a factory outlet. In the only photograph I had of her, a snapshot, she squinted blurrily at the camera, one hand on the Cyclone fence and the other on my father's new riding lawn mower. This, ostensibly, was the reason that the photo had been sent me, my mother having some notion that I would be interested in the new acquisition; I'd kept it because it was the only picture I had of her, kept it tucked inside a Webster's dictionary (under M for Mother) on my desk. But one night I rose from my bed, suddenly consumed with fear that Bunny would find it while snooping around my room. No hiding place seemed safe enough. Finally I burned it in an ashtray.

They were unpleasant enough, these private inquisitions, but I cannot find words to adequately express the torments I suffered when he chose to ply this art of his in public. Bunny's dead now, **requiescat in pace,** but so long as I live I will never forget a particular interlude of sadism to which he subjected me at the twins' apartment.

A few days earlier, Bunny had been grilling me about where I'd gone to prep school. I don't know why I couldn't just have admitted the truth, that I'd gone to the public school in Plano. Francis had gone to any number of wildly exclusive schools in England and

Switzerland, and Henry had been at corre-
spondingly exclusive American ones before he
dropped out entirely in the eleventh grade; but
the twins had only gone to a little country day
school in Roanoke, and even Bunny's own hal-
lowed Saint Jerome's was really only an expensive remedial school, the sort of place you see
advertised in the back of **Town and Country**
as offering specialized attention for the academic underachiever. My own school was not
particularly shameful in this context, yet I
evaded the question long as I could till finally,
cornered and desperate, I had told him I'd
gone to Renfrew Hall, which is a tennis-y, indifferent sort of boys' school near San Francisco. That had seemed to satisfy him, but
then, to my immense discomfort, and in front
of everybody, he brought it up again.

"So you were at Renfrew," he said chummily,
turning to me and popping a handful of pistachios in his mouth.

"Yes."

"When'd ya graduate?"

I offered the date of my real high school
graduation.

"Ah," he said, chomping busily on his nuts.
"So you were there with Von Raumer."

"What?"

"Alec. Alec Von Raumer. From San Fran.

Friend of Cloke's. He was in the room the other day and we got talking. Lots of old Renfrew boys at Hampden, he says."

I said nothing, hoping he'd leave it at that.

"So you know Alec and all."

"Uh, slightly," I said.

"Funny, he said he didn't remember you," said Bunny, reaching over for another handful of pistachios without taking his eyes off me. "Not at all."

"It's a big school."

He cleared his throat. "Think so?"

"Yes."

"Von Raumer said it was tiny. Only about two hundred people." He paused and threw another handful of pistachios into his mouth, and chewed as he talked. "What dormitory did you say you were in?"

"You wouldn't know it."

"Von Raumer told me to make a point of asking you."

"What difference does it make?"

"Oh, it's nothing, nothing at all, old horse," said Bunny pleasantly. "Just that it's pretty damn peculiar, **n'est-ce pas**? You and Alec being there together for four years, in a tiny place like Renfrew, and he never laid eyes on you even once?"

"I was only there for two years."

"How come you're not in the yearbook?"

"I am in the yearbook."

"No you're not."

The twins looked stricken. Henry had his back turned, pretending not to listen. Now he said, quite suddenly and without turning around: "How do **you** know if he was in the yearbook or not?"

"I don't think I've ever been in a yearbook in my life," said Francis nervously. "I can't stand to have my picture taken. Whenever I try to—"

Bunny paid no attention. He leaned back in his chair.

"Come on," he said to me. "I'll give you five dollars if you can tell me the name of the dorm you lived in."

His eyes were riveted on mine; they were bright with a horrible relish. I said something incoherent and then in consternation got up and went into the kitchen to get a glass of water. Leaning on the sink, I held the glass to my temple; from the living room, Francis whispered something indistinct but angry, and then Bunny laughed harshly. I poured the water down the sink and turned on the tap so I wouldn't have to listen.

———

How was it that a complex, a nervous and delicately calibrated mind like my own, was able to adjust itself perfectly after a shock like the murder, while Bunny's eminently more sturdy and ordinary one was knocked out of kilter? I still think about this sometimes. If what Bunny really wanted was revenge, he could have had it easily enough and without putting himself at risk. What did he imagine was to be gained from this slow and potentially explosive kind of torture, had it, in his mind, some purpose, some goal? Or were his own actions as inexplicable to him as they were to us?

Or perhaps they weren't so inexplicable as that. Because the worst thing about all of this, as Camilla once remarked, was not that Bunny had suffered some total change of personality, some schizophrenic break, but rather that various unpleasant elements of his personality which heretofore we had only glimpsed had orchestrated and magnified themselves to a startling level of potency. Distasteful as his behavior was, we had seen it all before, only in less concentrated and vitriolic form. Even in the happiest times he'd made fun of my California accent, my secondhand overcoat and my room barren of tasteful **bibelots**, but in such an ingenuous way I couldn't possibly do anything but laugh. ("Good Lord, Richard," he would say, picking up one of my old wingtips and poking his finger through the hole in the bottom. "What is it with you California kids? Richer you are, the more shoddy

you look. Won't even go to the barber. Before
I know it, you'll have hair down to your shoulders and be skulking around in rags like
Howard Hughes.") It never occurred to me to
be offended; this was Bunny, my friend, who
had even less pocket money than I did and a
big rip in the seat of his trousers besides. A
good deal of my horror at his new behavior
sprang from the fact that it was so similar to
the old and frankly endearing way he used to
tease me, and I was as baffled and enraged
at his sudden departure from the rules as
though—if we had been in the habit of doing
a little friendly sparring—he had boxed me
into the corner and beaten me half to death.

To compound this—all these unpleasant
recollections to the contrary—so much remained of the old Bunny, the one I knew and
loved. Sometimes when I saw him at a distance—fists in pockets, whistling, bobbing
along with his springy old walk—I would have
a strong pang of affection mixed with regret. I
forgave him, a hundred times over, and never
on the basis of anything more than this: a
look, a gesture, a certain tilt of his head. It
seemed impossible then that one could ever be
angry at him, no matter what he did. Unfortunately, these were often the moments when he
chose to attack. He would be amiable, charming, chatting in his old distracted manner

when, in the same manner and without missing a beat, he would lean back in his chair and come out with something so horrendous, so backhanded, so unanswerable, that I would vow not to forget it, and never to forgive him again. I broke that promise many times. I was about to say that it was a promise I finally had to keep, but that's not really true. Even today I cannot muster anything resembling anger for Bunny. In fact, I can't think of much I'd like better than for him to step into the room right now, glasses fogged and smelling of damp wool, shaking the rain from his hair like an old dog and saying: "Dickie, my boy, what you got for a thirsty old man to drink tonight?"

One likes to think there's something in it, that old platitude **amor vincit omnia**. But if I've learned one thing in my short sad life, it is that that particular platitude is a lie. Love doesn't conquer everything. And whoever thinks it does is a fool.

———

Camilla he tormented simply because she was a girl. In some ways she was his most vulnerable target—through no fault of her own, but simply because in Greekdom, generally speaking, women are lesser creatures, better seen than heard. This prevailing sentiment among the Argives is so pervasive that it lingers in the bones of the language itself; I can think of no better illustration of this than the fact that in Greek grammar, one of the very first axioms I learned is that men have friends, women have relatives, and animals have their own kind.

Bunny, through no impulse toward Hellenic purity but simply out of mean-spiritedness, championed this view. He didn't like women, didn't enjoy their company, and even Marion, his self-proclaimed **raison d'être**, was tolerated as grudgingly as a concubine. With Camilla he was forced to assume a slightly more paternalistic stance, beaming down at her with the condescension of an old papa toward a dimwit child. To the rest of us he complained that Camilla was out of her league, and a hindrance to serious scholarship. We all found this pretty funny. To be honest, none of us, not even the brightest of us, were destined for academic achievement in subsequent years, Francis being too lazy, Charles too diffuse, and Henry too erratic and generally strange, a sort of Mycroft Holmes of classical philology. Camilla was no different, secretly preferring, as I did, the easy delights of English literature to the coolie labor of Greek. What was laughable was that poor Bunny should display concern about anyone else's intellectual capacities.

Being the only female in what was basically a boys' club must have been difficult for her. Miraculously, she didn't compensate by becoming hard or quarrelsome. She was still a girl, a slight lovely girl who lay in bed and ate chocolates, a girl whose hair smelled like hyacinth and whose scarves fluttered jauntily in the breeze. But strange and marvelous as she was, a wisp of silk in a forest of black wool, she was not the fragile creature one would have her seem. In many ways she was as cool and competent as Henry; tough-minded and solitary in her habits, and in many ways as aloof. Out in the country it was not uncommon to discover that she had slipped away, alone, out to the lake, maybe, or down to the cellar, where once I found her sitting in the big marooned sleigh, reading, her fur coat thrown over her knees. Things would have been terribly strange and unbalanced without her. She was the Queen who finished out the suit of dark Jacks, dark King, and Joker.

If I found the twins so fascinating, I think it was because there was something a tiny bit inexplicable about them, something I was often on the verge of grasping but never quite did. Charles, kind and slightly ethereal soul that he was, was something of an enigma but Camilla was the real mystery, the safe I could never crack. I was never sure what she thought about anything, and I knew that Bunny found her even harder to read than I did. In good times he'd often offended her clumsily, without meaning to; as soon as things turned bad, he tried to insult and belittle her in a variety of ways, most of which struck wide of the mark. She was impervious to slights about her appearance; met his eye, unblinking, as he told the most vulgar and humiliating jokes; laughed if he attempted to insult her taste or her intelligence; ignored his frequent discourses, peppered with erudite quotations he must have gone to great trouble to dig up, all to the effect that all women were categorically inferior to himself: not designed—as he was—for Philosophy, and Art, and Higher Reasoning, but to attract a husband and to Tend the Home.

Only once did I ever see him get to her. It was over at the twins' apartment, very late. Charles, fortunately, was out with Henry getting ice; he'd had a lot to drink and if he'd been around things would almost certainly have gotten out of hand. Bunny was so drunk he could hardly sit up. For most of the evening, he'd been in a passable mood, but then, without warning, he turned to Camilla and said: "How come you kids live together?"

She shrugged, in that odd, one-shouldered way the twins had.

"Huh?"

"It's convenient," said Camilla. "Cheap."

"Well, I think it's pretty damned peculiar."

"I've lived with Charles all my life."

"Not much privacy, is there? Little place like this? On top of each other all the time?"

"It's a two-bedroom apartment."

"And when you get lonesome in the middle of the night?"

There was a brief silence.

"I don't know what you're trying to say," she said icily.

"Sure you do," said Bunny. "Convenient as hell. Kinda classical, too. Those Greeks carried on with their brothers and sisters like nobody's—whoops," he said, retrieving the whiskey glass which was about to fall off the arm of his chair. "Sure, it's against the law and stuff," he said. "But what's that to you. Break one, you might as well break 'em all, eh?"

I was stunned. Francis and I gaped at him as he unconcernedly drained his glass and reached for the bottle again.

To my utter, utter surprise, Camilla said tartly: "You mustn't think I'm sleeping with my brother just because I won't sleep with **you**."

Bunny laughed a low, nasty laugh. "You couldn't pay me to sleep with you, girlie," he said. "Not for all the tea in China."

She looked at him with absolutely no expression in her pale eyes. Then she got up and went into the kitchen, leaving Francis and me to one of the more torturous silences I have ever experienced.

———

Religious slurs, temper tantrums, insults, coercion, debt: all petty things, really, irritants—too minor, it would seem, to move five reasonable people to murder. But, if I dare say it, it wasn't until I had helped to kill a man that I realized how elusive and complex an act a murder can actually be, and not necessarily attributable to one dramatic motive. To ascribe it to such a motive would be easy enough. There was one, certainly. But the instinct for self-preservation is not so compelling an instinct as one might think. The danger which he presented was, after all, not immediate but slow and simmering, a sort which can, at least in the abstract, be postponed or diverted in any number of ways. I can easily imagine us there, at the appointed time and place, anxious suddenly to reconsider, perhaps even to grant a disastrous last-minute reprieve. Fear for our own lives might have induced us to lead him to the gallows and slip the noose around his neck, but a more urgent impetus was necessary to make us actually go ahead and kick out the chair.

Bunny, unawares, had himself supplied us with such an impetus. I would like to say I was driven to what I did by some overwhelming, tragic motive. But I think I would be lying if I told you that; if I led you to believe that on that Sunday afternoon in April, I was actually being driven by anything of the sort.

An interesting question: what was I thinking, as I watched his eyes widen with startled incredulity (**"come on, fellas, you're joking, right?"**) for what would be the very last time? Not of the fact that I was helping to save my friends, certainly not; nor of fear; nor guilt. But little things. Insults, innuendos, petty cruelties. The hundreds of small, unavenged humiliations which had been rising in me for months. It was of them I thought, and nothing more. It was because of them that I was able to watch him at all, without the slightest tinge of pity or regret, as he teetered on the cliff's edge for one long moment—arms flailing, eyes rolling, a silent-movie comedian slipping on a banana peel—before he toppled backwards, and fell to his death.

———

Henry, I believed, had a plan. What it was I didn't know. He was always disappearing on mysterious errands, and perhaps these were only more of the same; but now, anxious to believe that someone, at least, had the situation in hand, I imbued them with a certain hopeful significance. Not infrequently he refused to answer his door, even late at night when a light was burning and I knew he was at home; more than once he appeared late for dinner with wet shoes, and windblown hair, and mud on the cuffs of his neat dark trousers. A stack of mysterious books, in a Near Eastern language which looked like Arabic and bearing the stamp of the Williams College Library, materialized in the back seat of his car. This was doubly puzzling, as I did not think he read Arabic; nor, to my knowledge, did he have borrowing privileges at the Williams College Library. Glancing surreptitiously at the back pocket of one of them, I found the card was still in it, and that the last person to check it out was an F. Lockett, back in 1929.

Perhaps the oddest thing of all, though, I saw one afternoon when I'd hitched a ride into Hampden with Judy Poovey. I wanted to take some clothes to the cleaners and Judy, who was going into town, offered to drive me; we'd done our errands, not to mention an awful lot of cocaine in the parking lot of Burger King, and we were stopped in the Corvette at a red light, listening to terrible music ("Free Bird") on the Manchester radio station, and Judy rattling on, like the senseless cokehead she was, about these two guys she knew who'd had sex in the Food King ("Right in the store! In the frozen food aisle!"), when she glanced out her window and laughed. "Look," she said. "Isn't that your friend Four Eyes over there?"

Startled, I leaned forward. There was a tiny head shop directly across the street—bongs, tapestries, canisters of Rush, and all sorts of herbs and incense behind the counter. I'd never seen anyone in it before except the sad old hippie in granny glasses, a Hampden graduate, who owned it. But now to my astonishment I saw Henry—black suit, umbrella and all—among the celestial maps and unicorns. He was standing at the counter looking at a sheet of paper. The hippie started to say something but Henry, cutting him short, pointed to something behind the counter. The hippie shrugged and took a little bottle off the shelf. I watched them, half-breathless.

"What do you think **he's** doing in there, trying to harass that poor old Deadhead? That's a shitty store, by the way. I went in there once for a pair of scales and they didn't even have any, just a bunch of crystal balls and shit. You know that set of green plastic scales I— Hey, you're not **listening**," she said when she saw I was still staring out the window. The hippie had leaned down and was rummaging under the counter. "You want me to honk or something?"

"No," I shouted, edgy from the cocaine, and pushed her hand away from the horn.

"Oh, **God**. Don't scare me like that." She pressed her hand to her chest. "Shit. I'm speeding my brains out. That coke was cut with meth or something. Okay, okay," she said irritably, as the light turned green and the gas truck behind us began to honk.

———

Stolen Arabic books? A head shop in Hampden town? I couldn't imagine what Henry was doing, but as disconnected as his actions seemed, I had a childlike faith in him and, as confidently as Dr. Watson observing the actions of his more illustrious friend, I waited for the design to manifest itself.

Which it did, in a certain fashion, in a couple of days.

On a Thursday night, around twelve-thirty, I was in my pajamas and attempting to cut my own hair with the aid of a mirror and some nail scissors (I never did a very good job; the finished product was always very thistly and childish, **à la** Arthur Rimbaud) when there was a knock at the door. I answered it with scissors and mirror in hand. It was Henry. "Oh, hello," I said. "Come in."

Stepping carefully over the tufts of dusty brown hair, he sat down at my desk. Inspecting my profile in the mirror, I went back to work with the scissors. "What's up?" I said, reaching over to snip off a long clump by my ear.

"You studied medicine for a while, didn't you?" he said.

I knew this to be a prelude to some health-related inquiry. My one year of pre-med had provided scanty knowledge at best, but the others, who knew nothing at all of medicine and regarded the discipline **per se** as less a science than a kind of sympathetic magic, constantly solicited my opinion on their aches and pains as respectfully as savages consulting a witch doctor. Their ignorance ranged from the touching to the downright shocking; Henry, I suppose because he'd been ill so often, knew more than the rest of them but occasionally even he would startle one with a perfectly serious question about humors or spleen.

"Are you sick?" I said, one eye on his reflection in the mirror.

"I need a formula for dosage."

"What do you mean, a formula for dosage? Dosage of what?"

"There is one, isn't there? Some mathematical formula which tells the proper dose to administer according to height and weight, that sort of thing?"

"It depends on the drug," I said. "I can't tell

you something like that. You'd have to look it up in a **Physicians' Desk Reference**."

"I can't do that."

"They're very simple to use."

"That's not what I mean. It's not in the **Physicians' Desk Reference**."

"You'd be surprised."

For a moment there was no sound except the grinding of my scissors. At last he said: "You don't understand. This isn't something doctors generally use."

I brought down my scissors and looked at his reflection in the mirror.

"Jesus, Henry," I said. "What have you got? Some LSD or something?"

"Let's say I do," he said calmly.

I put down the mirror and turned to stare at him. "Henry, I don't think that's a good idea," I said. "I don't know if I ever told you this but I took LSD a couple of times. When I was a sophomore in high school. It was the worst mistake I ever made in my—"

"I realize that it's hard to gauge the concentration of such a drug," he said evenly. "But say we have a certain amount of empirical evidence. Let's say we know, for instance, that x amount of the drug in question is enough to affect a seventy-pound animal and another, slightly larger amount is sufficient to kill it.

I've figured out a rough formula, but still we are talking about a very fine distinction. So, knowing this much, how do I go about calculating the rest?"

I leaned against my dresser and stared at him, my haircut forgotten. "Let's see what you have," I said.

He looked at me intently for a moment or two, then reached into his pocket. When his hand opened, I couldn't believe my eyes, but then I stepped closer. A pale, slender-stemmed mushroom lay across his open palm.

"**Amanita caesaria,**" he said. "Not what you think," he added when he saw the look on my face.

"I know what an amanita is."

"Not all amanitae are poisonous. This one is harmless."

"What is it?" I said, taking it from his hand and holding it to the light. "A hallucinogen?"

"No. Actually they are good to eat—the Romans liked them a great deal—but people avoid them as a rule because they are so easily confused with their evil twin."

"Evil twin?"

"**Amanita phalloides,**" said Henry mildly. "Death cap."

I didn't say anything for a moment.

"What are you going to do?" I finally asked.

"What do you think?"

I got up, agitated, and walked to my desk. Henry put the mushroom back in his pocket and lit a cigarette. "Do you have an ashtray?" he said courteously.

I gave him an empty soda can. His cigarette was nearly finished before I spoke. "Henry, I don't think this is a good idea."

He raised an eyebrow. "Why not?"

Why not, he asks me. "Because," I said, a little wildly, "they can trace poison. Any kind of poison. Do you think if Bunny keels over dead, people won't find it peculiar? Any idiot of a coroner can—"

"I know that," said Henry patiently. "Which is why I'm asking you about the dosage."

"That has nothing to do with it. Even a tiny amount can be—"

"—enough to make one extremely ill," Henry said, lighting another cigarette. "But not necessarily lethal."

"What do you mean?"

"I mean," he said, pushing his glasses up on the bridge of his nose, "that strictly in terms of virulence there are any number of excellent poisons, most of them far superior to this. The woods will be soon full of foxglove and monkshood. I could get all the arsenic I needed from flypaper. And even herbs that aren't common here—good God, the Borgias would have wept to see the health-food store I found in Brattleboro last week. Hellebore, mandrake, pure oil of wormwood. . . . I suppose people will buy anything if they think it's natural. The wormwood they were selling as organic insect repellent, as if that made it safer than the stuff at the supermarket. One bottle could have killed an army." He toyed with his glasses again. "The problem with these things—excellent though they are—is one, as you said, of administration. Amatoxins are messy, as poisons go. Vomiting, jaundice, convulsions. Not like some of the little Italian comfortives, which are relatively quick and kind. But, on the other hand, what could be easier to give? I'm not a botanist, you know. Even mycologists have a hard time telling amanitae apart. Some handpicked mushrooms . . . a few bad ones get mixed in the lot . . . one friend gets dreadfully ill and the other . . . ?" He shrugged.

We looked at each other.

"How can you be sure you won't get too much yourself?" I asked him.

"I suppose I can't be, really," he said. "My own life must be plausibly in danger, so you can see I have a delicate margin to work with. But still, chances are excellent that I can bring it off. All I have to worry about is myself, you know. The rest will take care of itself."

I knew what he meant. The plan had several grave flaws, but this was its genius: if anything could be relied upon with almost mathematical certainty, it was that Bunny, at any given meal, would somehow manage to eat almost twice as much as anyone else.

Henry's face was pale and serene through the haze of his cigarette. He put his hand in his pocket and produced the mushroom again.

"Now," he said. "A single cap, roughly this size, of **A. phalloides** is enough to make a healthy seventy-pound dog quite ill. Vomiting, diarrhea, no convulsions that I saw. I don't think there was anything as severe as liver dysfunction but I suppose we will have to leave that to the veterinarians. Evidently—"

"Henry, how do you **know** this?"

He was silent for a moment. Then he said: "Do you know those two horrible boxer dogs who belong to the couple who live upstairs?"

It was dreadful but I had to laugh, I couldn't help it. **"No,"** I said. "You didn't."

"I'm afraid I did," he said dryly, mashing out his cigarette. "One of them is fine, unfortunately. The other one won't be dragging garbage up on **my** front porch anymore. It was dead in twenty hours, and only of a slightly larger dose—the difference perhaps of a gram. Knowing this, it seems to me that I should be able to prescribe how much poison each of us should get. What worries me is the variation in concentration of poison from one mushroom to the next. It's not as if it's measured out by a pharmacist. Perhaps I'm wrong—I'm sure you know more about it than I do—but a mushroom that weighs two grams might well have just as much as one that weighs three, no? Hence my dilemma."

He reached into his breast pocket and took out a sheet of paper covered with numbers. "I hate to involve you in this, but no one else knows a thing about math and I'm far from reliable myself. Will you have a look?"

Vomiting, jaundice, convulsions. Mechanically, I took the sheet of paper from him. It was covered with algebraic equations, but at the moment algebra was frankly the last thing on my mind. I shook my head and was on the point of handing it back when I looked up at him and something stopped me. I was in the position, I realized, to put an end to this, now, right here. He really did need my help, or else he wouldn't have come to me; emotional appeals, I knew, were useless but if I pretended that I knew what I was doing I might be able to talk him out of it.

I took the paper to my desk and sat down with a pencil and forced myself through the tangle of numbers step by step. Equations about chemical concentration were never my strong point in chemistry, and they are difficult enough when you are trying to figure a fixed concentration in a suspension of distilled water; but this, dealing as it did with varying concentrations in irregularly shaped objects, was virtually impossible. He had probably used all the elementary algebra he knew in figuring this, and as far as I could follow him he hadn't done a bad job; but this wasn't a problem that could be worked with algebra, if it could be worked at all. Someone with three or four years of college calculus might have been able to come up with something that at least looked more convincing; by tinkering, I was able to narrow his ratio slightly but I had forgotten most of the little calculus I knew and the answer I wound up with, though probably closer than his own, was far from correct.

I put down my pencil and looked up. The business had taken me about half an hour. Henry had got a copy of Dante's **Purgatorio** from my bookshelf and was reading it, absorbed.

"Henry."

He glanced up absently.

"Henry, I don't think this is going to work."

He closed the book on his finger. "I made a

mistake in the second part," he said. "Where the factoring begins."

"It's a good try, but just by looking at it I can tell that it's insolvable without chemical tables and a good working knowledge of calculus and chemistry proper. There's no way to figure it otherwise. I mean, chemical concentrations aren't even measured in terms of grams and milligrams but in something called moles."

"Can you work it for me?"

"I'm afraid not, though I've done as much as I can. Practically speaking, I can't give you an answer. Even a math professor would have a tough time with this one."

"Hmn," said Henry, looking over my shoulder at the paper on the desk. "I'm heavier than Bun, you know. By twenty-five pounds. That should count for something, shouldn't it?"

"Yes, but the difference of size isn't large enough to bank on, not with a margin of error potentially this wide. Now, if you were fifty pounds heavier, maybe . . ."

"The poison doesn't take effect for at least twelve hours," he said. "So even if I overdose I'll have a certain advantage, a grace period. With an antidote on hand for myself, just in case . . ."

"An antidote?" I said, jarred, leaning back in my chair. "Is there such a thing?"

"Atropine. It's in deadly nightshade."

"Well, Jesus, Henry. If you don't finish yourself off with one you will with the other."

"Atropine's quite safe in small amounts."

"They say the same about arsenic but I wouldn't like to try it."

"They are exactly opposite in effect. Atropine speeds the nervous system, rapid heartbeat and so forth. Amatoxins slow it down."

"That still sounds fishy, a poison counteracting a poison."

"Not at all. The Persians were master poisoners, and they say—"

I remembered the books in Henry's car. "The Persians?" I said.

"Yes. According to the great—"

"I didn't know you read Arabic."

"I don't, at least not well, but they're the great authorities on the subject and most of the books I need haven't been translated. I've been going through them as best I can with a dictionary."

I thought about the books I had seen, dusty, bindings crumbled with age. "When were these things written?"

"Around the middle of the fifteenth century, I should say."

I put down my pencil. "Henry."

"What?"

"You should know better than that. You can't rely on something that old."

"The Persians were master poisoners. These are practical handbooks, how-tos if you will. I don't know of anything quite like them."

"Poisoning people is quite a different matter from curing them."

"People have used these books for centuries. Their accuracy is beyond dispute."

"Well, I have as much respect for ancient learning as you do, but I don't know that I'd want to stake my life on some home remedy from the Middle Ages."

"Well, I suppose I can check it somewhere else," he said, without much conviction.

"Really. This is too serious a matter to—"

"Thank you," he said smoothly. "You've been a great help." He picked up my copy of **Purgatorio** again. "This isn't a very good translation, you know," he said, leafing through it idly. "Singleton is the best if you don't read Italian, quite literal, but you lose all the **terza rima**, of course. For that you should read the original. In very great poetry the music often comes through even when one doesn't know the language. I loved Dante passionately before I knew a word of Italian."

"Henry," I said, in a low, urgent voice.

He glanced over at me, annoyed. "Anything I do will be dangerous, you know," he said.

"But nothing is any good if you die."

"The more I hear about luxury barges, the

less terrible death begins to seem," he said. "You've been quite a help. Good night."

Early the next afternoon, Charles dropped by for a visit. "Gosh, it's hot in here," he said, shouldering off his wet coat and throwing it over the back of a chair. His hair was damp, his face flushed and radiant. A drop of water trembled at the end of his long, fine nose. He sniffed and wiped it away. "Don't go outside, whatever you do," he said. "It's terrible out. By the way, you haven't seen Francis, have you?"

I ran a hand through my hair. It was a Friday afternoon, no class, and I hadn't been out of my room all day, nor had I slept much the night before. "Henry stopped by last night," I said.

"Really? What did he have to say? Oh, I almost forgot." He reached in the pocket of his overcoat and pulled out a bundle wrapped in napkins. "I brought you a sandwich since you weren't at lunch. Camilla said the lady in the dining hall saw me stealing it and she made a black mark by my name on a list."

It was cream cheese and marmalade, I knew without looking. The twins were fanatical about them but I didn't like them much. I unwrapped a corner of it and took a bite, then set it down on my desk. "Have you talked to Henry recently?" I said.

"Just this morning. He drove me to the bank."

I picked up the sandwich and took another bite. I hadn't swept, and my hair still lay in clumps on the floor. "Did he," I said, "say anything about—"

"About what?"

"About asking Bunny to dinner in a couple of weeks?"

"Oh, that," said Charles, lying back on my bed and propping his head up with pillows. "I thought you knew about that already. He's been thinking about that for a while."

"What do **you** think?"

"I think he's going to have a hell of a hard time finding enough mushrooms to even make him sick. It's just too early. Last week he made Francis and me go out and help him, but we hardly found a thing. Francis came back really excited, saying, 'Oh, my God, look, I found all these mushrooms,' but then we looked in his bag and it was just a bunch of puffballs."

"So you think he'll be able to find enough?"

"Sure, if he waits awhile. I know you don't have a cigarette, do you?"

"No."

"I wish you smoked. I don't know why you don't. You weren't an athlete in high school or anything, were you?"

"No."

"That's why Bun doesn't smoke. Some clean-living type of football coach got to him at an impressionable age."

"Have you seen Bun lately?"

"Not too much. He was at the apartment last night, though, and stayed forever."

"This isn't just hot air?" I said, looking at him closely. "You're really going to go through with it?"

"I'd rather go to jail than know that Bunny was going to be hanging around my neck for the rest of my life. And I'm not too keen on going to jail, either, now that I think about it. You know," he said, sitting up on my bed and bending over double, as if from a pain in his stomach, "I really wish you had some cigarettes. Who's that awful girl who lives down the hall from you—Judy?"

"Poovey," I said.

"Go knock on her door, why don't you, and ask her if she'll give you a pack. She looks like the sort who keeps cartons in her room."

———

It was getting warmer. The dirty snow was pockmarked from the warm rain, and melting in patches to expose the slimy, yellowed grass beneath it; icicles cracked and plunged like daggers from the sharp peaks of the roofs.

"We might be in South America now," Camilla said one night while we were drinking bourbon from teacups in my room and listening to rain dripping from the eaves. "That's funny, isn't it?"

"Yes," I said, though I hadn't been invited.

"I didn't like the idea then. Now I think we might've got by all right down there."

"I don't see how."

She leaned her cheek on her closed fist. "Oh, it wouldn't have been so bad. We could have slept in hammocks. Learned Spanish. Lived in a little house with chickens in the yard."

"Got sick," I said. "Been shot."

"I can think of worse things," she said, with a brief sideways glance that pierced me to the heart.

The windowpanes rattled in a sudden gust.

"Well," I said, "I'm glad you didn't go."

She ignored this remark and, looking out the dark window, took another sip from the teacup.

———

It was by now the first week of April, not a pleasant time for me or anyone. Bunny, who had been relatively calm, was now on a rampage because Henry refused to drive him down to Washington, D.C., to see an exhibit of World War I biplanes at the Smithsonian. The twins were getting calls twice daily from an ominous B. Perry at their bank, and Henry from a D. Wade at his; Francis's mother had discovered his attempt to withdraw money from the trust fund, and each day brought a fresh volley of communication from her. "Good God," he muttered, having torn open the latest arrival and scanned it with disgust.

"What does she say?"

" 'Baby. Chris and I are so concerned about you,' " Francis read in a deadpan voice. " 'Now I do not pretend to be an authority on Young People and maybe you are going through something I am too old to understand but I have always hoped you would be able to go to Chris with your problems.' "

"Chris has a lot more problems than you do, it seems to me," I said. The character that Chris played on "The Young Doctors" was sleeping with his brother's wife and involved in a baby-smuggling ring.

"I'll say Chris has problems. He's twenty-six years old and married to my mother, isn't he? 'Now I even hate to bring this up,' " he read, " 'and I wouldn't have suggested it had not Chris insisted but you know, dear, how he loves you and he says he has seen this type of thing so often before in show business you know. So I phoned the Betty Ford Center and precious, what do you think? They have a nice little room waiting just for you, dear'—no, let me finish," he said, when I started to laugh. " 'Now I know you'll hate the idea but really you needn't be ashamed, it's a Disease, baby, that's what they told me when I went and it made me feel so much better you cannot imagine. Of course I don't know what it is you're taking but really, darling, let's be practical, whatever it is it must be frightfully expensive mustn't it and I have to be quite honest with you and tell you that we simply cannot afford it, not with your grandpa the way he is and the taxes on the house and everything . . .' "

"You ought to go," I said.

"Are you kidding? It's in Palm Springs or someplace like that and besides I think they lock you up and make you do aerobics. She watches too much television, my mother," he said, glancing at the letter again.

The telephone began to ring.

"Goddammit," he said in a tired voice.

"Don't answer it."

"If I don't she'll call the police," he said, and picked up the receiver.

I let myself out (Francis pacing back and forth: "**Funny?** What do you mean, I **sound funny?**") and walked to the post office, where in my box I found, to my surprise, an elegant little note from Julian asking me to lunch the next day.

Julian, on special occasions, sometimes had lunches for the class; he was an excellent cook and, when he was a young man living off his trust fund in Europe, had the reputation of being an excellent host as well. This was, in fact, the basis of his acquaintance with most of the famous people in his life. Osbert Sitwell, in his diary, mentions Julian Morrow's "sublime little **fêtes**," and there are similar references in the letters of people ranging from Charles Laughton to the Duchess of Windsor to Gertrude Stein; Cyril Connolly, who was notorious for being a hard guest to please, told Harold Acton that Julian was the most gracious American that he had ever met—a double-edged compliment, admittedly—and Sara Murphy, no mean hostess herself, once wrote him pleading for his recipe for **sole véronique**. But though I knew that Julian frequently invited Henry for lunches **à deux**, I had never before received an invitation to dine alone with him, and I was both flattered and vaguely worried. At that time, anything even slightly out of the ordinary seemed ominous to me, and, pleased as I was, I could not but feel that he might have an objective other than the pleasure of my company. I took the invitation home and studied it. The airy, oblique style in which it was written did little to dispel my feeling that there was more in it than met the eye. I phoned the switchboard and left a message for him to expect me at one the next day.

———

"Julian doesn't know anything about what happened, does he?" I asked Henry when next I saw him alone.

"What? Oh, yes," said Henry, glancing up from his book. "Of course."

"He knows you killed that guy?"

"Really, you needn't be so loud," said Henry sharply, turning in his chair. Then, in a quieter voice: "He knew what we were trying to do. And approved. The day after it happened, we drove out to his house in the country. Told him what happened. He was delighted."

"You told him everything?"

"Well, I saw no point in worrying him, if that's what you mean," said Henry, adjusting his glasses and going back to his book.

————

Julian, of course, had made the lunch himself, and we ate at the big round table in his office. After weeks of bad nerves, bad conversation, and bad food in the dining hall, the prospect of a meal with him was immensely cheering; he was a charming companion and his dinners, though deceptively simple, had a sort of Augustan wholesomeness and luxuriance which never failed to soothe.

There was roasted lamb, new potatoes, peas with leeks and fennel; a rich and almost maddeningly delicious bottle of Château Latour. I was eating with better appetite than I had had in ages when I noticed that a fourth course had appeared, with unobtrusive magic, at my elbow: mushrooms. They were pale and slender-stemmed, of a type I had seen before, steaming in a red wine sauce that smelled of coriander and rue.

"Where did you get these?" I said.

"Ah. You're quite observant," he said, pleased. "Aren't they marvelous? Quite rare. Henry brought them to me."

I took a quick swallow of my wine to hide my consternation.

"He tells me—may I?" he said, nodding at the bowl.

I passed it to him, and he spooned some of them onto his plate. "Thank you," he said. "What was I saying? Oh, yes. Henry tells me that this particular sort of mushroom was a great favorite of the emperor Claudius. Interesting, because you remember how Claudius died."

I did remember. Agrippina had slipped a poisoned one into his dish one night.

"They're quite good," said Julian, taking a bite. "Have you gone with Henry on any of his collecting expeditions?"

"Not yet. He hasn't asked me to."

"I must say, I never thought I cared very much for mushrooms, but everything he's brought me has been heavenly."

Suddenly I understood. This was a clever piece of groundwork on Henry's part. "He's brought them to you before?" I said.

"Yes. Of course I wouldn't trust just anyone with this sort of thing, but Henry seems to know an amazing lot about it."

"I believe he probably does," I said, thinking of the boxer dogs.

"It's remarkable how good he is at anything he tries. He can grow flowers, repair clocks like a jeweler, add tremendous sums in his head. Even if it's something as simple as bandaging a cut finger he manages to do a better job of it." He poured himself another glass of wine. "I gather that his parents are disappointed that he's decided to concentrate so exclusively on the classics. I disagree, of course, but in a certain sense it is rather a pity. He would have made a great doctor, or soldier, or scientist."

I laughed. "Or a great spy," I said.

Julian laughed too. "All you boys would be excellent spies," he said. "Slipping about in casinos, eavesdropping on heads of state. Really, won't you try some of these mushrooms? They're glorious."

I drank the rest of my wine. "Why not," I said, and reached for the bowl.

———

After lunch, when the dishes had been cleared away and we were talking about nothing in particular, Julian asked, out of the blue, if I'd noticed anything peculiar about Bunny recently.

"Well, no, not really," I said, and took a careful sip of tea.

He raised an eyebrow. "No? I think he's behaving **very** strangely. Henry and I were talking only yesterday about how brusque and contrary he's become."

"I think he's been in kind of a bad mood."

He shook his head. "I don't know. Edmund is such a simple soul. I never thought I'd be surprised at anything he did or said, but he and I had a very odd conversation the other day."

"Odd?" I said cautiously.

"Perhaps he'd only read something that disturbed him. I don't know. I am worried about him."

"Why?"

"Frankly, I'm afraid he might be on the verge of some disastrous religious conversion."

I was jarred. "Really?" I said.

"I've seen it happen before. And I can think of no other reason for this sudden interest in **ethics**. Not that Edmund is profligate, but really, he's one of the least **morally** concerned boys I've ever known. I was very startled when he began to question me—in all earnestness—about such hazy concerns as Sin and Forgiveness. He's thinking of going into the Church, I just know it. Perhaps that girl has something to do with it, do you suppose?"

He meant Marion. He had a habit of attributing all of Bunny's faults indirectly to her—his laziness, his bad humors, his lapses of taste. "Maybe," I said.

"Is she a Catholic?"

"I think she's Presbyterian," I said. Julian had a polite but implacable contempt for Judeo-Christian tradition in virtually all its forms. He would deny this if confronted, citing evasively his affection for Dante and Giotto, but anything overtly religious filled him with a pagan alarm; and I believe that like Pliny, whom he resembled in so many respects, he secretly thought it to be a degenerate cult carried to extravagant lengths.

"A Presbyterian? Really?" he said, dismayed.

"I believe so."

"Well, whatever one thinks of the Roman Church, it is a worthy and powerful foe. I could accept that sort of conversion with grace. But I shall be very disappointed indeed if we lose him to the Presbyterians."

————

In the first week of April the weather turned suddenly, unseasonably, insistently lovely. The sky was blue, the air warm and windless, and the sun beamed on the muddy ground with all the sweet impatience of June. Toward the fringe of the wood, the young trees were yellow with the first tinge of new leaves; woodpeckers laughed and drummed in the copses and, lying in bed with my window open, I could hear the rush and gurgle of the melted snow running in the gutters all night long.

In the second week of April everyone waited anxiously to see if the weather would hold. It did, with serene assurance. Hyacinth and daffodil bloomed in the flower beds, violet and periwinkle in the meadows; damp, bedraggled white butterflies fluttered drunkenly in the hedgerows. I put away my winter coat and overshoes and walked around, nearly light-headed with joy, in my shirtsleeves.

"This won't last," said Henry.

———

In the third week of April, when the lawns were green as Heaven and the apple blossoms had recklessly blown, I was reading in my room on a Friday night, with the windows open and a cool, damp wind stirring the papers on my desk. There was a party across the lawn, and laughter and music floated through the night air. It was long after midnight. I was nodding, half-asleep over my book, when someone bellowed my name outside my window.

I shook myself and sat up, just in time to see one of Bunny's shoes flying through my open window. It hit the floor with a thud. I jumped up and leaned over the sill. Far below, I saw his staggering, shaggy-headed figure, attempting to steady itself by clutching at the trunk of a small tree.

"What the hell's wrong with you?"

He didn't reply, only raised his free hand in a gesture half wave, half salute, and reeled out of the light. The back door slammed, and a few moments later he was banging on the door of my room.

When I opened it he came limping in, one shoe off and one shoe on, leaving a muddy trail of macabre, unmatched footprints behind him. His spectacles were askew and he stank of whiskey. "Dickie boy," he mumbled.

The outburst beneath my window seemed to have exhausted him and left him strangely uncommunicative. He tugged off his muddy sock and tossed it clumsily away from him. It landed on my bed.

By degrees, I managed to extricate from him the evening's events. The twins had taken him to dinner, afterwards to a bar in town for more drinks; he'd then gone alone to the party across the lawn, where a Dutchman had tried to make him smoke pot and a freshman girl had given him tequila from a thermos. ("Pretty little gal. Sort of a Deadhead, though. She was wearing clogs, you know those things? And a tie-dyed T-shirt. I can't stand them. 'Honey,' I said, 'you're such a cutie, how come you want to get yourself up in that nasty stuff?' ") Then, abruptly, he broke off this narrative and lurched away—leaving the door of my room open behind him—and I heard the sound of noisy, athletic vomiting.

He was gone a long time. When he returned he smelled sour, and his face was damp and very pale; but he seemed composed. "Whew," he said, collapsing in my chair and mopping his forehead with a red bandanna. "Musta been something I ate."

"Did you make it to the bathroom?" I asked uncertainly. The vomiting had sounded ominously near my own door.

"Naw," he said, breathing heavily. "Ran in the broom closet. Get me a glass of water, wouldja."

In the hall, the door to the service closet hung partly open, providing a coy glimpse of the reeking horror within. I hurried past it to the kitchen.

Bunny looked at me glassily when I came back in. His expression had changed entirely, and something about it made me uneasy. I gave him the water and he took a large, greedy gulp.

"Not too quick," I said, alarmed.

He paid no attention and drank the rest in a swallow, then set the glass on the desk with a trembling hand. Beads of sweat stood out on his forehead.

"Oh, my God," he said. "Sweet Jesus."

Uneasily, I crossed to my bed and sat down, trying to think of some neutral subject, but before I could say anything he spoke again.

"Can't stomach it any longer," he mumbled. "Just can't. Sweet Italian Jesus."

I didn't say anything.

Shakily, he passed a hand over his forehead. "You don't even know what the devil I'm talking about, do you?" he said, with an oddly nasty tone in his voice.

Agitated, I recrossed my legs. I'd seen this coming, seen it coming for months and dreaded it. I had an impulse to rush from the room, just leave him sitting there, but then he buried his face in his hands.

"All true," he mumbled. "All true. Swear to God. Nobody knows but me."

Absurdly, I found myself hoping it was a false alarm. Maybe he and Marion had broken up. Maybe his father had died of a heart attack. I sat there, paralyzed.

He dragged his palms down over his face, as

if he were wiping water from it, and looked up at me. "You don't have a clue," he said. His eyes were bloodshot, uncomfortably bright. "Boy. You don't have a fucking clue."

I stood up, unable to bear it any longer, and looked around my room distractedly. "Uh," I said, "do you want an aspirin? I meant to ask you earlier. If you take a couple now you won't feel so bad in the—"

"You think I'm crazy, don't you?" Bunny said abruptly.

Somehow I'd always known it was going to happen this way, the two of us alone, Bunny drunk, late at night. . . . "Why no," I said. "All you need is a little—"

"You think I'm a lunatic. Bats in the belfry. **Nobody listens to me,**" he said, his voice rising.

I was alarmed. "Calm down," I said. "I'm listening to you."

"Well, listen to this," he said.

———

It was three in the morning when he stopped talking. The story he told was drunken and garbled, out of sequence and full of vituperative, self-righteous digressions; but I had no problem understanding it. It was a story I'd already heard. For a while we sat there, mute. My desk light was shining in my eyes. The party across the way was still going strong and a faint but boisterous rap song throbbed obtrusively in the distance.

Bunny's breathing had become loud and asthmatic. His head fell on his chest, and he woke with a start. "What?" he said, confused, as if someone had come up behind him and shouted in his ear. "Oh. Yes."

I didn't say anything.

"What do you think about that, eh?"

I was unable to answer. I'd hoped, faintly, that he might have blacked it all out.

"Damndest thing. Fact truer than fiction, boy. Wait, that's not right. How's it go?"

"Fact stranger than fiction," I said mechanically. It was fortunate, I suppose, that I didn't have to make an effort to look shaken up or stunned. I was so upset I was nearly sick.

"Just goes to show," said Bunny drunkenly. "Could be the guy next door. Could be anybody. Never can tell."

I put my face in my hands.

"Tell anybody you want," Bunny said. "Tell the goddamn mayor. I don't care. Lock 'em right up in that combination post office and jail they got down by the courthouse. Thinks he's so smart," he muttered. "Well, if this wasn't Vermont he wouldn't be sleeping so well at night, let me tell you. Why, my dad's best friends with the police commissioner in Hartford. **He** ever finds out about this—**geez**. He and Dad were at school together. Used to date his daughter in the tenth grade. . . ." His head was drooping and he shook himself again. "Jesus," he said, nearly falling out of his chair.

I stared at him.

"Give me that shoe, would you?"

I handed it to him, and his sock too. He looked at them for a moment, then stuffed them in the outside pocket of his blazer. "Don't let the bedbugs bite," he said, and then he was gone, leaving the door of my room open behind him. I could hear his peculiar limping progress all the way down the stairs.

The objects in the room seemed to swell and recede with each thump of my heart. In a horrible daze, I sat on my bed, one elbow on the windowsill, and tried to pull myself together. Diabolical rap music floated from the opposite building, where a couple of shadowy figures were crouched on the roof, throwing empty beer cans at a disconsolate band of hippies huddled around a bonfire in a trash can, trying to smoke a joint. A beer can sailed from the roof, then another, which hit one of them on the head with a tinny sound. Laughter, aggrieved cries.

I was gazing at the sparks flying from the garbage can when suddenly I was struck by a harrowing thought. Why had Bunny decided to come to my room instead of Cloke's, or

Marion's? As I looked out the window the answer was so obvious it gave me a chill. It was because my room was by far the closest. Marion lived in Roxburgh, on the other end of campus, and Cloke's was on the far side of Durbinstall. Neither place was readily apparent to a drunk stumbling out into the night. But Monmouth was scarcely thirty feet away, and my own room, with its conspicuously lighted window, must have loomed in his path like a beacon.

I suppose it would be interesting to say that at this point I felt torn in some way, grappled with the moral implications of each of the courses available to me. But I don't recall experiencing anything of the sort. I put on a pair of loafers and went downstairs to call Henry.

The pay phone in Monmouth was on a wall by the back door, too exposed for my taste, so I walked over to the Science Building, my shoes squelching on the dewy grass, and found a particularly isolated booth on the third floor near the chemistry labs.

The phone must've rung a hundred times. No answer. Finally, in exasperation, I pressed down the receiver and dialed the twins. Eight rings, nine; then, to my relief, Charles's sleepy hello.

"Hi, it's me," I said quickly. "Something happened."

"What?" he said, suddenly alert. I could hear him sitting up in bed.

"He told me. Just now."

There was a long silence.

"Hello?" I said.

"Call Henry," said Charles abruptly. "Hang up the phone and call him right now."

"I already did. He's not answering the phone."

Charles swore under his breath. "Let me think," he said. "Oh, hell. Can you come over?"

"Sure. Now?"

"I'll run down to Henry's and see if I can get him to the door. We should be back by the time you get here. Okay?"

"Okay," I said, but he'd already hung up.

———

When I got there, about twenty minutes later, I met Charles coming from the direction of Henry's, alone.

"No luck?"

"No," he said, breathing hard. His hair was rumpled and he had a raincoat on over his pajamas.

"What'll we do?"

"I don't know. Come upstairs. We'll think of something."

We had just got our coats off when the light in Camilla's room came on and she appeared in the doorway, blinking, cheeks aflame. "Charles? What are **you** doing here?" she said when she saw me.

Rather incoherently, Charles explained what had happened. With a drowsy forearm she shielded her eyes from the light and listened. She was wearing a man's nightshirt, much too big for her, and I found myself staring at her bare legs—tawny calves, slender ankles, lovely, dusty-soled boy-feet.

"Is he there?" she said.

"I know he is."

"You sure?"

"Where else would he be at three in the morning?"

"Wait a second," she said, and went to the telephone. "I just want to try something." She dialed, listened for a moment, hung up, dialed again.

"What are you doing?"

"It's a code," she said, the receiver cradled between shoulder and ear. "Ring twice, hang up, ring again."

"Code?"

"Yes. He told me once— Oh, hello, Henry," she said suddenly, and sat down.

Charles looked at me.

"Well, I'll be damned," he said quietly. "He must have been awake the whole time."

"Yes," Camilla was saying; she stared at the

floor, bobbing the foot of her crossed leg idly up and down. "That's fine. I'll tell him."

She hung up. "He says to come over, Richard," she said. "You should leave now. He's waiting for you. Why are you looking at me like that?" she said crossly to Charles.

"Code, eh?"

"What about it?"

"You never told me about it."

"It's stupid. I never thought to."

"What do you and Henry need a secret code for?"

"It's not a secret."

"Then why didn't you tell me?"

"Charles, don't be such a baby."

———

Henry—wide awake, no explanations—met me at the door in his bathrobe. I followed him into the kitchen, and he poured me a cup of coffee and sat me down. "Now," he said, "tell me what happened."

I did. He sat across the table, smoking cigarette after cigarette with his dark blue eyes fastened on mine. He interrupted with questions only once or twice. Certain parts he asked me to repeat. I was so tired that I rambled a bit, but he was patient with my digressions.

By the time I finished, the sun was up and the birds were singing. Spots were swimming in front of my eyes. A damp, cool breeze shifted in the curtains. Henry switched off the lamp and went to the stove and began, rather mechanically, to make some bacon and eggs. I watched him move around the dim, dawn-lit kitchen in his bare feet.

While we ate, I looked at him curiously. He was pale, and his eyes were tired and preoccupied, but there was nothing in his expression that gave me any indication what he might be thinking.

"Henry," I said.

He started. It was the first time either of us had said a word for half an hour or more.

"What are you thinking about?"

"Nothing."

"If you've still got the idea of poisoning him—"

He glanced up with a quick flash of anger that surprised me. "Don't be absurd," he snapped. "I wish you'd shut up a minute and let me think."

I stared at him. Abruptly he stood up and went to pour himself some more coffee. For a moment he stood with his back to me, hands braced on the counter. Then he turned around.

"I'm sorry," he said wearily. "It's just not very pleasant to look back on something that one has put so much effort and thought into, only to realize it's completely ridiculous. Poisoned mushrooms. The whole idea is like something from Sir Walter Scott."

I was taken aback. "But I thought it was kind of a good idea," I said.

He rubbed his eyes with his thumb and forefinger. "Too good," he said. "I suppose that when anyone accustomed to working with the mind is faced with a straightforward action, there's a tendency to embellish, to make it overly clever. On paper there's a certain symmetry. Now that I'm faced with the prospect of executing it I realize how hideously complicated it is."

"What's wrong?"

He adjusted his glasses. "The poison is too slow."

"I thought that's what you wanted."

"There are half a dozen problems with it. Some of them you pointed out. Control of the dose is risky, but time, I think, is the real concern. From my standpoint the longer the better, but still . . . A person can do an awful lot of talking in twelve hours." He was quiet for a moment. "It's not as if I haven't seen this all along. The idea of killing him is so repellent that I haven't been able to think of it as anything but a chess-problem. A game. You have no idea how much thought I've put into this.

Even to the strain of poison. It's said to make the throat swell, do you know that? Victims are said to be struck dumb, unable to name their poisoner." He sighed. "Too easy to beguile myself with the Medicis, the Borgias, all those poisoned rings and roses. . . . It's possible to do that, did you know? To poison a rose, then present it as a gift? The lady pricks her finger, then falls dead. I know how to make a candle that will kill if burned in a closed room. Or how to poison a pillow, or a prayer book . . ."

I said: "What about sleeping pills?"

He glanced at me, annoyed.

"I'm serious. People die from them all the time."

"Where are we going to get sleeping pills?"

"This is Hampden College. If we want sleeping pills, we can get them."

We looked at each other.

"How would we give them?" he said.

"Tell him they're Tylenol."

"And how do we get him to swallow nine or ten Tylenol?"

"We could break them open in a glass of whiskey."

"You think Bunny is likely to drink a glass of whiskey with a lot of white powder at the bottom?"

"I think he's just as apt to do that as eat a dish of toadstools."

There was a long silence, during which a bird trilled noisily outside the window. Henry closed his eyes for a long moment and rubbed his temple with his fingertips.

"What are you going to do?" I said.

"I think I'm going to go out and run a few errands," he said. "I want you to go home and go to sleep."

"Do you have any ideas?"

"No. But there's something I want to look into. I'd drive you back to school, but I don't think it's a good idea for us to be seen together just now." He began to fish in the pocket of his bathrobe, pulling out matches, pen nibs, his blue enamel pillbox. Finally he found a couple of quarters and laid them on the table. "Here," he said. "Stop at the newsstand and buy a paper on your way home."

"Why?"

"In case anyone should wonder why you're wandering around at this hour. I may have to talk to you tonight. If I don't find you in, I'll leave a message that a Doctor Springfield called. Don't try to get in touch with me before then, unless of course you have to."

"Sure."

"I'll see you later, then," he said, starting out

of the kitchen. Then he turned in the door and looked at me. "I'll never forget this, you know," he said matter-of-factly.

"It's nothing."

"It's everything and you know it."

"You've done me a favor or two yourself," I said, but he had already started out and didn't hear me. At any rate, he didn't answer.

———

I bought a newspaper at the little store down the street and walked back to school through the dank, verdant woods, off the main path, stepping over the boulders and rotting logs that occasionally blocked my way.

It was still early when I got to campus. I went in the back door of Monmouth and, pausing at the top of the stairs, I was startled to see the house chairperson and a flock of girls in housecoats, huddled around the broom closet and conversing in varying tones of shrill outrage. When I tried to brush past them, Judy Poovey, clad in a black kimono, grabbed my arm. "Hey," she said. "Somebody puked in this broom closet."

"It was one of those goddamned freshmen," said a girl at my elbow. "They get stinking drunk and come to the upperclass suites to barf."

"Well, I don't know who did it," the house

chairperson said, "but whoever it was, they had spaghetti for dinner."

"Hmnn."

"That means they're not on the meal ticket, then."

I pushed through them to my room, locking the door behind me, and went, almost immediately, to sleep.

———

I slept all day, face down in the pillow, a comfortable dead-man's float only remotely disturbed by a chill undertow of reality—talk, footsteps, slamming doors—which threaded fitfully through the dark, blood-warm waters of dream. Day ran into night, and still I slept, until finally the rush and rumble of a flushing toilet rolled me on my back and up from sleep.

The Saturday night party had already started, in Putnam House next door. That meant dinner was over, the snack bar was closed, and I'd slept at least fourteen hours. My house was deserted. I got up and shaved and took a hot bath. Then I put on my robe and, eating an apple I'd found in the house kitchen, walked downstairs in my bare feet to see if any messages had been left for me by the phone.

There were three. Bunny Corcoran, at a quarter to six. My mother, from California, at eight-forty-five. And a Dr. H. Springfield, D.D.S., who suggested I visit at my earliest convenience.

———

I was famished. When I got to Henry's, I was glad to see that Charles and Francis were still picking at a cold chicken and some salad.

Henry looked as if he hadn't slept since I'd seen him last. He was wearing an old tweed jacket with sprung elbows, and there were grass stains on the knees of his trousers; khaki gaiters were laced over his mud-caked shoes. "The plates are in the sideboard, if you're hungry," he said, pulling out his chair and sitting down heavily, like some old farmer just home from the field.

"Where have you been?"

"We'll talk about it after dinner."

"Where's Camilla?"

Charles began to laugh.

Francis put down his chicken leg. "She's got a date," he said.

"You're kidding. With who?"

"Cloke Rayburn."

"They're at the party," Charles said. "He took her out for drinks before and everything."

"Marion and Bunny are with them," Francis said. "It was Henry's idea. Tonight she's keeping an eye on you-know-who."

"You-know-who left a message for me on the telephone this afternoon," I said.

"You-know-who has been on the warpath all day long," said Charles, cutting himself a slice of bread.

"Not now, please," said Henry in a tired voice.

After the dishes were cleared Henry put his elbows on the table and lit a cigarette. He needed a shave and there were dark circles under his eyes.

"So what's the plan?" said Francis.

Henry tossed the match into the ashtray. "This weekend," he said. "Tomorrow."

I paused with my coffee cup halfway to my lips.

"Oh my God," said Charles, disconcerted. "So soon?"

"It can't wait any longer."

"How? What can we do on such short notice?"

"I don't like it either, but if we wait we won't have another chance until next weekend. If it comes to that, we may not have another chance at all."

There was a brief silence.

"This is for real?" said Charles uncertainly. "This is, like, a definite thing?"

"Nothing is definite," said Henry. "The circumstances won't be entirely under our control. But I want us to be ready should the opportunity present itself."

"This sounds sort of indeterminate," said Francis.

"It is. It can't be any other way, unfortunately, as Bunny will be doing most of the work."

"How's that?" said Charles, leaning back in his chair.

"An accident. A hiking accident, to be precise." Henry paused. "Tomorrow's Sunday."

"Yes."

"So tomorrow, if the weather's nice, Bunny will more likely than not go for a walk."

"He doesn't always go," said Charles.

"Say he does. And we have a fairly good idea of his route."

"It varies," I said. I had accompanied Bunny on a good many of those walks the term before. He was apt to cross streams, climb fences, make any number of unexpected detours.

"Yes, of course, but by and large we know it," said Henry. He took a piece of paper from his pocket and spread it on the table. Leaning over, I saw it was a map. "He goes out the back door of his house, circles behind the tennis courts, and when he reaches the woods, heads not towards North Hampden but east, towards Mount Cataract. Heavily wooded, not much hiking out that way. He keeps on till he hits that deer path—you know the one I mean, Richard, the trail marked with the white boulder—and bears hard southeast. That runs for three-quarters of a mile and then forks—"

"But you'll miss him if you wait there," I said. "I've been with him on that road. He's as apt to turn west here as to keep heading south."

"Well, we may lose him before then if it comes to that," said Henry. "I've known him to ignore the path altogether and keep heading east till he hits the highway. But I'm counting on the likelihood he won't do that. The weather's nice—he won't want such an easy walk."

"But the second fork? You can't say where he'll go from there."

"We don't have to. You remember where it comes out, don't you? The ravine."

"Oh," said Francis.

There was a long silence.

"Now, listen," said Henry, taking a pencil from his pocket. "He'll be coming in from school, from the south. We can avoid his route entirely and come in on Highway 6, from the west."

"We'll take the car?"

"Partway, yes. Just past that junkyard, before the turnoff to Battenkill, there's a gravel road.

I'd thought it might be a private way, in which case we'd have to avoid it, but I went down to the courthouse this afternoon and found that it's just an old logging road. Comes to a dead end in the middle of the woods. But it should take us directly to the ravine, within a quarter mile. We can walk the rest of the way."

"And when we get there?"

"Well, we wait. I made Bunny's walk to the ravine from school twice this afternoon, there and back, and timed it both ways. It'll take him at least half an hour from the time he leaves his room. Which gives us plenty of time to go around the back way and surprise him."

"What if he doesn't come?"

"Well, if he doesn't, we've lost nothing but time."

"What if one of us goes with him?"

He shook his head. "I've thought of that," he said. "It's not a good idea. If he walks into the trap himself—alone, of his own volition—there's not much way it can be traced to us."

"If this, if that," said Francis sourly. "This sounds pretty haphazard to me."

"We want something haphazard."

"I don't see what's wrong with the first plan."

"The first plan is too stylized. Design is inherent in it through and through."

"But design is preferable to chance."

Henry smoothed the crumpled map against

the table with the flat of his palm. "There, you're wrong," he said. "If we attempt to order events too meticulously, to arrive at point X via a logical trail, it follows that the logical trail can be picked up at point X and followed back to us. Reason is always apparent to a discerning eye. But luck? It's invisible, erratic, angelic. What could possibly be better, from our point of view, than allowing Bunny to choose the circumstances of his own death?"

Everything was still. Outside, the crickets shrieked with rhythmic, piercing monotony.

Francis—his face moist and very pale—bit his lower lip. "Let me get this straight. We wait at the ravine and just hope he happens to stroll by. And if he does, we push him off—right there in broad daylight—and go back home. Am I correct?"

"More or less," said Henry.

"What if he doesn't come by himself? What if somebody else wanders by?"

"It's no crime to be in the woods on a spring afternoon," Henry said. "We can abort at any time, up to the moment he goes over the edge. And that will only take an instant. If we happen across anybody on the way to the car—I think it improbable, but if we should—we can always say there's been an accident, and we're going for help."

"But what if someone sees us?"

"I think that extremely unlikely," said Henry, dropping a lump of sugar into his coffee with a splash.

"But possible."

"Anything is possible, but probability will work for us here if only we let it," said Henry. "What are the odds that some previously un-detected someone will stumble into that very isolated spot, during the precise fraction of a second it will take to push him over?"

"It might happen."

"Anything **might** happen, Francis. He **might** be hit by a car tonight, and save us all a lot of trouble."

A soft, damp breeze, smelling of rain and ap-ple blossoms, blew through the window. I had broken out in a sweat without realizing it and the wind on my cheek made me feel clammy and light-headed.

Charles cleared his throat and we turned to look at him.

"Do you know . . ." he said. "I mean, are you sure it's high enough? What if he—"

"I went out there today with a tape mea-sure," Henry said. "The highest point is forty-eight feet, which should be ample. The trickiest part will be to get him there. If he falls from one of the lower points, he'll end up with nothing worse than a broken leg. Of course, a lot will rest on the fall itself. Backwards seems better than forward for our purposes."

"But I've heard of people falling from airplanes and not dying," said Francis. "What if the fall doesn't kill him?"

Henry reached behind his spectacles and rubbed an eye. "Well, you know, there's a little stream at the bottom," he said. "There's not much water, but enough. He'll be stunned, no matter what. We'd have to drag him there, hold him face-down for a bit—shouldn't think that'd take more than a couple of minutes. If he was conscious, maybe a couple of us could even go down and walk him over. . . ."

Charles passed a hand over his damp, flushed forehead. "Oh, Jesus," he said. "Oh my God. Just listen to us."

"What's the matter?"

"Are we insane?"

"What are you talking about?"

"We're insane. We've lost our minds. How can we possibly **do** this?"

"I don't like the idea any more than you do."

"This is crazy. I don't even know how we can talk about this. We've got to think of something else."

Henry took a sip of his coffee. "If you can think of anything," he said, "I'd be delighted to hear it."

"Well—I mean, why can't we just **leave**? Get in the car tonight and drive away?"

"And go where?" Henry said flatly. "With what money?"

Charles was silent.

"Now," said Henry, drawing a line on the map with a pencil. "I think it will be fairly easy to get away without being seen, though we should be especially careful about turning into the logging road and coming out of it onto the highway."

"Will we use my car or yours?" said Francis.

"Mine, I think. People tend to look twice at a car like yours."

"Maybe we should rent one."

"No. Something like that might ruin everything. If we keep it as casual as possible, no one will give us a second glance. People don't pay attention to ninety percent of what they see."

There was a pause.

Charles coughed slightly. "And after?" he said. "We just go home?"

"We just go home," said Henry. He lit a cigarette. "Really, there's nothing to worry about," he said, shaking out the match. "It seems risky, but if you look at it logically it couldn't be safer. It won't look like a murder at all. And who knows we have reason to kill him? I know, I know," he said impatiently when I tried to interrupt. "But I should be extremely surprised if he's told anyone else."

"How can you say what he's done? He could have told half the people at the party."

"But I'm willing to bank on the odds he hasn't. Bunny's unpredictable, of course, but at this point his actions still make a kind of rudimentary horse sense. I had very good reason to think he'd tell you first."

"And why's that?"

"Surely you don't think it an accident that, of all the people he might have told, he chose to come to you?"

"I don't know, except that I was handier than anyone else."

"Who else could he tell?" said Henry impatiently. "He'd never go to the police outright. He stands to lose as much as we do if he did. And for the same reason he doesn't dare tell a stranger. Which leaves an extremely limited range of potential confidants. Marion, for one. His parents for another. Cloke for a third. Julian as an outside possibility. And you."

"And what makes you think he hasn't told Marion, for instance?"

"Bunny might be stupid, but not **that** stupid. It would be all over school by lunch the next day. Cloke's a poor choice for different reasons. He isn't quite so apt to lose his head but he's untrustworthy all the same. Skittish and irresponsible. And very much out for his own interests. Bunny likes him—admires him too, I think—but he'd never go to him with something like this. And he wouldn't tell his parents, not in a million years. They'd stand behind him, certainly, but without a doubt they'd go right to the police."

"And Julian?"

Henry shrugged. "Well, he might tell Julian. I'm perfectly willing to concede that. But he hasn't told him yet, and I think the chances are he won't, at least not for a while."

"Why not?"

Henry raised an eyebrow at me. "Because who do you think Julian would be more apt to believe?"

No one said a thing. Henry drew deeply on his cigarette. "So," he said, and exhaled. "Process of elimination. He hasn't told Marion or Cloke, for fear of their telling other people. He hasn't told his parents, for the same reason, and probably won't except as a last resort. So what possibilities does that leave him? Only two. He could tell Julian—who wouldn't believe him—or you, who might believe him and wouldn't repeat it."

I stared at him. "Surmise," I said at last.

"Not at all. Do you think, if he'd told anyone else, we'd be sitting here now? Do you think now, once he's told you, that he'd be foolhardy enough to tell a third party before he even knows what your response will be? Why do you suppose he called you this afternoon? Why do you suppose he's pestered the rest of us all day?"

I didn't answer him.

"Because," said Henry, "he was testing the waters. Last night he was drunk, full of himself. Today he's not quite sure what you think. He wants another opinion. And he'll look to your response for the cue."

"I don't understand," I said.

Henry took a sip of his coffee. "What don't you understand?"

"Why you're in such a goddamned rush to kill him if you think he won't tell anyone but me."

He shrugged. "He hasn't told anyone **yet**. Which is not to say he won't, very soon."

"Maybe I could dissuade him."

"That's frankly not a chance I'm willing to take."

"In my opinion, you're talking about taking a much greater one."

"Look," said Henry evenly, raising his head and fixing me with a bleary gaze. "Forgive me for being blunt, but if you think you have any influence over Bunny you're sadly mistaken. He's not particularly fond of you, and, if I may speak plainly, as far as I know he never has been. It would be disastrous if you of all people tried to intercede."

"I was the one he came to."

"For obvious reasons, none of them very sentimental." He shrugged. "As long as I was sure he hadn't told anyone, we might have waited indefinitely. But you were the alarm bell, Richard. Having told you—nothing happened, he'll think, it wasn't so bad—he'll find it twice as easy to tell a second person. And a third. He's taken the first step on a downward slope. Now that he has, I feel that we're in for an extremely rapid progression of events."

My palms were sweating. In spite of the open window, the room seemed close and stuffy. I could hear everybody breathing; quiet, measured breaths that came and went with awful regularity, four sets of lungs, eating at the thin oxygen.

Henry folded his fingers and flexed them, at arm's length, until they cracked. "You can go now, if you like," he said to me.

"Do you want me to?" I said rather sharply.

"You can stay or not," he said. "But there's no reason why you must. I wanted to give you a rough idea, but in a certain sense the fewer details you know, the better." He yawned. "There were some things you had to know, I suppose, but I feel I've done you a disservice by involving you this far."

I stood up and looked around the table.

"Well," I said. "Well well well."

Francis raised an eyebrow at me.

"Wish us luck," said Henry.

I clapped him awkwardly on the shoulder. "Good luck," I said.

Charles—out of Henry's line of vision—caught my eye. He smiled and mouthed the words: **I'll call you tomorrow, okay?**

Suddenly, and without warning, I was overcome by a rush of emotion. Afraid I would say or do something childish, something I'd regret, I got into my coat and drank the rest of my coffee in a long gulp and left, without even the most perfunctory of goodbyes.

———

On my way home through the dark woods, my head down and my hands in my pockets, I ran virtually headlong into Camilla. She was very drunk and in an exhilarated mood.

"Hello," she said, linking her arm through mine and leading me back in the direction from which I'd just come. "Guess what. I had a date."

"So I heard."

She laughed, a low, sweet chortle that warmed me to my heart. "Isn't that funny?" she said. "I feel like such a spy. Bunny just went home. Now the problem is, I think Cloke kind of likes me."

It was so dark I could hardly see her. The weight of her arm was wonderfully comfortable, and her gin-sweet breath was warm on my cheek.

"Did Cloke behave himself?" I said.

"Yes, he was very nice. He bought me dinner and some red drinks that tasted like Popsicles."

We emerged from the woods into the deserted, blue-lit streets of North Hampden. Everything was silent and strange in the moonlight. A faint breeze tinkled in the wind chimes on someone's porch.

When I stopped walking, she tugged at my arm. "Aren't you coming?" she said.

"No."

"Why not?"

Her hair was tousled, and her lovely mouth was stained dark by the Popsicle drink, and just by looking at her I could tell she didn't have the faintest idea what was going on at Henry's.

She would go with them tomorrow. Somebody would probably tell her that she didn't have to go, but she would end up going with them anyway.

I coughed. "Look," I said.

"What?"

"Come home with me."

She lowered her eyebrows. "Now?"

"Yes."

"Why?"

The wind chimes tinkled again; silvery, insidious.

"Because I want you to."

She gazed at me with vacant, drunken composure, standing coltlike on the outer edge of her black-stockinged foot so the ankle was twisted inward in a startling, effortless L.

Her hand was in mine. I squeezed it hard. Clouds were racing across the moon.

"Come on," I said.

She raised up on tiptoe and gave me a cool, soft kiss that tasted of Popsicles. **Oh, you,** I thought, my heart beating fast and shallow.

Suddenly, she broke away. "I've got to go," she said.

"No. Please don't."

"I've got to. They'll wonder where I am."

She gave me a quick kiss, then turned and started down the street. I watched her until she reached the corner, then dug my hands in my pockets and started back home.

———

I woke the next day with a start, to chill sunlight and the thump of a stereo down the hall. It was late, noon, afternoon maybe; I reached for my watch on the night table and started again, more violently this time. It was a quarter of three. I jumped out of bed and began to dress, in great haste, without bothering to shave or even comb my hair.

Pulling on my jacket in the hall, I saw Judy Poovey walking briskly towards me. She was all dressed up, for Judy, and she had her head to the side attempting to fasten an earring.

"You coming?" she said when she saw me.

"Coming where?" I said, puzzled, my hand still on the doorknob.

"What is it with you? Do you live on Mars or what?"

I stared at her.

"The party," she said impatiently. "Swing into Spring. Up behind Jennings. It started an hour ago."

The edges of her nostrils were inflamed and rabbity, and she reached up to wipe her nose with a red-taloned hand.

"Let me guess what you've been doing," I said.

She laughed. "I have lots more. Jack Teitelbaum drove to New York last weekend and came back with a ton. And Laura Stora has Ecstasy, and that creepy guy in Durbinstall basement—you know, the chemistry major—just cooked up a big batch of meth. You're trying to tell me you didn't know about this?"

"No."

"Swing into Spring is a **big deal**. Everybody's

been getting ready for months. Too bad they didn't have it yesterday, though, the weather was so great. Did you go to lunch?"

She meant had I been outside yet that day. "No," I said.

"Well, I mean, the weather's okay, but it's a little cold. I walked outside and went, like, oh shit. Anyway. You coming?"

I looked at her blankly. I'd run out of my room without the slightest idea where I was going. "I need to get something to eat," I said at last.

"That's a good idea. Last year I went and I didn't eat anything before and I smoked pot and drank, like, thirty martinis. I was all right and everything but **then** I went to Fun O'Rama. Remember? That carnival they had—well, I guess you weren't here then. Anyway. **Big** mistake. I'd been drinking all day and I had a sunburn and I was with Jack Teitelbaum and all those guys. I wasn't going to go, you know, on a ride and then I thought, okay. The Ferris wheel. I can go on the Ferris wheel no problem. . . ."

I listened politely to the rest of her story which ended, as I knew it would, with Judy being pyrotechnically ill behind a hot-dog stand.

"So this year, I was like, no way. Stick with coke. Pause that refreshes. By the way, you ought to get that friend of yours—you know, what's his name—**Bunny,** and make him come with you. He's in the library."

"What?" I said, suddenly all ears.

"Yeah. Drag him out. Make him do some bong hits or something."

"He's in the library?"

"Yeah. I saw him through the window of the reading room a little while ago. Doesn't he have a car?"

"No."

"Well, I was thinking, maybe he could drive us. Long walk to Jennings. Or I don't know, maybe it's just me. I swear, I'm so out of shape, I have to start doing Jane Fonda again."

———

By now it was three. I locked the door and walked to the library, nervously jangling my key in my pocket.

It was a strange, still, oppressive day. The campus seemed deserted—everyone was at the party, I supposed—and the green lawn, the gaudy tulips, were hushed and expectant beneath the overcast sky. Somewhere a shutter creaked. Above my head, in the wicked black claws of an elm, a marooned kite rattled convulsively, then was still. **This is Kansas,** I thought. **This is Kansas before the cyclone hits.**

The library was like a tomb, illumined from within by a chill fluorescent light that, by contrast, made the afternoon seem colder and grayer than it was. The windows of the reading room were bright and blank; bookshelves, empty carrels, not a soul.

The librarian—a despicable woman named Peggy—was behind the desk reading a copy of **Woman's Day**, and didn't look up. The Xerox machine hummed quietly in the corner. I climbed the stairs to the second floor and went around behind the foreign language section to the reading room. It was empty, just as I'd thought, but at one of the tables near the front there was an eloquent little nest of books, wadded paper, and greasy potato-chip bags.

I went over for a closer look. It had the air of fairly recent abandonment; there was a can of grape soda, three-quarters drunk, still sweating and cool to the touch. For a moment I wondered what to do—perhaps he'd only gone to the bathroom, perhaps he'd be back any second—and I was about to leave when I saw the note.

Lying on top of a volume of the **World Book Encyclopedia**, a grubby piece of lined paper was folded in half, with "Marion" written on the outer edge in Bunny's tiny, crabbed hand. I opened it and read it quickly:

old Gal

Bored stiff. Walked down to the
party to get a brewski. See ya later.

    B

I refolded the note and sat down hard on the
arm of Bunny's chair. Bunny went on his
walks, when he went, around one in the afternoon. It was now three. He was at the Jennings
party. They'd missed him.

I went down the back steps and out the basement door, then over to Commons—its red
brick facade flat as a stage backdrop against the
empty sky—and called Henry from the pay
phone. No answer. No answer at the twins',
either.

Commons was deserted except for a couple
of haggard old janitors and the red-wigged
lady who sat at the switchboard and knitted all
weekend, paying no attention to the incoming
calls. As usual, the lights were blinking frantically and she had her back to them, as oblivious as that ill-omened wireless operator on the
Californian the night the **Titanic** went down.
I walked past her down the hall to the vending
machines, where I got a cup of watery instant
coffee before going down to try the phone
again. Still no answer.

I hung up and wandered back to the deserted common room, with a copy of an alumni magazine I'd found in the post office tucked under my arm, and sat in a chair by the window to drink my coffee.

Fifteen minutes passed, then twenty. The alumni magazine was depressing. Hampden graduates never seemed to do anything after they got out of school but start little ceramics shops in Nantucket or join ashrams in Nepal. I tossed it aside and stared blankly out the window. The light outside was very strange. Something about it intensified the green of the lawn so all that vast expanse seemed unnatural, luminous somehow, and not quite of this world. An American flag, stark and lonely against the violet sky, whipped back and forth on the brass flagpole.

I sat and stared at it for a minute and then, suddenly, unable to bear it a moment longer, I put on my coat and started out towards the ravine.

————

The woods were deathly still, more forbidding than I had ever seen them—green and black and stagnant, dark with the smells of mud and rot. There was no wind; not a bird sang, not a leaf stirred. The dogwood blossoms were poised, white and surreal and still against the darkening sky, the heavy air.

I began to hurry, twigs cracking beneath my feet and my own hoarse breath loud in my ears, and before long the path emerged into the clearing. I stood there, half-panting, and it was a moment or so before I realized that nobody was there.

The ravine lay to the left—raw, treacherous, a deep plunge to the rocks below. Careful not to get too near the edge, I walked to the side for a closer look. Everything was absolutely still. I turned again, towards the woods from which I had just come.

Then, to my immense surprise, there was a soft rustle and Charles's head rose up out of nowhere. "Hi!" he called, in a glad whisper. "What in the world—?"

"Shut up," said an abrupt voice, and a moment later Henry materialized as if by magic, stepping towards me from the underbrush.

I was speechless, agog. He blinked at me, irritated, and was about to speak when there was a sudden crackle of branches and I turned in amazement just in time to see Camilla, clad in khaki trousers, clambering down the trunk of a tree.

"What's going on?" I heard Francis say, somewhere very close. "Can I have a cigarette now?"

Henry didn't answer. "What are you doing here?" he said in a very annoyed tone of voice.

"There's a party today."

"What?"

"A party. He's there now." I paused. "He's not going to come."

"See, I told you," said Francis, aggrieved, stepping gingerly from the brush and wiping his hands. Characteristically, he was not dressed for the occasion and had on sort of a nice suit. "Nobody listens to me. **I** said we should have left an hour ago."

"How do you know he's at the party?" said Henry.

"He left a note. In the library."

"Let's go home," said Charles, wiping a muddy smudge off his cheek with the heel of his hand.

Henry wasn't paying any attention to him. "Damn," he said, and shook his head quickly, like a dog shaking off water. "I'd so hoped we'd be able to get it over with."

There was a long pause.

"I'm hungry," said Charles.

"Starving," Camilla said absently, and then her eyes widened. "Oh, **no**."

"What is it?" said everyone at once.

"Dinner. Tonight's Sunday. He's coming to our house for dinner tonight."

There was a gloomy silence.

"I never thought about it," Charles said. "Not once."

"I didn't either," said Camilla. "And we don't have a thing to eat at home."

"We'll have to stop at the grocery store on the way back."

"What can we get?"

"I don't know. Something quick."

"I can't believe you two," Henry said crossly. "I reminded you of this last night."

"But we **forgot**," said the twins, in simultaneous despair.

"How could you?"

"Well, if you wake up intending to murder someone at two o'clock, you hardly think what you're going to feed the corpse for dinner."

"Asparagus is in season," said Francis helpfully.

"Yes, but do they have it at the Food King?"

Henry sighed and started off towards the woods.

"Where are you going?" Charles said in alarm.

"I'm going to dig up a couple of ferns. Then we can leave."

"Oh, let's just forget about it," said Francis, lighting a cigarette and tossing away the match. "Nobody's going to see us."

Henry turned around. "Somebody might. If they do, I certainly want to have an excuse for having been here. And pick up that match," he said sourly to Francis, who blew out a cloud of smoke and glared at him.

It was getting darker by the minute and cold, too. I buttoned my jacket and sat on a damp rock that overlooked the ravine, staring at the muddy, leaf-clogged rill that trickled below and half-listening to the twins argue about what they were going to make for dinner. Francis leaned against a tree, smoking. After a while he put out the cigarette on the sole of his shoe and came over to sit beside me.

Minutes passed. The sky was so overcast it was almost purple. A wind swayed through a luminous clump of birches on the opposite bank, and I shivered. The twins were arguing monotonously. Whenever they were in moods like this—disturbed, upset—they tended to sound like Heckle and Jeckle.

All of a sudden Henry emerged from the woods in a flurry of underbrush, wiping his dirt-caked hands on his trousers. "Somebody's coming," he said quietly.

The twins stopped talking and blinked at him.

"What?" said Charles.

"Around the back way. Listen."

We were quiet, looking at each other. A chilly breeze rustled through the woods and a gust of white dogwood petals blew into the clearing.

"I don't hear anything," Francis said.

Henry put a finger to his lips. The five of us stood poised, waiting, for a moment longer. I took a breath, and was about to speak when all of a sudden I did hear something.

Footsteps, the crackle of branches. We looked at one another. Henry bit his lip and glanced quickly around. The ravine was bare, no place to hide, no way for the rest of us to run across the clearing and into the woods without making a lot of noise. He was about to say something when all of a sudden there was a crash of bushes, very near, and he stepped out of the clearing between two trees, like someone ducking into a doorway on a city street.

The rest of us, stranded in the open, looked at each other and then at Henry—thirty feet away, safe at the shady margin of the wood. He waved at us impatiently. I heard the sudden crunch of footsteps on gravel and, hardly aware of what I was doing, turned away spasmodically and pretended to inspect the trunk of a nearby tree.

The footsteps approached. Prickles rising on the nape of my neck, I bent to scrutinize the tree trunk more closely: silvery bark, cool to the touch, ants marching out of a fissure in a glittering black thread.

Then—almost before I noticed it—the footsteps stopped, very near my back.

I glanced up and saw Charles. He was staring straight ahead with a ghastly expression on his face and I was on the verge of asking him what was the matter when, with a sick, incredulous rush of disbelief, I heard Bunny's voice directly behind me.

"Well, I'll be damned," he said briskly. "What's this? Meeting of the Nature Club?"

I turned. It was Bunny, all right, all six-foot-three of him, looming up behind me in a tremendous yellow rain slicker that came almost to his ankles.

There was an awful silence.

"Hi, Bun," said Camilla faintly.

"Hi yourself." He had a bottle of beer—a Rolling Rock, funny I remember that—and he turned it up and took a long, gurgling pull. "Phew," he said. "You people sure do a lot of sneaking around in the woods these days. You know," he said, poking me in the ribs, "I've been trying to get ahold of you."

The abrupt, booming immediacy of his presence was too much for me to take. I stared at him, dazed, as he drank again, as he lowered the bottle, as he wiped his mouth with the back of his hand; he was standing so close I could feel the heaviness of his rich, beery breaths.

"Aaah," he said, raking the hair back from his eyes, and belched. "So what's the story, deerslayers? You all just felt like coming out here to study the vegetation?"

There was a rustle and a slight, deprecating cough from the direction of the woods.

"Well, not exactly," said a cool voice.

Bunny turned, startled—I did, too—just in time to see Henry step out of the shadows.

He came forward and regarded Bunny pleasantly. He was holding a garden trowel and his hands were black with mud. "Hello," he said. "This is quite a surprise."

Bunny gave him a long, hard look. "Jesus," he said. "What you doing, burying the dead?"

Henry smiled. "Actually, it's very lucky you happened by."

"This some kind of convention?"

"Why, yes," said Henry agreeably, after a pause. "I suppose one might call it that."

"One **might**," said Bunny mockingly.

Henry bit his lower lip. "Yes," he said, in all seriousness. "One might. Though it's not the term I would use myself."

Everything was very still. From somewhere far away, in the woods, I heard the faint, inane laughter of a woodpecker.

"Tell me," Bunny said, and I thought I detected for the first time a note of suspicion.

"Just what the Sam Hill **are** you guys doing out here anyway?"

The woods were silent, not a sound.

Henry smiled. "Why, looking for new ferns," he said, and took a step towards him.

BOOK II

Dionysus [is] the Master of Illusions, who could make a vine grow out of a ship's plank, and in general enable his votaries to see the world as the world's not.

—E. R. DODDS,
The Greeks and the Irrational

CHAPTER
6

JUST FOR the record, I do not consider myself an evil person (though how like a killer that makes me sound!). Whenever I read about murders in the news I am struck by the dogged, almost touching assurance with which inter-state stranglers, needle-happy pediatricians, the depraved and guilty of all descriptions fail to recognize the evil in themselves; feel compelled, even, to assert a kind of spurious decency. "Basically I am a very good person." This from the latest serial killer—destined for the chair, they say—who, with incarnadine axe, recently dispatched half a dozen registered nurses in Texas. I have followed his case with interest in the papers.

But while I have never considered myself a very good person, neither can I bring myself to believe that I am a spectacularly bad one. Perhaps it's simply impossible to think of one-self in such a way, our Texan friend being a case in point. What we did was terrible, but still I don't think any of us were bad, exactly;

chalk it up to weakness on my part, hubris on Henry's, too much Greek prose composition—whatever you like.

I don't know. I suppose I should have had a better idea of what I was letting myself in for. Still, the first murder—the farmer—seemed to have been so simple, a dropped stone falling to the lakebed with scarcely a ripple. The second one was also easy, at least at first, but I had no inkling how different it would be. What we took for a docile, ordinary weight (gentle plunk, swift rush to the bottom, dark waters closing over it without a trace) was in fact a depth charge, one that exploded quite without warning beneath the glassy surface, and the repercussions of which may not be entirely over, even now.

Towards the end of the sixteenth century, the Italian physicist Galileo Galilei did a variety of experiments on the nature of falling bodies, dropping objects (so they say) from the Tower of Pisa in order to measure the rate of acceleration as they fell. His findings were as follows: That falling bodies acquire speed as they fall. That the farther a body falls, the faster it moves. That the velocity of a falling body equals the acceleration due to gravity multiplied by the time of the fall in seconds. In short, that given the variables in our case, our particular falling body was traveling at a speed greater than thirty-two feet per second when it hit the rocks below.

You see, then, how quick it was. And it is impossible to slow down this film, to examine individual frames. I see now what I saw then, flashing by with the swift, deceptive ease of an accident: shower of gravel, windmilling arms, a hand that claws at a branch and misses. A barrage of frightened crows explodes from the underbrush, cawing and dark against the sky. Cut to Henry, stepping back from the edge. Then the film flaps up in the projector and the screen goes black. **Consummatum est.**

If, lying in my bed at night, I find myself unwilling audience to this objectionable little documentary (it goes away when I open my eyes but always, when I close them, it resumes tirelessly at the very beginning), I marvel at how detached it is in viewpoint, eccentric in detail, largely devoid of emotional power. In that way it mirrors the remembered experience more closely than one might imagine. Time, and repeated screenings, have endowed the memory with a menace the original did not possess. I watched it all happen quite calmly— without fear, without pity, without anything but a kind of stunned curiosity—so that the impression of the event is burned indelibly upon my optic nerves, but oddly absent from my heart.

It was many hours before I was cognizant of what we'd done; days (months? years?) before I began to comprehend the magnitude of it. I suppose we'd simply thought about it too much, talked of it too often, until the scheme ceased to be a thing of the imagination and took on a horrible life of its own. . . . Never, never once in any immediate sense, did it occur to me that any of this was anything but a game. An air of unreality suffused even the most workaday details, as if we were plotting not the death of a friend but the itinerary of a fabulous trip that I, for one, never quite believed we'd ever really take.

What is unthinkable is undoable. That is something that Julian used to say in our Greek class, and while I believe he said it in order to encourage us to be more rigorous in our mental habits, it has a certain perverse bearing on the matter at hand. The idea of murdering Bunny was horrific, impossible; nonetheless we dwelt on it incessantly, convinced ourselves there was no alternative, devised plans which seemed slightly improbable and ridiculous but which actually worked quite well when put to the test. . . . I don't know. A month or two before, I would have been appalled at the idea of any murder at all. But that Sunday afternoon, as I actually stood watching one, it seemed the easiest thing in the world. How quickly he fell; how soon it was over.

———

This part, for some reason, is difficult for me to write, largely because the topic is inextricably associated with too many nights like this one (sour stomach, wretched nerves, clock inching tediously from four to five). It is also discouraging, because I recognize attempts at analysis are largely useless. I don't know why we did it. I'm not entirely sure that, circumstances demanding, we wouldn't do it again. And if I'm sorry, in a way, that probably doesn't make much difference.

I am sorry, as well, to present such a sketchy and disappointing exegesis of what is in fact the central part of my story. I have noticed that even the most garrulous and shameless of murderers are shy about recounting their crimes. A few months ago, in an airport bookstore, I picked up the autobiography of a notorious thrill killer and was disheartened to find it entirely bereft of lurid detail. At the points of greatest suspense (rainy night; deserted street; fingers closing around the lovely neck of Victim Number Four) it would suddenly, and not without some coyness, switch to some entirely unrelated matter. (Was the reader aware that an IQ test had been given him in prison? That his score had been gauged as being close to that of Jonas Salk?) By far the major portion of the book was devoted to spinsterish discourses on prison life—bad food, hijinks in the exercise yard, tedious little jailbird hobbies. It was a waste of five dollars.

In a certain way, though, I know how my colleague feels. Not that everything "went black," nothing of the sort; only that the event itself is cloudy because of some primitive, numbing effect that obscured it at the time; the same effect, I suppose, that enables panicked mothers to swim icy rivers, or rush into burning houses, for a child; the effect that occasionally allows a deeply bereaved person to make it through a funeral without a single tear. Some things are too terrible to grasp at once. Other things—naked, sputtering, indelible in their horror—are too terrible to really ever grasp at all. It is only later, in solitude, in memory, that the realization dawns: when the ashes are cold; when the mourners have departed; when one looks around and finds oneself—quite to one's surprise—in an entirely different world.

————

When we got back to the car it had not yet begun to snow, but already the woods shrank beneath the sky, hushed and waiting, as if they could sense the weight of the ice that would be on them by nightfall.

"Christ, look at this mud," said Francis as we bounced through yet another pothole, brown spray striking the window with a thick **rataplan**.

Henry shifted down into first.

Another pothole, one that rattled the teeth in my head. As we tried to come out of it the tires whined, kicking up fresh splatters of mud, and we fell back into it with a jolt. Henry swore, and put the car in reverse.

Francis rolled down his window and craned his head outside to see. "Oh, Jesus," I heard him say. "Stop the car. There's no way we're going to—"

"We're not stuck."

"Yes we are. You're making it worse. **Christ,** Henry. Stop the—"

"Shut up," Henry said.

The tires whined in the back. The twins, sitting on either side of me, turned to look out the rear window at the muddy spray. Abruptly, Henry shifted into first, and with a sudden leap that made my heart glad we were clear of the hole.

Francis slumped back in his seat. He was a cautious driver, and riding in the car with Henry, even in the most propitious of circumstances, made him nervous.

———

Once in town, we drove to Francis's apartment. The twins and I were to split up and walk home—me to campus, the twins to their apartment—while Henry and Francis took care of the car. Henry turned off the engine. The silence was eerie, jolting.

He looked at me in the rear-view mirror. "We need to talk a minute," he said.

"What is it?"

"When did you leave your room?"

"About a quarter of three."

"Did anyone see you?"

"Not really. Not that I know of."

Cooling down after its long drive, the car ticked and hissed and settled contentedly on its frame. Henry was silent for a moment, and he was about to speak when Francis suddenly pointed out the window. "Look," he said. "Is that **snow**?"

The twins leaned low to see. Henry, biting his lower lip, paid no attention. "The four of us," he said, at last, "were at a matinee at the Orpheum in town—a double feature that ran from one o'clock to four-fifty-five. Afterwards we went on a short drive, returning"—he checked his watch—"at five-fifteen. That accounts for us, all right. I'm not sure what to do about you."

"Why can't I say I was with you?"

"Because you weren't."

"Who'll know the difference?"

"The ticket girl at the Orpheum, that's who. We went down and bought tickets for the afternoon show, paid for them with a hundred-dollar bill. She remembers us, I can assure you of that. We sat in the balcony and slipped out the emergency exit about fifteen minutes into the first movie."

"Why couldn't I have met you there?"

"You could have, except you don't have a car. And you can't say you took a cab because that can be easily checked. Besides, you were out walking around. You say you were in Commons before you met us?"

"Yes."

"Then I suppose there's nothing you can say except that you went straight home. It's not an ideal story, but at this point you don't have any alternative to speak of. We'll have to imagine you met up with us at some point **after** the movie, in the quite likely event that someone has seen you. Say we called you at five o'clock and met you in the parking lot. You rode with us to Francis's—really, this doesn't follow very smoothly, but it'll have to do—and walked home again."

"All right."

"When you get home, check downstairs in case any phone messages were left for you between three-thirty and five. If there were, we'll have to think of some reason why you didn't take the calls."

"Look, you guys," Charles said. "It's **really snowing**."

Tiny flakes, just visible at the tops of the pines.

"One more thing," said Henry. "We don't want to behave as if we're waiting around to hear some momentous piece of news. Go home. Read a book. I don't think we ought to try to contact one another tonight—unless, of course, it's absolutely necessary."

"I've never seen it snow this late in the year." Francis was looking out the window. "Yesterday it was nearly seventy degrees."

"Were they predicting it?" Charles said.

"Not that I heard."

"Christ. Look at this. It's almost Easter."

"I don't see why you're so excited," Henry said crossly. He had a pragmatic, farmer-like knowledge of how weather conditions affected growth, germination, blooming times, et cetera. "It's just going to kill all the flowers."

———

I walked home fast, because I was cold. A November stillness was settling like a deadly oxymoron on the April landscape. Snow was falling in earnest now—big silent petals drifting through the springtime woods, white bouquets segueing into snowy dark: a nightmarish topsy-turvy land, something from a story book. My path took me beneath a row of apple trees, full-blown and luminous, shivering in the twilight like an avenue of pale umbrellas. The big white flakes wafted through them, dreamy and soft. I did not stop to look, however, only hurried beneath them even faster. My winter in Hampden had given me a horror of snow.

There were no messages for me downstairs. I went up to my room, changed my clothes, couldn't decide what to do with the ones I'd taken off, thought of washing them, wondered if it might look suspicious, finally stuffed them all at the very bottom of my laundry bag. Then I sat down on my bed and looked at the clock.

It was time for dinner and I hadn't eaten all day but I wasn't hungry. I went to the window and watched the snowflakes whirl in the high arcs of light above the tennis courts, then crossed over and sat upon my bed again.

Minutes ticked by. Whatever anesthesia had carried me through the event was starting to wear off and with each passing second the thought of sitting around all night, alone, was seeming more and more unbearable. I turned on the radio, switched it off, tried to read.

When I found I couldn't hold my attention on one book I tried another. Scarcely ten minutes had passed. I picked up the first book and put it down again. Then, against my better judgment, I went downstairs to the pay phone and dialed Francis's number.

He answered on the first ring. "Hi," he said, when I told him it was me. "What is it?"

"Nothing."

"Are you sure?"

I heard Henry murmuring in the background. Francis, his mouth away from the receiver, said something that I couldn't catch.

"What are you guys doing?" I said.

"Not much. Having a drink. Hold on a second, would you?" he said, in response to another murmur.

There was a pause, an indistinct exchange, and then Henry's brisk voice came on the line. "What's the matter? Where are you?" he said.

"At home."

"What's wrong?"

"I just wondered if maybe I could come over for a drink or something."

"That's not a good idea. I was just leaving when you called."

"What are you going to do?"

"Well, if you want to know the truth, I'm going to take a bath and go to bed."

The line was silent for a moment.

"Are you still there?" Henry said.

"Henry, I'm going crazy. I don't know what I'm going to do."

"Well, do anything you like," Henry said amiably. "As long as you stick pretty close to home."

"I don't see what difference it would make if I—"

"When you're worried about something," said Henry abruptly, "have you ever tried thinking in a different language?"

"What?"

"It slows you down. Keeps your thoughts from running wild. A good discipline in any circumstance. Or you might try doing what the Buddhists do."

"What?"

"In the practice of Zen there is an exercise called **zazen**—similar, I think, to the Theravadic practice of **vipassana**. One sits facing a blank wall. No matter the emotion one feels, no matter how strong or violent, one remains motionless. Facing the wall. The discipline, of course, is in continuing to sit."

There was a silence, during which I struggled for language to adequately express what I thought of this goofball advice.

"Now, listen," he continued, before I could

say anything. "I'm exhausted. I'll see you in class tomorrow, all right?"

"**Henry,**" I said, but he'd hung up.

In a sort of trance, I walked upstairs. I wanted a drink badly but I had nothing to drink. I sat down on my bed and looked out the window.

My sleeping pills were all gone. I knew they were gone but I went to my bureau and checked the bottle just in case. It was empty except for some vitamin C tablets I'd got from the infirmary. Little white pills. I poured them on my desk, arranged them in patterns and then I took one, hoping that the reflex of swallowing would make me feel better, but it didn't.

I sat very still, trying not to think. It seemed as if I was waiting for something, I wasn't sure what, something that would lift the tension and make me feel better, though I could imagine no possible event, in past, present, or future, that would have either effect. It seemed as if an eternity had passed. Suddenly, I was struck by a horrible thought: **is this what it's like? Is this the way it's going to be from now on?**

I looked at the clock. Scarcely a minute had gone by. I got up, not bothering to lock the door behind me, and went down the hall to Judy's room.

By some miracle, she was in—drunk, putting on lipstick. "Hi," she said, without glancing away from the mirror. "Want to go to a party?"

I don't know what I said to her, something about not feeling well.

"Have a bagel," she said, turning her head from side to side and examining her profile.

"I'd rather a sleeping pill, if you've got one."

She screwed the lipstick down, snapped on the top, then opened the drawer of her dressing table. It was not actually a dressing table but a desk, college-issue, just like the one in my room; but like some savage unable to understand its true purpose—transforming it into a weapon rack, say, or a flower-decked fetish—she had painstakingly turned it into a cosmetics area, with a glass top and a ruffled satin skirt and a three-way mirror on the top that lit up. Scrabbling through a nightmare of compacts and pencils, she pulled out a prescription bottle, held it to the light, tossed it into the trash can and selected a new one. "This'll do," she said, handing it to me.

I examined the bottle. There were two drab tablets at the bottom. All the label said was FOR PAIN.

I said, annoyed, "What is this? Anacin or something?"

"Try one. They're okay. This weather's pretty wild, huh?"

"Yeah," I said, swallowing a pill and handing the bottle back.

"Don't worry, keep it," she said, already returned to her toilette. "Man. All it does here is fucking **snow**. I don't know why the hell I ever came here. You want a beer?"

She had a refrigerator in her room, in the closet. I fought my way through a jungle of belts and hats and lacy shirts to get to it.

"No, I don't want one," she said when I held one out to her. "Too fucked up. You didn't go to the party, did you?"

"No," I said, and then stopped, the beer bottle at my lips. There was something about the taste of it, the smell, and then I remembered: Bunny, the beer on his breath; spilled beer foaming on the ground. The bottle clattering after him down the slope.

"Smart move," said Judy. "It was cold and the band stunk. I saw your friend, what's-his-name. The Colonel."

"What?"

She laughed. "You know. Laura Stora calls him that. She used to live next door to him and he irritated the shit out of her playing these John Philip Sousa marching records all the time."

She meant Bunny. I set the bottle down.

But Judy, thank God, was busy with the eyebrow pencil. "You know," she said, "I think

Laura has an eating disorder, not anorexia, but that Karen Carpenter thing where you make yourself puke. Last night I went with her and Trace to the Brasserie, and, I'm totally serious, she stuffed herself until she could not breathe. Then she went in the men's room to barf and Tracy and I were looking at each other, like, is this **normal**? Then Trace told me, well, you remember that time Laura was supposedly in the hospital for mono? Well. The **story** is that **actually** . . ."

She rattled on. I stared at her, lost in my own awful thoughts.

Suddenly I realized she'd stopped talking. She was looking at me expectantly, waiting for a reply.

"What?" I said.

"I said, isn't that the most retarded thing you ever heard?"

"Ummmm."

"Her parents just must not give a shit." She closed the makeup drawer and turned to face me. "Anyway. You want to come to this party?"

"Whose is it?"

"Jack Teitelbaum's, you airhead. Durbinstall basement. Sid's band is supposed to play, and Moffat's back on the drums. And somebody said something about a go-go dancer in a cage. Come on."

For some reason I was unable to answer her.

Unconditional refusal to Judy's invitations was a reflex so deeply ingrained that it was hard to force myself to say yes. Then I thought of my room. Bed, bureau, desk. Books lying open where I'd left them.

"Come on," she said coquettishly. "You never go out with me."

"All right," I said at last. "Let me get my coat."

———

Only much later did I find out what Judy had given me: Demerol. By the time we got to the party it had started to kick in. Angles, colors, the riot of snowflakes, the din of Sid's band—everything was soft and kind and infinitely forgiving. I noted a strange beauty in the faces of people previously repulsive to me. I smiled at everyone and everyone smiled back.

Judy (Judy! God bless her!) left me with her friend Jack Teitelbaum and a fellow named Lars and went off to get us a drink. Everything was bathed in a celestial light. I listened to Jack and Lars talk about pinball, motorcycles, female kick-boxing, and was heartwarmed at their attempts to include me in the conversation. Lars offered me a bong hit. The gesture was, to me, tremendously touching and all of a sudden I realized I had been wrong about these people. These were good people, common people; the salt of the earth; people whom I should count myself fortunate to know.

I was trying to think of some way to vocalize this epiphany when Judy came back with the drinks. I drank mine, wandered off to get another, found myself roaming in a fluid, pleasant daze. Someone gave me a cigarette. Jud and Frank were there, Jud with a cardboard crown from Burger King on his head. This crown was oddly flattering to him. Head thrown back and howling with laughter, brandishing a tremendous mug of beer, he looked like Cuchulain, Brian Boru, some mythic Irish king. Cloke Rayburn was shooting pool in the back room. Just outside his line of vision, I watched him chalk the cue, unsmiling, and bend over the table so his hair fell in his face. **Click.** The colored balls spun out in all directions. Flecks of light swam in my eyes. I thought of atoms, molecules, things so small you couldn't even see them.

Then I remember feeling dizzy, pushing through the crowd to try to get some air. I could see the door propped invitingly with a cinder block, could feel a cold draft on my face. Then—I don't know, I must've blacked out, because the next thing I knew my back was against a wall, in an entirely different place, and a strange girl was talking to me.

Gradually I understood that I must have been standing there with her for some time. I blinked, and struggled gamely to bring her into focus. Very pretty, in a snub-nosed, good-natured way; dark hair, freckles, light blue eyes. I had seen her earlier, somewhere, in line at the bar maybe, had seen her without paying her much attention. And now here she was again, like an apparition, drinking red wine from a plastic cup and calling me by name.

I couldn't make out what she was saying, though the timbre of her voice was clear even over the noise: cheerful, raucous, oddly pleasant. I leaned forward—she was a small girl, barely five feet—and cupped a hand to my ear. "What?" I said.

She laughed, stretched up on tiptoe, brought her face close to mine. Perfume. Hot thunder of whisper against my cheek.

I grabbed her by the wrist. "It's too noisy," I said in her ear; my lips brushed against her hair. "Let's go outside."

She laughed again. "But we just came in," she said. "You said you were freezing."

Hmmn, I thought. Her eyes were pale, bored, regarding me with a kind of intimate amusement in the jaded light.

"Somewhere quiet, I mean," I said.

She turned up her glass and looked at me

through the bottom of it. "Your room or mine?"

"Yours," I said, without a moment's hesitation.

———

She was a good girl, a good sport. Sweet chuckles in the dark and her hair falling across my face, funny little catches in her breath like the girls back in high school. The warm feel of a body in my arms was something I'd almost forgotten. How long since I'd kissed anyone that way? Months, and more months.

Strange to think how simple things could be. A party, some drinks, a pretty stranger. That was the way most of my classmates lived—talking rather self-consciously at breakfast about their liaisons of the previous night, as if this harmless, homey little vice, which fell somewhere below drink and above gluttony in the catalogue of sins, was somehow the abyss of depravity and dissipation.

Posters; dried flowers in a beer mug; the luminous glow of her stereo in the dark. It was all too familiar from my suburban youth, yet now seemed unbelievably remote and innocent, a memory from some lost Junior Prom. Her lip gloss tasted like bubble gum. I buried my face in the soft, slightly acrid-smelling flesh of her neck and rocked her back and forth—babbling, mumbling, feeling myself fall down and down, into a dark, half-forgotten life.

———

I woke at two-thirty—according to the flashing, demonic red of a digital clockface—in an absolute panic. I'd had a dream, nothing scary really, in which Charles and I were on a train, trying to evade a mysterious third passenger. The cars were packed with people from the party—Judy, Jack Teitelbaum, Jud in his cardboard crown—as we lurched through the aisles. Throughout the dream, however, I'd had a feeling that it was all unimportant, that I actually had a far more pressing worry if only I could remember it. Then I did remember, and the shock of it woke me up.

It was like waking from a nightmare to a worse nightmare. I sat up, heart pounding, slapping at the blank wall for the light switch until the terrible realization dawned on me that I was not in my own room. Strange shapes, unfamiliar shadows, crowded horribly around me; nothing offered any clue to my whereabouts, and for a few delirious moments I wondered if I was dead. Then I felt the sleeping body next to mine. Instinctively I recoiled, and then I prodded it gently with my elbow. It didn't move. I lay in bed for a minute or two, trying to collect my thoughts; then I got up, found my clothes, dressed as best as I could in the dark, and left.

Stepping outside, I slipped on an icy step and pitched, face-forward, into more than a foot of snow. I lay still for a moment, then raised myself to my knees and looked about in disbelief. A few snowflakes were one thing, but I had not thought it possible for weather to change as suddenly and violently as this. The flowers were buried, and the lawn; everything had disappeared. An expanse of clean, unbroken snow stretched blue and twinkling as far as I could see.

My hands were raw and my elbow felt bruised. With some effort, I got to my feet. When I turned to see where I'd come from, I was horrified to realize I'd just walked out of Bunny's own dorm. His window, on the ground floor, stared back at me black and silent. I thought of his spare glasses lying on the desk; the empty bed; the family photographs smiling in the dark.

When I got back to my room—by a confused, circular route—I fell on my bed without taking off my coat or shoes. The lights were on, and I felt weirdly exposed and vulnerable but I didn't want to turn them off. The bed was rocking a little, like a raft, and I kept a foot on the floor to steady it.

Then I fell asleep, and slept very soundly for

a couple of hours until I was awakened by a knock at the door. Seized by fresh panic, I fought to sit up in the tangle of my coat, which had somehow got twisted around my knees and seemed to be attacking me with the force of a living creature.

The door creaked open. Then no sound at all. "What the hell is wrong with you?" said a sharp voice.

Francis was in the doorway. He stood with one black-gloved hand on the knob, looking at me like I was a lunatic.

I stopped struggling and fell back on my pillow. I was so glad to see him I felt like laughing, and I was so doped up I probably did. **"François,"** I said idiotically.

He shut the door and came over to my bed, where he stood looking down at me. It was really him—snow in his hair, snow on the shoulders of his long black overcoat. "Are you okay?" he said, after a long, derisive pause.

I rubbed my eyes and tried again. "Hi," I said. "I'm sorry. I'm fine. Really."

He stood looking at me with no expression and did not answer. Then he took off his coat and laid it over the back of a chair. "Do you want some tea?" he said.

"No."

"Well, I'm going to go make some, if you don't mind."

By the time he was back I was more or less myself. He put the kettle on the radiator and helped himself to some tea bags from my bureau drawer. "Here," he said. "You can have the good teacup. There wasn't any milk in the kitchen."

It was a relief to have him there. I sat up and drank my tea and watched him take off his shoes and socks. Then he put them by the radiator to dry. His feet were long and thin, too long for his slim, bony ankles; he flexed his toes, looked up at me. "It's an awful night," he said. "Have you been outside?"

I told him a little about my night, omitting the part about the girl.

"Gosh," he said, reaching up to loosen his collar. "I've just been sitting in my apartment. Giving myself the creeps."

"Heard from anyone?"

"No. My mother called around nine; I couldn't talk to her. Told her I was writing a paper."

For some reason my eyes strayed to his hands, fidgeting unconsciously on the top of my desk. He saw that I saw, forced them down, palms flat. "Nerves," he said.

We sat for a while without saying anything. I put my teacup on the windowsill and leaned back. The Demerol had set off some kind of weird Doppler effect in my head, like the whine of car tires speeding past and receding in the distance. I was staring across the room in a daze—how long, I don't know—when gradually I became aware that Francis was looking at me with an intent, fixed expression on his face. I mumbled something and got up and went to the bureau to get an Alka-Seltzer.

The sudden movement made me feel light-headed. I was standing there dully, wondering where I'd put the box, when all of a sudden I became aware that Francis was immediately behind me, and I turned around.

His face was very close to mine. To my surprise he put his hands on my shoulders and leaned forward and kissed me, right on the mouth.

It was a real kiss—long, slow, deliberate. He'd caught me off balance and I grabbed his arm to keep from falling; sharply, he drew in his breath and his hands went down to my back and before I knew it, more from reflex than anything else, I was kissing him, too. His tongue was sharp. His mouth had a bitter, mannish taste, like tea and cigarettes.

He pulled away, breathing hard, and leaned to kiss my throat. I looked rather wildly around the room. **God,** I thought, **what a night**.

"Look, Francis," I said, "cut it out."

He was undoing the top button of my collar.

"You idiot," he said, chuckling. "Did you know your shirt's on inside-out?"

I was so tired and drunk I started to laugh. "Come on, Francis," I said. "Give me a break."

"It's fun," he said. "I promise you."

Matters progressed. My jaded nerves began to stir. His eyes were magnified and wicked behind his pince-nez. Presently he took them off and dropped them on my bureau with an absent clatter.

Then, quite unexpectedly, there was another knock at the door. We sprang apart. His eyes were wide. We stared at each other, and then the knock came again.

Francis swore under his breath, bit his lip. I, panic-stricken, buttoning my shirt as fast as my numb fingers would go, started to say something but he made a quick, shushing gesture at me with his hand.

"But what if it's—?" I whispered.

I had been about to say "What if it's Henry?" But what I was actually thinking was "What if it's the cops?" Francis, I knew, was thinking the same thing.

More knocking, more insistent this time.

My heart was pounding. Bewildered with fear, I crossed to my bed and sat down.

Francis ran a hand through his hair. "Come in," he called.

I was so upset that it took me a moment to

realize it was only Charles. He was leaning with one elbow against the door frame, his red scarf slung into great careless loops around his neck. When he stepped in my room I saw immediately that he was drunk. "Hi," he said to Francis. "What the hell are you doing here?"

"You scared us to death."

"I wish I'd known you were coming. Henry called and got me out of bed."

The two of us looked at him, waiting for him to explain. He jostled off his coat and turned to me with a watery, intense gaze. "You were in my dream," he said.

"What?"

He blinked at me. "I just remembered," he said. "I had a dream tonight. You were in it."

I stared at him. Before I had a chance to tell him he was in my dream, too, Francis said impatiently: "Come on, Charles. What's the matter?"

Charles ran a hand through his windblown hair. "Nothing," he said. He reached into his coat pocket and pulled out a sheaf of papers folded lengthwise. "Did you do your Greek for today?" he asked me.

I rolled my eyes. Greek had been about the last thing on my mind.

"Henry thought you might have forgot. He called and asked me to bring mine for you to copy, just in case."

He was very drunk. He wasn't slurring his words, but he smelled of whiskey and he was extremely unsteady on his feet. His face was flushed and radiant as an angel's.

"You talked to Henry? Has he heard anything?"

"He's very annoyed about this weather. Nothing's turned up that he knows of. Gosh, it's hot in here," he said, shouldering off his jacket.

Francis, sitting in his chair by the window with an ankle balanced upon the opposite kneecap and his teacup balanced on his bare ankle, was looking at Charles rather narrowly.

Charles turned, reeling slightly. "What are you looking at?" he said.

"Do you have a bottle in your pocket?"

"No."

"Nonsense, Charles, I can hear it sloshing."

"What difference does it make?"

"I want a drink."

"Oh, all right," said Charles, irritated. He reached into the inside pocket of the jacket and brought out a flat pint bottle. "Here," he said. "Don't be a pig."

Francis drank the rest of his tea and reached for the bottle. "Thanks," he said, pouring the remaining inch or so into his teacup. I looked at him—dark suit, sitting very straight with his legs now crossed at the knee. He was the picture of respectability except that his feet were bare. All of a sudden I found myself able to see him as the world saw him, as I myself had seen him when I first met him—cool, well-mannered, rich, absolutely beyond reproach. It was such a convincing illusion that even I, who knew the essential falseness of it, felt oddly comforted.

He drank the whiskey down in a swallow. "We need to sober you up, Charles," he said. "We've got class in a couple of hours."

Charles sighed and sat on the foot of my bed. He looked very tired, a regard which manifested itself not in dark circles, or pallor, but a dreamy and bright-cheeked sadness. "I know," he said. "I hoped the walk might do the trick."

"You need some coffee."

He wiped his damp forehead with the heel of his hand. "I need more than coffee," he said.

I smoothed out the papers and went over to my desk and began to copy out my Greek.

Francis sat down on the bed next to Charles. "Where's Camilla?"

"Asleep."

"What'd you two do tonight? Get drunk?"

"No," said Charles tersely. "Cleaned house."

"No. Really."

"I'm not kidding."

I was still so dopey that I couldn't make any sense of the passage I was copying, only a sentence here and there. **Being weary from the march, the soldiers stopped to offer sacrifices at the temple. I came back from that country and said that I had seen the Gorgon, but it did not make me a stone.**

"Our house is full of tulips, if you want any," said Charles inexplicably.

"What do you mean?"

"I mean, before the snow got too deep, we went outside and brought them in. Everything's full of them. The water glasses, even."

Tulips, I thought, staring at the jumble of letters before me. Had the ancient Greeks known them under a different name, if they'd had tulips at all? The letter **psi**, in Greek, is shaped like a tulip. All of a sudden, in the dense alphabet forest of the page, little black tulips began to pop up in a quick, random pattern like falling raindrops.

My vision swam. I closed my eyes. I sat there for a long time, half-dozing, until I became aware that Charles was saying my name.

I turned in my chair. They were leaving. Francis was sitting on the side of my bed, lacing his shoes.

"Where are you going?" I said.

"Home to dress. It's getting late."

I didn't want to be alone—quite the contrary—but I felt, unaccountably, a strong desire to be rid of them both. The sun was up.

Francis reached over and turned off the lamp. The morning light was sober and pale and made my room seem horribly quiet.

"We'll see you in a little while," he said, and then I heard their footsteps dying on the stair. Everything was faded and silent in the dawn— dirty teacups, unmade bed, snowflakes floating past the window with an airy, dangerous calm. My ears rang. When I turned back to my work, with trembling, ink-stained hands, the scratch of my pen on the paper rasped loud in the stillness. I thought of Bunny's dark room and of the ravine, miles away; of all those layers of silence on silence.

———

"And where is Edmund this morning?" said Julian as we opened our grammars.

"At home, I suppose," said Henry. He'd come in late and we hadn't had a chance to talk. He seemed calm, well rested, more than he had any right to be.

The others were surprisingly calm as well. Even Francis and Charles were well dressed, freshly shaven, very much their unconcerned old selves. Camilla sat between them, with her elbow propped negligently on the table and her chin in her hand, tranquil as an orchid.

Julian arched an eyebrow at Henry. "Is he ill?"

"I don't know."

"This weather may have slowed him a bit. Perhaps we should wait a few minutes."

"I think that's a good idea," said Henry, going back to his book.

———

After class, once we were away from the Lyceum and near the birch grove, Henry glanced around to make sure that no one was within earshot; we all leaned close to hear what he was going to say but at just that moment, as we were standing in a huddle and our breath was coming out in clouds, I heard someone call my name and there, at a great distance, was Dr. Roland, tottering through the snow like a lurching corpse.

I disengaged myself and went to meet him. He was breathing hard and, with a good deal of coughing and hawing, he began to tell me about something he wanted me to have a look at in his office.

There was nothing I could do but go with him, adjusting my pace to his leaden shuffle. Once inside, he paused several times on the stair to remark upon scraps of debris that the janitor had missed, feebly kicking at them with his foot. He kept me for half an hour. When I finally escaped, with my ears ringing and an armful of loose papers struggling to fly away in the wind, the birch grove was empty.

I don't know what I'd expected, but the

world certainly hadn't been kicked out of its orbit overnight. People were hurrying to and fro, on their way to class, everything business as usual. The sky was gray and an icy wind was blowing off Mount Cataract.

I bought a milk shake at the snack bar and then went home. I was walking down the hall to my suite when I ran headlong into Judy Poovey.

She glared at me. She looked like she had an evil hangover and there were black circles under her eyes.

"Oh, hello," I said, edging past. "Sorry."

"Hey," she said.

I turned around.

"So you went home with Mona Beale last night?"

For a second I didn't know what she meant. "What?"

"How was it?" she said bitchily. "Was she good?"

Taken aback, I shrugged and started down the hall.

To my annoyance she followed and caught me by the arm. "She's got a boyfriend, do you know that? You better hope nobody tells him."

"I don't care."

"Last term he beat up Bram Guernsey because he thought Bram was hitting on her."

"She was the one who was hitting on **me**."

She gave me a catty, sideways look. "Well, I mean, she's kind of a slut."

———

Just before I woke up, I had a terrible dream.

I was in a large, old-fashioned bathroom, like something from a Zsa Zsa Gabor movie, with gold fixtures and mirrors and pink tile on the walls and floor. A bowl of goldfish stood on a spindly pedestal in the corner. I went over to look at them, my footsteps echoing on the tile, and then I became aware of a measured plink plink plink, coming from the faucet of the tub.

The tub was pink, too, and it was full of water, and Bunny, fully clad, was lying motionless at the bottom of it. His eyes were open and his glasses were askew and his pupils were different sizes—one large and black, the other scarcely a pinpoint. The water was clear, and very still. The tip of his necktie undulated near the surface.

Plink, plink, plink. I couldn't move. Then, suddenly, I heard footsteps approaching, and voices. With a rush of terror I realized I had to hide the body somehow, where I didn't know; I plunged my hands into the icy water and grasped him beneath the arms and tried to pull him out, but it was no good, no good; his head lolled back uselessly and his open mouth was filling with water. . . .

Struggling against his weight, reeling back-
ward, I knocked the fishbowl from its pedestal
and it crashed to the floor. Goldfish flopping
all around my feet, amidst the shards of broken glass. Someone banged on the door. In my
terror I let go of the body and it fell back into
the tub with a hideous slap and a spray of water and I woke up.

It was almost dark. There was a horrible, erratic thumping in my chest, as if a large bird
were trapped inside my ribcage and beating itself to death. Gasping, I lay back on my bed.

When the worst of it was over I sat up. I was
trembling all over and drenched in sweat.
Long shadows, nightmare light. I could see
some kids playing outside in the snow, silhou-
etted in black against the dreadful, salmon-
colored sky. Their shouts and laughter had, at
that distance, an insane quality. I dug the heels
of my hands hard into my eyes. Milky spots,
pinpoints of light. **Oh, God,** I thought.

———

Bare cheek on cold tile. The roar and rush of
the toilet was so loud I thought it would swallow me. It was like all the times I'd ever been
sick, all the drunken throw-ups I'd ever had
in the bathrooms of gas stations and bars.
Same old bird's-eye view: those odd little
knobs at the base of the toilet that you never
notice at any other time; sweating porcelain,

the hum of pipes, that long burble of water as it spirals down.

While I was washing my face, I began to cry. The tears mingled easily with the cold water, in the luminous, dripping crimson of my cupped fingers, and at first I wasn't aware that I was crying at all. The sobs were regular and emotionless, as mechanical as the dry heaves which had stopped only a moment earlier; there was no reason for them, they had nothing to do with me. I brought my head up and looked at my weeping reflection in the mirror with a kind of detached interest. **What does this mean?** I thought. I looked terrible. Nobody else was falling apart; yet here I was, shaking all over and seeing bats like Ray Milland in **The Lost Weekend**.

A cold draft was blowing in the window. I felt shaky but oddly refreshed. I ran myself a hot bath, throwing in a good handful of Judy's bath salts, and when I got out and put on my clothes I felt quite myself again.

Nihil sub sole novum, I thought as I walked back down the hall to my room. Any action, in the fullness of time, sinks to nothingness.

————

They were all there when I arrived at the twins' for dinner that night, gathered around the radio and listening to the weather forecast as if to some wartime bulletin from the front. "For the long-range outlook," said an announcer's spry voice, "expect cool weather on Thursday, with cloudy skies and a possibility of showers, leading into warmer weather for the—"

Henry snapped off the radio. "If we're lucky," he said, "the snow will be gone tomorrow night. Where were you this afternoon, Richard?"

"At home."

"I'm glad you're here. I want you to do a little favor for me, if you don't mind."

"What is it?"

"I want to drive you downtown after dinner so you can see those movies at the Orpheum and tell us what they're about. Do you mind?"

"No."

"I know this is an imposition on a school night, but I really don't think it's wise for any of the rest of us to go back again. Charles has offered to copy out your Greek for you if you like."

"If I do it on that yellow paper you use," said Charles, "with your fountain pen, he'll never know the difference."

"Thanks," I said. Charles had a rather startling talent for forgery which, according to Camilla, dated from early childhood—expert report-card signatures by the fourth grade, entire excuse notes by the sixth. I was always getting him to sign Dr. Roland's name to my time sheets.

"Really," said Henry, "I hate to ask you to do this. I think they're dreadful movies."

They were pretty bad. The first was a road movie from the early seventies, about a man who leaves his wife to drive cross-country. On the way he gets sidetracked into Canada and becomes involved with a bunch of draft dodgers; at the end he goes back to his wife and they renew their vows in a hippie ceremony. The worst thing was the soundtrack. All these acoustic guitar songs with the word "freedom" in them.

The second film was more recent. It was about the Vietnam War and was called **Fields of Shame**—a big-budget movie with a lot of stars. The special effects were a bit realistic for my taste, though. People getting their legs blown off and so forth.

When I got out, Henry's car was parked down the street with the lights off. Upstairs at Charles and Camilla's, everyone was sitting around the kitchen table with their sleeves rolled up, deep in Greek. When we came in they began to stir, and Charles got up and made a pot of coffee while I read my notes. Both movies were rather plotless and I had a hard time communicating the gist of them.

"But these are **terrible**," said Francis. "I'm

embarrassed that people will think we went to see such bad movies."

"But wait," said Camilla.

"I don't get it, either," Charles said. "Why did the sergeant bomb the village where the good people lived?"

"Yes," Camilla said. "Why? And who was that kid with the puppy who just wandered up in the middle of it? How did he know Charlie Sheen?"

———

Charles had done a beautiful job on my Greek, and I was looking it over before class the next day when Julian came in. He paused in the doorway, looked at the empty chair and laughed. "Goodness," he said. "Not **again**."

"Looks like it," said Francis.

"I must say, I hope our classes haven't become as tedious as all that. Please tell Edmund that, should he choose to attend tomorrow, I shall make an effort to be especially engaging."

———

By noon it was apparent that the weather forecast was in error. The temperature had dropped ten degrees, and more snow fell in the afternoon.

The five of us were to go out to dinner that night, and when the twins and I showed up at Henry's apartment, we found him looking especially glum. "Guess who just phoned me," he said.

"Who?"

"Marion."

Charles sat down. "What did she want?"

"She wanted to know if I'd seen Bunny."

"What'd you say?"

"Well, of course I said I hadn't," Henry said irritably. "They were supposed to meet on Sunday night and she hasn't seen him since Saturday."

"Is she worried?"

"Not particularly."

"Then what's the problem?"

"Nothing." He sighed. "I just hope the weather breaks tomorrow."

———

But it didn't. Wednesday dawned bright and cold and two more inches of snow had accumulated in the night.

"Of course," said Julian, "I don't mind if Edmund misses a class now and then. But three in a row. And you know what a hard time he has catching up."

———

"We can't go on like this much longer," said Henry at the twins' apartment that night, as we were smoking cigarettes over uneaten plates of bacon and eggs.

"What can we do?"

"I don't know. Except he's been missing now for seventy-two hours, and it'll start to look funny if we don't act worried pretty soon."

"No one else is worried," said Charles.

"No one else sees as much of him as we do. I wonder if Marion's home," he said, glancing at the clock.

"Why?"

"Because maybe I should give her a call."

"For God's sake," said Francis. "Don't drag **her** into it."

"I have no intention of dragging her into anything. I just want to make it plain to her that none of us have seen Bunny for three days."

"And what do you expect her to do about it?"

"I hope she'll call the police."

"Have you lost your mind?"

"Well, if she doesn't, we're going to have to," said Henry impatiently. "The longer he's gone, the worse it will look. I don't want a big ruckus, people asking questions."

"Then why call the police?"

"Because if we go to them soon enough, I doubt there'll be any ruckus at all. Perhaps they'll send one or two people out here to poke around, thinking it's probably a false alarm—"

"If no one's found him yet," I said, "I don't

see what makes you think that a couple of traffic cops from Hampden will do any better."

"No one's found him because no one's looking. He's not half a mile away."

It took whoever answered a long time to bring Marion to the telephone. Henry stood patiently, gazing down at the floor; gradually his eyes began to wander, and after about five minutes he made an exasperated noise and looked up. "My goodness," he said. "What's taking them so long? Let me have a cigarette, would you, Francis?"

He had it in his mouth and Francis was lighting it for him when Marion came on the line. "Oh, hello, Marion," he said, exhaling a cloud of smoke and turning his back to us. "I'm glad I caught you. Is Bunny there?"

A slight pause. "Well," said Henry, reaching for the ashtray, "do you know where he is, then?"

"Well, frankly," he said at last, "I was going to ask you the same thing. He hasn't been in class for two or three days."

Another long silence. Henry listened, his face pleasantly blank. Then, all of a sudden, his eyes widened. "What?" he said, a little too sharply.

All of us were jarred awake. Henry wasn't looking at any of us but at the wall above our heads, his blue eyes round and glassy.

"I see," he said finally.

More talk on the other end.

"Well, if he happens to stop by, I'd appreciate it if you would ask him to call me. Let me give you my number."

When he hung up he had a strange look on his face. We all stared at him.

"Henry?" said Camilla. "What is it?"

"She's angry. Not worried a bit. Expecting him to walk in the door any moment. I don't know," he said, staring at the floor. "This is very peculiar, but she said that a friend of hers—a girl named Rika Thalheim—saw Bunny standing around outside the First Vermont Bank this afternoon."

We were too stunned to say anything. Francis laughed, a short, incredulous laugh.

"My God," said Charles. "That's impossible."

"It certainly is," Henry said dryly.

"Why would somebody just make that up?"

"I can't imagine. People think they see all kinds of things, I suppose. Well, of course, she **didn't** see him," he added testily to Charles, who looked rather troubled. "But I don't know what we should do now."

"What do you mean?"

"Well, we can't very well call and report him missing when somebody **saw** him six hours ago."

"So what are we going to do? Wait?"

"No," said Henry, biting his lower lip. "I'll have to think of something else."

———

"Where on earth is Edmund?" said Julian on Thursday morning. "I don't know how long he plans on being absent, but it is very thoughtless of him not to have got in touch with me."

No one answered him. He looked up from his book, amused at our silence.

"What's wrong?" he said teasingly. "All these shameful faces. Perhaps," he said more coolly, "some of you are ashamed at how insufficiently you were prepared for yesterday's lesson."

I saw Charles and Camilla exchange a look. For some reason, this week of all weeks, Julian had loaded us down with work. We'd all managed, somehow or other, to bring in the written assignments; but no one had kept up with the reading, and in class the day before there had been several excruciating silences which not even Henry had been able to break.

Julian glanced down at his book. "Perhaps, before we begin," he said, "one of you should go call Edmund on the telephone and ask him to join us if he's at all able. I don't mind if he hasn't read his lesson, but this is an important class and he ought not to miss it."

Henry stood up. But then Camilla said, quite unexpectedly, "I don't think he's at home."

"Then where is he? Out of town?"

"I'm not sure."

Julian lowered his reading glasses and looked at her over the tops of them. "What do you mean?"

"We haven't seen him for a couple of days."

Julian's eyes widened with childish, theatrical surprise; not for the first time, I thought how much he was like Henry, that same strange mixture of chill and warmth. "Indeed," he said. "**Most** peculiar. And you have no idea where he might be?"

The mischievous, open-ended note in his voice made me nervous. I stared at the aqueous, rippling circles of light that the crystal vase cast over the tabletop.

"No," said Henry. "We're a bit puzzled."

"I should think so." His eyes met Henry's, for a long, strange moment.

He knows, I thought, with a rush of panic. **He knows we're lying. He just doesn't know what we're lying about.**

———

After lunch, after my French class, I sat on the top floor of the library with my books spread across the table in front of me. It was a strange, bright, dreamlike day. The snowy lawn—peppered with the toylike figures of distant people—was as smooth as sugar frosting on a birthday cake; a tiny dog ran, barking, after a ball; real smoke threaded from the dollhouse chimneys.

This time, I thought, **a year ago.** What had I been doing? Driving a friend's car up to San Francisco, standing around in the poetry sections of bookstores worrying about my application to Hampden. And now here I was, sitting in a cold room in strange clothes and wondering if I might go to prison.

Nihil sub sole novum. A pencil sharpener complained loudly somewhere. I put my head down on my books—whispers, quiet footsteps, the smell of old paper in my nostrils. Several weeks earlier, Henry had become angry when the twins were voicing moral objections at the idea of killing Bunny. "Don't be ridiculous," he snapped.

"But how," said Charles, who was close to tears, "how can you **possibly justify** cold-blooded murder?"

Henry lit a cigarette. "I prefer to think of it," he had said, "as redistribution of matter."

———

I woke, with a start, to find Henry and Francis standing over me.

"What is it?" I said, rubbing my eyes and looking up at them.

"Nothing," said Henry. "Will you come with us to the car?"

Sleepily I followed them downstairs, where the car was parked in front of the bookstore.

"What's the matter?" I said after we had got in.

"Do you know where Camilla is?"

"Isn't she at home?"

"No. Julian hasn't seen her, either."

"What do you want with her?"

Henry sighed. It was cold inside the car, and his breath came out white. "Something's up," he said. "Francis and I saw Marion at the guard booth with Cloke Rayburn. They were talking to some people from Security."

"When?"

"About an hour ago."

"You don't think they've done anything, do you?"

"We shouldn't jump to conclusions," said Henry. He was looking out at the roof of the bookstore, which was sheeted in ice and glittered in the sun. "What we want is for Camilla to drop in on Cloke and see if she can find out what's going on. I'd go myself, except I hardly know him."

"And he hates me," said Francis.

"I know him a little."

"Not well enough. He and Charles are on

fairly good terms, but we can't find him, either."

I unwrapped a Rolaids tablet from a roll in my pocket and began to chew on it.

"What's that you're eating?" said Francis.

"Rolaids."

"I'll have one of those, if you don't mind," Henry said. "I guess we should drive by the house again."

————

This time Camilla came to the door, opening it only a crack and looking out warily. Henry started to say something, but she gave him a sharp warning glance. "Hello," she said. "Come in."

We followed her inside without a word, down the dark hall into the living room. There, with Charles, was Cloke Rayburn.

Charles stood up nervously; Cloke stayed where he was and looked at us with sleepy, in-scrutable eyes. He had a sunburn and he needed a shave. Charles raised his eyebrows at us and mouthed the word "stoned."

"Hello," said Henry after a pause. "How are you?"

Cloke coughed—a deep, nasty-sounding rasp—and shook a Marlboro from a pack on the table before him. "Not bad," he said. "You?"

"Fine."

He stuck the cigarette in the corner of his mouth, lit it, coughed again. "Hey," he said to me. "How's it going?"

"Pretty good."

"You were at that party at Durbinstall on Sunday."

"Yes."

"Seen Mona?" he said without any inflection whatever.

"No," I said brusquely, and was suddenly aware that everyone was looking at me.

"Mona?" said Charles, after a puzzled silence.

"This girl," Cloke said. "Sophomore. Lives in Bunny's house."

"Speaking of whom," said Henry.

Cloke leaned back in his chair and fixed Henry with a bloodshot, heavy-lidded gaze. "Yeah," he said. "We were just talking about Bun. You haven't seen him the last couple days, have you?"

"No. Have you?"

Cloke didn't say anything for a moment. Then he shook his head. "No," he said hoarsely, reaching for an ashtray. "I can't figure out where the hell he is. Last time I saw him was Saturday night, not that I thought about it or anything until today."

"I talked to Marion last night," Henry said.

"I know," said Cloke. "She's kind of worried. I saw her in Commons this morning and she told me he hasn't been in his room for like five days. She thought maybe he was at home or something, but she called his brother Patrick. Who says he ain't in Connecticut. And she talked to Hugh, too, and he says he's not in New York, either."

"Did she speak to his parents?"

"Well, shit, she wasn't trying to get him in trouble."

Henry was silent for a moment. Then he said: "Where do you think he is?"

Cloke looked away, shrugged uneasily.

"You've known him longer than I have. He's got a brother at Yale, doesn't he?"

"Yeah. Brady. Business school. But Patrick said he'd just talked to Brady, you know?"

"Patrick lives at home, right?"

"Yeah. He's got some kind of business thing he's working on, a sporting goods store or something, trying to get it off the ground."

"And Hugh's the lawyer."

"Yes. He's the oldest. He's at Milbank Tweed in New York."

"What about the other brother—the married one?"

"Hugh's the married one."

"But isn't there another one who's married, too?"

"Oh. Teddy. I **know** he's not there."

"Why?"

"The T-man lives with his in-laws. I don't think they get along too well."

There was a long silence.

"Can you think of anyplace he might be?" said Henry.

Cloke leaned forward, his long, dark hair falling in his face, and knocked the ash off his cigarette. He had a troubled, secretive expression, and after a few moments he looked up. "Have you noticed," he said, "that Bunny's had an awful lot of **cash** around the last two or three weeks?"

"What do you mean?" said Henry, a trifle sharply.

"You know Bunny. He's broke all the time. Lately, though, he's had all this money. Like, a **lot**. Maybe his grandmother sent it to him or something, but you can be damn sure he didn't get it from his parents."

There was another long silence. Henry bit his lip. "What are you trying to get at?" he said.

"You have noticed it, then."

"Now that you mention it, I have."

Cloke shifted uncomfortably in his chair. "This is off the record, now," he said.

With a sinking feeling in my chest, I sat down.

"What is it?" Henry said.

"I don't know if I should even mention it."

"If you think it important, by all means do," Henry said curtly.

Cloke took a last draw on his cigarette and ground it out with a deliberate, corkscrewing movement. "You know," he said, "that I deal a little coke now and then, don't you? Not much," he said hastily, "just a few grams here and there. Just for me and my friends. But it's easy work and I can make a little money at it, too."

We all looked at each other. This was no news at all. Cloke was one of the biggest drug dealers on campus.

"So?" said Henry.

Cloke looked surprised. Then he shrugged. "So," he said, "I know this Chinaman down on Mott Street in New York, kind of a scary guy, but he likes me and he'll pretty much give me however much I can scrape up the cash for. Blow, mostly, sometimes a little pot as well but that's kind of a headache. I've known him for years. We even did a little business when Bunny and I were at Saint Jerome's." He paused. "Well. You know how broke Bunny always is."

"Yes."

"Well, he's always been real interested in the whole thing. Quick money, you know. If he'd ever had the cash I might've cut him in on it—

on the financial end, I mean—but he never did and besides, Bunny has no business being mixed up in a deal like this." He lit another cigarette. "Anyway," he said. "That's why I'm worried."

Henry frowned. "I'm afraid I don't follow."

"This was a bad mistake I guess but I let him ride down with me a couple weeks ago."

We had already heard about this excursion to New York. Bunny had bragged about it incessantly. "And?" said Henry.

"I don't know. I'm just kind of worried, is all. He knows where the guy lives—right?—and he's got all this money, so when I was talking to Marion, I just—"

"You don't think he went down there by himself?" said Charles.

"I don't know. I sure hope not. He never actually met the guy or anything."

"Would Bunny do something like that?" said Camilla.

"Frankly," said Henry, unhooking his glasses and giving them a quick swipe with his handkerchief, "it strikes me as just the type of stupid thing that Bunny would do."

Nobody said anything for a moment. Henry glanced up. His eyes without the glasses were blind, unwavering, strange. "Does Marion know about this?" he said.

"No," said Cloke. "And I'd just as soon you didn't tell her, okay?"

"Do you have any other reason for thinking this?"

"No. Except where else **could** he be? And Marion told you about Rika Thalheim seeing him at the bank on Wednesday?"

"Yes."

"That's kind of weird but not really, not if you think about it. Say he went down to New York with a couple hundred dollars, right? And talking like he had a lot more where that came from. These guys'll chop you up and put you in a garbage bag for twenty bucks. I mean, I don't know. Maybe they told him to go back home and close out his account and come back with all he had."

"Bunny doesn't even have a bank account."

"That you know of," Cloke pointed out.

"You're perfectly right," said Henry.

"Can't you just call down there?" Charles said.

"Who'm I gonna call? The guy's unlisted and he doesn't hand out business cards, all right?"

"Then how do you get in touch with him?"

"I have to call a third guy."

"Then call him," said Henry calmly, putting the handkerchief back in his pocket and hooking the glasses back over his ears.

"They're not going to tell me anything."

"I thought they were such good chums of yours."

"What do you think?" said Cloke. "You think these people are running some kind of a scout troop down there? Are you kidding? These are real guys. Doing **real shit**."

For one horrible instant I thought that Francis was going to laugh aloud but somehow he managed to turn it into a theatrical battery of coughs, hiding his face behind his hand. With barely a glance Henry slapped him, hard, on the back.

"Then what do you suggest we do?" Camilla said.

"I don't know. I'd like to get into his room, see if he took a suitcase or anything."

"Isn't it locked?" Henry said.

"Yes. Marion tried to get Security to open it for her and they wouldn't do it."

Henry bit his lower lip. "Well," he said slowly, "it wouldn't be so very hard to get in in spite of that, would it?"

Cloke put out his cigarette and looked at Henry with new interest. "No," he said. "It wouldn't."

"There's the ground floor window. The storm windows have been taken off."

"I know I could handle the screens."

The two of them stared at each other.

"Maybe," Cloke said, "I should go down and try it now."

"We'll go with you."

"Man," said Cloke, "we can't **all** go."

I saw Henry cut his eyes at Charles; Charles, behind Cloke's back, acknowledged the glance. "I'll go," he said suddenly, in a voice that was too loud, and tossed off the rest of his drink.

"Cloke, how on earth did you get mixed up in something like this?" Camilla said.

He laughed condescendingly. "It's nothing," he said. "You have to meet these guys on their own ground. I don't let them give me shit or anything."

Inconspicuously, Henry slipped behind Cloke's chair to where Charles stood, and leaned over and whispered something in his ear. I saw Charles nod tersely.

"Not that they don't try to fuck with you," said Cloke. "But I know how they think. Now Bunny, he doesn't have a clue, he thinks it's some kind of a game with hundred-dollar bills just lying on the ground, waiting for some stupid kid to come along and pick them up. . . ."

By the time he stopped talking, Charles and Henry had completed whatever business they'd been discussing and Charles had gone to the closet for his overcoat. Cloke reached for his sunglasses and stood up. He had a faint, dry smell of herbs, an echo of the pothead smell that always lingered in the dusty corridors of Durbinstall: patchouli oil, clove cigarettes, incense.

Charles wound the scarf around his neck. His expression was at once casual and turbulent; his eyes were distant and his mouth was steady, but his nostrils flared slightly with his breathing.

"Be careful," Camilla said.

She was talking to Charles, but Cloke turned and smiled. "Piece of cake," he said.

———

She walked with them to the door. As soon as she shut it behind them she turned around.

Henry put a finger to his lips.

We listened to their footsteps going down the stairs, and were quiet until we heard Cloke's car start. Henry went to the window and pulled aside a shabby lace curtain. "They're gone," he said.

"Henry, are you sure this is a good idea?" said Camilla.

He shrugged, still looking at the street below. "I don't know," he said. "I had to play that one by ear."

"I wish **you'd** gone. Why didn't you go with him?"

"I would have, but this is better."

"What did you say to him?"

"Well, it should be pretty obvious even to Cloke that Bunny isn't out of town. Everything he owns is in that room. Money, extra glasses, winter coat. Odds are that Cloke will want to leave, and not say anything, but I told Charles to insist that they at least call Marion over for a look. If **she** sees—well. She doesn't know a thing about Cloke's problems and wouldn't care if she did. Unless I'm mistaken she'll call the police, or Bunny's parents at the very least, and I doubt Cloke will be able to stop her."

"They won't find him today," said Francis. "It'll be dark in a couple of hours."

"Yes, but if we're lucky they'll start looking first thing tomorrow."

"Do you think anyone will want to talk to us about it?"

"I don't know," said Henry abstractedly. "I don't know how they go about such things."

A thin ray of sun struck the prisms of a candelabrum on the mantelpiece, throwing brilliant, trembling shards of light that were distorted by the slant of the dormer walls. All of a sudden, images from every crime movie I'd ever seen began to pop into my mind—the windowless room, the harsh lights and narrow hallways, images which did not seem so much theatrical or foreign as imbued with the indelible quality of memory, of experience lived. **Don't think, don't think,** I told myself, looking fixedly at a bright, cold pool of sunlight soaking into the rug near my feet.

Camilla tried to light a cigarette, but one match and then another went out. Henry took the box from her and struck one himself; it flared up high and strong and she leaned close to it, one hand cupped around the flame and the other resting upon his wrist.

———

The minutes crept by with a torturous slowness. Camilla brought a bottle of whiskey into the kitchen and we sat around the table playing euchre, Francis and Henry against Camilla and me. Camilla played well—this was her game, her favorite—but I wasn't a good partner and we lost trick after trick to the others.

The apartment was very still: clink of glasses, ruffle of cards. Henry's sleeves were rolled above his elbows and the sun glinted metallic off Francis's pince-nez. I did my best to concentrate on the game but again and again I found myself staring, through the open door, at the clock on the mantel in the next room. It was one of those bizarre pieces of Victorian bric-a-brac that the twins were so fond of—a white china elephant with the clock balanced in a howdah, and a little black mahout in gilt turban and breeches to strike the hours. There was something diabolical about the mahout, and every time I looked up I found him grinning at me in an attitude of cheerful malice.

I lost count of the score, lost count of the games. The room grew dim.

Henry laid down his cards. "March," he said.

"I'm sick of this," said Francis. "Where is he?"

The clock ticked loudly, a jangling, arrhythmic tick. We sat in the fading light, the cards forgotten. Camilla took an apple from a bowl on the counter and sat in the windowsill, eating it morosely and looking down at the street below. A fiery outline of twilight shone around her silhouette, burned red-gold in her hair, grew diffuse in the fuzzy texture of the woolen skirt pulled carelessly about her knees.

"Maybe something went wrong," Francis said.

"Don't be ridiculous. What could go wrong?"

"A million things. Maybe Charles lost his head or something."

Henry gave him a fishy look. "Calm down," he said. "I don't know where you get all these Dostoyevsky sorts of ideas."

Francis was about to reply when Camilla jumped up. "He's coming," she said.

Henry stood up. "Where? Is he alone?"

"Yes," said Camilla, running to the door.

She ran down to meet him on the landing and in a few moments the two of them were back.

Charles's eyes were wild and his hair was disordered. He took off his coat, threw it on a chair, flung himself on the couch. "Somebody make me a drink," he said.

"Is everything all right?"

"Yes."

"What happened?"

"Where's that drink?"

Impatiently, Henry splashed some whiskey in a dirty glass and shoved it at him. "Did it go well? Did the police come?"

Charles took a long swallow, winced and nodded.

"Where's Cloke? At home?"

"I guess."

"Tell us everything from the first."

Charles finished the glass and set it down. His face was a damp, feverish red. "You were right about that room," he said.

"What do you mean?"

"It was eerie. Terrible. Bed unmade, dust everywhere, half an old Twinkie lying on his desk and ants crawling all over it. Cloke got scared and wanted to leave, but I called Marion before he could. She was there in a few minutes. Looked around, seemed kind of stunned, didn't say much. Cloke was very agitated."

"Did he tell her about the drug business?"

"No. He hinted at it, more than once, but she wasn't paying much attention to him." He looked up. "You know, Henry," he said abruptly, "I think we made a bad mistake by not going down there first. We should've gone through that room ourselves before either of them even saw it."

"Why do you say that?"

"Look what I found." He pulled a piece of paper from his pocket.

Henry took it from him quickly and looked it over. "How did you get this?"

He shrugged. "Luck. It was on top of his desk. I slipped it off the first chance I had."

I looked over Henry's shoulder. It was a Xerox of a page of the Hampden **Examiner**. Wedged between a column by the Home Extension Service and a chopped-off ad for garden hoes, there was a small but conspicuous headline.

MYSTERIOUS DEATH IN
BATTENKILL COUNTY

Battenkill County Sheriff Department, along with Hampden police, are still investigating the brutal November 12 homicide of Harry Ray McRee. The mutilated corpse of Mr. McRee, a poultry farmer and former member of the Egg Producers Association of Vermont, was found upon his Mechanicsville farm. Robbery did not appear to be a motive, and though Mr. McRee was known to have several enemies, both in the chicken-and-egg business and in Battenkill county at large, none of these are suspects in the slaying.

Horrified, I leaned closer—the word **mutilated** had electrified me, it was the only thing I could see on the page—but Henry had turned the paper over and begun to study the other side. "Well," he said, "at least this isn't a photocopy of a clipping. Odds are he did this at the library, from the school's copy."

"I hope you're right but that doesn't mean it's the only copy."

Henry put the paper in the ashtray and struck the match. When he touched it to the edge a bright red seam crawled up the side, then licked suddenly over the whole thing; the words were illumined for a moment before they curled and darkened. "Well," he said, "it's too late now. At least you got this one. What happened next?"

"Well, Marion left. She went next door to Putnam House and came back with a friend."

"Who?"

"I don't know her. Uta or Ursula or something. One of those Swedish-looking girls who wears fishermen's sweaters all the time. Anyway, she had a look around, too, and Cloke was just sitting there on the bed smoking a cigarette and looking like his stomach hurt him, and finally she—this Uta or whatever—suggested we go upstairs and tell Bunny's house chairperson."

Francis started laughing. At Hampden, the house chairpeople were who you complained to if your storm windows didn't work or someone was playing their stereo too loud.

"Well, it's a good thing she did or we might still be standing there," said Charles. "It was that loud, red-haired girl who wears hiking boots all the time—what's her name? Briony Dillard?"

"Yes," I said. Besides being a house chairperson and a vigorous member of the student council, she was also the president of a leftist group off campus, and was always trying to mobilize the youth of Hampden in the face of crushing indifference.

"Well, she barged right in and got the show on the road," said Charles. "Took our names. Asked a bunch of questions. Herded Bunny's neighbors into the hall and asked **them** questions. Called Student Services, then Security. Security said they would send somebody over"—he lit a cigarette—"but it really wasn't their jurisdiction, a student disappearance, and that she should call the police. Will you get me another drink?" he said, turning abruptly to Camilla.

"And they came?"

Charles, cigarette balanced between his first and middle fingers, wiped the sweat from his forehead with the heel of his hand. "Yes," he said. "Two of them. And a couple of security guards as well."

"What did they do?"

"The security guards didn't do anything. But the policemen were actually kind of efficient. One of them looked around the room while the other herded everybody in the hall and started asking questions."

"What kind of questions?"

"Who'd seen him last and where, how long he'd been gone, where he might be. It all sounds pretty obvious but that was the first time anyone had even asked."

"Did Cloke say anything?"

"Not much. It was very confused, a lot of people around, most of them dying to tell what they knew, which was nothing. No one paid any attention to me at all. This lady who'd come down from Student Services kept trying to butt in, acting very officious and saying it wasn't a police matter, that the school would handle it. Finally one of the policemen got mad. 'Look,' he said, 'what's the matter with you people? This boy's been missing for a solid week and nobody's even mentioned it till now. This is serious business and if you want my two cents, I think the school may be at fault.' Well, that really got the lady from Student Services going and then, all of a sudden, the policeman in the room came out with Bunny's wallet.

"Everything got very quiet. There was two hundred dollars in it, and all of Bunny's ID. The policeman who'd found it said, 'I think we'd better contact this boy's family.' Everyone started whispering. The lady from Student Services got very white and said she'd go up to her office and get Bunny's file immediately. The policeman went with her.

"By this time the hall was absolutely mobbed. They'd trickled in from outdoors and were hanging around to see what was going on. The first policeman told them to go home and mind their own business, and Cloke slid away in the confusion. Before he left, he pulled me aside and told me again not to mention that drug business."

"I hope you waited until you were told you could leave."

"I did. It wasn't much longer. The policeman wanted to talk to Marion, and he told me and this Uta we could go home once he'd taken our names and stuff. That was about an hour ago."

"Then why are you just getting back?"

"I'm coming to that. I didn't want to run into anybody on the way home, so I cut across the back of campus, down behind the faculty offices. That was a big mistake. I hadn't even got to the birch grove when that troublemaker from Student Services—the lady who started the fight—saw me from out the window of the Dean's office and called for me to come in."

"What was she doing in the Dean's office?"

"Using the WATS line. They had Bunny's father on the telephone—he was yelling at everybody, threatening to sue. The Dean of Studies was trying to calm him down, but Mr. Corcoran kept asking to talk to someone he knew. They'd tried to get you on another line, Henry, but you weren't home."

"Had he asked to talk to me?"

"Apparently. They were about to send someone up to the Lyceum for Julian, but then this lady saw me out the window. There were about a million people there—the policeman, the Dean's secretary, four or five people from down the hall, that nutty lady who works in Records. Next door, in the admissions office, somebody was trying to get hold of the President. There were some teachers hanging around, too. I guess the Dean of Studies was in the middle of a conference when the lady from Student Services came bursting in with the policeman. Your friend was there, Richard. Doctor Roland.

"Anyway. The crowd parted when I came in and the Dean of Studies handed me the telephone. Mr. Corcoran calmed down when he realized who I was. Got all confidential and asked me if this wasn't some type of frat stunt."

"Oh, God," said Francis.

Charles looked at him out of the corner of his eye. "He asked about you. 'Where's the old Carrot-Top,' he said."

"What else did he say?"

"He was very nice. Asked about you all, really. Said to tell everybody that he said hi."

There was a long, uncomfortable pause.

Henry bit his lower lip and went to the liquor cabinet to pour himself a drink. "Did anything," he said, "come up about that bank business?"

"Yes. Marion gave them the girl's name. By the way"—when he looked up, his eyes were distracted, blank—"I forgot to tell you earlier, but Marion gave your name to the police. Yours too, Francis."

"Why?" said Francis, alarmed. "What for?"

"Who were his friends? They wanted to know."

"But why **me**?"

"Calm down, Francis."

The light in the room was gone. The skies were lilac-colored and the snowy streets had a surreal, lunar glow. Henry turned on the lamp. "Do you think they'll start looking tonight?"

"They'll look for him, certainly. Whether they'll look in the right place is something else."

No one said anything for a moment. Charles, thoughtfully, rattled the ice in his glass. "You know," he said, "we've done a terrible thing."

"We had to, Charles, as we have all discussed."

"I know, but I can't stop thinking about Mr. Corcoran. The holidays we've spent at his house. And he was so sweet on the telephone."

"We're all a lot better off."

"Some of us are, you mean."

Henry smiled acidly. "Oh, I don't know," he said. "Πελλαίου βοῦς μέγας εἰν ᾽Αίδη."

This was something to the effect that, in the Underworld, a great ox costs only a penny, but I knew what he meant and in spite of myself I laughed. There was a tradition among the ancients that things were very cheap in Hell.

———

When Henry left, he offered to drive me back to school. It was late, and when we pulled up behind the dormitory I asked him if he wanted to come to Commons and have some dinner.

We stopped in the post office so Henry could check his mail. He went to his mailbox only about every three weeks so there was quite a stack waiting for him; he stood by the trash can, going through it indifferently, throwing half the envelopes away unopened. Then he stopped.

"What is it?"

He laughed. "Look in your mailbox. It's a faculty questionnaire. Julian's up for review."

They were closing the dining hall by the time we arrived, and the janitors had already started to mop the floor. The kitchen was closed, too, so I went to ask for some peanut butter and bread while Henry made himself a cup of tea. The main dining room was deserted. We sat at a table in the corner, our reflections mirrored in the black of the plate-glass windows. Henry took out a pen and began to fill out Julian's evaluation.

I looked at my own copy while I ate my sandwich. The questions were ranked from one—poor to five—excellent: **Is this faculty member prompt? Well-prepared? Ready to offer help outside the classroom?** Henry, without the slightest pause, had gone down the list and circled all fives. Now I saw him writing the number 19 in a blank.

"What's that for?"

"The number of classes I've taken with Julian," he said, without looking up.

"You've taken **nineteen classes** with Julian?"

"Well, that's tutorials and everything," he said, irritated.

For a moment there was no sound except the scratching of Henry's pen and the distant crash of dish racks in the kitchen.

"Does everybody get these, or just us?" I said.

"Just us."

"I wonder why they even bother."

"For their records, I suppose." He had turned to the last page, which was mostly blank. **Please elaborate here on any additional compliments or criticisms you may have of this teacher. Extra sheets of paper may be attached if necessary.**

His pen hovered over the paper. Then he folded the sheet and pushed it aside.

"What," I said, "aren't you going to write anything?"

Henry took a sip of his tea. "How," he said, "can I possibly make the Dean of Studies understand that there is a divinity in our midst?"

———

After dinner, I went back to my room. I dreaded the thought of the night ahead, but not for the reasons one might expect—that I was worried about the police, or that my conscience bothered me, or anything of the sort. Quite the contrary. By that time, by some purely subconscious means, I had developed a successful mental block about the murder and everything pertaining to it. I talked about it in select company but seldom thought of it when alone.

What I did experience when alone was a sort of general neurotic horror, a common attack of nerves and self-loathing magnified to the power of ten. Every cruel or fatuous thing I'd ever said came back to me with an amplified clarity, no matter how I talked to myself or jerked my head to shake the thoughts away: old insults and guilts and embarrassments stretching clear back to childhood—the crippled boy I'd made fun of, the Easter chick I'd squeezed to death—paraded before me one by one, in vivid and mordant splendor.

I tried to work on Greek but it wasn't much good. I would look up a word in the lexicon only to forget it when I turned to write it down; my noun cases, my verb forms, had left me utterly. Around midnight I went downstairs and called the twins. Camilla answered the phone. She was sleepy, a little drunk and getting ready for bed.

"Tell me a funny story," I said.

"I can't think of any funny stories."

"**Any** story."

"Cinderella? The Three Bears?"

"Tell me something that happened to you when you were little."

So she told me about the only time she remembered seeing her father, before he and her mother were killed. It was snowing, she said, and Charles was asleep, and she was standing in her crib looking out the window. Her father was out in the yard in an old gray sweater, throwing snowballs against the side of the fence. "It must have been about the middle of the afternoon. I don't know what he was doing there. All I know is that I saw him, and I wanted to go out **so** bad, and I was trying to climb out of my crib and go to him. Then my grandmother came in and put the bars up so I couldn't get out, and I started to cry. My uncle Hilary—he was my grandmother's brother, he lived with us when we were little—came in the room and saw me crying. 'Poor little girl,' he said. He rummaged around in his pockets, and finally he found a tape measure and gave it to me to play with."

"A tape measure?"

"Yes. You know, the ones that snap in when

you push a button. Charles and I used to fight over it all the time. It's still at home some- where."

———

Late the next morning I woke with an unpleas- ant start to a knock at my door.

I opened it to find Camilla, who looked as if she'd dressed in a hurry. She came in and locked the door behind her while I stood blinking sleepily in my bathrobe. "Have you been outside today?" she said.

A spider of anxiety crawled up the back of my neck. I sat down on the side of my bed. "No," I said. "Why?"

"I don't know **what's** going on. The police are talking to Charles and Henry, and I don't even know where Francis is."

"What?"

"A policeman came by and asked for Charles around seven this morning. He didn't say what he wanted. Charles got dressed and they went off together and then, at eight, I got a call from Henry. He asked if I'd mind if he was a little late this morning? And I asked what he was talking about, because we hadn't planned to meet. 'Oh, thanks,' he said, 'I knew you'd un- derstand, the police are here about Bunny, you see, and they want to ask some questions.' "

"I'm sure it'll be all right."

She ran a hand through her hair, in an exasperated gesture reminiscent of her brother. "But it's not just that," she said. "There are people all over the place. Reporters. Police. It's like a madhouse."

"Are they looking for him?"

"I don't know **what** they're doing. They seem to be headed up towards Mount Cataract."

"Maybe we should leave campus for a while."

Her pale, silvery glance skittered anxiously around my room. "Maybe," she said. "Get dressed and we'll decide what to do."

———

I was in the bathroom scraping a quick razor over my face when Judy Poovey came in and rushed over so fast I cut my cheek. "Richard," she said, her hand on my arm. "Have you heard?"

I touched my face and looked at the blood on my fingertips, then glanced at her, annoyed. "Heard what?"

"About Bunny," she said, her voice hushed and her eyes wide.

I stared at her, not knowing what she was going to say.

"Jack Teitelbaum told me. Cloke was talking to him about it last night. I never heard of anybody just, like, **vanishing**. It's too weird. And Jack was saying, well, if they haven't found him by now. . . . I mean, I'm sure he's all right and everything," she said when she saw the way I was looking at her.

I couldn't think of anything to say.

"If you want to stop by or anything, I'll be at home."

"Sure."

"I mean, if you want to talk or something. I'm always there. Just stop by."

"Thanks," I said, a little too abruptly.

She looked up at me, her eyes large with compassion, with understanding of the solitude and incivility of grief. "It'll be okay," she said, giving my arm a squeeze, and then she left, pausing in the door for a sorrowful backwards glance.

———

Despite what Camilla had said, I was unprepared for the riot of activity outside. The parking lot was full and people from Hampden town were everywhere—factory workers mostly, from the looks of them, some with lunch boxes, others with children—beating the ground with sticks and making their way towards Mount Cataract in broad, straggling lines as students milled about and looked at them curiously. There were policemen, deputies, a state trooper or two; on the lawn, parked beside a couple of official-looking vehicles, was a remote radio-station hookup, a concessions truck, and a van from ActionNews Twelve.

"What are all these people doing here?" I said.

"Look," she said. "Is that Francis?"

Far away, in the busy multitude, I saw a flash of red hair, the conspicuous line of muffled throat and black greatcoat. Camilla stuck up her hand and yelled to him.

He shouldered his way through a bunch of cafeteria workers who had come outside to see what was going on. He was smoking a cigarette; there was a newspaper tucked under his arm. "Hello," he said. "Can you believe this?"

"What's going on?"

"A treasure hunt."

"What?"

"The Corcorans put up a big reward in the night. All the factories in Hampden are closed. Anybody want some coffee? I have a dollar."

We picked our way to the concessions truck, through a sparse, gloomy gathering of janitors and maintenance men.

"Three coffees, two with milk, please," said Francis to the fat woman behind the counter.

"No milk, just Cremora."

"Well, then, just black, I guess." He turned to us. "Have you seen the paper this morning?"

It was a late edition of the Hampden **Examiner**. In a column on the first page was a blurry, recent photograph of Bunny and under it this caption: POLICE, KIN, SEEK YOUTH, 24, MISSING IN HAMPDEN.

"Twenty-four?" I said, startled. The twins and I were twenty years old, and Henry and Francis were twenty-one.

"He failed a grade or two in elementary school," said Camilla.

"Ahh."

> Sunday afternoon Edmund Corcoran, a Hampden College student known to his family and friends as "Bunny," attended a campus party which he apparently left some time in the middle of the afternoon in order to meet his girlfriend Marion Barnbridge of Rye, New York, also a student at Hampden. That was the last that anyone has seen of Bunny Corcoran.
>
> The concerned Barnbridge, along with friends of Corcoran's, yesterday alerted state and local police, who put out a Missing Persons Bulletin. Today the search begins in the Hampden area. The missing youth is described as
> (See p. 5)

"Are you finished?" I asked Camilla.
"Yes. Turn the page."

being six feet, three inches tall, weighing 190 pounds, with sandy blond hair and blue eyes. He wears glasses, and when last seen was wearing a gray tweed sports coat, khaki pants, and a yellow rain slicker.

"Here's your coffee, Richard," said Francis, turning gingerly with a cup in either hand.

At St. Jerome's preparatory school in College Falls, Massachusetts, Corcoran was active in varsity sports, lettering in hockey, lacrosse and crew and leading his football team, the Wolverines, to a state championship when he captained during senior year. At Hampden Corcoran served as a volunteer fire marshall. He studied literature and languages, with a concentration in Classics, and was described by fellow students as "a scholar."

"Ha," said Camilla.

Cloke Rayburn, a school friend of Corcoran's and one of those who first notified police, said that Corcoran "is a real straight guy—definitely not mixed up in drugs or anything like that."

Yesterday afternoon, after growing suspicious, he broke into Corcoran's dormitory room, and subsequently notified police.

"That's not right," Camilla said. "He didn't call them."

"There's not a word about Charles."

"Thank God," she said, in Greek.

Corcoran's parents, Macdonald and Katherine Corcoran of Shady Brook, Connecticut, arrive in Hampden today to assist in the search for the youngest of their five children. (See "A Family Prays," p. 10.) In a telephone interview Mr. Corcoran, who is president of the Bingham Bank and Trust Company and a member of the Board of Directors of the First National Bank of Connecticut, said, "There's not much we can do down here. We want to assist if we can." He said that he had spoken to his son by telephone a week before the disappearance and had noticed nothing unusual.

Of her son, Katherine Corcoran said:

"Edmund is a very family-oriented type person. If anything was wrong I know he would have told Mack or myself."

A reward of fifty thousand dollars is being offered for information leading to the whereabouts of Edmund Corcoran, provided through contributions from the Corcoran family, the Bingham Bank and Trust Company, and the Highland Heights Lodge of the Loyal Order of the Moose.

The wind was blowing. With Camilla's help, I folded the newspaper and handed it back to Francis. "Fifty thousand dollars," I said. "That's a lot of money."

"And you wonder why you see all these people from Hampden town up here this morning?" said Francis, taking a sip of his coffee. "Gosh, it's cold out here."

We turned and started back towards Commons. Camilla said to Francis: "You know about Charles and Henry, don't you?"

"Well, they told Charles they might want to talk to him, didn't they?"

"But Henry?"

"I wouldn't waste my time worrying about him."

Commons was overheated and surprisingly

empty. The three of us sat on a clammy, black vinyl couch and drank our coffee. People drifted in and out, bringing blasts of cold air from outdoors; some of them came over to ask if there was any news. Jud "Party Pig" MacKenna, as Vice-president of the Student Council, came over with his empty paint can to ask if we would like to donate to an emergency search fund. Between us, we contributed a dollar in change.

We were talking to Georges Laforgue, who was telling us enthusiastically and at great length about a similar disappearance at Brandeis when suddenly, from nowhere, Henry appeared behind him.

Laforgue turned. "Oh," he said coldly when he saw who it was.

Henry inclined his head slightly. **"Bonjour, Monsieur Laforgue,"** he said. **"Quel plaisir de vous revoir."**

Laforgue, with a flourish, took a handkerchief from his pocket and blew his nose for what seemed about five minutes; then, refolding the handkerchief into fussy little squares, he turned his back on Henry and resumed his story. It happened, in this case, that the student had simply gone off to New York City on the bus without telling anybody.

"And this boy—Birdie, is it?"

"Bunny."

"Yes. This boy has been away for far less long. He will appear again, of his own accord, and everyone will feel very foolish." He lowered his voice. "I believe that the school is afraid of a lawsuit, and that perhaps is why they lost their sense of proportion, no? Please do not repeat me."

"Of course not."

"My position is delicate with the Dean, you understand."

———

"I'm a bit tired," Henry said later, in the car, "but there's nothing to worry about."

"What'd they want to know?"

"Nothing much. How long had I known him, was he acting strangely, did I know any reason why he might have decided to leave school. Of course, he **has** been acting strangely the last few months, and I said so. But I also said I hadn't seen very much of him lately, which is true." He shook his head. "Honestly. **Two hours**. I don't know if I could've made myself go through with this if I'd known what nonsense we were letting ourselves in for."

———

We stopped by the twins' apartment and found Charles asleep on the couch, sprawled on his stomach in his shoes and overcoat, one arm dangling over the edge so that three or four inches of wrist and an equal amount of cuff were exposed.

He woke with a start. His face was puffy and the ridged pattern from the sofa cushions was printed deeply on his cheek.

"How did it go?" said Henry.

Charles sat up a bit and rubbed his eyes. "All right, I guess," he said. "They wanted me to sign some thing that said what happened yesterday."

"They visited me as well."

"Really? What'd they want?"

"The same questions."

"Were they nice to you?"

"Not particularly."

"God, they were **so nice** to me down at the police station. They even gave me breakfast. Coffee and jelly doughnuts."

———

This was a Friday, which meant no classes, and that Julian was not in Hampden but at home. His house was not far from where we were— halfway to Albany, where we'd driven to have pancakes at a truck stop—and after lunch Henry suggested, quite out of the blue, that we drive by and see if he was there.

I had never been in Julian's house, had never even seen it, though I assumed the rest of them had been there a hundred times. Actually—

Henry being of course the notable exception—Julian did not allow many visitors. This was not so surprising as it sounds; he kept a gentle but firm distance between himself and his students; and though he was much more fond of us than teachers generally are of their pupils, it was not, even with Henry, a relationship of equals, and our classes with him ran more along the lines of benevolent dictatorship than democracy. "I am your teacher," he once said, "because I know more than you do." Though on a psychological level his manner was almost painfully intimate, superficially it was businesslike and cold. He refused to see anything about any of us except our most engaging qualities, which he cultivated and magnified to the exclusion of all our tedious and less desirable ones. While I felt a delicious pleasure in adjusting myself to fit this attractive if inaccurate image—and, eventually, in finding that I had more or less become the character which for a long time I had so skillfully played—there was never any doubt that he did not wish to see us in our entirety, or see us, in fact, in anything other than the magnificent roles he had invented for us: **genis gratus, corpore glabellus, arte multiscius, et fortuna opulentus**—smooth-cheeked, soft-skinned, well-educated, and rich. It was his odd blindness, I think, to all problems of a personal nature which made him able at the end to transmute even Bunny's highly substantive troubles into spiritual ones.

I knew then, and know now, virtually nothing about Julian's life outside of the classroom, which is perhaps what lent such a tantalizing breath of mystery to everything he said or did. No doubt his personal life was as flawed as anyone's, but the only side of himself he ever allowed us to see was polished to such a high gloss of perfection that it seemed when he was away from us he must lead an existence too rarefied for me to even imagine.

So, naturally, I was curious to see where he lived. It was a large stone house, set on a hill, miles off the main road and nothing but trees and snow as far as one could see—imposing enough, but not half so Gothic and monstrous as Francis's. I had heard marvelous tales of his garden, also of the inside of the house—Attic vases, Meissen porcelain, paintings by Alma-Tadema and Frith. But the garden was covered with snow, and Julian, apparently, was not at home; at least he didn't answer the door.

Henry looked back down the hill to where we waited in the car. He reached into his pocket for a piece of paper and scribbled a note that he folded and wedged in the crack of the door.

"Are there students out with the search parties?" Henry asked on the way back to Hampden. "I don't want to go down there if we'll be making ourselves conspicuous. But on the other hand, it does seem rather callous, don't you think, to just go home?"

He was quiet a moment, thinking. "Maybe we should have a look," he said. "Charles, you've done quite enough for one day. Maybe you should just go home."

———

After we dropped the twins off, the three of us went on to campus. I had expected that by now the search party would have grown tired and gone home but I was surprised to find the enterprise busier than ever. There were policemen, college administrators, Boy Scouts, maintenance workers and security guards, about thirty Hampden students (some in an official, student-councily-looking group, the rest just along for the ride), and mobs of townspeople. It was a large assembly, but as the three of us looked down at it from the top of the rise, it seemed oddly muffled and small in the great expanse of snow.

We went down the hill—Francis, sulky because he hadn't wanted to come, followed two or three paces behind—and wandered through the crowd. No one paid us the least bit of attention. Behind me I heard the indistinct, aborted garble of a walkie-talkie; and, startled, I walked backwards into the Chief of Security.

"Watch it," he shouted. He was a squat, bulldoggish man with liver spots on his nose and jowls.

"Sorry," I said hastily. "Can you tell me what—"

"College kids," he muttered, turning his head away as if to spit. "Stumbling around, getting in the way, don't know what the hell you're supposed to do."

"Well, that's what we're trying to find out," snapped Henry.

The guard turned quickly, and somehow his gaze landed not on Henry but on Francis, who was standing staring into space. "So it's you, is it?" he said with venom. "Mr. Off-Campus who thinks he can park in the faculty parking lot."

Francis started, a wild look in his eye.

"Yes, **you.** You know how many unpaid violations you're carrying? **Nine.** I turned your registration in to the Dean just last week. They can put you on probation, hold your transcripts, what have you. Suspend your library privileges. If it was up to me they'd put you in jail."

Francis gaped at him. Henry caught him by the sleeve and pulled him away.

A long, straggly line of townspeople was

crunching through the snow, some of them swiping listlessly at the ground with sticks. We walked to the end of the queue, then fell into step with them.

The knowledge that Bunny's body actually lay about two miles to the southwest did not lend much interest or urgency to the search, and I plodded along in a daze, my eyes on the ground. At the front of the rank an authoritative cluster of state troopers and policemen marched ahead, heads bent, talking in low voices as a barking German shepherd dog circled around them at a trot. The air had a heavy quality and the sky over the mountains was overcast and stormy. Francis's coat whipped out behind him in theatrical billows; he kept glancing furtively around to see if his inquisitor was anywhere nearby and from time to time he emitted a faint, self-pitying cough.

"Why the hell haven't you paid those parking tickets?" Henry whispered to him.

"Leave me alone."

We crept through the snow for what seemed like hours, until the energetic needle pricks in my feet subsided to an uncomfortable numbness; heavy boots of policemen, crunching black in the snow, night sticks swinging ponderously from heavy belts. A helicopter overhead swooped in with a roar over the trees, hovered above us for a moment, then darted back the way it had come. The light was thinning and people were trailing up the trampled hillside towards home.

"Let's go," said Francis, for the fourth or fifth time.

We were starting away at last when a strolling policeman stopped in front of our path. "Had enough?" he said, smiling, a big red-faced guy with a red moustache.

"I believe so," said Henry.

"You kids know that boy?"

"As a matter of fact, we do."

"No ideas where he might of went off to?"

If this was a movie, I thought, looking pleasantly into the pleasant beefy face of the policeman—**if this was a movie, we'd all be fidgeting and acting really suspicious.**

"How much does a television cost?" said Henry on the way home.

"Why?"

"Because I'd like to see the news tonight."

"I think they're kind of expensive," said Francis.

"There's a television in the attic of Monmouth," I said.

"Does it belong to anyone?"

"I'm sure it does."

"Well," said Henry, "we'll take it back when we're finished with it."

Francis kept watch while Henry and I went up to the attic and searched through broken lamps, cardboard boxes, ugly Art I oil paintings. Finally we found the television behind an old rabbit hutch and carried it down the stairs to Henry's car. On the way over to Francis's, we stopped by for the twins.

"The Corcorans have been trying to get in touch with you this afternoon," said Camilla to Henry.

"Mr. Corcoran's called half a dozen times."

"Julian called, too. He's very upset."

"And Cloke," said Charles.

Henry stopped. "What did he want?"

"He wanted to make sure that you and I hadn't said anything about drugs when we talked to the police this morning."

"What did you tell him?"

"I said I hadn't, but I didn't know about you."

"Come on," said Francis, glancing at his watch. "We're going to miss it if you don't hurry."

———

We put the television on Francis's dining room table and fooled around with it until we got a decent picture. The final credits of "Petticoat Junction" were rolling past, over shots of the Hooterville water tower, the Cannonball express.

The news was next. As the theme song died

away, a small circle appeared in the left-hand corner of the newscaster's desk; within it was a stylized picture of a policeman shining a flashlight and holding a straining dog back by a leash and, underneath, the word MANHUNT.

The newscaster looked at the camera. "Hundreds search and thousands pray," she said, "as the hunt for Hampden College student Edmund Corcoran begins in the Hampden area."

The picture shifted to a pan of a thickly wooded area; a line of searchers, filmed from behind, beat in the underbrush with sticks, while the German shepherd dog we had seen earlier laughed and barked at us from the screen.

"Where are you guys?" said Camilla. "Are you in there somewhere?"

"Look," said Francis. "There's that horrible man."

"One hundred volunteers," said the voice-over, "arrived this morning to help Hampden College students in the search for their classmate, who has been missing since Sunday afternoon. Until now there have been no leads in the search for the twenty-four-year-old Edmund Corcoran, of Shady Brook, Connecticut, but ActionNews Twelve has just received an important phone tip which authorities think may provide a new angle in the case."

"What?" said Charles, to the television set.

"We go now to Rick Dobson, live on the scene."

The picture switched to a man in a trench coat, holding a microphone and standing in front of what appeared to be a gas station.

"I know that place," said Francis, leaning forward. "That's Redeemed Repair on Highway 6."

"Ssh," somebody said.

The wind was blowing hard. The microphone shrieked, then died down with a sputtering noise. "This afternoon," the reporter said, chin low, "at one-fifty-six p.m., Action-News Twelve received an important piece of information which may provide a break for police in the recent Hampden missing-persons case."

The camera pulled back to reveal an old man in coveralls, a woolen cap, and a greasy dark windbreaker. He was staring to the side in a fixed manner; his head was round and his face as bland and untroubled as a baby's.

"I am now with William Hundy," the reporter said, "co-owner of Redeemed Repair in Hampden, a member of the Hampden County Rescue Squad who has just come forward with this information."

"Henry," said Francis. I was startled to see that his face had all of a sudden got very white.

Henry reached in his pocket for a cigarette. "Yes," he said tersely. "I see."

"What's the matter?" I said.

Henry tamped the cigarette down on the side of the pack. He didn't take his eyes from the screen. "That man," he said, "fixes my car."

"Mr. Hundy," said the reporter, "will you tell us what you saw on Sunday afternoon?"

"Oh, my God," said Charles.

"Hush," said Henry.

The mechanic glanced shyly at the camera, and then away. "Sunday afternoon," he said, in a nasal Vermont voice, "there was a cream-colored LeMans, few years old, pulled up to that pump over there." Awkwardly, as an afterthought, he raised his arm and pointed somewhere off camera. "It was three men, two in the front seat, one in the back. Out-of-towners. Seemed in a hurry. Wouldn't have thought a thing of it except that boy was with them. I recognized him when I saw his picture in the paper."

My heart had nearly stopped—**three men, white car**—but then the details registered. We were four, with Camilla, too, and Bunny hadn't been anywhere near the car on Sunday. And Henry drove a BMW, which was far from a Pontiac.

Henry had stopped tapping the unlit cigarette on the side of the pack; it dangled loosely between his fingers.

"Although no ransom note has been received by the Corcoran family, authorities have not yet ruled out the possibility of kidnapping. This is Rick Dobson, reporting live from ActionNews Twelve."

"Thank you, Rick. If any of our viewers have further information on this or any other story, they are urged to call our Tips Line, 363-TIPS, between the hours of nine and five. . . .

"Today the Hampden County School Board took a vote on what may be the most controversial . . ."

We stared at the television in astonished silence for what seemed several minutes. Finally the twins looked at each other and started to laugh.

Henry shook his head, still looking incredulously at the screen. **"Vermonters,"** he said.

"Do you know this man?" said Charles.

"I've taken my car to him for the last two years."

"Is he crazy?"

He shook his head again. "Crazy, lying, out for the reward. I don't know what to say. He always seemed sane enough, though he did drag me off in a corner once and start talking about Christ's kingdom on earth."

"Well, for whatever reason," said Francis, "he's done us a tremendous favor."

"I don't know," said Henry. "Kidnapping is a serious crime. If this turns into a criminal investigation they may stumble across something we'd rather they didn't know."

"How could they? What does any of this have to do with us?"

"I don't mean anything big. But there are a great many little things which would be just as damning if anyone took the trouble to add them up. I was a fool to put those plane tickets on my credit card, for instance. We'd have a difficult time explaining **that**. And your trust fund, Francis? And our bank accounts? Massive withdrawals over the last six months, and nothing to show for it. Bunny's got an awful lot of new clothes hanging in his closet that he couldn't possibly have paid for himself."

"Somebody would have to dig pretty deep to find that."

"Someone would only have to make two or three well-placed phone calls."

Just then the telephone rang.

"Oh, God," Francis wailed.

"Don't answer it," said Henry.

But Francis picked it up anyway, as I knew he would. "Yes," he said carefully. Pause. "Well, hello to you too, Mr. Corcoran," he said, sitting down and giving us the OK signal with thumb and forefinger. "Have you heard any-thing?"

A very long pause. Francis listened atten-tively for some minutes, looking at the floor and nodding; after a while he began to bob his foot up and down impatiently.

"What's going on?" Charles whispered.

Francis held the phone away from his ear and made a gabby mouth sign with his hand.

"I know what he wants," Charles said bleakly. "He wants us to come over to his hotel and have dinner."

"Actually, sir, we've already had our dinner," Francis was saying. ". . . No, of course not. . . . Yes. Oh, yes sir, I've been trying to get in touch with you, but you know how confused things are. . . . Certainly. . . ."

Finally he hung up. We stared at him.

He shrugged. "Well," he said, "I tried. He's expecting us at the hotel in twenty minutes."

"Us?"

"I'm not going by myself."

"Is he alone?"

"No." Francis had drifted into the kitchen; we could hear him opening and shutting cabi-nets. "It's the whole crew except for Teddy, and they're expecting him any minute."

There was a slight pause.

"What are you doing in there?" said Henry.

"Making myself a drink."

"Make me one, too," said Charles.

"Scotch all right?"

"I'd rather bourbon if you've got it."

"Make that two," said Camilla.

"Just bring the whole bottle in, why don't you," Henry said.

———

After they left, I lay on Francis's couch, smoking his cigarettes and drinking his Scotch, and watched "Jeopardy." One of the contestants was from San Gilberto, which is really close to where I grew up, only five or six miles away. All those suburbs tend to run into one another out there, so you can't always tell where one ends and the next begins.

After that came a made-for-television movie. It was about the threat of the earth colliding with another planet and how all the scientists in the world united to avert the catastrophe. A hack astronomer, who is constantly on talk shows and whose name you would probably recognize, played himself in a cameo role.

For some reason, I felt uneasy about watching the news alone when it came on at eleven, so I turned to PBS and watched something called "History of Metallurgy." It was actually quite interesting, but I was tired and a bit drunk, and I fell asleep before it ended.

———

When I awoke, a blanket had been thrown over me, and the room was blue with a cold dawn light. Francis sat in the windowsill with his back to me; he was wearing his clothes from the night before and he was eating maraschino cherries from a jar balanced on his knee.

I sat up. "What time is it?"

"Six," he said without turning around, his mouth full.

"Why didn't you wake me up?"

"I didn't get in until four-thirty. Too drunk to drive you home. Want a cherry?"

He was still drunk. His collar was open and his clothes disordered; his voice was flat and toneless.

"Where were you all night?"

"With the Corcorans."

"Not **drinking**."

"Of course."

"Till four?"

"They were still going at it when we left. There were five or six cases of beer in the bathtub."

"I didn't know it was going to be a frivolous occasion."

"It was donated by the Food King," said Francis. "The beer, I mean. Mr. Corcoran and Brady got hold of some of it and brought it to the hotel."

"Where are they staying?"

"I don't know," he said dully. "Terrible place. One of those big flat motels with a neon sign and no room service. All the rooms were connected. Hugh's children screaming and throwing potato chips, the television going in every room. It was hell. . . . Really," he said humorlessly as I started to laugh, "I think I could get through anything after last night. Survive a nuclear war. Fly a plane. Somebody—one of those damned toddlers, I guess—got my favorite scarf off the bed and wrapped up part of a chicken leg in it. That nice silk one with the pattern of clocks on it. It's just ruined."

"Were they upset?"

"Who, the Corcorans? Of course not. I don't think they even noticed."

"I don't mean about the scarf."

"Oh." He got another cherry from the jar. "They were all upset I suppose, in a way. Nobody talked about much else but they didn't seem out of their **minds** or anything. Mr. Corcoran would act all sad and worried for a while, then the next thing you knew he'd be playing with the baby, giving everybody beer."

"Was Marion there?"

"Yes. Cloke, too. He went for a drive with Brady and Patrick and came back reeking of pot. Henry and I sat on the radiator all night and talked to Mr. Corcoran. I guess Camilla went over to say hello to Hugh and his wife and got trapped. I don't even know what happened to Charles."

After a moment or so, Francis shook his head. "I don't know," he said. "Does it ever strike you, in a horrible sort of way, how **funny** this is?"

"Well, it's not all that funny really."

"I guess not," he said, lighting a cigarette with shaky hands. "And Mr. Corcoran said the National Guard is coming up today, too. What a mess."

For some time I had been staring at the jar of cherries without realizing fully what they were. "Why are you eating those?" I said.

"I don't know," he said, staring down at the jar. "They taste really bad."

"Throw them away."

He struggled with the window sash. It sailed up with a grinding noise.

A blast of icy air hit me in the face. "Hey," I said.

He threw the jar out the window and then leaned on the sash with all his weight. I went over to help him. Finally, it crashed down, and the draperies floated down to rest placidly by the windows. The cherry juice had left a spattered red trajectory on the snow.

"Kind of a Jean Cocteau touch, isn't it?"

Francis said. "I'm exhausted. If you don't mind, I'm going to have a bath now."

———

He was running the water and I was on my way out when the phone rang.

It was Henry. "Oh," he said. "I'm sorry. I thought I dialed Francis."

"You did. Hold on a second." I put down the phone and called for him.

He came in in his trousers and undershirt, his face half-lathered, a razor in his hand. "Who is it?"

"Henry."

"Tell him I'm in the bath."

"He's in the bath," I said.

"He is not in the bath," said Henry. "He is standing in the room with you. I can hear him."

I gave Francis the telephone. He held it away from his face so he wouldn't get any soap on the receiver.

I could hear Henry talking indistinctly. After a moment, Francis's sleepy eyes widened.

"Oh, no," he said. "Not me."

Henry's voice again, curt and businesslike.

"No. I mean it, Henry. I'm tired and I'm going to sleep and there's no way—"

Suddenly, his face changed. To my great surprise he cursed loudly and slammed down the receiver so hard that it jangled.

"What is it?"

He was staring at the phone. "God damn him," he said. "He hung up on me."

"What's the matter?"

"He wants us to go out with that damn search party again. **Now**. I'm not like he is. I can't just **stay up** for five or six days at a—"

"Now? But it's so early."

"It started an hour ago, so he says. Damn him. Doesn't he ever sleep?"

———

We had not spoken about the incident in my room several nights before and, in the drowsy silence of the car, I felt the need to make things plain.

"You know, Francis," I said.

"What?"

It seemed the best thing was just to come right out and say it. "You know," I said, "I'm really not attracted to you. I mean, not that—"

"Isn't that interesting," he said coolly. "I'm really not attracted to you, either."

"But—"

"You were there."

We drove the rest of the way to school in a not very comfortable silence.

———

Unbelievably, things had escalated even more during the night. There now were hundreds of people: people in uniforms, people with dogs and bullhorns and cameras, people buying sweet rolls from the concessions truck and trying to peek into the dark windows of the news vans—three of them, one from a station in Boston—parked on Commons lawn, along with the overflow of vehicles from the parking lot.

We found Henry on the front porch of Commons. He was reading, with absorbed interest, a tiny, vellum-bound book written in some Near Eastern language. The twins—sleepy, red-nosed, rumpled—were sprawled on a bench like a couple of teenagers, passing a cup of coffee back and forth.

Francis half nudged, half kicked the toe of Henry's shoe.

Henry started. "Oh," he said. "Good morning."

"How can you even say that? I haven't had a wink of sleep. I haven't eaten anything in about three days."

Henry marked his place with a ribbon and slipped the book in his breast pocket. "Well," he said amiably, "go get a doughnut, then."

"I don't have any money."

"I'll give you the money, then."

"I don't want a goddamn doughnut."

I went over and sat down with the twins.

"You missed quite a time last night," said Charles to me.

"So I hear."

"Hugh's wife showed us baby pictures for an hour and a half."

"Yes, at least," said Camilla. "And Henry drank a beer from a can."

Silence.

"So what did you do?" Charles said.

"Nothing. Watched a movie on TV."

They both perked up. "Oh, really? The thing about the planets colliding?"

"Mr. Corcoran had it on but somebody switched channels before it was over," said Camilla.

"How'd it end?"

"What's the last part you saw?"

"They were in the mountain laboratory. The young enthusiastic scientists had all ganged up on that cynical old scientist who didn't want to help."

I was explaining the **dénouement** when Cloke Rayburn abruptly shouldered through the crowd. I stopped talking, thinking he was headed for the twins and me, but instead he only nodded to us and walked up to Henry, who now was standing on the edge of the porch.

"Listen," I heard him say. "I didn't get a chance to talk to you last night. I got hold of those guys in New York and Bunny hasn't been there."

Henry didn't say anything for a moment. Then he said: "I thought you said you couldn't get in touch with them."

"Well, it's possible, it's just like a big headache. But they hadn't seen him, anyway."

"How do you know?"

"What?"

"I thought you said you couldn't believe a word they said."

He looked startled. "I did?"

"Yes."

"Hey, listen to me," said Cloke, taking off his sunglasses. His eyes were bloodshot and pouchy. "These guys are telling the truth. I didn't think of this before—well, I guess it hasn't been that long—but anyway, the story's all over the New York papers. If they really did something to him, they wouldn't be sticking around their apartment taking phone calls from me. . . . What is it, man?" he said nervously when Henry didn't respond. "You didn't say anything to anybody, did you?"

Henry made an indistinct noise in the back of his throat, which might have meant anything.

"What?"

"No one has asked," said Henry.

There was no expression on his face. Cloke,

his discomfiture evident, waited for him to continue. Finally, he put on his sunglasses again in a slightly defensive manner.

"Well," he said. "Um. Okay, then. See you later."

After he'd gone Francis turned to Henry, a bemused look on his face. "What on earth are you up to?" he said.

But Henry didn't answer.

———

The day passed like a dream. Voices, dogs barking, the whap of a helicopter overhead. The wind was strong and the roar of it in the trees was like an ocean. The helicopter had been sent from the New York State Police headquarters in Albany; it had, we were told, a special infrared heat sensor. Someone had also volunteered something called an "ultra-light" aircraft which swooped overhead, barely clearing the tops of the trees. There were real ranks now, squadron leaders with bullhorns; we marched over the snowy hills wave upon wave.

Cornfields, pastures, knolls heavy with undergrowth. As we approached the base of the mountain the land took a downward slope. A thick fog lay in the valley below, a smoldering cauldron of white from which only the treetops protruded, stark and Dantesque. By degrees, we descended, and the world sank from view. Charles, beside me, stood out sharp and almost hyper-realistic with his ruddy cheeks and labored breaths but further down, Henry had become a wraith, his large form light and strangely insubstantial in the mist.

When the ground rose several hours later, we came up on the rear of another, smaller party. In it were some people I was surprised and somehow touched to see. There was Martin Hoffer, an old and distinguished composer on the music faculty; the middle-aged lady who checked IDs in the lunch line, looking inexplicably tragic in her plain cloth coat; Dr. Roland, the blares of his nose-blowing audible even at a distance.

"Look," said Charles. "That's not Julian, is it?"

"Where?"

"Surely not," said Henry.

But it was. Rather characteristically, he pretended not to see us until we were so close it was impossible for him to ignore us any longer. He was listening to a tiny, fox-faced lady whom I knew to be a housekeeper in the dorms.

"Goodness," he said, when she had finished talking, drawing back in mock surprise. "Where did you come from? Do you know Mrs. O'Rourke?"

Mrs. O'Rourke smiled shyly. "I seen all of you before," she said. "The kids think the maids don't notice them, but I know you all by sight."

"Well, I should hope so," said Charles. "You haven't forgotten me, have you? Bishop House, number ten?"

He said this so warmly that she flushed with pleasure.

"Sure," she said. "I remember you. You was the one was always running off with my broom."

During this exchange Henry and Julian were talking softly. "You should have told me before now," I heard Julian say.

"We did tell you."

"Well, you did, but still. Edmund's missed class before," said Julian, looking distressed. "I thought he was playing sick. People are saying that he's been kidnapped but I think that's rather silly, don't you?"

"I'd rather one of mine be kidnapped than out in this snow for six days," said Mrs. O'Rourke.

"Well, I certainly hope that nothing has happened to him. You know, don't you, that his family is here? Have you seen them?"

"Not today," said Henry.

"Of course, of course," said Julian hastily. He disliked the Corcorans. "I haven't been to see them either, it's really not the time to intrude. . . . This morning I did run into the father quite by accident, and one of the brothers as well. He had a baby with him. Riding it on his shoulders as if they were on their way to a picnic."

"Little one like him had no business being out in this weather," said Mrs. O'Rourke. "Hardly three years old."

"Yes, I'm afraid I agree. I can't imagine why anyone would have a baby along on something like this."

"I certainly wouldn't have let one of mine yell and carry on like that."

"Perhaps it was cold," murmured Julian. The tone he used was a delicate cue that he had tired of the subject and wished to stop talking about it.

Henry cleared his throat. "Did you talk to Bunny's father?" he said.

"Only for a moment. He—well, I suppose we all have different ways of handling these things. . . . Edmund looks a great deal like him, doesn't he?"

"All the brothers do," said Camilla.

Julian smiled. "Yes! And so many of them! Like something from a fairy story. . . ." He glanced at his watch. "Goodness," he said, "it's late."

Francis started from his morose silence. "Are

you leaving now?" he asked Julian anxiously. "Do you want me to drive you?"

This was a blatant attempt at escape. Henry's nostrils flared, not so much in anger as in a kind of exasperated amusement: he gave Francis a dirty look, but then Julian, who was gazing into the distance and quite unaware of the drama which hinged on his reply, shook his head.

"No, thank you," he said. "Poor Edmund. I'm really quite worried, you know."

"Just think how his parents must feel," said Mrs. O'Rourke.

"Yes," said Julian, in a tone of voice which managed to convey at once both sympathy with and distaste for the Corcorans.

"I'd be wild if it was me."

Unexpectedly, Julian shuddered and turned up the collar of his coat. "Last night I was so upset I could hardly sleep," he said. "He's such a sweet boy, so silly; I'm really very fond of him. If anything should have happened to him I don't know if I could bear it."

He was looking over the hills, at all that grand cinematic expanse of men and wilderness and snow that lay beneath us; and though his voice was anxious there was a strange dreamy look on his face. The business had upset him, that I knew, but I also knew that there was something about the operatic sweep of the search which could not fail to appeal to him and that he was pleased, however obscurely, with the aesthetics of the thing.

Henry saw it, too. "Like something from Tolstoy, isn't it?" he remarked.

Julian looked over his shoulder, and I was startled to see that there was real delight on his face.

"Yes," he said. "Isn't it, though?"

———

At about two in the afternoon, two men in dark overcoats walked up to us from nowhere.

"Charles Macaulay?" said the shorter of the two. He was a barrel-chested fellow with hard, genial eyes.

Charles, beside me, stopped and looked at him blankly.

The man reached in his breast pocket and flipped out a badge. "Agent Harvey Davenport, Northeast Regional Division, FBI."

For a moment I thought Charles might lose his composure. "What do you want?" he said, blinking.

"We'd like to talk to you, if you don't mind."

"It won't take long," said the taller man. He was an Italian with stooped shoulders and a sad, doughy nose. His voice was soft and pleasant.

Henry, Francis, Camilla had all stopped and were staring at the strangers with varying degrees of interest and alarm.

"Besides," said Davenport snappily. "Good to get out of the cold for a minute or two. Bet you're freezing your balls off, huh?"

———

After they left, the rest of us were bristling with anxiety, but of course we couldn't talk and so we continued to shuffle along, eyes on the ground and half afraid to look up. Soon it was three o'clock, then four. Things were far from over, but at the first premature signs that the day's search was breaking up we headed rapidly and silently for the car.

———

"What do you suppose they want with him?" said Camilla for about the tenth time.

"I don't know," said Henry.

"He gave them a statement already."

"He gave the police one. Not these people."

"What difference does it make? Why would they want to talk to him?"

"I don't know, Camilla."

———

When we got to the twins' apartment we were relieved to find Charles there, alone. He was lying on the couch, a drink on the table beside him, talking to his grandmother on the telephone.

He was a little drunk. "Nana says hi," he said to Camilla when he got off the phone. "She's all worried. Some bug or something has got up into her azaleas."

"What's that all over your hands?" said Camilla sharply.

He held them out, palms up, none too steadily. The tips of the fingers were black. "They took my fingerprints," he said. "It was kind of interesting. I'd never had it done before."

For a moment we were all too shocked to say anything. Henry stepped forward, took one of his hands and examined it beneath the light. "Do you know why they did it?" he said.

Charles wiped his brow with the back of his free wrist. "They've sealed off Bunny's room," he said. "Some people are in there dusting for prints and putting things in plastic bags."

Henry dropped his hand. "But why?"

"I don't know why. They wanted the fingerprints of everybody who'd been in the room on Thursday and touched things."

"What good will that do? They don't have Bunny's fingerprints."

"Apparently they do have them. Bunny was in the Boy Scouts and his troop went in and was fingerprinted for some kind of Law Enforcement badge, years ago. They're still on file somewhere."

Henry sat down. "Why did they want to talk to you?"

"That was the first thing they asked me."

"What?"

" 'Why do you think we want to talk to you.' " He dragged the heel of his hand down the side of his face. "These people are smart, Henry," he said. "A lot smarter than the police."

"How did they treat you?"

Charles shrugged. "The one called Davenport was pretty brusque. The other one—the Italian—was nicer, but he scared me. Didn't say much, just listened. He's much more clever than the other one. . . ."

"Well?" said Henry impatiently. "What is it?"

"Nothing. We . . . I don't know. We've got to be really careful, that's all. They tried to trip me up more than once."

"What do you mean?"

"Well, when I told them Cloke and I had gone down to Bunny's room around four on Thursday, for instance."

"That's when you did go," said Francis.

"I know that. But the Italian—really, he's a very pleasant man—began to look all concerned. 'Can that be right, son?' he said. 'Think.' I was really confused, because I **knew** we went at four, and then Davenport said, 'You'd better think about it, because your buddy Cloke told us you two were down at that room for a solid hour before you called anybody.' "

"They wanted to see if you and Cloke had anything to hide," Henry said.

"Maybe. Maybe they just wanted to see if I would lie about it."

"Did you?"

"No. But if they'd asked me something a little touchier, and I was kind of scared . . . You don't realize what it's like. There are two of them, and only one of you, and you don't have much time to think. . . . I know, I know," he said despairingly. "But it's not **like** the police. These small-town cops don't actually expect to find anything. They'd be shocked to know the truth, probably wouldn't believe it if you told them. But these guys . . ." He shuddered. "I never realized, you know, how much we rely on appearances," he said. "It's not that we're so smart, it's just that we don't **look** like we did it. We might as well be a bunch of Sunday-school teachers as far as everyone else is concerned. But these guys won't be taken in by that." He picked up his glass and took a drink. "By the way," he said, "they asked a million questions about your trip to Italy."

Henry glanced up, startled. "Did they ask at all about the finances? Who paid for it?"

"No." Charles finished off the glass and rattled the ice around for a moment. "I was terrified they would. But I think they were kind of overly impressed by the Corcorans. I think if I told them that Bunny never wore the same pair of underpants twice they would probably believe me."

"What about that Vermonter?" Francis said. "The one on television last night?"

"I don't know. They were a lot more interested in Cloke than anything else, it seemed to me. Maybe they just wanted to make sure his story matched up with mine, but there were a couple of really strange questions that—I don't know. I wouldn't be surprised if he's going around telling people this theory of his, that Bunny was kidnapped by drug dealers."

"Certainly not," said Francis.

"Well, he told **us**, and we're not even his friends. Though the FBI men seem to think he and I are on intimate terms."

"I hope you took pains to correct them," said Henry, lighting a cigarette.

"I'm sure Cloke would have set them straight on that account."

"Not necessarily," said Henry. He shook out his match and threw it in an ashtray; then he inhaled deeply on his cigarette. "You know," he said, "I thought at first that this association with Cloke was a great misfortune. Now I see it's one of the best things that could have happened to us."

Before anyone could ask him what he meant, he glanced at his watch. "Goodness," he said. "We'd better go. It's almost six."

———

On the way to Francis's, a pregnant dog ran across the road in front of us.

"That," said Henry, "is a very bad omen."

But of what he wouldn't say.

———

The news was just beginning. The anchorman glanced up from his papers, looking grave but at the same time very pleased. "The frantic search—thus far a fruitless one—continues, for missing Hampden College student Edward Corcoran."

"Gosh," said Camilla, reaching into her brother's coat pocket for a cigarette. "You'd think they'd get his name right, don't you?"

The picture cut to an aerial shot of snowy hills, dotted like a war map with pinprick figures, Mount Cataract looming lopsided and huge in the foreground.

"An estimated three hundred searchers," said the voice-over, "including National Guard, police, Hampden firefighters and Central Vermont Public Service employees, combed the hard-to-reach area on this, Day Two of the search. In addition, the FBI has launched an investigation of its own in Hampden today."

The picture wobbled, then switched abruptly to a lean, white-haired man in a cowboy hat who the caption informed us was Dick Postonkill, Hampden County sheriff. He was talking, but no sound came from his mouth; searchers milled curiously in the snowy background, raising on tiptoe to jeer silently at the camera.

After a few moments, the audio lurched on with a jerky, garbled sound. The sheriff was in the middle of a sentence.

"—to remind hikers," he said, "to go out in groups, stay on the trail, leave a projected itinerary and carry plenty of warm clothing in case of sudden drops in temperature."

"That was Hampden County sheriff Dick Postonkill," said the anchorman brightly, "with a few tips for our viewers on winter hiking safety." He turned, and the camera zoomed in on him at a different angle. "One of the only leads so far in the Corcoran disappearance case has been provided by William Hundy, a local businessman and ActionNews Twelve viewer, who phoned our TIPS line with information regarding the missing youth. Today Mr. Hundy has been cooperating with state and local authorities in providing a description of Corcoran's alleged abductors. . . ."

" 'State and local,' " said Henry.

"What?"

"Not federal."

"Of course not," said Charles. "Do you think the FBI is going to believe some dumb story that a Vermonter made up?"

"Well, if they don't, why are they here?" said Henry.

This was a disconcerting thought. In the brilliant, delayed-tape noontime sun, a group of men hurried down the courthouse steps. Mr. Hundy, his head down, was among them. His hair was slicked back and he wore, in lieu of his service station uniform, a baby-blue leisure suit.

A reporter—Liz Ocavello, a sort of local celebrity, with her own current-issues program and a segment called "Movie Beat" on the local news—approached, microphone in hand. "Mr. Hundy," she said. "Mr. Hundy."

He stopped, confused, as his companions walked ahead and left him standing alone on the steps. Then they realized what was going on and came back up to huddle around him in an official-looking cluster. They grabbed Hundy by the elbows and made as if to hustle him away but he hung back, reluctant.

"Mr. Hundy," said Liz Ocavello, nudging her way in. "I understand you have been working today with police artists on composite drawings of the persons you saw with the missing boy on Sunday."

Mr. Hundy nodded rather briskly. His shy, evasive manner of the day before had given way to a slightly more assertive stance.

"Could you tell us what they looked like?"

The men surged around Mr. Hundy once more, but he seemed entranced by the camera. "Well," he said, "they wasn't from around here. They was . . . dark."

"Dark?"

They now were tugging him down the steps, and he glanced back over his shoulder, as if sharing a confidence. "Arabs," he said. "You know."

Liz Ocavello, behind her glasses and her big anchorwoman hairdo, accepted this disclosure so blandly that I thought I'd heard it wrong. "Thank you, Mr. Hundy," she said, turning away, as Mr. Hundy and his friends disappeared down the steps. "This is Liz Ocavello at the Hampden County Courthouse."

"Thanks, Liz," the newscaster said cheerily, swiveling in his chair.

"Wait," said Camilla. "Did he say what I thought he said?"

"What?"

"**Arabs?** He said Bunny got in a car with some **Arabs?**"

"In a related development," the anchorman

said, "area churches have joined hands in a prayer effort for the missing boy. According to Reverend A. K. Poole of First Lutheran, several churches in the tri-state area, including First Baptist, First Methodist, Blessed Sacrament and Assembly of God, have offered up their—"

"I wonder what this mechanic of yours is up to, Henry," said Francis.

Henry lit a cigarette. He had smoked it halfway down before he said: "Did they ask you anything about Arabs, Charles?"

"No."

"But they just said on television that Hundy's not dealing with the FBI," Camilla said.

"We don't know that."

"You don't think it's all some kind of setup?"

"I don't know what to think."

The picture on the set had changed. A thin, well-groomed woman in her fifties—Chanel cardigan, pearls at the neckline, hair brushed into a stiff, shoulder-length flip—was talking, in a nasal voice which was oddly familiar.

"Yes," she said; where had I heard that voice before? "The people of Hampden are ever so kind. When we arrived at our hotel, late yesterday afternoon, the concierge was waiting for—"

"Concierge," said Francis, disgusted. "They don't have a concierge at the Coachlight Inn."

I studied this woman with new interest. "That's Bunny's mother?"

"That's right," said Henry. "I keep forgetting. You haven't met her."

She was a slight woman, corded and freckled around the neck the way women of that age and disposition often are; she bore little resemblance to Bunny but her hair and eyes were the same color as his and she had his nose: a tiny, sharp, inquisitive nose which harmonized perfectly with the rest of her features but had always looked slightly incongruous on Bunny, stuck as it was like an afterthought in the middle of his large, blunt face. Her manner was haughty and distracted. "Oh," she said, twisting a ring on her finger, "we've had a deluge, indeed, from all over the country. Cards, calls, the most glorious flowers—"

"Do they have her doped up or something?" I said.

"What do you mean?"

"Well, she doesn't seem very upset, does she?"

"Of course," said Mrs. Corcoran reflectively, "of course, we're all just out of our **minds**, really. And I certainly hope that no mother will ever have to endure what I have for the past few nights. But the weather does seem to be breaking, and we've met so many lovely people, and the local merchants have all been generous in so many little ways. . . ."

"Actually," said Henry, when the station cut to a commercial, "she photographs rather well, doesn't she?"

"She looks like a tough customer."

"She's from Hell," Charles said drunkenly.

"Oh, she's not that bad," said Francis.

"You just say that because she kisses up to you all the time," Charles said. "Because of your mother and stuff."

"Kiss up? What are you talking about? Mrs. Corcoran doesn't **kiss up** to me."

"She's awful," Charles said. "It's a horrible thing to tell your kids that money's the only thing in the world, but it's a disgrace to work for it. Then toss 'em out without a penny. She never gave Bunny one red—"

"That's Mr. Corcoran's fault, too," said Camilla.

"Well, yeah, maybe. I don't know. I just never met such a bunch of greedy, shallow people. You look at them and think, oh, what a tasteful, attractive family but they're just a bunch of **zeros**, like something from an ad. They've got this room in their house," Charles said, turning to me, "called the Gucci Room."

"What?"

"Well, they painted it with a **da**do, sort of,

those awful Gucci stripes. It was in all kinds of magazines. **House Beautiful** had it in some ridiculous article they did on Whimsy in Decorating or some absurd idea—you know, where they tell you to paint a giant lobster or something on your bedroom ceiling and it's supposed to be very witty and attractive." He lit a cigarette. "I mean, that's exactly the kind of people **they** are," he said. "All surface. Bunny was the best of them by a long shot but even he—"

"I hate Gucci," said Francis.

"Do you?" said Henry, glancing up from his reverie. "Really? I think it's rather grand."

"Come on, Henry."

"Well, it's so expensive, but it's so ugly too, isn't it? I think they make it ugly on purpose. And yet people buy it out of sheer perversity."

"I don't see what you think is grand about that."

"Anything is grand if it's done on a large enough scale," said Henry.

———

I was walking home that night, paying no attention to where I was going, when a large, sulky fellow approached me near the apple trees in front of Putnam House. He said: "Are you Richard Papen?"

I stopped, looked at him, said that I was.

To my astonishment, he punched me in the face, and I fell backwards in the snow with a thump that knocked me breathless.

"Stay away from Mona!" he shouted at me. "If you go near her again, I'll kill you. You understand me?"

Too stunned to reply, I stared up at him. He kicked me in the ribs, hard, and then trudged sullenly away—footsteps crunching through the snow, a slamming door.

I looked up at the stars. They seemed very far away. Finally, I struggled to my feet—there was a sharp pain in my ribs, but nothing seemed broken—and limped home in the dark.

I woke late the next morning. My eye hurt when I rolled on my cheek. I lay there for a while, blinking in the bright sun, as confused details of the previous night floated back to me like a dream; then I reached for my watch on the night table and saw that it was late, almost noon, and why had no one been by to get me?

I got up, and as I did my reflection rose to meet me, head-on in the opposite mirror; it stopped and stared—hair on end, mouth agog in idiotic astonishment—like a comic book character konked on the head with an anvil, chaplet of stars and birdies twittering about the brow. Most startling of all, a splendid dark cartoon of a black eye was stamped in a ring on my eye socket, in the richest inks of Tyrian, chartreuse, and plum.

———

I brushed my teeth, dressed, and hurried outside, where the first familiar person I spotted was Julian on his way up to the Lyceum.

He drew back from me in innocent, Chaplinesque surprise. "Goodness," he said, "what happened to you?"

"Have you heard anything this morning?"

"Why, no," he said, looking at me curiously. "That eye. You look as if you were in a barroom brawl."

Any other time I would have been too embarrassed to tell him the truth, but I was so sick of lying that I had an urge to come clean, on this small matter at least. So I told him what had happened.

I was surprised at his reaction. "So it **was** a brawl," he said, with childish delight. "How **thrilling**. Are you in love with her?"

"I'm afraid I don't know her too well."

He laughed. "Dear me, you **are** being truthful today," he said, with remarkable perspicuity. "Life has got awfully dramatic all of a sudden, hasn't it? Just like a fiction. . . . By the way, did I tell you that some men came round to see me yesterday afternoon?"

"Who were they?"

"There were two of them. At first I was rather anxious—I thought they were from the State Department, or worse. You've heard of my problems with the Israami government?"

I am not sure what Julian thought the Israami government—terrorist state though it is—should want to do with him, but his fear of it came from his having taught its exiled crown princess about ten years before. After the revolution she'd been forced into hiding, had ended up somehow at Hampden College; Julian taught her for four years, in private tutorials supervised by the former Israami minister of education, who would occasionally fly in from Switzerland, with gifts of caviar and chocolates, to make sure that the curriculum was suitable for the heir apparent to his country's throne.

The princess was fabulously rich. (Henry had caught a glimpse of her once—dark glasses, full-length marten coat—clicking rapidly down the stairs of the Lyceum with her bodyguards at her heels.) The dynasty to which she belonged traced its origins to the Tower of Babel, and had accumulated a monstrous amount of wealth since then, a good deal of which her surviving relatives and associates had managed to smuggle out of the country. But there was a price on her head, as a result of which she'd been isolated, overprotected, and largely friendless, even while a teenager at Hampden. Subsequent years had made her a recluse. She moved from place to place, terrified of assassins; her whole family—except for a cousin or two and a little half-wit brother who was in an institution—had been picked off one by one over the years and even the old Minister of Education, six months after the princess was graduated from college, had died of a sniper's bullet, sitting in the garden of his own little red-roofed house in Montreux.

Julian was uninvolved in Isrami politics despite his fondness for the princess and his sympathy—on principle—with royalists instead of revolutionaries. But he refused to travel by airplane or accept packages COD, lived in fear of unexpected visitors, and had not been abroad in eight or nine years. Whether these were reasonable precautions or excessive ones I do not know, but his connection with the princess did not seem a particularly strong one and I, for one, suspected that the Isramic jihad had better things to do than hunting down Classics tutors in New England.

"Of course, they weren't from the State Department at all but they were connected with the government in some way. I have a sixth sense about such things, isn't that curious? One of the men was an Italian, very charming, really . . . courtly, almost, in a funny sort of way. I was rather puzzled by it all. They said that Edmund was on drugs."

"What?"

"Do you think that odd? I think it **very** odd."

"What did you say?"

"I said **certainly not**. I may be flattering myself, but I do think I know Edmund rather well. He's really quite timid, puritanical, almost. . . . I can't imagine him doing anything of the sort and besides, young people who take drugs are always so bovine and prosaic. But do you know what this man said to me? He said that with young people, **you can never tell**. I don't think that's right, do you? Do you think that's right?"

We walked through Commons—I could hear the crash of plates overhead in the dining hall—and, on the pretext of having business on that end of campus, I walked on with Julian to the Lyceum.

That part of school, on the North Hampden side, was usually peaceful and desolate, the snow trackless and undisturbed beneath the pines until spring. Now it was trampled and littered like a fairgrounds. Someone had run a Jeep into an elm tree—broken glass, twisted fender, horrible splintered wound gaping yellow in the trunk; a foul-mouthed group of townie kids slid and shrieked down the hillside on a piece of cardboard.

"Goodness," said Julian, "those poor children."

I left him at the back door of the Lyceum and walked to Dr. Roland's office. It was a Sunday, he wasn't there; I let myself in and locked the door behind me and spent the afternoon in happy seclusion: grading papers, drinking muddy drip coffee from a mug that said RHONDA, and half-listening to the voices from down the hall.

I have the idea that those voices were in fact audible, and that I could have understood what they were saying if I'd paid any attention, but I didn't. It was only later, after I'd left the office and forgotten all about them, that I learned whom they belonged to, and that maybe I hadn't been quite so safe that afternoon as I'd thought.

———

The FBI men, said Henry, had set up a temporary headquarters in an empty classroom down the hall from Dr. Roland's office, and that was where they talked to him. They hadn't been twenty feet from where I sat, were even drinking the same muddy coffee from the same pot I'd made in the teachers' lounge. "That's odd," said Henry. "The first thing I thought of when I tasted that coffee was you."

"What do you mean?"

"It tasted strange. Burnt. Like your coffee."

The classroom (Henry said) had a blackboard covered with quadratic equations, and two full ashtrays, and a long conference table at which the three of them sat. There was also a laptop computer, a litigation bag with the FBI insignia in yellow, and a box of maple sugar candies—acorns, wee pilgrims, in fluted paper cups. They belonged to the Italian. "For my kids," he said.

Henry, of course, had done marvelously. He didn't say so, but then he didn't have to. He, in some senses, was the author of this drama and he had waited in the wings a long while for this moment, when he could step onto the stage and assume the role he'd written for himself: cool but friendly; hesitant; reticent with details; bright, but not as bright as he really was. He'd actually enjoyed talking to them, he told me. Davenport was a Philistine, not worth mentioning, but the Italian was somber and polite, quite charming. ("Like one of those old Florentines Dante meets in Purgatory.") His name was Sciola. He was very interested in the trip to Rome, asked a lot of questions about it, not so much as investigator as fellow tourist. ("Did you boys happen to go out to the, what do you call it, San Prassede, out there around the train station? With that little chapel out on the side?") He spoke Italian, too, and he and Henry had a brief and happy conversation which was cut short by the irritated Davenport, who didn't understand a word and wanted to get down to business.

Henry was none too forthcoming, with me at least, about what that business actually was. But he did say that whatever track they were on, he was pretty sure it wasn't the right one. "What's more," he said, "I think I've figured out what it is."

"What?"

"Cloke."

"They don't think Cloke killed him?"

"They think Cloke knows more than he's telling. And they think his behavior is questionable. Which, as a matter of fact, it is. They know all kinds of things that I'm sure he didn't tell them."

"Like what?"

"The logistics of his drug business. Dates, names, places. Things that happened before he even came to Hampden. And they seemed to be trying to tie some of it up with me, which of course they weren't able to do in any kind of satisfactory way. Goodness. They even asked about **my** prescriptions, painkillers I got from the infirmary my freshman year. There were file folders all over the place, data that no single person has access to—medical histories, psychological evaluations, faculty comments, work samples, grades. . . . Of course, they made a point of letting me see they had all these things. Trying to intimidate me, I suppose. I know pretty much exactly what my records say, but Cloke's . . . bad grades, drugs, suspensions—I'd be willing to bet he's left quite a little trail of paper behind him. I don't know if it's the records **per se** that have made them curious, or if it was something Cloke himself had said when he talked to them; but mostly what they wanted from me—and from Julian, and from Brady and Patrick Corcoran, to whom they spoke last night—were details of Bunny's association with Cloke. Julian, of course, didn't know anything about it. Brady and Patrick apparently told them plenty. And I did, too."

"What are you talking about?"

"Well, I mean, Brady and Patrick were out in the parking lot of the Coachlight Inn smoking pot with him night before last."

"But what did you tell them?"

"What Cloke told us. About the drug business in New York."

I leaned back in my chair. "Oh, my God," I said. "Are you sure you know what you're doing?"

"Of course," said Henry serenely. "It was what they wanted to hear. They'd been circling around it all afternoon, when finally I decided to let it slip, they pounced. . . . I expect Cloke is in for an uncomfortable day or two but really, I think this is very fortunate for us. We couldn't have asked for anything better to keep them busy until the snow melts—and have you noticed how bright it's been the last couple of days? I think the roads are already starting to clear."

———

My black eye was the source of much interest, speculation, and debate—I told Francis that the FBI men had done it just to watch his eyes get round—but not nearly so much as was an article in the Boston **Herald**. They'd sent a reporter up the day before, as had the New York **Post** and the New York **Daily News**, but the **Herald** reporter had scooped them all.

DRUGS MAY BE INVOLVED
IN VERMONT DISAPPEARANCE

Federal agents investigating the April 24 disappearance of Edmund Corcoran, a twenty-four-year-old Hampden

College student who has been the subject of an intensive manhunt in Vermont for the past three days, have
found that the missing youth may
have been involved with drugs. Federal
authorities who searched Corcoran's
room discovered drug paraphernalia
and heavy cocaine residue. Though
Corcoran had no known history of
drug abuse, sources close to the boy
say that the normally extroverted Corcoran had become moody and with-
drawn in the months prior to the
disappearance. (See "What Your Child
Won't Tell You," p. 6.)

We were puzzled by this account, though
everyone else on campus seemed to know all
about it. I got the story from Judy Poovey.

"You know what it was they found in his
room? It was, like, this mirror that belonged to
Laura Stora. I bet everybody in Durbinstall has
done coke off that thing. Really old, with little
grooves carved in the side, Jack Teitelbaum
used to call it the Snow Queen because you
could always scrape up a line or two if you
were desperate or something. And sure, I guess
it's technically her mirror, but really it's kind of
public property and she said she hadn't even
seen it in about a million years, somebody

took it from a living room in one of the new houses in March. Bram Guernsey said that Cloke said it wasn't in Bunny's room when he was there before, that the Feds had planted it, but then Bram said that Cloke thought this whole thing was some kind of a setup. A frame. Like in 'Mission: Impossible,' he meant, or one of those paranoia books by Philip K. Dick. He told Bram he thought the Feebies had a hidden camera planted somewhere in Durbinstall, all this wild stuff. Bram says it's because Cloke is afraid to go to sleep and been up on crystal meth for forty-eight hours. He sits around in his room with the door locked and does lines and listens to this song by the Buffalo Springfield, over and over . . . you know that one? 'Something's happening here . . . what it is ain't exactly clear. . . .' It's weird. People get upset, all of a sudden they want to listen to old hippie garbage they would never listen to if they were in their right mind, when my cat died I had to go out and borrow all these Simon and Garfunkel records. Anyway." She lit a cigarette. "How did I get off on this? Right, Laura's freaking out, somehow they traced the mirror to her and she's already on probation, you know, had to do all this community service last fall because Flipper Leach got in trouble and ratted on Laura and Jack Teitelbaum—oh, you remember all that stuff, don't you?"

"I never heard of Flipper Leach."

"Oh, you know Flipper. She's a bitch. Everybody calls her Flipper because she flipped over her dad's Volvo, like, four times freshman year."

"I don't understand what this Flipper person has to do with this."

"Well, she doesn't have anything to do with it, Richard, you're just like that guy in 'Dragnet' that always wants the facts. It's just that Laura is freaking out, okay, and Student Services is threatening to call her parents unless she tells them how that mirror got in Bunny's room, which she doesn't even have a fucking **clue**, and, get this, those FBI men found out about the Ecstasy she had at Swing into Spring last week and they want her to give up the names. I said, 'Laura, don't do it, it'll be just like that thing with Flipper and everybody'll hate you and you'll have to transfer to another school.' It's like Bram was saying—"

"Where is Cloke now?"

"That's what I was going to tell you if you'd shut up a minute. Nobody knows. He was really wigged out and asked if he could borrow Bram's car last night, to leave school, but this morning the car was back in the parking lot with the keys in it and nobody's seen him and he's not in his room and something weird is happening there, too, but for sure I don't know what it is. . . . I just won't even do meth anymore. Heebiejeebieville. By the way, I've been meaning to ask you, what did you do to your eye?"

————

Back at Francis's with the twins—Henry was having lunch with the Corcorans—I told them what Judy had told me.

"But I know that mirror," said Camilla.

"I do, too," said Francis. "Spotty old dark one. Bunny's had it in his room for a while."

"I thought it was his."

"I wonder how he got hold of it."

"If the girl left it in a living room," said Charles, "he probably just found it and took it."

This was highly probable. Bunny had had a mild tendency towards kleptomania, and was apt to pocket any small, valueless articles that caught his eye—nail clippers, buttons, spools of tape. These he hid around his room in jumbled little nests. It was a vice he practiced in secret, but at the same time he had felt no compunction about quite openly carrying away objects of greater value which he found unattended. He did this with such assurance and authority—tucking bottles of liquor or unguarded boxes from the florist under his arm and walking away without a backwards glance—that I wondered if he knew it was stealing. I once heard him explaining vigorously and quite unselfconsciously to Marion what he thought ought to be done to people who stole food from house refrigerators.

———

As bad as things were for Laura Stora, they were worse for the luckless Cloke. We were to discover later that he had not brought Bram Guernsey's car back of his own volition, but had been impelled to do so by the FBI agents, who had had him pulled over before he was ten miles out of Hampden. They took him back to the classroom where they had set up headquarters, and kept him there for most of Sunday night, and while I don't know what they said to him, I do know that by Monday morning he had requested to have an attorney present at the interview.

———

Mrs. Corcoran (said Henry) was burned up that anyone had dared suggest Bunny was on drugs. At lunch at the Brasserie, a reporter had edged up to the Corcoran table to ask if they had any comment to make about the "drug paraphernalia" found in Bunny's room.

Mr. Corcoran, startled, had lowered his eyebrows impressively and said, "Well, of course, haw, ahem," but Mrs. Corcoran, sawing at her steak **au poivre** with subdued violence, launched without even looking up into a tart diatribe. Drug paraphernalia, as they chose to call it, was not drugs, and it was a pity the press chose to level accusations at persons not present to defend themselves, and she was having a hard enough time as it was without having strangers imply that her son was a drug kingpin. All of which was more or less reasonable and true, and which the **Post** reported dutifully the next day word for word, alongside an unflattering picture of Mrs. Corcoran with her mouth open and a headline which read: MOM SEZ: NOT MY KID.

———

On Monday night, about two in the morning, Camilla asked me to walk her home from Francis's. Henry had left around midnight; and Francis and Charles, who'd been drinking hard since four o'clock, showed no signs of slowing down. They were entrenched in Francis's kitchen with the lights turned out, preparing, with what I felt was alarming hilarity, a series of hazardous cocktails called "Blue Blazers" which involved ignited whiskey poured back and forth in a flaming arc between two pewter mugs.

At her apartment Camilla—shivering, preoccupied, her cheeks fever-red from the cold—

asked me upstairs for a cup of tea. "I wonder if we should have left them there," she said, switching on the lamp. "I'm afraid they're going to set themselves on fire."

"They'll be all right," I said, though the same thought had occurred to me.

We drank our tea. The lamplight was warm and the apartment still and snug. At home in bed, in my private abyss of longing, the scenes I dreamed of always began like this: drowsy drunken hour, the two of us alone, scenarios in which invariably she would brush against me as if by chance, or lean conveniently close, cheek touching mine, to point out a passage in a book; opportunities which I would seize, gently but manfully, as exordium to more violent pleasures.

The teacup was too hot; it burned my fingertips. I set it down and looked at her—oblivious, smoking a cigarette, scarcely two feet away. I could lose myself forever in that singular little face, in the pessimism of her beautiful mouth. **Come here, you. Let's shut the light out, shall we?** When I imagined these phrases cast in her voice, they were almost intolerably sweet; now, sitting right beside her, it was unthinkable that I should voice them myself.

And yet: why should it be? She had been party to the killing of two men; had stood calm as a Madonna and watched Bunny die. I remembered Henry's cool voice, scarcely six weeks earlier. **There was a certain carnal element to the proceedings, yes.**

"Camilla?" I said.

She glanced up, distracted.

"What really happened, that night in the woods?"

I think I had been expecting, if not surprise, at least a show of it. But she didn't blink. "Well, I don't remember an awful lot," she said slowly. "And what I do remember is almost impossible to describe. It's all much less clear than it was even a few months ago. I suppose I should have tried to write it down or something."

"But what **do** you remember?"

It was a moment before she answered. "Well, I'm sure you've heard it all from Henry," she said. "It seems a bit silly to even say it aloud. I remember a pack of dogs. Snakes twining around my arms. Trees on fire, pines bursting into flames like enormous torches. There was a fifth person with us for part of the time."

"A fifth person?"

"It wasn't always a person."

"I don't know what you mean."

"You know what the Greeks called Dionysus. πογυειδής. The Many-Formed One. Sometimes it was a man, sometimes a woman. And sometimes something else. I—I'll tell you something that I do remember," she said abruptly.

"What?" I said, hopeful at last for some passionate, back-clawing detail.

"That dead man. Lying on the ground. His stomach was torn open and steam was coming out of it."

"His **stomach**?"

"It was a cold night. I'll never forget the smell of it, either. Like when my uncle used to cut up deer. Ask Francis. He remembers, too."

I was too horrified to say anything. She reached for the teapot and poured a bit more into her cup. "Do you know," she said, "why I think we're having such bad luck this time around?"

"What?"

"Because it's terrible luck to leave a body unburied. That farmer they found straightaway, you know. But remember poor Palinurus in the **Aeneid**? He lingered around and haunted them for the longest time. I'm afraid that none of us are going to have a good night's sleep until Bunny's in the ground."

"That's nonsense."

She laughed. "In the fourth century B.C., the sailing of the entire Attic fleet was delayed just because a soldier sneezed."

"You've been talking too much to Henry."

She was silent for a moment. Then she said:

"Do you know what Henry made us do, a couple of days after that thing in the woods?"

"What?"

"He made us kill a piglet."

I was not shocked so much by this statement as by the eerie calm with which she delivered it. "Oh, my God," I said.

"We cut its throat. Then we took turns holding it over each other, so it bled on our heads and hands. It was awful. I nearly got sick."

It seemed to me that the wisdom of deliberately covering oneself with blood—even pig blood—immediately after committing a murder was questionable, but all I said was: "Why did he want to do that?"

"Murder is pollution. The murderer defiles everyone he comes into contact with. And the only way to purify blood is through blood. We let the pig bleed on us. Then we went inside and washed it off. After that, we were okay."

"Are you trying to tell me," I said, "that—"

"Oh, don't worry," she said hastily. "I don't think he plans on doing anything like that this time."

"Why? Didn't it work?"

She failed to catch the sarcasm of this. "Oh, no," she said. "I think it **worked**, all right."

"Then why not do it again?"

"Because I think Henry has got the idea that it might upset you."

There was the fumble of a key in the lock, and a few moments later Charles plunged through the door. He shouldered his coat off and let it fall in a heap on the rug.

"Hello, hello," he sang, lurching inside and shedding his jacket in the same fashion. He had not come into the living room, but made an abrupt turn into the hallway which led to bedrooms and bath. A door opened, then another. "Milly, my girl," I heard him call. "Where are you, honey?"

"Oh, dear," said Camilla. Out loud, she said: "We're in here, Charles."

Charles reappeared. His tie was now loosened and his hair was wild. "Camilla," he said, leaning against the doorframe, "Camilla," and then he saw me.

"You," he said, not too politely. "What are **you** doing here?"

"We're just having some tea," said Camilla. "Would you like some?"

"No." He turned and disappeared into the hall again. "Too late. Going to bed."

A door slammed. Camilla and I looked at each other. I stood up.

"Well," I said, "better be heading home."

———

There were still search parties, but the number of participating townspeople had shrunk dramatically, and almost no students remained at all. The operation had turned tight, secretive, professional. I heard the police had brought in a psychic, a fingerprint expert, a special team of bloodhounds trained at Dannemora. Perhaps because I imagined that I was tainted with a secret pollution, imperceptible to most but perhaps discernible to the nose of a dog (in movies, the dog is always the first to know the suave and unsuspected vampire for what it is), the thought of the bloodhounds made me superstitious and I tried to stay as far away from dogs as I could, all dogs, even the dopey Labrador mutts who belonged to the ceramics teacher and were always running around with their tongues hanging out, looking for a game of Frisbee. Henry—imagining, perhaps, some trembling Kassandra gibbering prophecies to a chorus of policemen—was far more concerned about the psychic. "If they're going to find us out," he said, with glum certainty, "that's how it's going to happen."

"Certainly you don't believe in that stuff."

He gave me a look of indescribable contempt.

"You amaze me," he said. "You think nothing exists if you can't see it."

The psychic was a young mother from upstate New York. An electrical shock from some jumper cables had put her into a coma from which she emerged, three weeks later, able to "know" things by handling an object or touching a stranger's hand. The police had used her successfully in a number of missing-person cases. Once she had found the body of a strangled child by merely pointing to an area on a surveyor's map. Henry, who was so superstitious that he sometimes left a saucer of milk outside his door to appease any malevolent spirits who might happen to wander by, watched her, fascinated, as she walked alone on the edge of campus—thick glasses, suburban car coat, red hair tied up in a polka-dot scarf.

"It's unfortunate," he said. "I don't dare risk meeting her. But I should like to talk to her very much."

The majority of our classmates, however, were thrown into an uproar by the information—accurate or not, I still don't know—that the Drug Enforcement Agency had brought in agents and was conducting an undercover investigation. Théophile Gautier, writing about the effect of Vigny's **Chatterton** on the youth of Paris, said that in the nineteenth-century night one could practically hear the crack of the solitary pistols: here, now, in Hampden, the night was alive with the flushing of toilets. Pillheads, cokeheads staggered around glassy-eyed, dazed at their sudden losses. Someone flushed so much pot down one of the toilets in the sculpture studio they had to get somebody in from the Water Department to dig up the septic tank.

———

About four-thirty on Monday afternoon, Charles showed up at my room. "Hello," he said. "Want to get something to eat?"

"Where's Camilla?"

"Somewhere, I don't know," he said, his pale glance skittering across my room. "Do you want to come?"

"Well . . . sure," I said.

He brightened. "Good. I've got a taxi downstairs."

———

The taxi driver—a florid man named Junior who'd driven Bunny and me into town that first fall afternoon, and who in three days would be driving Bunny back to Connecticut for the last time, this time in a hearse—looked back at us in the rear-view mirror as we pulled out onto College Drive. "You boys going to the Brassiere?" he said.

He meant the Brasserie. It was the little joke he always had with us. "Yes," I said.

"No," said Charles quite suddenly. He was slouched down childishly low against the door, staring straight ahead and drumming on the armrest with his fingers. "We want to go to 1910 Catamount Street."

"Where's that?" I said to him.

"Oh, I hope you don't mind," he said, almost looking at me but not quite. "Just feel like a change. It's not far and besides, I'm sick of the food at the Brasserie, aren't you?"

———

The place where we wound up—a bar called the Farmer's Inn—was not remarkable for its food, or its decor—folding chairs and Formica tables—or for its sparse clientele, which was mostly rural, drunken, and over sixty-five. It was, in fact, inferior to the Brasserie in every respect but one, which was that really very sizable shots of off-brand whiskey could be got at the bar for fifty cents each.

We sat at the end of the bar by the television set. A basketball game was on. The barmaid—in her fifties, with turquoise eye shadow and lots of turquoise rings to match—looked us over, our suits and ties. She seemed startled by Charles's order of two double whiskeys and a club sandwich. "What the hey," she said, in a voice like a macaw. "They're letting you boys have a snort now and then, huh?"

I didn't know what she meant—was this some dig at our clothes, at Hampden College, did she want to see our IDs? Charles, who only the moment before had been sunk in gloom, glanced up and fixed her with a smile of great warmth and sweetness. He had a way with waitresses. They always hovered over him in restaurants and went to all kinds of special trouble on his behalf.

This one looked at him—pleased, incredulous—and barked with laughter. "Well, ain't that a kick," she said hoarsely, reaching with a heavily ringed hand for the Silva-Thin burning in the ashtray beside her. "And here I thought you Mormon kids that went around wasn't even suppose to drink Coca-Cola."

As soon as she sauntered back to the kitchen to turn in our order ("Bill!" we heard her saying, behind the swinging doors. "Hey, Bill! Listen to this!"), the smile faded from Charles's face. He reached for his drink and offered a humorless shrug when I tried to catch his eye.

"Sorry," he said. "I hope you don't mind coming here. It's cheaper than the Brasserie and we won't see anybody."

He was not in a mood to talk—ebullient sometimes, he could also be as mute and sulky as a child—and he drank steadily, with both his elbows on the bar and his hair falling down in his face. When his sandwich came he picked it apart, ate the bacon and left the rest, while I drank my drink and watched the Lakers. It was weird to be there, in that clammy dark bar in

Vermont, and watching them play. Back in California, at my old college, they'd had a pub called Falstaff's with a wide-screen television; I'd had a dopey friend named Carl who used to drag me there to drink dollar beer and watch basketball. He was probably there now, on a redwood bar stool, watching this exact game.

I was thinking these depressing thoughts and others like them, and Charles was on his fourth or fifth whiskey when somebody started switching the television with a remote control: "Jeopardy," "Wheel of Fortune," "MacNeil/ Lehrer," at last a local talk show. It was called "Tonight in Vermont." The set was styled after a New England farmhouse, with mock Shaker furniture and antique farm equipment, pitch-forks and so forth, hanging from the clapboard backdrop. Liz Ocavello was the host. In imita-tion of Oprah and Phil, she had a question-and-answer period at the end of each show, generally not too lively since her guests tended to be pretty tame—the State Commissioner for Veterans' Affairs, Shriners announcing a blood drive ("What's that address again, Joe?").

Her guest that evening, though it was several moments before I realized it, was William Hundy. He had on a suit—not the blue leisure suit but an old one the likes of which a rural preacher might wear—and he was talking authoritatively, for some reason I did not immediately understand, about Arabs and OPEC. "That OPEC," he said, "is the reason we don't have Texaco filling stations anymore. I remember when I was a boy it was Texaco stations all over the place but these Arabs, it was some kind of, what you call, leverage buyout—"

"Look," I said to Charles, but by the time I'd got him to glance up from his stupor they'd switched back to "Jeopardy."

"What?" he said.

"Nothing."

"Jeopardy," "Wheel of Fortune," back to "MacNeil/Lehrer" for kind of a long time until someone yelled, "Turn that shit off, Dotty."

"Well, what you want to watch, then?"

" **'Wheel of Fortune,'** " shouted a hoarse chorus.

But "Wheel of Fortune" was going off the air (Vanna blowing a glittery kiss) and the next thing I knew we were back in the simulated farmhouse with William Hundy. He was talking now about his appearance the previous morning on the "Today" show.

"Look," said someone, "there's that guy runs Redeemed Repair."

"**He** don't run it."

"Who does, then?"

"Him and Bud Alcorn both do."

"Aw, shut up, Bobby."

"Naw," said Mr. Hundy, "didn't see Willard Scott. Reckon I wouldn't have known what to say if I had. It's a big operation they got there, course it don't look so big on the TV."

I kicked Charles's foot.

"Yeah," he said, without interest, and brought his glass up with an unsteady hand.

I was surprised to see how outspoken Mr. Hundy had become in just four days. I was even more surprised to see how warmly the studio audience responded to him—asking concerned questions on topics ranging from the criminal justice system to the role of the small businessman in the community, roaring with laughter at his feeble jokes. It seemed to me that such popularity could only be incidental to what he had seen, or claimed to see. His stunned and stuttering air was gone. Now, with his hands folded over his stomach, answering questions with the pacific smile of a pontiff granting dispensations, he was so perfectly at his ease that there was something palpably dishonest about it. I wondered why no one else, apparently, could see it.

A small, dark man in shirtsleeves, who had been waving his hand in the air for some time, was finally called upon by Liz and stood up.

"My name is Adnan Nassar and I am Palestin-ian-American," he said in a rush. "I came to this country from Syria nine years ago and have since then earned American citizenship and am assistant manager of the Pizza Pad on Highway 6."

Mr. Hundy put his head to the side. "Well, Adnan," he said cordially, "I expect that story would be pretty unusual in your own country. But here, that's the way the system works. For everybody. And that's regardless of your race or the color of your skin." Applause.

Liz, microphone in hand, made her way down the aisle and pointed at a lady with a bouffant hairdo, but the Palestinian angrily waved his arms and the camera shifted back to him.

"That is not the point," he said. "I am an Arab and I resent the racial slurs you make against my people."

Liz walked back to the Palestinian and put her hand on his arm, Oprah-style, to comfort him. William Hundy, sitting in his mock-Shaker chair on the podium, shifted slightly as he leaned forward. "You like it here?" he said shortly.

"Yes."

"You want to go back?"

"Now," Liz said loudly. "Nobody is trying to say that—"

"Because the boats," said Mr. Hundy, even louder, **"run both ways."**

Dotty, the barmaid, laughed admiringly and took a drag off her cigarette. "That's telling him," she said.

"Where your family comes from?" said the Arab sarcastically. "You American Indian or what?"

Mr. Hundy did not appear to have heard this. "I'll **pay** for you to go back," he said. "How much is a one-way ticket to Baghdad going for these days? If you want me to, I'll—"

"I think," Liz said hastily, "that you've misunderstood what this gentleman is trying to say. He's just trying to make the point that—" She put her arm around the Palestinian's shoulders and he threw it off in a rage.

"All night long you say offensive things about Arabs," he screamed. "You don't know what Arab is." He beat on his chest with his fist. "I know it, in my heart."

"You and your buddy Saddam Hussein."

"How dare you say we are all greedy, driving big cars? This is very offensive to me. I am Arabic and I conserve the natural resource—"

"By setting fire to all them oil wells, eh?"

"—by driving a Toyota Corolla."

"I wasn't talking about you **in particular**," said Hundy. "I was talking about them OPEC creepos and them sick people kidnapped that boy. You think they're driving around in Toyota Corollas? You think we condone terrorism here? Is that what they do in your country?"

"You lie," shouted the Arab.

For a moment, in confusion, the camera went to Liz Ocavello; she was staring, without seeing, right out of the screen and I knew she was thinking exactly what I was thinking, **oh, boy, oh, boy, here it comes . . .**

"It ain't a lie," said Hundy hotly. "I know. I been in the service station business for thirty years. You think I don't remember, when Carter was President, you had us over such a barrel, back in nineteen and seventy-five? And now all you people coming over here, acting like you own the place, with all your chick peas and your filthy little pocket breads?"

Liz was looking to the side, trying to mouth instructions.

The Arab screamed out a frightful obscenity.

"Hold it! Stop!" shouted Liz Ocavello in despair.

Mr. Hundy leapt to his feet, eyes blazing, pointing a trembling forefinger into the audience. **"Sand niggers!"** he shouted bitterly. **"Sand niggers! Sand—"**

The camera jerked away and panned wildly to the side of the set, a tangle of black cables, hooded lights. It wavered in and out of focus and then, with a jerk, a commercial for McDonald's came on the screen.

"Whooo-hoo," someone shouted appreciatively.

There was scattered clapping.

"Did you hear that?" said Charles, after a pause.

I had forgotten all about him. His voice was slurred and his hair fell sweaty across his forehead. **"Be careful,"** I said to him in Greek, and nodded towards the barmaid. **"She can hear you."**

He mumbled something, wobbling on his bar stool, all padded glitter-vinyl and chrome.

"Let's go. It's late," I said, fumbling in my pocket for money.

Unsteadily, his gaze locked on mine, he leaned over and caught hold of my wrist. The light from the jukebox caught and glinted in his eyes, making them strange, crazed, the luminous killer eyes that sometimes glow unexpectedly from a friend's face in a snapshot.

"Shut up, old man," he said. "Listen."

I pulled my hand away and swung round on the stool but just as I did it I heard a long, dry rumble. Thunder.

We looked at each other.

"It's raining," he whispered.

———

All that night it fell, warm rain, dripping from the eaves and pattering at my window, while I lay flat on my back with my eyes wide open, listening.

All that night it rained and all the next morning: warm, gray, coming down soft and steady as a dream.

———

When I woke up I knew they were going to find him that day, knew it in my stomach from the moment I looked out my window at the snow, rotten and pocky, patches of slimy grass and everywhere drip drip drip.

It was one of those mysterious, oppressive days we sometimes had at Hampden, where the mountains that lowered at the horizon were swallowed up in fog and the world seemed light and empty, dangerous somehow. Walking around campus, the wet grass squishing beneath your feet, you felt as if you were in Olympus, Valhalla, some old abandoned land above the clouds; the landmarks that you knew—clocktower, houses—floating up like memories from a former life, isolated and disconnected in the mist.

Drizzle and damp. Commons smelled like wet clothes, everything dark and subdued. I found Henry and Camilla upstairs at a table by the window, a full ashtray between them,

Camilla with her chin propped in her hand and a cigarette burning low between her ink-stained fingers.

The main dining room was on the second floor, in a modern addition that jutted over a loading dock in the back. Huge, rain-splashed panes of glass—tinted gray, so they made the day seem drearier than it was—walled us in on three sides and we had a prime view of the loading dock itself, where the butter and egg trucks pulled up early in the morning, and of the slick black road that wound through the trees and disappeared in the mist in the direction of North Hampden.

There was tomato soup for lunch, coffee with skim milk because they were out of plain. Rain pittered against the plate glass windows. Henry was distracted. The FBI had paid him another visit the night before—what they wanted he didn't say—and he was talking on and on in a low voice about Schliemann's **Ilios**, the fingertips of his big square hands poised on the table's edge as if it were a Ouija board. When I'd lived with him over the winter, he would sometimes go on for hours in these didactic monologues, reeling off a pedantic and astonishingly accurate torrent of knowledge with the slow, transfixed calm of a subject under hypnosis. He was talking about the excavation of Hissarlik: "a terrible place, a cursed place," he said dreamily—cities and cities buried beneath each other, cities torn down, cities burnt and their bricks melted to glass . . . a terrible place, he said absently, a cursed place, nests of tiny brown adders of the sort that the Greeks call **antelion** and thousands and thousands of little owl-headed death gods (goddesses, really, some hideous prototype of Athena) staring fanatical and rigid from the engraved illustrations.

I didn't know where Francis was, but there was no need to ask about Charles. The night before I'd had to bring him home in a taxi, help him upstairs and into bed, where, judging from the condition in which I'd left him, he still was now. Two cream cheese and marmalade sandwiches lay wrapped in napkins by Camilla's plate. She hadn't been there when I brought Charles home, and she looked like she'd just got out of bed herself: tousle-haired, no lipstick, wearing a gray wool sweater that came down past her wrists. Smoke drifted from her cigarette in wisps that were the color of the sky outside. A tiny white speck of a car came singing down the wet road from town, far away, twisting with the black curves and growing larger by the moment.

It was late. Lunch was over, people were leaving. A misshapen old janitor trudged in with mop and pail and began, with weary grunting noises, to slop water on the floor by the beverage center.

Camilla was staring out the window. Suddenly, her eyes got wide. Slowly, incredulously, she raised her head; and then she was scrambling out of her chair, craning to see.

I saw, too, and jumped forward. An ambulance was parked directly beneath us. Two attendants, pursued by a pack of photographers, hurried past with their heads bent against the rain and a stretcher between them. The form upon it was covered with a sheet but, just before they shoved it through the double doors (long, easy motion, like bread sliding into the oven) and slammed them shut, I saw, hanging down from the edge, five or six inches of yellow rain slicker.

Shouts, far away, downstairs in Commons; doors slamming, a growing confusion, voices shouting down voices and then one hoarse voice, rising above the others: "Is he living?"

Henry took a deep breath. Then he closed his eyes; and exhaling sharply, a hand to his chest, he fell back in his chair as if he'd been shot.

———

This is what happened.

At about one-thirty on Tuesday afternoon,

Holly Goldsmith, an eighteen-year-old freshman from Taos, New Mexico, decided to take
her golden retriever, Milo, for a walk.

Holly, who studied modern dance, knew of
the search for Bunny but like most students of
her year had not participated in it, taking advantage of the unexpected recess to catch up
on sleep and study for midterms. Quite understandably, she did not wish to run into a search
party while on her outing. Therefore she
decided to take Milo out behind the tennis
courts to the ravine, since it had been can-
vassed days before and was, besides, a spot of
which the dog was especially fond.

This is what Holly said:

"When we were out of sight of campus, I
unhooked Milo's leash so he could run around
by himself. He likes to do that. . . .

"So I was just standing there [at the edge of
the ravine] waiting for him. He'd scrambled
over the embankment and was running
around and barking, usual stuff. I'd forgot his
tennis ball that day. I thought it was in my
pocket but it wasn't, so I went off and found a
few sticks to throw to him. When I came back
to the edge of the embankment, I saw he had
something in his teeth, shaking it from side to
side. He wouldn't come when I called him. I
thought he had a rabbit or something. . . .

"I guess Milo had dug him up, his head and

his, um, chest, I guess—I couldn't see very well. It was the glasses I noticed . . . slipped off one [ear] and kind of flopping back and forth like . . . yes, please . . . licking his face . . . I thought for a moment he was . . ." [unintelligible].

———

The three of us went rapidly downstairs (gaping janitor, cooks peeping from the kitchen, the cafeteria ladies in their nurse cardigans leaning over the balustrade) past the snack bar, past the post office where for once the red-wigged lady at the switchboard had put aside her afghan and her bag of variegated yarns and was standing in the doorway, crumpled Kleenex in hand, following us curiously with her eyes as we rushed through the hall and into the main room of Commons, where stood a cluster of grim-looking policemen, the sheriff, the game warden, security guards, a strange girl crying and someone taking pictures and everybody talking at once until someone looked up at us and shouted: "Hey! You! Didn't you know the boy?"

Flashbulbs went off everywhere and there was a riot of microphones and camcorders in our faces.

"How long had you known him?"

". . . drug-related incident?"

". . . traveled across Europe, is that right?"

Henry passed a hand over his face; I'll never forget the way he looked, white as talc, beads of sweat on his upper lip and the light bouncing off his glasses ... "Leave me alone," he muttered, seizing Camilla by the wrist and trying to push through to the door.

They crowded forward to block his path.

". . . care to comment . . . ?"

". . . best friends?"

The black snout of a camcorder was thrust in his face. With a sweep of his arm Henry knocked it away and it fell on the floor with a loud crack, batteries rolling in all directions. The owner—a fat man in a Mets cap—shrieked, stooped partway to the floor in consternation, then sprang up, cursing, as if to grab the retreating Henry by the collar. His fingers brushed the back of Henry's jacket and Henry turned, surprisingly quick.

The man shrank. It was funny, but people never seemed to notice at first glance how big Henry was. Maybe it was because of his clothes, which were like one of those lame but curiously impenetrable disguises from a comic book (why does no one ever see that "bookish" Clark Kent, without his glasses, is Superman?). Or maybe it was a question of his making people see. He had the far more remarkable talent of making himself invisible—in a room, in a

car, a virtual ability to dematerialize at will—
and perhaps this gift was only the converse of
that one: the sudden concentration of his wandering molecules rendering his shadowy form
solid, all at once, a metamorphosis startling to
the viewer.

———

The ambulance had gone. The roads stretched
out slick and empty in the drizzle. Agent Davenport was hurrying up the steps to Commons, head down, black shoes slapping on the
wet marble. When he saw us, he stopped. Sciola, behind him, climbed laboriously up the
last two or three steps, bracing his knee with
his palm. He stood behind Davenport and regarded us for a moment, breathing hard. "I'm
sorry," he said.

An airplane went by overhead, invisible
above the clouds.

"He is dead, then," said Henry.

"Afraid so."

The buzz of the airplane receded in the
damp, windy distance.

"Where was he?" said Henry at last. He was
pale, pale and sweaty at the temples but perfectly composed. There was a flat sound in his
voice.

"In the woods," said Davenport.

"Not far," Sciola said, rubbing with a

knuckle at his pouchy eye. "Half a mile from here."

"Were you there?"

Sciola stopped rubbing his eye. "What?"

"Were you there when they found him?"

"We were at the Blue Ben having some lunch," said Davenport briskly. He was breathing heavily through the nostrils and his ginger brush cut was beaded with droplets of condensed mist. "We went down for a look. Right now we're on the way to see the family."

"Don't they know?" said Camilla, after a shocked pause.

"It's not that," said Sciola. He was patting his chest, fumbling gently with long yellow fingers in the pocket of his overcoat. "We're taking them a release form. We'd like to send him down to the lab in Newark, have some tests run. Cases like this, though"—his hand closed upon something, very slowly he drew out a crumpled pack of Pall Malls—"cases like this, it's hard to get the family to sign. Can't say I blame them. These folks have been waiting around a week already, the family's all together, they're going to want to go ahead and bury him and get it over with. . . ."

"What happened?" said Henry. "Do you know?"

Sciola rummaged for a light, found it, got

his cigarette lit after two or three tries. "Hard to say," he said, letting the match fall, still burning, from his fingers. "He was at the bottom of a drop-off with a broken neck."

"You don't think he might have killed himself?"

Sciola's expression did not change, but a wisp of smoke curled from his nostrils in a manner subtly indicative of surprise. "Why do you say that?"

"Because someone inside said it just now."

He glanced over at Davenport. "I wouldn't pay any attention to these people, son," he said. "I don't know what the police are going to find, and it's going to be their decision, you understand, but I don't think they'll rule it a suicide."

"Why?"

He blinked at us placidly, his eyes balled and heavy-lidded like a tortoise's. "There's no indication of it," he said. "That I'm aware. The sheriff thinks maybe he was out there, he wasn't dressed warm enough, the weather got bad and maybe he was just in too big of a hurry to get home. . . ."

"And they don't know for sure," said Davenport, "but it looks like he might've been drinking."

Sciola made a weary, Italianate gesture of resignation. "Even if he wasn't," he said. "The ground was muddy. It was raining. It could've been dark for all we know."

Nobody said anything for several long moments.

"Look, son," said Sciola, not unkindly. "It's just my opinion, but if you ask me, your friend didn't kill himself. I saw the place he went over. The brush at the edge was all, you know—" He made a feeble, flicking gesture at the air.

"Torn up," said Davenport brusquely. "Dirt under his nails. When that kid went down he was grabbing at anything he could get ahold of."

"Nobody's trying to say how it happened," said Sciola. "I'm just saying, don't believe everything you hear. That's a dangerous place up there, they ought to fence it off or something. . . . Maybe you'd better sit down a minute, you think, honey?" he said to Camilla, who was looking a bit green.

"The college is going to get stuck either way," said Davenport. "From the way that lady in Student Services was talking I can already see them trying to dodge liability. If he got drunk at that college party . . . There was a suit like this up in Nashua, where I'm from, about two years ago. A kid got drunk at some fraternity party, passed out in a snowbank, they didn't find him till the plows came through. I guess it all depends on how drunk they were and where they got their last drink but even if he wasn't drunk it looks pretty bad for the college, doesn't it? Kid's off at school, he has an accident like this right on the campus? All due respect to the parents, but I've met them, and they're the type's gonna sue."

"How do **you** think it happened?" said Henry to Sciola.

This line of questioning did not seem to me to be a wise one, especially here, now, but Sciola grinned, a gaunt, toothy expanse, like an old dog or an opossum—too many teeth, discolored, stained. "Me?" he said.

"Yes."

He didn't say anything for a moment, just took a drag of his cigarette and nodded. "It doesn't make any difference what I think, son," he said after a pause. "This isn't a federal case."

"What?"

"He means it's not a federal case," Davenport said sharply. "There's no federal offense committed here. It's for the local cops to decide. The reason they called us up here in the first place was because of that nut, you know, from the gas station, and he didn't have anything to do with it. D.C. faxed us a lot of information on him before we came. You want to know what kind of a nut he is? He used to send all this crank mail to Anwar Sadat in the 1970s. Ex-Lax, dog turds, mail order catalogues with pictures of nude Oriental women in them. Nobody paid much attention to him, but when Mr. Sadat was assassinated in, when was it, '82, the CIA ran a check on Hundy and it was the Agency made available the files we saw. Never been arrested or anything but what a nut. Runs up thousand-dollar phone bills making prank calls to the Middle East. I saw this letter he wrote to Golda Meir where he called her his kissing cousin. . . . I mean, you have to be suspicious when somebody like him steps forward. Seemed harmless enough, wasn't even after the reward—we had an undercover approach him with a phony check, he wouldn't touch it. But it's the ones like him that you've really got to wonder. I remember Morris Lee Harden back in '78, seemed like the sweetest thing going, repairing all those clocks and watches and giving them to the poor kids, but I'll never forget the day they went out behind that jewelry shop of his with the backhoe. . . ."

"These kids don't remember Morris, Harv," said Sciola, letting the cigarette fall from his fingers. "That was before their time."

We stood there a moment or two longer, an awkward semicircle on the flagstones, and just as it seemed that everyone was going to open his mouth at once and say he had to be going,

I heard a strange, choked noise from Camilla. I looked over at her in amazement. She was crying.

For a moment, no one seemed to know what to do. Davenport gave Henry and me a disgusted look and turned half away as if to say: **this is all your fault**.

Sciola, blinking in slow, somber consternation, twice reached to put his hand upon her arm, and on the third try his slow fingertips finally made contact with her elbow. "Dear," he said to her, "dear, you want us to drop you off home on our way?"

Their car—a car you'd expect, a black Ford sedan—was parked at the bottom of the hill, in the gravel lot behind the Science Building. Camilla walked ahead between the two of them. Sciola was talking to her, as soothingly as to a child; we could hear him above the crunching footsteps, the drip of water and the sift of wind in the trees overhead. "Is your brother at home?" he said.

"Yes."

He nodded slowly. "You know," he said, "I like your brother. He's a good kid. It's funny, but I didn't know a boy and a girl could be twins. Did you know that, Harv?" he said over her head.

"No."

"I didn't know it, either. Did you look more

alike when you were little kids? I mean, there's a family resemblance, but your hair's not even quite the same color. My wife, she's got some cousins, they're twins. They both look alike and they both work for the Welfare Department, too." He paused peacefully. "You and your brother, you get along pretty well, don't you?"

She made a muffled reply.

He nodded somberly. "That's nice," he said. "I bet you kids have some interesting stories. About ESP and things like that. My wife's cousins, they go to these twin conventions they have sometimes, you wouldn't believe the things they come back and tell us."

White sky. Trees fading at the skyline, the mountains gone. My hands dangled from the cuffs of my jacket as if they weren't my own. I never got used to the way the horizon there could just erase itself and leave you marooned, adrift, in an incomplete dreamscape that was like a sketch for the world you knew—the outline of a single tree standing in for a grove, lamp-posts and chimneys floating up out of context before the surrounding canvas was filled in—an amnesia-land, a kind of skewed Heaven where the old landmarks were recognizable but spaced too far apart, and disarranged, and made terrible by the emptiness around them.

An old shoe was lying on the asphalt in front of the loading dock, where the ambulance had been only minutes before. It wasn't Bunny's shoe. I don't know whose it was or how it got there. It was just an old tennis shoe lying on its side. I don't know why I remember that now, or why it made such an impression on me.

CHAPTER
7

ALTHOUGH BUNNY hadn't known many people at Hampden, it was such a small school that almost everyone had been aware of him in some way or other; people knew his name, knew him by sight, remembered the sound of his voice which was in many ways his most distinct feature of all. Odd, but even though I have a snapshot or two of Bunny it is not the face but the voice, the lost voice, which has stayed with me over the years—strident, garrulous, abnormally resonant, once heard it was not easily forgotten, and in those first days after his death the dining halls were strangely quiet without that great braying hee-haw of his echoing in its customary place by the milk machine.

It was normal, then, that he should be missed, even mourned—for it's a hard thing when someone dies at a school like Hampden, where we were all so isolated, and thrown so much together. But I was surprised at the wanton display of grief which spewed forth once his death became official. It seemed not only gratuitous, but rather shameful given the circumstances. No one had seemed very torn up by his disappearance, even in those grim final days when it seemed that the news when it came must certainly be bad; nor, in the public eye, had the search seemed much besides a massive inconvenience. But now, at news of his death, people were strangely frantic. Everyone, suddenly, had known him; everyone was deranged with grief; everyone was just going to have to try and get on as well as they could without him. "He would have wanted it that way." That was a phrase I heard many times that week on the lips of people who had absolutely no idea what Bunny wanted; college officials, anonymous weepers, strangers who clutched and sobbed outside the dining halls; from the Board of Trustees, who, in a defensive and carefully worded statement, said that "in harmony with the unique spirit of Bunny Corcoran, as well as the humane and progressive ideals of Hampden College," a large gift was being made in his name to the American Civil Liberties Union—an organization Bunny would certainly have abhorred, had he been aware of its existence.

I really could go on for pages about all the public histrionics in the days after Bunny's death. The flag flew at half-mast. The psychological counselors were on call twenty-four hours a day. A few oddballs from the Political Science department wore black armbands. There was an agitated flurry of tree plantings, memorial services, fund-raisers and concerts. A freshman girl attempted suicide—for entirely unrelated reasons—by eating poison berries from a bush outside the Music Building, but somehow this was all tied in with the general hysteria. Everyone wore sunglasses for days. Frank and Jud, taking as always the view that Life Must Go On, went around with their paint can collecting money for a Beer Blast to be held in Bunny's memory. This was thought to be in bad taste by certain of the school officials, especially as Bunny's death had brought to public attention the large number of alcohol-related functions at Hampden, but Frank and Jud were unmoved. "He would have wanted us to party," they said sullenly, which certainly was not the case; but then again, the Student Services office lived in mortal fear of Frank and Jud. Their fathers were on the lifetime board of directors; Frank's dad had donated money for a new library and Jud's had built the Science Building; theory had it that the two of them were unexpellable, and a reprimand from the Dean of Studies was not going to stop them from doing anything they felt like doing. So the Beer Blast went on, and was just the sort of tasteless and incoherent event you might expect—but I am getting ahead of my story.

Hampden College, as a body, was always strangely prone to hysteria. Whether from isolation, malice, or simple boredom, people there were far more credulous and excitable than educated people are generally believed to be, and this hermetic, overheated atmosphere made it a thriving black petri dish of melodrama and distortion. I remember well, for instance, the blind animal terror which ensued when some townie set off the civil defense sirens as a joke. Someone said it was a nuclear attack; TV and radio reception, never good there in the mountains, happened to be particularly bad that night, and in the ensuing stampede for the telephones the switchboard shorted out, plunging the school into a violent and almost unimaginable panic. Cars collided in the parking lot. People screamed, wept, gave away their possessions, huddled in small groups for comfort and warmth. Some hippies barricaded themselves in the Science Building, in the lone bomb shelter, and refused to let anyone in who didn't know the words to "Sugar Magnolia." Factions formed, leaders rose from the chaos. Though the world, in fact, was not destroyed, everyone had a marvelous time and people spoke fondly of the event for years afterward.

Though not nearly so spectacular, this manifestation of grief for Bunny was in many ways a similar phenomenon—an affirmation of community, a formulaic expression of homage and dread. **Learn by Doing** is the motto of Hampden. People experienced a sense of invulnerability and well-being by attending rap sessions, outdoor flute concerts; enjoyed having an official excuse to compare nightmares or break down in public. In a certain sense it was simply play-acting but at Hampden, where creative expression was valued above all else, play-acting was itself a kind of work, and people went about their grief as seriously as small children will sometimes play quite grimly and without pleasure in make-believe offices and stores.

The mourning of the hippies, in particular, had an almost anthropological significance. Bunny, in life, had been at almost perpetual war with them: the hippies contaminating the bathtub with tie-dye and playing their stereos loudly to annoy him; Bunny bombarding them with empty soda cans and calling Security whenever he thought they were smoking pot. Now that he was dead, they marked his passage to another plane in impersonal and almost tribal fashion—chanting, weaving mandalas, beating on drums, performing their own inscrutable and mysterious rites. Henry stopped to watch them at a distance, resting the ferrule of his umbrella on the toe of his khaki-gaitered shoe.

"Is 'mandala' a Pali word?" I asked him.

He shook his head. "No," he said. "Sanskrit. Means 'circle.' "

"So this is some Hindu kind of thing?"

"Not necessarily," he said, looking the hippies up and down as if they were animals in a zoo. "They have come to be associated with Tantrism—mandalas, that is. Tantrism acted as a kind of corrupting influence upon the Indian Buddhist pantheon, though of course elements of it were assimilated into and restructured by the Buddhist tradition, until, by A.D. 800, say, Tantrism had an academic tradition of its own—a corrupt tradition, to my way of thinking, but a tradition nonetheless." He paused, watching a girl with a tambourine twirling dizzily on the lawn. "But to answer your question," he said, "I believe that the mandala actually has quite a respectable place in the history of Theravada, Buddhism proper. One finds their features in reliquary mounds on the Gangetic plain and elsewhere from as early as the first century A.D."

Reading back over this, I feel that in some respects I've done Bunny an injustice. People really did like him. No one had known him all that well but it was a strange feature of his personality that the less one actually knew him, the more one felt one did. Viewed from a distance, his character projected an impression of solidity and wholeness which was in fact as insubstantial as a hologram; up close, he was all motes and light, you could pass your hand right through him. If you stepped back far enough, however, the illusion would click in again and there he would be, bigger than life, squinting at you from behind his little glasses and raking back a dank lock of hair with one hand.

A character like his disintegrates under analysis. It can only be defined by the anecdote, the chance encounter or the sentence overheard. People who had never once spoken to him suddenly remembered, with a pang of affection, having seen him throwing sticks to a dog or stealing tulips from a teacher's garden. "He **touched people's lives**," said the college president, leaning forward to grip the podium with both his hands; and though he was to repeat the exact phrase, in the exact way, two months later at a memorial service for the freshman girl (who'd fared better with a single-edged razor blade than with the poison berries), it was, in Bunny's case at least, strangely true. He **did** touch people's lives, the lives of strangers, in an entirely unanticipated way. It was they who really mourned him—or what they thought was him—with a grief that was no less sharp for not being intimate with its object.

It was this unreality of character, this cartoonishness if you will, which was the secret of his appeal and what finally made his death so sad. Like any great comedian, he colored his environment wherever he went; in order to marvel at his constancy you wanted to see him in all sorts of alien situations: Bunny riding a camel, Bunny babysitting, Bunny in space. Now, in death, this constancy crystallized and became something else entirely: he was an old familiar jokester cast—with surprising effect— in the tragic role.

————

When the snow finally melted it went as quickly as it had come. In twenty-four hours it was all gone except for some lovely shady patches in the woods—white-laced branches dripping rain holes in the crust—and the slushy gray piles at the roadside. Commons lawn stretched out wide and desolate like some Napoleonic battlefield: churned, sordid, roiled with footprints.

It was a strange, fragmented time. In the

days before the funeral none of us saw each other very much. The Corcorans had spirited Henry back to Connecticut with them; Cloke, who seemed to me close on the verge of a nervous breakdown, went uninvited to stay at Charles and Camilla's, where he drank Grolsch beer by the six-pack and fell asleep on the couch with lighted cigarettes. I myself was encumbered with Judy Poovey and her friends Tracy and Beth. At mealtimes they came regularly to fetch me ("Richard," Judy would say, reaching across the table to squeeze my hand, "you **must eat**") and for the rest of the time I was captive to little activities they planned for me—drive-in movies and Mexican food, going to Tracy's apartment for Margaritas and MTV. Though I didn't mind the drive-ins, I did not care for the continual parade of nachos and tequila-based drinks. They were crazy about something called Kamikazes, and liked to dye their Margaritas a horrifying electric blue.

Actually, I was often glad of their company. Despite her faults, Judy was a kindly soul, and she was so bossy and talkative that I felt oddly safe with her. Beth I disliked. She was a dancer, from Santa Fe, with a rubbery face and an idiotic giggle and dimples all over when she smiled. At Hampden she was thought something of a beauty but I loathed her lolloping, spaniel-like walk and her little-girl voice—very affected, it seemed to me—which degenerated frequently into a whine. She had also had a nervous breakdown or two, and sometimes, in repose, she got a kind of walleyed look that made me nervous. Tracy was great. She was pretty and Jewish, with a dazzling smile and a penchant for Mary Tyler Moore mannerisms like hugging herself or twirling around with her arms outstretched. The three of them smoked a lot, told long boring stories ("So, like, our plane just sat on the runway for **five hours**") and talked about people I didn't know. I, the absentminded bereaved, was free to stare peacefully out the window. But sometimes I grew tired of them, and if I complained of a headache or said I wanted to go to sleep, Tracy and Beth would disappear with pre-arranged swiftness and there I would be, alone with Judy. She meant well, I suppose, but the type of comfort she wished to offer did not much appeal to me and after ten or twenty minutes alone with her I was ready again for any amount of Margaritas and MTV at Tracy's.

Francis, alone of us all, was unencumbered and occasionally he stopped by to see me. Sometimes he found me alone; when he did not he would sit stiffly in my desk chair and pretend, Henrylike, to examine my Greek books until even dimwit Tracy got the hint and left. As soon as the door closed and he heard footsteps on the stairs he would shut the book on his finger and lean forward, agitated and blinking. Our main worry at the time was the autopsy Bunny's family had requested; we were shocked when Henry, in Connecticut, got us word that one was in progress, by slipping away from the Corcorans' house one afternoon to call Francis from a pay phone, under the flapping banners and striped awnings of a used-car lot, with a highway roaring in the background. He'd overheard Mrs. Corcoran tell Mr. Corcoran that it was all for the best, that otherwise (and Henry swore he'd heard this very distinctly) **they'd never know for sure.**

Whatever else one may say about guilt, it certainly lends one diabolical powers of invention; and I spent two or three of the worst nights I had, then or ever, lying awake drunk with a horrible taste of tequila in my mouth and worrying about clothing filaments, fingerprints, strands of hair. All I knew about autopsies was what I had seen on reruns of "Quincy," but somehow it never occurred to me that my information might be inaccurate because it came from a TV show. Didn't they research these things carefully, have a consulting physician on the set? I sat up, turned on the lights; my mouth was stained a ghastly blue. When the drinks came up in the bathroom they were brilliant-hued, perfectly clear, a rush of vibrant acid turquoise the color of Ty-D-Bol.

But Henry, free as he was to observe the Corcorans in their own habitat, soon figured out what was going on. Francis was so impatient with his happy news that he did not even wait for Tracy and Judy to leave the room but told me immediately, in sloppily inflected Greek, while sweet dopey Tracy wondered aloud at our wanting to keep up our schoolwork at a time like this.

"Do not fear," he said to me. **"It is the mother. She is concerned with the dishonor of the son having to do with wine."**

I did not understand what he meant. The form of "dishonor" ($\alpha\tau\iota\mu\acute{\iota}\alpha$) that he used also meant "loss of civil rights." **"Atimia?"** I repeated.

"Yes."

"But rights are for living men, not for the dead."

"Οἰμοι," he said, shaking his head. "Oh, dear. No. No."

He cast about, snapping his fingers, while Judy and Tracy looked on in interest. It is harder to carry on a conversation in a dead language than you might think. **"There has been much rumor,"** he said at last. **"The mother** grieves. **Not for her son,**" he added hastily, when he saw I was about to speak, **"for she is a wicked woman. Rather she grieves for the shame which has fallen on her house."**

"What shame is this?"

"Οινον," he said impatiently. "Φάρμακον. **She seeks to show that his corpse does not hold wine**" (and here he employed a very elegant and untranslatable metaphor: dregs in the empty wineskin of his body).

"And why, pray tell, does she care?"

"Because there is talk among the citizens. It is shameful for a young man to die while drunk."

This was true, about the talk at least. Mrs. Corcoran, who previously had put herself at the disposal of anyone who would listen, was angry at the unflattering position in which she now found herself. Early articles, which had depicted her as "well-dressed," "striking," the family "perfect," had given way to snide and vaguely accusatory ones of the ilk of MOM SEZ: NOT MY KID. Though there was only a poor beer bottle to suggest the presence of alcohol, and no real evidence of drugs at all, psychologists on the evening news spoke of dysfunctional families, the phenomenon of denial, pointed out that addictive tendencies were often passed from parent to child. It was a hard blow. Mrs. Corcoran, leaving Hampden, walked through the crush of her old pals the reporters with her eyes averted and her teeth clenched in a brilliant hateful smile.

Of course, it **was** unfair. From the news accounts one would have thought Bunny the most stereotypical of "substance abusers" or "troubled teens." It did not matter a whit that everyone who knew him (including us: Bunny was no juvenile delinquent) denied this; no matter that the autopsy showed only a tiny percentage of blood alcohol and no drugs at all; no matter that he was not even a teenager: the rumors—wheeling vulture-like in the skies above his corpse—had finally descended and sunk in their claws for good. A paragraph which blandly stated the results of the autopsy appeared in the back of the Hampden **Examiner**. But in college folklore he is remembered as a stumbling teen inebriate; his beery ghost is still evoked in darkened rooms, for freshmen, along with the car-crash decapitees and the bobby soxer who hanged herself in Putnam attic and all the rest of the shadowy ranks of the Hampden dead.

———

The funeral was set for Wednesday. On Monday morning I found two envelopes in my mailbox: one from Henry, the other from Julian. I opened Julian's first. It was postmarked New York and was written hastily, in the red pen he used for correcting our Greek.

> Dear Richard—How very unhappy I am this morning, as I know I will be for many mornings to come. The news of our friend's death has saddened me greatly. I do not know if you have tried to reach me, I have been away, I have not been well, I doubt if I shall return to Hampden until after the funeral—
>
> How sad it is to think that Wednesday will be the last time that we shall all be together. I hope this letter finds you well. It brings love.

At the bottom were his initials.

Henry's letter, from Connecticut, was as stilted as a cryptogram from the western front.

> Dear Richard,
>
> I hope you are well. For several days I have been at the Corcorans' house. Although I feel I am less comfort to them than they, in their bereavement, can recognize, they have allowed me to be of help to them in many small household matters.

Mr. Corcoran has asked me to write to Bunny's friends at school and extend an invitation to spend the night before the funeral at his house. I understand you will be put up in the basement. If you do not plan to attend, please telephone Mrs. Corcoran and let her know.

I look forward to seeing you at the funeral if not, as I hope, before.

There was no signature, but instead a tag from the **Iliad**, in Greek. It was from the eleventh book, when Odysseus, cut off from his friends, finds himself alone and on enemy territory:

Be strong, saith my heart; I am a soldier;
I have seen worse sights than this.

———

I rode down to Connecticut with Francis. Though I'd expected the twins to come with us, instead they went a day earlier with Cloke—who, to everyone's surprise, had received a personal invitation from Mrs. Corcoran herself. We had thought he would not be invited at all. After Sciola and Davenport caught him trying to leave town, Mrs. Corcoran had refused to even speak to him. ("She's saving face," said Francis.) At any rate, he'd got the personal invitation, and there had also been invitations—relayed through Henry—for Cloke's friends Rooney Wynne and Bram Guernsey.

Actually, the Corcorans had invited quite a few people from Hampden—dorm acquaintances, people I didn't know Bunny even knew. A girl named Sophie Dearbold, whom I knew slightly from French class, was to ride down with Francis and me.

"How did Bunny know her?" I asked Francis on the way to her dorm.

"I don't think he did, not well. He did have a crush on her, though, freshman year. I'm sure Marion won't like it a bit that they've asked her."

Though I'd feared that the ride down might be awkward, in fact it was a wonderful relief to be around a stranger. We almost had fun, with the radio going and Sophie (brown-eyed, gravel-voiced) leaning on folded arms over the front seat talking to us, and Francis in a better mood than I'd seen him in in ages. "You look like Audrey Hepburn," he told her, "you know that?" She gave us Kools and cinnamon gumballs, told funny stories. I laughed and looked out the window and prayed we'd miss our turn. I had never been to Connecticut in my life. I had never been to a funeral, either.

Shady Brook was on a narrow road that veered off sharply from the highway and twisted along for many miles, over bridges, past farmland and horse pastures and fields. After a time the rolling meadows segued into a golf course. SHADY BROOK COUNTRY CLUB, said the wood-burned sign that swung in front of the mock-Tudor clubhouse. The houses began after that—large, handsome, widely spaced, each set on its own six or seven acres of land.

The place was like a maze. Francis looked for numbers on the mailboxes, nosing into one false trail after another and backing out again, cursing, grinding the gears. There were no signs and no apparent logic to the house numbers, and after we'd poked around blind for about half an hour, I began to hope that we would never find it at all, that we could just turn around and have a jolly ride back to Hampden.

But of course we did find it. At the end of its own cul-de-sac, it was a large modern house of the "architectural" sort, bleached cedar, its split levels and asymmetrical terraces self-consciously bare. The yard was paved with black cinder, and there was no greenery at all except a few gingko trees in postmodern tubs, placed at dramatic intervals.

"Wow," said Sophie, a true Hampden girl, ever dutiful in homage to the New.

I looked over at Francis and he shrugged.

"His mom likes modern architecture," he said.

———

I had never seen the man who answered the door but with a sick, dreamlike feeling I recognized him instantly. He was big and red in the face, with a heavy jaw and a full head of white hair; for a moment he stared at us, his smallish mouth fallen open into a tight, round o. Then, surprisingly boyish and quick, he sprang forward and seized Francis's hand. "Well," he said. "Well, well, well." His voice was nasal, garrulous, Bunny's voice. "If it's not the old Carrot Top. How are you, boy?"

"Pretty good," said Francis, and I was a little surprised at the depth and warmth with which he said it, and the strength with which he returned the handshake.

Mr. Corcoran slung a heavy arm around his neck and pulled him close. "This one's my boy," he said to Sophie and me, reaching up to tousle Francis's hair. "All my brothers were redheads and out of my boys there's not an honest-to-god redhead in the bunch. Can't understand it. Who are you, sweetheart?" he said to Sophie, disengaging his arm and reaching for her hand.

"Hi. I'm Sophie Dearbold."

"Well, you're mighty pretty. Isn't she pretty, boys. You look just like your aunt Jean, honey."

"What?" said Sophie, after a confused pause.

"Why, your **aunt**, honey. Your daddy's sister. That pretty Jean Lickfold that won the ladies' golf tournament out at the club last year."

"No, sir. **Dear**bold."

"Dearfold. Well, isn't that strange. I don't know of any Dearfolds around here. Now, I used to know a fellow name of Breedlow, but that must have been, oh, twenty years ago. He was in business. They say he embezzled a cool five million from his partner."

"I'm not from around here."

He cocked an eyebrow at her, in a manner reminiscent of Bunny. "No?" he said.

"No."

"Not from Shady Brook?" He said it as if he could hardly believe it.

"No."

"Then where you from, honey? Greenwich?"

"Detroit."

"Bless your heart then. To come all this way."

Sophie, smiling, shook her head and started to explain when, with absolutely no warning, Mr. Corcoran flung his arms around her and burst into tears.

We were frozen with horror. Sophie's eyes, over his heaving shoulder, were round and aghast as if he'd run her through with a knife.

"Oh, darling," he wailed, his face buried deep in her neck. "Honey, how are we going to get along without him?"

"Come on, Mr. Corcoran," said Francis, tugging at his sleeve.

"We loved him a lot, honey," sobbed Mr. Corcoran. "Didn't we? He loved you, too. He would have wanted you to know that. You know that, don't you, dear?"

"Mr. Corcoran," said Francis, grabbing him by the shoulders and shaking him hard. **"Mr. Corcoran."**

He turned and fell back against Francis, bellowing.

I ran around to the other side and managed to get his arm around my neck. His knees sagged; he almost pulled me down but somehow, staggering beneath his weight, Francis and I got him to his feet and together we maneuvered him inside and weaved down the hall with him ("Oh, shit," I heard Sophie murmur, **"shit."**) and got him into a chair.

He was still crying. His face was purple. When I reached down to loosen his collar he grabbed me by the wrist. "Gone," he wailed, looking me straight in the eye. **"My baby."**

His gaze—helpless, wild—hit me like a blackjack. Suddenly, and for the first time, really, I was struck by the bitter, irrevocable truth of it; the evil of what we had done. It was like running full speed into a brick wall. I let go his collar, feeling completely helpless. I wanted to die. "Oh, God," I mumbled, "God help me, I'm sorry—"

I felt a fierce kick in my anklebone. It was Francis. His face was as white as chalk.

A shaft of light splintered painfully in my vision. I clutched the back of the chair, closed my eyes and saw luminous red as the rhythmic noise of his sobs fell over and over again, like a bludgeon.

Then, very abruptly, they stopped. Everything was quiet. I opened my eyes. Mr. Corcoran—leftover tears still rolling down his cheeks but his face otherwise composed—was looking with interest at a spaniel puppy who was gnawing furtively at the toe of his shoe.

"Jennie," he said severely. **"Bad** girl. Didn't Mama put you out? Huh?"

With a cooing, baby noise, he reached down and scooped up the little dog—its feet paddling furiously in midair—and carried her out of the room.

"Now, go on," I heard him say airily. "Scat."

A screen door creaked somewhere. In a moment he was back: calm now, beaming, a dad from an ad.

"Any of you kids care for a beer?" he said.

We were all agog. No one answered him. I stared at him, trembling, ashen-faced.

"Come on, guys," he said, and winked. "No takers?"

At last, Francis cleared his throat with a rasping sound. "Ah, I believe I'd like one, yes."

There was a silence.

"Me, too," said Sophie.

"Three?" said Mr. Corcoran to me jovially, holding up three fingers.

I moved my mouth but no sound came out of it.

He put his head to the side, as if fixing me with his good eye. "I don't think we've met, have we, son?"

I shook my head.

"Macdonald Corcoran," he said, leaning forward to offer his hand. "Call me Mack."

I mumbled my own name.

"What's that?" he said brightly, hand to ear.

I said it again, louder this time.

"Ah! So you're the one from California! Where's your tan, son?" He laughed loudly at his joke and went to fetch the beers.

I sat down hard, exhausted and almost sick. We were in an overscaled, **Architectural Digest** sort of room, big and loft-like, with skylights and a fieldstone fireplace, chairs upholstered in white leather, kidney-shaped coffee table—modern, expensive, Italian stuff. Running along the back wall was a long glass trophy case filled with loving cups, ribbons, school and sports memorabilia; in ominous proximity were several large funeral wreaths which, in conjunction with the trophies, gave that corner of the room a Kentucky Derby sort of look.

"This is a beautiful space," said Sophie. Her voice echoed amid the sharp surfaces and the polished floor.

"Why, thank you, honey," Mr. Corcoran said from the kitchen. "We were in **House Beautiful** last year, and the Home section of the **Times** the year before that. Not quite what I'd pick myself, but Kathy's the decorator in the family, y'know."

The doorbell rang. We looked at each other. Then it rang again, two melodious chimes, and Mrs. Corcoran clicked through from the back of the house and past us without a word or a glance.

"Henry," she called. "Your guests are here." Then she opened the front door. "Hello," she said to the delivery boy who was standing outside. "Which one are you? Are you from Sunset Florists?"

"Yes, ma'am. Please sign."

"Now wait just a minute. I called you people

earlier. I want to know why you delivered all these **wreaths** here while I was out this morning."

"I didn't deliver them. I just came on shift."

"You're with Sunset Florists, aren't you?"

"Yes, ma'am." I felt sorry for him. He was a teenager, with blotches of flesh-colored Clearasil scattered over his face.

"I asked **specifically** that only floral arrangements and house plants be sent here. These wreaths should all be down at the funeral home."

"I'm sorry, lady. If you want to call the manager or something—"

"I'm afraid you don't understand. I don't want these wreaths in my house. I want you to pack them right back up in your truck and take them to the funeral home. And don't try to give me that one, either," she said as he held up a gaudy wreath of red and yellow carnations. "Just tell me who it's from."

The boy squinted at his clipboard. " 'With sympathy, Mr. and Mrs. Robert Bartle.' "

"Ah!" said Mr. Corcoran, who had come back with the beers; he had them all clasped together in his hands, very clumsily, without a tray. "That from Betty and Bob?"

Mrs. Corcoran ignored him. "I guess you can go ahead and bring in those ferns," she said to the delivery boy, eyeing the foil-wrapped pots with loathing.

After he had gone Mrs. Corcoran began to inspect the ferns, lifting up the fronds to check for dead foliage, making notes on the backs of the envelopes with a tiny silver screw-point pencil. To her husband she said: "Did you see that wreath the Bartles sent?"

"Wasn't that nice of them."

"No, in fact I don't think it appropriate for an employee to send something like that. I wonder, is Bob thinking about asking you for a raise?"

"Now, hon."

"I can't believe these plants, either," she said, jabbing a forefinger into the soil. "This African violet is almost dead. Louise would be humiliated if she knew."

"It's the thought that counts."

"I know, but still, if I've learned one thing from this it is never to order flowers from Sunset Florists again. All the things from Tina's Flowerland are so much nicer. **Francis,**" she said, in the same bored tone and without looking up. "You haven't been to see us since last Easter."

Francis took a sip of his beer. "Oh, I've been fine," he said stagily. "How are you?"

She sighed and shook her head. "It's been

terribly hard," she said. "We're all trying to take things one day at a time. I never realized before how very difficult it can be for a parent to just **let go** and . . . Henry, is that you?" she said sharply at the sound of some scuffling on the landing.

A pause. "No, Mom, just me."

"Go find him, Pat, and tell him to get down here," she said. Then she turned back to Francis. "We got a lovely spray of Easter lilies from your mother this morning," she said to him. "How is she?"

"Oh, she's fine. She's in the city now. She was really upset," he added uncomfortably, "when she heard about Bunny." (Francis had told me she was hysterical on the telephone and had to go take a pill.)

"She is such a lovely person," said Mrs. Corcoran sweetly. "I was so sorry when I heard she'd been admitted to the Betty Ford Center."

"She was only there for a couple of days," said Francis.

She raised an eyebrow. "Oh? She made that much progress, did she? I've always heard it was an excellent place."

Francis cleared his throat. "Well, she mainly went out there for a rest. Quite a number of people do that, you know."

Mrs. Corcoran looked surprised. "Oh, you don't mind talking about it, do you?" she said.

"I don't think you should. I think it's very modern of your mother to realize that she needed help. Not so long ago one simply didn't admit to problems of that nature. When I was a girl—"

"Well, well, speak of the Devil," boomed Mr. Corcoran.

Henry, in a dark suit, was creaking down the stairs with a stiff, measured tread.

Francis stood up. I did, too. He ignored us.

"Come on in here, son," said Mr. Corcoran. "Grab yourself a brewski."

"Thank you, no," said Henry.

Up close, I was startled to see how pale he was. His face was leaden and set and beads of perspiration stood out on his forehead.

"What you boys been doing up there all afternoon?" Mr. Corcoran said through a mouthful of ice.

Henry blinked at him.

"Huh?" said Mr. Corcoran pleasantly. "Looking at girlie magazines? Building yourselves a ham radio set?"

Henry passed a hand—which, I saw, trembled slightly—over his forehead. "I was reading," he said.

"Reading?" said Mr. Corcoran, as if he'd never heard of such a thing.

"Yes, sir."

"What is it? Something good?"

"The **Upanishads**."

"Well aren't you smart. You know, I've got a whole shelf of books down in the basement if you want to take a look. Even have a couple old Perry Masons. They're pretty good. Exactly like the TV show, except Perry gets a little sexy with Della and sometimes he'll say 'damn' and stuff."

Mrs. Corcoran cleared her throat.

"Henry," she said smoothly, reaching for her drink, "I'm sure the **young people** would like to see where they'll be staying. Maybe they have some luggage in the car."

"All right."

"Check the downstairs bathroom to make sure there are enough washcloths and towels. If there aren't, get some from the linen closet in the hall."

Henry nodded but before he could answer Mr. Corcoran suddenly came up behind him. "This boy," he said, slapping him on the back—I saw Henry's neck clench and his teeth sink into his lower lip—"is **one in a million.** Isn't he a prince, Kathy?"

"He has certainly been quite a help," said Mrs. Corcoran coolly.

"You bet your boots he has. I don't know what we would've done this week without him. You kids," said Mr. Corcoran, a hand clamped on Henry's shoulder, "better hope you've got friends like this one. They don't come along like this every day. No, sir. Why, I'll never forget, it was Bunny's first night at Hampden, he called me up on the telephone. 'Dad,' he said to me, 'Dad, you ought to see this nut they gave me for a roommate.' 'Stick it out, son,' I told him, 'give it a chance' and before you could spit it was Henry this, Henry that, he's changing his major from whatever the hell it was to ancient Greek. Tearing off to Italy. Happy as a clam." The tears were welling in his eyes. "Just goes to show," he said, shaking Henry's shoulder with a kind of rough affection. "**Never judge a book by its cover.** Old Henry here may look like he's got a stick up his butt but there never breathed a finer fella. Why, just about the last time I spoke to the old Bunster he was all excited about taking off to France with this guy in the summer—"

"Now, Mack," said Mrs. Corcoran, but it was too late. He was crying again.

It was not as bad as the first time but still it was bad. He threw his arms around Henry and sobbed in his lapel while Henry just stood there, gazing off into the distance with a haggard, stoic calm.

Everyone was embarrassed. Mrs. Corcoran began to pick at the house plants and I, ears burning, was staring at my lap when a door slammed and two young men sauntered into the wide, high-raftered hall. There was no mistaking for an instant who they were. The light was behind them, I couldn't see either of them very well but they were laughing and talking and, oh, God, what a bright sudden stab in my heart at the echo of Bunny which rang—harsh, derisive, vibrant—through their laughter.

They ignored their father's tears and marched right up to him. "Hey, Pop," said the eldest. He was curly haired, about thirty, and looked very much like Bunny in the face. A baby wearing a little cap that said Red Sox was perched high on his hip.

The other brother—freckled, thinner, with a too-dark tan and black circles under his blue eyes—took the baby. "Here," he said. "Go see Grandpa."

Mr. Corcoran stopped crying instantly, in mid-sob; he held the baby high in the air and looked up at it adoringly. "Champ!" he shouted. "Did you go for a ride with Daddy and Uncle Brady?"

"We took him to McDonald's," said Brady. "Got him a Happy Meal."

Mr. Corcoran's jaw dropped in wonder. "Did you eat it all?" he asked the baby. "All that Happy Meal?"

"Say yes," cooed the baby's father. " **'Yes, Drampaw.' "**

"That's baloney, Ted," said Brady, laughing. "He didn't eat a bite of it."

"He got a prize in the box, though, didn't you? Didn't you? Huh?"

"Let's see it," said Mr. Corcoran, busily prying the baby's fingers from around it.

"Henry," said Mrs. Corcoran, "perhaps you'll help the young lady with her bags and show her to her room. Brady, you can take the boys downstairs."

Mr. Corcoran had got the prize—a plastic airplane—away from the baby and was making it fly back and forth.

"Look!" he said, in a tone of hushed awe.

"Since it's only for a night," Mrs. Corcoran said to us, "I'm sure that no one will mind doubling up."

As we were leaving with Brady, Mr. Corcoran plumped the baby down on the hearth rug and was rolling around, tickling him. I could hear the baby's high screams of terror and delight all the way down the stairs.

———

We were to stay in the basement. Along the back wall, near the Ping-Pong and pool tables, several army cots had been set up, and in the corner was a pile of sleeping bags.

"Isn't this wretched," said Francis as soon as we were alone.

"It's just for tonight."

"I can't sleep in rooms with lots of people. I'll be up all night."

I sat down on a cot. The room had a damp, unused smell and the light from the lamp over the pool table was greenish and depressing.

"It's dusty, too," said Francis. "I think we ought to just go check into a hotel."

Sniffing noisily, he complained about the dust as he searched for an ashtray but deadly radon could have been seeping into the room, it didn't matter to me. All I wondered was how, in the name of Heaven and a merciful God, was I going to make it through the hours ahead. We had been there only twenty minutes and already I felt like shooting myself.

He was still complaining and I was still sunk in despair when Camilla came down. She was wearing jet earrings, patent-leather shoes, a natty, closely cut black velvet suit.

"Hello," Francis said, handing her a cigarette. "Let's go check into the Ramada Inn."

As she put the cigarette between her parched lips I realized how much I'd missed her for the last few days.

"Oh, you don't have it so bad," she said. "Last night **I** had to sleep with **Marion**."

"Same room?"

"Same **bed**."

Francis's eyes widened with admiration and

horror. "Oh, really? Oh, I say. That's awful," he said in a hushed, respectful voice.

"Charles is upstairs with her now. She's hysterical because somebody asked that poor girl who rode down with you."

"Where's Henry?"

"Haven't you seen him yet?"

"I saw him. I didn't **talk** to him."

She paused to blow out a cloud of smoke. "How does he seem to you?"

"I've seen him looking better. Why?"

"Because he's sick. Those headaches."

"One of the **bad** ones?"

"That's what he says."

Francis looked at her in disbelief. "How is he up and walking around, then?"

"I don't know. He's all doped up. He has his pills and he's been taking them for days."

"Well, where is he now? Why isn't he in bed?"

"I don't know. Mrs. Corcoran just sent him down to the Cumberland Farms to get that damn baby a quart of milk."

"Can he **drive**?"

"I have no idea."

"Francis," I said, "your cigarette."

He jumped up, grabbed for it too quickly and burned his fingers. He'd laid it on the edge of the pool table and the coal had burned down to the wood; a charred spot was spreading on the varnish.

"Boys?" Mrs. Corcoran called from the head of the stairs. "Boys? Do you mind if I come down to check the thermostat?"

"Quick," Camilla whispered, mashing out her cigarette. "We're not supposed to smoke down here."

"Who's there?" said Mrs. Corcoran sharply. "Is something burning?"

"No, ma'am," Francis said, wiping at the burned spot and scrambling to hide the cigarette butt as she came down the steps.

———

It was one of the worst nights of my life. The house was filling with people and the hours passed in a dreadful streaky blur of relatives, neighbors, crying children, covered dishes, blocked driveways, ringing telephones, bright lights, strange faces, awkward conversations. Some swinish, hard-faced man trapped me in a corner for hours, boasting of bass tournaments and businesses in Chicago and Nashville and Kansas City until finally I excused myself and locked myself in an upstairs bathroom, ignoring the beating and piteous cries of an unknown toddler who pled, weeping, for admittance.

Dinner was set out at seven, an unappetizing combination of gourmet carry-out—orzo salad, duck in Campari, miniature **foie gras** tarts—and food the neighbors had made: tuna casseroles, gelatin molds in Tupperware, and a frightful dessert called a "wacky cake" that I am at a loss to even describe. People roamed with paper plates. It was dark outside and raining. Hugh Corcoran, in shirtsleeves, went around with a bottle freshening drinks, nudging his way through the dark, murmuring crowd. He brushed by me without a glance. Of all the brothers, he bore the strongest resemblance to Bunny (Bunny's death was starting to seem some horrible kind of generative act, more Bunnys popping up everywhere I looked, Bunnys coming out of the woodwork), and it was akin to looking into the future and seeing what Bunny would have looked like at thirty-five, just as looking at his father was like seeing him at sixty. I knew him and he didn't know me. I had a strong, nearly irresistible urge to take him by the arm, say something to him, what I didn't know: just to see the brows drop abruptly in the way I knew so well, to see the startled expression in the naive, muddy eyes.

It was I killed the old pawnbroker woman and her sister Lizaveta with an axe and robbed them.

Laughter, vertigo. Strangers kept wandering up and talking at me. I disengaged myself from one of Bunny's teenaged cousins—who, upon hearing I was from California, had begun to ask me a lot of very complicated questions about surfing—and, swimming through the bobbling crowd, found Henry. He was standing by himself in front of some glass doors, his back to the room, smoking a cigarette.

I stood beside him. He didn't look at me or speak. The doors faced out on a barren, flood-lit terrace—black cinder, privet in concrete urns, a statue artfully broken in white pieces on the ground. Rain slanted in the lights, which were angled to cast long, dramatic shadows. The effect was fashionable, post-nuclear but ancient, too, like some pumice-strewn courtyard from Pompeii.

"That is the ugliest garden I have ever seen," I said.

"Yes," said Henry. He was very pale. "Rubble and ash."

People laughed and talked behind us. The lights, through the rain-spattered window, cast a pattern of droplets trickling down his face.

"Maybe you'd better lie down," I said after a while.

He bit his lip. The ash on his cigarette was about an inch long. "I don't have any more medicine," he said.

I looked at the side of his face. "Can you get along?"

"I guess I'll have to, won't I?" he said without moving.

———

Camilla locked the door of the bathroom behind us and the two of us, on our hands and knees, began to rummage through the mess of prescription bottles under the sink.

" 'For high blood pressure,' " she read.

"No."

" 'For asthma.' "

There was a knock on the door.

"Somebody's in here," I yelled.

Camilla's head was wedged all the way in the cabinet by the water pipes, so that her rear end stuck out. I could hear the medicine bottles clinking. " 'Inner ear'?" she said, her voice muffled. " 'One cap twice daily'?"

"Let's see."

She handed me some antibiotics, at least ten years old.

"This won't do," I said, edging closer. "Do you see anything with a no-refill sticker? From a dentist, maybe?"

"No."

" 'May Cause Drowsiness'? 'Do Not Drive or Operate Heavy Machinery'?"

Someone knocked on the door again and rattled the knob. I knocked back, then reached up and turned on both taps full-blast.

Our findings were not good. If Henry had been suffering from poison ivy, hay fever, rheumatism, pinkeye, we would have been in luck but the only painkiller they had was Excedrin. Out of sheer desperation I took a handful, also two ambiguous capsules that had a Drowsiness sticker but which I suspected of being antihistamines.

I'd thought our mystery guest had left, but venturing out I was annoyed to find Cloke lurking outside. He gave me a contemptuous look that turned to a stare when Camilla— hair tousled, tugging at her skirt—stepped out behind me.

If she was surprised to see him, she didn't show it. "Oh, hello," she said to him, reaching down to dust off her knees.

"Hi." He glanced away in a studied, off-handed manner. We all knew Cloke was sort of interested in her, but even if he hadn't been, Camilla was not exactly the sort of girl one expected to find making out with someone in a locked bathroom.

She brushed past us and headed downstairs. I started down, too, but Cloke coughed in a significant manner and I turned around.

He leaned back against the wall, looking at me as if he'd had me figured out from the day I was born. "So," he said. His shirt was un-ironed and his shirttails were out; and though his eyes were red, I didn't know if he was stoned or just tired. "How's it going?"

I paused on the landing. Camilla was at the

foot of the steps, out of earshot. "All right," I said.

"What's the story?"

"What?"

"Better not let Kathy catch you guys screwing around in her bathroom. She'll make you walk to the bus station."

His tone was neutral. Still, I was reminded of the business with Mona's boyfriend the week before. Cloke, however, presented little or nothing in the way of physical threat and besides, he had problems enough of his own.

"Look," I said, "you've got it wrong."

"I don't care. I'm just telling you."

"Well, **I'm** telling **you**. Believe it or not, I don't care."

Cloke fished lazily in his pocket, came out with a pack of Marlboros so crumpled and flat that it did not seem possible that a cigarette could be inside it. He said: "I thought she was seeing somebody."

"For God's sake."

He shrugged. "It's no business of mine," he said, extracting one crooked cigarette and crushing the empty pack in his hand. "People were bothering me at school, so I was staying on their couch before we came down here. I've heard her talking on the phone."

"And saying what?"

"Oh, nothing, but like two or three in the

morning, whispering, you've got to wonder." He smiled bleakly. "I guess she thinks I'm passed out but to tell you the truth I haven't been sleeping all that well. . . . Right," he said, when I didn't answer. "You don't know a thing about it."

"I don't."

"Sure."

"I really don't."

"So what were you doing in there?"

I looked at him for a moment, and then I took out a handful of pills and held them out on my open palm.

He leaned forward, brows knit, and then, quite suddenly, his foggy eyes became intelligent and alert. He selected a capsule and held it up to the light in businesslike fashion. "What is it?" he said. "Do you know?"

"Sudafed," I said. "Don't bother. There's nothing in there."

He chuckled. "Know why?" he said, looking at me for the first time with real friendliness. "That's because you were looking in the wrong place."

"What?"

He glanced over his shoulder. "Down the hall. Off the master bedroom. I would have told you if you'd asked."

I was startled. "How do you know?"

He pocketed the capsule and raised an eye-brow at me. "I practically grew up in this house," he said. "Old Kathy is on about six-teen different types of dope."

I looked back at the closed door of the mas-ter bedroom.

"No," he said. "Not now."

"Why not?"

"Bunny's grandma. She has to lie down after she eats. We'll come up later."

———

Things downstairs had cleared out some, but not much. Camilla was nowhere in sight. Charles, bored and drunk, his back in a corner, was holding a glass to his temple as a tearful Marion babbled away—her hair pulled back in one of those tremendous preppy bows from the Talbots catalogue. I hadn't had a chance to speak to him because she had shadowed him almost constantly since we arrived; why she had latched so firmly on to him I don't know, except that she wasn't talking to Cloke, and Bunny's brothers were either married or en-gaged, and of the remaining males in her age group—Bunny's cousins, Henry and me, Bram Guernsey and Rooney Wynne—Charles was by far the best looking.

He glanced at me over her shoulder. I didn't have the stomach to go over and rescue him, and I looked away; but just then a toddler—fleeing his grinning, jug-eared brother—slid into my legs and almost knocked me down.

They dodged round me in circles. The smaller one, terrified and shrieking, dove to the floor and grabbed my knees. "Butthole," he sobbed.

The other one stopped and took a step backwards, and there was something nasty and almost lascivious about the look on his face. "Oh, Dad," he sang, his voice like spilled syrup. **"Oh, Daa-yid."**

Across the room, Hugh Corcoran turned, glass in hand. "Don't make me come over there, Brandon," he said.

"But Corey called you a butthole, **Daa-yid**."

"**You're** a butthole," sobbed the little one. "You you you."

I pried him off my leg and went looking for Henry. He and Mr. Corcoran were in the kitchen, surrounded by a semicircle of people: Mr. Corcoran, who had his arm around Henry, looked as if he'd had a few too many.

"Now Kathy and I," he said, in a loud, didactic voice, "have **always opened our home to young people**. Always an extra place at the table. First thing you know, they'd be coming to Kathy and me with their problems, too. Like this guy," he said, jostling Henry. "I'll never forget the time he came up to me one night after supper. He said, 'Mack'—all the kids call me Mack—'I'd like to ask your advice about something, man to man.' 'Well, before you start, son,' I said, 'I want to tell you just one thing. I think I know boys pretty well. I raised five of 'em myself. And I had four brothers when I was coming up, so I guess you might call me a pretty good authority on boys in general. . . .' "

He rambled on with this fraudulent recollection while Henry, pale and ill, endured his prods and backslaps as a well-trained dog will tolerate the pummeling of a rough child. The story itself was ludicrous. It had a dynamic and strangely hot-headed young Henry wanting to rush out and buy a used single-engine airplane against the advice of his parents.

"But this guy was determined," said Mr. Corcoran. "He was going to get that plane or bust. After he'd told me all about it I sat there for a minute and then I took a deep breath and I said, 'Henry, son, she sounds like a beaut, but I'm still going to have to be a square and agree with your folks. Let me tell you why that is.' "

"Hey, Dad," said Patrick Corcoran, who had just come in to fix himself another drink. He was slighter than Bun, heavily freckled, but had Bunny's sandy hair and his sharp little nose. "Dad, you're all mixed up. That didn't happen to Henry. That was Hugh's old friend Walter Ballantine."

"Bosh," said Mr. Corcoran.

"Sure it was. And he ended up buying the plane anyway. Hugh?" he shouted into the next room. "Hugh, do you remember Walter Ballantine?"

"Sure," said Hugh, and appeared in the doorway. He had by the wrist the kid Brandon, who was twisting and trying furiously to get away. "What about him?"

"Didn't Walter wind up buying that little Bonanza?"

"It wasn't a Bonanza," said Hugh, ignoring with a glacial calm the thrashing and yelps of his son. "It was a Beechcraft. No, I know what you're thinking," he said, as both Patrick and his father started to object. "I drove out to Danbury with Walter to look at a little converted Bonanza, but the guy wanted way too much. Those things cost a fortune to maintain, and there was plenty wrong with it, too. He was selling it because he couldn't afford to keep it."

"What about this Beechcraft, then?" said Mr. Corcoran. His hand had slipped from Henry's shoulder. "I've heard that's an excellent little outfit."

"Walter had some trouble with it. Got it

through an ad in the **Pennysaver**, off some retired congressman from New Jersey. He'd used it to fly around in while he was campaigning and—"

Gasping, he lurched forward as with a sudden wrench the kid broke free of him and shot across the room like a cannonball. Evading his father's tackle, he sidestepped Patrick's block as well and, glancing back at his pursuers, slammed right into Henry's abdomen.

It was a hard blow. The kid began to cry. Henry's jaw dropped and every ounce of blood drained from his face. For a moment I was sure he would fall, but somehow he drew himself upright, with the dignified, massive effort of a wounded elephant, while Mr. Corcoran threw back his head and laughed merrily at his distress.

———

I had not entirely believed Cloke about the drugs to be found upstairs, but when I went up with him again I saw he had told the truth. There was a tiny dressing room off the master bedroom, and a black lacquer vanity with lots of little compartments and a tiny key, and inside one of the compartments was a ballotin of Godiva chocolates and a neat, well-tended collection of candy-colored pills. The doctor who had prescribed them—E. G. Hart, M.D., and apparently a more reckless character than his prim initials would suggest—was a generous fellow, particularly with the amphetamines. Ladies of Mrs. Corcoran's age usually went in pretty heavily for the Valium and so forth but she had enough speed to send a gang of Hell's Angels on a cross-country rampage.

I was nervous. The room smelled like new clothes and perfume; big disco mirrors on the wall reproduced our every move in paranoiac multiple-image; there was no way out and no possible excuse for being there should anyone happen in. I kept an eye on the door while Cloke, with admirable efficiency, went swiftly through the bottles.

Dalmane. Yellow and orange. Darvon. Red and gray. Fiorinal. Nembutal. Miltown. I took two from each of the bottles he gave me.

"What," he said, "don't you want more than that?"

"I don't want her to miss anything."

"Shit," he said, opening another bottle and pouring half the contents into his pocket. "Take what you want. She'll think it was one of her daughters-in-law or something. Here, have some of this speed," he said, tapping most of the rest of the bottle on my palm. "It's great stuff. Pharmaceutical. During exams you can get ten or fifteen dollars a hit for this, easy."

I went downstairs, the right-hand pocket of my jacket full of ups and the left full of downs. Francis was standing at the foot of the steps. "Listen," I said, "do you know where Henry is?"

"No. Have you seen Charles?"

He was half-hysterical. "What's wrong?" I said.

"He stole my car keys."

"What?"

"He took the keys out of my coat pocket and left. Camilla saw him pulling out of the drive-way. He had the **top** down. That car stalls in the rain, anyway, but if—shit," he said, running a hand through his hair. "You don't know anything about it, do you?"

"I saw him about an hour ago. With Marion."

"Yes, I talked to her too. He said he was going out for cigarettes, but that was an hour ago. You did see him? You haven't talked to him?"

"No."

"Was he drunk? Marion said he was. Did he look drunk to you?"

Francis looked pretty drunk himself. "Not very," I said. "Come on, help me find Henry."

"I told you. I don't know where he is. What do you want him for?"

"I have something for him."

"What is it?" he said in Greek. **"Drugs?"**

"Yes."

"Well, give me something, for God's sake," he said, swaying forward, pop-eyed.

He was far too drunk for sleeping pills. I gave him an Excedrin.

"Thanks," he said, and swallowed it with a big sloppy drink of his whiskey. "I hope I die in the night. Where do you suppose he went, anyway? What time is it?"

"About ten."

"You don't suppose he decided to drive **home**, do you? Maybe he just took the car and went back to Hampden. Camilla said certainly not, not with the funeral tomorrow, but I don't know, he's just **disappeared**. If he really just went for cigarettes, don't you think he'd be back by now? I can't imagine where else he would have gone. What do you think?"

"He'll turn up," I said. "Look, I'm sorry, I've got to go. I'll see you later."

I looked all over the house for Henry and found him sitting by himself on an army cot, in the basement, in the dark.

He looked at me out of the corner of his eye, without moving his head. "What is that?" he said, when I offered him a couple of capsules.

"Nembutal. Here."

He took them from me and swallowed them without water. "Do you have any more?"

"Yes."

"Give them to me."

"You can't take more than two."

"Give them to me."

I gave them to him. "I'm not kidding, Henry," I said. "You'd better be careful."

He looked at them, then reached in his pocket for the blue enamel pillbox and put them carefully inside it. "I don't suppose," he said, "you would go upstairs and get me a drink."

"You shouldn't be drinking on top of those pills."

"I've been drinking already."

"I know that."

There was a brief silence.

"Look," he said, pushing his glasses up on the bridge of his nose. "I want a Scotch and soda. In a tall glass. Heavy on the Scotch, light on the soda, lots of ice, a glass of plain water, no ice, on the side. That's what I want."

"I'm not going to get it for you."

"If you don't go up and get it for me," he said, "I'll just have to go up and get it my-self."

I went up to the kitchen and got it for him, except I made it a good deal heavier on the soda than I knew he wanted me to.

"That's for Henry," said Camilla, coming into the kitchen just as I'd finished the first glass and was filling the second with water from the tap.

"Yes."

"Where is he?"

"Downstairs."

"How's he doing?"

We were alone in the kitchen. With my eyes on the empty doorway, I told her about the lacquer chest.

"That sounds like Cloke," she said, laughing. "He's really pretty decent, isn't he? Bun always said he reminded him of you."

I was puzzled and a bit offended by this last. I started to say something about it, but instead I set down the glass and said, "Who do you talk to on the telephone at three in the morning?"

"What?"

Her surprise seemed perfectly natural. The problem was that she was such an expert actress it was impossible to know if it was genuine.

I held her gaze. She met it unblinking, brows knit, and just when I thought she'd been silent a beat too long, she shook her head and laughed again. "What's wrong with you?" she said. "What are you talking about?"

I laughed too. It was impossible to outfox her at this game.

"I'm not trying to put you on the spot," I

said. "But you need to be careful what you say on the telephone when Cloke's in your house."

She looked blank. "I am careful."

"I hope you are, because he's been listening."

"He couldn't have heard anything."

"Well, that's not for want of trying."

We stood looking at each other. There was a heart-stopping, ruby-red pinprick of a beauty mark just beneath her eye. On an irresistible impulse I leaned down and gave her a kiss.

She laughed. "What was that for?" she said.

My heart—which, thrilled at my daring, had held its breath for a moment or two—began suddenly to beat quite wildly. I turned and busied myself with the glasses. "Nothing," I said, "you just looked pretty," and I might have said something else had Charles—dripping wet—not burst through the kitchen door, Francis hard at his heels.

"Why didn't you just **tell** me?" said Francis in an angry whisper. He was flushed and trembling. "Never mind that the seats are soaked, and will probably mildew and rot, and that I've got to drive back to Hampden tomorrow. But never mind about that. I don't care. What I can't believe is that you went up, you **deliberately** went looking for my coat, you took the keys and—"

"I've seen you leave the top down in the rain before," said Charles curtly. He was at the counter, his back to Francis, pouring himself a drink. His hair was plastered to his head and a small puddle was forming round him on the linoleum.

"What," said Francis, through his teeth. **"I never."**

"Yes you have," said Charles, without turning around.

"Name one time."

"Okay. What about that afternoon you and I were in Manchester, and it was about two weeks before school started, and we decided to go to the Equinox House for—"

"That was a **summer afternoon**. It was **sprinkling**."

"It was not. It was raining hard. You just don't want to talk about that now because that was the afternoon you tried to get me to—"

"You're crazy," said Francis. "That doesn't have anything to do with this. It's dark as hell and **pouring** rain and you're drunk out of your skull. It's a miracle you didn't kill somebody. Where the hell did you go for those cigarettes, anyway? There's not a store around here for—"

"I'm not drunk."

"Ha, ha. Tell me. Where'd you get those cigarettes? I'd like to know. I bet—"

"I said I'm not drunk."

"Yeah, sure. I bet you didn't even buy any

cigarettes. If you did, they must be soaking wet. Where are they, anyway?"

"Leave me alone."

"No. Really. Show them to me. I'd like to see these famous—"

Charles slammed down his glass and spun around. **"Leave me alone,"** he hissed.

It was not the tone of his voice, exactly, as much as the look on his face which was so terrible. Francis stared, his mouth fallen slightly open. For about ten long seconds there was no sound but the rhythmic tick tick tick of the water dripping from Charles's sodden clothes.

I took Henry's Scotch and soda, lots of ice, and his water, no ice, and walked past Francis, out the swinging door and down to the basement.

———

It rained hard all night. My nose tickled from the dust in the sleeping bag, and the basement floor—which was poured concrete beneath a thin, comfortless layer of indoor-outdoor carpeting—made my bones ache whichever way I turned. The rain drummed on the high windows, and the floodlights, shining through the glass, cast a pattern on the walls as if dark rivulets of water were streaming down them from ceiling to floor.

Charles snored on his cot, his mouth open;

Francis grumbled in his sleep. Occasionally a car swooshed by in the rain and its headlights would swing round momentarily and illuminate the room—the pool table, the snowshoes on the wall and the rowing machine, the armchair in which Henry sat, motionless, a glass in his hand and the cigarette burning low between his fingers. For a moment his face, pale and watchful as a ghost's, would be caught in the headlights and then, very gradually, it would slide back into the dark.

———

In the morning I woke up sore and disoriented to the sound of a loose shutter banging somewhere. The rain was falling harder than ever. It lashed in rhythmic waves against the windows of the white, brightly lit kitchen as we guests sat around the table and ate a silent, cheerless breakfast of coffee and Pop Tarts.

The Corcorans were upstairs, dressing. Cloke and Bram and Rooney drank coffee with their elbows on the table and talked in low voices. They were freshly showered and shaven, cocky in their Sunday suits but uneasy, too, as if they were about to go to court. Francis—puff-eyed, his stiff red hair full of absurd cowlicks—was still in his bathrobe. He had got up late and was in a state of barely contained outrage because all the hot water in the downstairs tank was gone.

He and Charles were across the table from each other, and took great pains to avoid looking in the other's direction. Marion—red-eyed, her hair in hot curlers—was sullen and silent, too. She was dressed very smartly, in a navy suit, but with fuzzy pink slippers over her fleshtone nylons. Every now and then she would reach up and put her hands on the rollers to see if they were cooling off.

Henry, among us, was the only pallbearer—the other five being family friends or business associates of Mr. Corcoran's. I wondered if the coffin was very heavy and, if so, how Henry would manage. Though he emitted a faint, ammoniac odor of sweat and Scotch he did not look at all drunk. The pills had sunk him into a glassy, fathomless calm. Threads of smoke floated up from a filterless cigarette whose coal burned dangerously near his fingertips. It was a state which might have seemed a suspiciously narcotic one except that it differed so little from his customary manner.

It was a little after nine-thirty by the kitchen clock. The funeral was set for eleven. Francis went off to dress and Marion to take her rollers out. The rest of us were still sitting around the kitchen table, awkward and inert, pretending to enjoy our second and third cups of coffee when Teddy's wife marched in. She was a hard-faced, pretty litigation lawyer who smoked constantly and wore her blond hair in a China chop. With her was Hugh's wife: a small, mild-mannered woman who looked far too young and frail to have borne as many children as she had. By an unfortunate coincidence, both of them were named Lisa, which made for a lot of confusion around the house.

"Henry," said the first Lisa, leaning forward and jamming out her half-smoked Vantage so it crooked at a right angle in the ashtray. She was wearing Giorgio perfume and far too much of it. "We're driving to the church now to arrange the flowers in the chancel and collect the cards before the service starts. Ted's mother"—both Lisas disliked Mrs. Corcoran, a feeling which was heartily reciprocated—"said you should drive over with us so that you can meet with the pallbearers. Okay?"

Henry, the light winking off the steel rims of his glasses, gave no indication of having heard her. I was about to kick him under the table when, very slowly, he looked up.

"Why?" he said.

"The pallbearers are supposed to meet in the vestibule at ten-fifteen."

"Why?" repeated Henry, with Vedic calm.

"I don't know why. I'm just telling you what she said. This stuff is planned out like synchronized swimming or some damn thing. Are you ready to go, or do you need a minute?"

"Now, Brandon," said Hugh's wife weakly to her little son, who had run into the kitchen and was attempting to swing from his mother's arms like an ape. "Please. You're going to hurt Mother. **Brandon.**"

"Lisa, you shouldn't let him hang all over you like that," said the first Lisa, glancing at her watch.

"**Please,** Brandon. Mother's got to go now."

"He's too big to act like that. You know he is. If I were you, I would just take him in the bathroom and tear him up."

———

Mrs. Corcoran came down about twenty minutes later, in black crepe de chine, riffling through a quilted-leather clutch. "Where is everybody?" she said when she saw only Camilla, Sophie Dearbold and me loafing by the trophy case.

When no one answered her, she paused on the stair, annoyed. "Well?" she said. "Has everybody left? Where's Francis?"

"I think he's dressing," I said, glad she'd asked something I could answer without having to lie. From where she stood on the stairs she could not see what the rest of us saw, quite clearly, through the glass doors of the living room: Cloke and Bram and Rooney, Charles with them, all of them standing around under the sheltered part of the terrace getting stoned.

It was odd to see Charles of all people smoking pot and the only reason I could think why he was doing it was because he thought it would brace him up, the way a stiff drink might. If so, I felt certain he was in for a nasty surprise. When I was twelve and thirteen I used to get high at school every day—not because I liked it, it broke me out in cold sweats and panic— but because in the lower grades it was such a fabulous prestige to be thought a pothead, also because I was so expert at hiding the paranoiac flulike symptoms it gave me.

Mrs. Corcoran was looking at me as if I'd uttered some Nazi oath. **"Dressing?"** she said.

"I think so."

"Isn't he even dressed by now? What's everybody been doing all morning?"

I didn't know what to say. She was drifting down the stairs a step at a time, and now that her head was free of the balustrade, she had an unimpeded view of the patio doors—rain-splashed glass, oblivious smokers beyond—if she chose to look that way. We were all transfixed with suspense. Sometimes mothers didn't know what pot was when they saw it, but Mrs. Corcoran looked like she would know, all right.

She snapped the clutch bag shut and looked around with a sweeping, raptor-like gaze—the only thing about her, surely, that could remind me of my father, and it did.

"Well?" she said. "Would **somebody** tell him to hurry up?"

Camilla jumped up. "I'll get him, Mrs. Corcoran," she said, but once she was around the corner she scooted over to the terrace door.

"Thank you, dear," said Mrs. Corcoran. She had found what she wanted—her sunglasses—and she put them on. "I don't know what it is with you young people," she said. "I don't mean you **in particular**, but this is a very difficult time and we're all under a great deal of stress and we must try to make things go as smoothly as they possibly can."

Cloke looked up, bloodshot and uncomprehending, at Camilla's soft rap on the glass. Then he looked past her into the living room, and all of a sudden his face changed. **Shit,** I saw him say, noiselessly, and a cloud of smoke escaped from his mouth.

Charles saw, too, and almost choked. Cloke snatched the joint from Bram and pinched it out with thumb and forefinger.

Mrs. Corcoran, in big black sunglasses, remained thankfully unaware of this drama unfolding behind her back. "The church is a bit of a drive, you know," she said as Camilla circled behind her and went to fetch Francis.

"Mack and I will go ahead in the station wagon, and you people can follow either us or the boys. I think you'll have to go in three cars, though maybe you can squeeze into two— **Don't run in Grandmother's house,**" she snapped at Brandon and his cousin Neale, who'd darted past her on the stairs and clattered into the living room. They wore little blue suits with snap-on bow ties, and their Sunday shoes made a terrific racket on the floor.

Brandon, panting, dodged behind the sofa. "He hit me, Grandma."

"He called me a bootywipe."

"Did not."

"Did too."

"**Boys,**" she thundered. "You ought to be **ashamed** of yourselves." She paused dramatically, to observe their silent, stricken faces. "Your Uncle Bunny is dead and do you know what that means? It means that he is **gone forever**. You will never see him again **as long as you live**." She glared at them. "Today is a very special day," she said. "It is a day for remembering him. You ought to be sitting quietly somewhere thinking about all the nice things he used to do for you instead of running around and scuffing up this pretty new floor that Grandmother just had refinished."

There was a silence. Neale kicked sullenly at

Brandon. "One time Uncle Bunny called me a bastard," he said.

I wasn't sure if she really didn't hear him or if she chose not to; the fixed expression on her face made me think maybe the latter, but then the terrace doors slid open and Cloke came in with Charles and Bram and Rooney.

"Oh. So there you are," said Mrs. Corcoran suspiciously. "What are you doing out there in the rain?"

"Fresh air," said Cloke. He looked really stoned. The tip of a Visine bottle stuck out from the handkerchief pocket of his suit.

They all looked really stoned. Poor Charles was bug-eyed and sweating. This was probably more than he'd bargained for: bright lights, too high, having to deal with a hostile adult.

She looked at them. I wondered if she knew. For a moment I thought she'd say something, but instead she reached out and grabbed hold of Brandon's arm. "Well, you should all get a move on," she said curtly, leaning down to run a hand through his mussed hair. "It's getting late and I've been led to expect that there might be a little problem with **seating**."

———

The church had been built in seventeen-something, according to the National Register of Historic Places. It was an age-blacked, dungeonlike building with its own rickety little graveyard in the back, set on a rolling country lane. When we arrived, damp and uncomfortable from Francis's sodden car seats, cars lined the road on both sides, as if for a rural dance or bingo night, sloping gently into the grassy ditch. A gray drizzle was falling. We parked near the country club, which was down a bit, and hiked the quarter-mile silently, in the mud.

The sanctuary was dim, and stepping inside I was blinded by a dazzle of candles. When my eyes cleared I saw iron lanterns, clammy stone floors, flowers everywhere. Startled, I noticed that one of the arrangements, quite near the altar, was wired in the shape of the number 27.

"I thought he was twenty-four," I whispered to Camilla.

"No," she said, "that's his old football number."

The church was packed. I looked for Henry but didn't see him; saw someone I thought was Julian but realized it wasn't when he turned around. For a moment we stood there in a knot, confused. There were metal folding chairs along the back wall to accommodate the crowd, but then someone spotted a half-empty pew and we headed for that: Francis and Sophie, the twins, and me. Charles, who stuck close to Camilla, was plainly freaking out. The doomy horrorhouse atmosphere of the church was not helping at all and he stared at his surroundings with frank terror, while Camilla took his arm and tried to nudge him down the row. Marion had disappeared to sit with some people who'd driven down from Hampden, and Cloke and Bram and Rooney had simply disappeared, somewhere between car and church.

———

It was a long service. The minister, who took his ecumenical and—some felt—slightly impersonal remarks from Saint Paul's sermon on Love from First Corinthians, talked for about half an hour. ("Didn't you feel that was a **very** inappropriate text?" said Julian, who had a pagan's gloomy view of death coupled with a horror of the non-specific.) Next was Hugh Corcoran ("He was the best little brother a guy could have"); then Bunny's old football coach, a dynamic Jaycee type who talked at length of Bunny's team spirit, telling a rousing anecdote about how Bunny had once saved the day against a particularly tough team from "lower" Connecticut. ("That means black," whispered Francis.) He wound up his story by pausing and staring at the lectern for a count of ten; then he looked up frankly. "I don't know," he said, "a whole lot about Heaven. My business is teaching boys to play a game and play it hard. Today we're here to honor a boy who's been taken out of the game early. But that's not to say that while he was out on the field, **he didn't give us all he had**. That's not to say he wasn't a winner." A long, suspenseful pause. "Bunny Corcoran," he said gruffly, "was a winner."

A long, solitary wail went up from somebody towards the middle of the congregation.

Except in the movies **(Knute Rockne, All-American)** I don't know if I've ever seen such a bravura performance. When he sat down, half the place was in tears—the coach included. No one paid much attention to the final speaker, Henry himself, who went to the podium and read, inaudibly and without comment, a short poem by A. E. Housman.

The poem was called "With Rue My Heart Is Laden." I don't know why he chose that particular one. We knew that the Corcorans had asked him to read something and I expected that they had trusted him to choose something appropriate. It would have been so easy for him to choose something else, though, something you would think he would pick, for Christ's sake, from **Lycidas** or the **Upanishads** or anything, really—certainly not that poem, which Bunny had known by heart. He'd been very fond of the corny old poems he'd learned in grade school: "The Charge of the Light Brigade," "In Flanders Fields," a lot of strange old sentimental stuff whose authors and titles I never even knew. The rest of us, who were snobs about such things, had thought this a shameful taste, akin to his taste for King Dons and Hostess Twinkies. Quite often I had heard Bunny say this Housman aloud—seriously when drunk, more mockingly when sober—so that the lines for me were set and hardened in the cadence of his voice; perhaps that is why hearing it then, in Henry's academic mono-tone (he was a terrible reader) there with the guttering candles and the draft shivering in the flowers and people crying all around, enkin-dled in me such a brief and yet so excruciating pain, like one of those weirdly scientific Japa-nese tortures calibrated to extract the greatest possible misery in the smallest space of time.

It was a very short poem.

> With rue my heart is laden
> For golden friends I had,
> For many a rose-lipt maiden
> And many a lightfoot lad.
> By brooks too broad for leaping
> The lightfoot boys are laid;
> The rose-lipt girls are sleeping
> In fields where roses fade.

———

During the closing prayer (overly long) I felt myself swaying, so much so that the sides of my new shoes dug in the tender spot beneath my anklebones. The air was close; people were crying; there was an insistent buzz which came in close to my ear and then receded. For a moment I was afraid I would black out. Then I realized the buzz actually came from a large wasp flying in erratic darts and circles over our heads. Francis, by flailing at it uselessly with the memorial service bulletin, had succeeded in enraging it; it dove towards the weeping Sophie's head but, finding her unresponsive, turned in midair and lit on the back of the pew to collect its wits. Stealthily Camilla leaned to one side and began to slip off her shoe, but before she could, Charles had killed it with a resounding thwack from **The Book of Common Prayer**.

The pastor, at a key point in his prayer, started. He opened his eyes and his glance fell on Charles, still wielding the guilty prayerbook. **"That they may not languish in unavailing grief,"** he said in a slightly amplified voice, "nor sorrow as those who have no hope, but through their tears look always up to Thee. . . ."

Quickly I bowed my head. The wasp still clung with one black feeler to the edge of the pew. I stared down at it and thought of Bunny, poor old Bunny, expert killer of flying pests, stalking houseflies with a rolled-up copy of the Hampden **Examiner**.

———

Charles and Francis, who weren't speaking before the service, had managed somehow to make up during the course of it. After the final **amen**, in silent, perfect sympathy, they ducked into an empty corridor off the side aisle. I caught a glimpse of them speeding wordlessly down it before they turned into the men's room, Francis stopping for one last nervous glance behind and already reaching in his coat pocket for what I knew was there—the flat pint bottle of something or other I'd seen him take from the glove compartment.

It was a muddy, black day in the churchyard. The rain had stopped but the sky was dark and the wind was blowing hard. Someone was ringing the church bell and not doing a very good job of it; it clanged unevenly to and fro like a bell at a seance.

People straggled to their cars, dresses billowing, holding hats to head. A few paces in front of me Camilla struggled on tiptoe to pull down her umbrella, which dragged her along in little skipping steps—Mary Poppins in her black funeral dress. I stepped up to help her, but before I got there the umbrella blew inside out. For a moment it had a horrible life of its own, squawking and flapping its spines like a pterodactyl; with a sudden sharp cry she let it go and immediately it sailed ten feet in the air, somersaulting once or twice before it caught in the high branches of an ash tree.

"Damn," she said, looking up at it and then down at her finger, from which a thin seam of blood sprang. "Damn, damn, damn."

"Are you okay?"

She stuck the injured finger in her mouth. "It's not that," she said peevishly, glancing up at the branches. "This is my favorite umbrella."

I fished around in my pocket, gave her my handkerchief. She shook it out and held it to her finger **(flutter of white, blown hair, darkening sky)** and as I watched time stopped and I was transfixed by a bright knife of memory: the sky was the same thundery gray as it had been then, new leaves, her hair had blown across her mouth just so . . .

(flutter of white)

(. . . at the ravine. She'd climbed down with Henry and was back at the top before him, the rest of us waiting at the edge, cold wind, jitters, springing to hoist her up; dead? is he . . . ? **She took a handkerchief from her pocket and wiped her muddy hands, not looking at any of us, really, her hair blowing back light against the sky and**

**her face a blank for just about any emotion
one might care to project. . . .)**

Behind us someone said, very loudly, "Dad?"

I jumped, startled and guilty. It was Hugh.
He was walking briskly, half-running, and in
a moment had caught up with his father.
"Dad?" he said again, placing a hand on his father's slumping shoulder. There was no response. He shook him gently. Up ahead,
the pallbearers (Henry indistinct, somewhere
among them) were sliding the casket into the
open doors of the hearse.

"Dad," said Hugh. He was tremendously agitated. "**Dad**. You gotta listen to me for a sec."

The doors slammed. Slowly, slowly, Mr.
Corcoran turned. He was carrying the baby
they called Champ but today its presence
seemed to offer him little comfort. The expression on his big slack face was haunted and lost.
He stared at his son as if he had never seen him
before.

"**Dad,**" said Hugh. "Guess who I just saw.
Guess who came. **Mr. Vanderfeller,**" he said
urgently, pressing his father's arm.

The syllables of this illustrious name—one
which the Corcorans invoked with very nearly
as much respect as that of God Almighty—
had when uttered aloud a miraculous effect
of healing on Mr. Corcoran. "Vanderfeller's
here?" he said, looking around. "Where?"

This august personage, who loomed large in the collective unconscious of the Corcorans, was the head of a charitable foundation—endowed by his even more august grandpapa—which happened to own a controlling interest in the stock of Mr. Corcoran's bank. This entailed board meetings, and occasional social functions, and the Corcorans had an endless store of "delightful" anecdotes about Paul Vanderfeller, of how European he was, what a celebrated "wit," and though the witticisms they found frequent occasion to repeat seemed poor things to me (the guards up at the security booth at Hampden were cleverer) they made the Corcorans rock with urbane and apparently quite sincere laughter. One of Bunny's favorite ways to start a sentence had been to let drop, quite casually: "When Dad was lunching with Paul Vanderfeller the other day . . ."

And here he was, the great one himself, scorching us all with his rays of glory. I glanced in the direction Hugh indicated to his father and saw him—an ordinary-looking man with the good-natured expression of someone used to being constantly catered to; late forties; nicely dressed; nothing particularly "European" about him except his ugly eyeglasses and the fact that he was considerably below the average height.

An expression of something very like tenderness spread itself across Mr. Corcoran's face. Without a word he thrust the baby at Hugh and hurried off across the lawn.

———

Maybe it was because the Corcorans were Irish, maybe it was that Mr. Corcoran was born in Boston, but the whole family seemed to feel, somehow, that it had a mysterious affinity with the Kennedys. It was a resemblance they tried to cultivate—especially Mrs. Corcoran, with her hairdo and faux-Jackie glasses—but it also had some slight physical basis: in Brady and Patrick's toothy, too-tanned gauntness there was a shadow of Bobby Kennedy while the other brothers, Bunny among them, were built on the Ted Kennedy model, much heavier, with little round features bunched in the middle of their faces. It would not have been difficult to mistake any of them for minor clan members, cousins perhaps. Francis had told me of walking into a fashionable, very crowded restaurant in Boston once, with Bunny. There was a long wait, and the waiter had asked for a name: "Kennedy," Bun said briskly, rocking back on his heels, and the next instant half the staff was scrambling to clear a table.

And maybe it was these old associations which were clicking around in my mind or maybe it was that the only funerals I had ever seen were televised events, affairs of state: in any case, the funeral procession—long, black, rain-splashed cars, Mr. Vanderfeller's Bentley among them—was linked for me in dreamlike fashion to another funeral and another, far more famous motorcade. Slowly we rolled along. Open cars of flowers—like convertibles in some nightmare Rose Parade—crept behind the curtained hearse. Gladiola, dyed chrysanthemum, sprays of palm. The wind was blowing hard, and garish petals shook loose and tumbled back among the cars, sticking to the damp windshields like bits of confetti.

———

The cemetery was on a highway. We pulled over and got out of the Mustang (flat clack of car doors) and stood blinking on the littered shoulder. Cars whooshed past on the asphalt, not ten feet away.

It was a big cemetery, windy and flat and anonymous. The stones were laid out in rows like tract homes. The uniformed driver of the funeral-home Lincoln walked around to open the door for Mrs. Corcoran. She was carrying—I didn't know why—a small bouquet of rosebuds. Patrick offered her an arm and she slipped a gloved hand in the crook of his elbow, inscrutable behind her dark glasses, calm as a bride.

The back doors of the hearse were opened and the coffin slid out. Silently, the party drifted after it as it was borne aloft into the open field, bobbing across the sea of grass like a little boat. Yellow ribbons fluttered gaily from the lid. The sky was hostile and enormous. We passed one grave, a child's, from which grinned a faded plastic jack-o'-lantern.

A green striped canopy, of the sort used for lawn parties, was set up over the grave. There was something vacuous and stupid about it, flapping out there in the middle of nowhere, something empty, banal, brutish. We stopped, stood, in awkward little groups. Somehow I had thought there would be more than this. Bits of litter chewed up by the mowers lay scattered on the grass. There were cigarette butts, a Twix wrapper, recognizable.

This is stupid, I thought, with a sudden rush of panic. **How did this happen?**

Traffic washed past up on the expressway.

The grave was almost unspeakably horrible. I had never seen one before. It was a barbarous thing, a blind clayey hole with folding chairs for the family teetering on one side and raw dirt heaped on the other. **My God,** I thought. I was starting to see everything, all at once, with a blistering clarity. Why bother with the coffin, the awning or any of it if they were just going to dump him, shovel the dirt in, go home? Was this all there was to it? To get rid of him like a piece of garbage?

Bun, I thought, **oh, Bun, I'm sorry.**

The minister ran through the service fast, his bland face tinted green beneath the canopy. Julian was there—I saw him now, looking towards the four of us. First Francis, and then Charles and Camilla, moved to go stand with him but I didn't care, I was in a daze. The Corcorans sat very quietly, hands in laps: **how can they just sit there?** I thought, **by that awful pit, do nothing?** It was Wednesday. On Wednesdays at ten we had Greek Prose Composition and that was where we all ought to have been now. The coffin lay dumbly by the grave. I knew they wouldn't open it, but I wished they would. It was just starting to dawn on me that I would never see him again.

The pallbearers stood in a dark row behind the coffin, like a chorus of elders in a tragedy. Henry was the youngest one. He stood there quietly, his hands folded before him—big, white, scholarly hands, capable and well-kept, the same hands that had dug in Bunny's neck for a pulse and rolled his head back and forth on its poor broken stem while the rest of us leaned over the edge, breathless, watching. Even from that distance we could see the terrible angle of his neck, the shoe turned the wrong way, the trickle of blood from nose and mouth. He pulled back the eyelids with his thumb, leaning close, careful not to touch the eyeglasses which were skewed on top of Bunny's head. One leg jerked in a solitary spasm which quieted gradually to a twitch and then stopped. Camilla's wristwatch had a second hand. We saw them silently conferring. Climbing up the hill after her, bracing his knee with his palm, he'd wiped his hands on his trousers and answered our clamorous whispers—**dead? is he—?**—with the brief impersonal nod of a doctor. . . .

—O Lord we beseech you, that while we lament the departure of our brother Edmund Grayden Corcoran your servant out of this life, we bear in mind that we are most certainly ready to follow him. Give us grace to make ready for that last hour, and protect us against a sudden and unprovided death. . . .

He hadn't seen it coming at all. He hadn't even understood, there wasn't time. Teetering back as if on the edge of the swimming pool: comic yodel, windmilling arms. Then the surprised nightmare of falling. Someone who didn't know there was such a thing in the world as Death; who couldn't believe it even when he saw it; had never dreamed it would come to him.

Flapping crows. Shiny beetles crawling in the undergrowth. A patch of sky, frozen in a cloudy retina, reflected in a puddle on the ground. Yoo-hoo. Being and nothingness.

. . . I am the Resurrection and the life; he who believeth in Me, even if he die, shall live; and whosoever liveth and believeth in Me shall never die. . . .

The pallbearers lowered the coffin into the grave with long, creaking straps. Henry's muscles quivered with the effort; his jaw was clenched tight. Sweat had soaked through to the back of his jacket.

I felt in the pocket of my jacket to make sure the painkillers were still there. It was going to be a long ride home.

The straps were pulled up. The minister blessed the grave and then sprinkled it with holy water. Dirt and dark. Mr. Corcoran, his face buried in his hands, sobbed monotonously. The awning rattled in the wind.

The first spadeful of earth. The thud of it on the hollow lid gave me a sick, black, empty feeling. Mrs. Corcoran—Patrick on one side, sober Ted on the other—stepped forward. With a gloved hand she tossed the little bouquet of roses into the grave.

Slowly, slowly, with a drugged, fathomless calm, Henry bent and picked up a handful of dirt. He held it over the grave and let it trickle from his fingers. Then, with terrible composure, he stepped back and absently dragged the hand across his chest, smearing mud upon his lapel, his tie, the starched immaculate white of his shirt.

I stared at him. So did Julian, and Francis, and the twins, with a kind of shocked horror. He seemed not to realize he had done anything out of the ordinary. He stood there perfectly still, the wind ruffling his hair and the dull light glinting from the rims of his glasses.

CHAPTER

8

MY MEMORIES of the Corcorans' post-funeral get-together are very foggy, due possibly to the handful of mixed painkillers I swallowed on the way there. But even morphia could not fully dull the horror of this event. Julian was there, which was something of a blessing; he drifted through the party like a good angel, making graceful small talk, knowing exactly the right thing to say to everyone, and behaving with such heavenly charm and diplomacy towards the Corcorans (whom he in fact disliked and vice versa) that even Mrs. Corcoran was mollified. Besides—the pinnacle of glory as far as the Corcorans were concerned—it turned out that he was an old acquaintance of Paul Vanderfeller's, and Francis, who happened to be nearby, said he hoped he never forgot the expression on Mr. Corcoran's face when Vanderfeller recognized Julian and greeted him ("European-style," as Mrs. Corcoran was heard explaining to a neighbor) with an embrace and a kiss on the cheek.

The little Corcorans—who seemed oddly elated by the morning's sad events—skidded around in hilarious spirits: throwing croissants, shrieking with laughter, chasing through the crowd with a horrible toy that made an explosive noise like a fart. The caterers had screwed up as well—too much liquor, not enough food, a recipe for certain trouble. Ted and his wife fought without stopping. Bram Guernsey was sick on a linen sofa. Mr. Corcoran swung to and fro between euphoria and the wildest of despairs.

After a bit of this, Mrs. Corcoran went up to the bedroom, and came down again with a look on her face that was terrible to see. In low tones, she told her husband that there had been "a burglary," a remark which—repeated by a well-meaning eavesdropper to his neighbor—spread rapidly around the room and generated a flurry of unwanted concern. When had it happened? What was missing? Had the police been called? People abandoned their conversations and gravitated towards her in a murmuring swarm. She evaded their questions masterfully, with a martyred air. No, she said, there was no point in calling the police: the missing items were small things, of sentimental value, and of no use to anyone but herself.

Cloke found occasion to leave not long after this. And though no one said much about it,

Henry too had left. Almost immediately after the funeral he'd collected his bags, got in his car, and driven away, with only the most perfunctory of goodbyes to the Corcorans and without a word to Julian, who was very anxious to talk to him. "He looks wretched," he said to Camilla and me (I unresponsive, deep in my Dalmane stupor). "I believe he should see a doctor."

"The last week has been hard on him," said Camilla.

"Certainly. But I think Henry is a more sensitive fellow than we often give him credit for being. In many ways it's hard to imagine that he'll ever get over this. He and Edmund were closer than I think you realize." He sighed. "That was a peculiar poem he read, wasn't it? I would have suggested something from the **Phaedo**."

———

Things started to break up around two in the afternoon. We could have stayed for supper, could have stayed—if Mr. Corcoran's drunken invitations held true (Mrs. Corcoran's frosty smile behind his back informed us that they did not)—indefinitely, friends of the family, sleeping on our very own cots down in the basement; welcome to join in the life of the Corcoran household and share freely in its daily joys and sorrows: family holidays, babysitting the little ones, pitching in occasionally with the household chores, working together, **as a team** (he emphasized) which was the Corcoran way. It would not be a soft life—he was not soft with his boys—but it would be an almost unbelievably enriching one in terms of things like character, and pluck, and fine moral standards, the latter of which he did not expect that many of our parents had taken the trouble to teach us.

It was four o'clock before we finally got away. Now, for some reason, it was Charles and Camilla who weren't speaking. They'd fought about something—I'd seen them arguing in the yard—and all the way home, in the back seat, they sat side by side and stared straight ahead, their arms folded across their chests in what I am sure they did not realize was a comically identical fashion.

———

It felt as if I'd been away longer than I had. My room seemed abandoned and small, like it had stood empty for weeks. I opened the window and lay on my unmade bed. The sheets smelled musty. It was twilight.

Finally it was over but I felt strangely let down. I had classes on Monday: Greek and French. I hadn't been to French in nearly three weeks and the thought of it gave me a twinge of anxiety. Final papers. I rolled over on my stomach. Exams. And summer vacation in a month and a half, and where on earth was I going to spend it? Working for Dr. Roland? Pumping gas in Plano?

I got up and took another Dalmane and lay down again. Outside it was nearly dark. Through the walls I could hear my neighbor's stereo: David Bowie. "This is Ground Control to Major Tom . . ."

I stared at the shadows on the ceiling.

In some strange country between dream and waking, I found myself in a cemetery, not the one Bunny was buried in but a different one, much older, and very famous—thick with hedges and evergreens, its cracked marble pavilions choked with vines. I was walking along a narrow flagstone path. As I turned a corner, the white blossoms of an unexpected hydrangea—luminous clouds, floating pale in the shadows—brushed against my cheek.

I was looking for the tomb of a famous writer—Marcel Proust, I think, or maybe George Sand. Whoever it was, I knew they were buried in that place, but it was so overgrown I could hardly see the names on the stones, and it was getting dark besides.

I found myself at the top of a hill in a dark grove of pines. A smudged, smoky valley lay far beneath. I turned and looked back the way I'd come: a prickle of marble spires, dim mausoleums, pale in the growing darkness. Far be-low, a tiny light—a lantern, maybe, or a flash-light—bobbed towards me through the crowd of gravestones. I leaned forward to see more clearly, and then was startled by a crash in the shrubbery behind me.

It was the baby the Corcorans called Champ. It had tumbled the length of its body and was trying to stagger to its feet; after a moment it gave up and lay still, barefoot, shivering, its belly heaving in and out. It was wearing noth-ing but a plastic diaper and there were long ugly scratches on its arms and legs. I stared at it, aghast. The Corcorans were thoughtless but this was unconscionable; **those monsters,** I thought, **those imbeciles, they just went off and left it here all by itself.**

The baby was whimpering, its legs mottled blue with cold. Clutched in one fat starfish of a hand was the plastic airplane which had come with its Happy Meal. I bent down to see if it was okay but as I did I heard, very near, the wry, ostentatious clearing of a throat.

What happened next took place in a flash. Looking over my shoulder I had only the most fleeting impression of the figure looming be-hind me, but the glimpse I got struck me stumbling backwards, screaming, falling down and down and down until at last I hit my own bed, which rushed up from the dark to meet me. The jolt knocked me awake. Trembling, I lay flat on my back for a moment, then scrambled for the light.

Desk, door, chair. I lay back, still trembling. Though his features had been clotted and ruined, with a thick, scabbed quality that I did not like to remember even with the light on—still, I had known very well who it was, and in the dream he knew I knew.

———

After what we'd been through in the previous weeks, it was no wonder we were all a little sick of one another. For the first few days we stayed pretty much to ourselves, except in class and in the dining halls; with Bun dead and buried, I suppose, there was much less to talk about, and no reason to stay up until four or five in the morning.

I felt strangely free. I took walks; saw some movies by myself; went to an off-campus party on Friday night, where I stood on the back porch of some teacher's house and drank beer and heard a girl whisper about me to another girl, "He looks so sad, don't you think?" It was a clear night, with crickets and a million stars. The girl was pretty, the bright-eyed, ebullient type I always go for. She struck up a conversation, and I could have gone home with her; but it was enough just to flirt, in the tender, uncertain way tragic characters do in films (shell-shocked veteran or brooding young widower; attracted to the young stranger yet haunted by a dark past which she in her innocence cannot share) and have the pleasure of watching the stars of empathy bloom in her kind eyes; feeling her sweet wish to rescue me from myself (and, oh, my dear, I thought, if you knew what a job you'd be taking on, if you only knew!); knowing that if I wanted to go home with her, I could.

Which I did not. Because—no matter what kindhearted strangers thought—I was in need of neither company nor comfort. All I wanted was to be alone. After the party I didn't go to my room but to Dr. Roland's office, where I knew no one would think to look for me. At night and on weekends it was wonderfully quiet, and once we got back from Connecticut I spent a great deal of time there—reading, napping on his couch, doing his work and my own.

At that time of night, even the janitors had left. The building was dark. I locked the office door behind me. The lamp on Dr. Roland's desk cast a warm, buttery circle of light and, after turning the radio on low to the classical station in Boston, I settled on the couch with my French grammar. Later, when I got sleepy, there would be a mystery novel, a cup of tea if I felt like it. Dr. Roland's bookshelves glowed warm and mysterious in the lamplight. Though I wasn't doing anything wrong, it seemed to me that I was sneaking around somehow, leading a secret life which, pleasant though it was, was bound to catch up with me sooner or later.

———

Between the twins, discord still reigned. At lunch they would sometimes arrive as much as an hour apart. I sensed that the fault lay with Charles, who was surly and uncommunicative and—as lately was par for the course—drinking a little more than was good for him. Francis claimed to know nothing about it, but I had an idea he knew more than he was saying.

I had not spoken to Henry since the funeral nor even seen him. He didn't show up at meals and wasn't answering the telephone. At lunch on Saturday, I said: "Do you suppose Henry's all right?"

"Oh, he's fine," said Camilla, busy with knife and fork.

"How do you know?"

She paused, the fork in mid-air; her glance was like a light turned suddenly into my face. "Because I just saw him."

"Where?"

"At his apartment. This morning," she said, going back to her lunch.

"So how is he?"

"Okay. A little shaky still, but all right."

Beside her, chin in hand, Charles glowered down at his untouched plate.

———

Neither of the twins was at dinner that night. Francis was talkative and in a good mood. Just back from Manchester and loaded with shopping bags, he showed me his purchases one by one: jackets, socks, suspenders, shirts in half a dozen different stripes, a fabulous array of neckties, one of which—a greeny-bronze silk with tangerine polka dots—was a present for me. (Francis was always generous with his clothes. He gave Charles and me his old suits by the armload; he was taller than Charles, and thinner than both of us, and we would have them altered by a tailor in town. I still wear a lot of those suits: Sulka, Aquascutum, Gieves and Hawkes.)

He had been to the bookstore, too. He had a biography of Cortés; a translation of Gregory of Tours; a study of Victorian murderesses, put out by the Harvard University Press. He had also bought a gift for Henry: a corpus of Mycenaean inscriptions from Knossos.

I looked through it. It was an enormous book. There was no text, only photograph after photograph of broken tablets with the inscriptions—in Linear B—reproduced in fac-simile in the bottom. Some of the fragments had only a single character.

"He'll like this," I said.

"Yes, I think he will," said Francis. "It was the most boring book I could find. I thought I might drop it off after dinner."

"Maybe I'll come along," I said.

Francis lit a cigarette. "You can if you like. I'm not going in. I'm just going to leave it on the porch."

"Oh, well, then," I said, oddly relieved.

———

I spent all day Sunday in Dr. Roland's office, from ten in the morning on. Around eleven that night I realized I'd had nothing to eat all day, nothing but coffee and some crackers from the Student Services office, so I got my things, locked up, and walked down to see if the Rathskeller was still open.

It was. The Rat was an extension of the snack bar, with lousy food mostly but there were a couple of pinball machines, and a juke-box, and though you couldn't buy any kind of a real drink there they would give you a plastic cup of watered-down beer for only sixty cents.

That night it was loud and very crowded. The Rat made me nervous. To people like Jud and Frank, who were there every time the doors opened, it was the nexus of the universe.

They were there now, at the center of an enthusiastic table of toadies and hangers-on, playing, with froth-mouthed relish, some game which apparently involved their trying to stab each other in the hand with a piece of broken glass.

I pushed my way to the front and ordered a slice of pizza and a beer. While I was waiting for the pizza to come out of the oven, I saw Charles, alone, at the end of the bar.

I said hello and he turned halfway. He was drunk; I could see it in the way he was sitting, not in an inebriated manner **per se** but as if a different person—a sluggish, sullen one— had occupied his body. "Oh," he said. "Good. It's you."

I wondered what he was doing in this obnoxious place, by himself, drinking bad beer when at home he had a cabinet full of the best liquor he could possibly want.

He was saying something I couldn't make out over the music and shouting. "What?" I said, leaning closer.

"I said, could I borrow some money."

"How much?"

He did some counting on his fingers. "Five dollars."

I gave it to him. He was not so drunk that he was able to accept it without repeated apologies and promises to repay it.

"I meant to go to the bank on Friday," he said.

"It's okay."

"No, really." Carefully, he took a crumpled check from his pocket. "My Nana sent me this. I can cash it on Monday no problem."

"Don't worry," I said. "What are you doing here?"

"Felt like going out."

"Where's Camilla?"

"Don't know."

He was not so drunk, now, that he couldn't make it home on his own; but the Rat didn't close for another two hours, and I didn't much like the idea of his staying on by himself. Since Bunny's funeral several strangers—including the secretary in the Social Sciences office—had approached me and tried to pick me for information. I had frozen them out, a trick I'd learned from Henry (no expression, pitiless gaze, forcing intruder to retreat in embarrassment); it was a nearly infallible tactic but dealing with these people when you were sober was one thing, and quite another if you were drunk. I wasn't drunk, but I didn't feel like hanging around the Rat until Charles got ready to leave, either. Any effort to draw him away would, I knew, serve only to entrench him further; when he was drunk he had a perverse way of always wanting to do exactly the opposite of what anyone suggested.

"Does Camilla know you're here?" I asked him.

He leaned over, palm on the bar to brace himself. "What?"

I asked him again, louder this time. His face darkened. "None of her business," he said, and turned back to his beer.

My food came. I paid for it and told Charles, "Excuse me, I'll be right back."

The men's room was in a dank, smelly hallway that ran perpendicular to the bar. I turned down it, out of Charles's view, to the pay phone on the wall. Some girl was on it, though, talking in German. I waited for ages, and was just about to leave when finally she hung up, and I dug in my pocket for a quarter and dialed the twins' number.

The twins weren't like Henry; if they were home, they would generally answer the phone. But no one did answer. I dialed again and glanced at my watch. Eleven-twenty. I couldn't think where Camilla would be, that time of night, unless she was on her way over to get him.

I hung up the phone. The quarter tinkled into the slot. I pocketed it and headed back to Charles at the bar. For a moment I thought he had just moved somewhere into the crowd, but after standing there a moment or two I realized I wasn't seeing him because he wasn't there. He had drunk the rest of his beer and left.

———

Hampden, suddenly, was green as Heaven again. Most of the flowers had been killed by the snow except the late bloomers, honeysuckle and lilac and so forth, but the trees had come back bushier than ever, it seemed, deep and dark, foliage so dense that the way that ran through the woods to North Hampden was suddenly very narrow, green pushing in on both sides and shutting out the sunlight on the dank, buggy path.

On Monday I arrived at the Lyceum a little early and, in Julian's office, found the windows open and Henry arranging peonies in a white vase. He looked as if he'd lost ten or fifteen pounds, which was nothing to someone Henry's size but still I saw the thinness in his face and even in his wrists and hands; it wasn't that, though, but something else, indefinable, that somehow had changed since I had seen him last.

Julian and he were talking—in jocular, mocking, pedantic Latin—like a couple of priests tidying the vestry before a mass. A dark smell of brewing tea hung strong in the air.

Henry glanced up. **"Salve, amice,"** he said, and a subtle animation flickered in his rigid features, usually so locked up, and distant: **"Valesne? Quid est rei?"**

"You look well," I said to him, and he did.

He inclined his head slightly. His eyes, which had been murky and dilated while he was ill, were now the clearest of blues.

"Benigne dicis," he said. "I feel much better."

Julian was clearing away the last of the rolls and jam—he and Henry had had breakfast together, quite a large one from the looks of it—and he laughed and said something I didn't quite catch, some Horatian-sounding tag about meat being good for sorrow. I was glad to see that he seemed quite his bright, serene old self. He'd been almost inexplicably fond of Bunny, but strong emotion was distasteful to him, and a display of feeling normal by modern standards would to him have seemed exhibitionist and slightly shocking: I was fairly sure this death had affected him more than he let show. Then again, I suspect that Julian's cheery, Socratic indifference to matters of life and death kept him from feeling too sad about anything for very long.

Francis arrived, and then Camilla; no Charles, he was probably in bed with a hangover. We all sat down at the big round table.

"And now," said Julian, when everything was quiet, "I hope we are all ready to leave the phenomenal world and enter into the sublime?"

———

Those days, I took an enormous relish in my new-found freedom. Now it appeared that we were safe, a huge darkness had lifted from my mind. The world was a fresh and wonderful place to me, green and bracing and entirely new, and I looked at it now with fresh new eyes.

I went on a lot of long walks by myself, through North Hampden, down to the Battenkill River. I liked especially going to the little country grocery in North Hampden (whose ancient proprietors, mother and son, were said to have been the inspiration for a famous and frequently anthologized horror story from the 1950s) to buy a bottle of wine, and wandering down to the riverbank to drink it, then roaming around drunk all the rest of those glorious, golden, blazing afternoons—a waste of time, I was behind in school, there were papers to write and exams coming up but still I was young; the grass was green and the air was heavy with the sound of bees and I had just come back from the brink of Death itself, back to the sun and air. Now I was free; and my life, which I had thought was lost, stretched out indescribably precious and sweet before me.

On one of those afternoons I wandered by Henry's house and found him in his back yard digging a flower bed. He had on his gardening clothes—old trousers, shirtsleeves rolled up past the elbow—and in the wheelbarrow were tomato plants and cucumber, flats of strawberry and sunflower and scarlet geranium. Three or four rosebushes with their roots tied in burlap were propped against the fence.

I let myself in through the side gate. I was quite drunk. "Hello," I said, "hello, hello, hello."

He stopped and leaned on his shovel. A pale flush of sunburn glowed on the bridge of his nose.

"What are you doing?" I said.

"Putting out some lettuces."

There was a long silence, in which I noticed the ferns he'd dug up the afternoon we killed Bunny. Spleenwort, I remembered him calling them; Camilla had remarked on the witchiness of the name. He had planted them on the shady side of the house, near the cellar, where they grew dark and foamy in the cool.

I lurched back a bit, caught myself on the gatepost. "Are you going to stay here this summer?" I said.

He looked at me closely, dusted his hands on his trousers. "I think so," he said. "What about you?"

"I don't know," I said. I hadn't mentioned it to anyone, but only the day before I had put in an application at the Student Services office for an apartment-sitting job, in Brooklyn, for a history professor who was studying in England over the summer. It sounded ideal—a rent-free place to stay in, nice part of Brooklyn, and no duties except watering the plants and taking care of a pair of Boston terriers, who couldn't go to England because of the quarantine. My experience with Leo and the mandolins had made me wary, but the clerk had assured me that no, this was different, and she'd shown me a file of letters from happy students who had previously held the job. I had never been to Brooklyn and didn't know a thing about it but I liked the idea of living in a city—any city, especially a strange one—liked the thought of traffic and crowds, of working in a bookstore, waiting tables in a coffee shop, who knew what kind of odd, solitary life I might slip into? Meals alone, walking the dogs in the evenings; and nobody knowing who I was.

Henry was still looking at me. He pushed his glasses up on his nose. "You know," he said, "it's pretty early in the afternoon."

I laughed. I knew what he was thinking: first Charles, now me.

"I'm okay," I said.

"Are you?"

"Of course."

He went back to his work, sticking the shovel into the ground, stepping down hard on one side of the blade with a khaki-gaitered foot. His suspenders made a black X across his back. "Then you can give me a hand with these lettuces," he said. "There's another spade in the toolshed."

———

Late that night—two a.m.—my house chairperson pounded on my door and yelled that I had a phone call. Dazed with sleep, I put on my bathrobe and stumbled downstairs.

It was Francis. "What do you want?" I said.

"Richard, I'm having a heart attack."

I looked with one eye at my house chairperson—Veronica, Valerie, I forget her name—who was standing by the phone with her arms folded over her chest, head to one side in an attitude of concern. I turned my back. "You're all right," I said into the receiver. "Go back to sleep."

"Listen to me." His voice was panicky. "I'm having a heart attack. I think I'm going to die."

"No you're not."

"I have all the symptoms. Pain in the left arm. Tightness in chest. Difficulty breathing."

"What do you want me to do?"

"I want you to come over here and drive me to the hospital."

"Why don't you call the ambulance?" I was so sleepy my eyes kept closing.

"Because I'm scared of the ambulance," said Francis, but I couldn't hear the rest because Veronica, whose ears had pricked up at the word **ambulance**, broke in excitedly.

"If you need a paramedic, the guys up at the security booth know CPR," she said eagerly. "They're on call from midnight to six. They also run a van service to the hospital. If you want me to I'll—"

"I don't need a paramedic," I said. Francis was repeating my name frantically at the other end.

"Here I am," I said.

"Richard?" His voice was weak and breathy. "Who are you talking to? What's wrong?"

"Nothing. Now listen to me—"

"Who said something about paramedic?"

"Nobody. Now listen. **Listen,**" I said, as he tried to talk over me. "Calm down. Tell me what's wrong."

"I want you to come over. I feel really bad. I think my heart just stopped beating for a moment. I—"

"Are drugs involved?" said Veronica in a confidential tone.

"Look," I said to her, "I wish you'd be quiet and let me hear what this person is trying to say."

"Richard?" said Francis. "Will you just come get me? Please?"

There was a brief silence.

"All right," I said, "give me a few minutes," and I hung up the phone.

———

At Francis's apartment I found him dressed except for his shoes, lying on his bed. "Feel my pulse," he said.

I did, to humor him. It was quick and strong. He lay there limply, eyelids fluttering. "What do you think is wrong with me?" he said.

"I don't know," I said. He was a bit flushed but he really didn't look that bad. Still—though it would be insane, I knew, to mention it at that moment—it was possible that he had food poisoning or appendicitis or something.

"Do you think I should go into the hospital?"

"You tell me."

He lay there a moment. "I don't know. I really think I should," he said.

"All right, then. If it'll make you feel better. Come on. Sit up."

———

He was not too ill to smoke in the car all the way to the hospital.

We circled around the drive and pulled up by the wide floodlit entrance marked **Emergency**. I stopped the car. We sat there for a moment.

"Are you sure you want to do this?" I said.

He looked at me with astonishment and contempt.

"You think I'm **faking**," he said.

"No I don't," I said, surprised; and, to be honest, the thought hadn't occurred to me. "I just asked you a question."

He got out of the car and slammed the door.

———

We had to wait about half an hour. Francis filled out his chart and sat sullenly reading back issues of **Smithsonian** magazine. But when the nurse finally called his name, he didn't stand up.

"That's you," I said.

He still didn't move.

"Well, go on," I said.

He didn't answer. He had a sort of wild look in his eye.

"Look here," he finally said. "I've changed my mind."

"What?"

"I said I've changed my mind. I want to go home."

The nurse was standing in the doorway, listening to this exchange with interest.

"That's stupid," I said to him, irritated. "You've waited this long."

"I changed my mind."

"You were the one who wanted to come."

I knew this would shame him. Annoyed, avoiding my gaze, he slammed down his magazine and stalked through the double doors without looking back.

———

About ten minutes later an exhausted-looking doctor in a scrub shirt poked his head into the waiting room. I was the only person there.

"Hi," he said curtly. "You with Mr. Abernathy?"

"Yes."

"Would you step back with me for a moment, please?"

I got up and followed him. Francis was sitting on the edge of an examining table, fully clad, bent almost double and looking miserable.

"Mr. Abernathy will not put on a gown," said the doctor. "And he won't let the nurse take any blood. I don't know how he expects us to examine him if he won't cooperate."

There was a silence. The lights in the examining room were very bright. I was horribly embarrassed.

The doctor walked over to a sink and began to wash his hands. "You guys been doing any drugs tonight?" he said casually.

I felt my face getting red. "No," I said.

"A little cocaine? Some speed, maybe?"

"No."

"If your friend here took something, it would help a lot if we knew what it was."

"Francis," I said weakly, and was silenced by a glare of hatred: **et tu, Brute**.

"How dare you," he snapped. "I didn't take anything. You know very well I didn't."

"Calm down," said the doctor. "Nobody's accusing you of anything. But your behavior is a little irrational tonight, don't you think?"

"No," said Francis, after a confused pause.

The doctor rinsed his hands and dried them on a towel. "No?" he said. "You come here in the middle of the night saying you're having a heart attack and then you won't let anyone near you? How do you expect me to know what is wrong with you?"

Francis didn't answer. He was breathing hard. His eyes were cast downward and his face was a bright pink.

"I'm not a mind reader," the doctor said at last. "But in my experience, somebody your age saying they're having a heart attack, it's one of two things."

"What?" I finally said.

"Well. Amphetamine poisoning, for one."

"It's not that," Francis said angrily, glancing up.

"All right, all right. Something else it could be is a panic disorder."

"What's that?" I said, carefully avoiding looking in Francis's direction.

"Like an anxiety attack. A sudden rush of fear. Heart palpitations. Trembling and sweating. It can be quite severe. People often think they're dying."

Francis didn't say anything.

"Well?" said the doctor. "Do you think that might be it?"

"I don't know," said Francis, after another confused pause.

The doctor leaned back against the sink. "Do you feel afraid a lot?" he said. "For no good reason you can think of?"

———

By the time we left the hospital, it was a quarter after three. Francis lit a cigarette in the parking lot. In his left hand he was grinding a piece of paper on which the doctor had written the name of a psychiatrist in town.

"Are you mad?" he said when we were in the car.

It was the second time he had asked. "No," I said.

"I know you are."

The streets were dream-lit, deserted. The car top was down. We drove past dark houses, turned onto a covered bridge. The tires thumped on the wooden planks.

"Please don't be mad at me," said Francis.

I ignored him. "Are you going to see that psychiatrist?" I said.

"It wouldn't do any good. I know what's bothering me."

I didn't say anything. When the word **psychiatrist** had come up, I had been alarmed. I was not a great believer in psychiatry but still, who knew what a trained eye might see in a personality test, a dream, even a slip of the tongue?

"I went through analysis when I was a kid," Francis said. He sounded on the verge of tears. "I guess I must've been eleven or twelve. My mother was on some kind of Yoga kick and she yanked me out of my old school in Boston and packed me off to this terrible place in Switzerland. The Something Institute. Everyone wore sandals with socks. There were classes in dervish dancing and the Kabbalah. All the White Level—that was what they called my grade, or form, whatever it was—had to do Chinese **Quigong** every morning and have four hours of Reichian analysis a week. I had to have six."

"How do you analyze a twelve-year-old kid?"

"Lots of word association. Also weird games they made you play with anatomically correct dolls. They'd caught me and a couple of little French girls trying to sneak off the grounds— we were half-starved, macrobiotic food, you know, we were only trying to get down to the **bureau de tabac** to buy some chocolates but of course they insisted it had somehow been some sort of sexual incident. Not that they minded that sort of thing but they liked you to tell them about it and I was too ignorant to oblige. The girls knew more about such matters and had made up some wild French story to please the shrink—**ménage à trois** in some haystack, you can't imagine how sick they thought I was for repressing this. Though I would've told them anything if I thought they'd send me home." He laughed, without much humor. "God. I remember the head of the Institute asking me once what character from fiction I most identified with, and I said Davy Balfour from **Kidnapped**."

We were rounding a corner. Suddenly, in the wash of the headlights, a large animal loomed in my path. I hit the brakes hard. For half a moment I found myself looking through the windshield at a pair of glowing eyes. Then, in a flash, it bounded away.

We sat for a moment, shaken, at a full stop.

"What was that?" said Francis.

"I don't know. A deer maybe."

"That wasn't a deer."

"Then a dog."

"It looked like some kind of a cat to me."

Actually, that was what it had looked like to me too. "But it was too big," I said.

"Maybe it was a cougar or something."

"They don't have those around here."

"They used to. They called them catamounts. Cat-o-the-Mountain. Like Catamount Street in town."

The night breeze was chilly. A dog barked somewhere. There wasn't much traffic on that road at night.

I put the car in gear.

———

Francis had asked me not to tell anyone about our excursion to the emergency room but at the twins' apartment on Sunday night I had a little too much to drink and I found myself telling the story to Charles in the kitchen after dinner.

Charles was sympathetic. He'd had some drinks himself but not as many as me. He was wearing an old seersucker suit which hung very loosely on him—he, too, had lost some weight—and a frayed old Sulka tie.

"Poor François," he said. "He's such a fruit-cake. Is he going to see that shrink?"

"I don't know."

He shook a cigarette from a pack of Lucky Strikes that Henry had left on the counter. "If I were you," he said, tapping the cigarette on the inside of his wrist and craning to make sure that no one was in the hall, "if I were you, I would advise him not to mention this to Henry."

I waited for him to continue. He lit the cigarette and blew out a cloud of smoke.

"I mean, I've been drinking a bit more than I should," he said quietly. "I'm the first to admit that. But my God, I was the one who had to deal with the cops, not him. I'm the one who has to deal with **Marion**, for Christ sake. She calls me almost every night. Let **him** try talking to her for a while and see how he feels. . . . If I wanted to drink a bottle of whiskey a day I don't see what he could say about it. I told him it was none of his business, and none of his business what you did, either."

"Me?"

He looked at me with a blank, childish expression. Then he laughed.

"Oh, you hadn't heard?" he said. "Now it's you, too. Drinking too much. Wandering around drunk in the middle of the day. Rolling down the road to ruin."

I was startled. He laughed again at the look on my face but then we heard footsteps and the tinkle of ice in an advancing cocktail—

Francis. He poked his head into the doorway and began to gabble good-naturedly about something or other, and after a few minutes we picked up our drinks and followed him back to the living room.

———

That was a cozy night, a happy night; lamps lit, sparkle of glasses, rain falling heavy on the roof. Outside, the treetops tumbled and tossed, with a foamy whoosh like club soda bubbling up in the glass. The windows were open and a damp cool breeze swirled through the curtains, bewitchingly wild and sweet.

Henry was in excellent spirits. Relaxed, sitting in an armchair with his legs stretched out in front of him, he was alert, well rested, quick with a laugh or a clever reply. Camilla looked enchanting. She wore a narrow sleeveless dress, salmon-colored, which exposed a pair of pretty collarbones and the sweet frail vertebrae at the base of her neck—lovely kneecaps, lovely ankles, lovely bare, strong-muscled legs. The dress exaggerated her spareness of body, her unconscious and slightly masculine grace of posture; I loved her, loved the luscious, stuttering way she would blink while telling a story, or the way (faint echo of Charles) that she held a cigarette, caught in the knuckles of her bitten-nailed fingers.

She and Charles seemed to have made up.

They didn't talk much, but the old silent thread of twinship seemed in place again. They perched on the arms of each other's chairs, and fetched drinks back and forth (a peculiar twin-ritual, complex and charged with meaning). Though I did not fully understand these ob-servances, they were generally a sign that all was well. She, if anything, seemed the more conciliatory party, which seemed to disprove the hypothesis that he was at fault.

The mirror over the fireplace was the center of attention, a cloudy old mirror in a rosewood frame; nothing remarkable, they'd got it at a yard sale, but it was the first thing one saw when one stepped inside and now even more conspicuous because it was cracked—a dra-matic splatter that radiated from the center like a spider's web. How that had happened was such a funny story that Charles had to tell it twice, though it was his reenactment of it that was funny, really—spring housecleaning, sneezing and miserable with dust, sneezing himself right off his stepladder and landing on the mirror, which had just been washed and was on the floor.

"What I don't understand," said Henry, "is how you got it back up again without the glass falling out."

"It was a miracle. I wouldn't touch it now. Don't you think it looks kind of wonderful?"

Which it did, there was no denying it, the spotty dark glass shattered like a kaleidoscope and refracting the room into a hundred pieces.

Not until it was time to leave did I discover, quite by accident, how the mirror had actually been broken. I was standing on the hearth, my hand resting on the mantel, when I happened to look into the fireplace. The fireplace did not work. It had a screen and a pair of andirons, but the logs that lay across them were furry with dust. But now, glancing down, I saw something else: silver sparkles, bright-needled splinters from the broken mirror, mixed with large, unmistakable shards of a gold-rimmed highball glass, the twin of the one in my own hand. They were heavy old glasses, an inch thick at the bottom. Someone had thrown this one hard, with a pretty good arm, from across the room, hard enough to break it to pieces and to shatter the looking-glass behind my head.

———

Two nights later, I was woken again by a knock at my door. Confused, in a foul temper, I switched on the lamp and reached blinking for my watch. It was three o'clock. "Who's there?" I said.

"Henry," came the surprising reply.

I let him in, somewhat reluctantly. He didn't

sit down. "Listen," he said. "I'm sorry to disturb you, but this is very important. I have a favor to ask of you."

His tone was quick and businesslike. It alarmed me. I sat down on the edge of my bed.

"Are you listening to me?"

"What is it?" I said.

"About fifteen minutes ago I got a call from the police. Charles is in jail. He has been arrested for drunk driving. I want you to go down and get him out."

A prickle rose on the nape of my neck. "What?" I said.

"He was driving my car. They got my name from the registration sticker. I have no idea what kind of condition he's in." He reached into his pocket and handed me an unsealed envelope. "I expect it's going to cost something to get him out, I don't know what."

I opened the envelope. Inside was a check, blank except for Henry's signature, and a twenty-dollar bill.

"I already told the police that I lent him the car," said Henry. "If there's any question about that, have them call me." He was standing by the window, looking out. "In the morning I'll get in touch with a lawyer. All I want you to do is get him out of there as soon as you can."

It took a moment or two for this to sink in.

"What about the money?" I said at last.

"Pay them whatever it costs."

"I mean this twenty dollars."

"You'll have to take a taxi. I took one over here. It's waiting downstairs."

There was a long silence. I still wasn't awake. I was sitting there in just an undershirt and a pair of boxer shorts.

While I dressed, he stood at the window looking out at the dark meadow, hands clasped behind his back, oblivious to the jangle of clothes-hangers and my clumsy, sleep-dazed fumbling through the bureau drawers—serene, preoccupied; lost, apparently, in his own abstract concerns.

———

It wasn't until I'd dropped Henry off and was being driven, at a rapid clip, towards the dark center of town, that I realized how poorly I had been apprised of the situation I was heading into. Henry hadn't told me a thing. Had there been an accident? For that matter, was anyone hurt? Besides, if this was such a big deal—and it **was** Henry's car, after all—why wasn't he coming, too?

A lone traffic light rocked on a wire over the empty intersection.

The jail, in Hampden town, was in an annex of the courthouse. It was also the only building in the square that had any lights on that time of night. I told the taxi driver to wait and went inside.

Two policemen were sitting in a large, well-lit room. There were many filing cabinets, and metal desks behind partitions; an old-fashioned water cooler; a gumball machine from the Civitan Club ("Your Change Changes Things"). I recognized one of the policemen—a fellow with a red moustache—from the search parties. The two of them were eating fried chicken, the sort you buy from under heat lamps in convenience stores, and watching "Sally Jessy Raphael" on a portable black-and-white TV.

"Hi," I said.

They looked up.

"I came to see about getting my friend out of jail."

The one with the red moustache wiped his mouth on a paper napkin. He was big and pleasant-looking, in his thirties. "That's Charles Macaulay, I bet," he said.

He said this as if Charles were an old friend of his. Maybe he was. Charles had spent a lot of time down here when the stuff with Bunny was going on. The cops, he said, had been nice to him. They'd sent out for sandwiches, bought him Cokes from the machine.

"You're not the guy I talked to on the phone," said the other policeman. He was large and relaxed, about forty, with gray hair and a froglike mouth. "Is that your car out there?"

I explained. They ate their chicken and listened: big, friendly guys, big police .38s on their hips. The walls were covered in government-issue posters: FIGHT BIRTH DEFECTS, HIRE VETERANS, REPORT MAIL FRAUD.

"Well, you know, we can't let you have the car," said the policeman with the red moustache. "Mr. Winter is going to have to come down here and pick it up himself."

"I don't care about the car. I just want to get my friend out of jail."

The other policeman looked at his watch. "Well," he said, "come back in about six hours, then."

Was he joking? "I have the money," I said.

"We can't set bail. The judge will have to do that at the arraignment. Nine o'clock in the morning."

Ar**raign**ment? My heart pumped. What the hell was that?

The cops were looking at me blandly as if to say, "Is that all?"

"Can you tell me what happened?" I said.

"What?"

My voice sounded flat and strange to me. "What exactly did he do?"

"State trooper pulled him over out on Deep Kill Road," said the gray-haired policeman. He said it as if he were reading it. "He was obviously intoxicated. He agreed to a Breathalyzer and failed it when it was administered. The trooper brought him down here and we put him in the lock-up. That was about two-twenty-five a.m."

Things still weren't clear, but for the life of me I couldn't think of the right questions to ask. Finally I said, "Can I see him?"

"He's fine, son," said the policeman with the red moustache. "You can see him first thing in the morning."

All smiles, very friendly. There was nothing more to say. I thanked them and left.

———

When I got outside the cab was gone. I still had fifteen dollars from Henry's twenty but to call another cab I'd have to go back inside the jail and I didn't want to do that. So I walked down Main Street to the south end, where there was a pay phone in front of the lunch counter. It didn't work.

So tired I was almost dreaming, I walked back to the square—past the post office, past the hardware store, past the movie theater with its dead marquee: plate glass, cracked sidewalks, stars. Mountain cats in bas-relief prowled the friezes of the public library. I walked a long way, till the stores got sparse and the road was dark, walked on the deep singing

shoulder of the highway till I got to the Greyhound bus station, sad in the moonlight, the
first glimpse I'd ever had of Hampden. The
terminal was closed. I sat outside, on a wooden
bench beneath a yellow light bulb, waiting for
it to open so I could go in and use the phone
and have a cup of coffee.

The clerk—a fat man with lifeless eyes—
came to unlock the place at six. We were the
only people there. I went into the men's room
and washed my face and had not one cup of
coffee but two, which the clerk sold me grudgingly from a pot he'd brewed on a hot plate behind the counter.

The sun was up, it was hard to see much
through the grime-streaked windows. Defunct
timetables papered the walls; cigarette butts
and chewing gum were stomped deep into the
linoleum. The doors of the phone booth were
covered in fingerprints. I closed them behind
me and dialed Henry's number, half-expecting
he wouldn't answer but to my surprise he did,
on the second ring.

"Where are you? What's the matter?"
he said.

I explained what had happened. Ominous
silence on the other end.

"Was he in a cell by himself?" he said at last.

"I don't know."

"Was he conscious? I mean, could he talk?"

"I don't know."

Another long silence.

"Look," I said, "he's going before the judge at nine. Why don't you meet me at the courthouse."

Henry didn't answer for a moment. Then he said: "It's best if you handle it. There are other considerations involved."

"If there are other considerations I'd appreciate knowing what they are."

"Don't be angry," he said quickly. "It's just that I've had to deal with the police so much. They know me already, and they know him too. Besides"—he paused—"I am afraid that I'm the last person Charles wants to see."

"And why is that?"

"Because we quarreled last night. It's a long story," he said as I tried to interrupt. "But he was very upset when I saw him last. And of all of us, I think you're on the best terms with him at the moment."

"Hmph," I said, though secretly I was mollified.

"Charles is very fond of you. You know that. Besides, the police don't know who you are. I don't think they'll be likely to associate you with that other business."

"I don't see that it matters at this point."

"I am afraid that it does matter. More than you might think."

There was a silence, during which I felt acutely the hopelessness of ever trying to get to the bottom of anything with Henry. He was like a propagandist, routinely withholding information, leaking it only when it served his purposes. "What are you trying to say to me?" I said.

"Now's not the time to discuss it."

"If you want me to go down there, you'd better tell me what you're talking about."

When he spoke, his voice was crackly and distant. "Let's just say that for a while things were much more touch-and-go than you realized. Charles has had a hard time. It's no one's fault really but he's had to shoulder more than his share of the burden."

Silence.

"I am not asking much of you."

Only that I do what you tell me, I thought as I hung up the telephone.

———

The courtroom was down the hall from the cells, through a pair of swinging doors with windows at the top. It looked very much like what I'd seen of the rest of the courthouse, circa 1950 or so, with pecky linoleum tiles and paneling that was yellowed and sticky-looking with honey-colored varnish.

I had not expected so many people would be there. There were two tables before the judge's bench, one with a couple of state troopers, the other with three or four unidentified men; a court reporter with her funny little typewriter; three more unidentified men in the spectators' area, sitting well apart from each other, as well as a poor haggard lady in a tan raincoat who looked like she was getting beat up by somebody on a pretty regular basis.

We rose for the judge. Charles's case was called first.

He padded through the doors like a sleepwalker, in his stocking feet, a court officer following close behind him. His face was blurry and thick. They'd taken his belt and tie as well as his shoes and he looked a little like he was in his pajamas.

The judge peered down at him. He was sour-faced, about sixty, with a thin mouth and big meaty jowls like a bloodhound's. "You have an attorney?" he said, in a strong Vermont accent.

"No, sir," said Charles.

"Wife or parent present?"

"No, sir."

"Can you post bail?"

"No, sir," Charles said. He looked sweaty and disoriented.

I stood up. Charles didn't see me but the judge did. "Are you here to post bail for Mr. Macaulay?" he said.

"Yes, I am."

Charles turned to stare, lips parted, his expression as blank and trancelike as a twelve-year-old's.

"It'll be five hundred dollars you can pay it at the window down the hall to your left," said the judge in a bored monotone. "You'll have to appear again in two weeks and I suggest you bring a lawyer. Do you have a job for which you need your vehicle?"

One of the shabby middle-aged men at the front spoke up. "It's not his car, Your Honor."

The judge glowered at Charles, suddenly fierce. "Is that correct?" he said.

"The owner was contacted. A Henry Winter. Goes to school up at the college. He says he lent the vehicle to Mr. Macaulay for the evening."

The judge snorted. To Charles he said gruffly: "Your license is suspended pending resolution and have Mr. Winter here on the twenty-eighth."

———

The whole business was amazingly quick. We were out of the courthouse by ten after nine.

The morning was damp and dewy, cold for May. Birds chattered in the black treetops. I was reeling with fatigue.

Charles hugged himself. "Christ, it's cold," he said.

Across the empty streets, across the square, they were just pulling the blinds up at the bank. "Wait here," I said. "I'll go call a cab."

He caught me by the arm. He was still drunk, but his night of boozing had done more damage to his clothes than to anything else; his face was fresh and flushed as a child's. "Richard," he said.

"What?"

"You're my friend, aren't you?"

I was in no mood to stand around on the courthouse steps and listen to this sort of thing. "Sure," I said, and tried to disengage my arm.

But he only clutched me tighter. "Good old Richard," he said. "I know you are. I'm so glad it was you who came. I just want you to do me this one little favor."

"What's that?"

"Don't take me home."

"What do you mean?"

"Take me to the country. To Francis's. I don't have the key but Mrs. Hatch could let me in or I could bust a window or something—no, **listen.** Listen to this. I could get in through the basement. I've done it millions of times. Wait," he said as I tried to interrupt again.

"You could come, too. You could swing by school and get some clothes and—"

"Hold on," I said, for the third time. "I can't take you anywhere. I don't have a car."

His face changed, and he let go my arm. "Oh, right," he said with sudden bitterness. "Thanks a lot."

"Listen to me. I **can't**. I don't have a car. I came down here in a taxicab."

"We can go in Henry's."

"No we can't. The police took the keys."

His hands were shaking. He ran them through his disordered hair. "Then come home with me. I don't want to go home by myself."

"All right," I said. I was so tired I was seeing spots. "All right. Just wait. I'll call a cab."

"No. No cab," he said, lurching backwards. "I don't feel so hot. I think I'd rather walk."

———

This walk, from the courthouse steps to Charles's apartment in North Hampden, was not an inconsiderable one. It was three miles, at least. A good portion of it lay along a stretch of highway.

Cars whooshed past in a rush of exhaust. I was dead tired. My head ached and my feet were like lead. But the morning air was cool and fresh and it seemed to bring Charles around a little. About halfway, he stopped at the dusty roadside window of a Tastee Freeze, across the highway from the Veterans Hospital, and bought an ice cream soda.

Our feet crunched on the gravel. Charles smoked a cigarette and drank his soda through a red-and-white-striped straw. Blackflies whined around our ears.

"So you and Henry had an argument," I said, just for something to say.

"Who told you? Him?"

"Yes."

"I couldn't remember. It doesn't matter. I'm tired of him telling me what to do."

"You know what I wonder," I said.

"What?"

"Not why he tells us what to do. But why we always do what he says."

"Beats me," said Charles. "It's not as if much good has come of it."

"Oh, I don't know."

"Are you kidding? The idea of that fucking bacchanal in the first place—who thought of that? Whose idea was it to take Bunny to Italy? Who the hell wrote that diary and left it lying around? The son of a bitch. I blame every bit of this on him. Besides, you have no idea how close they were to finding us out."

"Who?" I said, startled. "The police?"

"The people from the FBI. There was a lot towards the end we didn't tell the rest of you. Henry made me swear not to tell."

"Why? What happened?"

He threw down his cigarette. "Well, I mean, they had it confused," he said. "They thought Cloke was mixed up in it, they thought a lot of things. It's funny. We're so used to Henry. We don't realize sometimes how he looks to other people."

"What do you mean?"

"Oh, I don't know. I can think of a million examples." He laughed sleepily. "I remember last summer, when Henry was so gung-ho about renting a farmhouse, driving with him to a realtor's office upstate. It was perfectly straightforward. He had a specific house in mind—big old place built in the 1800s, way out on some dirt road, tremendous grounds, servants' quarters, the whole bit. He even had the cash in hand. They must've talked for two hours. The realtor called up her manager at home and asked him to come down to the office. The manager asked Henry a million questions. Called every one of his references. Everything was in order but even then they wouldn't rent it to him."

"Why?"

He laughed. "Well, Henry looks a bit too good to be true, doesn't he? They couldn't believe someone his age, a college student, would pay so much for a place that big and isolated, just to live all by himself and study the Twelve Great Cultures."

"What? They thought he was some kind of a crook?"

"They thought he wasn't entirely above-board, let's put it that way. Apparently the men from the FBI thought the same thing. They didn't think he killed Bunny, but they thought he knew something he wasn't telling. Obviously there had been a disagreement in Italy. Marion knew that, Cloke knew it, even Julian did. They even tricked me into admitting it, though I didn't tell that to Henry. If you ask me, I think what they really thought was that he and Bunny had some money sunk in Cloke's drug-dealing business. That trip to Rome was a big mistake. They could've done it inconspicuously but Henry spent a fortune, throwing money around like crazy, they lived in a **palazzo**, for Christ sake. People remembered them everywhere they went. I mean, you know Henry, that's just the way he is but you have to look at it from their point of view. That illness of his must've looked pretty suspicious, too. Wiring a doctor in the States for Demerol. Plus those tickets to South America. Putting them on his credit card was about the stupidest thing he ever did."

"They found out about that?" I said, horrified.

"Certainly. When they suspect somebody is dealing drugs, the financial records are the first thing they check—and good God, of all places, South America. Luckily Henry's dad really does own some property down there. Henry was able to cook up something fairly plausible—not that they believed him; it was more a matter of their not being able to disprove it."

"But I don't understand where they got this stuff about drugs."

"Imagine how it looked to them. On one hand, there was Cloke. The police knew he was dealing drugs on a pretty substantial scale; they also figured he was probably the middleman for somebody a lot bigger. There was no obvious connection between that and Bunny, but then there was Bunny's best friend, with **all** this money, they can't tell quite where it's coming from. And during those last months Bunny was throwing around plenty of money himself. Henry was giving it to him, of course, but they didn't know that. Fancy restaurants. Italian suits. Besides. Henry just **looks** suspicious. The way he acts. Even the way he dresses. He looks like one of those guys with horn-rimmed glasses and armbands in a gangster movie, you know, the one who cooks the books for Al Capone or something." He lit another cigarette. "Do you remember the night before they found Bunny's body?" he said. "When you and I went to that awful bar, the one with the TV, and I got so drunk?"

"Yes."

"That was one of the worst nights of my life. It looked pretty bad for both of us. Henry was almost sure he was going to be arrested the next day."

I was so appalled that for a moment I couldn't speak. "Why, for God's sake?" I said at last.

He drew deeply on his cigarette. "The FBI men came to see him that afternoon," he said. "Not long after they'd taken Cloke into custody. They told Henry they had enough probable cause to arrest half a dozen people, including himself, either for conspiracy or withholding evidence."

"Christ!" I said, dumbfounded. "Half a dozen people? Who?"

"I don't know exactly. They might've been bluffing but Henry was worried sick. He warned me they'd probably be coming over to my place and I just had to get out of there, I couldn't sit around waiting for them. He made me promise not to tell you. Even Camilla didn't know."

There was a long pause.

"But they didn't arrest you," I said.

Charles laughed. I noticed that his hands still shook a little. "I think we have dear old Hampden College to thank for that," he said. "Of course, a lot of the stuff didn't tie up; they figured that out from talking to Cloke. But still they knew they weren't getting the truth and they probably would've kept after it if the college had been a little more cooperative. Once Bunny's body was found, though, the administration just wanted to hush it up. Too much bad publicity. Freshman applications had gone down something like twenty percent. And the town police—whose business it was, really—are very cooperative about such things. Cloke was in a lot of trouble, you know— some of that drug stuff was serious, they could've thrown him in jail. But he got off with academic probation and fifty hours of community service. It didn't even go on his school record."

It took me some moments to digest this. Cars and trucks whooshed past.

After a while Charles laughed again. "It's funny," he said, pushing his fists deep in his pockets. "We thought we were putting our ace man up front but if one of the rest of us had handled it it would've been much better. If it had been you. Or Francis. Even my sister. We could have avoided half of this."

"It doesn't matter. It's over now."

"No thanks to him. **I** was the one who had to deal with the police. He takes the credit, but it was me who actually had to sit around that goddamned station all hours drinking coffee and trying to make them like me, you know, trying to convince them we were all just a bunch of regular kids. Same with the FBI, and that was even worse. Being the front for everybody, you know, always on guard, having to say exactly the right thing and doing my best to size up things from their point of view, and you had to hit exactly the right note with these people, too, you couldn't drop it for a second, trying to be all communicative and open yet concerned, too, you know, and at the same time not at all nervous, though I could hardly pick up a cup without being afraid of spilling it and a couple of times I was so panicky I thought I was just going to black out or break down or something. Do you know how hard that was? Do you think Henry would lower himself to do something like that? No. It was all right, of course, for **me** to do it but he couldn't be bothered. Those people had never seen anything like Henry in their lives. I'll tell you the sort of thing he worried about. Like if he was carrying around the right **book**, if Homer would make a better impression than Thomas Aquinas. He was like something from another planet. If he was the only one they'd had to deal with he would have landed us all in the gas chamber."

A lumber truck rattled past.

"Good God," I finally said. I was quite shaken. "I'm glad I didn't know."

He shrugged. "Well, you're right. It all came out okay. But I still don't like the way he tries to lord it over me."

We walked for a long time without saying anything.

"Do you know where you're going to spend the summer?" said Charles.

"I haven't thought about it much," I said. I hadn't heard anything about the situation in Brooklyn, which tended to make me think it had fallen through.

"I'm going to Boston," Charles said. "Francis's great-aunt has an apartment on Marlborough Street. Just a few doors from the Public Garden. She goes to the country in the summer and Francis said if I wanted to stay there, I could."

"Sounds nice."

"It's a big place. If you wanted, you could come too."

"Maybe."

"You'd like it. Francis will be in New York but he'll come up sometimes. Have you ever been to Boston?"

"No."

"We'll go to the Gardner Museum. And the piano bar at the Ritz."

He was telling me about a museum they had at Harvard, some place where they had a million different flowers all made of colored glass, when all of a sudden, with alarming swiftness, a yellow Volkswagen swooped from the opposite lane and ground to a stop beside us.

It was Judy Poovey's friend Tracy. She rolled down her window and gave us a brilliant smile. "Hi, guys," she said. "Want a ride?"

———

She dropped us off at Charles's place. It was ten o'clock. Camilla wasn't home.

"God," said Charles, shouldering off his jacket. It fell, in a heap, on the floor.

"How do you feel?"

"Drunk."

"Want some coffee?"

"There's some in the kitchen," Charles said, yawning and running a hand through his hair. "Mind if I have a bath?"

"Go ahead."

"I'll be out in a minute. That cell was filthy. I think I might have fleas."

He was more than a minute. I could hear him sneezing, running the hot and cold taps, humming to himself. I went into the kitchen and poured myself a glass of orange juice and put some raisin bread in the toaster.

While looking through the cabinet for coffee, I found a half-full jar of Horlick's malted milk. The label stared at me like a reproach. Bunny was the only one of us who ever drank malted milk. I pushed it to the rear of the cabinet, behind a jug of maple syrup.

The coffee was ready and I was on my second batch of toast when I heard a key in the lock, the front door opening. Camilla stuck her head into the kitchen.

"Hi, you," she said. Her hair was untidy and her face pale and watchful; she looked like a little boy.

"Hi yourself. Want some breakfast?"

She sat down at the table beside me. "How did it go?" she said.

I told her. She listened attentively, reached out and took a triangle of buttered toast from my plate and ate it as she listened.

"Is he all right?" she said.

I didn't know exactly how she meant it, "all right." "Sure," I said.

There was a long silence. Very faintly, on a downstairs radio, a sprightly female voice sang a song about yogurt, backed by a chorus of mooing cows.

She finished her toast and got up to pour herself some coffee. The refrigerator hummed.

I watched her rummage in the cabinet for a cup.

"You know," I said, "you ought to throw away that jar of malted milk you have in there."

It was a moment before she answered. "I know," she said. "In the closet there's a scarf he left the last time he was here. I keep running across it. It still smells like him."

"Why don't you get rid of it?"

"I keep hoping I won't have to. I hope one day I'll open the closet door and it'll be gone."

"I thought I heard you," said Charles, who had been standing in the kitchen door for I didn't know how long. His hair was wet and all he had on was a bathrobe and in his voice was still a trace of that liquory thickness I knew so well. "I thought you were in class."

"Small class. Julian let us out early. How do you feel?"

"Fabulous," said Charles, padding into the kitchen, his moist feet tracking prints that evaporated instantly on the shiny, tomato-red linoleum. He came up behind her and laid his hands on her shoulders; bending low, he put his lips close to the nape of her neck. "How about a kiss for your jailbird brother?" he said.

She turned halfway, as if to touch her lips to his cheek, but he slid a palm down her back and tipped her face up to his and kissed her full on the mouth—not a brotherly kiss, there was no mistaking it for that, but a long, slow, greedy kiss, messy and voluptuous. His bathrobe fell slightly open as his left hand sank from her chin to neck, collarbone, base of throat, his fingertips just inside the edge of her thin polka-dot shirt and trembling over the warm skin there.

I was astounded. She didn't flinch, didn't move. When he came up for breath she pulled her chair in close to the table and reached for the sugar bowl as if nothing had happened. Spoon tinkled against china. The smell of Charles—damp, alcoholic, sweet with the linden-water he used for shaving—hung heavy in the air. She brought the cup up and took a sip and it was only then I remembered: Camilla didn't like sugar in her coffee. She drank it unsweetened, with milk.

I was astounded. I felt I should say something—anything—but I couldn't think of a thing to say.

It was Charles who finally broke the silence. "I'm starving to death," he said, retying the knot of his bathrobe and pottering over to the refrigerator. The white door opened with a bark. He stooped to look in, his face radiant in the glacial light.

"I think I'm going to make some scrambled eggs," he said. "Anyone else want some?"

———

Late that afternoon, after I'd gone home and had a shower and a nap, I went to visit Francis.

"Come in, come in," he said, waving me in frenetically. His Greek books were spread out on the desk; a cigarette burned in a full ashtray. "What happened last night? Was Charles **arrested**? Henry wouldn't tell me a thing. I got part of the story from Camilla but she didn't know the details. . . . Sit down. Do you want a drink? What can I get for you?"

It was always fun to tell Francis a story. He leaned forward and hung on every word, reacting at appropriate intervals with astonishment, sympathy, dismay. When I was finished he bombarded me with questions. Normally, enjoying his rapt attention, I would have strung it out much longer, but after the first decent pause I said, "Now I want to ask you something."

He was lighting a fresh cigarette. He clicked shut the lighter and brought his eyebrows down. "What is it?"

Though I had thought of various ways to phrase this question, it seemed, in the interests of clarity, most expedient to come to the point. "Do you think Charles and Camilla ever sleep together?" I said.

He had just drawn in a big lungful of smoke.

At my question it spurted out his nose the wrong way.

"Do you?"

But he was coughing. "What makes you ask something like that?" he finally said.

I told him what I'd seen that morning. He listened, his eyes red and streaming from the smoke.

"That's nothing," he said. "He was probably still drunk."

"You haven't answered my question."

He laid the burning cigarette in the ashtray. "All right," he said, blinking. "If you want my opinion. Yes. I think sometimes they do."

There was a long silence. Francis closed his eyes, rubbed them with thumb and forefinger.

"I don't think it's anything that happens too frequently," he said. "But you never know. Bunny always claimed he walked in on them once."

I stared at him.

"He told Henry, not me. I'm afraid I don't know the details. Apparently he had the key and you remember how he used to barge in without knocking— Come now," he said. "You must have had some idea."

"No," I said, though actually I had, from the time I'd first met them. I'd attributed this to my own mental perversity, some degenerate vagary of thought, a projection of my own desire—because he was her brother, and they did look an awful lot alike, and the thought of them together brought, along with the predictable twinges of envy, scruple, surprise, another very much sharper one of excitement.

Francis was looking at me keenly. Suddenly I felt he knew exactly what I was thinking.

"They're very jealous of each other," he said. "He much more so than she. I always thought it was a childish, charming thing, you know, all verbal rough-and-tumble, even Julian used to tease them about it—I mean, I'm an only child, so is Henry, what do we know about such things? We used to talk about what fun it would be to have a sister." He chuckled. "More fun than either of us imagined, it seems," he said. "Not that I think it's so terrible, either— from a moral standpoint, that is—but it's not at all the casual, good-natured sort of thing that one might hope. It runs a lot more deep and nasty. Last fall, around the time when that farmer fellow . . ."

He trailed away, sat smoking for some moments, an expression of frustration and vague irritation on his face.

"Well?" I said. "What happened?"

"Specifically?" He shrugged. "I can't tell you. I remember hardly anything that happened that night, which isn't to say the tenor of it isn't clear enough. . . ." He paused; started to speak but thought better of it; shook his head. "I mean, after that night it was obvious to everyone," he said. "Not that it wasn't before. It's just that Charles was so much worse than anyone had expected. I . . ."

He sat staring into space for a moment. Then he shook his head and reached for another cigarette.

"It's impossible to explain," he said. "But one can also look at it on an extremely simple level. They were always keen on each other, those two. And I'm no prude, but this jealousy I find astounding. One thing I'll say for Camilla, she's more reasonable about that sort of thing. Perhaps she has to be."

"What sort of thing?"

"About Charles going to bed with people."

"Who's he been to bed with?"

He brought up his glass and took a big drink. "Me for one," he said. "That shouldn't surprise you. If you drank as much as he does, I daresay I would have been to bed with you, too."

Despite the archness of his tone—which normally would have irritated me—there was a melancholy undertone in his voice. He drained off the rest of the whiskey and set the glass down on the end table with a bang. He said, after a pause: "It hasn't happened often.

Three or four times. The first time when I was a sophomore and he was a freshman. We were up late, drinking in my room, one thing led to another. Loads of fun on a rainy night, but you should have seen us at breakfast the next morning." He laughed bleakly. "Remember the night Bunny died?" he said. "When I was in your room? And Charles interrupted us at that rather unfortunate moment?"

I knew what he was going to tell me. "You left my room with him," I said.

"Yes. He was awfully drunk. Actually a little **too** drunk. Which was quite convenient for him as he pretended not to remember it the next day. Charles is very prone to these attacks of amnesia after he spends the night at my house." He looked at me out of the corner of his eye. "He denies it all quite convincingly and the thing is, he expects me to play along with him, you know, pretend it never happened," he said. "I don't even think he does it out of guilt. As a matter of fact he does it in this particularly light-hearted way which infuriates me."

I said: "You like him a lot, don't you?"

I don't know what made me say this. Francis didn't blink. "I don't know," he said coldly, reaching for a cigarette with his long, nicotine-stained fingers. "I like him well enough, I suppose. We're old friends. Certainly I don't fool myself that it's more than that. But I've had a lot of fun with him, which is a great deal more than you can say about Camilla."

That was what Bunny would have called a shot across the bow. I was too surprised to even answer.

Francis—though his satisfaction was evident—did not acknowledge his point. He leaned back in his chair by the window; the edges of his hair glowed metallic red in the sun. He said: "It's unfortunate, but there it is. Neither one cares about anybody but himself—or herself, as the case may be. They like to present a unified front but I don't even know how much they care about each other. Certainly they take a perverse pleasure in leading one on—yes, she does lead you on," he said when I tried to interrupt, "I've seen her do it. And the same with Henry. He used to be crazy about her, I'm sure you know that; for all I know he still is. As for Charles—well, basically, he likes girls. If he's drunk, I'll do. But— just when I've managed to harden my heart, he'll turn around and be so **sweet**. I always fall for it. I don't know why." He was quiet for a moment. "We don't run much to looks in my family, you know, all knuckles and cheekbones and beaky noses," he said. "Maybe that's why I tend to equate physical beauty with qualities with which it has absolutely nothing to do. I see a pretty mouth or a moody pair of eyes and imagine all sorts of deep affinities, private kinships. Never mind that half a dozen jerks are clustered round the same person, just because they've been duped by the same pair of eyes." He leaned over and energetically stubbed out his cigarette. "She'd behave a lot more like Charles if she were allowed to; he's so possessive, though, he keeps her reeled in pretty tight. Can you imagine a worse situation? He watches her like a hawk. And he's also rather poor—not that it matters much," he said hastily, realizing to whom he was speaking, "but he's quite self-conscious about it. Very proud of his family, you know, very well aware that he himself is a sot. There's something kind of Roman about it, all this regard he puts in his sister's honor. Bunny wouldn't go near Camilla, you know, he would hardly even **look** at her. He used to say that she wasn't his type but I think the old Dutchman in him just knew she was bad medicine. My God . . . I remember once, a long time ago, we had dinner at a ridiculous Chinese restaurant in Bennington. The Lobster Pagoda. It's closed now. Red bead curtains and a shrine to the Buddha with an artificial waterfall. We drank a lot of drinks with umbrellas in them and Charles was **horribly** drunk—not that it was his fault, really; we were all drunk, the cocktails are always too strong in a place like that and besides, you never know quite what they put in them, do you? Outside, they had a footbridge to the parking lot that went over a moat with tame ducks and goldfish. Somehow Camilla and I got separated from everyone else, and we were waiting there. Comparing fortunes. Hers said something like 'Expect a kiss from the man of your dreams,' which was too good to pass up, so I—well, we were both drunk, and we got a little carried away—and then Charles barreled out of nowhere and grabbed me by the back of the neck and I thought he was going to throw me over the rail. Bunny was there, too, he pulled him off, and Charles had the sense to say he'd been joking but he wasn't, he **hurt** me, twisted my arm behind my back and damn near pulled it out of the socket. I don't know where Henry was. Probably looking at the moon and reciting some poem from the T'ang Dynasty."

Subsequent events had knocked it from my mind, but the mention of Henry made me think of what Charles had told me that morning about the FBI—and of another question, this one regarding Henry too. I was wondering if this was the time to bring up either of them when Francis said, abruptly and in a tone suggestive of bad news to follow, "You know, I was at the doctor's today."

I waited for him to go on. He didn't.

"What for?" I finally said.

"Same stuff. Dizziness. Chest pains. I wake up in the night and can't get my breath. Last week I went back to the hospital and let them run some tests but nothing turned up. They referred me to this other fellow. A neurologist."

"And?"

He shifted restlessly in his chair. "He didn't find anything. None of these hick doctors are any good. Julian gave me the name of a man in New York; he was the one who cured the Shah of Isram, you know, of that blood disease. It was in all the papers. Julian says he's the best diagnostician in the country and one of the best in the world. He's booked two years in advance but Julian says maybe if he calls him, he might agree to see me."

He was reaching for another cigarette, and the last, untouched, was still smoldering in the ashtray.

"The way you smoke," I said, "no wonder you're short of breath."

"That has nothing to do with it," he said irritably, tamping the cigarette on the back of his wrist. "That's just what these stupid Vermonters tell you. Stop smoking, cut out booze and coffee. I've been smoking half my life. You think I don't know how it affects me? You don't get these nasty cramping pains in your chest from cigarettes, nor from having a few drinks, either. Besides, I have all these other symptoms. Heart palpitations. Ringing in the ears."

"Smoking can have totally weird effects on your body."

Francis frequently made fun of me when I used some phrase he perceived as Californian. **"Totally weird?"** he said maliciously, mimicking my accent: suburban, hollow, flat. **"Rilly?"**

I looked at him slouching in his chair: polka-dot tie, narrow Bally shoes, foxy narrow face. His grin was foxy too, and showed too many teeth. I was sick of him. I stood up. The room was so smoky that my eyes watered. "Yeah," I said. "I've got to go now."

Francis's snide expression faded. "You're mad, aren't you?" he said anxiously.

"No."

"Yes you are."

"No, I'm not," I said. These sudden, panicky attempts at conciliation annoyed me more than his insults.

"I'm sorry. Don't listen to me. I'm drunk, I'm sick, I didn't mean it."

Without warning I had a vision of Francis—twenty years later, fifty years, in a wheelchair. And of myself—older, too, sitting around with him in some smoky room, the two of us repeating this exchange for the thousandth time. At one time I had liked the idea, that the act, at least, had bound us together; we were not ordinary friends, but friends till-death-do-us-part. This thought had been my only comfort in the aftermath of Bunny's death. Now it made me sick, knowing there was no way out. I was stuck with them, with all of them, for good.

———

On the walk home from Francis's—head down, sunk in a black, inarticulate tangle of anxiety and gloom—I heard Julian's voice saying my name.

I turned. He was just coming out of the Lyceum. At the sight of his quizzical, kindly face—so sweet, so agreeable, so glad to see me—something wrenched deep in my chest.

"Richard," he said again, as if there were no one on earth he could possibly be so delighted to see. "How are you?"

"Fine."

"I'm just going over to North Hampden. Will you walk with me?"

I looked at the innocent, happy face and thought: **If he only knew. It would kill him.**

"Julian, I'd love to, thanks," I said. "But I have to be getting home."

He looked at me closely. The concern in his eyes made me nearly sick with self-loathing.

"I see so little of you these days, Richard," he said. "I feel that you're becoming just a shadow in my life."

The benevolence, the spiritual calm, that radiated from him seemed so clear and true that, for a dizzying moment, I felt the darkness lift almost palpably from my heart. The relief was such that I almost broke down sobbing; but then, looking at him again, I felt the whole poisonous weight come crashing back down, full force.

"Are you sure you're all right?"

He can never know. We can never tell him.

"Oh. Sure I am," I said. "I'm fine."

———

Though the fuss about Bunny had mostly blown over, the college had still not returned quite to normal—and not at all in the new "Dragnet" spirit of drug enforcement which had spread across campus. Gone were the nights when, on one's way home from the Rathskeller, it was not unheard-of to see an occasional teacher standing under the bare light bulb of Durbinstall basement—Arnie Weinstein, say, the Marxist economist (Berkeley, '69), or the haggard, scraggle-haired Englishman who taught classes in Sterne and Defoe.

Long gone. I had watched grim security men dismantling the underground laboratory, hauling out cartons of beakers and copper piping, while Durbinstall's head chemist—a small, pimple-faced boy from Akron named Cal Clarken—stood by and wept, still in his trademark high-top sneakers and lab coat. The anthropology teacher who for twenty years had taught "Voices and Visions: The Thought of Carlos Castaneda" (a course which featured, at its conclusion, a mandatory campfire ritual at which pot was smoked) announced quite suddenly that he was leaving for Mexico on sabbatical. Arnie Weinstein took to frequenting the townie bars, where he attempted to discuss Marxist theory with hostile countermen. The scraggle-haired Englishman had returned to his primary interest, which was chasing girls twenty years younger than himself.

As part of the new "Drug Awareness" policy, Hampden was hosting an intercollege tournament, in game-show format, which tested students' knowledge about drugs and alcohol. The questions were developed by the National Council for Alcoholism and Substance Abuse.

The shows were moderated by a local TV personality (Liz Ocavello) and were broadcast live on Channel 12.

Unexpectedly, the quizzes proved wildly popular, though not in the spirit the sponsors might have hoped. Hampden had assembled a crack team which—like one of those commando forces in the movies, made up of desperate fugitives, men with freedom to gain and nothing to lose—proved virtually invincible. It was an all-star lineup: Cloke Rayburn; Bram Guernsey; Jack Teitelbaum; Laura Stora; none other than the legendary Cal Clarken heading the team. Cal was participating in hopes of being allowed back into school next term; Cloke and Bram and Laura as part of their required hours of community service; Jack was merely along for the ride. Their combined expertise was nothing short of stunning. Together, they led Hampden to victory after crashing victory over Williams, Vassar, Sarah Lawrence, fielding with dazzling speed and skill such questions as: Name five drugs in the Thorazine family, or: What are the effects of PCP?

But—even though business had been seriously curtailed—I was not surprised to find that Cloke was still plying his trade, though a good bit more discreetly than he had used to in the old days. One Thursday night before a party I went down to Judy's room to ask for an aspirin and, after a brief but mysterious inquisition from behind the locked door, found Cloke inside, shades pulled, busy with her mirror and her druggist's scales.

"Hi," he said, ushering me quickly inside and locking the door behind me again. "What can I do for you tonight?"

"Uh, nothing, thanks," I said. "I'm just looking for Judy. Where is she?"

"Oh," he said, crossing back to his work. "She's in the costume shop. I thought she probably sent you over. I like Judy but she's got to make such a big production of everything, which is definitely not cool. Not cool"—carefully, he tapped a measure of powder into an open fold of paper—"at all." His hands trembled; it was evident that he had been dipping pretty freely into his own wares. "But I had to toss my own scales, you know, after all that shit happened and what the fuck am I supposed to do? Go up to the infirmary? She was running around all day, at lunch and stuff, rubbing her nose and saying, '**Gram**ma's here, **Gram**ma's here,' lucky nobody knew what the fuck she was talking about, but still." He nodded at the open book beside him—Janson's **History of Art**, which was cut practically to tatters. "Even these fucking bindles. She got fixated on the idea that I had to make these fancy ones, Jesus, open them up and there's a fucking Tintoretto on the inside. And gets pissed if I cut them out so that the cupid's butt or whatever isn't, like, right in the center. How's Camilla?" he said, glancing up.

"Fine," I said. I didn't want to think about Camilla. I didn't want to think of anything having to do with Greek or Greek class, either one.

"How's she liking her new place?" said Cloke.

"What?"

He laughed. "Don't you know?" he said. "She moved."

"What? Where to?"

"Don't know. Down the street, probably. Stopped by to see the twins—hand me that blade, would you?—stopped by to see them yesterday and Henry was helping her put her stuff in boxes." He had abandoned his work at the scales and was now cutting out lines on the mirror. "Charles is going to Boston for the summer and she's staying here. Said she didn't want to stay there alone and it was too much of a pain to sublet. Sounds like there are going to be a lot of us here this summer." He offered me the mirror and a rolled-up twenty. "Bram and I are looking for a place right now."

"This is very good," I said, half a minute or so later, just as the first euphoric sparkle was starting to hit my synapses.

"Yeah. It's **excellent**, isn't it? Especially after that awful shit of Laura's that was going around. Those FBI guys analyzed it and said it was about eighty percent talcum powder or something." He wiped his nose. "Did they ever come talk to you, by the way?"

"The FBI? No."

"I'm surprised. After all that lifeboat shit they were feeding everybody."

"What are you talking about?"

"Christ. They were saying all kinds of weird stuff. There was a conspiracy going on. They knew that Henry and Charles and I were involved. We were all in bad trouble and there was only room for one guy on the lifeboat out. And that guy was going to be the guy that talked first." He sniffed again, and rubbed his nose with his knuckle. "In a way, it got worse **after** my dad sent the lawyer up. 'Why do you need a lawyer if you're innocent,' all that kind of shit. Thing is, even the fucking **lawyer** couldn't figure out what they were trying to get me to confess to. They kept saying that my friends—Henry and Charles—had ratted on me. That **they** were the guilty ones, and if I didn't start talking I might get blamed for something I didn't even do."

My heart was pounding, and not just from the cocaine. "Talking?" I said. "About what?"

"Search me. My lawyer said not to worry,

that they were full of shit. I talked to Charles and he said they were giving him the same line, too. And I mean—I know you like Henry but I think he got pretty flipped out by the whole thing."

"What?"

"Well, I mean, he's so straight, probably never even had an overdue library book, and out of the blue here comes the fucking FBI all over him. I don't know what the hell he told them, but he was trying to point them in any direction but towards himself."

"Like what direction?"

"Like me." He reached for a cigarette. "And, I hate to say it, but I think towards you."

"Me?"

"I never brought your name up, man. I hardly fucking know you. But they got it from somewhere. And it wasn't from me."

"You mean they actually **mentioned my name**?" I said, after a stunned silence.

"Maybe Marion gave it to them or something, I don't know. God knows, they had Bram's name, Laura's, even Jud MacKenna's. . . . Yours was only once or twice, towards the end there. Don't ask me why, but I had the idea the Feebies went over to talk to you. I guess that would've been the night before they found Bunny's body. They were coming over to talk to Charles again, I know that, but Henry called and tipped him off that they were on the way. That was when I was staying over at the twins'. Well, **I** didn't want to see them, either, so I headed over to Bram's, and Charles I guess just went to some townie bar and got completely fucked up."

My heart was thumping so wildly I thought it would burst in my chest like a red balloon. Had Henry got scared, tried to sic the FBI on me? That didn't make sense. There was no way, at least that I could see, he could set me up without incriminating himself. Then again (**paranoia,** I thought, **I have to stop this**), maybe it was no coincidence that Charles had stopped by my room that night on his way to the bar. Maybe he had been apprised of the whole thing and—unbeknownst to Henry— had come over and successfully lured me out of harm's way.

"You look like you could use a drink, man," said Cloke presently.

"Yeah," I said. I had been sitting for a long time without saying anything. "Yeah, I guess I could."

"Why don't you go to the Villager tonight? Thirsty Thursday. Two for the price of one."

"Are you going?"

"Everybody's going. Shit. You're trying to tell me you never went to Thirsty Thursday before?"

———

So I went to Thirsty Thursday, with Cloke and Judy, with Bram and Sophie Dearbold and some friends of Sophie's, and a lot of other people I didn't even know, and though I don't know what time I got home I didn't wake up till six the next evening, when Sophie knocked at my door. My stomach hurt and my head was splitting in two, but I put on my robe and let her in. She had just got out of ceramics class and was wearing a T-shirt and faded old jeans. She had brought me a bagel from the snack bar.

"Are you okay?" she said.

"Yes," I said, though I had to hold on to the back of my chair to stand up.

"You were really drunk last night."

"I know," I said. Getting out of bed had made me feel, suddenly, much worse. Red spots jumped in front of my eyes.

"I was worried. I thought I'd better come check on you." She laughed. "Nobody's seen you all day. Somebody told me they saw the flag at the guard booth at half-mast and I was afraid you might be dead."

I sat on the bed, breathing hard, and stared at her. Her face was like a half-remembered fragment of dream—**bar?** I thought. There had been the bar—Irish whiskeys and a pin-ball game with Bram, Sophie's face blue in the sleazy neon light. More cocaine, cut into lines with a school ID, off the side of a compact-disc case. Then a ride in the back of someone's truck, a Gulf sign on the highway, someone's apartment? The rest of the evening was black. Vaguely I remembered a long, earnest conversation with Sophie, standing by an ice-filled sink in someone's kitchen (MeisterBrau and Genesee, MOMA calendar on the wall). Certainly—a coil of fear wrenched in my stomach—certainly I hadn't said anything about Bunny. Certainly not. Rather frantically, I searched my memory. Certainly, if I had, she would not be in my room now, looking at me the way she was, would not have brought me this toasted bagel on a paper plate, the smell of which (it was an onion bagel) made me want to retch.

"How did I get home?" I said, looking up at her.

"Don't you remember?"

"No." Blood hammered nightmarishly in my temples.

"Then you **were** drunk. We called a cab from Jack Teitelbaum's."

"And where did we go?"

"Here."

Had we slept together? Her expression was neutral, offering no clue. If we had, I wasn't sorry—I liked Sophie, I knew she liked me, she was one of the prettiest girls at Hampden besides—but this was the kind of thing you like to know for sure. I was trying to think how I could ask her, tactfully, when someone knocked at the door. The raps were like gun shots. Sharp pains ricocheted through my head.

"Come in," said Sophie.

Francis stuck his head around the door. "Well, look at this, would you," he said. He liked Sophie. "It's the car trip reunion and nobody asked me."

Sophie stood up. "Francis! Hello! How've you been?"

"Good, thanks. I haven't talked to you since the funeral."

"I know. I was thinking about you just the other day. How have you been?"

I lay back on the bed, my stomach boiling. The two of them were conversing animatedly. I wished they would both leave.

"Well well," said Francis after a long interlude, peering over Sophie's shoulder at me. "What's wrong with tiny patient?"

"Too much to drink."

He came over to the bed. He seemed, up close, slightly agitated. "Well, I hope you've learned your lesson," he said brightly and then, in Greek, added: **"Important news, my friend."**

My heart sank. I had screwed up. I had been careless, talked too much, said something weird. "What have I done?" I said.

I had said it in English. If Francis was flustered, he didn't look it. "I haven't the slightest idea," he said. "Do you want some tea or something?"

I tried to figure out what he was trying to say. The pounding agony in my head was such that I couldn't concentrate on anything. Nausea swelled in a great green wave, trembled at the crest, sank and rolled again. I felt saturated with despair. Everything, I thought tremulously, everything would be okay if only I could have a few moments of quiet and if I lay very, very still.

"No," I said finally. "Please."

"Please what?"

The wave swelled again. I rolled over on my stomach and gave a long, miserable moan.

Sophie caught on first. "Come on," she said to Francis, "let's go. I think we ought to let him go back to sleep."

———

I fell into a tormented half-dreaming state from which I woke, several hours later, to a soft knock. The room was now dark. The door creaked open and a flag of light fell in from the corridor. Francis slipped in and closed the door behind him.

He switched on the weak reading lamp on my desk and pulled the chair over to my bed. "I'm sorry but I've got to talk to you," he said. "Something very odd has happened."

I had forgotten my earlier fright; it came back in a sick, bilious wash. "What is it?"

"Camilla has **moved**. She's moved out of the apartment. All her things are gone. Charles is there right now, drunk nearly out of his mind. He says she's living at the Albemarle Inn. Can you imagine? The Albemarle?"

I rubbed my eyes, trying to collect my thoughts. "But I knew that," I said finally.

"You did?" He was astonished. "Who told you?"

"I think it was Cloke."

"**Cloke?** When was this?"

I explained, as far as memory allowed. "I forgot about it," I said.

"For**got**? How could you forget something like that?"

I sat up a bit. Fresh pain surged through my head. "What difference does it make?" I said, a little angrily. "If she wants to leave I don't blame her. Charles will just have to straighten up. That's all."

"But the Albemarle?" said Francis. "Do you have any idea how expensive it is?"

"Of course I do," I said irritably. The Albe-

marle was the nicest inn in town. Presidents
had stayed there, and movie stars. "So what?"

Francis put his head in his hands. "Richard,"
he said, "you're dense. You must have brain
damage."

"I don't know what you're talking about."

"How about two hundred dollars a night?
Do you think the twins have that kind of
money? Who the hell do you think is paying
for it?"

I stared at him.

"Henry, that's who," said Francis. "He came
over when Charles was out and moved her
there, lock, stock and barrel. Charles came
home and her things were gone. Can you
imagine? He can't even get in touch with her,
she's registered under a different name. Henry
won't tell him anything. For that matter, he
won't tell me anything, either. Charles is absolutely beside himself. He asked me to call
Henry and see if I could get anything out of
him, I couldn't, of course, he was like a brick
wall."

"What's the big deal? Why are they making
such a secret of it?"

"I don't know. I don't know Camilla's side
but I think Henry is being very foolish."

"Maybe she has reasons of her own."

"She doesn't think that way," said Francis,

exasperated. "I know Henry. This is just the sort of thing he'd do and it's just the way he'd do it. But even if there's a good reason it's the wrong way to go about it. **Especially** now. Charles is in a state. Henry should know better than to antagonize him after the other night."

Uncomfortably, I thought of the walk home from the police station. "You know, there's something I've meant to tell you," I said, and I told him about Charles's outburst.

"Oh, he's mad at Henry all right," said Francis tersely. "He's told me the same thing—that Henry pushed it all off on him, basically. But what does he expect? When you get down to it, I don't think Henry asked all that much of him. That's not the reason he's angry. The real reason is Camilla. Do you want to know my theory?"

"What?"

"I think Camilla and Henry have been slipping around with each other for quite some time. I think Charles has been suspicious for a while but until lately he didn't have any proof. Then he found something out. I don't know what, exactly," he said, raising his hand as I tried to interrupt, "but it's not hard to imagine. I think it's something he found out down at the Corcorans'. Something he saw or heard. And I think it must've happened before we arrived. The night before they left for Connecticut with Cloke, everything seemed fine, but you remember what Charles was like when we got there. And by the time we left they weren't even speaking."

I told Francis what Cloke had said to me in the upstairs hallway.

"God knows what happened, then, if Cloke was smart enough to catch on," said Francis. "Henry was sick, probably wasn't thinking too clearly. And the week we came back, you know, when he holed up in his apartment, I think Camilla was there a lot. She was there, I know, the day I went to take him that Mycenaean book and I think she might have even spent the night a couple of times. But then he got well and Camilla came home and for a while after that, things were okay. Remember? Around the time you took me to the hospital?"

"I don't know about that," I said. I told him about the glass I had seen lying broken in the fireplace at the twins' apartment.

"Well, who knows what was really happening. At least they **seemed** better. And Henry was in good spirits too. Then there was that quarrel, the night Charles ended up in jail. Nobody seems to want to say exactly what **that** was all about but I'll bet it had something to do with her. And now this. Good God. Charles is in a bloody rage."

"Do you think he's sleeping with her? Henry?"

"If he's not, he's certainly done everything he possibly can to convince Charles that he is." He stood up. "I tried to call him again before I came over here," he said. "He wasn't in. I expect he's over at the Albemarle. I'm going to drive by and see if his car is there."

"There must be some way you can find out what room she's in."

"I've thought about that. I can't get anything out of the desk clerk. Maybe I'd have better luck talking to one of the maids, but I'm afraid I'm not very good at that sort of thing." He sighed. "I wish I could see her for just five minutes."

"If you find her, do you think you can talk her into coming home?"

"I don't know. I must say, I wouldn't care to be living with Charles right now. But I still think everything would be okay if Henry would just keep out of it."

———

After Francis left I fell asleep again. When I woke up it was four in the morning. I had slept for nearly twenty-four hours.

The nights that spring were unusually cold; this one was colder than most and the heat was on in the dormitories—steam heat, full blast, which made it unbearably stuffy even with the windows open. My sheets were damp with sweat. I got up and stuck my head out the window and took a few breaths. The chill air was so refreshing that I decided to put on some clothes and go for a walk.

The moon was full and very bright. Everything was silent except for the chirp of the crickets and the full foamy toss of the wind in the trees. Down at the Early Childhood Center, where Marion worked, the swings creaked gently to and fro, and the corkscrewed slide gleamed silver in the moonlight.

The most striking object in the playground was without question the giant snail. Some art students had built it, modeling it after the giant snail in the movie of **Doctor Dolittle**. It was pink, made of fiberglass, nearly eight feet tall, with a hollow shell so kids could play inside. Silent in the moonlight, it was like some patient prehistoric creature that had crawled down from the mountains: dumb, lonely, biding its time, untroubled by the articles of playground equipment which surrounded it.

Access to the snail's interior was gained by a child-sized tunnel, maybe two feet high, at the base of the tail. From this tunnel, I was extremely startled to see protruding a pair of adult male feet, shod in some oddly familiar brown-and-white spectator shoes.

On hands and knees, I leaned forward

and stuck my head in the tunnel and was overwhelmed by the raw, powerful stink of whiskey. Light snores echoed in the close, boozy darkness. The shell, apparently, had acted as a brandy snifter, gathering and concentrating the vapors until they were so pungent I felt nauseated just to breathe them.

I caught and shook a bony kneecap. "Charles." My voice boomed and reverberated in the dark interior. **"Charles."**

He began to flounder wildly, as if he had waked to find himself in ten feet of water. At length, and after repeated assurances that I was who I said I was, he fell on his back again, breathing hard.

"Richard," he said thickly. "Thank God. I thought you were some kind of creature from space."

At first it had been completely dark inside but now my eyes had adjusted I was aware of a faint, pinkish light, moonlight, just enough to see by, glowing through the translucent walls. "What are you doing here?" I asked him.

He sneezed. "I was depressed," he said. "I thought if I slept here it might make me feel better."

"Did it?"

"No." He sneezed again, five or six times in a row. Then he slumped back on the floor.

I thought of the nursery-school kids, hud-

dled round Charles the next morning like Lil-
liputians round the sleeping Gulliver. The lady
who ran the Childhood Center—a psychiatrist, whose office was down the hall from Dr.
Roland's—seemed to me a pleasant, grand-
motherly sort, though who could predict how
she'd react to finding a drunk passed out on
her playground. "Wake up, Charles," I said.

"Leave me alone."

"You can't sleep here."

"I can do whatever I want," he said
haughtily.

"Why don't you come home with me? Have
a drink."

"I'm fine."

"Oh, come on."

"Well—just one."

He bumped his head, hard, while crawling
out. The little kids were certainly going to love
that smell of Johnnie Walker when they came
to school in a few hours.

He had to lean on me on the way up the hill
to Monmouth House.

"Just one," he reminded me.

———

I was not in terrific shape myself and had a
hard time hauling him up the stairs. Finally I
reached my room and deposited him on my
bed. He offered little resistance and lay there,
mumbling, while I went down to the kitchen.

My offer of a drink had been a ruse. Quickly I searched the refrigerator but all I could find was a screw-top bottle of some syrupy Kosher stuff, strawberry-flavored, which had been there since Hanukkah. I'd tasted it once, with the idea of stealing it, and hurriedly spit it out and put the bottle back on the shelf. That had been months ago. I slipped it under my shirt; but when I got upstairs, Charles's head had rolled back against the wall where the headboard should have been and he was snoring.

Quietly, I put the bottle on my desk, got a book, and left. Then I went to Dr. Roland's office, where I lay reading on the couch with my jacket thrown over me until the sun came up, and I turned off the lamp and went to sleep.

———

I woke around ten. It was Saturday, which surprised me a little; I'd lost track of the days. I went to the dining hall and had a late breakfast of tea and soft-boiled eggs, the first thing I'd eaten since Thursday. When I went to my room to change, around noon, Charles was still asleep in my bed. I shaved, put on a clean shirt, got my Greek books and went back to Dr. Roland's.

I was ridiculously behind in my studies but not (as is often the case) so far behind as I'd thought. The hours went by without my noticing them. When I got hungry, around six, I went to the refrigerator in the Social Sciences office and found some leftover hors d'oeuvres and a piece of birthday cake, which I ate from my fingers off a paper plate at Dr. Roland's desk.

Since I wanted a bath, I came home around eleven, but when I unlocked the door and turned on the light, I was startled to find Charles still in my bed. He was sleeping, but the bottle of Kosher wine on the desk was half-empty. His face was flushed and pink. When I shook him, he felt as though he had a good deal of fever.

"Bunny," he said, waking with a start. "Where did he go?"

"You're dreaming."

"But he was here," he said, looking wildly round. "For a long time. I saw him."

"You're dreaming, Charles."

"But I **saw him**. He was here. He was sitting on the foot of the bed."

I went next door to borrow a thermometer. His temperature was nearly a hundred and three. I gave him two Tylenol and a glass of water and left him, rubbing his eyes and talking nonsense, to go downstairs and call Francis.

Francis wasn't home. I decided to try Henry. To my surprise it was Francis, not Henry, who answered the phone.

"Francis? What are you doing over there?" I said.

"Oh, hello, Richard," said Francis. He said it in a stagy way, as if for Henry's benefit.

"I guess you can't really talk now."

"No."

"Look here. I need to ask you something." I explained to him about Charles, playground and all. "He seems pretty sick. What do you think I should do?"

"The snail?" said Francis. "You found him inside that giant snail?"

"Yes. What should I do? I'm kind of worried."

Francis put his hand over the receiver. I could hear a muffled discussion. In a moment Henry came on the line. "Hello, Richard," he said. "What's the matter?"

I had to explain all over again.

"How high, did you say? A hundred and three?"

"Yes."

"That's rather a lot, isn't it?"

I said that I thought it was.

"Did you give him some aspirins?"

"A few minutes ago."

"Well, then, why don't you wait and see. I'm sure he's fine."

This was exactly what I wanted to hear.

"You're right," I said.

"He probably caught cold sleeping out of doors. I'm sure he'll be better in the morning."

———

I spent the night on Dr. Roland's couch, and after breakfast, came back to my room with blueberry muffins and a half-gallon carton of orange juice which, with extraordinary difficulty, I had managed to steal from the buffet in the dining hall.

Charles was awake, but feverish and vague. From the state of the bedclothes, which were tumbled and tossed, blanket trailing on the floor and the stained ticking of the mattress showing where he'd pulled the sheets loose, I gathered he'd not had a very good night of it. He said he wasn't hungry, but he managed a few limp little sips of the orange juice. The rest of the Kosher wine had disappeared, I noticed, in the night.

"How do you feel?" I asked him.

He lolled his head on the crumpled pillow. "Head hurts," he said sleepily. "I had a dream about Dante."

"Alighieri?"

"Yes."

"What?"

"We were at the Corcorans' house," he mumbled. "Dante was there. He had a fat friend in a plaid shirt who yelled at us."

I took his temperature; it was an even hundred. A bit lower, but still kind of high for the first thing in the morning. I gave him some more aspirin and wrote down my number at Dr. Roland's in case he wanted to call me, but when he realized I was leaving, he rolled his head back and gave me such a dazed and hopeless look that it stopped me cold in the middle of my explanation about how the switchboard re-routed calls to administrative offices on the weekends.

"Or, I could stay here," I said. "If I wouldn't be bothering you, that is."

He pushed up on his elbows. His eyes were bloodshot and very bright. "Don't go," he said. "I'm scared. Stay a little while."

He asked me to read to him, but I didn't have anything around but Greek books, and he didn't want me to go to the library. So we played euchre on a dictionary balanced on his lap, and when that started to prove a bit much we switched to Casino. He won the first couple of games. Then he started losing. On the final hand—it was his deal—he shuffled the cards so poorly they were coming up in virtually exact sequence, which should not have made for very challenging play but he was so absentminded he kept trailing when he could easily have built or taken in. When I was reaching to increase a build, my hand brushed against his and I was taken aback by how dry and hot it was. And though the room was warm, he was shivering. I took his temperature. It had shot back to a hundred and three.

I went downstairs to call Francis, but neither he nor Henry was in. So I went back upstairs. There was no doubt about it: Charles looked terrible. I stood in the door looking at him for a moment, and then I said, "Wait a minute" and went down the hall to Judy's room.

I found her lying on her bed, watching a Mel Gibson movie on a VCR she'd borrowed from the video department. She was managing somehow to polish her fingernails, smoke a cigarette, and drink a Diet Coke all at the same time.

"Look at Mel," she said. "Don't you just love him? If he called up and asked me to marry him I would do it in, like, one second."

"Judy, what would you do if you had a hundred and three degrees of fever?"

"I would go to the fucking doctor," she said without looking away from the TV.

I explained about Charles. "He's really sick," I said. "What do you think I should do?"

She fanned a red taloned hand in the air, drying it, her eyes still fixed on the screen. "Take him to the emergency room."

"You think?"

"You're not going to find any doctors on Sunday afternoon. Want to use my car?"

"That would be great."

"Keys are on the desk," she said absently. "Bye."

———

I drove Charles to the hospital in the red Corvette. He was bright-eyed and quiet, staring straight ahead, his right cheek pressed to the cool window-glass. In the waiting room, while I looked through magazines I'd seen before, he sat without moving, staring at a faded color photograph from the 1960s which hung opposite, of a nurse who had a white-nailed finger pressed to a white-lipsticked, vaguely pornographic mouth, in a sexy injunction to hospital silence.

The doctor on duty was a woman. She'd been with Charles for only about five or ten minutes when she came from the back with his chart; leaning over the counter, she consulted briefly with the receptionist, who indicated me.

The doctor came over and sat beside me. She was like one of those cheery young physicians in Hawaiian shirts and tennis shoes that you see on TV shows. "Hello," she said. "I've just been looking at your friend. I think we're going to have to keep him with us for a couple of days."

I put down my magazine. This I hadn't expected. "What's wrong?" I said.

"It looks like bronchitis, but he's very dehydrated. I want to put him on an IV. Also we need to get that fever down. He'll be okay, but he needs rest and a good strong series of antibiotics, and to get those working as soon as we can we should give him those intravenously, too, for the first forty-eight hours at least. You both in school up at the college?"

"Yes."

"Is he under a lot of stress? Working on his thesis or something?"

"He works pretty hard," I said cautiously. "Why?"

"Oh, nothing. It just looks like he hasn't been eating properly. Bruises on his arms and legs, which look like a C deficiency, and he may be running low on some of the B vitamins as well. Tell me. Does he smoke?"

I couldn't help but laugh. At any rate, she wouldn't let me see him; she said she wanted to get some blood work done before the lab technicians left for the day, so I drove to the twins' apartment to gather some of his things. The place was ominously neat. I packed pajamas, toothbrush, shaving kit, and a couple of paperback books (P. G. Wodehouse, who I thought might cheer him up) and left the suitcase with the receptionist.

———

Early the next morning, before I left for Greek, Judy knocked at my door and told me I had a call downstairs. I thought it was Francis or Henry—both of whom I'd tried to reach repeatedly the night before—or maybe even Camilla, but it was Charles.

"Hello," I said. "How are you feeling?"

"Oh, very well." His voice had a strange, forced note of cheeriness. "It's quite comfortable here. Thanks for bringing the suitcase by."

"No problem. Do you have one of those beds you can crank up and down?"

"As a matter of fact I do. Listen. I want to ask you something. Will you do me a favor?"

"Sure."

"I'd like you to get a couple of things for me." He mentioned a book, and letter paper, and a bathrobe which I would find hanging on the inside of his closet door—"Also," he said hurriedly, "there's a bottle of Scotch. You'll find it in the drawer of my night table. Do you think you can get it out this morning?"

"I have to go to Greek."

"Well, after Greek, then. What time do you think you'll be here?"

I told him I would have to see about borrowing a car.

"Don't worry about that. Take a taxi. I'll give you the money. I really appreciate this, you know. What time should I expect you? Ten-thirty? Eleven?"

"Probably more like eleven-thirty."

"That's fine. Listen. I can't talk, I'm in the patients' lounge. I have to get back to bed before they miss me. You will come, won't you?"

"I'll be there."

"Bathrobe and letter paper."

"Yes."

"And the Scotch."

"Of course."

———

Camilla was not at class that morning, but Francis and Henry were. Julian was there when I arrived, and I explained that Charles was in the hospital.

Though Julian could be marvelously kind in difficult circumstances of all sorts, I sometimes got the feeling that he was less pleased by kindness itself than by the elegance of the gesture. But at this news he appeared genuinely concerned. "Poor Charles," he said. "It's not **serious**, is it?"

"I don't think so."

"Is he allowed any visitors? I shall telephone him this afternoon. Can you think of anything he might like? Food is so dreadful in the hospital. I remember years ago, in New York, when a dear friend of mine was in Columbia Presbyterian—in the bloody Harkness Pavilion, for goodness' sake—the chef at the old Le Chasseur used to send her dinner to her every single day. . . ."

Henry, across the table, was absolutely inscrutable. I tried to catch Francis's glance; he slid me a quick look, bit his lip and glanced away.

". . . and flowers," said Julian, "you've never seen so many flowers, she had so many I could only suspect that she was sending at least some of them to herself." He laughed. "Anyway. I suppose there's no need to ask where Camilla is this morning."

I saw Francis's eyes snap open. For a moment I was startled too, before I realized that he'd assumed—naturally, of course—that she was at the hospital with Charles.

Julian's eyebrows went down. "What's wrong?" he said.

The utter blankness which met this question made him smile.

"It doesn't do to be too Spartan about these things," he said kindly, after a very long pause; and I was grateful to see that, as usual, he was projecting his own tasteful interpretation upon the confusion. "Edmund was your friend. I too am very sorry that he is dead. But I think you are grieving yourselves sick over this, and not only does that not help him, it hurts you. And besides, is death really so terrible a thing?

It seems terrible to you, because you are young, but who is to say he is not better off now than you are? Or—if death is a journey to another place—that you will not see him again?"

He opened his lexicon and began to search for his place. "It does not do to be frightened of things about which you know nothing," he said. "You are like children. Afraid of the dark."

———

Francis didn't have his car with him, so after class I got Henry to drive me to Charles's apartment. Francis—who came too—was nervous and on edge, chain-smoking and pacing in the foyer while Henry stood in the bedroom door and watched me get Charles's things: quiet, expressionless, his eyes following me with an abstract calculation that entirely precluded the possibility of my asking him about Camilla—which I had determined to do as soon as we were alone—or, in fact, of asking practically anything at all.

I got the book, the letter paper, the bathrobe. The Scotch I hesitated over.

"What's the matter?" said Henry.

I put the bottle back in the drawer and shut it. "Nothing," I said. Charles, I knew, would be furious. I would have to think of a good excuse.

He nodded at the closed drawer. "Did he ask you to bring that to him?" he said.

I did not feel like discussing Charles's personal business with Henry. I said: "He asked for cigarettes, too, but I don't think he ought to have them."

Francis had been pacing in the hall outside, prowling restlessly back and forth like a cat. During this exchange he paused in the door. Now I saw him dart a quick worried glance at Henry. "Well, you know . . . ?" he said hesitantly.

Henry said to me: "If he wants it—the bottle, that is—I think you'd better go ahead and take it to him."

His tone annoyed me. "He's sick," I said. "You haven't even seen him. If you think you're doing him a favor by—"

"Richard, he's right," said Francis nervously, tapping a cigarette ash into his cupped palm. "I know about this a little bit. Sometimes, if you drink, it's dangerous to stop too suddenly. Makes you sick. People can die of it."

I was shocked by this. Charles's drinking had never seemed so bad as all that. I did not comment on this, though, only said: "Well, if he's that bad off, he'll do a lot better in the hospital, won't he?"

"What do you mean?" said Francis. "Do you want them to put him in a detox? Do you know what that's like? When my mother came off drink that first time, she was out of her head. Seeing things. Wrestling with the nurse and yelling nutty stuff at the top of her lungs."

"Hate to think of Charles having DTs in the Catamount Memorial Hospital," said Henry. He went to the night table and got the bottle. It was a fifth, a little less than half full. "This will be cumbersome for him to hide," he said, holding it up by the neck.

"We could pour it into something else," said Francis.

"It would be easier, I think, if we bought him a new one. Less chance of it leaking all over everything. And if we get him one of those flat ones he can keep it under his pillow without much trouble."

———

It was a drizzly morning, overcast and gray. Henry didn't go with us to the hospital. He had us drop him off at his apartment—he had some excuse, plausible enough, I can't remember what it was—and when he got out of the car he gave me a hundred-dollar bill.

"Here," he said. "Give Charles my love. Will you buy some flowers for him or something?"

I looked at the bill, momentarily stunned. Francis snatched it from me and pushed it back at him. "Come on, Henry," he said, with an anger that surprised me. "Stop it."

826   THE SECRET HISTORY

"I want you to have it."

"**Right**. We're supposed to get him a hundred dollars' worth of flowers."

"Don't forget to stop at the package store," said Henry coldly. "Do what you like with the rest of the money. Just give him the change, if you want. I don't care."

He pushed the money at me again and shut the car door, with a click that was more contemptuous than if he'd slammed it. I watched his stiff square back receding up the walk.

———

We bought Charles's whiskey—Cutty Sark, in a flat bottle—and a basket of fruit, and a box of petit-fours, and a game of Chinese checkers, and, instead of cleaning out the day's stock of carnations at the florist's downtown, an Oncidium orchid, yellow with russet tiger-stripes, in a red clay pot.

On the way to the hospital, I asked Francis what had happened over the weekend.

"Too upsetting. I don't want to talk about it now," he said. "I did see her. Over at Henry's."

"How is she?"

"Fine. A little preoccupied but fine, basically. She said she didn't want Charles to know where she was and that was all there was to it. I wish I could've talked to her alone, and of course Henry didn't leave the room for a second." Restlessly, he felt in his pocket for a cigarette. "This may sound crazy," he said, "but before I saw her I'd been a little worried, you know? That something maybe had happened to her."

I didn't say anything. The same thought had crossed my mind, more than once.

"I mean—not that I thought Henry would **kill** her or anything, but you know—it was strange. Her disappearing like that, without a word to anybody. I—" He shook his head. "I hate to say this, but sometimes I wonder about Henry," he said. "Especially with things like— well, you know what I mean?"

I didn't answer. Actually I did know what he meant, quite well. But it was too horrible for either of us to come out and say.

———

Charles had a semi-private room. He was in the bed nearer the door, separated by a curtain from his roommate: the Hampden County postmaster, as we later discovered, who was in for a prostate operation. On his side there were a lot of FTD flower arrangements, and corny get-well cards taped to the wall, and he was propped up in bed talking with some noisy family members: food smells, laughter, every- thing cheery and snug. More of his visitors trailed in after Francis and me, stopping, for an instant, to peer curiously over the curtain at Charles: silent, alone, flat on his back with an

IV in his arm. His face was puffy and his skin rough and coarse-looking, broken out in some kind of a rash. His hair was so dirty it looked brown. He was watching cartoons on television, violent ones, little animals that looked like weasels cracking up cars and bashing each other on the head.

He struggled to sit up when we stepped into his partition. Francis drew the curtain behind us, practically in the faces of the postmaster's inquisitive visitors, a pair of middle-aged ladies, who were dying to get a good look at Charles and one of whom had craned around and cawed "Good morning!" through the gap in the curtain, in the hopes of initiating conversation.

"Dorothy! Louise!" someone called from the other side. "Over here!"

There were rapid footsteps on the linoleum and henlike clucks and cries of greeting.

"Damn them," said Charles. He was very hoarse and his voice was little more than a whisper. "He's got people there all the time. They're always coming in and out and trying to look at me."

By way of distraction, I presented Charles with the orchid.

"Really? You bought that for me, Richard?" He seemed touched. I was going to explain that it was from all of us—without coming out and mentioning Henry, exactly—but Francis shot me a warning look and I kept my mouth shut.

We unloaded the sack of presents. I'd half expected him to pounce on the Cutty Sark and tear it open in front of us, but he only thanked us and put the bottle in the compartment underneath his upright gray-plastic bed tray.

"Have you talked to my sister?" he said to Francis. He said it in a very cold way, as if he were saying **Have you talked to my lawyer?**

"Yes," Francis said.

"She's all right?"

"Seems to be."

"What does she have to say for herself?"

"I don't know what you mean."

"I hope you told her I said go to hell."

Francis didn't answer. Charles picked up one of the books I had brought him and began to leaf through it sporadically. "Thanks for coming," he said. "I'm kind of tired now."

———

"He looks awful," said Francis in the car.

"There's got to be some way they can patch this up," I said. "Surely we can get Henry to call him and apologize."

"What good do you think that's going to do? As long as Camilla's at the Albemarle?"

"Well, she doesn't know he's in the hospital, does she? This is kind of an emergency."

"I don't know."

The windshield wipers ticked back and forth. A cop in a rain slicker was directing traffic at the intersection. It was the cop with the red moustache. Recognizing Henry's car, he smiled at us and beckoned for us to go through. We smiled and waved back, happy day, two guys on a ride—then drove for a block or two in grim, superstitious silence.

"There's got to be something we can do," I said at last.

"I think we had better stay out of it."

"You can't tell me that if she knew how sick he was, she wouldn't be over at the hospital in five minutes."

"I'm not kidding," said Francis. "I think we both had better just stay out of it."

"Why?"

But he only lit another cigarette and wouldn't say anything else, no matter how I grilled him.

———

When I got back to my room I found Camilla sitting at my desk, reading a book. "Hi," she said, glancing up. "Your door was open. I hope you don't mind."

Seeing her was like an electric shock. Unexpectedly I felt a surge of anger. Rain was blowing through the screen and I walked across the room to shut the window.

"What are you doing here?" I said.

"I wanted to talk to you."

"About what?"

"How's my brother?"

"Why don't you go see him yourself?"

She put down the book—**ah, lovely,** I thought helplessly, I loved her, I loved the very sight of her: she was wearing a cashmere sweater, soft gray-green, and her gray eyes had a luminous celadon tint. "You think you have to take sides," she said. "But you don't."

"I'm not taking sides. I just think whatever you're doing, you picked a bad time to do it."

"And what would be a good time?" she said. "I want you to see something. Look."

She held up a piece of the light hair near her temples. Underneath was a scabbed spot about the size of a quarter where someone had, apparently, pulled a handful of hair out by the roots. I was too startled to say a thing.

"And this." She pushed up the sleeve of her sweater. The wrist was swollen and a bit discolored, but what horrified me was a tiny, evil burn on the underside of the forearm: a cigarette burn, gouged deep and ugly in the flesh.

It was a moment before I found my voice. "Good God, Camilla! Charles did this?"

She pulled the sleeve down. "See what I mean?" she said. Her voice was unemotional; her expression watchful, almost wry.

"How long has this been going on?"

She ignored my question. "I know Charles," she said. "Better than you do. Staying away, just now, is much wiser."

"Whose idea was it that you stay at the Albemarle?"

"Henry's."

"How does he fit into this?"

She didn't answer.

A horrible thought flashed across my mind. "**He** didn't do this to you, did he?" I said.

She looked at me in surprise. "No. Why would you think that?"

"How am I supposed to know what to think?"

The sun came suddenly from behind a rain cloud, flooding the room with glorious light that wavered on the walls like water. Camilla's face burst into glowing bloom. A terrible sweetness boiled up in me. Everything, for a moment—mirror, ceiling, floor—was unstable and radiant as a dream. I felt a fierce, nearly irresistible desire to seize Camilla by her bruised wrist, twist her arm behind her back until she cried out, throw her on my bed: strangle her, rape her, I don't know what. And then the cloud passed over the sun again, and the life went out of everything.

"Why did you come here?" I said.

"Because I wanted to see you."

"I don't know if you care what I think"—I hated the sound of my voice, was unable to control it, everything I said was coming out in the same haughty, injured tone—"I don't know if you care what I think, but I think you're making things worse by staying at the Albemarle."

"And what do **you** think I should do?"

"Why don't you stay with Francis?"

She laughed. "Because Charles bullies poor Francis to death," she said. "Francis means well. I know that. But he couldn't stand up to Charles for five minutes."

"If you asked him, he'd give you the money to go somewhere."

"I know he would. He offered to." She reached in her pocket for a cigarette; with a pang I saw they were Lucky Strikes, Henry's brand.

"You could take the money and stay wherever you like," I said. "You wouldn't have to tell him where."

"Francis and I have gone over all this." She paused. "The thing is, I'm afraid of Charles. And Charles is afraid of Henry. That's really all there is to it."

I was shocked by the coldness with which she said this.

"So is that it?" I said.

"What do you mean?"

"You're protecting your own interests?"

"He tried to kill me," she said simply. Her eyes met mine, candid and clear.

"And is Henry not afraid of Charles too?"

"Why should he be?"

"You know."

Once she realized what I meant, I was startled how quickly she leapt to his defense. "Charles would never do that," she said, with childlike swiftness.

"Let's say he did. Went to the police."

"But he **wouldn't**."

"How do you know?"

"And implicate the rest of us? Himself, too?"

"At this point, I think he might not care."

I said this intending to hurt her, and with pleasure I saw that I had. Her startled eyes met mine. "Maybe," she said. "But you've got to remember, Charles is **sick** now. He's not himself. And the thing is, I believe he knows it." She paused. "I love Charles," she said. "I love him, and I know him better than anybody in the world. But he's been under an awful lot of pressure, and when he's drinking like this, I don't know, he just becomes a different person. He won't listen to anybody; I don't know if he even remembers half the things he does. That's why I thank God he's in the hospital. If he has to stop for a day or two, maybe he'll start thinking straight again."

What would she think, I wondered, if she knew that Henry was sending him whiskey.

"And do you think Henry really has Charles's best interest at heart?" I said.

"Of course," she said, startled.

"And yours too?"

"Certainly. Why shouldn't he?"

"You do have a lot of faith in Henry, don't you," I said.

"He's never let me down."

For some reason, I felt a fresh swell of anger. "And what about Charles?" I said.

"I don't know."

"He'll be out of the hospital soon. You'll have to see him. What are you going to do then?"

"Why are you so angry at me, Richard?"

I glanced at my hand. It was trembling. I hadn't even realized it. I was trembling all over with rage.

"Please leave," I said. "I wish you'd go."

"What's wrong?"

"Just go. Please."

She got up and took a step towards me. I stepped away. "All right," she said, "all right," and she turned around and left.

———

It rained all day and the rest of the night. I took some sleeping pills and went to the movies: Japanese film, I couldn't seem to follow it. The characters loitered in deserted rooms, no one talking, everything silent for whole minutes except the hiss of the projector and rain pounding on the roof. The theater was empty except for a shadowy man in the back. Dust motes floated in the projector beam. It was raining when I came out, no stars, sky black as the ceiling of the movie house. The marquee lights melted on the wet pavement in long white gleams. I went back inside the glass doors to wait for my taxi, in the carpeted, popcorn-smelling lobby. I called Charles on the pay phone, but the hospital switchboard wouldn't put me through: it was past visiting hours, she said, everyone was sleeping. I was still arguing with her when the taxi pulled up at the curb, long slants of rain illumined in the headlights and the tires throwing up low fans of water.

———

I dreamed about the stairs again that night. It was a dream I'd had often in the winter but seldom since. Once more, I was on the iron stairs at Leo's—rusted thin, no railing—except now they stretched down into a dark infinity and the steps were all different sizes: some tall, some short, some as narrow as the width of my shoe. The drop was bottomless on either side. For some reason, I had to hurry, though I was terrified of falling. Down and down. The stairs got more and more precarious, until finally they weren't even stairs at all; farther down—and for some reason this was always the most terrifying thing of all—a man was going down them, far ahead of me, really fast. . . .

I woke around four, couldn't get back to sleep. Too many of Mrs. Corcoran's tranquilizers: they'd started to backfire in my system, I was taking them in the daytime now, they wouldn't knock me out anymore. I got out of bed and sat by the window. My heartbeat trembled in my fingertips. Outside the black panes, past my ghost in the glass (**Why so pale and wan, fond lover?**) I heard the wind in the trees, felt the hills crowding around me in the dark.

I wished I could stop myself from thinking. But all sorts of things had begun to occur to me. For instance: why had Henry let me in on this, only two months (it seemed years, a lifetime) before? Because it was obvious, now, that his decision to tell me was a calculated move. He had appealed to my vanity, allowing me to think I'd figured it out by myself (**good for you,** he'd said, leaning back in his chair; I could still remember the look on his face as he'd said it, **good for you, you're just as smart as I'd thought you were**); and I had congratulated myself in the glow of his praise, when in fact—I saw this now, I'd been too vain to see it then—he'd led me right to it, coaxing and flattering all the way. Perhaps—the thought crawled over me like a cold sweat—perhaps even my preliminary, accidental discovery had been engineered. The lexicon that had been misplaced, for instance: had Henry stolen it, knowing I'd come back for it? And the messy apartment I was sure to walk into; the flight numbers and so forth left deliberately, so it now seemed, by the phone; both were oversights unworthy of Henry. Maybe he'd wanted me to find out. Maybe he'd divined in me—correctly—this cowardice, this hideous pack instinct which would enable me to fall into step without question.

And it wasn't just a question of having kept my mouth shut, I thought, staring with a sick feeling at my blurred reflection in the windowpane. **Because they couldn't have done it without me**. Bunny had come to me, and I had delivered him right into Henry's hands. And I hadn't even thought twice about it.

"You were the alarm bell, Richard," Henry had said. "I knew if he told anybody, he'd tell you first. And now that he has, I feel that we're in for an extremely rapid progression of events."

An extremely rapid progression of events. My flesh crawled, remembering the ironic, almost humorous twist he'd put on the last words—oh, God, I thought, my God, how could I have listened to him? He was right, too, about the rapid part at least. Less than twenty-four hours later, Bunny was dead. And though I hadn't done the actual pushing—which had seemed an essential distinction at the time—now that didn't matter much anymore.

I was still trying to force back the blackest thought of all; the merest suggestion of it sent the rat's feet of panic skittering up my spine. Had Henry intended to make me the patsy if his plan had fallen through? If so, I wasn't quite sure how he'd meant to manage it, but if he'd felt like doing it, there was no doubt in my mind he would have been able to. So much of what I knew was only secondhand, so much of it was only what he'd told me; there was an awful lot, when you got right down to it, that I didn't even know. And—though the immediate danger was apparently gone—there was no guarantee that it wouldn't surface again a year, twenty years, fifty years from now. I knew, from television, that there was no statute of limitations on murder. New evidence discovered. The case reopened. You read about these things all the time.

It was still dark. Birds were chirping in the eaves. I pulled out my desk drawer and counted the rest of the sleeping pills: candy-colored pretties, bright on a sheet of typing paper. There were still quite a lot of them, plenty for my purposes. (Would Mrs. Corcoran feel better if she knew this twist: that her stolen pills had killed her son's killer?) So easy, to feel them go down my throat: but blinking in the glare of my desk lamp, I was struck with a wave of revulsion so strong it was almost nausea. Horrific as it was, the present dark, I was afraid to leave it for the other, permanent dark—jelly and bloat, the muddy pit. I had seen the shadow of it on Bunny's face—stupid terror; the whole world opening upside down; his life exploding in a thunder of crows and the sky expanding empty over his stomach like a white ocean. Then nothing. Rotten stumps, sowbugs crawling in the fallen leaves. Dirt and dark.

I lay on my bed. I felt my heart limping in my chest, and was revolted by it, a pitiful muscle, sick and bloody, pulsing against my ribs. Rain streamed down the windowpanes. The lawn outside was sodden, swampy. When the sun came up, I saw, in the small, cold light of dawn, that the flagstones outside were covered with earthworms: delicate, nasty, hundreds of them, twisting blind and helpless on the rain-dark sheets of slate.

———

In class on Tuesday, Julian mentioned he'd spoken to Charles on the telephone. "You're right," he murmured. "He doesn't sound well. Very groggy and confused, don't you think? I suppose they have him under sedation?" He smiled, sifting through his papers. "Poor Charles. I asked where Camilla was—I wanted to get her on the line, I couldn't make any sense of what he was trying to tell me—and he said"—(here his voice changed slightly, in imitation of Charles, a stranger might assume; but it was really Julian's own voice, cultured and purring, only raised slightly in tone, as if he could not bear, even in mimicry, to substantively alter its own melodious cadence)—"he said, in the most melancholy voice, 'She's hiding from me.' He was dreaming, of course. I thought it was rather sweet. So, to humor him, I said, 'Well, then. You must hide your eyes and count to ten and she'll come back.' "

He laughed. "But he got angry at me. It was really rather charming of him. 'No,' he said, 'no she won't.' 'But you're **dreaming,**' I said to him. 'No,' he said, 'no I'm not. It's not a dream. It's real.' "

———

The doctors couldn't figure out quite what was wrong with Charles. They'd tried two antibiotics over the course of the week, but the infection—whatever it was—didn't respond. The third try was more successful. Francis, who went to see him Wednesday and Thursday, was told that Charles was improving, and that if everything went well he could come home over the weekend.

About ten o'clock on Friday, after another sleepless night, I walked over to Francis's. It was a hot, overcast morning, trees shimmering in the heat. I felt haggard and exhausted. The warm air vibrated with the thrum of wasps and the drone of lawn mowers. Swifts chased and chittered, in fluttering pairs, through the sky.

My head hurt. I wished I had a pair of sunglasses. I wasn't supposed to meet Francis until eleven-thirty but my room was a wreck, I hadn't done laundry in weeks; it was too hot to do anything more taxing than lie on my tangled bed, and sweat, and try to ignore the bass of my neighbor's stereo thumping through the wall. Jud and Frank were building some enormous, ramshackle, modernistic structure out on Commons lawn, and the hammers and the power drills had started early in the morning. I didn't know what it was—I had heard, variously, that it was a stage set, a sculpture, a Stonehenge-type monument to the Grateful Dead—but the first time I had looked out my window, dazed with Fiorinal, and seen the upright support posts rising stark from the lawn, I was flooded with black, irrational terror: **gibbets,** I thought, **they're putting up gibbets, they're having a hanging on Commons**

lawn. . . . The hallucination was over in a moment, but in a strange way it had persisted, manifesting itself in different lights like one of those pictures on the cover of horror paperbacks in the supermarket: turned one way, a smiling blond-haired child; turned the other, a skull in flames. Sometimes the structure was mundane, silly, perfectly harmless; though early in the morning, say, or around twilight, the world would drop away and there loomed a gallows, medieval and black, birds wheeling low in the skies overhead. At night, it cast its long shadow over what fitful sleep I was able to get.

The problem, basically, was that I had been taking too many pills; the ups now, periodically, mixed with the downs, because though the latter had ceased to put me effectively to sleep, they hung me over in the daytime, so that I wandered in a perpetual twilight. Unmedicated sleep was impossible, a fairy tale, some remote childhood dream. But I was running low on the downs; and though I knew I could probably get some more, from Cloke, or Bram, or somebody, I'd decided to cut them out for a couple of days—a good idea, in the abstract, but it was excruciating to emerge from my eerie submarine existence into this harsh stampede of noise and light. The world jangled with a sharp, discordant clarity: green everywhere, sweat and sap, weeds pushing through the spattered cracks of the old marble sidewalk; veined white slabs, heaved and buckled by a century's worth of hard January freezes. A millionaire had put them down, those marble walks, a man who summered in North Hampden and threw himself from a window on Park Avenue in the 1920s. Behind the mountains the sky was overcast, dark as slate. There was pressure in the air; rain coming, sometime soon. Geraniums blazed from the white housefronts, the red of them, against the chalky clapboard, fierce and harrowing.

I turned down Water Street, which ran north past Henry's house, and as I approached I saw a dark shadow in the back of his garden. **No**, I thought.

But it was. He was on his knees with a pail of water, and a cloth, and as I drew nearer I saw that he was washing not the flagstones, as I'd thought at first, but a rosebush. He was bent over it, polishing the leaves with meticulous care, like some crazed gardener from **Alice in Wonderland**.

I thought that any moment he must stop, but he didn't, and finally I let myself in through the back gate. "Henry," I said. "What are you doing?"

He glanced up, calmly, not at all surprised to see me. "Spider mites," he said. "We've had a damp spring. I've sprayed them twice, but to get the eggs off it's best to wash them by hand." He dropped the cloth in the pail. I noted, not for the first time lately, how well he looked, how his stiff sad manner had relaxed into a more natural one. I had never thought Henry handsome—indeed, I'd always thought that only the formality of his bearing saved him from mediocrity, as far as looks went—but now, less rigid, and locked-up in his movements, he had a sure, tigerish grace the swiftness and ease of which surprised me. A lock of hair blew upon his forehead. "This is a Reine des Violettes," he said, indicating the rosebush. "A lovely old rose. Introduced in 1860. And that is a Madame Isaac Pereire. The flowers smell of raspberries."

I said: "Is Camilla here?"

There was no trace of emotion upon his face, or of any effort to conceal it. "No," he said, turning back to his work. "She was sleeping when I left. I didn't want to wake her."

It was shocking to hear him speak of her with such intimacy. Pluto and Persephone. I looked at his back, prim as a parson's, tried to imagine the two of them together. His big white hands with the square nails.

Henry said, unexpectedly: "How is Charles?"

"All right," I said, after an awkward pause.

"He'll be coming home soon, I suppose."

A dirty tarpaulin flapped loudly on the roof. He kept working. His dark trousers, with the suspenders crossed over his white-shirted back, gave him a vaguely Amish appearance.

"Henry," I said.

He didn't look up.

"Henry, it's none of my business, but I hope for God's sake you know what you're doing," I said. I paused, expecting some response, but there was none. "You haven't seen Charles, but I have, and I don't think you realize the shape he's in. Ask Francis, if you don't believe me. Even Julian's noticed. I mean, I've tried to tell you, but I just don't think you understand. He's out of his mind, and Camilla has no idea, and I don't know what we'll do when he gets home. I'm not even sure he'll be able to stay by himself. I mean—"

"I'm sorry," interrupted Henry, "but would you mind handing me those shears?"

There was a long silence. Finally, he reached over and got them himself. "All right," he said pleasantly. "Never mind." Very conscientiously, he parted the canes and clipped one in the middle, holding the shears at a careful slant, taking care not to injure a larger cane adjacent to it.

"What the hell is wrong with you?" I had a hard time keeping my voice down. There were windows open in the upstairs apartment that faced the back; I heard people talking, listening to the radio, moving around. "Why do you have to make things so hard for everybody?" He didn't turn around. I grabbed the shears from his hand and threw them, with a clatter, on the bricks. **"Answer me,"** I said.

We looked at each other for a long moment. Behind his glasses, his eyes were steady and very blue.

Finally, he said, quietly: "Tell me."

The intensity of his gaze frightened me. "What?"

"You don't feel a great deal of emotion for other people, do you?"

I was taken aback. "What are you talking about?" I said. "Of course I do."

"Do you?" He raised an eyebrow. "I don't think so. It doesn't matter," he said, after a long, tense pause. "I don't, either."

"What are you trying to get at?"

He shrugged. "Nothing," he said. "Except that my life, for the most part, has been very stale and colorless. Dead, I mean. The world has always been an empty place to me. I was incapable of enjoying even the simplest things. I felt dead in everything I did." He brushed the dirt from his hands. "But then it changed," he said. "The night I killed that man."

I was jarred—a little spooked, as well—at so blatant a reference to something referred to, by mutual agreement, almost exclusively with codes, catchwords, a hundred different euphemisms.

"It was the most important night of my life," he said calmly. "It enabled me to do what I've always wanted most."

"Which is?"

"To live without thinking."

Bees buzzed loudly in the honeysuckle. He went back to his rosebush, thinning the smaller branches at the top.

"Before, I was paralyzed, though I didn't really know it," he said. "It was because I thought too much, lived too much in the mind. It was hard to make decisions. I felt immobilized."

"And now?"

"Now," he said, "now, I know that I can do anything that I want." He glanced up. "And, unless I'm very wrong, you've experienced something similar yourself."

"I don't know what you're talking about."

"Oh, but I think you do. That surge of power and delight, of confidence, of control. That sudden sense of the richness of the world. Its infinite possibility."

He was talking about the ravine. And, to my horror, I realized that in a way he was right. As ghastly as it had been, there was no denying that Bunny's murder had thrown all subsequent events into a kind of glaring Technicolor. And, though this new lucidity of vision was frequently nerve-wracking, there was no denying that it was not an altogether unpleasant sensation.

"I don't understand what this has to do with anything," I said, to his back.

"I'm not sure that I do, either," he said, assessing the balance of his rosebush, then removing, very carefully, another cane in the center. "Except that there's not much which matters a great deal. The last six months have made that plain. And lately it has seemed important to find a thing or two which do. That's all."

As he said this, he trailed away. "There," he said at last. "Does that look all right? Or do I need to open it up more in the middle?"

"Henry," I said. "Listen to me."

"I don't want to take off too much," he said vaguely. "I should have done this a month ago. The canes bleed if they're pruned this late, but better late than never, as they say."

"Henry. **Please**." I was on the verge of tears. "What's the matter with you? Have you lost your mind? Don't you understand what's going on?"

He stood up, dusted his hands on his trousers. "I have to go in the house now," he said.

I watched him hang the shears on a peg, then walk away. At the last, I thought he was going to turn and say something, goodbye, anything. But he didn't. He went inside. The door shut behind him.

———

I found Francis's apartment darkened, razor slits of light showing through the closed venetian blinds. He was asleep. The place smelled sour, and ashy. Cigarette butts floated in a gin glass. There was a black, bubbled scorch in the varnish of the night table beside his bed.

I pulled the blinds to let some sun in. He rubbed his eyes, called me a strange name. Then he recognized me. "Oh," he said, his face screwed up, albino-pale. "**You**. What are you doing here?"

I reminded him that we had agreed to visit Charles.

"What day is it?"

"Friday."

"Friday." He slumped back down in the bed. "I hate Fridays. Wednesdays, too. Bad luck. Sorrowful Mystery on the Rosary." He lay in bed, staring at the ceiling. Then he said: "Do you get the sense something really awful is about to happen?"

I was alarmed. "No," I said, defensively, though this was far from true. "What do you think's going to happen?"

"I don't know," he said without moving. "Maybe I'm wrong."

"You should open a window," I said. "It smells in here."

"I don't care. I can't smell. I've got a sinus infection." Listlessly, with one hand, he groped for his cigarettes on the night table. "Jesus, I'm depressed," he said. "I can't handle seeing Charles right now."

"We've got to."

"What time is it?"

"About eleven."

He was silent for a moment, then said: "Look here. I've got an idea. Let's have some lunch. Then we'll do it."

"We'll worry about it the whole time."

"Let's ask Julian, then. I'll bet he'll come."

"Why do you want to ask Julian?"

"I'm depressed. Always nice to see him, anyway." He rolled over on his stomach. "Or maybe not. I don't know."

Julian answered the door—just a crack, as he had the very first time I'd knocked—and opened it wide when he saw who it was. Immediately Francis asked him if he wanted to come to lunch.

"Of course. I'd be delighted." He laughed. "This has been an odd morning indeed. **Most** peculiar. I'll tell you about it on the way."

Things which were odd, by Julian's definition, often turned out to be amusingly mundane. By his own choice, he had so little contact with the outside world that he frequently considered the commonplace to be bizarre: an automatic-teller machine, for instance, or some new peculiarity in the supermarket—cereal shaped like vampires, or unrefrigerated yogurt sold in pop-top cans. All of us enjoyed hearing about these little forays of his into the twentieth century, so Francis and I pressed him to tell us what now had happened.

"Well, the secretary from the Literature and Languages Division was just here," he said. "She had a letter for me. They have in and out boxes, you know, in the literature office—one can leave things to be typed or pick up messages there, though I never do. Anyone with whom I have the slightest wish to talk knows to reach me here. This letter"—he indicated it, lying open on the table beside his reading glasses—"which was meant for me, somehow wound up in the box of a Mr. Morse, who apparently is on sabbatical. His son came round to pick up his mail this morning and found it had been put by mistake into his father's slot."

"What kind of letter?" said Francis, leaning closer. "Who's it from?"

"Bunny," Julian said.

A bright knife of terror plunged through my

heart. We stared at him, dumbstruck. Julian smiled at us, allowing a dramatic pause for our astonishment to blossom to the full.

"Well, of course, it's not **really** from Edmund," he said. "It's a forgery, and not a very clever one. The thing is typewritten, and there's no signature or date. That doesn't seem quite legitimate, does it?"

Francis had found his voice. "Typewritten?" he said.

"Yes."

"Bunny didn't own a typewriter."

"Well, he was my student for nearly four years, and he never handed in anything typewritten to **me**. As far as I'm aware, he didn't know how to type-write at all. Or did he?" he said, looking up shrewdly.

"No," said Francis, after an earnest, thoughtful pause, "no, I think you're right"; and I echoed this, though I knew—and Francis knew, too—that as a matter of fact Bunny had known how to type. He didn't have a typewriter of his own—this was perfectly true; but he frequently borrowed Francis's, or used one of the sticky old manuals in the library. The fact was—though neither of us was about to point it out—that none of us, ever, gave typed things to Julian. There was a simple reason for this. It was impossible to write in Greek alphabet on an English typewriter; and though

Henry actually had somewhere a little Greek-alphabet portable, which he had purchased on holiday in Mykonos, he never used it because, as he explained to me, the keyboard was different from the English and it took him five minutes to type his own name.

"It's terribly sad that someone would want to play a trick like this," Julian said. "I can't imagine who would do such a thing."

"How long had it been in the mailbox?" Francis said. "Do you know?"

"Well, that's another thing," Julian said. "It might have been put in at any time. The secretary said that Mr. Morse's son hadn't been to check his father's box since March. Which means, of course, that it might have been slipped in yesterday." He indicated the envelope, on the table. "You see. There's only my name, typewritten, on the front, no return address, no date, of course no postmark. Obviously it's the work of a crank. The thing is, though, I can't imagine why anyone would play such a cruel joke. I'd almost like to tell the Dean, though goodness knows I don't want to stir things up again after all that fuss."

Now that the first, horrible shock was over, I was starting to breathe a bit easier. "What sort of a letter is it?" I asked him.

Julian shrugged. "You can have a look at it, if you like."

I picked it up. Francis looked at it over my shoulder. It was single-spaced, on five or six small sheets of paper, some of which looked not unlike some writing paper which Bunny used to have. But though the sheets were roughly the same size, they didn't all match. I could tell, by the way the ribbon had struck a letter sometimes half-red and half-black, that it had been written on the typewriter in the all-night study room.

The letter itself was disjointed, incoherent, and—to my astonished eyes—unquestionably genuine. I skimmed it only briefly, and remember so little about it that I am unable to reproduce it here, but I do remember thinking that if Bunny wrote it, he was a lot closer to a breakdown than any of us had thought. It was filled with profanities of various sorts which it was difficult, even in the most desperate of circumstances, to imagine Bunny using in a letter to Julian. It was unsigned, but there were several clear references which made it plain that Bunny Corcoran, or someone purporting to be him, was the author. It was badly spelled, with a great many of Bunny's characteristic errors, which fortunately couldn't have meant much to Julian, as Bunny was such a poor writer that he usually had someone else go over his work before he handed it in. Even I might have had doubts about the authorship, the

thing was so garbled and paranoid, if not for
the reference to the Battenkill murder: "He"—
(Henry, that is, or so the letter ran approxi-
mately at one point)—"is a fucking Monster.
He has killed a man and he wants to kill Me,
too. Everybody is in on it. The man they killed
in October, in Battenkill county. His name
was McRee. I think they beat him to death I
am not sure." There were other accusations—
some of them true (the twins' sexual practices),
some not; all of which were so wild that they
only served to discredit the whole. There was
no mention of my name. The whole thing had
a desperate, drunken tone that was not unfamiliar. Though this didn't occur to me until
later, I now believe he must have gone to the
all-night study room and written it on the
same night that he came drunk to my room—
either directly before or after, probably after—
in which case it was a pure stroke of luck
we didn't run into each other when I was on
my way to the Science Building to telephone
Henry. I remember only one other thing,
which was its closing line, and the only thing I
saw which struck a pang at me: "Please Help
me, this is why I wrote you, you are the only
person that can."

"Well, I don't know who wrote this," said
Francis at last, his tone offhand and perfectly

casual, "but whoever they were, they certainly couldn't spell."

Julian laughed. I knew he didn't have the slightest idea that the letter was real.

Francis took the letter and shuffled ruminatively through the pages. He stopped at the next-to-last sheet—which was of a slightly different color than the rest—and idly turned it over. "It seems that—" he said, and then stopped.

"Seems that what?" said Julian pleasantly.

There was a slight pause before Francis continued. "Seems that whoever wrote this needed a new typewriter ribbon," he said; but that was not what he was thinking, or I was thinking, or what he had been about to say. That had been struck from his mind when, turning the irregular sheet over, the two of us saw, with horror, what was on the back of it. It was a sheet of hotel stationery, engraved, at the top, with the address and letterhead of the Excelsior: the hotel where Bunny and Henry had stayed in Rome.

Henry told us, later, head in hands, that Bunny had asked him to buy him another box of stationery the day before he died. It was expensive stuff, white cream laid, imported from England; the best they had at the store in town. "If only I'd bought it for him," he said.

"He asked me half a dozen times. But I figured, there wasn't much point, you see. . . ." The sheet from the Excelsior wasn't quite so heavy, or fine. Henry speculated—probably correctly—that Bunny had got to the bottom of the box, so he rooted around in his desk and found that piece, roughly the same size, and turned it over to use the back.

I tried not to look at it, but it kept obtruding at the corners of my vision. A palace, drawn in blue ink, with flowing script like the script on an Italian menu. Blue edges on the paper. Unmistakable.

"To tell you the truth," said Julian, "I didn't even finish reading it. Obviously the perpetrator of this is quite disturbed. One can't say, of course, but I think it must have been written by another student, don't you?"

"I can't imagine that a member of the faculty would write something like this, if that's what you mean," said Francis, turning the letterhead back over. We didn't look at each other. I knew exactly what he was thinking: **how can we steal this page? how can we get it away?**

To distract Julian's attention, I walked to the window. "It's a beautiful day, isn't it?" I said, my back to both of them. "It's hard to believe there was snow on the ground hardly a month ago. . . ." I babbled on, hardly aware of what I was saying, and afraid to look around.

"Yes," said Julian politely, "yes, it is lovely out," but his voice came not from where I was expecting it but farther away, near the bookcase. I turned and saw that he was putting on his coat. From the look on Francis's face, I knew he hadn't succeeded. He was turned halfway, watching Julian from the corner of his eye; for a moment, when Julian turned his head to cough, it seemed like he was going to be able to get away with it but no sooner had he pulled the page out than Julian turned around, and he had no choice but to casually place it where it had been, as if the pages were out of order and he was simply rearranging them.

Julian smiled at us, by the door. "Are you boys ready?" he said.

"Certainly," said Francis, with more enthusiasm than I knew he felt. He laid the letter, folded, back on the table and the two of us followed him out, smiling and talking, though I could see the tension in the back of Francis's shoulders and I was biting the inside of my bottom lip with frustration.

———

It was a miserable lunch. I remember hardly anything about it except that it was a very bright day, and we sat at a table too close to the window, and the glare in my eyes only increased my confusion and discomfort. And all the time we talked about the letter, the letter, the letter. Might whoever sent it have a grudge against Julian? Or was someone angry at us? Francis was more composed than me, but he was downing the glasses of house wine one after another, and a light sweat had broken out on his forehead.

Julian thought the letter was a fake. That was obvious. But if he saw the letterhead, the game was up, because he knew as well as we did that Bunny and Henry had stayed at the Excelsior for a couple of weeks. Our best hope was that he would simply throw it away, without showing it to anyone else or examining it further. But Julian liked intrigue, and secrecy, and this was the sort of thing that could keep him speculating for days. ("**No.** Could it have been a faculty member? Do you think?") I kept thinking about what he'd said earlier, about showing it to the Dean. We would have to get hold of it somehow. Break in his office, maybe. But even assuming he left it there, in a place where we could find it, that meant waiting six or seven hours.

I drank a good deal during lunch, but by the time we were finished I was still so nervous that I had brandy with my dessert instead of coffee. Twice, Francis slipped away to telephone. I knew he was trying to get Henry, to ask him to go over to the office and nip the letter while we had Julian captive at the Brasserie; I knew also, from his tense smiles when he returned, that he wasn't having any luck. After the second time he came back, an idea occurred to me: if he could leave to telephone, why couldn't he just go out the back and get in his car and go get it himself? I would have slipped out and done it myself if I had only had the car keys. Too late—as Francis was paying the check—I realized what I should have said: that I'd left something in the car and needed the keys to go unlock the door and get it.

On the way back to school, in the charged silence, I realized that something we had always relied on was the ability to communicate whenever we wanted. Always, previously, in an emergency we could throw out something in Greek, under the guise of an aphorism or quotation. But now that was impossible.

Julian didn't invite us back up to his office. We watched him going up the walk, waved as he turned at the back door to the Lyceum. It was, by now, about one-thirty in the afternoon.

———

We sat motionless in the car for a moment after he disappeared. Francis's chummy, goodbye smile had died on his face. Suddenly, and with a violence that frightened me, he leaned down and banged his forehead on the steering wheel. "Shit!" he yelled. "Shit! Shit!"

I grabbed his arm and shook it. "Shut up," I said.

"Oh, shit," he wailed, rolling his head back, the heels of his hands pressed to his temples. "Shit. This is it, Richard."

"Shut up."

"It's over. We've had it. We're going to jail."

"Shut up," I said again. His panic, oddly, had sobered me. "We've got to figure out what to do."

"Look," said Francis. "Let's just go. If we leave now we can be in Montreal by dark. Nobody will ever find us."

"You're not making any sense."

"We'll stay in Montreal a couple of days. Sell the car. Then take the bus to, I don't know, Saskatchewan or something. We'll go to the weirdest place we can find."

"Francis, I wish you would calm down for a minute. I think we can handle this."

"What are we going to do?"

"Well, first, I think, we've got to find Henry."

"Henry?" He looked at me in amazement. "What makes you think he'll be any help? He's so whacked-out, he doesn't know which way—"

"Doesn't he have a key to Julian's office?"

He was quiet a moment. "Yes," he said. "Yes, I think he does. Or he used to."

"There you go," I said. "We'll find Henry and drive him over here. He can make some excuse to get Julian out of the office. Then one of us can slip up the back stairs with the key."

———

It was a good plan. The only problem was, running Henry down wasn't so easy as we'd hoped. He wasn't at his apartment, and when we went by the Albemarle, his car wasn't there.

We drove back to campus to check the library, then back to the Albemarle. This time Francis and I got out of the car and walked around the grounds.

The Albemarle had been built in the nineteenth century, as a retreat for rich convalescents. It was shady and luxurious, with tall shutters and a big, cool porch—everyone from Rudyard Kipling to FDR had stayed there—but it wasn't much bigger than a big private house.

"You tried the desk clerk?" I asked Francis.

"Don't even think about it. They're registered under a phony name, and I'm sure Henry gave the innkeeper some story, because when I tried to talk to her the other night she clammed up in a second."

"Is there any way we can get in past the lobby?"

"I have no idea. My mother and Chris stayed here once. It isn't that big a place. There's only one set of stairs that I know of, and you have to walk past the desk to get to them."

"What about downstairs?"

"The thing is, I think they're on an upper floor. Camilla said something about carrying bags upstairs. There might be fire stairs, but I wouldn't know how to go about finding them."

We stepped up onto the porch. Through the screen door we could see a dark, cool lobby and, behind the desk, a man of about sixty, his half-moon glasses pulled low on his nose, reading a copy of the Bennington **Banner**.

"Is that the guy you talked to?" I whispered.

"No. His wife."

"Has he seen you before?"

"No."

I pushed open the door and stuck my head in for a moment, then went inside. The innkeeper glanced from his paper and gave us a supercilious up-and-down look. He was one of those prissy retirees one sees frequently in New England, the sort who subscribe to antique magazines and carry those canvas tote bags they give as gift premiums on public TV.

I gave him my best smile. Behind the desk, I noticed, was a pegboard with room keys. They were arranged in tiers according to floor. There were three keys—2-B, -C, and -E—missing on the second floor, and only one—3-A—on the third.

He was looking at us frostily. "How may I help you?" he said.

"Excuse me," I said, "but do you know if our parents have arrived yet from California?"

He was surprised. He opened a ledger. "What's the name?"

"Rayburn. Mr. and Mrs. Cloke Rayburn."

"I don't see a reservation."

"I'm not sure they made one."

He looked at me over the tops of his glasses. "Generally, we require a reservation, with deposit, at least forty-eight hours in advance," he said.

"They didn't think they'd need one this time of year."

"Well, there's no guarantee that there'll be room for them when they arrive," he said curtly.

I would have liked to have pointed out that his inn was more than half-empty, and that I didn't see the guests exactly fighting to get in, but I smiled again and said, "I guess they'll have to take their chances, then. Their plane got into Albany at noon. They should be here any minute."

"Well, then."

"Do you mind if we wait?"

Obviously, he did. But he couldn't say so. He nodded, his mouth pursed—thinking, no doubt, about the lecture on reservation policy he would deliver to my parents—and, with an ostentatious rattle, went back to his paper.

We sat down on a cramped Victorian sofa, as far from the desk as possible.

Francis was jittery and kept glancing around. "I don't want to stay here," he whispered, his lips barely moving, close to my ear. "I'm afraid the wife will come back."

"This guy is from hell, isn't he?"

"She's worse."

The innkeeper was, very pointedly, not looking in our direction. In fact, his back was to us. I put my hand on Francis's arm. "I'll be right back," I whispered. "Tell him I went looking for the men's room."

The stairs were carpeted and I managed to get up them without making much noise. I hurried down the corridor until I saw 2-C, and 2-B next to it. The doors were blank and foreboding, but this was no time to hesitate. I knocked on 2-C. No answer. I knocked again, louder this time. "Camilla!" I said.

At this, a small dog began to raise a racket, down the hall in 2-E. **Nix that,** I thought, and was about to knock on the third door, when suddenly it opened and there stood a middle-aged lady in a golfing skirt. "Excuse me," she said. "Are you looking for someone?"

It was funny, I thought, as I shot up the last flight of stairs, but I'd had a premonition they'd be on the top floor. In the corridor I passed a gaunt, sixtyish woman—print dress, harlequin glasses, sharp nasty face like a poodle—carrying a stack of folded towels. "Wait!" she yelped. "Where are you going?"

But I was already past her, down the hall, banging at the door of 3-A. "Camilla!" I shouted. "It's Richard! Let me in!"

And then, there she was, like a miracle: sunlight streaming behind her into the hall, barefoot and blinking with surprise. "Hello," she said, "hello! What are you doing here?" And, behind my shoulder, the innkeeper's wife: "What do you think you're doing here? Who are you?"

"It's all right," Camilla said.

I was out of breath. "Let me in," I gasped.

She pulled the door shut. It was a beautiful room—oak wainscoting, fireplace, only one bed, I noticed, in the room beyond, bedclothes tangled at the foot. . . . "Is Henry here?" I said.

"What's wrong?" Bright circles of color burned high in her cheeks. "It's Charles, isn't it? What's happened?"

Charles. I'd forgotten about him. I struggled

to catch my breath. "No," I said. "I don't have time to explain. We've got to find Henry. Where is he?"

"Why"—she looked at the clock—"I believe he's at Julian's office."

"Julian's?"

"Yes. What's the matter?" she said, seeing the astonishment on my face. "He had an appointment, I think, at two."

———

I hurried downstairs to get Francis before the innkeeper and his wife had a chance to compare notes.

"What should we do?" said Francis on the drive back to school. "Wait outside and watch for him?"

"I'm afraid we'll lose him. I think one of us better run up and get him."

Francis lit a cigarette. The match flame wavered. "Maybe it's okay," he said. "Maybe Henry managed to get hold of it."

"I don't know," I said. But I was thinking the same thing. If Henry saw the letterhead, I was pretty sure he'd try to take it, and I was pretty sure he'd be more efficient about it than Francis or me. Besides—it sounded petty but it was true—Henry was Julian's favorite. If he put his mind to it, he could coerce away the whole letter on some pretext of giving it to the police, having the typing analyzed, who knew what he might come up with?

Francis glanced at me sideways. "If Julian found out about this," he said, "what do you think he would do?"

"I don't know," I said, and I didn't. It was such an unthinkable prospect that the only responses I could imagine him having were melodramatic and improbable. Julian suffering a fatal heart attack. Julian weeping uncontrollably, a broken man.

"I can't believe he'd turn us in."

"I don't know."

"But he couldn't. He **loves** us."

I didn't say anything. Regardless of what Julian felt for me, there was no denying that what I felt for him was love and trust of a very genuine sort. As my own parents had distanced themselves from me more and more— a retreat they had been in the process of effecting for many years—it was Julian who had grown to be the sole figure of paternal benevolence in my life, or, indeed, of benevolence of any sort. To me, he seemed my only protector in the world.

"It was a mistake," said Francis. "He has to understand."

"Maybe," I said. I couldn't conceive of his finding out, but as I tried to visualize myself

explaining this catastrophe to someone, I realized that we would have an easier time explaining it to Julian than to anyone else. Perhaps, I
thought, his reaction would be similar to my
own. Perhaps he would see these murders as a
sad, wild thing, haunted and picturesque ("I've
done everything," old Tolstoy used to boast,
"I've even killed a man"), instead of the basically selfish, evil act which it was.

"You know that thing Julian used to say,"
said Francis.

"Which thing?"

"About a Hindu saint being able to slay a
thousand on the battlefield and it not being a
sin unless he felt remorse."

I had heard Julian say this, but had never understood what he meant. "We're not Hindus,"
I said.

———

"Richard," Julian said, in a tone which simultaneously welcomed me and let me know that
I had come at a bad time.

"Is Henry here? I need to talk to him about
something."

He looked surprised. "Of course," he said,
and opened the door.

Henry was sitting at the table where we did
our Greek. Julian's empty chair, on the side by
the window, was pulled close to his. There
were other papers on the table but the letter

was in front of them. He glanced up. He did not look pleased to see me.

"Henry, may I speak to you?"

"Certainly," he said coldly.

I turned, to step into the hall, but he didn't make a move to follow. He was avoiding my eye. **Damn him,** I thought. He thought I was trying to continue our earlier conversation in the garden.

"Could you come out here for a minute?" I said.

"What is it?"

"I need to tell you something."

He raised an eyebrow. "You mean, it's something you want to tell me in **private**?" he said.

I could have killed him. Julian, politely, had been pretending not to follow this exchange, but his curiosity was aroused by this. He was standing, waiting, behind his chair. "Oh, dear," he said. "I hope nothing's wrong. Shall I leave?"

"Oh, no, Julian," said Henry, looking not at Julian but at me. "Don't bother."

"Is everything all right?" Julian asked me.

"Yes, yes," I said. "I just need to see Henry for a second. It's kind of important."

"Can't it wait?" said Henry.

The letter was spread out on the table. With horror, I saw that he was turning through it slowly, like a book, pretending to examine the pages one by one. He hadn't seen the letter-head. He didn't know it was there.

"Henry," I said. "It's an emergency. I have to talk to you **right now**."

He was struck by the urgency in my voice. He stopped, and pivoted in his chair to look at me—they were both staring now—and as he did, as part of the motion of turning, he turned over the page in his hand. My heart did a somersault. There was the letterhead, face-up on the table. White palace drawn in blue curlicues.

"All right," said Henry. Then, to Julian: "I'm sorry. We'll be back in a moment."

"Certainly," said Julian. He looked grave and concerned. "I hope nothing's the matter."

I wanted to cry. I had Henry's attention; I had it, now, but I didn't want it. The letterhead lay exposed on the table.

"What's wrong?" said Henry, his eyes locked on mine.

He was attentive, poised as a cat. Julian was looking at me too. The letter lay on the table, between them, directly in Julian's line of vi-sion. He had only to glance down.

I darted my eyes at the letter, then at Henry. He understood in an instant, turned smooth but fast; but he wasn't fast enough, and in that split-second, Julian looked down—casually, just an afterthought, but a second too soon.

I do not like to think about the silence that followed. Julian leaned over and looked at the letterhead for a long time. Then he picked up the page and examined it. **Excelsior. Via Veneto.** Blue-inked battlements. I felt curiously light and empty-headed.

Julian put on his glasses and sat down. He looked through the whole thing, very carefully, front and back. I heard kids laughing, faintly, somewhere outside. At last he folded the letter and put it in the inside pocket of his jacket.

"Well," he said at last. "Well, well, well."

As is true of most incipient bad things in life, I had not really prepared myself for this possibility. And what I felt, standing there, was not fear or remorse but only terrible, crushing humiliation, a dreadful, red-faced shame I hadn't felt since childhood. And what was even worse was to see Henry, and to realize that he was feeling the same thing, and if anything, more acutely than myself. I hated him—was so angry I wanted to kill him—but somehow I was not prepared to see him like that.

Nobody said anything. Dust motes floated in a sunbeam. I thought of Camilla at the Albemarle, Charles in the hospital, Francis waiting trustfully in the car.

"Julian," said Henry, "I can explain this."

"Please do," said Julian.

His voice chilled me to the bone. Though he

and Henry had in common a distinct coldness
of manner—sometimes, around them, the
very temperature seemed almost to drop—I
had always thought Henry's coldness essential,
to the marrow, and Julian's only a veneer for
what was, at bottom, a warm and kind-hearted
nature. But the twinkle in Julian's eye, as I
looked at him now, was mechanical and dead.
It was as if the charming theatrical curtain had
dropped away and I saw him for the first time
as he really was: not the benign old sage, the
indulgent and protective good-parent of my
dreams, but ambiguous, a moral neutral,
whose beguiling trappings concealed a being
watchful, capricious, and heartless.

Henry started to talk. It was so painful to
hear him—Henry!—stumble over his words
that I am afraid I blocked out much of what he
said. He began, in typical fashion, by attempting to justify himself but that soon faltered in
the white glare of Julian's silence. Then—I still
shudder to remember it—a desperate, pleading note crept into his voice. "I disliked having to lie, of course"—disliked! as if he were
talking about an ugly necktie, a dull dinner
party!—"we never **wanted** to lie to you, but it
was necessary. That is, I felt it was necessary.
The first matter was an accident; there was no
use in worrying you about it, was there? And
then, with Bunny . . . He wasn't a happy per-

son in those last months. I'm sure you know that. He was having a lot of personal problems, problems with his family. . . ."

He went on and on. Julian's silence was vast, arctic. A black buzzing noise echoed in my head. **I can't stand this,** I thought, **I've got to leave,** but still Henry talked, and still I stood there, and the sicker and blacker I felt to hear Henry's voice and to see the look on Julian's face.

Unable to stand it, I finally turned to go. Julian saw me do it.

Abruptly, he cut Henry off. "That's enough," he said.

There was an awful pause. I stared at him. **This is it,** I thought, with a kind of fascinated horror. **He won't listen anymore. He doesn't want to be left alone with him.**

Julian reached into his pocket. The expression on his face was impossible to read. He took the letter out and handed it to Henry. "I think you'd better keep this," he said.

He didn't get up from the table. The two of us left his office without a word. Funny, when I think about it now. That was the last time I ever saw him.

———

Henry and I didn't speak in the hallway. Slowly, we drifted out, eyes averted, like strangers. As I went down the stairs he was standing by the windowsill on the landing, looking out, blind and unseeing.

———

Francis was panic-stricken when he saw the look on my face. "Oh, no," he said. "Oh, my God. What's happened?"

It was a long time before I could say anything. "Julian saw it," I said.

"What?"

"He saw the letterhead. Henry's got it now."

"How'd he get it?"

"Julian gave it to him."

Francis was jubilant. "He gave it to him? He gave Henry the letter?"

"Yes."

"And he's not going to tell anyone?"

"No, I don't think so."

He was startled by the gloom in my voice.

"But what's the matter?" he said shrilly. "You got it, didn't you? It's okay. Everything's all right now. Isn't it?"

I was staring out the car window, at the window of Julian's office.

"No," I said, "no, I don't really think that it is."

———

Years ago, in an old notebook, I wrote: "One of Julian's most attractive qualities is his inability to see anyone, or anything, in its true light." And under it, in a different ink, "maybe one of my most attractive qualities, as well (?)"

It has always been hard for me to talk about Julian without romanticizing him. In many ways, I loved him the most of all; and it is with him that I am most tempted to embroider, to flatter, to basically reinvent. I think that is because Julian himself was constantly in the process of reinventing the people and events around him, conferring kindness, or wisdom, or bravery, or charm, on actions which contained nothing of the sort. It was one of the reasons I loved him: for that flattering light in which he saw me, for the person I was when I was with him, for what it was he allowed me to be.

Now, of course, it would be easy for me to veer to the opposite extreme. I could say that the secret of Julian's charm was that he latched on to young people who wanted to feel better than everybody else; that he had a strange gift for twisting feelings of inferiority into superiority and arrogance. I could also say that he did this not through altruistic motives but selfish ones, in order to fulfill some egotistic impulse of his own. And I could elaborate on this at some length and with, I believe, a fair degree of accuracy. But still that would not explain the fundamental magic of his personality or

why—even in the light of subsequent events—
I still have an overwhelming wish to see him
the way that I first saw him: as the wise old
man who appeared to me out of nowhere on a
desolate strip of road, with a bewitching offer
to make all my dreams come true.

But even in fairy tales, these kindly old gentlemen with their fascinating offers are not always what they seem to be. That should not be
a particularly difficult truth for me to accept at
this point but for some reason it is. More than
anything I wish I could say that Julian's face
crumbled when he heard what we had done. I
wish I could say that he put his head on the
table and wept, wept for Bunny, wept for us,
wept for the wrong turns and the life wasted:
wept for himself, for being so blind, for having
over and over again refused to see.

And the thing is, I had a strong temptation
to say he had done these things anyway,
though it wasn't at all the truth.

George Orwell—a keen observer of what lay
behind the glitter of constructed facades, social
and otherwise—had met Julian on several occasions, and had not liked him. To a friend he
wrote: "Upon meeting Julian Morrow, one has
the impression that he is a man of extraordinary sympathy and warmth. But what you call
his 'Asiatic serenity' is, I think, a mask for great

coldness. The face one shows him he invariably reflects back at one, creating the illusion
of warmth and depth when in fact he is brittle
and shallow as a mirror. Acton"—this, apparently, Harold Acton, who was also in Paris
then and a friend to both Orwell and Julian—
"disagrees. But I think he is not a man to be
trusted."

I have thought a great deal about this passage, also about a particularly shrewd remark
once made by, of all people, Bunny. "Y'know,"
he said, "Julian is like one of those people
that'll pick all his favorite chocolates out of the
box and leave the rest." This seems rather enigmatic on the face of it, but actually I cannot
think of a better metaphor for Julian's personality. It is similar to another remark made to
me once by Georges Laforgue, on an occasion
when I had been extolling Julian to the skies.
"Julian," he said curtly, "will never be a scholar
of the very first rate, and that is because he is
only capable of seeing things on a selective
basis."

When I disagreed—strenuously—and asked
what was wrong with focusing one's entire attention on only two things, if those two things
were Art and Beauty, Laforgue replied: "There
is nothing wrong with the love of Beauty.
But Beauty—unless she is wed to something

more meaningful—is always superficial. It is not that your Julian chooses solely to concentrate on certain, exalted things; it is that he chooses to ignore others equally as important."

It's funny. In retelling these events, I have fought against a tendency to sentimentalize Julian, to make him seem very saintly—basically to falsify him—in order to make our veneration of him seem more explicable; to make it seem something more, in short, than my own fatal tendency to try to make interesting people good. And I know I said earlier that he was perfect but he wasn't perfect, far from it; he could be silly and vain and remote and often cruel and still we loved him, in spite of, because.

———

Charles was released from the hospital the following day. Despite Francis's insistence that he come to his house for a while, he insisted on going home to his own apartment. His cheeks were sunken; he'd lost a lot of weight and he needed a haircut. He was sullen and depressed. We didn't tell him what had happened.

I felt sorry for Francis. I could tell he was worried about Charles, and upset that he was so hostile and uncommunicative. "Would you like some lunch?" he asked him.

"No."

"Come on. Let's go to the Brasserie."

"I'm not hungry."

"It'll be good. I'll buy you one of those roulage things you like for dessert."

We went to the Brasserie. It was eleven o'clock in the morning. By an unfortunate coincidence, the waiter sat us at the table by the window where Francis and I had sat with Julian less than twenty-four hours before. Charles wouldn't look at a menu. He ordered two Bloody Marys and drank them in quick succession. Then he ordered a third.

Francis and I put down our forks and exchanged an uneasy glance.

"Charles," Francis said, "why don't you get an omelet or something?"

"I told you I'm not hungry."

Francis picked up a menu and gave it a quick once-over. Then he motioned to the waiter.

"I said I'm **not fucking hungry**," said Charles without looking up. He was having a hard time keeping his cigarette balanced between his first and middle fingers.

Nobody had much to say after that. We finished eating and got the check, not before Charles had time to finish his third Bloody Mary and order a fourth. We had to help him to the car.

I was not much looking forward to going to Greek class, but when Monday rolled around I got up and went anyway. Henry and Camilla arrived separately—in case Charles decided to show up, I think—which, thank God, he didn't. Henry, I noticed, was puffy and very pale. He stared out the window and ignored Francis and me.

Camilla was nervous—embarrassed, maybe, by the way Henry was acting. She was anxious to hear about Charles and asked a number of questions, to most of which she didn't receive any response at all. Soon it was ten after; then fifteen.

"I've never known Julian to be this late," said Camilla, looking at her watch.

Suddenly, Henry cleared his throat. His voice was strange and rusty, as if fallen into disuse. "He's not coming," he said.

We turned to look at him.

"What?" said Francis.

"I don't think he's going to come today."

Just then we heard footsteps, and a knock at the door. It wasn't Julian, but the Dean of Studies. He creaked open the door and looked inside.

"Well, well," he said. He was a sly, balding man in his early fifties who had a reputation for being kind of a smart-aleck. "So this is what the Inner Sanctum looks like. The Holy of Holies. I've never once been allowed up here."

We looked at him.

"Not bad," he said ruminatively. "I remember about fifteen years ago, before they built the new Science Building, they had to stick some of the counselors up here. This one psychologist liked to leave her door open, thought it gave things a friendly feeling. 'Good morning,' she'd say to Julian whenever he walked past her door, 'have a nice day.' Can you believe that Julian phoned Channing Williams, my wicked predecessor, and threatened to quit unless she was moved?" He chuckled. " 'That dreadful woman.' That's what he called her. 'I can't bear that dreadful woman accosting me every time I happen to walk by.' "

This was a story which had some currency around Hampden, and the Dean had left some of it out. The psychologist had not only left her own door open but also had tried to get Julian to do the same.

"To tell the truth," said the Dean, "I'd expected something a little more classical. Oil lamps. Discus throwing. Nude youths wrestling on the floor."

"What do you want?" said Camilla, not very politely.

He paused, caught short, and gave her an oily smile. "We need to have a little talk," he said. "My office has just learned that Julian has been called away from school very suddenly. He has taken an indefinite leave of absence and does not know when he might return. Needless to say"—a phrase he delivered with sarcastic delicacy—"this puts you all in a rather interesting position in terms of academics, especially as it is only three weeks until the end of term. I understand that he was not in the habit of giving a written examination?"

We stared at him.

"Did you write papers? **Sing songs?** How was he accustomed to determining your final grade?"

"An oral examination for the tutorials," Camilla said, "as well as a term paper for the Civilization class." She was the only one of us who was collected enough to speak. "For the composition classes, an extended translation, English to Greek, from a passage of his choosing."

The Dean pretended to ponder this. Then he took a breath and said: "The problem you face, as I'm sure you're aware, is that we currently have no other teacher able to take over your class. Mr. Delgado has a reading knowledge of Greek, and though he says he'd be happy to look at your written work he is teaching a full load this term. Julian himself was most unhelpful on this point. I asked him to suggest a possible replacement and he said there wasn't any that he knew of."

He took a piece of paper from his pocket. "Now here are the three possible alternatives which occur to me. The first is for you to take incompletes and finish the course work in the fall. The thing is, however, I'm far from certain that Literature and Languages will be hiring another Classics teacher. There is so little interest in the subject, and the general consensus seems to be that it should be phased out, especially now that we're attempting to get the new Semiotics department off the ground."

He took a deep breath. "The second alternative is for you to take incompletes and finish the work in summer school. The third possibility is that we bring in—mind you, on a **temporary** basis—a substitute teacher. Understand this. At this point in time it is extremely doubtful that we will continue to offer the degree in Classics at Hampden. For those of you who choose to remain with us, I feel sure that the English department can absorb you with minimal loss of credit hours, though I think each of you in order to fulfill the department requirements are looking at two semesters of work above and beyond what you might've anticipated for graduation. At any rate." He looked at his list. "I am sure you have heard of Hackett, the preparatory school for boys," he said. "Hackett has extensive offerings in the field of Classics. I contacted the headmaster this morning and he said he would be happy to send a master over twice a week to supervise you. Though this might seem the best option from your perspective, it would by no means be ideal, relying, as it does, upon the auspices of the—"

It was at this moment that Charles chose to come crashing through the door.

He lurched in, looked around. Though he might not have been intoxicated technically, that very instant, he had been so recently enough for this to be an academic point. His shirttails hung out. His hair fell in long dirty strings over his eyes.

"What?" he said, after a moment. "Where's Julian?"

"Don't you knock?" said the Dean.

Charles turned, unsteadily, and looked at him.

"What's this?" he said. "Who the hell are you?"

"I," said the Dean sweetly, "am the Dean of Studies."

"What have you done with Julian?"

"He has left you. And somewhat in the lurch

if I dare say it. He has been called very suddenly from the country and doesn't know—or hasn't thought—about his return. He gave me to understand that it was something with the State Department, the Isrami government and all that. I think we are fortunate not to have had more problems of this nature, with the princess having gone to school here. One thinks at the time only of the prestige of such a pupil, alas, and not for an instant of the possible repercussions. Though I can't for the life of me imagine what the Isramis would want with Julian. Hampden's own Salman Rushdie." He chuckled appreciatively, then consulted his sheet again. "At any rate. I have arranged for the master from Hackett to meet with you tomorrow, here, at three p.m. I hope there is no conflict of schedule for anyone. If that happens to be the case, however, it would be well for you to re-evaluate your priorities, as this is the only time that he will be available to answer your . . ."

I knew that Camilla hadn't seen Charles in well over a week, and I knew she couldn't have been prepared to see him looking so bad, but she was gazing at him with an expression not so much of surprise as of panic, and horror. Even Henry looked taken aback.

". . . and, of course, this will entail a certain spirit of compromise on your parts too, as—"

"What?" said Charles, interrupting him. "What did you say? You said Julian's **gone**?"

"I must compliment you, young man, on your grasp of the English language."

"What happened? He just picked up and left?"

"In essence, yes."

There was a brief pause. Then Charles said, in a loud, clear voice: "Henry, why do I think for some reason that this is all your fault?"

There followed a long and not too pleasant silence. Then Charles spun and stormed out, slamming the door behind him.

The Dean cleared his throat.

"As I was **saying**," he continued.

———

It is strange, but true, to relate, that at this point in time I was still capable of being upset by the fact that my career at Hampden had pretty much gone down the drain. When the Dean had said "two extra semesters," my blood ran cold. I knew, with the certainty I knew that night follows day, there was no way I could get my parents to make their measly, but quite necessary, contribution for an extra year. I'd lost time already, in three changes of major, in the transfer from California, and I'd lose even more if I transferred again—assuming that I could even get into another school, that I could get another scholarship, with my spotty records, with my spotty grades: why, I asked myself, oh, why, had I been so foolish, why hadn't I picked something and stuck with it, how was it that I could currently be at the end of my third year of college and have basically nothing to show for it?

What made me angrier was that none of the others seemed to care. To them, I knew, this didn't make the slightest bit of difference. What was it to them if they had to go an extra term? What did it matter, if they failed to graduate, if they had to go back home? At least they had homes to go to. They had trust funds, allowances, dividend checks, doting grandmas, well-connected uncles, loving families. College for them was only a way station, a sort of youthful diversion. But this was my main chance, the only one. And I had blown it.

I spent a frantic couple of hours pacing in my room—that is, I'd come to think of it as "mine" but it wasn't really, I had to be out in three weeks, already it seemed to be assuming a heartless air of impersonality—and drafting a memo to the financial aid office. The only way I could finish my degree—in essence, the only way I could ever acquire the means to support myself in any passably tolerable fashion—was if Hampden agreed to shoulder the entire cost of my education during this additional year. I pointed out, somewhat aggressively, that it wasn't my fault Julian had decided to leave. I brought up every miserable commendation and award I'd won since the eighth grade. I argued that a year of classics could only bolster and enrich this now highly desirable course of study in English Literature.

Finally, my plea finished, and my handwriting a passionate scrawl, I fell down on my bed and went to sleep. At eleven o'clock I woke, made some changes, and headed for the all-night study room to type it up. On the way I stopped at the post office, where, to my immense gratification, a note in my box informed me that I had got the job apartment-sitting in Brooklyn, and that the professor wanted to meet with me sometime in the coming week to discuss my schedule.

———

Well, that's the summer taken care of, I thought.

It was a beautiful night, full moon, the meadow like silver and the housefronts throwing square black shadows sharp as cutouts on the grass. Most of the windows were dark: everyone sleeping, early to bed. I hurried across the lawn to the library, where the lights of the all-night study room—"The House of Eternal Learning," Bunny had called it in happier days—burned clear and bright on the top floor, shining yellow through the treetops. I

went up the outside stairs—iron stairs, like a
fire escape, like the steps in my nightmare—
my shoes clattering on the metal in a way that
might have given me the heebie-jeebies in a
less distracted mood.

Then, through the window, I saw a dark figure in a black suit, alone. It was Henry. Books
were piled in front of him but he wasn't working. For some reason, I thought of that February night I had seen him standing in the
shadows beneath the windows of Dr. Roland's
office, dark and solitary, hands in the pockets
of his overcoat and the snow whirling high in
the empty arc of the streetlights.

I closed the door. "Henry," I said. "Henry.
It's me."

He didn't turn his head. "I just got back
from Julian's house," he said, in a monotone.

I sat down. "And?"

"The place is shut up. He's gone."

There was a long silence.

"I find it very hard to believe he's done this,
you know." The light glinted off his spectacles;
beneath the dark, glossy hair his face was
deadly pale. "It's just such a cowardly thing to
have done. That's why he left, you know. Because he was afraid."

The screens were open. A damp wind rustled
in the trees. Beyond them clouds sailed over
the moon, fast and wild.

Henry took off his glasses. I never could get used to seeing him without them, that naked, vulnerable look he always had.

"He's a coward," he said. "In our circumstance, he would have done exactly what we did. He's just too much of a hypocrite to admit it."

I didn't say anything.

"He doesn't even care that Bunny is dead. I could forgive him if that was why he felt this way, but it isn't. He wouldn't care if we'd killed half a dozen people. All that matters to him is keeping his own name out of it. Which is essentially what he said when I talked to him last night."

"You went to see him?"

"Yes. One would hope that this matter would've seemed something more to him than just a question of his own comfort. Even to have turned us in would have shown some strength of character, not that I wanted to be turned in. But it's nothing but cowardice. Running away like this."

Even after all that had happened, the bitterness and disappointment in his voice cut me to the heart.

"Henry," I said. I wanted to say something profound, that Julian was only human, that he was old, that flesh and blood are frail and weak and that there comes a time when we have to transcend our teachers. But I found myself unable to say anything at all.

He turned his blind, unseeing eyes upon me. "I loved him more than my own father," he said. "I loved him more than anyone in the world."

The wind was up. A gentle pitter of rain swept across the roof. We sat there like that, not talking, for a very long time.

———

The next afternoon at three, I went to meet the new teacher.

When I stepped inside Julian's office I was shocked. It was completely empty. The books, the rugs, the big round table were gone. All that was left were the curtains on the windows and a tacked-up Japanese print that Bunny had given him. Camilla was there, and Francis, looking pretty uncomfortable, and Henry. He was standing by the window doing his best to ignore the stranger.

The teacher had dragged in some chairs from the dining hall. He was a round-faced, fair-haired man of about thirty, in turtleneck and jeans. A wedding band shone conspicuously on one pink hand; he had a conspicuous smell of after-shave. "Welcome," he said, leaning to shake my hand, and in his voice I heard the enthusiasm and condescension of a man accustomed to working with adolescents. "My name is Dick Spence. Yours?"

It was a nightmarish hour. I really don't have the heart to go into it: his patronizing tone at the start (handing out a page from the New Testament, saying, "Of course I don't expect you to pick up the **finer** points, if you can get the sense, it's okay with me"), a tone which metamorphosed gradually into surprise ("Well! Rather advanced, for undergraduates!") and defensiveness ("It's been quite a while since I've seen students at your level") and, ultimately, embarrassment. He was the chaplain at Hackett and his Greek, which he had mostly learned at seminary, was crude and inferior even by my standards. He was one of those language teachers who rely heavily on mnemonics. ("**Agathon.** Do you know how I remember that word? 'Agatha Christie writes **good** mysteries.' ") Henry's look of contempt was indescribable. The rest of us were silent and humiliated. Matters were not helped by Charles stumbling in—obviously drunk—about twenty minutes into the class. His appearance prompted a rehash of previous formalities ("Welcome! My name is Dick Spence. Yours?") and even, incredibly, a repetition of the **agathon** embarrassment.

———

When the lesson was over (teacher sneaking a look at his watch: "Well! Looks like we're running out of time here!") the five of us filed out in grim silence.

"Well, it's only two more weeks," said Francis, when we were outside.

Henry lit a cigarette. "I'm not going back," he said.

"Yeah," Charles said sarcastically. "That's right. **That'll** show him."

"But Henry," said Francis, "you've got to go."

He was smoking the cigarette with tight-lipped, resolute drags. "No, I don't," he said.

"Two weeks. That's it."

"Poor fellow," said Camilla. "He's doing the best he can."

"But that's not good enough for **him**," said Charles loudly. "Who does he expect? Fucking Richmond Lattimore?"

"Henry, if you don't go you'll fail," said Francis.

"I don't care."

"**He** doesn't have to go to school," said Charles. "**He** can do whatever he fucking pleases. He can fail every single fucking class and his dad'll still send him that fat allowance check every month—"

"Don't say 'fuck' anymore," said Henry, in a quiet but ominous voice.

"**Fuck?** What's the matter, Henry? You never heard that word before? Isn't that what you do to my sister every night?"

I remember, when I was a kid, once seeing my father strike my mother for absolutely no reason. Though he sometimes did the same thing to me, I did not realize that he did it sheerly out of bad temper, and believed that his trumped-up justifications ("You talk too much"; "Don't look at me like that") somehow warranted the punishment. But the day I saw him hit my mother (because she had re-marked, innocently, that the neighbors were building an addition to their house; later, he would claim she had provoked him, that it was a reproach about his abilities as wage earner, and she, tearfully, would agree) I realized that the childish impression I had always had of my father, as Just Lawgiver, was entirely wrong. We were utterly dependent on this man, who was not only deluded and ignorant, but incompetent in every way. What was more, I knew that my mother was incapable of standing up to him. It was like walking into the cockpit of an airplane and finding the pilot and co-pilot passed out drunk in their seats. And standing outside the Lyceum, I was struck with a black, incredulous horror, which in fact was not at all unlike the horror I had felt at twelve, sitting on a bar stool in our sunny little kitchen in Plano. **Who is in control here?** I thought, dismayed. **Who is flying this plane?**

———

And the thing of it was, that Charles and Henry had to appear together in court in less than a week, because of the business with Henry's car.

Camilla, I knew, was worried sick. She— whom I had never known to fear anything— was afraid now; and though in a certain perverse way I was pleased at her distress, there was no denying that if Henry and Charles— who practically came to blows each time they were in the same room—were going to be forced to appear before a judge, and with some show of cooperation and friendship, there could be no possible outcome but disaster.

Henry had hired a lawyer in town. The hope that a third party would be able to reconcile these differences had granted Camilla a small measure of optimism, but in the afternoon on the day of the appointment, I received a telephone call from her.

"Richard," she said. "I've got to talk to you and Francis."

Her tone frightened me. When I arrived at Francis's apartment, I found Francis badly shaken and Camilla in tears.

I had seen her cry only once before, and then

only, I think, from nerves and exhaustion. But this was different. She was blank and hollow-eyed, and there was despair in the set of her features.

"Camilla," I said. "What's wrong?"

She didn't answer immediately. She smoked one cigarette, then another. Little by little the story came out. Henry and Charles had gone to see the lawyer and Camilla, in capacity of peacemaker, had gone along. At first, it had seemed as if everything might be all right. Henry, apparently, had not hired the lawyer entirely from altruism but because the judge before whom they were to appear had a repu-tation for being tough on drunk drivers and there was a possibility—as Charles neither had a valid driver's license nor was covered on Henry's insurance—that Henry might lose his license or car or both. Charles, though he ob-viously felt himself martyred by the whole business, had nonetheless been willing to go along: not, as he told anyone who would lis-ten, because he had any affection for Henry but because he was sick of being blamed for things that weren't his fault, and if Henry lost his license he'd never hear the end of it.

But the meeting was a catastrophe. Charles, in the office, was sullen and uncommunica-tive. This was merely embarrassing but then—being prodded a bit too energetically by the attorney—he suddenly and quite without warning lost his head. "You should have heard him," said Camilla. "He told Henry he didn't care if he lost his car. He told him he didn't care if the judge put them both in jail for fifty years. And Henry—well, you can imagine how Henry reacted. He **blew up**. The lawyer thought they were out of their minds. He kept trying to get Charles to calm down, be reasonable. And Charles said: 'I don't care what happens to him. I don't care if he dies. I wish he was dead.' "

It got so bad, she said, the lawyer kicked them out of his office. Doors were opening up and down the hallway: an insurance agent, the tax assessor, a dentist in a white coat, all poking their heads out to see what the fuss was about. Charles stormed off—walked home, got a taxi, she didn't know what he'd done.

"And Henry?"

She shook her head. "He was in a rage," she said; her voice was exhausted, hopeless. "As I was following him to the car, the lawyer pulled me aside. 'Look here,' he said. 'I don't know what the situation is, but your brother is obviously quite disturbed. Please try to make him understand that if he doesn't cool down, he's going to be in a lot more trouble than he bargained for. This judge is not going to be particularly amenable to them even if they walk in there like a pair of lambs. Your brother is almost sure to be sentenced to an alcohol treatment program, which might not be a bad idea from what I've seen of him today. There's a pretty good chance that the judge will give him probation, which is not as easy as it sounds. And there's more than a gambler's chance that he's going to get either jail time or he's going to get put in a locked ward over at the detox center in Manchester.' "

She was extremely upset. Francis was ashen-faced.

"What does Henry say?" I asked her.

"He says he doesn't care about the car," she said. "He doesn't care about anything. 'Let him go to jail,' he says."

"You saw this judge?" Francis said to me.

"Yes."

"What was he like?"

"To tell you the truth, he looked like a pretty tough customer," I said.

Francis lit a cigarette. "What would happen," he said, "if Charles didn't show up?"

"I'm not sure. I'm almost certain they'd come looking for him."

"But if they couldn't find him?"

"What are you suggesting?" I said.

"I think we ought to get Charles out of town for a while," said Francis. He looked tense and worried. "School's almost over. It's not as if anything's keeping him here. I think we ought to pack him off to my mother and Chris in New York for a couple of weeks."

"The way he's acting now?"

"Drunk, you mean? You think my mother minds drunks? He'd be safe as a baby."

"I don't think," said Camilla, "you'd be able to get him to go."

"I could take him myself," said Francis.

"But what if he got away?" I pointed out. "Vermont is one thing but he could get into a hell of a lot of trouble in New York."

"All right," said Francis irritably, "all right, it was just an idea." He ran a hand through his hair. "You know what we could do? We could take him out to the country."

"To your place, you mean?"

"Yes."

"What would that accomplish?"

"Easy to get him there, for one thing. And once he's out there, what's he going to do? He won't have a car. It's miles from the road. You can't get a Hampden taxi driver to pick you up for love nor money."

Camilla was looking at him thoughtfully.

"Charles loves to go to the country," she said.

"I know," said Francis, pleased. "What could

be simpler? And we won't have to keep him there long. Richard and I can stay with him. I'll buy a case of champagne. We'll make it look like a party."

———

It was not easy to get Charles to come to the door. We knocked for what seemed like half an hour. Camilla had given us a key, which we didn't want to use unless we had to, but just as we were contemplating it the bolt snapped and Charles squinted at us through the crack.

He looked disordered, terrible. "What do you want?" he said.

"Nothing," said Francis, quite easily, despite a slight, stunned pause of maybe a second. "Can we come in?"

Charles looked back and forth at the two of us. "Is anybody with you?"

"No," Francis said.

He opened the door and let us in. The shades were pulled and the place had the sour smell of garbage. As my eyes adjusted to the dim I saw dirty dishes, apple cores and soup cans littering almost every conceivable surface. Beside the refrigerator, arranged with perverse neatness, stood a row of empty Scotch bottles.

A lithe shadow darted across the kitchen counter, twisting through the dirty pans and empty milk cartons: **Jesus**, I thought, **is that a rat?** But then it jumped to the floor, tail switching, and I saw it was a cat. Its eyes glowed at us in the dark.

"Found her in an empty lot," said Charles. His breath, I noticed, did not have an alcoholic odor but a suspiciously minty one. "She's not too tame." He pushed up the sleeve of his bathrobe and showed us a discolored, contaminated-looking crisscross of scratches on his forearm.

"Charles," said Francis, jingling his car keys nervously, "we stopped by because we're driving out to the country. Thought it might be nice to get away for a while. Do you want to come?"

Charles's eyes narrowed. He pushed down his sleeve. "Did Henry send you?" he said.

"God, no," said Francis, surprised.

"Are you sure?"

"I haven't seen him in days."

Charles still didn't look convinced.

"We're not even speaking to him," I said.

Charles turned to look at me. His gaze was watery and a little unfocused. "Richard," he said. "Hi."

"Hi."

"You know," he said, "I've always liked you a lot."

"I like you, too."

"You wouldn't go behind my back, would you?"

"Of course not."

"Because," he said, nodding at Francis, "because I know he would."

Francis opened his mouth, then shut it. He looked as if he'd been slapped.

"You underestimate Francis," I said to Charles, in a calm, quiet voice. It was a mistake the others often made with him, to try to reason with him in a methodical, aggressive way, when all he wanted was to be reassured like a child. "Francis likes you very much. He's your friend. So am I."

"Are you?" he said.

"Of course."

He pulled out a kitchen chair and sat down, heavily. The cat slunk over and began to twine round his ankles. "I'm afraid," he said hoarsely. "I'm afraid Henry's going to kill me."

Francis and I looked at each other.

"Why?" said Francis. "Why would he want to do that?"

"Because I'm in the way." He looked up at us. "He'd do it, too, you know," he said. "For two cents." He nodded at a small, unlabeled medicine bottle on the counter. "You see that?" he said. "Henry gave it to me. Couple of days ago."

I picked it up. With a chill I recognized the Nembutals I'd stolen for Henry at the Corcorans.

"I don't know what they are," said Charles, pushing the dirty hair from his eyes. "He told me they'd help me sleep. God knows I need something, but I'm afraid to take them."

I handed the bottle to Francis. He looked at it, then up at me, horrified.

"Capsules, too," said Charles. "No telling what he filled them with."

But he wouldn't even have to, that was the evil thing. I remembered, with a sick feeling, having tried to impress upon Henry how dangerous these were when mixed with liquor.

Charles passed a hand over his eyes. "I've seen him sneaking around here at night," he said. "Out back. I don't know what he's doing."

"Henry?"

"Yes. And if he tries anything with me," he said, "it'll be the worst mistake he ever made in his life."

We had less trouble enticing him to the car than I'd expected. He was in a rambling, paranoid humor and was somewhat comforted by our solicitude. He asked repeatedly if Henry knew where we were going. "You haven't talked to him, have you?"

"No," we assured him, "no, of course not."

He insisted on taking the cat with him. We had a terrible time catching it—Francis and I dodging round the dark kitchen, knocking dishes to the floor, trying to corner it behind the water heater while Charles stood anxiously by saying things like "Come on" and "Good kitty." Finally, in desperation, I seized it by a scrawny black hindquarter—it thrashed around and sank its teeth into my arm—and, together, we managed to wrap it up in a dish towel so that only its head stuck out, eyes bulging and ears flattened back against the skull. We gave the mummified, hissing bundle to Charles. "Now, hold her tight," Francis kept saying in the car, glancing anxiously back in the rear-view mirror, "watch out, don't let it get away—"

But, of course, it did get away, catapulting into the front seat and nearly running Francis off the road. Then, after scrabbling around under the brake and gas pedal—Francis aghast, attempting simultaneously to avoid touching it and to kick it away from him—it settled on the floorboard by my feet, succumbing to an attack of diarrhea before falling into a glaring, prickle-haired trance.

———

I had not been out to Francis's since the week before Bunny died. The trees in the drive were in full leaf and the yard was overgrown and dark. Bees droned in the lilacs. Mr. Hatch, mowing the lawn some thirty yards away, nodded and raised a hand at us.

The house was shadowy and cool. There were sheets on some of the furniture and dust balls on the hardwood floor. We locked the cat in an upstairs bathroom and Charles went down to the kitchen, to make himself something to eat, he said. He came back up with a jar of peanuts and a double martini in a water glass, which he carried into his room, and shut the door.

———

We didn't see an awful lot of Charles for the next thirty-six hours or so. He stayed in his room eating peanuts, and drinking, and looking out the window like the old pirate in **Treasure Island**. Once he came down to the library while Francis and I were playing cards, but he refused our invitation to join in and poked listlessly through the shelves, finally meandering upstairs without choosing a book. He came down for coffee in the mornings, in an old bathrobe of Francis's, and sat in the kitchen windowsill looking moodily over the lawn as if he were waiting for someone.

"When do you think is the last time he had a bath?" Francis whispered to me.

He had lost all interest in the cat. Francis sent Mr. Hatch out for some cat food and each morning and evening Francis let himself in the bathroom to feed it ("Get away," I heard him muttering, "get away from me, you devil.")

and came out again with a fouled crumple of newspaper, which he held from his body at arm's length.

———

About six o'clock in the afternoon of our third day there, Francis was up in the attic digging around for a jar of old coins his aunt had said he could have if he could find it, and I was lying on the couch downstairs drinking iced tea and trying to memorize the irregular subjunctive verbs in French (for my final exam was in less than a week) when I heard the phone ringing in the kitchen. I went to answer it.

It was Henry. "So there you are," he said.

"Yes."

There was a long, crackly silence. At last he said: "May I speak to Francis?"

"He can't come to the phone," I said. "What is it?"

"I suppose you've got Charles out there with you."

"Look here, Henry," I said. "What's the big idea giving Charles those sleeping pills?"

His voice came back at me brisk and cool. "I don't know what you're talking about."

"Yes you do. I saw them."

"Those pills you gave me, you mean?"

"Yes."

"Well, if he has them, he must have taken them from my medicine cabinet."

"He says you gave them to him," I said. "He thinks you're trying to poison him."

"That's nonsense."

"Is it?"

"He **is** there, isn't he?"

"Yes," I said, "we brought him out the day before yesterday . . ." and then I stopped, because it seemed to me that somewhere towards the beginning of this sentence I had heard a stealthy but distinct click, as of an extension being picked up.

"Well, listen," Henry said. "I'd appreciate it if you could keep him out there a day or two longer. Everyone seems to think this should be some big secret but believe me, I'm happy to have him out of the way for a while. If he doesn't come to court he'll be guilty by default, but I don't think there's an awful lot they can do to him."

It seemed I could hear breathing on the other end.

"What is it?" said Henry, suddenly wary.

Neither of us said anything for a moment.

"Charles?" I said. "Charles, is that you?"

Upstairs, the telephone slammed down.

I went up and knocked on Charles's door. No answer. When I tried the knob, it was locked.

"Charles," I said. "Let me in."

No answer.

"Charles, it wasn't anything," I said. "He called out of the blue. All I did was answer the phone."

Still no answer. I stood in the hall for a few minutes, the afternoon sun shining golden on the polished oak floor.

"Really, Charles, I think you're being a bit silly. Henry can't hurt you. You're perfectly safe out here."

"Bullshit," came the muffled reply from within.

There was nothing more to say. I went downstairs again, and back to the subjunctive verbs.

————

I must have fallen asleep on the couch, and I don't know how much later it was—not a whole lot later, because it was still light out— when Francis shook me awake, not too gently.

"Richard," he said. "Richard, you've got to wake up. Charles is gone."

I sat up, rubbed my eyes. "Gone?" I said. "But where could he go?"

"I don't know. He's not in the house."

"Are you sure?"

"I've looked everywhere."

"He's got to be around somewhere. Maybe he's in the yard."

"I can't find him."

"Maybe he's hiding."

"Get up and help me look."

I went upstairs. Francis ran outside. The screen door slammed behind him.

Charles's room was in disarray and a half-empty bottle of Bombay gin—from the liquor cabinet in the library—was on the night table. None of his things were gone.

I went through all the upstairs rooms, then up to the attic. Lampshades and picture frames, organdy party dresses yellowed with age. Gray wide-plank floors, so worn they were almost fuzzy. A shaft of dusty cathedral light filtered through the stained-glass porthole that faced the front of the house.

I went down the back staircase—low and claustrophobic, scarcely three feet wide—through the kitchen and butler's pantry, and out onto the back porch. Some distance away, Francis and Mr. Hatch were standing in the driveway. Mr. Hatch was talking to Francis. I had never heard Mr. Hatch say much of anything to anyone and he was plainly uncomfortable. He kept running a hand over his scalp. His manner was cringing and apologetic.

I met Francis on his way back to the house.

"Well," he said, "this is a hell of a note." He looked a bit stunned. "Mr. Hatch says he gave

Charles the keys to his truck about an hour and a half ago."

"What?"

"He said Charles came looking for him and said he had to run an errand. He promised to have the truck back in fifteen minutes."

We looked at each other.

"Where do you think he went?" I said.

"How should I know?"

"Do you think he just took off?"

"Looks that way, doesn't it?"

We went back in the house—dim now with twilight—and sat by the window on a long davenport that had a sheet thrown over it. The warm air smelled like lilac. Across the lawn, we could hear Mr. Hatch trying to get the lawn mower started up again.

Francis had his arms folded across the back of the davenport and his chin resting on his arms. He was looking out the window. "I don't know what to do," he said. "He's stolen that truck, you know."

"Maybe he'll be back."

"I'm afraid he'll have a wreck. Or a cop will pull him over. I'll bet you anything he's plastered. That's all he needs, getting stopped for drunk driving."

"Shouldn't we go look for him?"

"I wouldn't know where to start. He could be halfway to Boston for all we know."

"What else can we do? Sit around and wait for the phone to ring?"

———

First we tried the bars: the Farmer's Inn, the Villager, the Boulder Tap and the Notty Pine. The Notch. The Four Squires. The Man of Kent. It was a hazy, gorgeous summer twilight and the gravel parking lots were packed with trucks but none of the trucks was Mr. Hatch's.

Just for the hell of it, we drove by the State Liquor Store. The aisles were bright and empty, splashy rum displays ("Tropical Island Sweepstakes!") competing with somber, medicinal rows of vodka and gin. A cardboard cutout advertising wine coolers twirled from the ceiling. There were no customers, and a fat old Vermonter with a naked woman tattooed on his forearm was leaning against the cash register, passing time with a kid who worked at the Mini-Mart next door.

"So then," I heard him say in an undertone, "so then the guy pulls out a sawed-off shotgun. Emmett's standing here beside me, right where I am now. 'We don't have the key to the cashbox,' he says. And the guy pulls the trigger and I seen Emmett's brains"—he gestured—"splatter all over that wall back there. . . ."

We drove to campus, to the library ("He's not there," said Francis, "I'll bet a million dollars") and back to the bars again.

"He's left town," said Francis. "I know it."

"Do you think Mr. Hatch will call the police?"

"What would you do? If it was your truck? He won't do anything without talking to me, but if Charles isn't back, say, by tomorrow afternoon. . . ."

We decided to drive by the Albemarle. Henry's car was parked out front. Francis and I went in the lobby cautiously, not knowing quite how we were going to deal with the innkeeper, but, miraculously, there was no one at the desk.

We went upstairs to 3-A. Camilla let us in. She and Henry were eating their dinner, from room service—lamb chops, bottle of burgundy, yellow rose in a bud vase.

Henry was not pleased to see us. "What can I do for you?" he said, putting down his fork.

"It's Charles," said Francis. "He's gone AWOL."

He told them about the truck. I sat down beside Camilla. I was hungry and her lamb chops looked pretty good. She saw me looking at them and pushed the plate at me distractedly. "Here, have some," she said.

I did, and a glass of wine, too. Henry ate steadily as he listened. "Where do you think he's gone?" he said when Francis had finished.

"How the hell should I know?"

"You can keep Mr. Hatch from pressing charges, can't you?"

"Not if he doesn't get the truck back. Or if Charles cracks it up."

"How much could a truck like that possibly cost? Assuming your aunt didn't buy it for him in the first place."

"That's beside the point."

Henry wiped his mouth with a napkin and reached in his pocket for a cigarette. "Charles is getting to be quite a problem," he said. "You know what I've been thinking? I wonder how much it would cost to hire a private nurse."

"To get him off drink, you mean?"

"Of course. We can't send him to the hospital, obviously. Perhaps if we got a hotel room—not here, of course, but somewhere— and if we found some trustworthy person, maybe someone who didn't speak English all that well. . . ."

Camilla looked ill. She was slumped back in her chair. She said: "Henry, what are you going to do? Kidnap him?"

"**Kidnap** is not the word that I would use."

"I'm afraid he'll have a wreck. I think we ought to go look for him."

"We've looked all over town," said Francis. "I don't think he's in Hampden."

"Have you called the hospital?"

"No."

"What I think we really ought to do," said Henry, "is call the police. Ask if there have been any traffic accidents. Do you think Mr. Hatch will agree to say that he lent Charles the truck?"

"He did lend Charles the truck."

"In that case," said Henry, "there should be no problem. Unless, of course, he gets stopped for drunk driving."

"Or unless we can't find him."

"From my point of view," said Henry, "the best thing that Charles could do right now is to disappear entirely from the face of the earth."

Suddenly there was a loud, frenetic banging at the door. We looked at one other.

Camilla's face had gone blank with relief. "Charles," she said, **"Charles,"** and she jumped up from her chair and started to the door; but no one had locked it behind us, and before she got there it flew open with a crash.

It was Charles. He stood in the doorway, blinking drunkenly around the room, and I was so surprised and glad to see him that it was a moment before I realized that he had a gun.

He stepped inside and kicked the door shut behind him. It was the little Beretta that Francis's aunt kept in the night table, the one we'd used for target practice the fall before. We stared at him, thunderstruck.

At last Camilla said, and in a voice which was fairly steady: "Charles, what do you think you are doing?"

"Out of the way," said Charles. He was very drunk.

"So you've come to kill me?" said Henry. He was still holding his cigarette. He was remarkably composed. "Is that it?"

"Yes."

"And what do you suppose that will solve?"

"You've ruined my life, you son of a bitch." He had the gun pointed at Henry's chest. With a sinking feeling, I remembered what an expert shot he was, how he'd broken the rows of mason jars one by one.

"Don't be an idiot," Henry snapped; and I felt the first prickle of real panic at the back of my neck. This belligerent, bullying tone might work with Francis, maybe even with me, but it was a disastrous tack to take with Charles. "If anyone's to blame for your problems, it's you."

I wanted to tell him to shut up, but before I could say anything Charles lurched abruptly to the side, to clear his shot. Camilla stepped into his path. "Charles, give me the gun," she said.

He pushed the hair from his eyes with his forearm, holding the gun remarkably steady with his other hand. "I'm telling you, Milly." It was a pet name he had for her, one he seldom used. "You better get out of the way."

"Charles," said Francis. He was white as a ghost. "Sit down. Have some wine. Let's just forget about this."

The window was open and the chirrup of the crickets washed in harsh and strong.

"You bastard," said Charles, reeling backwards, and it was a moment before I realized, startled, that he was speaking not to Francis or Henry but to me. "I trusted you. You told him where I was."

I was too petrified to answer. I blinked at him.

"I knew where you were," said Henry coolly. "If you want to shoot me, Charles, go ahead and do it. It'll be the stupidest thing you ever did in your life."

"The stupidest thing I ever did in my life was listening to you," Charles said.

What happened next took place in an instant. Charles raised his arm; and quick as a flash, Francis, who was standing closest to him, threw a glass of wine in his face. At the same time Henry sprang from his chair and rushed in. There were four pops in rapid succession, like a cap gun. With the second pop, I heard a windowpane shatter. And with the third I was conscious of a warm, stinging sensation in my abdomen, to the left of my navel.

Henry was holding Charles's right forearm above his head with both hands, bending him backwards; Charles was struggling to get the gun with his left hand, but Henry twisted it from his wrist and it dropped to the carpet. Charles dove for it but Henry was too quick.

I was still standing. **I'm shot,** I thought, **I'm shot.** I reached down and touched my stomach. Blood. There was a small hole, slightly charred, in my white shirt: **my Paul Smith shirt,** I thought, with a pang of anguish. I'd paid a week's salary for it in San Francisco. My stomach felt very hot. Waves of heat radiating from the bull's-eye.

Henry had the gun. He twisted Charles's arm behind his back—Charles fighting, thrashing wildly about—and, nosing the pistol into his spine, shoved him away from the door.

I still hadn't quite grasped what had happened. **Maybe I should sit down,** I thought. Was the bullet still in me? Was I going to die? The thought was ridiculous; it didn't seem possible. My stomach burned but I felt oddly calm. Getting shot, I'd always thought, would hurt a lot more than this. Carefully, I stepped back, and felt the back of the chair I had been sitting in bump against my legs. I sat down.

Charles, despite having one arm pinned behind him, was trying to elbow Henry in the stomach with the other. Henry pushed him, staggering, across the room and into a chair. "Sit down," he said.

Charles tried to get up. Henry mashed him back down. He tried to get up a second time and Henry slapped him across the face with his open hand with a whack that was louder than the gunshots. Then, with the pistol on him, he stepped to the windows and drew the shades.

I put my hand over the hole in my shirt. Bending forward slightly, I felt a sharp pain. I expected everyone to stop and look at me. No one did. I wondered if I should call it to their attention.

Charles's head was rolled against the back of the chair. I noticed that there was blood on his mouth. His eyes were glassy.

Awkwardly—he was holding the gun in his good hand—Henry reached up and took off his spectacles and rubbed them on the front of his shirt. Then he hooked them over his ears again. "Well, Charles," he said. "You've done it now."

I heard some kind of commotion downstairs, through the open window—footsteps, voices, a door slamming.

"Do you think anybody heard?" said Francis anxiously.

"I should think they did," Henry said.

Camilla went over to Charles. Drunkenly, he made as if to push her away.

"Get away from him," Henry said.

"What are we going to do about this window?" said Francis.

"What are we going to do about **me**?" I said.

They all turned and looked at me.

"He **shot** me."

Somehow, this remark did not elicit the dramatic response I expected. Before I had the chance to elaborate, there were footsteps on the stairs and somebody banged at the door.

"What's going on in there?" I recognized the innkeeper's voice. "What's happening?"

Francis put his face in his hands. "Oh, shit," he said.

"Open up in there."

Charles, drunkenly, mumbled something and tried to raise his head. Henry bit his lip. He went to the window and looked out the corner of the shade.

Then he turned around. He still had the pistol. "Come here," he said to Camilla.

She looked at him in horror. So did Francis and I.

He beckoned to her with his gun arm. "Come here," he said. "Quick."

I felt faint. **What's he doing?** I thought, bewildered.

Camilla took a step away from him. Her gaze was terrified. "No, Henry," she said, "don't . . ."

To my surprise, he smiled at her. "You think I'd hurt you?" he said. "Come here."

She went to him. He kissed her between the eyes, then whispered something—what, I've always wondered—in her ear.

"I've got a key," the innkeeper yelled, pounding away at the door. "I'll use it."

The room was swimming. **Idiot,** I thought wildly, **just try the knob.**

Henry kissed Camilla again. "I love you," he said. Then he said, out loud: "Come in."

The door flew open. Henry raised the arm with the gun. **He's going to shoot them,** I thought, dazed; the innkeeper and his wife, behind him, thought the same thing, because they froze about three steps into the room—but then I heard Camilla scream, "**No, Henry!**" and, too late, I realized what he was going to do.

He put the pistol to his temple and fired, twice. Two flat cracks. They slammed his head to the left. It was the kick of the gun, I think, that triggered the second shot.

His mouth fell open. A draft, created by the open door, sucked the curtains into the gap of the open window. For a moment or two, they shuddered against the screen. Then they breathed out again, with something like a sigh; and Henry, his eyes squeezed tight, and his knees giving way beneath him, fell with a thud to the carpet.

EPILOGUE

Alas, poor gentleman,
He look'd not like the ruins of his youth
But like the ruins of those ruins.

—JOHN FORD,
The Broken Heart

I MANAGED to get out of taking my French exams the next week, due to the very excellent excuse of having a gunshot wound to the stomach.

They said at the hospital that I was lucky, and I suppose I was. The bullet drilled me clean through, missing my intestinal wall by a millimeter or two and my spleen by not much more, exiting about an inch and a half to the right of where it came in. I lay flat on my back in the ambulance, feeling the summer night flash by warm and mysterious—kids on bikes, moths haunting the street lamps—and wondering if this was what it was like, if life sped up when you were about to die. Bleeding richly. Sensations fading round the edges. I kept thinking how funny, this dark ride to the underworld, the tunnel illuminated by Shell Oil, Burger King. The paramedic riding in the back wasn't much older than I was; a kid, really, with bad skin and a downy little moustache. He had never seen a gunshot wound. He kept asking what it felt like? dull or sharp? an ache or burn? My head was spinning and naturally I could give him no kind of coherent answer but I remember thinking dimly that it was sort of like the first time I got drunk, or slept with a girl; not quite what one expected, really, but once it happened one realized it couldn't be any other way. Neon lights: Motel 6, Dairy Queen. Colors so bright, they nearly broke my heart.

Henry died, of course. With two bullets to the head I don't suppose he could have done much else. Still, he lived more than twelve hours, a feat which amazed the doctors. (I was under sedation, this is what they tell me.) Such grave wounds, they said, would have killed most people instantly. I wonder if that means he didn't want to die; and if so, why he shot himself in the first place. As bad as it looked, there in the Albemarle, I still think we could have patched it up somehow. It wasn't from desperation that he did it. Nor, I think, was it fear. The business with Julian was heavy on his mind; it had impressed him deeply. I think he felt the need to make a noble gesture, something to prove to us and to himself that it was in fact possible to put those high cold principles which Julian had taught us to use. **Duty, piety, loyalty, sacrifice.** I remember his reflection in the mirror as he raised the pistol to his head. His expression was one of rapt concentration, of triumph, almost, a high diver rushing to the end of the board; eyes tight, joyous, waiting for the big splash.

I think about it quite a bit, actually, that look on his face. I think about a lot of things. I think about the first time I ever saw a birch tree; about the last time I saw Julian; about the first sentence that I ever learned in Greek. Χαλεπά τά καλά. **Beauty is harsh**.

———

I did end up graduating from Hampden, with a degree in English literature. And I went to Brooklyn, with my guts taped up like a gangster ("Well!" said the professor, "this is Brooklyn Heights, not Bensonhurst!") and spent the summer drowsing on his rooftop deck, smoking cigarettes, reading Proust, dreaming about death and indolence and beauty and time. The gunshot healed, leaving a char mark on my stomach. I went back to school in the fall: a dry, gorgeous September, you wouldn't believe how beautiful the trees were that year: clear skies, littered groves, people whispering whenever I walked by.

Francis didn't come back to school that fall. Neither did the twins. The story at the Albemarle was simple, it told itself, really: suicidal Henry, struggle for the gun, leaving me wounded and him dead. In a way I felt this was unfair to Henry but in another it wasn't. And it made me feel better in some obscure way: imagining myself a hero, rushing fearlessly for the gun, instead of merely loitering in the bullet's path like the bystander which I so essentially am.

———

Camilla took Charles down to Virginia the day of Henry's funeral. It was, incidentally, the same day that Henry and Charles were to have appeared in court. The funeral took place in St. Louis. None of us was there but Francis. I was still in the hospital, half-delirious, still seeing the overturned wine glass rolling on the carpet and the oak-sprigged wallpaper at the Albemarle.

A few days before, Henry's mother had stopped in to see me, after she'd been down the hall to see her own son in the morgue. I wish I remembered more of her visit. All I remember is a pretty lady with dark hair and Henry's eyes: one of a stream of visitors, real and imagined, living and dead, who drifted in and out of my room, clustering around my bed at all hours. Julian. My dead grandfather. Bunny, indifferent, clipping his fingernails.

She held my hand. I had tried to save her son's life. There was a doctor in the room, a nurse or two. I saw Henry himself, over her shoulder, standing in the corner in his old gardening clothes.

It was only when I was leaving the hospital, and found the keys to Henry's car among my things, that I remembered something she'd tried to tell me. In going through Henry's affairs, she'd discovered that before he died, he was in the process of transferring the registration of his car to my name (which fit neatly with the official story—suicidal young man, giving away his possessions; no one, not even the police, ever tried to reconcile this generosity with the fact that, when Henry died, he believed himself in danger of losing the car). At any rate, the BMW was mine. She'd picked it out herself, she said, as a present for his nineteenth birthday. She couldn't bear to sell it, or to see it again. This she tried to tell me, crying softly in a chair beside my bed as Henry padded about in the shadows behind her; preoccupied, unnoticed by the nurses; rearranging, with meticulous care, a disordered vase of flowers.

———

You would think, after all we'd been through, that Francis and the twins and I would have kept in better touch over the years. But after Henry died, it was as if some thread which bound us had been abruptly severed, and soon after we began to drift apart.

Francis was in Manhattan the whole summer that I was in Brooklyn. During that time we talked on the telephone maybe five times and saw each other twice. Both times were in

a bar on the Upper East Side, directly downstairs from his mother's apartment. He didn't
like to venture far from home, he said; crowds
made him nervous; two blocks away, he said,
and he started to feel as though the buildings
were going to collapse on him. His hands fid-
geted around the ashtray. He was seeing a doctor. He was doing a lot of reading. The people
at the bar all seemed to know him.

The twins were in Virginia, sequestered at
their grandmother's, incommunicado. Camilla
sent me three postcards that summer and
called me twice. Then in October, when I was
back at school, she wrote to say that Charles
had stopped drinking, hadn't had a drop for
over a month. There was a Christmas card. In
February, a card on my birthday—conspicuously lacking in news of Charles. And then, after that, for a long time, nothing.

———

Around the time I graduated, there was a
sporadic renewal of communications. "Who
would've thought," wrote Francis, "that you'd
be the only one of us to make it out with a
diploma." Camilla sent her congratulations,
and called a couple of times. There was some
talk from both of them about coming up to
Hampden, to watch me walk down the aisle,
but this did not materialize and I was not very
surprised when it didn't.

I had started to date Sophie Dearbold, my senior year of school, and during my last term I moved into her apartment off-campus: on Water Street, just a few doors down from Henry's house, where his Madame Isaac Pereire roses were running wild in the back yard (he never lived to see them bloom, it occurs to me, those roses that smelled like raspberries) and where the boxer dog, sole survivor of his chemistry experiments, ran out to bark at me when I walked by. Sophie had a job, after school, with a dance company in Los Angeles. We thought we were in love. There was some talk of getting married. Though everything in my subconscious was warning me not to (at night I dreamed of car crashes, freeway snipers, the glowing eyes of feral dogs in suburban parking lots) I restricted my applications for graduate fellowships to schools in Southern California.

We hadn't been out there six months when Sophie and I broke up. I was uncommunicative, she said. She never knew what I was thinking. The way I looked at her sometimes, when I woke up in the morning, frightened her.

———

I spent all my time in the library, reading the Jacobean dramatists. Webster and Middleton, Tourneur and Ford. It was an obscure specialization, but the candlelit and treacherous uni-

verse in which they moved—of sin unpun-
ished, of innocence destroyed—was one I
found appealing. Even the titles of their
plays were strangely seductive, trapdoors to
something beautiful and wicked that trickled
beneath the surface of mortality: **The Malcontent. The White Devil. The Broken
Heart.** I pored over them, made notes in the
margins. The Jacobeans had a sure grasp of catastrophe. They understood not only evil, it
seemed, but the extravagance of tricks with
which evil presents itself as good. I felt they cut
right to the heart of the matter, to the essential
rottenness of the world.

I had always loved Christopher Marlowe,
and I found myself thinking a lot about him,
too. "Kind Kit Marlowe," a contemporary had
called him. He was a scholar, the friend of
Raleigh and of Nashe, the most brilliant and
educated of the Cambridge wits. He moved in
the most exalted literary and political circles;
of all his fellow poets, the only one to whom
Shakespeare ever directly alluded was he; and
yet he was also a forger, a murderer, a man of
the most dissolute companions and habits,
who "dyed swearing" in a tavern at the age of
twenty-nine. His companions on that day
were a spy, a pickpocket, and a "bawdy serv-
ing-man." One of them stabbed Marlowe, fa-

tally, just above the eye: "of which wound the aforesaid Christ. Marlowe died instantly."

I often thought of these lines of his, from **Doctor Faustus:**

> I think my master shortly means to die
> For he hath given me all his goods . . .

and of this one, spoken as an aside on the day that Faustus in his black robes went to the emperor's court:

> I'faith, he looks much like a conjurer.

———

When I was writing my dissertation, on Tourneur's **The Revenger's Tragedy**, I received the following letter from Francis.

> Dear Richard:
>
> I wish I could say that this is a difficult letter for me to write but in fact it is not. My life has been for many years in a process of dissolution and it seems to me that now, finally, it is time for me to do the honorable thing.
>
> So this is the last chance I will have to speak to you, in this world at least. What

I want to say to you is this. Work hard. Be happy with Sophie. [He did not know about our breakup.] Forgive me, for all the things I did but mostly for the ones that I did not.

Mais, vrai, j'ai trop pleuré! Les aubes sont navrantes. What a sad and beautiful line that is. I'd always hoped that someday I'd have the chance to use it. And maybe the dawns will be less harrowing in that country for which I shortly depart. Then again, the Athenians think death to be merely sleep. Soon I will know for myself.

I wonder if I will see Henry on the other side. If I do, I am looking forward to asking him why the hell he didn't just shoot us all and get it over with.

Don't feel too bad about any of this. Really.

Cheerily,
Francis

I had not seen him in three years. The letter was postmarked Boston, four days earlier. I dropped everything and drove to the airport and got on the first plane to Logan, where I found Francis in Brigham and Women's Hospital recuperating from two razor-blade cuts to the wrist.

He looked terrible. He was pale as a corpse. The maid, he said, had found him in the bathtub.

He had a private room. Rain was pounding on the gray windowpanes. I was terribly glad to see him and he, I think, to see me. We talked for hours, about nothing, really.

"Did you hear I'm going to get married?" he said presently.

"No," I said, startled.

I thought he was joking. But then he pushed up in his bed a bit and riffled through his night table and found a photograph of her, which he showed to me. Blue-eyed blonde, tastefully clad, built along the Marion line.

"She's pretty."

"She's stupid," said Francis passionately. "I hate her. Do you know what my cousins call her? The Black Hole."

"Why is that?"

"Because the conversation turns into a vacuum whenever she walks into the room."

"Then why are you going to marry her?"

For a moment he didn't answer. Then he

said: "I was seeing someone. A lawyer. He's a bit of a drunk but that's all right. He went to Harvard. You'd like him. His name is Kim."

"And?"

"And my grandfather found out. In the most melodramatic way you can possibly imagine."

He reached for a cigarette. I had to light it for him because of his hands. He had injured one of the tendons that led to his thumb.

"So," he said, blowing out a plume of smoke. "I have to get married."

"Or what?"

"Or my grandfather will cut me off without a cent."

"Can't you get by on your own?" I said.

"No."

He said this with such certainty that it irritated me.

"I do," I said.

"But you're used to it."

Just then the door to his room cracked open. It was his nurse—not from the hospital, but one that his mother had privately engaged.

"Mr. Abernathy!" she said brightly. "There's someone here who wants to see you!"

Francis closed his eyes, then opened them. "It's her," he said.

The nurse withdrew. We looked at each other.

"Don't do it, Francis," I said.

"I've got to."

The door opened, and the blonde in the photograph—all smiles—waltzed in, wearing a pink sweater with a pattern of snowflakes knit into it, and her hair tied back with a pink ribbon. She was actually quite pretty. Among her armload of presents were a teddy bear; jelly beans wrapped in cellophane; copies of **GQ, The Atlantic Monthly, Esquire:** good God, I thought, since when does Francis read magazines?

She walked over to the bed, kissed him briskly on the forehead. "Now, sweetie," she said to him, "I thought we'd decided not to smoke."

To my surprise, she plucked the cigarette from between his fingers and put it out in the ashtray. Then she looked over at me and beamed.

Francis ran a bandaged hand through his hair. "Priscilla," he said tonelessly, "this is my friend Richard."

Her blue eyes widened. "Hi!" she said. "I've heard so much about you!"

"And I about you," I said politely.

She pulled up a chair to Francis's bed. Pleasant, still smiling, she sat down.

And, as if by magic, the conversation stopped.

———

Camilla showed up in Boston the next day; she, too, had got a letter from Francis.

I was drowsing in the bedside chair. I'd been reading to Francis, **Our Mutual Friend**— funny, now I think about it, how much my time with Francis at the hospital in Boston was like the time that Henry spent at the hospital in Vermont with me—and when I woke up, awakened by Francis's exclamation of surprise, and saw her standing there in the dreary Boston light, I thought that I was dreaming.

She looked older. Cheeks a bit hollower. Different hair, cut very short. Without realizing it, I had come to think of her, too, as a ghost: but to **see** her, wan but still beautiful, in the flesh, my heart gave such a glad and violent leap that I thought it would burst, I thought I would die, right there.

Francis sat up in bed and held out his arms. "Darling," he said. "Come here."

———

The three of us were in Boston together for four days. It rained the whole time. Francis got out of the hospital on the second day—which, as it happened, was Ash Wednesday.

I had never been to Boston before; I thought it looked like the London I had never seen. Gray skies, sooty brick townhouses, Chinese magnolias in the fog. Camilla and Francis wanted to go to mass, and I went along with them. The church was crowded and drafty. I went to the altar with them to get ashes, shuffling along in the swaying line. The priest was bent, in black, very old. He made a cross on my forehead with the flat of his thumb. **Dust thou art, to dust thou shalt return.** I stood up again when it was time for communion, but Camilla caught my arm and hastily pulled me back. The three of us stayed in our seats as the pews emptied and the long, shuffling line started towards the altar again.

"You know," said Francis, on the way out, "I once made the mistake of asking Bunny if he ever thought about Sin."

"What did he say?" asked Camilla.

Francis snorted. "He said 'No, of course not. I'm not a **Catholic.**' "

We loitered all afternoon in a dark little bar on Boylston Street, smoking cigarettes and drinking Irish whiskey. The talk turned to Charles. He, it seemed, had been an intermittent guest at Francis's over the course of the past few years.

"Francis lent him quite a bit of money about two years ago," Camilla said. "It was good of him, but he shouldn't have done it."

Francis shrugged and drank off the rest of his glass. It was clear the subject made him un-comfortable. "I wanted to," he said.

"You'll never see it again."

"That's all right."

I was consumed with curiosity. "Where **is** Charles?"

"Oh, he's getting by," said Camilla. It was clear the topic made her uncomfortable, too. "He worked for my uncle for a little while. Then he had a job playing piano in a bar— which, as you can imagine, didn't work out so well. Our Nana was distraught. Finally she had to have my uncle tell him that if he didn't shape up, he was going to have to move out of the house. So he did. He got himself a room in town and went on working at the bar. But they finally fired him and he had to come home again. That was when he started coming up here. It was good of you," she said to Francis, "to put up with him the way you did."

He was staring down into his drink. "Oh," he said, "it's all right."

"You were very kind to him."

"He was my friend."

"Francis," said Camilla, "lent Charles the money to put himself into a treatment place. A hospital. But he only stayed about a week. He ran off with some thirty-year-old woman he met in the detox ward. Nobody heard from them for about two months. Finally the woman's husband—"

"She was married?"

"Yes. Had a baby, too. A little boy. Anyway, the woman's husband finally hired a private detective, and he tracked them down in San Antonio. They were living in this horrible place, a dump. Charles was washing dishes in a diner, and she—well, I don't know what **she** was doing. They were both in kind of bad shape. But neither of them wanted to come home. They were very happy, they said."

She paused to take a sip of her drink.

"And?" I said.

"And they're still down there," she said. "In Texas. Though they're not in San Antonio anymore. They were in Corpus Christi for a while. The last we heard they'd moved to Galveston."

"Doesn't he ever call?"

There was a long pause. Finally, she said: "Charles and I don't really talk anymore."

"Not at all?"

"Not really, no." She took another drink of her whiskey. "It's broken my Nana's heart," she said.

———

In the rainy twilight, we walked back to Francis's through the Public Gardens. The lamps were lit.

Very suddenly, Francis said: "You know, I keep expecting Henry to show up."

I was a bit unnerved by this. Though I hadn't mentioned it, I'd been thinking the same thing. What was more, ever since arriving in Boston I'd kept catching glimpses of people I thought were him: dark figures dashing by in taxicabs, disappearing into office buildings.

"You know, I thought I saw him when I was lying in the bathtub," said Francis. "Faucet dripping, blood all over the goddamned place. I thought I saw him standing there in his bathrobe—you know, that one with all the pockets that he kept his cigarettes and stuff in—over by the window, with his back half-turned, and he said to me, in this really disgusted voice: 'Well, Francis, I hope you're happy now.' "

We kept walking. Nobody said anything.

"It's funny," said Francis. "I have a hard time believing he's really dead. I mean—I know there's no way he could have **faked** dying—but, you know, if anybody could figure out how to come back, it's him. It's kind of like Sherlock Holmes. Going over the Reichenbach Falls. I keep expecting to find that it was all a trick, that he'll turn up any day now with some kind of elaborate explanation."

We were crossing a bridge. Yellow streamers

of lamplight shimmered bright in the inky water.

"Maybe it really was him that you saw," I said.

"What do you mean?"

"I thought I saw him too," I said, after a long, thoughtful pause. "In my room. While I was in the hospital."

"Well, you know what Julian would say," said Francis. "There **are** such things as ghosts. People everywhere have always known that. And we believe in them every bit as much as Homer did. Only now, we call them by different names. Memory. The unconscious."

"Do you mind if we change the subject?" Camilla said, quite suddenly. "Please?"

———

Camilla had to leave on Friday morning. Her grandmother wasn't well, she said, she had to get back. I didn't have to be back in California until the following week.

As I stood with her on the platform—she impatient, tapping her foot, leaning forward to look down the tracks—it seemed more than I could bear to see her go. Francis was around the corner, buying her a book to read on the train.

"I don't want you to leave," I said.

"I don't want to, either."

"Then don't."

"I have to."

We stood looking at each other. It was raining. She looked at me with her rain-colored eyes.

"Camilla, I love you," I said. "Let's get married."

She didn't answer for the longest time. Finally she said: "Richard, you know I can't do that."

"Why not?"

"I can't. I can't just pick up and go to California. My grandmother is old. She can't get around by herself anymore. She needs someone to look after her."

"So forget California. I'll move back East."

"Richard, you can't. What about your dissertation? School?"

"I don't care about school."

We looked at each other for a long time. Finally, she looked away.

"You should see the way I live now, Richard," she said. "My Nana's in bad shape. It's all I can do to take care of her, and that big house, too. I don't have a single friend my own age. I can't even remember the last time I read a book."

"I could help you."

"I don't want you to help me." She raised her head and looked at me: her gaze hit me hard and sweet as a shot of morphine.

"I'll get down on my knees if you want me to," I said. "Really, I will."

She closed her eyes, dark-lidded, dark shadows beneath them; she really was older, not the glancing-eyed girl I had fallen in love with but no less beautiful for that; beautiful now in a way that less excited my senses than tore at my very heart.

"I can't marry you," she said.

"Why not?"

I thought she was going to say, **Because I don't love you,** which probably would have been more or less the truth, but instead, to my surprise, she said: "Because I love Henry."

"Henry's dead."

"I can't help it. I still love him."

"I loved him, too," I said.

For just a moment, I thought I felt her waver. But then she looked away.

"I know you did," she said. "But it's not enough."

———

The rain stayed with me all the way back to California. An abrupt departure, I knew, would be too much; if I was to leave the East at all, I could do so only gradually and so I rented a car, and drove and drove until finally the landscape changed, and I was in the Midwest, and the rain was all I had left of Camilla's goodbye kiss. Raindrops on the windshield, radio stations fading in and out. Cornfields bleak in all those gray, wide-open reaches. I had said goodbye to her once before, but it took everything I had to say goodbye to her then, again, for the last time, like poor Orpheus turning for a last backwards glance at the ghost of his only love and in the same heartbeat losing her forever: **hinc illae lacrimae,** hence those tears.

———

I suppose nothing remains now but to tell you what happened, as far as I know, to the rest of the players in our story.

Cloke Rayburn, amazingly, ended up going to law school. He is now an associate in mergers and acquisitions at Milbank Tweed in New York, where, interestingly, Hugh Corcoran was just made partner. Word is Hugh got him the job. This might or might not be true, but I tend to think it is, as Cloke almost certainly did not distinguish himself wherever it was that he happened to matriculate. He lives not far from Francis and Priscilla, on Lexington and Eighty-first (Francis, by the way, is supposed to have an incredible apartment; Priscilla's dad, who's in real estate, gave it to them for a wedding present) and Francis, who still has trouble sleeping, says he runs into him every now and then in the wee hours of the morning at the Korean deli where they both buy their cigarettes.

Judy Poovey is now something of a minor celebrity. A certified Aerobics instructor, she appears regularly—with a bevy of other muscle-toned beauties—on an exercise program, "Power Moves!" on cable TV.

After school, Frank and Jud went in together and bought the Farmer's Inn, which has become the preferred Hampden hangout. Supposedly they're doing a great business. They have a lot of old Hampdenians working for them, including Jack Teitelbaum and Rooney Wynne, according to a feature article not long ago in the alumni magazine.

Somebody told me that Bram Guernsey was in the Green Berets, though I tend to think this is untrue.

Georges Laforgue is still on the Literature and Languages faculty at Hampden, where his enemies have still not managed to supplant him.

Dr. Roland is retired from active teaching. He lives in Hampden town, and has published a book of photographs of the college through the years, which has made him much sought-after as an after-dinner speaker at the various clubs in town. He was almost the cause of my not being admitted to graduate school by writing me a recommendation which—though it was a glowing one—repeatedly referred to me as "Jerry."

The feral cat that Charles found turned out, surprisingly, to be a rather good pet. He took up with Francis's cousin Mildred over the summer and in the fall made the move with her to Boston, where he now lives, quite contentedly, in a ten-room apartment on Exeter Street under the name of "Princess."

Marion is married now, to Brady Corcoran. They live in Tarrytown, New York—an easy commute for Brady into the city—and the two of them have a baby now, a girl. She has the distinction of being the first female born into the Corcoran clan for no one even knows how many generations. According to Francis, Mr. Corcoran is absolutely wild about her, to the exclusion of all his other children, grandchildren, and pets. She was christened Mary Katherine, a name which has fallen more and more into disuse, as—for reasons best known to themselves—the Corcorans have chosen to give her the nickname "Bunny."

Sophie I hear from now and again. She injured her leg and was out of commission with the dance company for a while, but recently she was given a big role in a new piece. We go out to dinner sometimes. Mostly when she calls it's late at night, and she wants to talk about her boyfriend problems. I like Sophie. I guess you could say she's my best friend here. But somehow I never really forgave her for making me move back to this godforsaken place.

I have not laid eyes on Julian since that last afternoon with Henry, in his office. Francis—with extraordinary difficulty—managed to get in touch with him a couple of days before Henry's funeral. He said that Julian greeted him cordially; listened politely to the news of Henry's demise; then said: "I appreciate it, Francis. But I'm afraid there's really nothing more that I can do."

About a year ago Francis repeated to me a rumor—which we subsequently found was complete romance—that Julian had been appointed royal tutor to the little crown prince of Suaoriland, somewhere in East Africa. But this story, though false, took on a curious life in my imagination. What better fate for Julian than someday being the power behind the Suaori throne, than transforming his pupil into a philosopher-king? (The prince in the fiction was only eight. I wonder what I should be now if Julian had got hold of me when I was only eight years old.) I like to think that maybe he—as Aristotle did—would bring up a man who would conquer the world.

But then, as Francis said, maybe not.

I don't know what happened to Agent Davenport—I expect he's still living in Nashua, New Hampshire—but Detective Sciola is dead. He died of lung cancer maybe three years ago. I discovered this from a public service announcement that I saw late one night on television. It shows Sciola standing, gaunt and Dantesque, against a black backdrop. "By the time you see this announcement," he says, "I will be dead." He goes on to say that it wasn't a career in law enforcement that killed him but two packs of cigarettes a day. I saw this at about three o'clock in the morning, alone in my apartment, on a black-and-white set with lots of interference. White noise and snow. He seemed to be speaking directly at me, right out of the television set. For a moment I was disoriented, seized by panic; could a ghost embody itself through wavelengths, electronic dots, a picture tube? What are the dead, anyway, but waves and energy? Light shining from a dead star?

That, by the way, is a phrase of Julian's. I remember it from a lecture of his on the **Iliad,** when Patroklos appears to Achilles in a dream. There is a very moving passage where Achilles—overjoyed at the sight of the apparition—tries to throw his arms around the ghost of his old friend, and it vanishes. **The dead appear to us in dreams,** said Julian, **because that's the**

only way they can make us see them; what we see is only a projection, beamed from a great distance, light shining at us from a dead star . . .

Which reminds me, by the way, of a dream I had a couple of weeks ago.

I found myself in a strange deserted city—an old city, like London—underpopulated by war or disease. It was night; the streets were dark, bombed-out, abandoned. For a long time, I wandered aimlessly—past ruined parks, blasted statuary, vacant lots overgrown with weeds and collapsed apartment houses with rusted girders poking out of their sides like ribs. But here and there, interspersed among the desolate shells of the heavy old public buildings, I began to see new buildings, too, which were connected by futuristic walkways lit from beneath. Long, cool perspectives of modern architecture, rising phosphorescent and eerie from the rubble.

I went inside one of these new buildings. It was like a laboratory, maybe, or a museum. My footsteps echoed on the tile floors. There was a cluster of men, all smoking pipes, gathered around an exhibit in a glass case that gleamed in the dim light and lit their faces ghoulishly from below.

I drew nearer. In the case was a machine revolving slowly on a turntable, a machine with metal parts that slid in and out and collapsed

956 THE SECRET HISTORY

in upon themselves to form new images. An Inca temple . . . click click click . . . the Pyramids . . . the Parthenon. History passing beneath my very eyes, changing every moment.

"I thought I'd find you here," said a voice at my elbow.

It was Henry. His gaze was steady and impassive in the dim light. Above his ear, beneath the wire stem of his spectacles, I could just make out the powder burn and the dark hole in his right temple.

I was glad to see him, though not exactly surprised. "You know," I said to him, "everybody is saying that you're dead."

He stared down at the machine. The Colosseum . . . click click click . . . the Pantheon. "I'm not dead," he said. "I'm only having a bit of trouble with my passport."

"What?"

He cleared his throat. "My movements are restricted," he said. "I no longer have the ability to travel as freely as I would like."

Hagia Sophia. St. Mark's, in Venice. "What is this place?" I asked him.

"That information is classified, I'm afraid."

I looked around curiously. It seemed that I was the only visitor. "Is it open to the public?" I said.

"Not generally, no."

I looked at him. There was so much I

wanted to ask him, so much I wanted to say; but somehow I knew there wasn't time and even if there was, that it was all, somehow, beside the point.

"Are you happy here?" I said at last.

He considered this for a moment. "Not particularly," he said. "But you're not very happy where you are, either."

St. Basil's, in Moscow. Chartres. Salisbury and Amiens. He glanced at his watch.

"I hope you'll excuse me," he said, "but I'm late for an appointment."

He turned from me and walked away. I watched his back receding down the long, gleaming hall.